TWO AGAINST ONE

They had Davy cornered, the river at his back. Giving as good as he got, he slowly retreated, cautious steps taking him into the reeds. Neither of the killers had connected but it was only a matter of time.

Grizwald and Zeist paused. They traded looks. Grizwald winked, then nodded and roared, "Now!"

Simultaneously, both men leaped. Two glistening knives sought Davy's heart. He tried to jump to the rear but his left foot became entangled and he crashed down among the reeds. Water splashed, soaking part of his pants and shirt. His coonskin cap slipped but did not fall.

Frantically, Davy surged upright. He knocked one knife away, then another. The pair were grinning, sure of themelves, confident that in another few moments he would be worm food.

The *Davy Crockett* Series:
#1: HOMECOMING
#2: SIOUX SLAUGHTER
#3: BLOOD HUNT

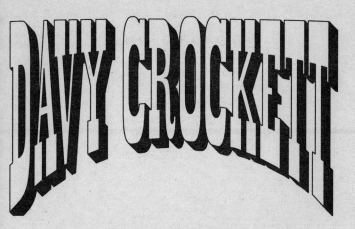

DAVY CROCKETT

MISSISSIPPI MAYHEM

David Thompson

LEISURE BOOKS   NEW YORK CITY

To Judy, Joshua and Shane.

A LEISURE BOOK®

July 1997

Published by

Dorchester Publishing Co., Inc.
276 Fifth Avenue
New York, NY 10001

Printed in the United States of America.

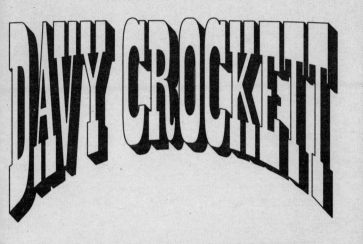

DAVY CROCKETT

MISSISSIPPI MAYHEM

Chapter One

"Look yonder!" Davy Crockett whooped. "We've struck it!"

His close friend and traveling companion, Flavius Harris, stared glumly at the broad expanse of water ahead. He did not share the brawny Irishman's enthusiasm. So what if they had found the mighty Mississippi? Rivers were all the same to him. A person could drown in any one of them.

Davy rose in his saddle for a better view. They were descending a low hill bordered by reeds. Across the river reared steep limestone bluffs. A few ducks were out in the middle of the river. As he scanned the waterway, a large fish leaped from the water, shimmering silver in the bright sunlight, and came down with a spectacular splash.

Excitement tingled Davy's scalp. He had never seen the Mississippi before. But he sure had heard a lot about it. Everyone had. "The Great River," the

7

David Thompson

Indians called it. One of the largest and longest in the whole world. Its northern reaches were largely unexplored. But at the southern end, cities and towns were sprouting faster than ripe seeds in a fertile field.

The third member of their party, a beefy specimen whose double chin was covered with stubble, pointed at the reeds and said, "The canoe is down there. We have to hide it or the savages will help themselves."

"Worthless vermin," muttered the fourth man, a skinny fellow whose grungy homespun clothes fitted his sour personality. "I wish to hell the government would exterminate every last one. It'd be doing us common folks a favor."

Davy made no comment. Experience had taught him that nothing he could say would change a bigot's mind.

Flavius regarded the pair with frank dislike. He didn't trust either as far as he could toss a bull buffalo. It surprised him that Davy had accepted their offer. But then, he had to keep in mind that his pard's hankering for adventure was as boundless as the ocean.

"Follow us," said Grizwald, the man with the stubble. "We'll take you right to it."

"Sure will," confirmed Zeist, the skinny one. His smirk revealed yellow teeth and a gap where two of his upper ones had been.

Davy moved his sorrel aside so the pair could pass. Across his thighs rested his Kentucky long rifle. Liz, he called it, in honor of his second wife, Elizabeth. Buckskins clothed his muscular frame. Atop his head perched a coonskin cap, a rarity there in Illinois, although not in his neck of the woods back in Tennessee.

Thinking of home brought a smile to his lips. If all went well, in a few short weeks he would be holding Elizabeth in his arms and have a swarm of young'uns underfoot. He could hardly wait.

Unknown to Davy, Flavius was also thinking about home. To him, it was beginning to seem as if they would never reach it. Their gallivant had turned into a trek of epic proportions.

Flavius had taken to fretting that his friend's wanderlust might well be the death of them. Here they were, hundreds of miles from Tennessee, deep in woods bordering the Mississippi where hostiles were known to lurk, about to embark on the most harebrained stunt Flavius had ever heard of. It was enough to give a grown man fits!

The game trail wound down to the shore. In a clear space adjoining the reeds, Grizwald and Zeist reined up. They slid off their mounts, waded into the cattails, and within moments returned dragging a long canoe, which they proceeded to haul onto dry land.

"Here it is, just like we promised," Grizwald said, adding proudly, "We built it our own selves."

Zeist licked his thin lips. "Do we have a deal or not, boys?"

Were it up to Flavius, he would have declined. Sadly, he held his tongue as Davy climbed down to examine the craft that was supposed to carry them all the way to St. Louis.

The canoe had been fashioned primarily from birch bark, the seams sealed with pine pitch. Davy had seen few better made, and confessed as much, mentioning, "It must have taken a long time to do the work."

"Oh, about four weeks," Grizwald said, even as Zeist declared, "Seven weeks, give or take." Startled, they exchanged troubled glances.

Suddenly Davy knew. They were lying. The pair of Peorians had not constructed the canoe at all. More than likely, they had done the very thing Grizwald accused the Indians of doing: They had stolen it from a local tribe.

"Who cares how long it was?" Zeist said irritably, and glanced longingly at the horses. "Are you willin' to trade, like we agreed? The canoe for your animals, in an even swap?"

Flavius could not keep silent. "I don't think it's a fair trade," he remarked. "Two horses are worth more than a single canoe."

Grizwald frowned. "Maybe so. But this canoe will get you to St. Louis faster than you could ride. And from St. Louis, it's a short jaunt to your homes."

Which was exactly the reason Davy cottoned to the notion of trading, and sailing on down the river. It promised new sights, new sounds. The lure of new land and new people. The idea was downright intoxicating. "I'm all for it," he announced, looking at his friend, "but we won't swap if you're dead set against making the trip."

Flavius squirmed, uncomfortable at having to render the final decision. Every instinct in his body screamed for him to refuse, but guilt assailed him at the prospect of denying Davy anything. "I reckon it won't be that bad," he reluctantly allowed.

Davy rose and extended his right hand toward Grizwald. "We have a deal, gentlemen. Let us strip off our saddles, then the horses are yours."

Smiling, Grizwald shook. As he did, he nodded at Zeist, who abruptly sidled to the left and elevated his rifle. "All right, bumpkins. The time has come. The first one who moves gets a lead ball in the brain."

Davy tensed to bring Liz into play, but Grizwald's

grip firmed, preventing him from using his right hand.

"Don't try it, Crockett. You'll be dead before you can take a step."

Flavius started to bring up his rifle, but the muzzle of Zeist's gun swung in his direction, changing his mind. At that range the man could hardly miss. "Hold on! What's this about?" Flavius demanded.

Chuckling, Grizwald let go of Davy and stepped back to bring his own rifle to bear. "I should think you would be able to figure it out for yourself, fat man. Your animals and your effects will fetch a pretty price."

"You aimed to kill us all along?" Flavius said. "That offer you made at the tavern was just a trick to get us out here so you can rub us out for our belongings?"

Zeist snickered and winked at Grizwald. "Smart one, ain't he? Makes you wonder how he manages to lace up his moccasins in the mornin'."

Davy needed to stall. "Others saw us with you," he said. "If something happens to us, they'll put two and two together."

"Hogwash," Grizwald replied. "In the first place, no one will ever find your bodies. We'll chop 'em up and leave the bits and pieces for the buzzards and other scavengers, like we've done a dozen times before." He paused, enjoying their plight. "In the second place, everyone in the tavern heard you say that you're bound for St. Louis. No one will think twice if you're never heard from again."

"That's right," Zeist said, eyes gleaming like those of a crazed raven. "The only friend you've got in these parts is John Kayne. And he went off on a trappin' expedition with a bunch of others."

Davy tensed to spring. The cutthroats were right

on all counts. But he would not stand there as meek as a little lamb and let himself be slaughtered. Even though he had as much chance of living as a wax cat in hell, he prepared to fling himself at the duo.

Flavius knew his friend well. They had been in plenty of scrapes, and not once, even when hopeless odds were stacked against them, had Davy given in. Among the people of the canebrake, the Crockett clan were notorious for their fighting spirit.

So Flavius figured the Irishman would try something. To help in that regard, he engineered a distraction, the only one he could come up with on the spur of the moment. Hoisting his right leg, he simply slid off the far side of his bay.

Flavius counted on neither of the men being willing to hurt the horse. Dead, it wouldn't fetch any money. But he counted wrongly. For as he dropped, Zeist snapped off a shot, narrowly missing the bay's neck.

Davy Crockett seized the moment. At the instant Zeist fired, Grizwald's gaze darted toward the bay. In a twinkling, Davy grabbed the barrel of Grizwald's rifle and yanked on it, while sidestepping. The rifle went off, spewing acrid smoke, the ball smashing into the ground in front of Davy's sorrel, which reared and nickered.

Venting a lusty oath, Grizwald clawed for a flintlock wedged under his leather belt.

Davy was not about to let him draw it. Wrenching the spent rifle from the scoundrel's grasp, Davy drove the stock up and in. It connected with Grizwald's mouth as the pistol leaped clear, pulping both lips and crunching teeth in a geyser of scarlet drops. The pistol fell.

"Lem! Help me!" Grizwald sputtered, tottering

backward and raising his arms to ward off another blow.

Flavius saw Lem Zeist pivot toward Davy and produce a long butcher knife. Davy was so intent on Grizwald that he failed to notice.

Rolling onto his side, Flavius extended his rifle between the prancing bay's legs, took a hasty bead, and fired just as Zeist cocked an arm to plunge the blade into Crockett's broad back. Because he aimed hastily, the shot caught Zeist high in the shoulder, not in the heart as Flavius wanted.

Jolted by the impact, Zeist fell to one knee, the knife plopping at his side.

Davy glimpsed all this while closing on Grizwald, who flourished a knife of his own. Discarding the rifle, Davy resorted to the tomahawk he had obtained during the Creek War. Constant practice had lent him the skill of a Creek, a skill he now relied on to parry a flurry of cuts and slashes meant to gut him or open his jugular.

Davy and Grizwald circled each other furiously, Grizwald with gore and pieces of teeth dribbling down his chin.

"You're dead, bastard!" the man blustered. "I'm going to skin you and make a possibles bag from your hide!"

Davy did not respond. Talking distracted a man when he needed to have his full wits about him. Blocking a thrust at his abdomen, he swiped at the cutthroat's head only to have the tomahawk met by Grizwald's knife. Steel rang, and his swing was deflected.

Over by the bay, Flavius had drawn one of his pistols, but he couldn't shoot. It was all he could do to keep from being trampled. Having a rifle discharged under its belly had panicked his bay, which was dancing about as if its legs were aflame. Rolling right and left, Flavius dodged a hailstorm of pounding hooves.

Zeist, meanwhile, had recovered enough to pick up his knife and rotate toward his companion. A sly look came over his face, and he coiled.

Davy continued to circle, seeking an opening. His adversary was skilled, though, and foiled him time and again. Inadvertently, they had wound up at the water's edge. High reeds flanked them as Grizwald, snarling fiercely, lunged at Davy's chest.

Davy threw himself backward. As he did, he collided with something or someone behind him. A knife speared under his left arm from behind, nearly slicing his hunting shirt. Down he went, a struggling form under him.

Realizing who it was, Davy flipped to the right. Zeist's knife whizzed past his ear. As he scrambled into a crouch, Grizwald attacked, his blade shearing space occupied by Davy's head a moment before.

Straightening, Davy battled both of them. They had him cornered, the river at his back. Giving as good as he got, he slowly retreated, cautious steps taking him into the reeds. Neither of the killers had connected, but it was only a matter of time.

A glance showed Davy his friend's plight. No help would come from that quarter unless Flavius rolled clear of the bay.

Grizwald and Zeist paused. They traded looks. Grizwald winked, then nodded and roared, "Now!"

Simultaneously, both men leaped. Two glistening knives sought Davy's heart. He tried to jump to the rear, but his left foot became entangled and he crashed down among the reeds. Water splashed, soaking part of his pants and shirt. His coonskin cap slipped but did not fall.

Frantically, Davy surged upright. He knocked one knife away, then another. The pair were grinning, sure of themselves, confident that in another few moments he would be worm food.

Despair welled up in Davy's breast. Despair that might have spelled doom for other men. Despair that would have weakened their limbs at the crucial moment.

But despair had the opposite effect on the Irishman from Tennessee. From infancy he had been taught to shun weakness, that human frailty was the bane of existence.

As Davy's pa had so often said, "Any man worthy of the name never gives up. A man has to have true grit, boy. Prove your mettle. Don't make me ashamed of you."

The Crockett outlook was reflected in the family motto: "Always be sure you're right, then go ahead."

So now, with two cutthroats thirsting to spill his blood, their knives weaving a threatening tapestry that inched ever closer, Davy Crockett called on the reserves of grit and willpower that had seen him safely through the Creek War and near-deadly bouts with a mysterious illness.

Gritting his teeth, Davy gave the pair a shock by doing that which they least anticipated. He attacked *them*. A bound put him between them. Whirling, he whipped the tomahawk at Zeist's thigh and had the satisfaction of hearing the skinny killer screech like a woman in labor. Twisting on the balls of his feet, he evaded Grizwald's blade, then arced the tomahawk into the Illinoisan's side.

Severely wounded, Grizwald staggered, clasping a hand to the spurting gash. "Damn you!" he raged.

Zeist was down, holding his leg and sobbing hysterically.

Davy backed off and palmed a pistol. His breath came in wracking gasps, his temples drummed to the beat of his racing pulse. As scrapes went, this one had been much too close to suit him.

Flavius finally pushed to his feet and rushed over. Covering the ruffians, he said, "Sorry. I darn near had my noggin caved in."

Davy nodded. No apology was needed. Some folks back home branded the Harris family no-account, but Flavius had proven time and again that he was willing to lay down his life for a true friend. No higher compliment could be paid a man.

Grizwald glowered. "If I'd been a shade quicker—" he said, then focused his spite on Zeist, who had not stopped blubbering like a five-year-old. "Shut up, fool!" he fumed. When his partner failed to heed, he kicked Zeist in the ribs. "You ain't worth the powder and lead it would take to shoot you!"

Warily, Davy collected their weapons and placed them in the center of the canoe. Next, he stripped off his saddle and the parfleches he used to store his effects and did the same with them. Returning, he trained his pistol on the now quiet cutthroats so Flavius could go add his belongings.

"What do you aim to do with us?" Grizwald demanded.

"A deal is a deal," Davy said. "We're taking the canoe and leaving our mounts."

"What about our guns and knives?"

Davy shook his head. "As my friend pointed out, our animals are worth more than the canoe. We'll make up the difference by taking your rifles and such."

Despite being covered, Grizwald bristled. "You can't do that, you son of a bitch! What if we run into hostiles on our way back to the settlement? We wouldn't stand a prayer unarmed."

"How much of a chance did you give us, mister?" Davy retorted sternly. "Be thankful I'm a man of my word. By rights, I should let the horses loose to roam. You certainly don't deserve them."

"Amen to that, brother," Flavius quipped. He was removing his saddle, slowly. Try as he might, he could not come up with a compelling reason to forget about the canoe trip and keep their horses.

Zeist had both hands clamped to his thigh. "What about me?" he whined. "I'm bleeding to death. You can't leave me like this!"

"Make a fire and cauterise the cut," Davy suggested. On several occasions he'd had to do likewise, the most notable instance being the time a black bear, presumed dead, had turned out to be very much alive.

"You're letting us keep our fire steel and tinder box?" Grizwald said sarcastically. "How generous."

Their shenanigans annoyed Davy. They didn't seem to realize how fortunate they were that he did not plant them six feet under. Given their crime, he would be thoroughly justified.

Toting them the fifty or sixty miles to Peoria wasn't practical. The fledgling settlement lacked a duly constituted arm of the law. There was not even a justice of the peace. To turn the pair over to the authorities entailed a trip to the nearest military post, a costly delay.

Davy would rather just be shed of the pair. His conscience was pricked, however, by the thought of their being free to commit more dastardly deeds later on. To nip their foul career in the bud, he proposed, "There's something you should know. At the first town I come to, I'm writing a letter to the commander of the garrison at Fort Dearborn."

Grizwald started. "You wouldn't!"

"I'm sure he'll be mighty interested in your antics," Davy said. "In fact, it wouldn't surprise me if he sent a patrol out after you boys."

Livid with fury, Grizwald clenched a fist. "If I ever run into you again, Crockett, I'll hack off your oysters and make you eat them!"

Davy took a step, jamming his pistol into the man's stomach, causing Grizwald to blanch and gulp. "I hope we do meet, mister. I'd sorely like to finish what I started."

His dander up, Davy shoved the cutthroat, then stalked to the canoe. Flavius had it fully loaded. To reach open water they would have to wade through forty feet of reeds. Davy grabbed an end, but his friend was not in any great hurry to leave.

"I hope we're not making a mistake, pard. Good horseflesh is hard to come by. And I'm right fond of that bay."

"Is this the same bay that's forever biting you? The same bay that tries to throw you whenever it thinks it can catch you unawares? The same bay that you once claimed we should carve up and eat?"

Flavius was unwilling to admit that he never had liked the critter. "You ought to know not to take me seriously when I'm raving like that," he responded lamely.

"Quit fretting," Davy said. "On our way downriver we'll keep our eyes skinned for bear and panther. With any luck we should collect enough peltries to pay for two new horses. And we'll sell the canoe in St. Louis for provision money."

"I'm not upset," Flavius lied. They both knew he was the world's worst worrier, a bad habit he had developed as a child and never outgrown. His pa claimed that his grandma was to blame. She had always been warning him against this, that, and the other.

Flavius blamed a massacre of close kin when he was only seven. His folks had gone to pay their respects, and Flavius had seen a corpse for the very first time. Actually, there had been five bodies, in various states of mutilation. For years afterward, nightmares about that day plagued him.

"Let's go," Davy said, raising his end of the canoe. Action was a sure cure for indecision. Once they were under way, Flavius was bound to perk up.

Against his better judgment, Flavius lifted. "All right. Let's do it before—" The distinct crack of a twig in the forest silenced him. It had been much too loud for a small animal to be responsible.

Davy had also heard the sound. Peering into the shadowy woodland, he beheld spectral shapes flitting toward the shore. Ten, possibly twelve, strung out in a ragged line. One crossed an open patch and was bathed by sunlight, clearly revealing bronzed limbs, buckskin leggins, moccasins, and a quiver full of deadly shafts.

"Indians!" Davy hollered, propelling the canoe into the reeds.

Ice congealed in Flavius's veins. Of all the fates that might befall a frontiersman, he dreaded most being captured and tortured. Stocky legs churning, he barreled into the cattails.

War whoops rent the air. Painted forms burst from the trees.

At the same moment, to the north, two canoes appeared—canoes filled with more warriors.

Chapter Two

As the first war whoops rang out, the sorrel and the bay nickered and bolted.

Griswald yelled for Zeist to help him catch them and bounded in pursuit. Managing to snag the sorrel's reins, he held on for dear life.

Zeist went after the bay, but his wounded leg hampered him. His outstretched hand missed its dangling reins and the horse raced off, swerving past a husky warrior who attempted to bar its path. It plunged into the undergrowth.

Davy Crockett and Flavius Harris barreled through the slippery reeds, pushing their canoe. Davy saw a warrior in the bow of the nearest Indian craft notch an arrow to a sinew string. As yet, the warriors were out of range, but that would not last long.

Warriors in both canoes were paddling in swift,

flawless rhythm, hurtling their craft through the water at unbelievable speed.

A scream drew Davy's attention to the shore where Grizwald had mounted the sorrel and was galloping madly southward, dodging warriors right and left.

The one who had screamed was Zeist. Five warriors ringed him. Terrified, he was beside himself, screeching and cursing while darting every which way in a vain bid to get past them. Whenever he drew close to one, the warrior would shove him back again.

Flavius could not take his eyes off the approaching canoes. He didn't see how Davy and he could escape. All the ghastly tales he had ever heard about the atrocities committed on captured whites flitted through his mind in riotous confusion. Some had been skinned alive, then staked out on anthills. Others had had their eyes gouged out, their tongues and ears cut off, and worse, before being killed. Some had been whittled down a small piece at a time, lingering in abject torment for days on end until their captors eventually put them out of their misery.

Goose bumps erupted all over Flavius. He could practically feel cold steel sliding into his flesh already. Shuddering, he tripped over a cattail and almost fell.

The sudden lurch threw Davy off balance. "Be careful!" he warned. A misstep now would prove costly. The two canoes were nearly in range, and the archer in the lead craft was taking precise aim.

A yip of triumph to the south heralded Griswald's escape. He had burst past the last of the Indians and was speeding along, bent low over the sorrel. Looking over a shoulder, he grinned, but his grin died seconds later when a feathered shaft streaked out of the blue and embedded itself in his back.

David Thompson

Stiffening, Grizwald flung his arms out wide. Just then the sorrel vaulted over a low log. Unable to hold on, Grizwald pitched off, landing on his shoulder. Weakly, he endeavored to regain his feet, but his legs wobbled and buckled. Looking up, he saw six warriors converging. The cry that issued from his throat was hideous to hear.

Zeist, meanwhile, had exhausted himself. On his knees, he blubbered piteously as the warriors toyed with him, lightly pricking him with knives.

"They're goners!" Flavius exclaimed, resisting a tidal wave of stark fear that threatened to engulf him. What was it Davy always said? So long as there was life, there was hope. Gulping, he helped plow the canoe through a thick cluster of reeds.

Ahead, open water beckoned. As Davy lowered the canoe and turned to climb in, an arrow sliced into the river inches from his leg. Tucking Liz to his shoulder, Davy cocked the hammer, sighted, then stroked the trigger.

The bowman in the lead canoe was nocking another shaft. The ball smashed into his chest. Catapulted to the rear, he bowled over one of the paddlers and both fell against a third. The canoe veered landward, the last man trying to straighten it as his companions untangled themselves.

Davy did not waste another precious second. Getting in, he traded his rifle for a paddle. "Hurry!" he urged.

Flavius set his rifle down and gripped the gunwales. He started to heave himself up over the side, but the canoe pitched perilously, almost spilling Davy.

"Get in the right way!"

Not having much experience with canoes, Flavius had completely forgotten that when a canoe was in the water, the safest means of entering was to rise up over the stern and gently slide in. Shifting around, he did just that, gouging his belly on the steeply upturned end. Once his knees were on the bottom, he scooped up a paddle. "Go! Go!"

Davy dipped his paddle into the Mississippi and their craft moved forward, gaining momentum rapidly. A check showed that the second warrior-laden canoe was flying toward them, all four bronzed Indians stroking in skillful unison. "Give me your rifle!"

Flavius did not ask why. Snatching Matilda, his rifle, up, he shoved it at his friend.

The warrior in the bow of the onrushing craft stiffened when Davy pointed the rifle. Lining up the front and rear sights, Davy waited a few more seconds before he fired. What he was attempting had rarely been done. If it didn't work, their prospects of getting away were slim.

Matilda roared. The lead warrior ducked, then smirked, thinking that Davy had missed. Suddenly he glanced down at the bow and bleated. Setting his paddle down, he bent to press both hands against the hole Davy's ball had made just below the waterline.

Flavius whooped for joy. That should keep the warriors busy for a spell. He matched his strokes to Davy's as their canoe angled southward under Davy's seasoned guidance. "We did it!"

"Did we?"

Flavius was afraid to look, but he did anyway. The first canoe was after them again. The man Davy had shot had been placed in the center and the remaining three were hell-bent for vengeance, paddling with savage vigor. "Damn!"

Davy threw every ounce of strength he had into each and every stroke. Because the current was sluggish close to the bank, he steered toward the middle.

An interesting observation provided insight into why they had been attacked. Davy noticed that the canoe they were in was an exact duplicate of those used by the Indians. Evidently, the warriors were members of the tribe Grizwald and Zeist had stolen it from.

Speaking of which, Davy twisted and discovered that the cutthroats were being tied, hand and feet. Grizwald resisted, but Zeist simply lay there, weeping forlornly.

Davy could not honestly say he was sorry for them. There was no telling how many innocents the pair had murdered. Justice had been served, wilderness fashion. Or, as the parson back home might put it, as they reaped, so had they sown.

"Davy!"

The other canoe was gaining fast. Grim bloodlust lit the swarthy faces of its occupants.

Davy pulled a pistol, but instead of aiming at one of the warriors, he aimed over their heads. He had no personal quarrel with these Indians. And ever since his involvement in the Creek War, where he had witnessed atrocities that curdled his blood, he had gone out of his way to avoid needless killing.

Back home, a few unfriendly types had spread the rumor that he had gone soft in the head, that he was willing to let the Indians be if they would let the whites be. Siding with Indians was highly unpopular; most folks shared the sentiments of Andrew Jackson, who wanted to get rid of every red man, woman, and child, either by relocating them if they would cooperate, or by much harsher measures if they would not.

But Davy had never been one to go along with the crowd for conformity's sake. He always settled in his own mind on the right course, then stuck to it, come what may.

So now, as the canoe full of hostile warriors bore down on them, Davy fired into the air above the first man's mane of black hair. The warrior slowed a trifle, then resumed stroking hard and fast again.

Davy sighed. Exchanging the spent pistol for his other flintlock, he aimed as best he could. The .55-caliber smoothbore thundered, spewing smoke and lead.

In the act of dipping his paddle, the warrior wrenched sharply around. His hand flew to his shoulder as he slumped, stunned. Without him to steer and help stroke, the canoe slanted to the right.

Flavius redoubled his efforts. Sweat broke out on his brow and his shoulders commenced to ache. Adopting a mechanical motion, he did not check behind them until they neared a bend.

The Indians in the first canoe had given up. They were heading for the shore. Those from the second canoe were already on land, surrounded by their fellows. Prominent among them were the slumped forms of Griswald and Zeist. Neither horse, Flavius was pleased to learn, had been caught.

Davy held to a steady pace for the next half hour. Only when he was convinced the Indians were definitely not after them did he straighten and say, "Take a breather. We'll let the current carry us for a spell."

None too soon, by Flavius's reckoning. His arms were leaden, his shoulders pricked by awful pangs. "If we ever make it home alive, I'm never setting foot out of Tennessee again," he vowed.

Davy made no such promise. Since he had been knee-high to a grasshopper, he'd been afflicted by a powerful hankering to always see what lay over the next hill. Wanderlust was in his blood.

David Thompson

Daniel Boone, it was claimed, had been the same. Some people just couldn't stay in one place for any length of time. The enticing allure of adventure forever goaded them on.

Now that they were safe, Davy took stock. They had their saddles. They had parfleches filled with jerked venison and pemmican. They had enough ammunition and powder to last until St. Louis if they conserved it wisely. All in all, they were doing right fine. He mentioned as much.

"I suppose," Flavius said flatly. He missed their horses something terrible. Gazing out over the gently rippling water, he shivered.

Water and Flavius did not mix. The deep, dank depths scared him. Next to being captured by hostiles and tortured, he most feared drowning. Several times he nearly had.

Unless someone had been through what Flavius had, they could never fully understand the queasy helplessness that came over those who were barely spared a watery grave when near deep water.

On occasion, Flavius still had bad dreams about sinking into a murky, clammy pool, about pumping his arms and legs for all he was worth and continuing to sink, sink, sink, about the excruciating pain that engulfed his lungs as the last air was expended, then the sickening sensation of water rushing into his mouth and down his throat as he gasped for salvation that wasn't there. He woke up in a cold sweat every time.

But Flavius was not going to tell Davy. He had an obligation to his friend to hold up his end of their partnership. He would not let Davy down.

The afternoon waxed and waned. Lulled by the warmth and serenity, Davy paddled slowly.

Wildlife was abundant. Ducks, geese, and various

other waterfowl thronged sections of the river. Fish constantly jumped. The croaking of frogs, the buzzing drone of insects, and the musical chirping of birds seldom ceased. From time to time the snarl of a cougar or the cough of a prowling bear punctuated the chorus.

The river itself meandered lazily. Snags and bars were common. Once, Davy spied a gigantic snake coiled on a jutting log. He had never seen the like. Over twelve feet long and as thick around as a man's thigh, it was a peculiar copper hue. It detected them and, hissing loudly, glided smoothly into the water. Glad he had reloaded his guns earlier, Davy gripped a pistol, but the snake did not reappear.

The reptile appalled Flavius. Where there were snakes, alligators might lurk. And next to being tortured by Indians or drowning, he most dreaded being torn apart by a wild animal.

Flavius had been told that the marshy country around the Mississippi Delta swarmed with gators. How far north the alligator population thrived, he did not know. But suffice it to say, he regarded every shadow and untoward ripple with keen suspicion.

Twilight lent the river a majestic glow. Davy sought a spot to land, and it was not long before a small clearing hove into view. Motioning to Flavius, he brought their craft to shore broadside, then hopped out and carefully eased the canoe out of the water.

Flavius was so glad to be on solid ground, he had to resist a temptation to hunker and kiss the soil. "I'll get the fire going," he volunteered.

Davy unloaded their effects. By then half the sun had vanished below the horizon. With darkness pending, he deemed it prudent to rely on their supplies for supper rather than go off into the woods after game.

Thanks to John Kayne, their friend from Peoria, they had enough coffee to last a good long while. Flavius filled their pot and soon had the brew steaming. His stomach rumbled like that of a bear fresh out of hibernation. To quiet it, he greedily munched on the pemmican given to them by Kayne's sister.

Flavius had watched her make it. Susan had pounded deer meat into a powder, then mixed it with hot fat. Berries had been added for flavor. When the mess cooled, she cut it into pieces for ease of packing.

Pemmican was on the tough side and not exactly tasty, even with the berries, but it could keep indefinitely. A little could keep a man alive for many days.

Davy found a log close to the clearing and dragged it near the fire. Propped against it, he quietly chewed as the day's tension drained away. "Still have regrets?" he asked.

"No," Flavius fibbed. To change the subject, he said, "I hope to heaven we don't tangle with any more hostiles. How many tribes live along the Mississippi, anyhow?"

"I don't rightly know," Davy confessed. "I think the ones who jumped us today were the Illinois tribe, but I could be wrong. Farther south live the Missouria and the Quapaw. South of them are the Chickasaws, the Chocktaws, and a whole passel of others that the whites know as much about as a frog does about bed sheets."

The news was not comforting. Flavius tilted his tin cup and savored a sip. "In other words, we'll have to be on our guard every minute until we reach St. Louis."

"More or less."

Mississippi Mayhem

The Irishman's casual attitude annoyed Flavius. He held his life too dear to be so nonchalant about possibly losing it. "Doesn't anything ever bother you?" he inquired.

"Why trouble our heads about things we have no control over?" Davy responded. "We have to take each day as it comes." The sage advice had been dispensed often by Davy's father, who had lost *his* father to a marauding war party.

People living on the frontier learned early in life never to take anything for granted. A man never knew from one day to the next if he would be alive to greet the next dawn. Indians, fierce beasts, illness, and accidents made it highly unlikely that any frontiersman would live to a ripe old age.

Women were equally plagued. They worked themselves to death for the sake of their families, bearing the greater burden of child nurturing and taking care of the home because the men were either off in the fields from dawn until dusk or hunting to put fresh meat on the table.

No one complained. It was the way things were. Everyone learned to accept their lot. Or, if they were too weak to bear the strain, they went off to live in big cities, where they only had to walk to the nearest general store or tavern to have their needs met.

Flavius finished his coffee and poured a second cup. This was his favorite time of the day, when they unwound after a long day's travel. When, for a few hours, at least, he need not dread that around the next bend waited some new menace that would make their lives a living hell. "How far is the nearest settlement?"

Davy pursed his lips. "I seem to recollect Kayne mentioned a new trading post about two hundred miles lower down. We'll find out soon enough."

Leaning back, he clasped his hands behind his head and admired the myriad of stars.

Davy never tired of the nightly celestial display. So many heavenly bodies, it took a man's breath away! He saw a shooting star and made a wish.

In the dark woods to the west a creature broke into a wavering howl.

Flavius started. "Coyotes, you think?"

"Wolves."

"Wonderful." Pulling his blanket tighter around his shoulders, Flavius anxiously regarded the encircling ebony wall of vegetation. Not long ago, when they were in *Nadowessioux* country, a nasty wolf with the disposition of a temperance crusader had nearly done him in.

The howl was answered to the north. A third wolf joined in east of the river. Soon the forest vibrated to lupine cries from all points of the compass. It was unnatural, profoundly eerie.

"I ain't never heard so many at one time," Flavius commented. "What are they up to?"

"Maybe it's their way of admiring the stars," Davy suggested, and received a look that implied he had left his sanity in Peoria. Chuckling, he ate the last bit of pemmican in his hand, then stretched out. "Take first watch. Wake me about midnight."

"Wouldn't you rather stay up and jaw?"

"No. We need to get an early start."

Throwing another branch on the fire, Flavius cradled his rifle. Out on the river something splashed loudly. He swung around, half expecting an alligator to lumber up out of the depths with its maw agape.

Get a grip on yourself! Flavius mentally chided himself. Never in all his born days had he been so jumpy! The river was probably to blame, he mused. Or was his unease due to the nagging, disquieting feeling that they were in for hard times?

Hours passed. The soothing warmth and crackle of the fire combined with a soft northwesterly breeze to entice Flavius into dozing off.

He dreamed that he was back in Tennessee, walking toward his cabin. The door flew open and out rushed Matilda, her hair flying as she ran toward him with her arms spread wide in welcome. He spread his to embrace her, tingling with thankfulness for her love and devotion. As they were about to embrace, she hauled off and smacked him across the cheek, rasping, "Where in the hell have you been? You told me that you'd be gone for three weeks, and it's been three *months!*"

Flavius sat bolt upright, blinking his eyes. The dream had been so real, he swore that his cheek stung. Rubbing it, he was surprised that the fire had burned so low. A look at the sky explained why.

He had been sound asleep for over two hours. A shudder coursed through him. Such negligence could get both of them killed. Davy would be as riled as a wet hen were he to find out.

Sitting up, Flavius stretched. A muffled noise from the river he dismissed as another fish. Then he heard an odd, rumbling snarl unlike any he had ever heard.

Whipping around, Flavius was flabbergasted to make out the vague silhouette of an enormous— thing—moving up the river. He assumed it must be a keelboat or a mackinaw. Yet if that was the case, why didn't the crew hail the camp?

His breath caught in his throat when part of the huge bulk moved, giving the impression of a living limb that had stroked the water.

Could it be? Is it alive? Flavius ticked off the possibilities: buffalo, elk, grizzly, black bear, maybe even a moose. Yet if so, it was the biggest damn critter he had ever set eyes on, and he wanted nothing to do with it.

He recalled the immense snake, sparking recollection of a conversation he'd once had with fellow frontiersmen at the Pork and Ale. Someone had mentioned that bears in virgin country were always bigger than those found in tamer parts. Another had pointed out the same was true with all kinds of wildlife, from panthers to raccoons, to frogs and salamanders.

Everyone speculated as to why. Davy had cleared his throat, and they hushed. As the premier hunter in their neck of the woods, his word on such matters was final.

Animals were larger in untamed country, he had said, because man had not yet moved in. Once that happened, the biggest bears and whatnot were always the first to fall to the guns of newly arrived settlers. As more and more homesteaders with hungry mouths to feed set down roots, it cut the odds of any wild creature living long enough to attain truly gigantic proportions.

Flavius heard a snort. The rustling in the river gradually faded. Soon the night returned to normal. He doubled the size of the fire as a precaution, eager for his turn at watch to be over.

Along about midnight, Flavius roused himself, stood, and crossed to the Irishman. As he bent to shake Davy's shoulder, his nerves, already frayed by the wolves and the thing in the river, were jarred by a new sound.

It came from the south, from the direction they were headed come morning. And it was unmistakably a scream, a scream of hair-raising terror torn from human lips.

Chapter Three

"Who do you reckon it could have been?" Flavius asked for the umpteenth time that morning.

"How would I know?" Davy responded a bit irritably. His friend had gone on and on about the scream for hours, and it was growing wearisome. "Use your head for more than something to keep your ears apart. I didn't hear the cry, remember?"

"I wish you had," Flavius said. Try as he might, he could not get that haunting wail out of his mind. It had pierced him to his core. He dearly desired to learn who had uttered it, and why.

Beads of sweat formed on Flavius's forehead. Idly, he rubbed his brow on his sleeve as he raised the paddle to stroke, then squinted at the blazing sun. The day had turned out to be a lot hotter than he had figured on, and the temperature was continuing to climb. "Uncommonly warm," he allowed.

David Thompson

"If you want to cool off, we'll stop and you can take a dip," Davy suggested.

"Not on your life," Flavius said, staring aghast at the murky depths of the broad river. Who knew what lurked down there!

Flavius had lost track of the number of snakes he'd seen since they started out, and he was nowhere near as sure as Davy that alligators were not found so far north. It would be just his luck to jump in and have a big old gator grab hold.

"Suit yourself," Davy said. In all their travels he had never seen his partner so nervous, and he was at a loss to know what to make of it. Given the hardships they had already encountered and survived, it was downright strange that Flavius would be bothered by a picayune thing like canoeing on down the Mississippi.

They were near the middle, where snags were fewer and where Davy could see both banks clearly. Ambush by hostiles was a constant threat. Once, half an hour ago, slender columns of spiraling smoke had been visible to the east. An Indian village, Davy guessed, and he was glad that no warriors appeared to challenge them.

Thanks to the sun beating down from directly overhead, and the gentle swish of their paddles, Davy had to fight off a wave of drowsiness. To his right a loud splash sounded.

"What was that?" Flavius asked anxiously.

"A fish, most likely."

Flavius grunted. It could just as well have been a snake, or an alligator. "Are we stopping soon to eat?" he asked eagerly. His stomach had a habit of rumbling like a volcano if he went more than four or five hours without food, and it was rumbling now.

"I was thinking we'd push on until late afternoon,"

Davy said. "Then I'll take Liz and see what I can rustle up for supper."

"Oh," Flavius said, as might someone who had just been sentenced to the gallows. "Well, if that's what you want, I guess it's fine by me."

A look showed Davy that it was *not* fine. "On second thought," he said, "a short rest can't hurt. Break out some pemmican when we land."

By adroitly handling his paddle, Davy steered them toward the west shoreline. Willows and maples grew thickly on a low bank worn in spots by erosion. Davy made for a gravel finger that jutted from under drooping limbs.

Insects droned without cease. Gaily colored butterflies flitted among spectacular flowers. Sparrows frolicked in the brush, and off in the woods a crow cawed.

Davy could see why some folks took a fancy to river life. The pulse of the current, combined with the throbbing rhythm of the many wild creatures that thronged its shores, instilled a powerful sense of being alive. A fragrant aroma filled his nostrils as he brought the canoe to a gradual stop broadside to the shaded gravel bar.

Flavius was quick to clamber out. Parfleche in hand, he knelt and treated himself to some pemmican. His mouth watered as he chewed slowly to savor the taste. "Too bad we couldn't trade for a heap more of this stuff," he mentioned, easing onto his back to rest.

Davy made no complaint about having to pull the canoe onto solid ground by his lonesome. When food was at stake, Flavius sometimes forgot himself. Turning, he scanned the teeming vegetation.

Movement at the edge of the bar glued his moccasins in place. Their commotion had drawn the interest of a river denizen. Already it was within striking distance of his companion. "Don't move!" he warned.

About to take another bite, Flavius gazed in the same direction as the Irishman, and went stiff in alarm. Crawling steadily toward him, its forked tongue darting in and out, was a whopper of a snake, olive in color, heavy-bodied, with a broad head much wider than the neck. Any hope Flavius had that it was harmless was dispelled by its vertical pupils, a telltale trait of the viper family.

"It's a water moccasin!" Davy confirmed in a whisper. The biggest he had ever come across, at least seven feet from nose to tail.

"Lordy!" Flavius breathed, and wished he hadn't when the cottonmouth suddenly stopped and reared its head as if to strike. Its tongue darted several times in rapid succession. The animal had sensed his presence and was testing the air.

Davy had left his rifle in the canoe. Not daring to make any sudden moves for fear of provoking the serpent into attacking Flavius, he sidled slowly to the right, a hand inching toward his waist. A few feet would give him an obstructed shot.

The cottonmouth coiled and hissed, opening its mouth wide to reveal the pale cotton lining—and its deadly tapered fangs.

Davy froze. Maybe the thing would crawl off if they didn't provoke it.

Flavius scarcely breathed, his skin tingling when the reptile moved toward him, its triangular head swiveling from side to side. *Why doesn't Davy shoot?* he wondered. Another few feet and it would be too late.

Davy's hand closed on a flintlock. The snake hissed again, showing those wicked fangs. Its eyes were fixed on him, not Flavius. That sparked an idea. Boldly taking another step to keep it riveted, he gestured, hoping to shoo it off. "Scat, you scaly devil!" he said. "Go find a frog!"

The sound of his voice had the opposite effect. Hissing louder than ever, the water moccasin coiled.

Flavius imagined its long teeth sinking into his body, and inadvertently shivered. Instantly, the cottonmouth reared and coldly eyed him. Its tongue was the only part of it that moved, as for the longest while it simply glared. Then the tail came up out of the river, and the serpent slid nearer.

Flavius choked down a scream. The thing was so close, he saw drops of liquid on its lower jaw. Were they water? Or venom? Biting his lower lip, he tried not to twitch as the creature crawled to within a few inches of his right side.

Davy had the flintlock halfway free. He could snap off a shot, but what if he missed or only wounded it?

The cottonmouth was still again, its head hovering over Flavius. Stinging sweat trickled into Flavius's eyes, but he refused to blink. To do so invited certain death.

Another pace put Davy at an angle where he could shoot without risk of harming his friend. Yet he hesitated.

Just then, accompanied by loud flapping, several crows took wing from trees lining the bank. One dipped low over the gravel bar.

In a blinding rush of speed, the water moccasin spun and knifed into the river, disappearing under the surface. Moments later it popped up yards downstream, moving rapidly away.

It all happened so fast that Flavius could hardly believe his good fortune. Rising on an elbow, he watched the serpent until it was lost among cattails.

David Thompson

"Good riddance," he muttered in relief. "But why did it run off like that?"

"Maybe it mistook the crow for a hawk or eagle," was Davy's best guess. In the past he had observed other snakes act the same way when the shadows of birds passed over them.

Flavius stood, his hunger all but forgotten, and scoured the shoreline for more serpents. "Let's head out," he proposed. "Filling my belly can wait."

Davy steadied the canoe while his friend climbed in. Pushing off, they sailed out to the center and pointed the bow southward. Time grew as sluggish as the river itself. Minutes went by, becoming an hour, then two.

Mechanically, Davy paddled on through the sweltering heat and muggy humidity. Dip, stroke, lift. Dip, stroke, lift. His shoulders grew mildly sore, his forearms painful.

A series of turns brought them to a long, straight stretch. Flavius saw an object he assumed was an alligator until closer examination showed it to be a log. "I can't wait to get back home where we belong," he said.

"That makes two of us," Davy said.

Presently, tendrils of smoke were silhouetted against the azure-blue vault of sky. Davy's eyes narrowed. A single campfire was to blame. It was on the east side, where Indian sign had been most prevalent. Resting the paddle across the gunwales, Davy picked up his rifle.

On a grassy point materialized a figure waving a flap of buckskin. Across the water boomed a resonant voice.

"Ho there, fellers! Come and light a spell! Coffee is on! And I've got fresh deer meat!"

Flavius spotted the hailer. The mention of food set

his stomach to growling once more. "What do you think?" he asked. "Is he on the level? Or is it a trap?"

"Only one way to find out," Davy said. Stroking briskly, he brought them within rifle range, then held the canoe steady while he scrutinized the forest.

The figure moved into the open. It was a white man with stringy gray hair and a salt-and-pepper beard. Buckskins adorned with exceptionally long whangs clothed his bony frame. Beadwork decorated his pants and sleeves. A beaver hat crowned his head, which he took off and waved in his other hand.

"Don't be shy, boys! It's good for these sore eyes to see a couple of young coons like yourselves!" The man stepped to the water's edge. "Tarnation! It's been ages since last I chawed with a white man."

Since the man did not have a long gun, Davy deemed it prudent to paddle closer. "What are you doing way out here by yourself?" he called out.

"This hoss has been to the Rockies trappin' beaver," was the reply. "Got me a bunch of peltries I'm fixin' to sell down to St. Louis. Gonna celebrate until I drop, I am!"

Davy's interest was piqued. Here was an opportunity to learn, firsthand, about a region he had long yearned to visit. One day, maybe, he would, along with California, the Oregon country, and Texas. Especially the last. Men claimed that Texas was a hunter's paradise, so rife with game that a man only had to step out his door to find something to shoot. "Let's do it," he said quietly, "but don't let your guard down."

The trapper beamed when they made for shore. "Yahoo!" he whooped while hopping into the air and smacking his heels together. "Company's a-callin', George! Ain't it grand!"

"Is he talking to himself or someone else?" Flavius said, wary of a trick.

Davy saw no sign of anyone besides the old-timer. As the canoe coasted to land, the man cheerily helped to pull it high enough so it wouldn't drift, then warmly clasped each of them in turn.

"Howdy, howdy, howdy!" the trapper enthused. "Tom Fitzgerald is my handle. What's yours?"

Answering, Davy noticed that the man's eyes were oddly mismatched. The right one was twice the size of the left, and was blue where the left one was brown. By an added quirk, the right was permanently angled to the side rather than straight ahead.

Tom Fitzgerald chuckled. "Don't pay my peepers no mind, boy. Been this way since I was born. My ma got kicked by a mule when she was carryin' me. George says that explains a lot."

"George?" Flavius said.

"My brother," Fitzgerald said.

Fingering his rifle, Flavius looked around. A small fire crackled a score of yards off. An open pack lay beside it. On a flat stone was a coffeepot; on another were strips of roasted meat. No one else was in evidence. "Where is he?"

Fitzgerald chortled. "Hell, sonny, old George has been dead nigh on thirty years. I talk to him in my head, sometimes, is all."

Davy studied the trapper anew. Tales were told of men who had gone off into the far mountains and returned drastically changed. Something happened to them in the remote vastness of the Rockies. The immensity, the loneliness, the savagery, it affected their minds; they were never the same again. "I suppose that can't hurt so long as George doesn't talk back," he joked.

Fitzgerald snickered. "I'll never tell," he said, ushering them toward his camp.

Flavius was uneasy. "Tell me, Mr. Fitzgerald—"

"Call me Tom, boy," the trapper interrupted. "Or Hoodoo Tom, if you want. That's what the mountaineers were partial to callin' me, the skunks."

Hoodoo meant "crazy." Flavius was having serious reservations. "We don't mean to be any bother, Tom. Maybe we should be on our way."

"And let all this meat go to waste?" Hoodoo Tom said, indicating the strips and a butchered deer lying in the shadows. "That'd be a shame. What do you say, Irish?"

Davy wondered how the man had guessed. "Bring on the victuals."

"Hallelujah! I'll fetch the fine china." Hoodoo Tom dashed into the woods, scampering from tree to tree like a squirrel gone amok.

When the man was beyond earshot, Flavius leaned toward Davy. "I'd rather we were on our way."

"Since when do you pass up food?"

"I don't trust this jasper."

Davy pointed at a fine Hawken rifle propped against a log. "He must trust us. He left his belongings here, didn't he?" Sitting, he patted the grass. "Make yourself comfortable. The worst that can happen is he'll talk us to death."

Soon their host jogged up bearing three flat pieces of bark. "Our china!" he said, passing them out. "Don't break the dishes or George will have a fit."

Davy joined the trapper in rowdy mirth, but Flavius merely smiled to be polite. He didn't like how Hoodoo Tom's oversize eye always seemed to be staring at him, even when the man was facing Davy.

"Are you boys bound for St. Louis too?" the trapper inquired while spearing a piece of meat with his

41

David Thompson

Green River knife and sliding it onto a makeshift plate.

"Yep," Davy said, and explained briefly. "You're the first white man we've come across since we struck the river."

"Really?" Hoodoo Tom bit off a mouthful of dripping venison and moaned in ecstasy. "Nothin' like whitetail. Not even buffler can shine with this." Chewing lustily, he commented, "Keelboats and mackinaws go up and down the Mississippi all the time. A few steamboats have tried it also, I hear. You're bound to run into one, sooner or later."

"Seen any big animals?" Flavius asked, recollecting the monster he had glimpsed the night before.

Hoodoo Tom grinned. "Boy, if I was to tell you about some of the critters I've come across, you'd brand me a liar. Why, once up to the geyser country, I saw me a—"

"Geysers?" Flavius cut in.

The trapper nodded while taking another hearty bite. "Seen 'em with my own eyes, I did. Spouts of hot water shootin' out of holes in the ground. Hundreds of feet high they go." He paused. "And there are pools of mud that bubble like stew in a pot and stink to high heaven. Mounds of dirt that look like beehives. Bears as big as elephants. And a lot more, besides."

Flavius could not help but chuckle. "Did you happen to see horses with wings and wolves that can sing?"

"Scoff if you like, youngster," Hoodoo Tom said. "But I know what I saw. John Colter told me about the place. Everyone knows that his word is his bond."

Colter's name was familiar to Davy. A famous frontiersman who had been on the Lewis and Clark expedition, Colter had visited parts of the country never set foot in by other whites.

"Go there yourself if you don't believe George and me," Hoodoo Tom was saying to Flavius. "You'll be eatin' crow, if'n you do."

Flavius realized that he had hurt the old-timer's feelings. To make amends, he remarked, "I'm not calling you a liar, friend. It's just that some folks like to tell tall tales for the fun of it, and you might be one of them."

Davy's mouth quirked upward. Flavius was referring to him, among others. The backwoodsmen of west Tennessee took great pride in their ability to spin yarns and boast. Under the influence of horns of liquor, informal matches were often held to determine which of them could outdo the other. And while he didn't like to brag, he was the generally acknowledged champion.

"I was speakin' with a straight tongue, young feller," Hoodoo Tom told Flavius.

Since it was plain the man was still peeved, Davy changed the subject. "Come across much Indian sign hereabouts?"

"Not for a couple of days," Hoodoo Tom said. "How about you? Any sign of a pack of Rees?"

The Rees were also known as Arikaras. A powerful tribe notorious for their dislike of whites, they dwelled in villages far up the Missouri River. Not the Mississippi. Davy brought that up, adding, "You have about as much chance of meeting up with a Ree here as you would a Comanche."

An enigmatic twinkle lit Hoodoo Tom's left eye. "I suppose," was all he said.

They finished their meal in silence. The trapper poured each of them a cup of coffee, filled his own battered tin cup, then sank back against the log with a sigh of contentment. "I'm about down to the last of my supplies," he revealed. "Another day or so and I'll be livin' off the land."

An idea occurred to Davy. "We have plenty, and we'd be glad to share. Since we're all heading for St. Louis, why not stick together? There's strength in numbers."

Flavius had his cup in front of his face or they would have seen his frown. Davy was entirely too friendly and generous, to his way of thinking. Inviting a stranger to join them was tantamount to asking for trouble. Hadn't Davy learned his lesson with Grizwald and Zeist?

Hoodoo Tom scratched his chin. "Hmmmmm. Your notion has merit, hoss. I'd hate for anything to happen to my plews after all I went through to get 'em."

Davy checked the vicinity. "Did you cache them somewhere?"

"I'll show you in a bit," Hoodoo Tom said. "First let's polish off this pot."

So they did, the trapper regaling them with stories of his sundry escapades in the Rockies, where the beaver were "as thick as fleas on a coon dog," where in winter it got so cold that a man's breath "plumb froze the moment he exhaled," and where the wind "howled constantly like a wolf with its paw caught in a trap," and was "enough to drive a man clear out of his mind."

When the coffee was gone, Hoodoo Tom rose stiffly and beckoned. Walking to a patch of high weeds growing rank along the river, he parted them. Hidden from prying eyes was a dugout twice as long as the canoe being used by Davy and Flavius. Two large bales of prime beaver hides occupied the bow; another had been placed at the stern. Next to it was a unique pack consisting of wolf hides stretched over a wooden frame. The top had been lashed tight with cord.

Hoodoo Tom bent to pat the craft. "Carved this my own self," he declared proudly. "Took me practically a week, workin' from before sunup until damn near midnight each and every day."

Davy had to admit the old-timer had done an outstanding job, worthy of a Creek Indian. "What happened to your packhorses?" he inquired.

The trapper glanced at him. "Who said I had any?"

"You had to tote these hides to the Mississippi somehow," Davy said. Now that he thought about it, it was strange that Hoodoo Tom had gone to so much bother when it would have been infinitely easier to float the hides down the Missouri River to its confluence with the Mississippi just a few miles above St. Louis.

Flavius hunkered to run his hand over the bale in the stern. The soft beaver fur tickled his palm. Innocently, he reached out to touch the wolf-hide pack.

"Don't you dare!" Hoodoo Tom snapped, swatting Flavius's arm aside. "That there contains my treasures. Ain't no one allowed to look inside except me."

Miffed, Flavius said, "I wasn't trying to take a peek." He rubbed his sore wrist and stepped back, grousing, "What do you have in there, anyway? Gold?"

The trapper squatted and embraced the pack as a man might a lover. "That's none of your business, hoss. Just don't let me catch you near it or George and me will skin you alive." His hand drifted to the hilt of his knife.

Davy moved between them, intent on being peacemaker. But as he did, three canoes flowed into sight around the bend hundreds of yards to the north. All three were filled with painted warriors bristling with weapons.

Chapter Four

"The Rees!" Hoodoo Tom gasped. "George and me are goners if they get their hands on us!" Whirling, he bolted for his camp.

Davy Crockett and Flavius Harris ducked. As yet, the warriors were unaware of their presence. Their canoe and Tom's dugout were close among the reeds, and the smoke from the trapper's fire had dwindled to barely noticeable wisps.

"Can they really be Arikaras?" Flavius whispered. He was no Indian expert, but from what he'd gleaned on their travels, the Rees had never, *ever* been this far from the tribe's homeland before. Which was just as well, because the Arikaras despised whites.

Word had it that their hatred stemmed from an incident in which a party of trappers sided with a band of Nadowessioux, or Sioux, as some called them, in a dispute with an Arikara band.

The two tribes had long been bitter enemies. By

not remaining neutral, those trappers had imperiled every white man who ventured into the wilderness after them, for the Rees had vowed that whites would no longer be welcome in their land. And it just so happened that the Missouri River, the gateway to the Rockies, passed smack dab through the middle of their territory.

A muted clank brought Flavius's recollection to an end. Hoodoo Tom, bearing his pack, coffeepot, and cups, was racing for his dugout. He made no effort to hide, so it was no surprise that one of the Ree warriors suddenly pointed and shouted. All three craft shot forward.

"Damn!" Davy declared. The fat was in the fire now. Dashing to the canoe, he climbed in, waited for Flavius to join him, and shoved off. A few strokes swept them into the current. "Paddle for your life!" he yelled.

Flavius needed no encouragement. The Arikaras were paddling like men possessed. Hatred distorted every face. A few sent arrows winging in their direction, but the range, as yet, was too great.

Hoodoo Tom had cleared the reeds and was propelling his dugout southward with surprising agility and speed. The bow of his craft nipped at the stern of theirs. He talked excitedly—to himself.

Flavius cocked an ear, but he could not hear what the addle-pated trapper was saying.

Davy was anxious to gain the next turn. Once around it, they would temporarily be safe from stray shafts. Eluding the Rees, though, posed a thornier problem. On open water it was impossible. "Stay close to shore!" he advised their newfound companion.

War whoops resounded off the walls of vegetation lining both banks. The Arikaras were bunched together, their sleek canoes knifing through the water with the grace of winsome swans.

The bend loomed. Davy leaned into his strokes, throwing all the power in his brawny body into every one. Hopefully, he scanned the next stretch of river. Cattails and low trees bordered it, offering no safe haven. "Keep at it!" he urged.

Flavius had broken out in a sweat and was breathing as heavily as a bellows. Over his shoulder he saw the old trapper keeping pace, a lopsided grin curling his features. It was almost as if Hoodoo Tom were enjoying himself. Crazy as a coot, Flavius thought.

Without warning, a snag appeared. Davy tried to steer wide but felt grating contact. The canoe tilted upward, its momentum carrying it up and over the submerged tree. For tense seconds he feared the collision would open a gaping hole in the keel, but the canoe made it over, righting itself with a splash that drenched him.

Flavius nearly fell out. Grabbing a gunwale, he clung on and hollered a warning to Hoodoo Tom. "Look out!"

The mountaineer never slowed. Wearing his inane grin, he powered his dugout at full speed, cackling with glee when it careened over the obstruction.

Davy was more alert for obstacles from then on. But despite his vigilance, repeatedly they came on snags so unexpectedly that there was little he could do other than pray their canoe stayed intact.

For more than ten minutes the chase continued, with the Rees neither gaining nor losing ground. Davy's shoulders began to ache. At that pace, it would not be long before creeping fatigue slowed them to a crawl, with disastrous results.

The fourth or fifth bend hove into sight. A check

showed that the Rees had adopted a regular, relaxed rhythm. They knew that they would overtake the smaller canoes eventually and were not about to exhaust themselves in the effort.

Davy's paddle sliced smoothly into the water. Past the turn was a short straight section, then another, sharper bend. Between the two lay the mouth of a narrow creek, one of hundreds that fed into the mighty river.

"Follow us!" Davy cried to Hoodoo Tom, and steered into the creek, past high cattails and lush grass. Hugging the steep north bank, which was shrouded in shadow, he brought the canoe to a stop and tucked at the waist.

Flavius did not need to be told what they were up to. Mimicking his friend, he shifted to see that the trapper had also caught on.

Paddles splashed beyond the mouth. Bronzed figures flashed past. Flavius counted five in each canoe, and was horrified to hear Hoodoo Tom laugh lightly. The fool would give them away if he wasn't careful!

Davy did not share the trapper's elation. They had earned a fleeting reprieve. Once past the next bend, the Arikaras were bound to realize that they had been duped, and backtrack. In order for his plan to succeed, he must now pursue the warriors as ardently as they had pursued him.

"Back into the Mississippi," Davy whispered, and dipped his paddle.

Experience had taught Flavius not to question the Irishman at times like this. Diligently, he helped bring their canoe around and barrel it through the reeds.

Turning the bow downstream, Davy hurtled after the war party. The three canoes had slowed to a turtle's crawl twenty yards from the bend. At least one warrior in each had stood to scour the waterway.

Davy made straight for them. It was madness, but sometimes only a mad act would suffice. The Rees were preoccupied with the river; not one had looked behind them.

The three canoes were spaced about two yards apart, barely enough space for what Davy had in mind. Facing Flavius and Hoodoo Tom, he pantomimed his intention. They nodded, the trapper snickering in anticipation.

Slowing dramatically, Davy slanted between the center canoe and the one on the left. Both were now virtually dead in the water. Many of the warriors were talking at once, creating quite a racket. Which suited Davy perfectly.

As his canoe glided into the gap, Davy shoved his paddle against the inner gunwale of the one on the left. The Ree craft tilted sharply. Some cried out. Two who were on their feet lost their balance, flailing their arms as they fell. Neither could stop his plunge. Their combined weight was sufficient to upend their canoe.

Flavius, meanwhile, gripped the stern of the center canoe and wrenched with all his might. Only one man was standing, and he pitched sideways, yelping. The warrior nearest the stern shifted, bringing up a war club. As the blow descended, the canoe went over, spilling all five warriors into the water.

Flavius swatted an outflung arm. Another warrior lunged, seeking to grasp their canoe, earning only a thump on the head. Then they were in the clear, moving rapidly, going faster with each heartbeat. Strident shouts and shaken fists testified to their success.

Davy looked for Hoodoo Tom. To his dismay, the trapper had not bothered to overturn the third craft.

Instead, he had drawn his Green River knife and slashed at each warrior as he sailed by.

Two were slumped over, their throats spurting. A third had a hand pressed to his scarlet side. The fourth's left hand was nearly severed. And the last man had taken a thrust in the chest.

Hoodoo Tom roared with mirth as he paddled out of their reach. "That'll teach you, you filthy red vermin! Next time stay on the Missouri, where you belong!"

Fury gushed in Davy. By wreaking bloody havoc, the trapper had ensured the Rees would never give up. As soon as the war party tended their wounded, they would strike out in pursuit.

With that in mind, Davy did not stop again until twilight claimed the river country. A barren finger of land offering an unobstructed view was the site he selected for their camp. All afternoon he had simmered, so no sooner was he on solid ground than he stormed over to the mountaineer.

"What got into you earlier? Why did you tear into those Arikaras instead of doing as I wanted?"

Hoodoo Tom's left eyebrow arched. "Who are you to tell me what to do? Those varmints have been doggin' my heels for weeks now. I can't wait to be shed of the whole bunch."

"Why have they been after you for so long?" Davy bluntly asked.

The trapper shrugged. "My hide is white, ain't it? Rees don't need more reason than that."

Davy was skeptical. Yes, the Arikaras went after every white man they saw. But none had ever traveled so far afield before. What had the trapper done to garner such fanatical spite?

"They're bound to give up, in time," Hoodoo Tom

said. "Not even those bloodthirsty butchers would dare get too close to St. Louis."

Flavius lived for that day. The pearl of the frontier, St. Louis boasted more taverns, saloons, and grog shops per square mile than any city except New Orleans. His first order of business would be to gorge himself on corn pone, johnnycakes, and ale. If he couldn't find corn pone, a huge pot of baked beans would do, maybe with a dozen hot biscuits as an added treat.

Stomach gurgling, Flavius sought wood for the fire. He kept his rifle handy in case game strayed by, but none did. Pemmican and jerked deer meat had to suffice. "I sure do miss Matilda's potpie," he commented.

Davy had more than food on his mind. He was debating whether to press on or wait for daylight. Navigating the river in the dark was a risky proposition. Normally, few attempted it. But the Rees just might be mad enough to try. He voiced his concern.

"Don't fret," Hoodoo Tom said confidently. "The Arikaras never fight at night. Most Injuns don't. Superstitious bunk, mostly."

"Even so, we'll take turns keeping watch," Davy said.

The evening was uneventful. An inky mantle claimed the woodland, luring nocturnal predators from their dens. Howls and snarls joined in savage cacophony, without end.

Flavius reclined on his side, stuck a finger in his ear, and was asleep within moments. He had the last shift, so he was not awakened until two in the morning. A stiff northwesterly breeze chilled him as he stretched and yawned. "Anything?"

"It's been as quiet as church when the parson asks us to pray," Davy said, stifling a yawn of his own. "I heard a big cat in the trees yonder, but it's kept its distance."

Flavius turned to add a branch to the low flames. None were left. "I should have gathered more," he said to himself.

"Want me to fetch a load?" Davy volunteered.

"I will," Flavius said, disguising his trepidation at having to traipse into the stygian forest. Truth was, he'd rather eat nails.

His boots made little sound on the soft earth. Flavius paused often to look and listen. From the river came soft splashing. On the bank, bullfrogs croaked. Everywhere, crickets sang.

Flavius remembered where he had seen a lot of dead limbs. Wending among the spectral trees, he placed each foot down with care. Rattlesnakes and water moccasins did most of their hunting at night. Copperheads might also be abroad.

The cough of a cougar stopped Flavius dead in his tracks. It was much too close. Flattening against a trunk, he probed the murky realm for a hint of its location. Painters, as some folks called them, attacked with blinding quickness, and in the dark they were virtually invisible.

After a suitable interval, Flavius walked on. Above him the canopy of branches blotted out the stars. To his rear the growth hid the river. It was like being at the bottom of a black pit, only worse.

He came to where he thought the dead limbs had been, but when he knelt and felt the ground, his fingers encountered grass. Positive he was close, he roved in an ever-widening circle. Soon it grew apparent that he was wide of the mark. Opting to return for a burning brand to light his way, Flavius headed for the river. Or where he believed the river to be.

He hiked for a score of yards without reaching the shoreline. That couldn't be, unless he had somehow got turned around. Stopping, he peered upward to take his bearings by the constellations, but the canopy combined with low clouds to foil him.

"Damn it all," Flavius muttered sourly. If it wasn't one thing, it was another. Licking a finger, he tested the breeze, which had been blowing from the northwest when he woke up. It was not as strong in the woods. Strong enough, however, to guide him in the right direction.

Two minutes of tramping blindly, of being scratched and poked by bushes and trees, of being snared by vines and roots, was enough to ball his stomach into a knot. He should have come on the Mississippi. Evidently the wind had shifted.

Flavius was lost. Quelling rising panic, he pondered. It was doubtful he was out of earshot of the camp. A holler would wake up the others. Pride, though, silenced him. No frontiersman worthy of the name would ever own up to becoming lost. What would Davy think? Not to mention Hoodoo Tom Fitzgerald, who would never let him hear the end of it!

Flavius pivoted on the ball of a foot, a full three hundred and sixty degrees. Dense vegetation hemmed him completely. And either the bullfrogs had fallen silent, or he was too far from the river to hear them.

Gnawing on his lower lip, Flavius stepped to a maple tree. He leaned his rifle against the trunk and jumped straight up, snagging a limb. His joy on seeing a pinpoint of light was boundless. It was smaller than he remembered the fire as being, but that was easily explained. The fire had burned lower in his absence.

Cheerfully, Flavius claimed his rifle and hurried toward the spot. Every so often he would hop up and down to verify that he had not strayed off track.

As the minutes piled on top of one another, doubt crept over him. He could not possibly have gone this far from the river, he reflected. Something was wrong.

Cautiously, Flavius edged on. The pinpoint of light grew. It was a fire, but it was set amid the trees. It was someone else's camp.

Indians! Flavius deduced, and halted. Whoever they were, they were bound to be unfriendly. Backing off, he retraced his steps until he came upon a clearing that he had not crossed earlier. At last he could read the stars.

The Big Dipper indicated the location of the North Star, which, in turn, confirmed that Flavius was well to the northeast of where he should be. To reach the Mississippi, he must go due southwest.

Flavius bent his steps accordingly. At the edge of the clearing he drew up short, startled by rustling in the brush. Something, or someone, was in there. Leveling his rifle, Flavius sidled to the left, toward a patch of weeds as high as his chest.

A figure flitted between trees, affording no more than a tantalizing glimpse of limbs and a breechclout. Flavius tried to take a bead, but the warrior was gone in the blink of an eye.

Another form rose to the right. Metal glittered dully in the starlight. Rotating, Flavius centered on the man's chest and would have fired if the apparition had not vanished.

A feeling came over Flavius that he was being surrounded. He had to get out of there while he still could. Facing due west, he charged into the growth, heedless of the limbs that tore at his face, his eyes.

56

Someone called out in a tongue Flavius had never heard before. It must have been a signal, because more shapes heaved up out of the ground. Bounding like bloodhounds, they converged.

Since all pretense at stealth had been dropped, Flavius broke into a run and cut to the right. Leaves slashed his cheek. The tip of a limb nearly gouged his eye out. Stung, bleeding, he stumbled over a small log.

As Flavius regained his balance, a vision solidified out of the night. It was a tall, stately woman in an exquisite buckskin dress decorated with hundreds of beads in many colors. Ivory teeth shone in a broad smile.

Dazzled, Flavius halted. It couldn't be another war party, not with women along. Or could it? Hadn't he heard tell that among some tribes, women *did* participate in raids? "I'm a friend," he blurted, lowering his muzzle to prove it.

A tree limb to his right creaked. Flavius glimpsed a tawny outline as he turned. Distracted, he had no idea someone had snuck up on him until bands of iron encircled his chest and he was hurled bodily to the earth.

They wanted him alive!

Fear lent Flavius the willpower needed to lash out, to kick his assailant in the stomach and send the warrior rolling. Shoving onto his knees, he wedged his rifle to his shoulder, only to have it knocked from his numb fingers by a heavy human battering ram who caught him squarely in the back.

His spine alive with pain, Flavius thudded onto his stomach. A foot slammed onto his lower back. Fingers made of stone seized his wrists.

Flavius had endured enough. "Let go of me!" he fumed, struggling to free himself. There were too many. Four had him pinned. Four more, including the woman, watched. "I don't mean any harm!" he declared, but he might as well have been speaking Greek.

A babble of voices presaged the arrival of a warrior bearing a torch. The man held it close to Flavius so the Indians could see his face. It worked both ways, the glow enabling Flavius to behold the handsome features and rippling muscles of his captors. They were unlike those of any Indians he had ever met.

"Please, you've got to believe me!" he tried one more time.

The Indians consulted. After much gesturing and heated debate, one pointed eastward. Flavius was lifted to his feet and stripped of his weapons. Some of the Indians assumed a single file in front of him; others did so behind. Stout warriors with chests as big around as barrels held on to his elbows and he was ushered from the clearing.

Flavius was in a quandary. To resist would be pointless. Yet he had to do something. They were taking him eastward, farther from the river. And farther from Davy.

Two additional torches had been lit. The illumination permitted the party to hold to a brisk pace.

Many an inquisitive glance was cast at Flavius, giving him the impression that his captors had not encountered many white men. That could work in his favor. The less contact they'd had, the less likely they were to make worm food of him on general principle.

They were relying on a narrow trail worn smooth by the passage of many feet over many years. Thick undergrowth walled the path on both sides. It occurred to Flavius that unless a person knew the path was there, they could pass within a few feet of it and not be the wiser. Was that by design?

Gradually, the eastern sky brightened. A pink streak heralded a new day. The torches were extinguished.

Flavius happened to be staring at the stately woman when she looked over her shoulder. "Where are you taking me?" he asked politely. "Who are you people?"

She gestured, signifying she did not comprehend.

The warriors became agitated when a sliver of gold crowned the eastern horizon. They moved twice as fast, apparently anxious to reach their destination before sunrise.

Flavius grew depressed. Even if Davy were to track him, it would take half a day. And another half a day for the trek back to the Mississippi.

That was more than enough time for the Arikaras to catch up. And it was all his fault. If he had the brains God gave a turnip, he would have yelled the moment he realized he was lost. He'd botched things badly this time around.

Despondent, Flavius plodded on through thinning foliage to the crest of a hill, one of half a dozen that formed a natural barrier around a lush valley watered by a glistening stream.

Out in the center of the valley were three gigantic knolls, almost hills in their own right. Or so Flavius thought until he noted their precise configurations, and people moving up and down them. One of the mounds was conical, one a rectangle, and the third bore the shape of a giant bird in flight.

Dumbfounded, Flavius let himself be hustled down the slope. In Tennessee and elsewhere were mounds just like these. No one knew who had built them, or why. Rumor had it that the Indians responsible had long since been wiped out. Obviously, that was not quite the case.

David Thompson

In the bright light of dawn, Flavius verified his first impression. His captors were remarkably unlike any Indians he knew of. The men were endowed with exceptional builds; the women were magnificently attractive. None, though, compared to a trio of bizarre figures moving from the conical mound to greet them.

They were men with *antlers*.

Chapter Five

Davy Crockett knew that something was terribly amiss when he opened his eyes to find the sun roosting on the rim of the world. Flavius was supposed to have awakened him well before sunrise.

Sitting up, Davy saw that the fire had died. The charred coals were cold to the touch, proof it had gone out hours ago. Flavius was too skittish of the dark to ever let that happen.

Hoodoo Tom snored lightly, blissfully unaware of the new development. Davy let the man sleep and rose to search the ground. He found where his friend had gone into the woods after more wood for the fire.

Cupping a hand to his mouth, Davy was about to shout when common sense overrode the impulse. If hostiles were abroad, shouting would draw them like a magnet.

Davy dashed to the camp and bent to shake Hoodoo Tom's shoulder. The man had to be the heaviest sleeper this side of the Mississippi. Except for a few grunts and snorts, the trapper slept on.

"Wake up, darn it!" Davy said. "Time's a-wasting. Those Rees will be along directly, and I don't want to be anywhere near here when they show."

At the mention of the Arikaras, Hoodoo Tom's eyelids snapped wide. "What's the fuss?" he asked.

Davy explained while placing their gear into the canoe. He concluded with, "I'm going after him. You're welcome to stay, or you can push on by your lonesome."

Hoodoo Tom slowly rose, grimacing as he stretched. "Tarnation! These old bones sure do creak in the mornin'!" Scratching his chin, he said, "I reckon I'll tag along with you, Tennessee. I've sort of taken a shine to your fat friend. And besides, you helped me against the stinkin' Rees."

"I'll be moving fast," Davy remarked.

"So? Don't let my gray hairs fool you, pup. I'll keep up. Just you watch."

Gripping the bow of the canoe, Davy said, "Give me a hand. We'll pull both into the trees. With any luck, if the Rees do catch up, they'll go right on by."

After both craft were concealed, Davy chopped a small leafy branch off a tree and obliterated the drag marks as best he could. The dugout was considerably heavier than the canoe, and no amount of swishing would erase the gouge in the soil. Gathering armfuls of leaves, he covered the mark from end to end, adding random stones and limbs to keep the leaves from blowing away. When he was done, he was satisfied the site would pass scrutiny from out on the river. A close inspection, though, would betray his handiwork. "It's the best I can do," he commented.

"Not bad, hoss," Hoodoo Tom said. "Now what say we go find your fat friend?"

"Don't call him that."

"What? Fat? Well, he is, ain't he?"

"He's heavier than most, but most of it is muscle," Davy said, hefting Liz as he entered the trees.

The trapper chuckled. "If'n you say so, young coon. I won't argue. But it seems to me that sayin' your pard is mostly muscle is a lot like sayin' a cow is mostly brains. And George agrees."

Davy held his temper. He had to remember that the man was not quite right in the head. When Davy had asked why he insisted on bringing the pack made from wolf skin, the old trapper had winked at him while adjusting the straps, and said, "I don't want any thievin' redskins to steal my treasures. Where I go, they go. When I die, I want 'em buried with me so I can fondle 'em in my grave."

Flavius had left a trail that any twelve-year-old from back home could follow. Davy moved swiftly. It was soon apparent that Flavius had grown lost and wandered in circles. Then Davy came to where his friend had made a beeline to the northeast. Flavius's long stride and steady gait were ample evidence that he had thought he was going in the right direction.

Davy sighed. Only once in his whole life had he ever been lost, and that when he was barely old enough to shave. His sense of direction had not failed him since. Others, though, were not so fortunate. Many a fellow frontiersman had felt harrowing fear at being adrift in the deep woods at one time or another.

Flavius had a knack for getting lost more often than most. Davy had taught him how to read the night sky, and how to tell the four points of the compass by day. He had also made it plain that certain wood lore taken for granted as true was not.

For instance, moss did not always grow on the

David Thompson

north side of trees. It grew on the shadiest, dankest side, and if that happened to be the east, west, or south, then that was where the moss grew.

Another fallacy was that the wind always blew from the west. Generally, it did, but it could switch to come from any direction at any time.

Flavius had shown great improvement recently. It was mildly annoying that *now*, of all times, he should get lost again.

Davy's annoyance changed to outright alarm in a small clearing where scuffle marks revealed his friend had been taken prisoner by Indians. A war party, Davy reckoned, until he discovered the moccasin prints of two women.

Hoodoo Tom studied them as well. "Mighty strange, hoss," he said. "No two tribes fashion their footwear exactly alike. I ain't never seen this style before, and I know most every kind there is." Brow furrowed, he gazed into the forest. "I wonder. Could those wild tales be true?"

"What tales?"

"Stories about the Old Ones, a tribe that used to call this region their own. Other Injuns came along and wiped 'em out. Or so most believe. But a few claim the tribe is still here, hidin' far back where no whites have ever gone."

"Has anyone actually seen them?"

"Two or three, as I recollect. About the same as have seen the Thunderbirds."

Davy had turned to hurry along the narrow trail. He paused. "The what?"

Hoodoo Tom peered skyward. "Giant birds, son. As big as a horse. Back in the old days they were a holy terror, killin' Injuns and whites alike. I talked to a 'breed once who swore some are still around. The *piasas*, he called 'em." He wagged a finger westward.

"In fact, on the river, not far from here, is a cliff where the Old Ones painted a likeness of one of these birds. The Sioux call 'em Thunderbirds."

Birds as big as horses? Davy shook his head and began to jog.

"I know what you're thinkin'," the trapper said, keeping up. "And I'd think it was nonsense, too, if not for the time I found a dead bull buffalo out on the prairie. Something had ripped that critter to shreds, tearin' off huge chunks of flesh. At first I thought wolves were to blame. Then I saw bird tracks, prints bigger than those of the buffalo."

"You're saying that one of these Thunderbirds killed a full-grown bull?"

"What else could it have been?" Hoodoo Tom said. "You should've seen the tracks! They were like an eagle's or hawk's, only ten times larger. Gave me goose bumps just to look at 'em."

A tall tale, if ever Davy had heard one. One eye on the trail, he forged eastward.

Hoodoo Tom was in a talkative mood. "That 'breed told me a lot about the Old Ones. How they used to be on friendly terms with the piasas, until one day some other Injuns attacked their village. After the battle, the ground was covered with the dead and dyin'. And that's when the piasas came. They ate the flesh and took a likin' to it. Ever after, the Thunderbirds have fed on us like we feed on rabbits."

"Is that so?"

"I swear by the Bible! The 'breed also told me that the name, piasa, comes from the Old Ones themselves. It means 'the bird that eats people,' or some such."

Davy did not encourage him by asking any more questions. The legend was interesting, but it was no more than that. He'd heard plenty of similar whoppers over the years, from reports of demons dwelling underground to fanciful accounts of hairy manlike beasts over seven feet tall roaming helter-skelter all over creation. Any sensible person took the reports with a grain of salt.

The sun rose ever higher. Thanks to the dense walls of vegetation, cool shade cloaked the trail. It was more like a tunnel, Davy mused. The ground had been well worn. Countless feet had passed along it over many years. Davy could not establish its age, but it had to be quite old.

Along about the middle of the morning, Davy rested briefly. He did so more for the old-timer's sake than his own. Doffing his coonskin cap, he wiped his forehead and listened to the merry chirps of playful sparrows.

Hoodoo Tom had removed his pack and was idly caressing it. "If it is the Old Ones we're up against, we'd best be careful," he said quietly. "Word has it that anyone who runs into 'em is never seen again."

"I'll keep that in mind."

The trapper tittered. "Don't be sassin' me, young coon. It ain't polite to mock your elders."

Davy was going to point out that it didn't matter which tribe had taken Flavius captive so long as they got him back safe and sound, when faint voices fell on his ears. Putting a finger to his lips, he rose.

The voices were growing closer.

A gap between trees afforded Davy a means of taking cover. Squeezing between them, he had to make room for the mountain man, who crouched at his side. Hardly were they settled before a pair of warriors walked into view to the east. And what warriors they were!

Raven hair ringed by decorated headbands fell past wide shoulders rippling with muscle. Broad chests were naked except for necklaces of finely wrought green stones, possibly gems. Loincloths that fell halfway to their knees and knee-high moccasins completed their apparel. Each held a war club bearing wicked spikes near the top.

The men were as unique as their garb. High brows, aquiline noses, and square jaws lent them superbly handsome aspects. Their thighs were as thick as tree stumps, their hands brawny, their builds hinting at immense latent strength.

Most macabre of all were their headdresses, which consisted of a pair of antlers attached to a kind of cap strapped tightly to their chins.

"Old Ones!" Hoodoo Tom whispered in Davy's ear.

Davy had to admit that he had never seen Indians like these. Actually, he had never even *heard* of any like them. They moved with supple grace, conversing softly, soon disappearing around the next bend to the west. Davy did not speak until a safe interval had gone by. "Sorry I doubted you, old-timer."

"Did you see those war clubs?" Hoodoo Tom said. "We call 'em eyedaggs, 'cause those spikes can gouge out an eyeball as pretty as you please."

"Their village must be nearby," Davy speculated. Since one man could move more stealthily than two, he suggested, "Maybe you should wait here for me."

"And miss out on all the fun? Not on your life, hoss. Lead on." Hoodoo Tom looked after the departed warriors. "Did you see the heads on them fellers? Wouldn't you like to have a head like that?"

"I'm happy with the one I've got," Davy said, sliding onto the trail. His soles made no sound on the packed earth. Even so, he stopped at each bend to make sure no one was approaching from the other side.

Half an hour of rapid travel did not turn up any

village. Just when Davy figured that he had misjudged, in the distance laughter tinkled.

"We've done it!" Hoodoo Tom whispered. "We've done what no other white man ever have! We've found the Old Ones!"

Davy advanced slowly, Liz leveled. They climbed a hill. Suddenly the forest ended, and before his wondering gaze unfolded a spectacle from the dawn of time. Amazed, he admired high grass-covered earthworks in a verdant valley, and noted figures moving about.

Hoodoo Tom was agog. "Lookee there! This explains all the peculiar mounds found in these parts, and elsewhere! The Old Ones are the builders! Just like that 'breed claimed."

Davy regained his wits and motioned to seek cover behind some bushes. In vain, he hunted for sign of Flavius among the villagers.

The mountaineer shrugged out of his pack. "Ain't very many of them, are there? That should make it easier for us."

Davy's eyes narrowed. Given the size of the mounds, he'd expect the valley to be crawling with inhabitants. Yet he counted less than three dozen, and not a single child anywhere. Why should that be?

In a field adjacent to a rectangular mound, a handful of women cultivated crops. Some men were doing work on the top of a cone. And six or seven warriors were gathered beside a birdlike earthwork.

"Where do they live?" Davy wondered. "I don't see any lodges? Do you?"

"Maybe in there," Hoodoo Tom said, pointing.

A woman had just emerged from an opening at the base of the rectangle. Carrying a clay vase or pot, she walked toward the stream bordering the village to the east.

Davy saw that the opening through which the woman came had vanished. Grass grew in its place. Watching closely, he learned the secret when a man walked up to the mound, parted a green hide or blanket, and went inside.

The rectangular mound was a giant lodge! The doorways were cleverly arranged so that from a distance they appeared to be part of the mound itself. What better defense than to hide right under the noses of their enemies?

Of course, the strategy would only work if the villagers had ample warning. So there must be lookouts. Davy surveyed the valley from end to end but did not spot any. And that bothered him.

"So what's your plan, hoss?" Hoodoo Tom asked.

"We wait until dark. Then I sneak on down there."

The trapper pursed his lips. "There you go again, thinkin' I ain't fit company. But I'm taggin' along anyhow. You'll need someone to cover your backside."

Davy made himself comfortable. They had a long wait ahead, and he wished he had brought pemmican. Sticking a blade of grass in his mouth, he chewed thoughtfully.

"I ain't complainin', mind you," Hoodoo Tom commented, "but this delay will likely spell trouble for us later on. Those Rees we walloped are liable to be ahead of us by the time we start on down the Mississippi again."

"It could work in our favor," Davy said.

"Maybe so. Maybe we'll spot 'em before they spot us. Or maybe they'll get tired of lookin' and head on up the Missouri when they get to where it flows into the Mississippi, down south a ways."

Davy doubted it. The Arikaras were not likely to give up, not after chasing the trapper overland hundreds of miles, clear to the northern reaches of the Mississippi. What motivated them? What had Hoodoo Tom done to earn their tireless pursuit? Fishing for information, he said casually, "Those Rees sure must hate you."

Hoodoo Tom laughed. "I reckon they do, at that. But they're not alone. The Blackfeet and the Crows ain't none too fond of me, neither."

"What did you do to get them so riled?" Davy inquired. Whatever answer he would have received was cut short by the abrupt appearance of two warriors on the trail. As silent as specters, the Old Ones had given no hint of their arrival.

Davy crouched, worried that the pair had overheard them, even though they had spoken in whispers. The two men were the same ones who had gone by earlier, only now they carried a slain doe, lashed to a long pole.

The Old Ones intently scanned the brush. They were suspicious, all right.

Davy reached for his tomahawk. If the pair ventured closer, he had to render them unconscious, or worse, without allowing them to cry out. A shout would bring the whole village on the run. It would also doom poor Flavius.

Hoodoo Tom drew a flintlock and curved his thumb around the hammer. "I can pick those buzzards off before they take a step," he boasted.

"No!" Davy whispered.

The foremost warrior tilted his head, as if he had heard. The man listened for a bit, then gave a shrug and addressed the other. They tramped down the slope, the doe swaying from side to side.

"You should've let me kill the varmints," Hoodoo Tom complained.

"And what about my friend?" Davy said.

"Oh. Him. I plumb forgot." Smirking, the trapper said, "I wouldn't want your partner to be harmed on my account."

The warriors bearing the deer were greeted by four others and a tall woman. In short order the doe had been butchered and was being roasted over an open fire. The entire tribe gathered, women bringing vegetables and other dishes.

"It's a celebration of some sort," Hoodoo Tom guessed.

Until sunset the Old Ones ate and drank and lounged and laughed. Davy counted thirty-one, six of them with white hair. But not a single child was present.

Torches were lit. A procession of six robed figures climbed recessed steps to the top of the birdlike mound and started a fire in the center. Forming a circle, they linked hands and commenced to chant.

Hoodoo Tom pried the bushes apart for a better look. "Must be callin' on the Great Mystery," he observed. "Pretty soon drums will start up, I bet. I ain't seen an Injun ceremony yet that didn't include 'em."

The mountain man was right. Shortly, the vibrant pulse of drumbeats rumbled across the valley. Not very loud initially, they rose in volume as the rest of the tribe assembled on the mound. Masked figures began to prance and dance in time to the tempo.

Hoodoo Tom was all teeth. "We're lookin' on something no other white men have ever witnessed."

Ordinarily, Davy would have shared the oldster's excitement. But he had Flavius to think of, and as yet, there had been no sign of him.

During the afternoon Davy had memorized the lay

of the land between the hill and the mounds, and the positions of the three mounds in relation to one another. Every tree, every shrub, every gully was equally important.

Stars speckled the heavens. The chanting rose to rival the drums as other Old Ones joined in.

Davy fidgeted with impatience but did not move yet. If the Creeks were any example, the ceremony would last until late. There was plenty of time.

Hoodoo Tom had acquired a wooden sliver and was picking at his yellow teeth. "This reminds me of the time I was spyin' on some Arapahos," he mentioned. "They'd traded for liquor, and by mornin' they were so fuddled, not one could stand."

"Why were you spying on them?" Davy asked, his gaze on the bird mound.

"One of the bastards had something I hankered after," Hoodoo Tom said, and patted his pack.

The crisp night air throbbed to the raw rhythm of the drums, the chorus swelling and tapering much like ocean surf. Most of the Old Ones were stomping their feet and parading clockwise around the fire. One, an ornately garbed figure wearing an immense headdress in the likeness of a bird of prey, was leaping and bounding in mad abandon that grew wilder and wilder.

"That feller must be actin' the part of a piasa," Hoodoo Tom said. "Saw some Cheyennes doing the same thing years ago. One of their warriors was dressed up as a white buffalo, complete with horns and a tail."

Davy stood. With all the Old Ones involved in the ceremony, he could check the lodge mound for Flavius. "I'm going," he announced.

"Wait for me," Hoodoo Tom said. To Davy's surprise, he left the pack where it was.

"You're not bringing it?"

"Hell, no. I don't want my treasures to fall into the hands of those heathens. George would never forgive me."

Rather than follow the trial, Davy angled to an oak partway down. Scattered trees and brush provided sufficient cover for him to reach the bottom undetected. He made no more noise than would a field mouse. Nor, to the man's credit, did Hoodoo Tom.

Flickering, writhing shapes were cast on the valley floor by the roaring fire atop the bird mound. The rectangular mound was on its left, and Davy swung wide to approach from the opposite side. He never took his eyes off the ceremony for long, for he never knew when one of the Old Ones might turn to stare across the valley.

As it was, Davy should have paid more attention to the shadowy base of the great lodge. For as he came within a stone's throw, a bulky silhouette detached itself from the mound.

Davy froze so unexpectedly that Hoodoo Tom bumped into him. They were in the open, the nearest cover twenty yards to their left. Exposed and vulnerable, they watched, aghast, as an antlered warrior moved toward them.

"We're goners!" the trapper whispered.

As if to accent the point, on top of the bird mound someone yelled shrilly and pointed in their direction.

Chapter Six

Flavius Harris was stupefied by the men with antlers until he realized the antlers were part of a headdress. A long exchange took place between the trio and those who had brought him to the village. Other Indians joined in. Soon he was surrounded by dozens.

Flavius stood quietly, smiling meekly at one and all to demonstrate his peaceable intentions. None returned his smile. But it was encouraging that they did not abuse him with taunts and blows. They acted more curious than anything else.

The hubbub died when a white-haired man arrived. He was dressed in a flowing robe adorned with the biggest feathers Flavius had ever beheld. Judging by the reception, Flavius figured that the newcomer must be a tribal leader.

The chief listened to the stately woman and another warrior, then stepped up to Flavius. Intense, smoldering eyes raked him from head to toe.

Gnarled fingers plucked at his hunting shirt, at his possibles bag, at his belt. Comments were made.

It was impossible for Flavius to determine whether the leader was kindly disposed, or otherwise. Smiling wider than ever, he tried to catch the man's eye, but the chief went on with the examination.

A warrior produced Flavius's weapons. His knife was openly admired. His pistols and rifle were treated with cold disdain, tinged with a smidgen of fear.

At a word from the leader, two antlered warriors clasped Flavius by the arms and ushered him to the rectangular mound. He thought they were going to take him to the top, but to his astonishment, they walked to the base and parted a cleverly disguised hanging.

It was a hide with the hair still on, dyed green to resemble grass. So expert was the dye job that even close up, Flavius mistook it for solid ground.

A warrior pushed him. Flavius nearly stumbled going through the doorway. A dank, earthy scent assailed his nostrils, mixed with an odor reminiscent of pine needles.

Sunlight streaming in revealed a small chamber with no other exit or opening of any kind. The flap was closed, plunging Flavius into inky gloom. Moving to the hide, he parted it just enough to see out.

The husky warriors had taken up posts, arms folded. Immobile as statues, they stared into the distance. Escaping was out of the question.

Flavius slumped to his knees. A fine pickle he was in! Somehow, he must convince these Indians that he meant no harm, and persuade them to let him go.

The morning dragged, weighted by millstones of tearing anxiety. The tribe went on about their daily activities. Women worked in a nearby field tilling the soil, or tanned hides, or sewed, or sat and talked. Warriors crafted weapons or sharpened knives or took part in an activity that prickled Flavius's scalp.

It started when the women filled a basket with overripe melons. A somber man carried it to an open space between the mounds. Twenty feet away, nine warriors lined up, their war clubs in hand.

The man snatched a melon, held it a moment, then yipped and threw it in a high arc. It was a signal for the first warrior to barrel forward, cocking his arm. As the melon swept lower, the warrior swung. His timing was impeccable. The club connected solidly, smashing the melon to bits.

And so it went. Each warrior had a turn, then moved to the end of the line to try again. Sometimes the melons were pulped. Sometimes they were impaled by the nasty spikes that protruded from the bent clubs. Not one warrior missed.

Flavius imagined what one of those clubs would do to his noggin, and gulped. Unarmed, he wouldn't last two seconds out there.

The practice session had been over about an hour when a familiar figure approached bearing a bowl and a jug or pitcher. It was the stately woman who had been with the party that captured him.

Seeking to earn her goodwill, Flavius held the hide aside and beamed. She hesitated, a glance at the guards giving her the confidence to pass through.

Flavius extended his hand. "Howdy, ma'am. Flavius Harris is my handle. Do you savvy English, by any miracle?"

The woman put the bowl and jug down in the center of the chamber. Her blank expression was an eloquent answer. Moving to the hide, she bunched it, looped an attached cord, then tied the cord to a peg in the wall, a peg Flavius had not known was there. She gestured for him to sit.

Vegetables and jerked deer meat filled the bowl. Flavius stuffed a tomato into his mouth and ate with relish. Lifting the jug, he sniffed. A taste of the cool water relieved his dry throat and mouth. "I'm grateful, ma'am," he said.

The woman stood near the doorway, quizzing him in her singsong tongue.

Frowning, Flavius shook his head. "I wish to high heaven I knew what you were saying," he said in earnest. Remembering Davy's encounter with the Sioux, he tried the finger language Davy had been taught.

Holding his right hand in front of his neck with the palm out and his index and second fingers pointed upward, Flavius raised his hand until his fingertips were as high as his head. It was the sign for "friend." Davy had made a point of teaching it to him, just in case.

The woman's eyebrows puckered and she tossed her head to show she did not understand.

Flavius did not give up. He clasped his hands in front of his body, the left hand down. This was sign talk for "peace." But again the woman indicated that she was at a loss. "Damn," he said aloud. "How am I ever going to convince you that I'm no threat to your people?"

The woman tapped a finger on her bosom and said the word "Illini."

"Is that your name?" Flavius said. Touching his chest, he repeated his first name several times.

Shifting, the woman pointed at one of the guards and said again, "Illini." Then at the other. "Illini."

Flavius caught on. It wasn't *her* handle. It was the name of her people. "Tennessean," he said, thumping himself, adding his full name for good measure.

With an effort, the woman pronounced, "Tennesseanflaviusharris." A tentative smile lit her lovely features.

Flavius did not have the heart to try to get it across that she had it all backward. "I reckon that'll have to do." Biting off a piece of jerky, he chewed while racking his brain for a means to communicate.

After saying something in her own language, the woman placed a finger against her forehead and said, several times, "Waneetoka."

"Is *that* your name?" Flavius said, and uttered it twice.

Again a smile lit the woman's face. Extending her arm, she indicated a white-haired warrior forty yards off, the same one who had inspected Flavius. "Matotonga."

"Matotonga," Flavius said.

Waneetoka faced the bird-shaped mound. Pointing at the top, she said soberly, "Piasa."

"Piasa."

The maiden bobbed her head at the sun, moved her left arm in an arc, and spoke at length. Flavius caught the words "Matotonga" and "piasa," but the rest was so much gibberish. He had the impression she was striving to tell him something important, and his failure to understand disappointed her.

Rather sadly, Waneetoka said, "Piasa," and fluttered her right hand as if it were a falling leaf. Suddenly she snatched at her left hand and tugged at it as if trying to tear it from her arm. Hopefully, she looked at him.

"My ears for a heel tap if I know what you mean," Flavius admitted.

Waneetoka came over, patted him on the shoulder, sighed loudly, and departed, leaving the food and drink. She left the flap open. Neither of the warriors bothered to close it.

Depressed, Flavius munched on his meal. He took his sweet time, stuffing the last of the jerky into a pocket to eat later. He also saved some water. There was no telling if or when his captors would see fit to feed him again.

The afternoon crawled by. The Illini stopped working at one point to congregate at the conical mound. Matotonga addressed them, twice pointing at the open doorway to Flavius's chamber.

Flavius grew edgy. The Illini had not harmed him or even threatened to, but he had a sneaking hunch he would not like what they had in mind.

Just then a strange thing happened. A frantic shout rang out. All eyes turned skyward, including those of the guards.

Flavius was more interested in a huge shadow rippling across the grassy tract to the northwest, a darkling silhouette like that of a bird, only ten times larger than the shadow of any hawk or eagle ever known. The shadow was so incredibly immense that Flavius decided it had to be a trick of the light. No real bird could be so enormous.

A hideous shriek sounded on high. A shriek like that of a red hawk, but so loud it hurt the ears. A shriek so inhuman and terrible, Flavius recoiled.

It had a similar effect on the Illini. They scattered, seeking cover. The warriors guarding Flavius nervously backed into the doorway.

Overcome by curiosity, Flavius stood and moved to the opening. Craning his neck, he glimpsed a gigantic aerial form as it soared over the rectangular mound. "What the devil?" he blurted.

A warrior grunted and pushed him back inside. Flavius took a step, eager for another glimpse, but both warriors raised their clubs, their meaning crystal clear.

The shrieking faded as its source flew south. After silence reigned, the guards went back out. A babble of excited voices drew Flavius to investigate. Most of the tribe had reassembled.

Matotonga, all smiles, was gesturing at the heavens, then at the birdlike mound. Flavius suspected that the mound and the creature that just flew over the village were somehow linked. And that the great bird's appearance had been taken by the Illini as a favorable omen.

Peace and quiet persisted thereafter. Flavius dozed, curled on his side. He slept fitfully. Any loud noises awakened him. A commotion late in the afternoon brought him to the door.

The village bustled with activity. People were going every which way. A constant flow of women proceeded to the top of the bird mound, carrying dead limbs. Firewood, Flavius reckoned.

A festive air animated the Illini. They went about their varied tasks happily, buzzing all the while.

It was hard to judge, but it must have been around four in the afternoon when Waneetoka approached with two other women in tow. One held a large bowl, the other had a cloth and a folded blanket.

Flavius patted his stomach, relishing another meal. Water was in the bowl, though. He stepped back as the women came in. The blanket was spread out, the bowl lowered beside it.

Waneetoka motioned for him to sit on the blanket. Flavius did so. The two maidens knelt on either side of him and the smaller of the two pressed her slender hand against his chest, pushing him onto his back.

When the other woman reached for the strap to his possibles bag and started to slide it over his head,

GET YOUR 4 FREE BOOKS NOW—
A VALUE BETWEEN $16 AND $20

Mail the Free Book Certificate Today!

FREE BOOKS CERTIFICATE!

YES! I want to subscribe to the Leisure Western Book Club. Please send my 4 FREE BOOKS. Then, each month, I'll receive the four newest Leisure Western Selections to preview FREE for 10 days. If I decide to keep them, I will pay the Special Members Only discounted price of just $3.36 each, a total of $13.44. This saves me between $3 and $6 off the bookstore price. There are no shipping, handling or other charges. There is no minimum number of books I must buy and I may cancel the program at any time. In any case, the 4 FREE BOOKS are mine to keep—at a value of between $17 and $20! Offer valid only in the USA.

Name_____

Address_____

City_____ State_____

Zip_____ Phone_____

Biggest Savings Offer!

For those of you who would like to pay us in advance by check or credit card—we've got an even bigger savings in mind. Interested? Check here. ☐

If under 18, parent or guardian must sign.
Terms, prices and conditions subject to change. Subscription subject to acceptance. Leisure Books reserves the right to reject any order or cancel any subscription.

GET FOUR BOOKS TOTALLY *FREE*—A VALUE BETWEEN $16 AND $20

Flavius slapped her hand. "Enough of that. You've taken everything else, but not this."

The woman called out. One of the guards filled the opening, his glare ample warning. Flavius took off the bag himself and gave it to the woman.

Embarrassed to his core, Flavius had to lie there while they stripped him nearly naked. They had trouble with his belt, having never worked a buckle before. At their prodding, he unfastened it, and soon his hunting shirt and moccasins had joined it on the floor.

The only female who had ever seen Flavius in his birthday suit was his wife. For a man to parade in the altogether in front of women he did not know was unthinkable. The canebrake stock from which he sprang were shy by nature and lived in dire dread of committing a mortal sin. So when the small Illini brazenly lowered her hands to his pants, he grabbed her wrists. "No, you don't! I draw the line here, missy!"

The woman yelled. Into the chamber rushed the guard, who elevated his war club.

"Bash my brains out if you like!" Flavius refused to be cowed. "But a man has got to have some dignity!"

The warrior took another step and would have swung if Waneetoka had not stepped between them. A flick of her arm, and the warrior reluctantly backed off. Kneeling, she gently pried Flavius's fingers from the other woman's wrists, then reached for his pants herself. Slowly, considerately, she peeled them from his body.

Flavius closed his eyes. If only this were a nightmare! If only he had never left Tennessee! In no time he was buck naked. Covering his manhood, he braced for the next indignity.

David Thompson

The feel of something hot on his chest made him yelp. Flavius sat up, or tried to, but the women would not permit it. Waneetoka had soaked the cloth in the bowl and was bathing him with hot water.

"Is this necessary?" Flavius squeaked. What possible purpose could they have for cleaning him up? Granted, it had been a while since his last bath, and maybe he was a mite whiffy, but it wasn't as if he smelled as bad as a buffalo in a wallow.

Waneetoka was most meticulous. She cleaned every square inch of skin, rubbing parts of him his own wife had never touched. Some men would have been aroused, but Flavius was so upset, his manhood shrank to the size of a shriveled carrot. His shame knew no bounds.

A brush was applied to his hair. Flavius couldn't remember the last time he had combed it, which accounted for the knots and tangles the woman had to deal with. He winced with each stroke.

Waneetoka finished bathing him. She rolled up his moccasins and possibles in his shirt, then rolled up the shirt in his pants. The bundle wound up by the entrance.

Flavius squirmed uncomfortably. The women rose, Waneetoka beckoning him to do likewise. Keeping a hand over his private part, he complied.

The small woman picked up the blanket and shook it. Boldly, she wrapped it around his waist, tucking the top in on itself to hold the blanket in place.

"Now what?" Flavius muttered. To his utter consternation, they wanted him to go outside. The guards were waiting, so he dared not dally.

No one paid much attention. Escorted by the warriors, Flavius shuffled toward the bird mound. He grasped the blanket so it wouldn't slip. Looking over his shoulder, he saw the two maidens leave. Wanee-toka lingered, gazing sorrowfully.

A series of shallow footholds had been gouged out of the sloped face of the earthwork. A warrior started up, and the other one poked Flavius with his club.

Flavius climbed carefully, taking little steps, afraid of losing his balance. With the blanket wrapped so tightly, his movement was limited anyway. Preoccupied with reaching the crest intact, he did not think to scan the valley until they were close to the top.

The vista took his breath away. Flavius had not fully appreciated how high the mound reared. From his lofty perch he could see for miles: the emerald sea of forest to the west, north, and east; the broken, speckled lowland to the south; the three spokes of the valley and the sparkling blue of the stream.

The warrior behind him jabbed him and motioned.

"All right. Hold your horses," Flavius complained. Scaling the final few steps, he discovered a rut eroded by the passage of countless feet over countless years. It brought him to the center of the mound, to a wide space corresponding to the belly of the giant bird. A mountain of firewood had been piled beside a broad fire pit charred black by previous fires. Off to the left sat large deer-hide drums.

The warrior poked him again.

Past the pit, four stakes had been pounded into the soil. The moment Flavius saw them, he halted, and was shoved with so much force, he tripped.

Roughly, the warriors seized him, focing him to lie down. The blanket was torn from his grasp. While one stood poised to strike, the other lashed his wrists and ankles to the stakes.

No! No! No! Flavius was tempted to scream. This

couldn't be happening! Surely the Illini did not intend to do what the stakes signified!

His circulation was cut off within moments. Numbness spread to his wrists, to his knees.

The blanket he had worn was thrown over him and spread out so that it entirely covered his body. Why, he could only guess. Then the warriors left.

Flavius listened to their footsteps grow fainter. Twisting his arms, he attempted to loosen his restraints. It restored enough circulation to flood him with pain, so he stopped.

The breeze ruffled the blanket but was not strong enough to blow it off. Flavius was glad. That huge bird might come back. Was that why the warriors had covered him?

Unbidden, every horror story he had ever heard about frontiersmen who met grisly ends by being tortured to death, paraded through his memory. The same fate, evidently, was in store for him.

Would he be equal to the occasion and die without crying out? Or would he weaken? Would he prove himself less than the man his father always wanted him to be?

As his pa had pointed out when he was a sprout, "A man can't always choose how his life will unfold, son, or the manner of his passing. But he can control how he meets that moment. Show the Harris backbone when your time comes. Don't be a coward."

Flavius had vowed to never let his pa down. But now, confronted by the imminent prospect of the worst sort of death, his resolve faltered. What if the Illini cut out his eyes? Or hacked off his tongue? Or his *manhood?* He had courage, but not *that* much.

He would cry out. He would blubber like a baby. He would beg for mercy. He just knew it.

The air grew chill. Through a fold in the blanket a

portion of the sky was visible. Twilight dimmed to night. Flavius lost all feeling in his limbs, and yearned to lose consciousness, as well. No such luck.

Shuffling footsteps announced the arrival of Illini. Flitting shades of lights hinted at torches. He heard voices and movement, and a noise that took him half a minute to identify as the clatter of dead tree limbs being tossed into the fire pit.

Flames engulfed the pyre with a whoosh. The light was so bright, it seemed to turn the night into day. Chanting broke out.

They were beginning the ceremony, whatever it was. Flavius vigorously bobbed his head, seeking to shift the blanket off his face so he could see. To his surprise, he succeeded, and regretted the move. He had been better off not knowing.

Six hooded figures ringed the fire pit, their hoods screening their faces from the dancing flames. Their guttural chants wafted on the wind, to be dimly echoed by the rampart of vegetation to the east. As they chanted, they hoisted their arms and jerked their bodies in odd, bird-type movements.

"Oh, God," Flavius whispered. Lying back, he stared blankly at the firmament. *Davy, where are you?* Crockett should have been there by now. Something must have happened to him.

The chanting grated on Flavius's nerves. But it was nothing compared to the stark dread inspired by the sound of more Illini climbing the mound.

One of the hooded figures moved to the drums. Hiking his sleeves, he brought the flat of his callused hands down on the skins in a staccato beat.

Turning his neck, Flavius saw Illini appear on the crest. They were dressed in their finest raiment. In somber procession they filed to the center, forming a circle. Some joined in the chant, then more, and more, until all of them were participating.

Flavius sought a friendly face in the crowd. Waneetoka was on his right. She studiously avoided looking at him, averting her face when he spotted her. In unison with the rest, she stomped her feet and moved clockwise around the fire pit—and him.

Soundlessly, the circle parted. Into the center pranced an Illini in the outlandish garb of an oversized bird. Mimicking the darting motion of a bird of prey on the attack, he leaped and bounded, flapping wings tied to his arms.

Birds again! Flavius thought. Everything the Illini did dealt with birds. They had built the massive bird mound. They wore feathers in their clothes. They imitated birds in their rituals. What connection did it all have to the huge bird that had flown over the village?

The prancing dancer hopped to the blanket and cast it off. For once, Flavius did not care that he was naked to the world. A jarring thought had petrified the blood in his veins. He remembered the pantomime Waneetoka had performed that afternoon with her hands. She had been striving to get an important point across, and now he knew what it was.

Just then the chanting died. Far to the northwest, so faint that Flavius would not have heard it if he had not been listening for it, the night was rent by a horrid shriek.

Chapter Seven

Davy Crockett snapped his rifle to his shoulder. Just in time, he realized that the warrior wearing the antler headdress was hurrying toward the bird mound, not toward Hoodoo Tom and him.

More shouts rose from the crest. Glancing up, Davy discovered that the Old Ones were pointing at the *sky*, not downward. Why would they do that? Pivoting, he scanned the starry canopy but saw nothing out of the ordinary.

Then a faint shriek wavered on the stiff breeze. The Old Ones fell silent. In the remote distance a speck appeared, a speck that expanded rapidly in size, blotting out stars. Its shrieks grew correspondingly louder.

Davy gaped as the ebony outline of an enormous bird took definite shape, a bird so gargantuan that it defied belief.

The creature swooped in low over the bird mound.

The glow cast by the fire etched a flashing image of wings as long as canoes, of a body as thick around as a bear's, of a great hooked beak and talons the size of a man's hand.

"It can't be!" Davy gasped.

The bird banked to make a pass over the village, voicing another unearthly cry.

Hoodoo Tom took an awestruck step backward. Forgetting himself, he flung an arm skyward and exclaimed, "The piasa! I told you! I was right about it!"

Davy lunged to clamp a hand over the trapper's mouth, but the harm had already been done.

The warrior moving toward the bird mound spun, spied them, and charged, voicing a war whoop that was drowned out by yet another thunderous shriek from the piasa or Thunderbird or whatever it was.

Davy palmed his tomahawk. There was still a chance. If he could dispatch the warrior without alerting the Old Ones up on the mound, his search for Flavius could continue. Risking a glance at the crest, he was momentarily riveted by the spectacle of the Thunderbird hovering fifty or sixty feet above the mound, its mighty wings beating fiercely, its talons extended, as if it were about to plunge straight down at prey. Incredibly, the Old Ones were not fleeing for their lives.

Insight flooded through Davy in a rush of cold terror. The bird mound! The feathered robes! He should have seen it sooner! The Old Ones weren't fleeing because they *wanted* the piasa there. The bonfire, the pounding of the drums, the loud chanting, they were all designed to lure the creature to the village. They were conducting a sacrifice! But the offering was certainly not one of their own.

Flavius! Davy thought, taking a few swift steps, forgetting all about the onrushing warrior. The blast of a rifle brought reality crashing down on his shoulders.

The warrior clutched at his chest, staggered a few yards, and toppled, voicing a vibrant death wail with his last breath. Up on the mound, the faces of the Old Ones nearest the rim bent down. And the piasa, with a cry different from its hunting shriek, wheeled abruptly up into the darkness. Gaining altitude with astounding speed, it flew to the northwest.

It's leaving, Davy realized. His elation, though, was short-lived. For with a roar of outrage and bloodlust, the Old Ones flooded over the side.

"Uh-oh," Hoodoo Tom said. "I think they're a mite mad at us, hoss."

Swearing, Davy whirled. "Come on!" he hollered, and ran westward. They had a substantial lead, but the Old Ones knew the lay of the land. Finding somewhere to hide was crucial. He bestowed a wistful glance at the bird mound, wondering if his hunch about his friend being up there was true.

The man who could confirm it gawked for joy as the Illini raged over the rim. Flavius thought his time had come when that demon bird hovered directly over him, about to plummet. He had grit his teeth to keep from screaming, and closed his eyes.

The rifle shot had sent a tingle down his spine. So far as he knew, the only guns in the whole village were his own, confiscated by the Illini. He had not seen any of the warriors carrying them, so the shot must mean someone else was there! And the only one he could think of was Davy!

Now the bird was gone, and the Illini, in their rabid fury at having their ceremony spoiled, were racing pell-mell down the mound, not bothering to leave a guard.

David Thompson

A hand fell on his shoulder. Startled, Flavius shifted. Waneetoka was next to him, sadness mirrored in her lovely eyes. She said something and nodded at the sky.

Flavius had to wet his lips before he could speak. "Will that monster come back? Is that what you're trying to tell me?" He strained, trying to rise higher. "Help me, please," he pleaded. "You're not like the rest. I can tell. Don't let me die like this."

Waneetoka looked at the rim. The last of her people were going down the steps. Reaching into the long sleeve of her feathered dress, she pulled out a slender knife and placed the carved hilt in his right hand.

"I can't move my arms," Flavius said. "You'll need to cut the rope for me."

Tenderly touching his cheek, Waneetoka rose and hastened toward the steps.

"Wait!" Flavius called. "Don't leave me like this! I can't do it myself!"

At the crest, Waneetoka paused. Smiling, she gave a little wave, then dipped from sight.

"No!" Flavius shouted. "For the love of God! Come back! Come back!"

All alone now, Flavius blinked away tears of frustration. He could barely feel the knife, his hand was so numb. Grunting with the exertion, he twisted so he could see the stake. As carefully as he could, he applied the sharp edge of the blade to the rope and began to saw back and forth.

His frustration mounted. He was so weak, the knife only sliced through a single strand of hemp.

"No, no, no," Flavius said in desperation. Unless he could restore his circulation, the gift was useless.

Flavius began to wrench his body from side to side as far as the ropes allowed. At first he felt little except a slight tingling in his shoulders. But the more he did it, the more sensation returned. The tingling became a dull ache. The dull ache became stabbing pain. The stabbing pain became acute agony that flared up both arms and down both legs.

The torment was nigh unendurable. Flavius clamped his jaws to keep from screaming. Deathly afraid that the Illini would return at any moment, he threw his whole weight into each twist, regardless of the result.

Much too slowly, feeling returned to his wrists and fingers. He wriggled his hands, clutching the knife as firmly as he could, fearful of dropping it.

At last Flavius applied the blade to the rope with renewed vigor. This time he sliced through a quarter of it with no problem. But the angle was such that cutting through the rest would take considerable effort.

Muscles lanced by searing pain, Flavius hacked repeatedly. Perspiration drenched him. His hand grew unbearably sore. His fingers began to lose their newfound strength. He was on the verge of collapsing when the last strand parted.

His right arm was free! His body demanded rest, but Flavius turned to his left wrist. He made short shrift of the rope, then propped himself up off the ground. A gust of cool wind invigorated him. Tucking at the waist, he slashed the hemp that bound both ankles.

Flavius rose unsteadily and took halting steps. Dizziness afflicted him, threatening to suck him down into a whirlpool of darkness. Resisting, he steeled his mind and made it to the top of the steps.

The body of a warrior lay sprawled in the open. To the west, the Illini were clustered, sweeping across the valley like a herd of buffalo gone amok. They were probably after Davy, Flavius mused.

The village appeared to be deserted. He descended, using his hands as well as his feet. At the bottom he leaned against the earthwork to catch his breath.

A distant cry galvanized Flavius into running to the great lodge. Whether the cry had been human or not was hard to judge. Either way, he had to get out of there while he still could.

His clothes were right where Waneetoka had placed them. After unwrapping the bundle, Flavius dressed and slipped his possibles bag over his shoulder. It was too bad he didn't have his pistols and Matilda!

Outdoors, Flavius breathed deeply. He started westward, halting when he recalled seeing one of the Illini carrying his guns toward the east end of the lodge.

Should he or shouldn't he? Flavius looked back, then sped east. At the base, he groped along the wall, seeking dyed hides. Finding one, he shoved it wide.

Bathed in the faint glow from the roaring fire was a spacious chamber filled with furnishings: mats, blankets, pottery vessels, baskets, a cradleboard, a long pestle, spoons, a bow and quiver, a pair of rackets like those the Seminoles used in ball games, and more. Nowhere did he see his belongings.

Flavius went on. His probing fingers roved over a depression as wide as a typical doorway, but it was solid earth. Had one of the chambers been filled in? The mystery would remain unsolved. He was running out of time.

At the next hanging, Flavius yanked, almost ripping it off. The chamber was similar to the other, only more lavishly adorned. Someone of importance lived here, perhaps Matotonga. Flavius scoured the interior and was about to back out when objects propped in a far corner caught his eye. They had a dull metallic sheen and poked above a blanket that had been draped over them.

His heart hammering, Flavius flung the blanket off. Underneath were Matilda, both of his flintlocks, his powder horn, and his ammo pouch. In addition, there were two other rifles, another set of pistols, as well as two more powder horns and ammunition pouches. Evidently, he was not the first white man the Illini had taken captive.

Flavius crammed all four pistols under his belt, slung his powder horn and ammo pouch across his chest, then grabbed Matilda and another Kentucky rifle. With renewed confidence, he bustled out and sprinted across the village.

Rather than go westward and maybe run into returning Illini, Flavius bore to the south, planning to turn west later.

Words could not describe how wonderful it felt to be alive! The air seemed fresher. The night seemed more filled with stars than ever before. His only regret now was that Davy was in the frying pan instead.

Davy Crockett shared those sentiments.

Loping along the narrow trail to the top of the hill, Davy stopped so Hoodoo Tom Fitzgerald could catch up. A hundred feet from the bottom, a tide of maddened Old Ones stormed in their wake, venting savage whoops. Farther back were several white-haired figures, elders whose stamina was not equal to the chase. Even farther away was a solitary runner, a woman, Davy thought.

Puffing like a steam engine, Hoodoo Tom clasped his ribs. "Whooee, boy! Them fellers sure can run! They must be part antelope."

"Hurry," Davy coaxed, moving toward the forest.

"Don't get your britches in an uproar," Hoodoo Tom said, and darted to the bushes they had hid behind all day. "I'm not leavin' without my treasures."

The Old Ones were almost to the bottom of the hill. In the lead were five or six of the fleetest warriors, who sensed their quarry was close and had pulled ahead.

"We don't have the time!" Davy warned.

Hoodoo Tom pushed through the weeds, hunting, hunting. "I know we left 'em here, somewhere. Where can they be?"

Davy drew a pistol. The warriors would soon be in range. "I'm leaving," he announced, "whether you come or not."

The trapper glanced sharply at him. "I thought we'd partnered up, boy. You ain't one those backstabbers, are you?"

"Come on!"

"Damn, but you're testy." Hoodoo Tom parted a patch of weeds. "Ah! Here are my little darlin's! George would never forgive me if I left 'em for the heathens to find." Leaning over, he shrugged into the pack, but it snagged on his left shoulder and would go no lower. "Tarnation. You'd think a man my age would know how to put on a backpack."

Three of the warriors were halfway up. Davy darted to the mountaineer, gripped the snagged strap, and pulled, nearly knocking the trapper off his feet.

"Careful, Tennessee! George don't like to be jostled."

Dave shoved, propelling the oldster toward the tree line. "Just run!" he said, and plunged into the benighted woods himself, dodging tree trunks and random obstacles, sacrificing stealth for speed.

Hoodoo Tom was breathing hard. "Damn, Irish!"

he complained. "A man could bust his neck this way!"

"Would you rather the Old Ones got their hands on you?"

That shut Hoodoo Tom up. On through an inky realm of stygian growth they fled, weaving around thickets and ducking low limbs and vaulting logs. Blackness cloaked them. It was their salvation and their bane. For no matter how agile they were, they could not avoid everything. Branches tore at them, thorns lashed them. They were jabbed and pricked.

A branch gashed Davy's face, nearly spearing an eye. He never broke stride. To their rear the undergrowth crashed and crunched. The Old Ones were not about to give up anytime soon. Whether he survived depended on his endurance. He simply had to outlast them. Him, and Hoodoo Tom.

Hoodoo Tom! Davy glanced both ways. The trapper was gone! Shocked, he slowed, checking behind him.

Forty feet away a brawny shape barreled toward him, a war club uplifted.

"Tom!" Davy bellowed. Receiving no answer, he resumed his flight. Whatever had happened, the trapper was on his own until Davy could shake the Old Ones. Which might prove to be more of a challenge than he had counted on. The warrior behind him was narrowing the distance at a rate that would put a Creek to shame.

Davy knuckled down, running flat out. It soon became apparent that he could not elude his bronzed pursuer. His only recourse was to turn at bay. But where?

A clearing mushroomed ahead. Davy reached the center and pivoted, discarding his spent rifle. Automatically, he grasped a pistol. A shot, though, would bring the others right to him. His hand switched to the tomahawk.

Out of the brush burst the Old One, war club sweeping down in a blow that would have caved in the thick skull of a grizzly bear. Davy countered with his tomahawk, the impact jolting his shoulder. Separating, they circled, taking each other's measure. Off in the woods, dry leaves crackled. Other Old Ones would soon show up.

The warrior feinted, rotated, and drove his war club at Davy's temple. Parrying, Davy skipped to the right and swung, down low.

The tomahawk sheared into the man's leg below the knee, clear to the bone. Blood spurted in a geyser. It had to hurt abominably, yet the warrior made no outcry. Nor did he slacken his attack. Shifting onto his good leg, he drove the war club at Davy's face, the spike lancing at Davy's left eye.

Davy barely evaded the blow. He felt the spike brush his coonskin cap as he brought the tomahawk around and in, burying it in the Old One's stomach.

A low grunt was the only sound the warrior uttered. Jerking backward, he pressed a hand over the wound, set himself, and waded in again with his war club flailing.

Davy backpedaled, countering, blocking, dodging, amazed his adversary could go on fighting. What manner of men and women were these Old Ones? How could they absorb so much punishment without complaint?

Thinking distracted him, and he paid for it. His heel caught on a clump of weeds. Before he could regain his balance, he fell, landing hard on his back.

Instantly, the warrior seized the advantage. He pounced and brought the war club down with both hands, seeking to prevail by sheer brute strength.

Davy did not even attempt to ward off the club. He rolled and heard it thud into the soil beside him. Kicking out, he sent the Old One flying. It bought him enough time to scramble erect.

Among the trees, dry brush crackled. More Old Ones were closing in, fast.

His foe hobbled toward him, warily, wagging the club. It dawned on Davy that maybe the warrior was deliberately stalling, holding him there until the others arrived.

Davy took the fight to the Old One, raining the tomahawk down again and again. The warrior retreated under the onslaught, favoring his hurt leg. Davy slid to the left, and when the warrior swung to confront him, he reversed direction, chopping into the wounded leg again, but this time into the thigh.

The leg gave way. The warrior pitched forward, flinging an arm out to grab Davy's shoulder. Davy swatted it off and sprang to his rifle. As he uncoiled, the Old One finally found his voice and yelled at the top of his lungs to bring the rest.

Davy ran past. It would have been child's play to finish the warrior off, but the man was down, helpless, and it had never been in Davy's nature to kill someone who could not defend himself.

The vegetation closed around him. Across the clearing, three warriors materialized. Even though the wounded man pointed, showing them which way to go, Davy did not regret his decision. A man had to draw the line somewhere, or he wasn't much of a man.

Davy ran and ran, his legs tired, his lungs strained. If he pushed himself to his limit, and they caught him, he would be overpowered in no time. Time to rethink his strategy. Where stamina had failed him, his wits had better not.

David Thompson

A large log loomed out of the night, too large to leap over in a single bound. Davy had to jump on top, swing himself over, and drop beyond.

The Old Ones were uncomfortably close, twenty yards off at the most.

Davy took a step, then stopped. The tree had been uprooted, most likely by a storm. As it fell, it had torn out a massive chunk of earth on which it was propped a foot or so off the ground. Diving flat, Davy crawled under. It was a snug fit, but no one would spot him. He hoped.

Moccasin-shod feet pattered lightly. Davy saw one pair approach the log. Another pair bore wide to the south. A third warrior went to the north. They were moving briskly, but the one coming toward him unaccountably slowed. Whispers were exchanged, and all three halted.

Davy knew what they were doing. They had lost track of him, so they were listening.

This was bad. When they did not hear anything, they would realize he had gone to ground and scour the area. As competent as they had proven to be, they were bound to find him.

More whispers. They fanned out, searching behind bushes and trees. The one nearest the log walked right up to it. His feet were so close, Davy could see the stitching along the edge of the sole.

The toes pointed toward the tree, then to the north, then to the south, proof the warrior was confused, that he had no idea where his prey had gotten to. Suddenly the feet vanished. The Old One had leaped onto the log.

Davy did not move, not even when an insect crawled onto his neck and up over his cheek, not even when tiny antenna or pincers brushed his eye.

A soft thud signaled that the warrior had dropped

to the opposite side of the log. His heels were inches from Davy's face. They rotated from right to left and back again. A whisper elicited a reply from the north.

The insect crawled onto the bridge of Davy's nose, then down over the end of his nose and *into* his right nostril. An irresistible urge to sneeze came over him, and he pinched his nose to stifle it. In doing so, he crushed the bug.

The movement, although slight, brought the warrior to a stop. The man's moccasins swung toward the log.

Had the warrior heard? Davy gripped a pistol, every nerve on edge as the Old One retraced his steps.

Off in the trees, a man called out softly. The warrior close to the log hesitated, but not for long. The crack of a twig catapulted him toward the source.

Davy exhaled, then disposed of the bits of bug. For the time being he was safe, which was small consolation. Flavius was still unaccounted for and might well be dead. Hoodoo Tom had disappeared and might be a captive. They were no better off than when he snuck into the village. All that effort for nothing. With the Old Ones aroused, it would be daylight before he dared poke his head out of his hiding place.

As if all that weren't enough to give a body gray hairs, he had to keep his eyes skinned for a creature more powerful and savage than any he had ever gone up against.

The Thunderbird.

Chapter Eight

It was dawn before Davy Crockett could leave his hiding place. The Old Ones roamed the forest until shortly before sunrise. Half a dozen times, searchers came within yards of the fallen tree.

No shots resounded the entire night long. No shouts shattered the quiet. Davy took that as a good omen, a sign that the Old Ones had not gotten their hands on Hoodoo Tom Fitzgerald.

As for Flavius, Davy didn't know what to think. Recalling the events of the previous afternoon, he recollected seeing a heavyset man that might have been Flavius climb to the top of the bird mound, along with two warriors. But since the man had worn a blanket, not buckskins, and since the distance had been too great for Davy to note more details, he'd assumed it was another Old One.

Where was Flavius now? That was the critical question. The ceremony had been spoiled. The piasa had flown off. So Flavius must still be in the tribe's clutches.

Davy's course, then, was clear. But the Old Ones were stirred up. Sneaking close to the village without being caught would be like trying to get close to a hive of riled hornets without being stung.

Still, he had to do it. If there was one trait his father had most impressed on him when he was knee-high to a calf, it was that "a Crockett never shirks his duty." Crocketts saw what had to be done, and they went out and did it.

John Crockett had certainly set a sterling example. As a frontier ranger during the war for independence, Davy's pa had risked life and limb more than once against British regulars, turncoat Americans, and bands of Indians partial to the English.

Was it any wonder freedom meant so much to the backwoods folk of Tennessee? And those of every other state, for that matter? Many of the heroes who had fought in the war were still alive, their sacrifice as fresh as the day they took up arms on behalf of the colonies.

But now, as Davy crawled out from under the tree and crept off through the forest, thoughts of freedom and the revolution were supplanted by the most basic of human instincts: self-preservation. His whole attention was focused on the thick vegetation, on shadows where warriors might lurk, on furtive movements and faint sounds.

Davy hiked for hundreds of yards without mishap. He had not realized how far he ran the night before, and seeing how rugged the land was in the full light of day, he marveled that he had not broken a leg, or worse.

His face grew hot. A burning sensation in his chest brought him to a stop. Alarmed, he leaned against a maple and touched a hand to his brow. Daily he dreaded that he would suffer another bout of the mysterious illness that had laid him low several times, once almost proving fatal.

No one could tell him what it was. None of the doctors he went to had been able to pinpoint the cause. Prolonged exertion brought it on, which was why he made a point of getting enough rest, and always eating enough.

But he had not slept last night. And his last meal had been two days ago.

Tensely, Davy waited. The first symptoms were always fever and weakness in his legs, weakness that spread rapidly throughout his body, rendering him helpless, so feeble he could barely lift a finger.

This time, fate spared him. His brow cooled. He could breathe again.

In a crouch, Davy moved on, veering to the south slope of the hill. It was choked with blackberry bushes. To reach the bottom he had to negotiate a thorny maze.

The screech of a blue jay brought him to his belly, and he did not go on until he was sure that the jay had not squawked at roving Old Ones.

The morning sun lent the valley a pristine quality that belied the horror spawned by darkness. Davy climbed into an oak. Here and there Old Ones moved about the village. Most were missing, perhaps asleep after their all-night search.

Descending, Davy worked his way along the tree line to more open, broken country. He was watching the mounds, and almost committed a serious blunder. Voices stopped him just as he stepped from cover. Quickly, he ducked behind a patch of weeds.

Sixty feet away were eight Old Ones. A husky warrior was on one knee, examining the ground. At a gesture from him, the war party filed southward at a brisk jog, the tracker well in the lead.

On hands and knees Davy advanced to the same spot. Their feet had tramped on the spoor they followed, but Davy found a partial print that spurred him into flying after them.

No two people made identical tracks. Footprints were as unique as signatures. And Davy knew the one he had found as well as he knew the back of his hand. Sometime during the night, Flavius had escaped! The Old Ones were in pursuit.

Being in the open bothered him. Davy constantly checked the sky for sign of the Thunderbird. Once, a large speck appeared and his heart skipped a beat. The speck was only an eagle, though.

Stands of trees were broken by meadows and gullies. The Old Ones forged silently on, pausing every so often for the tracker to examine the sign. A mile from the village the trail bore to the right.

Davy had figured it would, eventually. His friend was making for the Mississippi. Flavius enjoyed a substantial lead on the Old Ones, but now they picked up the pace, moving three times as fast as Flavius ever could. Davy was hard-pressed to keep up.

The broken country gave way to lowland, which in turn was bordered by marshy tracts that fringed the river. Stretches of shallow water had to be waded. Bogs and deep holes had to be avoided, along with scores of slithering snakes.

Judging by how adroitly the Old Ones wended through the marsh, they had been here before. All Davy had to do was walk where they walked, skirt whatever they skirted, and he was safe.

His main worry was that Flavius, who had covered

the same ground in the gloom of night, might not have fared as well.

Little did Davy know that his concern was justified.

At that moment, Flavius Harris was up to his chest in muck. Thick, clinging mud held him in a reeking vise that he could not, for the life of him, break.

Flavius stared forlornly at a low limb, just out of reach. Everything had been going so well until he blundered into the bog. In the dark, covered as it was with moss and tufts of grass, he had mistaken it for solid ground. Two steps was all it had taken to sink to the waist. Twisting, he had tried to regain the bank, but he could barely move his legs.

Flavius had sunk another four inches between then and daylight. Thankfully, he had not gone under any farther. Neither could he reach the limb, although he attempted over and over to snag it with his rifle.

Now Flavius licked his dry lips and squinted at the blazing sun. Exhaustion nipped at him. Drowsiness plagued him. His only consolation was that he had given the Illini the slip.

Plants growing along the edge of the bog rustled. A blunt brown head emerged, a snake whose red forked tongue darted in and out.

Flavius trained his rifle on it. This was the fourth or fifth he'd seen, but the others had not come so close. As the serpent slid forward, he cocked Matilda's trigger. Whether the reptile was poisonous or not, he had no idea. It was a snake. That was enough.

The thing glided out onto the bog. Slitted orbs regarded him coldly. Maybe it thought he was a small animal, since most of his body was under the muck. He sighted on the head.

Mississippi Mayhem

"Go away!"

At the sound of his voice, the serpent coiled.

"Shoo!" Flavius said. "Scat, or so help me, you're dead!" The other rifle, the one he had taken from the great lodge, lay on the bank six feet away, where he had thrown it after becoming stuck.

Tongue flicking, the snake sidled nearer.

"Suit yourself, damn you," Flavius said, and stroked the trigger. The retort rolled off across the marsh, startling storks into flight.

Well to the east, Davy Crockett stiffened. That had to be Flavius. The Old Ones were bound to have heard, and would go even faster. He broke into a run.

Flopped onto its back, the snake twisted and churned in the grip of death throes. Over five feet in length, its slender body bore speckled scales.

Five feet. Flavius gazed at the low branch, gauging the distance. Maybe. Just maybe.

Gingerly, dreading he would miss, he chucked his rifle to the bank beside the other one. Then he slid the strap to his possibles bag off his chest and shoulder.

The strap was about three feet long from the top of the bag to its end. Alone, it was not long enough to reach the branch. But what if he added another two feet or so of makeshift rope?

Flavius flipped the bag at the snake. Several tries later, he aligned it just right and slowly dragged the dead reptile toward him. Skin crawling, Flavius picked the serpent up. Its skin was silken smooth. Squeezing the jaws apart revealed fangs typical of vipers.

Swallowing, Flavius looped the body of the snake around the end of the strap to his bag. Gripping the viper below the head and tail, he swung his arm from side to side, gaining momentum, the leather bag rising higher and higher.

On the apex of a swing, Flavius angled the bag at the tree limb. It caught, drooping over the far side. Afraid it would slip off, he pulled with both hands. Bit by bit, the branch bent toward him, its leaves shaking.

Flavius froze when the bag started to slide. Once it was still, he tugged gently. The limb angled lower, but it was not yet close enough.

"Just a little farther," Flavius breathed. "Don't fail me now!"

His body quivering, Flavius transferred his right hand from the snake to the strap, then his left. The serpent plopped next to him. Using both arms, he brought the branch nearer. Thrusting against the muck, he grabbed the end and held on.

Would the limb hold? Flavius inched his hand higher. Tensing his shoulder, he cautiously eased his body toward solid footing. The branch creaked but did not break. Slipping the possibles bag over his shoulder, he wrapped his other hand around the limb.

Painstakingly, Flavius hiked himself higher while pulling landward. The muck clung to him like a glove. Each leg seemed to be encased in iron. He had to pull on one, then the other, alternating so the weight of both combined would not put undue stress on the branch.

The bank was tantalizingly close. Flavius flipped the possibles bag onto it. Muck held him from the knees down, but its grip was weakening.

"Come on!" Flavius spurred himself. He tried not to think of the consequences should the limb snap.

Another few inches were gained. Flavius probed

with his right foot and found firm purchase. Taking a gamble, he threw himself at the bank. The muck encasing his left leg was like solid stone. It held on, refusing to give. For awful moments he teetered. Gravity won, and Flavius pitched onto his face, spongy grass breaking his fall.

"Hallelujah!" Flavius whooped.

In his opinion he'd earned a rest, so for a spell he lay there, his head pillowed by an arm. But the random thought that another viper might come along was sufficient to counter his lethargy.

Sitting up, Flavius took stock. His buckskins were a muddy mess, the four pistols caked and useless, his knife coated thick. The ammo pouch and powder horn were dry, but only because he had knotted their straps so they were above the mud shortly after he'd stumbled into it.

Palming a convenient stick, Flavius scraped at the muck on his right leg. A dip in clean water was in order as soon as he quit the bogs.

To the west a quarter of a mile, through a line of trees, glimmered the surface of the broad Mississippi.

Flavius would be there before too long. He pried mud off his moccasins and stood. Deeper in the marsh, the growth crackled to the passage of an animal in a hurry. Flavius rose on the tips of his toes and saw several figures wading through cattails.

There was not another moment to lose. Tossing the stick, a rifle in each hand, Flavius dashed over the bank. He sloshed through an ankle-deep, insect-infested pool. Dragonflies buzzed his head. Butterflies flitted over flowers.

The Old Ones had caught up. Flavius had tried to conceal his trail, but he was not as skilled in that regard as his Irish friend.

Hugging cover, avoiding bogs and snakes, Flavius came to a particularly large pool. Twenty-five feet across, the surface was choked by lilies. Frogs lined its shore.

Nervously, Flavius waded in. A lily pad on his left stirred as something moved underneath. "Another danged serpent," he muttered. Or was it a lot worse? Were there gators in that neck of the woods?

Every step tested Flavius's courage. When his foot slipped on mud, he backpedaled, terrified of being sucked under. Turning wide of the spot, he pushed lilies aside with the stock of the spare rifle. A green frog swam frantically away, rear legs pumping. A tadpole, or a small fish, dived deep.

Flavius was a few feet from the water's edge when a mat of growth lining the shore bulged upward. The outline of a big creature took shape. Alligator or lizard or God-knew-what, Flavius didn't care. He was out of the pool in the blink of an eye.

The trees beckoned. Once among them, Flavius loaded both rifles. The pistols were too caked with mud to be of any use.

The Illini were after him. They were nearing the bog in which he had been caught. Suddenly an enormous shadow swept over the eight men and half of them glanced overhead. Flavius looked, but trees hid the sky.

Could it be? Flavius wondered. A shadow streaked over the treetops and he heard the pounding beat of mighty wings. Only one bird alive could make that much noise.

If the monster had shown up thirty seconds sooner, it would have spotted him crossing the pool.

Flavius turned to wade down river so the Illini couldn't track him, staying close to shore where the under growth would shelter him from their avian protector.

Or was the piasa more than that? Was the mound and their feathered garb and their fascination with the giant birds tribute paid an ally, or worship afforded a god?

The notion wasn't so far-fetched. Flavius had heard tell of tribes in South America that worshiped jaguars. And the Sioux regarded white buffalo as special.

Not losing sight of his pursuers, Flavius hastened away, pausing only to verify that none of the Illini had glimpsed him. That was when Davy appeared.

Keeping up with the band of Old Ones had proven a daunting chore. Davy had never met anyone who could move so swiftly for so long. They were tireless. Their feat was all the more daunting because the vegetation was unbearably thick, tearing at him like a thing alive.

He had lost sight of them for a while. Breaking from high grass, he saw them beside a bog, pointing and jabbering. Apprehensive that Flavius was trapped, or had already gone under, Davy moved closer. A high bank interposed. In order to see what they saw, he would have to scale a tree.

There was only one problem. Trees were few and far between, except on the other side of the marsh, and those that had taken root were short and gnarled and would not serve his purpose.

An Old One hollered. Another, linked by hand to several companions, waded down into the bog.

Davy had to see. A stunted tree on a knoll was his best bet. To reach it he crossed a pear-shaped pool that rose as deep as his waist. Leaning Liz against the trunk, he hoisted himself onto a low limb.

The warrior in the bog was probing its depths with a pole. Did they think Flavius was in there? Another warrior, the tracker, roved to the other side. Hunkering, he called out and pointed westward. The man in the bog was pulled out by his friends. Like a ravenous pack of wolves hot on a fresh scent, the Old Ones padded to the tracker. They consulted, then fanned out. Several kept glancing upward.

Why? Davy scanned the sky. Other than a few fluffy clouds and a flock of ducks on the wing, it was empty.

The tracker was threading slowly across the marsh. Davy would not lose them again. Dropping from the limb, he reclaimed Liz and paralleled the route taken by the Old Ones.

Deduction told Davy that his friend was nearby. Flavius's tracks had grown so fresh, the war party must be almost on top of him. Flavius was bound to put up a fight, and Davy needed to be ready to intervene.

An open tract unfolded before him. Scattered lilies dotted clear water no deeper than his knees. Briars and reeds separated him from the Old Ones, so he felt comfortable in venturing from concealment.

It would only take a minute to cross. What could happen in so short a time?

Davy moved slowly in order not to splash. Bypassing clusters of lilies where water moccasins might be hiding, he was halfway across before he realized that the Old Ones had stopped to study a grassy area fringing a pool. An opening in the brush revealed them. It also exposed him, and Davy immediately ran several yards, putting vegetation between them.

No one yelled. No war cries pealed.

Avoiding a large snapping turtle that fixed him with fierce eyes, Davy wiped a sleeve across his face.

The temperature had climbed dramatically. What he wouldn't give for a brief shower to cool things down.

As if in answer to his plea, the sunlight dimmed. A cloud had covered it, Davy reckoned. As he removed his coonskin cap, the breeze fanned his scalp. Stooping, he scooped a hand in the cool water and splashed it on his neck.

As Davy put his cap back on, someone appeared among the trees lining the Mississippi. Davy brought up his rifle. Stunned, he recognized Flavius. His fellow frontiersman was waving.

"What in the world?" Davy blurted, and motioned for Flavius to hide before the war party saw him.

Flavius waved again wildly. Davy took several strides, thinking that maybe his friend thought he was waving, too. Then it hit him. Flavius wasn't waving; he was frantically gesturing at the sky.

Too late, Davy saw that the shadow he mistook for a cloud had grown in size and was expanding by the second. The air pulsed to the swish of enormous wings as a shrill shriek drew his gaze to its source. Despite himself, he staggered backward.

The Thunderbird had found a new victim.

Chapter Nine

Twenty times larger than any eagle ever known, the aerial predator plummeted toward the Tennessean with its talons outstretched to rip and rend. It should not exist, yet it did. Legend made real. Monster given flesh. The piasa was a living wonder, so gargantuan, so dazzling, that Davy Crockett gaped at it in sheer astonishment.

Another hair-raising shriek snapped Davy out of his daze. He bolted to the right, spraying water everywhere. Twisting, he tried to bring up his rifle.

The Thunderbird was upon him. Its raking talons missed him by a few feet. Alighting in the pool, the creature snapped its beak at him while pumping its huge wings.

One of those wings caught Davy across the shoulders. It was like being kicked by a mule. Propelled toward the brush, he stumbled to his knees.

The piasa came after him, shrieking in baffled anger. Whereas in the air it was grace incarnate, on the ground the creature was awkward, ungainly, its short legs reducing its stride to small steps. Swaying from side to side, it extended its neck, its hooked beak seeking his flesh.

Davy scrambled upright and crashed through the reeds, into the briars. Barreling through them, scratched and bleeding, he turned to confront the Thunderbird.

Behind him, voices rose in alarm. Davy pivoted. In the extremity of the moment he had blundered on the Old Ones. But they had no interest in him. To a man, they gawked at the monstrosity smashing through the growth. Jabbering and pointing, they broke in fear, running every which way.

One collided with Davy, bounced off, and ran past the Thunderbird. Instantly, its iron beak swooped. A scream rattled from the warrior's throat as he was lifted bodily and shaken as a terrier might shake a rat.

Davy sped toward the river. Among the trees he stood a better chance of eluding the piasa. Some of the Old Ones felt the same way. They were also racing for the tree line.

A glance revealed that the Thunderbird had pinned the man it caught and was tearing at his abdomen. The bird jerked its head up, intestines dangling from its beak. The yells of the Old Ones turned it toward the river. Shrieking, it came after them.

Davy tripped. Flinging an arm out, he caught himself, heaved to his feet, and hurtled for cover. The bird made an awful racket, its feet pounding heavily, its wings fluttering.

The whole tableau was unreal. Yet it was happening. It was real, all right, but it was reality gone mad.

The wide eyes of the Old Ones showed that they

had no control over the creature they worshiped. They were just as likely to be its meal as a deer or elk or buffalo. Why they had not sought to slay the creature long ago, Davy could not fathom.

Flavius stepped into the open, Matilda tucked to his shoulder. He had seen the piasa circling high up in the sky, so high that it had been no more than a tiny speck, and he had tried to warn his friend. Then the monster had streaked down from the heavens like a living bolt of lightning. In dumbfounded horror Flavius had expected to see Davy torn limb from limb.

Now, with the bird hopping on the Irishman's heels, Flavius aimed at its chest, cocked Matilda, and fired.

At the crack of the rifle, the piasa slowed. Its head rose and it glared around. Suddenly straightening its wings, the bird bounded upward, flapped furiously, and rapidly gained altitude.

Flavius dashed to the spare rifle, propped against a bole. He brought it to his shoulder, but the monster flew above the trees, preventing him from getting a clear shot.

Davy paused next to him and clapped him on the shoulder. They traded looks that expressed their feelings at being reunited. Then Davy motioned at the milling Old Ones, who would not ignore them for long. "Let's get out of here!" he suggested.

They sped southward, staying among the trees where the Thunderbird was less likely to attack.

Flavius was overjoyed to be with Davy again. He couldn't wait to reclaim their canoe and sail on down the river, leaving this land of nightmare far behind. "Where's Hoodoo Tom?" he asked.

"I wish I knew," Davy said. His fervent hope was that the trapper had made it safely to their camp and was waiting for them to arrive. If not, he had an obligation to go back and hunt for him.

"How far do you reckon we are from the canoes?" Flavius asked. The farther they had to go, the higher the risk.

"I'm not sure," Davy conceded. To pinpoint their position, he needed to see the river. Veering toward it, he stopped under a willow growing a stone's throw from shore. Thirty feet out was one of the countless sandbars that lined the waterway.

No other landmarks were visible, but Davy seemed to recall passing that point, and made a calculated guess. "I'd say we have fourteen or fifteen miles to cover."

"That far?" Flavius said, aghast. It would take them the better part of the day.

"Afraid so."

Davy checked to their rear. The Old Ones had not given chase, which surprised him. Maybe, he reasoned, the Indians were as anxious to quit the area as they were. "We'll stay under the trees as much as possible," he proposed.

For nearly an hour the pair jogged steadily, until, on the bank of a creek that fed into the Mississippi, Davy halted to rest. Roosting on a handy log, he confirmed there were no openings in the foliage above.

Flavius seized the opportunity to clean the mud from his pistols and load all four. He related his ordeal, finishing with, "If it hadn't been for that maiden, I'd be a goner. Why do you suppose she went against the wishes of her own kith and kin?"

A bestial shriek brought Davy off the log. Where the creek widened at its junction with the river, a familiar shadow passed over the sunlit surface.

"Damn!" Flavius said. "It's still hunting us! What do we do?"

"We keep going. And never stray into the open."

Their trek proved daunting. Swampy stretches had to be crossed, deep creeks forded, tangled timber negotiated, always with an eye to the sky. Twice, the shrieks of the Thunderbird reminded them that it was still around.

It was late afternoon when Davy stopped beside a thickly weeded knoll. At the rate they were going, they would not reach the canoes until well after nightfall. "We'll rest a spell, then push on until we get there."

Flavius nodded and sank wearily against a tree. He had not slept since the night before last, and he did not know how much longer he could hold out. To make matters worse, he was hungry enough to eat a horse.

A beetle crawled past his leg. Remembering that some Indians ate insects, Flavius picked it up, regarded its hard wings and wriggling legs, and set it down, scrunching his face in distaste. He'd have to be half starved before he would pop one of those into his mouth.

Flavius sighed. Everything that could go wrong, had gone wrong. "Whose brainstorm was it, anyway, to take the river route?" he inquired innocently.

Davy did not take the bait.

"It sure enough wasn't *mine*," Flavius said. "If it was, I'd shoot myself in the leg so I'd suffer some for the grief I've caused my partner."

A retort was on the tip of Davy's tongue, but it died at the sight of furtive shapes bounding toward them from the north. "The Old Ones!" he exclaimed, rising.

"Who?" Flavius said, and saw the Indians himself. Snatching up his rifles, he headed across the creek. "They call themselves the Illini," he mentioned.

Davy wanted to kick himself for not being more

alert. The warriors were only seventy or eighty yards away. He sighted at the foremost, but held his fire. Better to wait until they were closer, when the shot counted more.

Again they fled. Hampered by the dense undergrowth and the weaving and wending of the Illini, Davy could not make an accurate count. Were there six? Or seven?

Flavius was not up to a sustained chase. His legs were leaden, his muscles sluggish. He concentrated solely on keeping up with Davy.

The land gradually rose. Rolling hills replaced the marsh, hills with slopes so steep that at the top of the first one, Flavius doubled over, wheezing like a bellows. "I can't go on like this," he gasped.

The warriors were at the bottom, spreading out. Davy needed to slow them down. Taking a hasty bead, he fired. The ball thudded into a tree inches from its intended target. All the Illinis promptly went to ground.

"Let's go," Davy urged. They could gain a bit if they flagged themselves.

Puffing, Flavius followed. Going down was a lot easier than climbing had been, but another hill had to be traversed, and then another, and another. His lungs were aflame with pain, his legs wobbly, when he cried, "I'm plumb tuckered out!" and staggered to a stop.

Below them was a gully that wound between the hills. Littered with pebbles, its steep sides afforded protection. "There!" Davy said. "We'll make a stand." Hurrying lower, he went over the rim in a rain of dirt and stones.

Flavius took his time. A sprained or busted ankle would be the death of him. Coughing, he swiped at the dust Davy had raised, then turned and peered over the shoulder-high rim. "Too bad Hoodoo Tom ain't here," he commented. He had scant fondness for the old-timer, but they could sure use another rifle.

Davy looked straight up. Trees grew close enough to the gully for overhanging limbs to partially shield them from the Thunderbird. It would have to be enough, because there was no time to seek a better spot.

Humans in antelope headdresses appeared on the hill's crest. Strung out in a line, they rushed lower, their tawny bodies visible now and then.

Flavius fixed Matilda on a tall warrior in the center. The man was armed with a bow, an arrow already nocked. Like the rest, he was scanning the opposite slope. It had not dawned on the Indians yet that their quarry had turned at bay.

Matilda spewed smoke and lead. Shot, the warrior clutched his ribs and fell headlong to the turf, rolling a dozen feet to come to rest against a pine.

Davy fired at the tracker. The man spun around, took three halting paces, then dived for cover. "He's only wounded," Davy groused at himself. Seldom did he miss a shot. He would *now*, of all times.

Yanking out the ramrod, Davy reloaded. First, he opened the powder horn and poured the proper amount of black powder down the muzzle. Next, he tamped a ball and patch into the barrel with the ramrod. Sliding the rod into its housing under the barrel, he propped Liz on the rim to steady his aim.

There was no one to shoot. None of the Old Ones had showed themselves.

"Where are they?" Flavius whispered.

"Working their way toward us" was Davy's guess. By creeping in close, the warriors could overwhelm them, engage in personal combat where their numbers gave the Illini a decided edge.

"They have to be there, somewhere," Flavius said anxiously. He looked for trembling leaves, rustling grass, bending boughs, anything. It was as if the earth had yawned wide and swallowed the war party whole.

Davy began to crawl from the gully. "Cover me," he said.

"Where in tarnation are you going?"

"To do the last thing they'd expect. I'm taking the fight to them." Sound logic, Davy believed. It would throw the Old Ones into confusion and deflect their attention from Flavius. Reaching a maple, he balanced on the balls of his feet.

Quiet reigned, quiet all the more unnatural because even the birds and other wildlife had stilled their tongues. Davy scoured the wooded slope. In this instance, the weapons the Illini were armed with would determine the tactics they adopted. Those with clubs would slink low to the ground so they could get close to the gully before charging, but those with bows needed to get higher in order to see *into* the gully to locate targets.

In the fork of a tree twenty feet off crouched a warrior, a long feathered shaft notched to a sinew string. The string twanged at the very instant Davy spotted the bowman. He ducked, the shaft thumping into the trunk above him and quivering loudly.

The Old One clawed at his quiver for another arrow. Davy centered on the man's torso. At the boom of his shot, the Illini was punched backward. Folded in half, he dropped like a rock, breaking a limb on his way down.

Another arrow flashed out of the vegetation, the barbed tip embedding itself a hand's width from

Davy's cheek. Skipping to the right, he circled a thicket and hunkered behind a stump. Three of the Illini had been hit, but that was no guarantee they were out of the fight. Wounded warriors were often as fierce as wounded panthers.

The rest would be more cautious. Try as he might, Davy could not locate a single one. He glanced toward the gully, but Flavius was no longer in sight. That bothered him. He reminded himself that Flavius was a grown man and could look out for his own hide. As silently as possible, he reloaded his rifle.

In the gully, Flavius thought he saw movement and swung Matilda, only to see a sparrow dart from a bush. He grinned at his jumpiness, and swallowed.

Where was Davy? Flavius wondered. He didn't like it that Crockett had gone into the trees. They should have stayed together so he could cover his friend's back, just like always. One day he wouldn't be on hand, and Davy would regret it.

The silence rattled his nerves. He'd much rather the Illini made a concerted rush. Being stalked by hostiles was worse than being attacked by a gator or a grizzly. A body never knew but when a knife might bury itself in his back, or a whizzing shaft would take out an eye.

Suddenly a shadow passed over him. Instinctively, Flavius ducked and whirled, tilting Matilda skyward in abject dread that the piasa was diving at him. But it was the sparrow, not the monster, winging up the slope. He sagged, his heart fluttering.

A scraping noise reminded Flavius that he should not take his eyes off the woods. Rising, he was startled witless to find himself staring a warrior in the face.

The man held a club. Whooping, he pounced.

Flavius had nowhere to go. Trapped in the narrow

gully, he could only retreat a few feet. The Illini crashed into him as Flavius brought up his rifle. They sprawled against the side, the war club ramming into the dirt next to Flavius's ear.

Swinging the stock up and around, Flavius clipped his foe on the jaw, jarring him. But it was not enough to force the man backward and give him room to draw his knife. The war club's second blow glanced off his shoulder.

Letting go of Matilda, Flavius grappled with the Illini. He clamped a hand on the man's wrist so the warrior could not swing the club. A knee caught him in the chest. A fist grazed his temple. A foot raked his shin. Still, he would not let go.

They turned this way and that, the Illini struggling to wrest his weapon free, Flavius doing all in his power to foil him.

A loose rock brought them both down. It was the warrior who slipped. Tottering, he grasped Flavius by the shoulder for support. But Flavius shrugged him off and the Illini's feet swept out from under him.

Flavius landed on top. Slamming his left knee into the man's gut while simultaneously gripping the war club and twisting sharply upward, he seized control of it. The Illini clutched at a knife hilt.

Hiking the club overhead, Flavius brought it down with all his strength onto the man's head. A crunch, a gurgled whine, and the muscular form became as limp as a wet rag.

Flavius cast the club down the gully, then rose unsteadily. Something buzzed by his right ear. An arrow overshot the gully by half a foot and sank into a tree trunk.

Hunkering, Flavius retrieved Matilda. He crabbed to the rim and peeked out, seeking the archer. He saw no one. Not the bowman, not any other Illini, nor his best friend.

"Davy, where the heck are you?" he whispered.

In the woods, the object of Flavius's anxiety was on his stomach, slinking toward a tree trunk half as wide as his cabin. He thought that he'd heard noises coming from the gully, but when he cocked his head, the only sound was the whispering breeze.

At the tree, Davy rose into a crouch. Somewhere a man groaned feebly. Propping his rifle against the bole, he jumped, wrapped both hands around a limb, and levered himself into a fork. Bending, he clasped Liz.

Davy carefully climbed higher, then moved around the trunk, stepping from limb to limb. He spotted the groaner. The bowman he had shot in the chest was flat on his back, a scarlet rivulet oozing from the wound to form a bright red puddle.

Where are the others? Davy clutched a limb above him so he could shift to another in front. To the southeast an Old One brandishing a bow briefly materialized, but melted into the vegetation a heartbeat later.

Davy stepped to another limb. Bushes rippled as the warrior slunk through them, but Davy could not see him clearly. Taking a bead on an opening the warrior would pass, he cocked the hammer and waited.

A scraping above him caused Davy to raise his head. It was hard to say who was more flabbergasted, he or the warrior clambering around the trunk higher up. They locked eyes. Davy snapped Liz upward, or tried to; the barrel struck another branch. As he changed position, the Illini shrieked like the Thunderbird, and sprang.

It was reckless. They were a good fifteen feet above the ground. A plunge from that height might not kill them, but suffering broken bones or internal bleeding was a distinct possibility.

Davy slid closer to the trunk to evade the warrior's outflung arms. Hampered by his precarious perch, he could not move fast enough. The warrior plowed into his right shoulder, bowling him over. Upended, Davy hurtled toward the hard earth below.

Exactly *how* hard the ground was, Davy found out. His left side absorbed the brunt. Pain flared in every sinew, along every bone. His consciousness spun. The world around him danced and dimmed. He was totally at the warrior's mercy. At any second a knife thrust or blow would finish him off.

Yet nothing happened.

By torturous degrees, Davy's awareness returned. The pain in his chest was terrible but bearable. Rolling onto his back, he tested his arms and legs. None appeared to be broken. His left side was numb, though, the sensation slowly coming back. Sitting up, he shook his head to dispel lingering cobwebs.

The Illini was also rising, sluggishly, befuddled, but rising nonetheless.

Davy groped for his rifle. Not finding it, he placed his hand on his tomahawk. Or where it should be, since the tomahawk was gone, too.

Teeth clenched, eyebrows knit, the Old One pushed to his knees. From a sheath attached to a cord he produced a glittering knife. His flinty eyes narrowed as he shuffled forward, growling words in his own tongue.

Davy shoved backward, wagging his arms to restore sensation and mobility. In his condition he was no match for the Illini, man to man. Drawing a pistol, he pointed it at the warrior's head.

The Old One froze.

"That's it," Davy said calmly. "Now do us both a favor. Round up your friends and cut out for your village. I'm sick and tired of all this bloodshed."

The Illini glanced at the flintlock, then at Davy.

"I just want to be left alone."

A sneer creased the warrior's countenance.

"Please," Davy said.

Like a cannonball exploding from a cannon, the man shot toward him. Davy's finger tightened, the crack of the smoothbore amplified by the trees.

Without delay, Davy located his rifle and the tomahawk and sprinted toward the gully. Enough was enough.

Flavius rotated when the undergrowth crackled. Assuming it to be a warrior, he was ready to shoot. He actually squeezed the trigger when a figure emerged—and gave silent thanks that he had neglected to pull back the hammer. "Lord Almighty!" he exclaimed. "Are you trying to get yourself shot?"

"We're leaving," Davy announced, sliding over the rim.

"What about the Illini? Won't they try to stop us?"

Davy contemplated the forest. Only one or two Old Ones were left unhurt. Surely, he thought, they were more interested in aiding their fellows than in exacting revenge. "Something tells me they won't." He scrambled up the other side.

"Wait for me!" Watching their backs, Flavius followed, tensed for a shower of arrows. It was the height of folly, in his view, to venture into the open. They would end up like porcupines.

His fears were unfounded. They were soon in

heavy cover, without a solitary shaft having whizzed down. Shaking his head in amazement, Flavius trudged in his friend's wake. So far, so good. But they had a long way to go, and a lot could happen.

Chapter Ten

Davy Crockett had never been so glad to see the sun go down. At last he could stop scanning the sky for the Thunderbird. Rubbing a kink in the back of his neck, he tramped to the river to take his first drink since morning.

"Is this smart?" Flavius asked. Being in the open made him nervous. So what if night had fallen? Maybe the piasa had eyes like an owl. He commented as much.

"I doubt it," Davy said, and cupped another handful to his mouth. "If the thing can see in the dark, the Illini wouldn't have staked you out next to that bonfire."

Flavius had told Davy all about his ordeal. "Maybe," he said, only half convinced. "And maybe they didn't build the fire just so the bird could see me. Maybe it was a signal for the piasa to come eat supper."

Mississippi Mayhem

A brisk wind from the northwest fanned the Mississippi as Davy straightened. Stars had blossomed in a cloudless sky. There was no moon, but the starlight was sufficient. "Anything is possible," he conceded. "But I say we stick to open ground to make better time. As it is, we won't reach the campsite until close to midnight."

"You know best," Flavius said with little conviction. He trusted the Irishman completely, but there were instances when that trust was stretched to the breaking point.

Davy cradled Liz and set off. He did not blame Flavius for being upset. His friend had suffered greatly on their gallivant—a journey Flavius undertook at his insistence. If he had not talked Flavius into tagging along, Flavius would be safe at home, seated in a rocking chair on the porch of his cabin, sipping from a jug.

Matilda had objected, as she always did. Unlike Davy's wife, who understood his restless craving to roam, Matilda believed that a husband should never leave his wife's side. Davy could still recollect her last words.

"It ain't right for the menfolks to go off whenever they feel like it and leave us women to fend for ourselves! While you're away having a grand time, we're taking care of the house and tending the kids and tilling the fields and doing all the work you *men* should be doing." She had crooked a finger at him. "If you ask me, David Crockett, these gallivants of yours are just an excuse to get out of doing your husbandly duty. Thank your lucky stars that Liz is your wife. If you were my man, I wouldn't let you get away with these shenanigans."

"As for you," Matilda said to Flavius, "the only reason I let you go is because it's best if this Irish vagabound doesn't go alone. Liz is a dear friend of mine, and she'd be brokenhearted if anything happened to him, perish forbid."

"Thank you, dear," Flavius had dutifully said. And away they rode.

Now, looking back, Davy regretted dragging Flavius along. The blame would fall on his shoulders should his friend be harmed. It was a burden he would rather not bear.

The wilderness was alive with sounds. Painters snarled and screamed. Bears growled and grunted. Wolves howled. Coyotes yipped. Owls voiced their eternal query. Occasionally, birds squawked.

Along the river frogs croaked in constant chorus, the deep throb of bullfrogs blended with the short throaty croaks of leopard frogs and the high chirps of tree frogs. Insects twittered and buzzed.

Often, from out on the water, came loud splashing. Some of the noises were undoubtedly fish. But the others? Once, Davy heard a sinuous swishing. Another time, a massive black shape swam northward, causing a wake that lapped small waves on the shore.

Flavius hated it. He couldn't shake the nagging dread that there might be other monsters out there besides the piasa, creatures no white man had ever set eyes on, horrid, vile beasts that would give a grown man nightmares.

Landmarks were few and far between. Most of the prominent ones Davy had memorized—a hill here, a lightning-charred tree there, elsewhere a gravel bar— were not visible at night. To mark their progress he kept track of the bends they passed and compared them to his recollection of the river's general course.

Judging by the position of the Big Dipper, it was close to one in the morning when Davy halted. Pointing at a finger of land that jutted into the river, he said softly, "I think that's where we camped."

"No sign of Hoodoo Tom," Flavius said. His main concern was their canoe. Without it, they were stranded.

"Keep your eyes skinned," Davy advised. Cat-footing into the trees, he prowled toward the spot where the campfire and their personal effects had been. The burnt remains of their fire stood out like a sore thumb, but of their packs and parfleches, there was no trace.

"Damn," Flavius whispered. "Someone must have come along and swiped our stuff. Now what are we going to do?"

"Check on the canoe."

To reach the high reeds fringing the site, they had to cross the clearing. Davy was midway when a twig crunched to his left. Spinning, he leveled his rifle at a shadowy silhouette creeping from cover.

"Don't shoot, hoss! It's me! Hoodoo Tom!"

The mountain man strode over, grinning from ear to ear. "It does this old coon good to see that you fellers made it! I was beginnin' to think I'd have to go on in the mornin' by my lonesome, and I was won-derin' what to do with your war sacks."

They shook. Flavius remembered the pemmican in one of his parfleches. "Where are our belongings?" he asked.

Hoodoo Tom jerked a thumb at the high grass. "I hid it all yonder in case any stinkin' Injuns came along." He nodded at the cattails. "The canoes are right where we left 'em."

"How long have you been back?" Davy inquired.

"Oh, hell. Since about four this afternoon, I'd say. I couldn't understand what was keepin' you. I gave the Old Ones the slip last night, soon after we got to the top of that hill."

"And you didn't think to wait for us?" Davy said accusingly.

The trapper recoiled as if he'd been slapped. "Hold on, young coon. I don't like what you're implyin'." He gestured angrily and said, "Those woods were swarmin' with Old Ones, remember? It wasn't as if I could holler your name to get your attention. I had no idea where you had gotten to, or that Harris was even alive. So I snuck toward the village for the treasure I hankered after, then circled to the river and lit a shuck." He smiled. "And here I am."

Davy had been about to sit on a log. Stiffening, he said, "Let me get this straight. You went back to the village *after* we were separated?"

"Pretty near to it, yes," Hoodoo Tom said. "The treasure I wanted was hard to come by."

"Show us," Flavius said, upset that the mountaineer valued his precious "treasures" more than his life, or Davy's.

The trapper shook his head. "I told you before, hoss, nobody takes a gander at 'em except me. For all I know, you might take a fancy to 'em and bash me over the head when my back is turned."

Flavius was not satisfied. "What are they? Jewelry you've stolen from Indians? Gold nuggets? Silver?"

"Better than that," Hoodoo Tom declared proudly.

"What can be better than gold?" Flavius said, confident he had hit the nail on the head. Some tribes were known to have secret sources of precious metals. And rumor had it that the Rockies were rich with veins of ore.

Snickering, Hoodoo Tom walked into the grass and lifted his wolfskin pack. "Wouldn't you like to know?" he bantered, patting it.

Davy did not care one way or the other. Disgusted, he got the fire going, a small one so as not to draw unwanted attention. Once their personal effects were lugged from hiding, he treated himself to jerky.

"Mmmmmm," Flavius moaned, devouring pemmican like there would be no tomorrow. He was positively famished.

"That has to last us until we reach St. Louis," Davy noted.

Being reminded of the immense distance they must cover dampened Flavius's spirits. He finished the piece he held and resisted the temptation to have another.

Their grizzled acquaintance poked a slim stick into the crackling flames. "It's sort of nice havin' you boys along," he commented. "Off in the mountains, I'd go months at a time without seein' another soul, let alone talkin' to one."

"Man wasn't meant to be alone," Davy said. "Why didn't you join a fur brigade?"

"And have to turn over most of my profits to the company?" Hoodoo Tom snorted. "Not on your life. I'd rather be a free trapper than a company man, any day. As for the loneliness, so what? Being alone never killed anyone."

"Do you plan to go back again next season?"

"You bet. I can only abide civilization for a little while before my feet get to itchin'. Especially city folks. Not one of 'em is sane, you know."

Davy looked at him. If ever there was a case of the pot calling the kettle black, this was it.

"Yessiree," Hoodoo Tom went on blithely. "I've always cottoned to the far places, to where a man can do as he pleases without havin' to justify himself to nosy neighbors and pushy politicians."

In that regard, they were a lot alike, and Davy said so.

"Hell, son. Anyone with half a brain thinks the

same." Hoodoo Tom leaned forward. "Do you know that in some cities back east a man can get arrested for spittin'? That's the gospel! The damned politicians went and passed a law against spittin'!" Sadly shaking his head, he continued. "The jackasses runnin' our country think they have the right to boss us around as they see fit. Don't do this! Don't do that! Why, in some places, like New York, they won't even let a man walk down the street with a pistol under his belt!"

"They say it's too risky," Flavius chimed in. "People might take to shooting on crowded streets."

"*Life* is a risk, mister," Hoodoo Tom declared bitterly. "As for the rest, politicians are always lookin' for the worst in folks. Never the best. That way they turn people against one another. Then they offer to keep the peace by makin' even more laws. And the people fall for it. It's downright pitiful!"

It shocked Davy to hear his own thoughts given voice by a man he deemed half crazy. "If enough decent men stand up for what's right, we can preserve our freedom."

"You're dreamin'," Hoodoo Tom responded. "The only way to stay free is at the point of a gun. Havin' their stupid laws shoved down their throats is the only surefire method to get politicians to own up to their mistakes."

"I hope you're wrong," Flavius said. Personally, he never paid much attention to politics. It was all so much hot air.

They made small talk for a while, and turned in. Each took a turn keeping watch, only this time Davy made certain enough wood was on hand to last the entire night.

He was last to stand guard. The morning chill gnawed at his joints, so he hunkered by the fire, rubbing his hands. Presently alternating bands of pink and yellow framed the horizon, harbingers of a new day.

Flavius did not sleep well. Fitful dreams plagued him, dreams of being tied down and helpless, and of an enormous winged terror with blazing eyes and molten talons. Small wonder he awoke at first light damp with perspiration.

"Are you all right?" Davy asked. "You've been tossing and groaning for hours."

"Fine," Flavius fibbed. To take his mind off the dreams, he offered to prepare their coffee.

Hoodoo Tom did not rouse until the fragrant aroma of the perking brew hung heavy in the air. Sniffing, he sat up and blinked. "Darn. I overslept. That's the trouble with easy livin'. It makes a person lazy."

By six o'clock the canoes were packed. Davy and Flavius pushed theirs into the water, climbed in, and steered into the current.

Dawn was magnificent, with scintillating shafts of sunlight sparkling among the trees, wisps of mist curling upward from the river, and Nature's children greeting the new day in typical noisy fashion.

A sense of tranquillity claimed Flavius. It lasted all of ten minutes. As they were passing rank reeds, a heron took hurried wing, flapping right over them.

Naturally, Flavius thought of the Thunderbird. Were they far enough south of its normal range to be safe? Or would the creature resume hunting them? "We should stay close to the bank," he said.

"As much as we can," Davy promised.

But the terrain did not cooperate. Limbs poked out from shore, snags dotted long stretches, sand and gravel bars had to be skirted. Whenever they paddled into the open, Flavius blanched and studied the sky.

David Thompson

Hoodoo Tom hummed and sang and whistled, as happy as a pig in mud. At noon he called their attention to a picturesque meadow adjoining the river. Grazing at the east end were four deer. "What say we treat ourselves to some fresh meat?"

"Let's!" Flavius exclaimed, stroking quickly landward. He was out of the canoe before it drifted to a stop.

The deer looked up, ears pricked. A buck tossed its head, flashed its white tail, and bounded into the undergrowth. Flavius aimed at a doe, but she melted into the greenery with the rest. "I'm going after them!"

"Wait!" Davy called, to no effect. By the time he slid out and dragged the canoe onto a grassy knob, his friend was a hundred yards off. He started to go after him.

"What's the matter, Tennessee?" Hoodoo Tom said, chuckling. "That boy need you to hold his hand in broad daylight?"

"He's a fine hunter," Davy replied, miffed.

"Then let him prove it."

Despite misgivings, Davy stayed. As he gathered wood and broke out his fire steel and flint, he caught Hoodoo Tom eyeing him oddly several times. Applying kindling, he bent to strike the steel against the flint. His gaze strayed backward, under his arm, and he saw the trapper's legs moving slowly toward him. Puzzled, he turned.

Hoodoo Tom stopped dead and grinned. "How's it comin'?" he asked much too casually.

Davy shifted so the man was in front of him. "I'll have it lit in a moment."

"Fine, fine." The mountain man fidgeted, his oversized right eye twitching.

"Something on your mind?" Davy asked.

"That's a fine nose you have."

Davy didn't think he had heard correctly. "My nose?"

"Yep. George thinks so, too. We noticed it right off. Saw a nose like that on a paintin' once, in Philadelphia. Some Greek feller, it was. Alex-somebody-or-other."

Davy could not help himself. "My nose?" he said again, touching it. He'd always assumed it was perfectly normal. No one had ever commented on its shape or size one way or the other before.

"And those high cheekbones, and that strong jawbone of yours," Hoodoo Tom said airily. "Shows character, and George and me are partial to character. I wouldn't've minded being born with a face like yours."

What was a man supposed to say to a compliment like that? Davy bent to the kindling, struck the steel and flint until a fiery spark caught. Then he blew lightly, fanning the hungry flames. When he looked up, he was surprised to find the trapper only a step away, one hand resting on the hilt of his knife.

The mountaineer backed off, smiling. "Sorry. Didn't mean to crowd you none."

Uneasiness gripped Davy. He rose, replaced the flint and fire steel in his possibles bag, and claimed Liz. For lack of anything else to say, he posed a question that had been nagging him. "How did your brother die, Tom?" He had a hunch that it might explain why Hoodoo Tom was forever talking about his brother as if George were still around.

To Davy's astonishment, Hoodoo Tom flushed red and coiled as if to attack. "What the hell business is it of yours? He's dead, his body long since buried. That's all that matters."

"Sorry," Davy said. He had not meant to ruffle the old-timer's feathers.

"Why should you be?" Hoodoo Tom snapped. "You didn't know him." He embraced the wolf-hide pack, holding it close as if for comfort. "The Lord knows he wasn't a saint, but he was fair enough, as brothers go."

Davy gazed across the meadow. It shouldn't take Flavius long to track down one of those deer, he mused. Once he heard the shot, he would go help butcher it.

Hoodoo Tom's eyes had misted over. "It's not as if I didn't care for him. We bickered a lot, but we were like two peas in a pod. He just shouldn't have argued with me, is all. I don't take to being pushed around. Not by my pa, not by George, not by anybody."

"He was bossy, was he?" Davy had no desire to pry into the man's personal affairs, but Hoodoo Tom seemed to want to talk.

"Not really, no. I reckon I was bossier. Usually he'd do whatever I told him. But that last time was different. He wouldn't see things my way." Hoodoo Tom sniffed. "That was right before he died."

"I'm sure he's forgiven you for any spats you had," Davy said to soothe the man.

Hoodoo Tom straightened. "You think so? I'd like to believe that. Yes, I truly would. But some things can't be forgave, and what I did was one of 'em. I'd wager my whole poke that he's up above the clouds somewhere, right this minute, cussin' a blue streak on my account."

Was cussing allowed in the Hereafter? Now, there was a question to boggle the mind. Davy began to pace, hoping to hear that shot soon.

"I don't suppose George would approve of my treasures, either," the mountain man said. "But then, he didn't want to eat that dead Injun, neither."

Davy stopped pacing. "You *ate* an Indian?"

"Had to. We got caught up in the Rockies by an early blizzard. No way down. Not enough food to last a month. We rationed it, of course, but the day came when we ran out. So we took to eatin' bark and weeds and such. About died, we did." Hoodoo Tom shuddered at the memory. "One mornin' I went off huntin' and found a frozen Injun up on the divide. A coyote was nibblin' on the fingers. That's what gave me the notion."

"To eat him?"

The trapper nodded. "It was the only way to survive. I dragged him to our cabin, but George didn't want no part of it. He'd rather starve, he said."

"But you went ahead."

"That I did. Took some doing, Crockett, I don't mind tellin' you. Made me so sick, at first, I thought I'd keel over. But do you know what?"

Davy's queasiness had grown to where he felt light-headed. "What?"

"After a few mouthfuls, the taste grows on you. Human flesh ain't half bad. Saltier than I figured, but it's a lot like painter meat."

Fighting to control his repugnance, Davy began to walk off in search of Flavius. But more revelations were to come.

"Have you ever ate a person, Tennessee?"

"Never."

"You would if it was that or die. George got off his high horse once I'd filled my belly. Oh, he threw up a few times before he could hold any down. Once he did, he wolfed that Injun's leg like a grizzly. I was so proud of him."

"Proud?"

"George was always too squeamish. Wouldn't do

this. Wouldn't do that. I had to talk myself hoarse plenty of times to get him to do something that needed doing. Like the time we stumbled on some Piegans camped up in the geyser country. He wanted to let them be. I had to point out that they were part of the Blackfoot Confederacy and had vowed to wipe out every white man west of the Mississippi before he would agree to sneak on into their camp and slit their throats while they slept." Hoodoo Tom sniffed. "Little things like that can be mighty aggravatin'."

The welcome crack of Flavius's rifle gave Davy an excuse to nod and leave. Revulsion washed over him in physical waves. There was a word for what the Fitzgeralds had done: cannibalism.

Hold it! Davy slowed, thinking back. The other day Hoodoo Tom had claimed his brother died thirty years ago. Yet that couldn't be true, not if they had been up in the mountains trapping beaver when the blizzard hit. Thirty years ago, there hadn't been any American trappers that far west.

Something wasn't quite right. Davy shrugged, reminding himself that he had no business prying. He'd settle for being shed of the cannibal soon. Real soon.

Chapter Eleven

Flavius Harris woke up the next morning refreshed both in body and soul. A fine meal of roast venison the evening before and a good night's sleep had him raring to go.

Davy Crockett, on the other hand, had not slept well at all. He could not shake the menacing image of Hoodoo Tom Fitzgerald slinking toward him while he had been hunched over the kindling. What would have happened if he had not turned around? Would Hoodoo Tom have buried that knife in his back?

Davy made it a point to arrange his blankets so he was facing the trapper, who stood watch first. He did not sleep a wink. Through slitted eyes Davy spied on their companion, who acted normally enough until it was about time to wake him. Then the mountaineer had started pacing and glancing at them while fingering the knife hilt.

Finally, Hoodoo Tom had nodded to himself, removed his hand from the weapon, and walked over to shake Davy's shoulder.

Sitting on a log, Davy sipped black coffee and pondered. He had always tended to give people the benefit of the doubt, but what should he do in this case? Was Hoodoo Tom a threat?

Undecided, Davy had awakened Flavius about two in the morning. His last words, whispered in Flavius's ear, were "Don't turn your back on our friend."

"Why? What's wrong?"

"I'm not sure. Maybe nothing."

Covering himself, Davy had tried to sleep. But every time he dozed, any little noise snapped him instantly alert. He was glad when dawn came.

Hoodoo Tom was in fine fettle. He whistled as he prepared breakfast, then took a deep breath and declared, "Smell that coffee? It's the one thing I missed most up in the mountains."

"I miss my wife's cooking," Flavius commented. "That woman makes the most delicious sweet cakes you ever bit into. And her pies melt in your mouth."

Hoodoo Tom laid a strip of deer meat in the skillet. "Never saw much sense in takin' a wife, myself. I can cook as well as any darned female, and I sew better than most. So what use are they?"

Davy resented the slur. His first wife had been the finest of ladies. His second was wonderfully loving, considerate, and warm. "They make us complete," he said.

The mountain man snickered, then winked at his pack of treasures. "Ain't that plumb silly, George?" To Davy, he said, "The way I see it, if the good Lord meant for us to go through life shackled to a female, we'd be joined at the waist with one when we're born."

Flavius laughed. "And you called Davy silly? How would we get around with four pairs of legs? The man would always want to go one way while the woman hankered to go another."

"Just my point," Hoodoo Tom said. "Females are contrary critters. I saw how my ma treated my pa. She nagged him something awful. Nothin' he ever did was good enough to suit her. And he couldn't take so much as a sip of liquor without her givin' him a tongue-lashin' that would flay an ox bare to the bone."

"Not all women are like that," Davy said defensively.

"It only takes one to make a feller's life miserable," Hoodoo Tom countered.

Davy did not speak again until the canoes were loaded and being slid into the Mississippi. "We'll follow you today," he told Hoodoo Tom.

"Whatever you want, young coon."

Flavius eased over the gunwale and applied his paddle. He could tell that something was bothering the Irishman, so when they were under way and the trapper was far enough ahead not to overhear, he cleared his throat. "Fess up, partner. What's eating at you?"

In low tones, Davy related his talk with Hoodoo Tom, ending with, "I reckon I should have let you know sooner, but after we toted that deer to camp, he was always close by."

"The man *ate* another human being!" Flavius breathed, revolted. As if talking to long-dead kin was not bad enough! He vowed to never turn his back on the trapper again. After further reflection he remarked, "Maybe we should part company with him."

Davy wanted to, but his conscience pricked him.

After all, the mountain man had not done them any harm. "We'll see," he said.

Flavius frowned. Sometimes he did not understand Crockett worth a hoot. What was there to think about? Having Hoodoo Tom around was like being in the company of a partially tamed grizzly. Bears and lunatics were notoriously unpredictable. At any moment he might lash out.

Davy scanned the sky only once the whole morning. Preoccupied with the trapper, he hardly gave the Thunderbird a thought. It had not appeared since the previous morning, and by now they were many miles from its customary haunts.

The Mississippi widened. Brightly plumed herons and ducks became more common. At one point they rounded a bend and came on a herd of elk swimming toward the west bank. Hoodoo Tom, cackling lustily, glided close enough to whack one on the rump. It snorted and plunged, sparking panic among the rest. Hoodoo Tom found the spectacle highly amusing.

The sun was poised overhead when a wide bend appeared. Hoodoo Tom moved closer to shore, as was their habit, and slowed. Suddenly he reversed his grip on his paddle and frantically brought his canoe sharply around, calling out in a low tone, "The Rees! The Rees!"

With all that had transpired the past couple of days, Davy had forgotten about the Arikaras. "Turn!" he said to Flavius.

"They're comin' up the river!" Hoodoo Tom informed them as he came alongside. "We have to hide!"

The shore was flat and open on both sides. Their only recourse was to hurry northward around the last turn they had passed and pray they were out of sight before the Arikaras showed. Bending to their paddles, they fairly flew.

Flavius glanced over his shoulder every few strokes. This was the last straw, as far as he was concerned. The Rees were after Hoodoo Tom, not them. Why should he and Davy stick their necks out on the madman's behalf? The trapper wouldn't even reveal *why* the Arikaras thirsted for his blood.

It was all the more unsettling because Flavius had figured the worst was over. They had given the Illini the slip, they had eluded the monstrous piasa. He had looked forward to some peace and quiet, for a change.

Their canoe outdistanced the trapper's. Davy pumped his arms, intent on the spur of land they must pass to be safe. It was over a hundred yards away. Then eighty, sixty, forty, twenty.

A triumphant screech signified failure. First one Ree canoe, then the other, swept into view. Four warriors manned each, and with practiced skill they powered forward, their canoes surging as if slung by slingshots.

"Damn!" Flavius fumed. Now they were in for it! Sheer luck had pulled them through the first clash. This time might be another story.

Hoodoo Tom laughed. "Here they come, boys! Let's make a stand and teach 'em what for!"

"Double damn!" Flavius declared. For two bits he would throttle the trapper himself. "What do we do, Davy?" he yelled.

Davy was thinking fast. Their choices were limited. Trying to outrun the Rees was hopeless. With four men to a canoe, the warriors would eventually overtake them. Beaching their canoes and fleeing into the forest was equally pointless. Even if they eluded the Rees, the outraged warriors might destroy their canoes and belongings, leaving them afoot with hundreds and hundreds of miles to cover. The only feasible course was to do exactly as Hoodoo Tom wanted.

"Head for shore!" Davy directed.

Their canoe grounded on gravel and they leaped out. Davy had to make another bound when Hoodoo Tom brought the dugout in so close to theirs that it nearly bowled him over.

The Rees', canoes were abreast of one another, two men in each paddling, two notching arrows. Hoodoo Tom sighted and fired, his ball splashing shy of the mark. "Son of a bitch!" he said. "My eyes ain't what they used to be!"

Davy had Liz. Flavius had Matilda and his spare rifle. Running to a low log flanked by cottonwoods, they hunkered behind it. "Wait for my say-so," Davy said.

Arrows cleaved the muggy air. One thudded into the soil near the log. Another missed Hoodoo Tom by a whisker as he hurriedly reloaded, brazenly standing out in the open.

"Take cover, you old coot!" Flavius hollered.

"I ain't scared of no mangy Rees!" Hoodoo Tom responded, and the very next second a shaft sheared into his thigh. Crying out, he staggered and would have fallen if not for his long gun. Shoving the stock against the ground, he used it as a crutch and hobbled toward them, swearing luridly.

The Arikara canoes were close enough. "Now," Davy said, aligning his sights on the bowman in the bow of the one on the left. As he placed his thumb on Liz's hammer, the warrior unexpectedly ducked below the gunwale.

Flavius's intended target did likewise. He shifted to shoot another, but that man also disappeared.

Even those paddling had bent low, exposing as little of themselves as they could and still steer the canoes.

"Shoot! Shoot!" Hoodoo Tom urged.

Davy picked a paddler whose shoulder was higher than any of the others. Sighting carefully, he held his breath to steady his aim, and fired. At the report, the warrior jerked up, clutched himself, and sagged against a gunwale, bleeding profusely.

"Again! Again!" Hoodoo Tom goaded. "Finish the bastard off! Kill him!"

Flavius aimed at the wounded warrior, but he could not bring himself to fire. Years ago, he would have slain the Rees without hesitation. But the warrior was defenseless, unable to harm them. Wryly, he reflected that the Irishman's highfalutin sense of moral rightness must be rubbing off on him. Which was a hell of a note.

Hoodoo Tom pranced on his good leg, wagging his rifle. "What are you waitin' for? Do it! Do it!" Seeing that they were not going to shoot, he cursed and set about reloading. "If you want something done, do it yourself!"

A warrior in the stern of the canoe on the right popped up and loosed a feathered streak that clipped the whangs on Hoodoo Tom's sleeve. Unperturbed, he poured powder down his gun, muttering spitefully, "Gonna slaughter 'em all! Damn me if I don't!"

Davy also started to reload. Realizing the canoes would reach shore before he could, he sprang erect and commanded, "Follow me!"

Flavius obeyed, but Hoodoo Tom stubbornly would not budge. Glaring defiantly at the Rees, his fingers flying, he roared, "Come and get me, you filthy heathens! I'll show you how a white man dies!"

Almost to cover, Davy paused. He owed the old-timer nothing. He was under no obligation to throw his life away for a man most would deem not worth saving. So why did he hesitate?

Flavius stopped and snatched at his friend's arm. "What are you waiting for?" he hollered. Already the canoes were grinding on the gravel. In another moment the warriors would spill out. "Let's go!"

"Who are we to judge?" Davy said, and threw himself toward Hoodoo Tom as the first Ree surged to his feet with a bow extended. Davy's pistol cracked a split moment before the man's fingers loosened on the arrow. Struck in the cheek, the Arikara catapulted over the side with a tremendous splash.

Flavius was beside himself. Another step or two and he would be among the trees. But he could never desert Davy, no matter what. The bond that existed between them had been cemented by shared hardships and joys too numerous to count. Or, put more simply, David Crockett was his one true friend, and a true friend was worth his weight in gold.

"Hell!" Flavius cried. Leaning the spare rifle against his leg, he jammed Matilda to his shoulder and sent a ball into the chest of a warrior stepping over the bow of the closest canoe.

The rest of the Arikaras swarmed onto land. Five were left. Animated by fury that contorted their painted features, they converged on the mountain man, the foremost raising a war club to bash Hoodoo Tom's brains out.

The trapper gave up trying to reload. Gripping the barrel of his rifle, he swung it like a club, momentarily fending the Rees off.

Davy reached the melee. Discarding his rifle and his spent pistol, he drew his second flintlock only to have it knocked from his hand by a blow from another warrior also armed with a club. Flourishing the tomahawk, Davy pivoted, then lunged.

The Arikara, exceptionally light on his feet, parried and danced to the left.

Flavius held back, raising the spare rifle. With it and the four pistols he could pick the warriors off. He quickly realized, though, that in the swirl of combat, none of the Rees were standing still long enough for him to fix a bead. He could not shoot without fear of hitting Davy or Hoodoo Tom. Seeing a burly warrior move toward Davy from the side, he lowered the rifle, drew two pistols, and charged into the fray.

Out of the corner of his eye Davy glimpsed Hoodoo Tom holding three of the Arikaras at bay. The oldster could not do so for long.

A swing of his foe's war club reminded Davy not to let himself be distracted. Blocking the club, he stepped to the right and cut at the warrior's hip. The man twisted and retreated a stride, unscathed.

"You lousy vermin!" Hoodoo Tom was railing. "I'll carve out your guts and eat 'em raw!"

Flavius had to skirt Davy for a clear shot at the Arikara sneaking toward him. The man was poised to plunge a keen blade into the Irishman's shoulders. Without an instant's hesitation, Flavius simultaneously squeezed both triggers.

At a range of less than two feet the twin balls smashed into the warrior's rib cage, lifted him off his feet, and flung him toward the river, where he crumpled like a paper doll to lie inert, staining the water a murky brown.

Flavius wanted to reload, but one of the other Rees was not going to let him. A savage war whoop tore from the man's throat as he pounced, his club sweeping down. It was all Flavius could do to avoid being split like a melon.

Davy had tangled with Indians before, but never any that fought with the unnatural ferocity of the

Arikaras. They battled like men possessed, demons made mortal. Why that should be was a mystery undoubtedly linked to Hoodoo Tom Fitzgerald.

The trapper had only two warriors to contend with now, and was still holding his own by swinging his rifle without cease.

Flavius ducked and weaved as his antagonist flailed brutally, nearly connecting time and again.

Davy yearned to help, but he had his own hands full. His wily adversary was not giving him a moment's respite. Blocking the blows had rendered his forearms and shoulders unbearably sore.

An opening presented itself when the Ree swung so violently, he overextended himself. Tucking, Davy tackled the warrior around the knees. They both toppled, landing in the river.

Davy had not realized they were so close. The water was shallow, but it got into his nose and mouth. Worse, as the warrior kicked free, some got into Davy's eyes. Blinded, he blinked to clear them and backpedaled in case the Ree attacked.

Flavius saw that Davy was in trouble, but he had problems of his own. He had tried to draw another pistol and been thwarted by the relentless pressure of the Arikara seeking to smash his skull. The club performed a tight arc, whistling past his ear. In retaliation, he flicked a punch that rocked the man on his heels.

Davy's eyes cleared just as his enemy closed in. Deliberately, he fell backward, sparing his cheek from being pulped. Flat on his back, he brought up the tomahawk to ward off a drive at his temple. The heavier war club nearly battered the tomahawk from his grasp.

Flavius spun to aid his friend and was taken by surprise by one of the two Rees who had been pressing Hoodoo Tom so hard. The warrior turned from the trapper to him, a knife gleaming in the sunshine.

At that very moment, Davy grabbed the wrist of his assailant, yanked the man toward him, rammed both feet into the warrior's stomach, and sent the Ree flying over his head.

There was a startled yelp. The Arikara Davy flipped collided with the warrior about to stab Flavius. They went down in a swirl of limbs.

The precious seconds Davy had bought enabled Flavius to whirl and unlimber a flintlock. He pointed it at the Arikara who had tried to cave his head in, and who was now almost on top of him. His thumb and finger moved quicker than the Ree, yet instead of a welcome blast, there was a dry click.

Flavius looked at the pistol. Either he had not primed it properly or it was fouled.

Smirking, the Arikara brought the war club down and around, aiming at Flavius's legs this time. Flavius darted to the right, but his luck had run out. The club glanced off his thigh, lancing him with agony. He tried to take another step, but his leg buckled and he landed on his knee.

The warrior had him. They both knew it. Aglow with feral glee, the Ree hiked his weapon for the fatal blow.

Davy Crockett had rolled to his feet and rotated to face the pair untangling themselves. He saw his friend's plight. His right arm whipped in a half-circle, and the tomahawk he needed to defend himself against his two foes flew neatly across the intervening space to bury itself in the neck of the man about to kill Flavius.

The stricken warrior clasped a hand over the gushing gash. On pure impulse he tried to complete his swing with his other arm. Losing strength with every spurt of blood, he crumpled in midswing.

Flavius was in the act of shoving erect. He thrust his hand out to ward off the falling body but forgot to take into account the warrior's club. Searing pain racked his head. Everything around him spun, then blurred, then faded to black. He felt himself pitch toward the ground, but he did not feel the impact.

"Flavius!" Davy cried, bounding toward him.

A bronzed hand lashed out, catching hold of Davy's ankle. He tripped, his elbows and knees absorbing the brunt. As he heaved onto his side to stand, the two warriors converged. The warrior with the club had lost it when he fell, but the Ree wielding the knife still had it.

Davy's own knife flashed. Steel rang on steel. He parried thrust after thrust, striving to keep an eye on both Arikaras at once. Under the circumstances, it was impossible.

The warrior with the knife speared it at Davy's jugular. Davy dodged, shifted, struck. He nicked the man's wrist, drawing blood, but that did not stop the Ree from weaving an intricate pattern of glittering steel designed to break through Davy's guard.

That was what Davy assumed, anyway. Then iron fingers closed on his neck from the rear, fingernails gouging into his flesh.

The other Arikara had gotten behind him! Davy clawed at the constricting fingers while warding off another savage onslaught by the first man's blade. He could not fight them both at once! He would be either stabbed or strangled unless he did something, and did it right away!

The Ree holding the knife cocked his arm, then lanced it at Davy's chest. With a monumental effort, Davy wrenched to the left. The blade sheared past. A shocked roar ensued as it sank into the Arikara seeking to throttle him.

The fingers on his throat slackened. Davy ripped free and pivoted. He slashed at the knife wielder's torso, but the man was pantherish quick.

Cold steel sought Davy's heart. Countering, he traded stabs. Neither of them inflicted a wound. They were too evenly matched, which explained why the Ree threw caution to the wind and suddenly barreled forward, risking everything in a bold gambit.

Davy seized the Ree's knife arm, and the Ree seized his. They struggled viciously, Davy forced steadily backward until his legs bumped against an obstacle.

It was the low log. Muscles surging, the Arikara slammed into Davy like an enraged bull and Davy keeled backward. His spine smashed onto the log. Nose to nose, straining and heaving, they slipped onto the grass.

Davy contrived to alight on his left side, but the warrior twisted, partially pinning him. The Arikara's blade inched toward his neck. Try though he may, Davy could not long resist the inevitable.

The warrior seemed to sense as much. Baring his teeth like a wolf would its fangs, he redoubled his efforts, throwing every ounce of bulging sinew into sinking his weapon in Davy's body.

Davy pretended to momentarily weaken. The Ree, hissing, reared to thrust his knife home. He barely noticed Davy's own knife held close to the grass. But in a tremendous burst of raw stamina, Davy arced the blade up and in.

A strangled groan escaped the Arikara. Davy shoved him off, looped an arm over the log, and stood. The other members of the war party were on the ground, dead or dying. "I'll be switched!" he declared wearily. "We beat them, boys."

But there was no one to hear.

Flavius was gone.

So was Hoodoo Tom Fitzgerald.

So was the dugout.

Chapter Twelve

Bewildered, Davy Crockett gazed out over the river. Sixty yards to the south Hoodoo Tom sat in the stern of the dugout, paddling in a frenzy. Slumped in front of him, still unconscious, was Flavius.

The trapper saw Davy and beckoned. "Come on, young coon! Don't keep me waitin'!" Cackling, he bent to the paddle again with an alacrity that belied his years.

"What's your hurry?" Davy shouted. "Where are you going?" His answer was another beckoning gesture and louder cackling.

Not knowing what to think, he collected his weapons and those Flavius had lost, piled them in the birch-bark canoe, and set out after the mountain man. With his lighter craft, he would overtake them in no time and demand an accounting.

It was surprising how swiftly Hoodoo Tom plied the river. Davy gained, but not nearly fast enough to suit him. Hoodoo Tom reached the bend, glanced back, and hollered, "Not quite good enough by half, Tennessee! Better luck in your next life!" With that, the dugout sailed on around the knob of land.

What was that all about? Davy wondered. Stroking evenly, he brought his canoe to the same point and swept into the next straight stretch of glistening waterway. He blinked, dumbfounded.

The dugout was gone!

Davy slowed, perplexed. There had not been enough time for the trapper to reach the next bend hundreds of yards off. Nor could the mountaineer have crossed to the west shore, rimmed by high cliffs. No, Hoodoo Tom had apparently entered one of three narrow tributaries on the left.

Fringed by heavy growth, including low-hanging limbs that dappled their surfaces with dark shadow, the tributaries were no more than twenty yards apart. Hoodoo Tom could have gone into any one.

Davy paddled to the first. A high bank thirty feet inland blocked his view, so he could not tell if it was the branch the trapper took. Advancing to the next, he found a wide patch of cattails blocking its mouth. None of the stems was bent or showed any other signs of being disturbed. Hoodoo Tom had not gone that way.

Stroking to the third creek, Davy angled into it. Almost immediately he had to negotiate a sharp turn. Ahead were more cattails. He was elated to discover some had been flattened by the passage of a heavy object.

"The dugout," Davy said to himself, and hastened on, the reeds rustling against the sides of his canoe. Soon he was in open water and increased his speed.

The tributary averaged five yards in width. Deep

pools were separated by channels where the depth varied from four to eight feet.

A series of turns to the left presently brought Davy to a confluence of the tributary with a wider waterway. He realized that he had misjudged.

The three creek mouths he had seen were in reality the single mouth of a broad river that merged with the Mississippi through a number of channels.

Davy scoured this new river but did not see the dugout. Sailing along the near bank, he searched for hiding places or breaks in the vegetation. Minutes crawled by, one after another, his anxiety mounting the farther he went.

Where could the trapper have gotten to? Why had he run off with Flavius? It defied logic. But so did everything else Hoodoo Tom did.

Trees grew right to the water's edge, blotting out whatever lay inland. Sheltered nooks were common, and in one, pulled onto shore and left right out in the open, was the dugout.

Davy blinked. He had not figured it would be this easy. Beaching his canoe beside the dugout, he climbed out. In his rush to catch up he had not loaded any of his guns, so he took his two pistols from the pile to do so. Suddenly, a loud groan, as of someone in great pain, issued from farther in the forest.

It must be Flavius! Davy thought, and raced pell-mell along a game trail. Moccasin prints confirmed that Hoodoo Tom had gone this way, carrying Flavius. Davy sprinted around a bend.

A hundred feet or so ahead was a small clearing. Directly over it hung the limb of a giant maple. And hanging from it by a stout rope bound around the ankles was a heavyset figure, arms dangling.

As if he had wings on his feet, Davy sped to his

friend. Flavius groaned again. Jamming his pistols under his wide belt, Davy grabbed Flavius around the shoulders to brace him, then reached higher to pry at the knots. They were too tight. Pulling his knife, he slashed at the rope. It parted, and he caught Flavius with both arms, lowering him gently to the grass.

Davy could not find evidence of any wounds other than a nasty welt on the brow. As he straightened, tittering laughter came from the direction of the river.

Davy jumped up. The wily trapper had outfoxed him, luring him to the clearing and doubling back! Although loath to leave his friend alone, he sprinted down the trail. Exploding out of the trees, he halted at the water's edge, baffled outrage seizing him.

Both the dugout and the canoe had been taken.

The river was empty in both directions. Davy guessed that Hoodoo Tom was hiding in one of the many nooks or in a patch of reeds. He roved the shore westward a short distance, then eastward for a quarter of a mile. Nothing.

Defeated, dejected, Davy bent his steps toward the clearing. Hoodoo Tom had hoodwinked them but good. All their belongings were gone—their rifles, their packs, their blankets, everything—and would probably be sold in St. Louis for a tidy sum.

Davy was not one to hold a grudge, but if he ever met up with Hoodoo Tom again, there would be hell to pay.

At least they were still alive, and as his pa had always said, where there was life, there was hope.

Rubbing a sore rib, Davy looked up. The clearing was in sight—but not Flavius. Figuring that his friend had revived and wandered off, Davy hollered several times. He received no reply.

"Flavius? Where are you?" Davy tried again, his gut balling into a knot. An awful premonition filled him with rising dread. He checked the grass. Furrows left by a heavy body being dragged led to the trees.

Flavius had not walked off under his own steam. Someone had hauled him off, possibly hostiles.

Crouching, Davy loaded both pistols. He sorely missed having his rifle; the flintlocks were only reliable at short range. Moving stealthily into the growth, he spotted a clear print in a bare spot. A chill gripped him.

Indians were not to blame. For a reason Davy could not begin to imagine, Hoodoo Tom had concealed the canoe and dugout somewhere and snuck on back. What was the mountain man up to? More than thievery was involved here. It was almost as if Hoodoo Tom were playing some sort of bizarre game with them.

Davy's nerves were stretched taut. So when a twig snapped to his right, he whirled, only to startle a small doe that bounded off. Licking his lips, Davy tracked the trapper deeper and deeper into the gloomy woods.

The man had not made any attempt to hide his trail, which was just as puzzling as everything else. It was almost as if Hoodoo Tom *wanted* Davy to hunt him down.

Abruptly, the drag marks ended. Davy glanced right and left, but the ground was undisturbed. Not a single footprint was evident. "This can't be," he whispered.

Seemingly on cue, tittering fluttered on the sluggish breeze. "Lose something, Tennessee?"

Davy whirled. The mountain man was northwest of him, approximately thirty yards away. It might as well have been a mile. The undergrowth was dense enough to hide a herd of buffalo. "Fitzgerald! What are you up to?"

"Ain't you guessed yet?" was the mocking response, a little farther to the west than before. "Folks must not be too bright down your way."

"Where's Flavius? Why did you take him?"

"He was the bait, pup." Hoodoo Tom's voice came from a different spot than the last time.

"Bait?" Davy repeated. It was obvious that the trapper was circling, to make it hard to pinpoint him.

"Lordy, you sure are a dumb cluck," Hoodoo Tom declared. "You must've been in the outhouse when God gave out brains."

"Tell me where Flavius is!"

Silence greeted the demand. When next Hoodoo Tom spoke, he had gone another ten yards. "Not likely, hoss. But I will make you a deal. If you beat me, I'll let you know where to find him. If I come out on top, then I'll do with your friend as I please." He paused. "The plumper they are, the tastier they are."

Horrified by the implication, Davy did not respond.

"The trick is to let the chunks simmer an hour or more," the madman elaborated. "They're downright juicy! I like to add onions when I can, and pepper, but not salt. The meat is salty enough on its own."

Davy found his voice. "You meant to do this all along?"

"No, not at first. Not until I took a shine to that nose of yours."

"You like to eat noses?"

Maniacal mirth scared a few sparrows into winging skyward. "Hell, boy! That's the craziest thing I ever heard! Who would do anything so disgustin'?" There was another pause while Hoodoo Tom traveled a dozen feet. "It's the whole head, hoss. The way the nose and the cheeks and the ears all fit together. Some are regular works of art. Treasures, I call 'em."

Davy shuddered, his palms growing slick on the stocks of his pistols. "Your brother?" he asked.

"What about him?"

"He didn't die thirty years ago. You killed him, didn't you? Not too long ago, up in the Rockies?"

Hoodoo Tom did not answer.

"You can't go on like this," Davy shouted. "Come to St. Louis with Flavius and me. Talk to a doctor, or a parson. There might be something they can do." He was stalling, grasping at straws, and the mountaineer knew it.

"Who are you tryin' to kid, Crockett? They'd bind me in chains, then put me in one of those places where they keep people who howl at the moon and talk to walls and such." Hoodoo Tom stopped. "My brother wanted to put me in one," he said softly. "Me! His own flesh and blood! I couldn't believe it!"

"So you murdered him."

"Not murder, no!" Hoodoo Tom said angrily. "I only did what I had to, what he made me do. And it's not as if he went to waste."

A sour sensation crept from Davy's stomach up his throat to his mouth. He glided soundlessly to the west, letting the mountain man's voice guide him.

"Just because a person doesn't see things the way everyone else does, just because he's a mite different, doesn't give anyone the right to judge him."

Davy moved faster, wary of dry grass and brush.

"My brother called me evil," Hoodoo Tom said sorrowfully. "How could he do that? We had the same ma, the same pa. We grew up side by side, doing the same things all boys do. I never harmed a soul in my life until after we ate that Injun, and we only ate him because we were about starved to death."

A vague shape hinted at the trapper's position. Not yet in range, Davy stalked toward it.

"What's evil, anyway? Look at Andrew Jackson. He's from your part of the country, ain't he? He's killed people in duels. He wiped out a heap of Injun women and brats durin' that war you fellers had with the Creeks. Yet has anybody ever called him evil? Does anyone want to throw him in chains?"

Davy was close enough to distinguish the mountain man's buckskins. He took deliberate aim.

"It's not a question of my being good or evil," Hoodoo Tom continued. "I'm just livin' my life as I see fit. And to hell with those who don't like it!"

Another step, and Davy saw the mountain man clearly. At the same instant, Hoodoo Tom saw him. He fired, but Hoodoo Tom dived and rolled into tall weeds. Davy dashed to them, squatted, and listened. All he heard was his own heavy breathing.

To the south of him, Hoodoo Tom snickered. "Nice try, cub. That'll teach me to prattle on like an old maid."

Davy extended his other pistol, hoping against hope for another shot. But Hoodoo Tom was not about to make the same mistake twice. Lowering onto his belly, Davy snaked to a wide tree trunk and rose onto his knees.

It was a war of wits now. Wits and wood lore. He must pit his skill against a man whose woodcraft rivaled an Indian's.

Standing, Davy peeked out. A rifle cracked, and a lead ball smashed into the bark so close to his cheek that he was stung by flying slivers. More laughter taunted him as he turned and ran.

"Is that the best you can do, hoss? You make more noise than a pregnant moose!"

Hoodoo Tom was enjoying himself immensely.

A rock outcropping gave Davy an idea. Climbing to a small ledge six feet up, he reloaded, then glued his eyes to the forest. He was not going to budge. Why expose himself, when it was smarter to let the trapper come to him?

All the birds and squirrels had fallen silent. Even the wind had died. It was so quiet, Davy could have heard a pin drop. No noise broke the stillness, though. Not so much as a leaf stirred.

Davy pursed his lips, thinking. He couldn't stay up there the rest of the day. There was Flavius to think of. Sliding to the left, he rose slightly higher. Several hundred feet distant was a meadow.

A rifle boomed, shockingly near. The ball spanged stone chips off a boulder at Davy's elbow. He fired at a mushrooming cloud of smoke, levered off the ledge, and dropped.

A pistol shot rang out. Davy clutched his stinging left shoulder and plunged into the trees. Fearful of being shot in the back, he weaved among the boles, not stopping until he came to the meadow.

Hunkering, Davy examined his shoulder. It had only been creased. It barely bled. Reloading, he crawled into the high grass.

The meadow was tear-shaped, hemmed by heavy timber on three sides, by a knoll to the south. In the center, Davy halted. Now no one could approach him without being seen or heard.

Evidently Hoodoo Tom was in no hurry to finish him off. Fifteen minutes elapsed. Half an hour. Davy grew impatient and had to resist an urge to sneak on back into the woods. When a bee alighted on his left hand, he stayed as rigid as a statue. It explored his knuckles, then flew off.

What was keeping the mountain man? Davy won-

David Thompson

dered. Removing his coonskin cap, he craned his neck. He guessed that Hoodoo Tom would come at him from out of the woods to the north, east, or west.

Behind him, to the *south*, a shot cracked. Davy spun, bringing up his flintlocks, but he did not shoot.

Brazenly standing on top of the knoll, which was well out of pistol range, Hoodoo Tom chuckled and lowered his smoking pistol. Making a show of tucking it under his belt, he casually raised his rifle and sighted down the barrel. "Now that I've got your attention, why don't you chuck those short guns and mosey on over here?"

What else could Davy do? There was nowhere to run, nowhere to hide. Setting the pistols down, he elevated both hands and complied.

Hoodoo Tom relaxed, chortling. "Yes, sir. This has been a grand day. I'm finally shed of those pesky Rees. Later on I get to eat until I burst. And I add another treasure to my pack." He hefted his rifle as Davy came to the base of the knoll. "That's far enough, hoss."

More upset that he had failed Flavius than at his own impending fate, Davy said, "We all go to our reward sooner or later. My only regret is that I won't be around when your past catches up with you. As it surely will."

"Wishful thinkin'," Hoodoo Tom said. He encompassed the western horizon with a sweep of his arm. "Think of it, friend. Thousands and thousands of square miles, they say, and not a lick of law anywhere. A man can do as he damn well pleases."

"You'll be caught," Davy insisted.

"Not if I'm careful. The mistake I made with the Rees was not buryin' the chief's body deep enough. A stinkin' mongrel sniffed it out. They put two and two together and lit out after me."

"So that's why they wouldn't give up."

"The way I see it," Hoodoo Tom declared, "I can go on treatin' myself to anyone who takes my fancy until I'm too old and feeble to lift a butcher knife."

Davy squared his shoulders. He was tired of being played for a fool. Tired of listening to the trapper babble on. And just plain *tired*. "What are you waiting for? Get it over with."

Hoodoo Tom cocked his head. "What's your rush, young coon? I don't mind chawin' with you a few minutes more. Then I'll go slit your friend's throat and bleed him dry before I carve him up like a turkey."

Beyond the knoll a tiny black dot appeared high in the sky, roving in circles. A hawk or eagle, Davy reckoned, and did not pay more attention. Of more immediate concern was preventing the lunatic from eating his best friend. "He's ill, you know. Has been for months."

"What's that?" Hoodoo Tom perked up.

"It's a sickness Flavius picked up in Florida during the Creek War," Davy fibbed. "Every now and then he breaks out in festering sores. They itch and hurt like the devil. And the doctors don't know what to do."

"So?"

"So if he winds up in your stomach, you could catch the same thing." Davy mentally crossed his fingers that the mountain man would fall for it.

"I don't believe you," Hoodoo Tom stated flatly. "I wasn't born yesterday."

The speck had swelled in proportions. Davy squinted over Hoodoo Tom's shoulder and felt a surge of disbelief. Keeping his face impassive, his tone neutral, he commented, "Our pasts have a way of catching up with us when we least expect it."

"Spare me a sermon," Hoodoo Tom snapped. "I heard it all from my brother."

The bird banked toward the meadow. It had seen them! Clasping his hands, Davy sank to his knees. "I'm begging you!" he cried out much more loudly than the short distance between them warranted. "Spare me! Spare Flavius! We'll never tell a soul about you! Honest!"

Hoodoo Tom scowled. "Get up, damn it! I credited you with more grit than this! It ain't fittin' to grovel."

"Please!" Davy shouted. The bird had dipped lower and was hurtling toward the meadow, skimming the tops of the trees. Its huge beak and gigantic talons stood out in stark relief.

"Quit your squawkin'!" Hoodoo Tom groused. "I have half a mind to truss you up and skin you alive. You don't deserve a manly death."

"But I don't want to die!" Davy yelled, flinging himself to the ground. "Spare me! Spare me!" Then, looking into the madman's mismatched eyes, he smiled.

Hoodoo Tom stiffened. "What the hell—?" he said, and finally heard the high-pitched whistle of rushing air sliced by gargantuan wings. Wheeling, he screeched, and threw up both arms. "Nooooooo!"

Feathered lightning streaked out of the blue. The Thunderbird's talons ripped into Hoodoo Tom's chest, rending flesh, crushing bones, even as he was yanked off his feet. Wings beating, the creature shot upward, carrying its prey as easily as an eagle might a fish.

Davy saw the lunatic struggle feebly, saw the great bird dip its head and tear at Hoodoo Tom's neck and shoulder. An arm was ripped off. Spraying scarlet, it fell end over end, crashing down amid the trees to the north.

The Thunderbird, venting a shriek, gained height. Presently it was lost in the distance.

Davy slowly stood. It had all occurred so astoundingly quickly, he could not quite accept it had happened. Rousing himself, he collected his pistols and lost no time returning to the spot where the drag marks disappeared. Closer inspection showed that Hoodoo Tom had lifted Flavius and taken a long bound behind a row of weeds. From there tracks led to a depression created by an uprooted tree.

Lying at the bottom, bound and gagged, was Flavius. The first words out of his mouth were "What's this all about? Who tied me up? And where's Hoodoo Tom?"

The last Flavius recollected was being struck by the war club. He listened, stupefied, as Davy related all that had transpired. When the Irishman was done, he said, "That bird did the world a favor. Some folks ought never to be born."

It took them two hours of hard searching to locate the canoe and dugout, cleverly concealed among reeds.

"What are we going to do with Fitzgerald's stuff?" Flavius asked.

Davy stepped to the dugout and lifted the wolfskin pack. "I know what I'm doing with this," he said, and swung his arms back to throw it.

"Wait!" Flavius exclaimed. "What's in there? Do you know?"

"Yes."

"I want to see."

Davy unfastened the cord at the top and upended the pack. Out tumbled the contents into the water, six, seven, eight of them, all told. Most had patches of skin and hair still attached. The freshest belonged to an Arikara chief, his glazed eyes not yet decayed.

"My God!" Flavius blurted, grasping the gunwale to steady himself. "My dear God!"

Bobbing like so many apples, the human heads were caught by the current and borne westward. One by one, they became waterlogged and sank, the last being that of a white man whose mouth gaped wide in the terror he had felt at the moment his own brother slew him.

Davy Crockett lowered himself into their canoe, picked up a paddle, and mustered a wan smile. "Let's go home."

DIABLO
DAVID ROBBINS

The wide-open boomtown of Diablo is a tinderbox in the blistering Arizona sun, just waiting for a spark to set it off. It looks like every prospector, gunman and hard-luck case west of the Mississippi has hit town, desperate to get what he can, and to hell with everyone else. The homesteaders hate the prospectors and the miners, and both sides hate the cowboys and the ranchers.

Lee Scurlock is the spark Diablo is dreading. He is riding to escape his past in the dirty Lincoln County War, and trying hard to mind his own business at the stage relay station when three cowboys take it into their heads to make trouble. When the shooting stops, one of the cowboys is dead, and Scurlock finds himself in some serious trouble–trouble that will follow him when he rides with the stage into the blazing man-made hell of...Diablo.

——4254-1 $4.50 US/$5.50 CAN

BLOOD HUNT

David Thompson

With only his oldest friend and his trusty long rifle for company, Davy Crockett explores the wild frontier looking for adventure, and has the strength and cunning to face any enemy. But even he may have met his match when he gets caught between two warring tribes on one side and a dangerous band of white men on the other—all of them willing to die—and kill—for a group of stolen women. It is up to Crockett to save the women, his friend and his own hide if he wants to live to explore another day.

_4229-0 $3.99 US/$4.99 CAN

Dorchester Publishing Co., Inc.
65 Commerce Road
Stamford, CT 06902

Please add $1.75 for shipping and handling for the first book and $.50 for each book thereafter. NY, NYC, PA and CT residents, please add appropriate sales tax. No cash, stamps, or C.O.D.s. All orders shipped within 6 weeks via postal service book rate. Canadian orders require $2.00 extra postage and must be paid in U.S. dollars through a U.S. banking facility.

Name_____
Address_____
City _____ State_____ Zip_____
I have enclosed $_____in payment for the checked book(s).
Payment <u>must</u> accompany all orders.□ Please send a free catalog.

DON'T MISS THESE OTHER GREAT STORIES IN

 **The Lost Wilderness Tales**

DODGE TYLER

In the days of the musket, the powder horn, and the flintlock, one pioneer ventures forth into the virgin land that will become the United States.

#6: *Death Trail.* The uneasy peace in Apache territory is shattered when a murderous bandit named Bear Killer begins a campaign to slaughter settlers and steal as much as he and his warriors can get their hands on. And when a Mexican family sets out on a journey to help a survivor of one of the vicious raids, they turn to the best guide in the territory...Dan'l Boone.

___4257-6 $4.99 US/$5.99 CAN

#5: *Apache Revenge.* A band of Apaches with blood in their eyes ride the warpath right to Dan'l's door, looking to avenge their humiliating defeat at his hands three years earlier. And when they capture Dan'l's niece as a trophy it beomes more than just a battle for Dan'l, it becomes personal. No matter where the warriors ride, the frontiersman swears to find them, to get the girl back–and to exact some vengeance of his own.

___4183-9 $4.99 US/$5.99 CAN

Dorchester Publishing Co., Inc.
65 Commerce Road
Stamford, CT 06902

Please add $1.75 for shipping and handling for the first book and $.50 for each book thereafter. NY, NYC, PA and CT residents, please add appropriate sales tax. No cash, stamps, or C.O.D.s. All orders shipped within 6 weeks via postal service book rate. Canadian orders require $2.00 extra postage and must be paid in U.S. dollars through a U.S. banking facility.

Name _____ ___ _____
Address _____.
City _____ State _____ Zip _____
I have enclosed $ _____ in payment for the checked book(s).
Payment <u>must</u> accompany all orders. ☐ Please send a free catalog.

A mighty hunter, intrepid guide, and loyal soldier, Dan'l Boone faced savage beasts, vicious foes, and deadly elements—and conquered them all. These are his stories—adventures that made Boone a man and a foundering young country a great nation.

DAN'L BOONE: THE LOST WILDERNESS TALES #1:

The colonists call the stalwart settler Boone. The Shawnees call him Sheltowee. Then the French lead a raid that ends in the death of Boone's young cousin, and they learn to call Dan'l their enemy. Stalking his kinsman's killers through the untouched wilderness, Boone lives only for revenge. And even though the frontiersman is only one man against an entire army, he will not rest until he defeats his murderous foes—or he himself goes to meet his Maker.

_3947-8 $4.99 US/$6.99 CAN

WILDERNESS DOUBLE EDITION

SAVE $$$!

Savage Rendezvous by David Thompson. In 1828, the Rocky Mountains are an immense, unsettled region through which few white men dare travel. Only courageous mountain men like Nathaniel King are willing to risk the unknown dangers for the freedom the wilderness offers. But while attending a rendezvous of trappers and fur traders, King's freedom is threatened when he is accused of murdering several men for their money. With the help of his friend Shakespeare McNair, Nate has to prove his innocence. For he has not cast off the fetters of society to spend the rest of his life behind bars.

And in the same action-packed volume...

Blood Fury by David Thompson. On a hunting trip, young Nathaniel King stumbles onto a disgraced Crow Indian. Attempting to regain his honor, Sitting Bear places himself and his family in great peril, for a war party of hostile Utes threatens to kill them all. When the savages wound Sitting Bear and kidnap his wife and daughter, Nathaniel has to rescue them or watch them perish. But despite his skill in tricking unfriendly Indians, King may have met an enemy he cannot outsmart.

_4208-8 $4.99 US/$5.99 CAN

Dorchester Publishing Co., Inc.
65 Commerce Road
Stamford, CT 06902

Please add $1.75 for shipping and handling for the first book and $.50 for each book thereafter. NY, NYC, PA and CT residents, please add appropriate sales tax. No cash, stamps, or C.O.D.s. All orders shipped within 6 weeks via postal service book rate. Canadian orders require $2.00 extra postage and must be paid in U.S. dollars through a U.S. banking facility.

Name _____

Address _____

City _____ State _____ Zip _____

I have enclosed $_____ in payment for the checked book(s). Payment <u>must</u> accompany all orders. ☐ Please send a free catalog.

BONNER'S STALLION
T. V. OLSEN

Winner of the Golden Spur Award

Bonner's life is the kind that makes a man hard, makes him love the high country, and makes him fear nothing but being limited by another man's fenceposts. Suddenly it looks as if his life is going to get even harder. He has already lost his woman. Now he is about to lose his son and his mountain ranch to a rich and powerful enemy—a man who hates to see any living thing breathing free. That is when El Diablo Rojo, the feared and hated rogue stallion, comes back into Bonner's life. He and Bonner have one thing in common...they are survivors.

___4276-2 $4.50 US/$5.50 CAN

BACK TO MALACHI

ROBERT J. CONLEY
THREE-TIME SPUR
AWARD-WINNER

Charlie Black is a young half-breed caught between two worlds. He is drawn to the promise of the white man's wealth, but torn by his proud heritage as a Cherokee. Charlie's pretty young fiancée yearns for the respectability of a Christian marriage and baptized children. But Charlie can't forsake his two childhood friends, Mose and Henry Pathkiller, who live in the hills with an old full-blooded Indian named Malachi. When Mose runs afoul of the law, Charlie has to choose between the ways of his fiancée and those of his friends and forefathers. He has to choose between surrender and bloodshed.

___4277-0 $3.99 US/$4.99 CAN

ODISEA

HOMERO

Odisea

Edición de José Luis Calvo

Traducción de José Luis Calvo

CATEDRA

LETRAS UNIVERSALES

Letras Universales
Asesores: Carmen Codoñer, Javier Coy
Antonio López Eire, Emilio Náñez
Francisco Rico, María Teresa Zurdo

Título original de la obra: Ὀδύσσεια

Diseño de cubierta: Diego Lara
Ilustración de cubierta: Dionisio Simón

© Ediciones Cátedra, S. A., 1987
Don Ramón de la Cruz, 67. 28001-Madrid
Depósito legal: M. 1.184-1987
ISBN: 84-376-0640-3
Printed in Spain
Impreso en Lavel
Los Llanos, nave 6. Humanes (Madrid)

INTRODUCCIÓN

Palas Atenea parte para amparar a Ulises (relieve en alabastro)

L A Odisea es una epopeya dramática que se compone de elementos muy dispares en perfecta fusión realizada por un poeta (quizá Homero), aproximadamente a finales del siglo VIII a.C.

La historia desnuda del poema, el héroe que después de muchos años de ausencia retorna a su hogar, que se encuentra en mala situación, se da a conocer a su esposa mediante una serie de pruebas y finalmente mata a los pretendientes de ésta, es en sí misma un cuento que se repite en diversos lugares y culturas.

Pero a este cuento se unen en la *Odisea* multitud de temas inspirados en el folklore mediterráneo y anatolio y otros tomados de la saga griega que, lejos de constituir un conglomerado inorgánico, forman una unidad narrativa y dramática debido a:

a) Su unión en torno a un héroe bien conocido del folklore griego: Odiseo o Ulises.

b) Su inclusión dentro de uno de los temas más celebrados de la épica griega: los *Nostoi* o *Regresos* de los héroes aqueos desde Troya; de esta forma la *Odisea* es el *Nostos* de Odiseo.

c) La inserción de todo este conjunto en las coordenadas sociales y políticas —principalmente, aunque no sólo— de la época correspondiente al ocaso del imperio micénico.

Merecería la pena, al hacer la introducción de la *Odisea,* analizar también estos elementos históricos aludidos en último lugar, pero voy a limitarme, por razones obvias, a contemplarla puramente como obra literaria.

Tampoco voy a referirme, con ser sumamente interesantes, a los componentes narrativos pertenecientes a otros folklores o a los elementos mágicos, etc., cuya exposición detallada y brillante se encuentra y puede fácilmente consultarse en obras como las de Rhys Carpenter, Germain o Stella[1].

LA ÉPICA COMO POESÍA ORAL

He señalado arriba que la *Odisea* es un cuento que incorpora otros cuentos. Sin embargo, por su lengua, metro, composición, época de creación e, incluso, por el espíritu de gran parte de ella es un poema épico. Y como epopeya voy a analizarla a continuación.

Ahora bien, antes de tratar de la estructura de la *Odisea* y los problemas de composición que presenta, será útil referirnos en general —y brevemente— a la técnica de la composición oral, pues su conocimiento es imprescindible para explicar algunos de estos problemas.

Al poeta épico se le denomina generalmente hoy con el nombre de poeta oral. Esta denominación, sumamente vaga, desde luego, se refiere a una de sus características más sobresalientes, esto es, que no se sirve de la escritura para componer sus poemas, sino sólo de su memoria, una memoria prodigiosa desarrollada mediante el ejercicio de toda una vida y que suele darse precisamente entre los pueblos iletrados.

Por otra parte, el poeta épico se diferencia del concepto que hoy tenemos de poeta, en el sentido de que no es un creador de palabras ni de frases, ni siquiera de temas, sino un *compositor* que maneja y combina elementos que ha heredado y que conserva en el almacén de su memoria.

Esto lo sabemos hoy gracias a los estudios que se han realizado sobre la naturaleza de la lengua épica. Gracias a éstos, hoy sabemos que ésta es una lengua formular. Cualquier lector de la *Odisea* observará enseguida que se repiten sin cesar sintagmas, frases, versos e, incluso, tiradas enteras de versos. An-

---

[1] R. Carpenter, *Folk Tale, Fiction and Saga in the Homeric Epics*, Berkeley, 1946; G. Germain, *Genèse de l'Odyssée*, París, 1954; Stella, *Il poema di Ulisse*, Florencia, 1955.

tiguamente se pensó que esto era un demérito desde el punto de vista estilístico (por lo que Homero cedió su puesto a Virgilio) y una razón para dudar seriamente de la unidad de autor de los poemas. Sólo después de los estudios de Witte[2], Meister[3] y Meillet[4], y especialmente los trabajos de Milman Parry[5], sabemos que la repetición no es un demérito estilístico, sino algo intrínseca y necesariamente unido al carácter oral de la Épica. El poeta épico tiene que operar —si quiere retener en su memoria millares de versos— con fórmulas fijas que pueden consistir desde un grupo de versos (la llamada *escena típica* de las que en la *Odisea* abundan, por ejemplo, la de preparación de un banquete) hasta un verso completo (por ejemplo, «cuando se mostró Eos, la que nace de la mañana, la de dedos de rosa»), una frase verbal (ejemplo, «le dirigió aladas palabras»), o una frase nominal compuesta de nombre propio y epíteto (ejemplo, «el sufridor Odiseo»), o nombre común y epíteto (ejemplo, «las cóncavas naves»), o incluso una palabra aislada cuando aparece sistemáticamente en un mismo lugar del verso.

Estas fórmulas han surgido y deben su firmeza gracias a la rígida estructura métrica del verso épico, el hexámetro.

Cuando la fórmula no es todo un verso, ésta suele llenar una de las varias secciones o unidades rítmicas en que se divide el hexámetro por causa de sus cesuras, siendo las más corrientes $-\cup\cup -\cup\cup -(\cup)$ (desde el comienzo del verso hasta la primera cesura principal $(\cup)\cup -\cup\cup -\cup\cup --$ (desde la primera principal hasta el fin del verso), $\cup\cup -\cup\cup --$ (desde la segunda cesura principal hasta el final), $-\cup\cup --$ (desde la diéresis bucólica hasta el final).

De esta forma el poeta épico puede formar un verso a base de la combinación de frases hechas. Ahora bien, esto implica que a menudo el uso del epíteto no es estilístico, sino métrico funcional, por lo que a menudo se aplican epítetos inadecua-

---

2 En *RE*, s. v. «Homeros, Sprache».

3 *Die homerische Kunstsprache*, Leizpig, 1921.

4 *Aperçu d'une histoire de la langue grecque*, París, 1942.

5 Entre las obras de este autor se pueden destacar *Les formules et la metrique d'Homère*, *L'Epithète traditionelle chez Homère* y *Studies in the Epic Technique of Oral Verse-Making*, hoy recogidas en A. Parry, *The making of Homeric Verse. The collected papers of Milman Parry*, Oxford, 1971.

dos al sustantivo o a la situación; así cuando a la madre del mendigo Iro se le llama «venerable» o «irreprochables» a los pretendientes. Por otra parte, como la lengua griega es flexiva, según el caso en que se encuentre un sustantivo, recibirá un epíteto u otro. Así, cuando la palabra «nave» va en dativo siempre lleva el epíteto «negra» νηὶ μελαίνη, en cambio, cuando va en genitivo, puede llevar el epíteto «equilibrada», εἴσσης, «bien curvada», ἀμφιελίσσης, o «de azuloscura proa», κυανοπρώροιο, según la posición que ocupe en el verso.

Pero es más, esta lengua formular de la épica se rige por dos leyes —descubiertas y ejemplificadas ampliamente por Parry—, que son la de economía y la de extensión. Por la primera, absolutamente necesaria para que el poeta pueda retener en su memoria todo el repertorio de fórmulas, suelen evitarse las fórmulas duplicadas (o sea, las que tengan la misma estructura métrica y contenido similar); por la segunda, la posibilidad de combinación de las fórmulas en *stock* es lo suficientemente amplia como para evitar una impresión de excesiva pesadez y repetición.

De todo esto se podría deducir que la originalidad del poeta épico es nula, ya que su composición es sumamente mecánica. Sin embago, no se le puede negar un cierto grado de originalidad. En el caso de cualquier poeta épico, ésta consiste en el empleo adecuado o brillante en un momento dado de una u otra fórmula. En el caso de Homero, la originalidad consiste, por un lado, en su concepción grandiosa de la épica, en haber pasado del poema pequeño al monumental, pero sobre todo en haber creado la épica dramática a partir del pequeño poema épico de dimensiones reducidas y carente de intención dramática.

En resumen, el poeta épico oral trabaja componiendo frases y versos con un material heredado que conserva en su memoria, un material sujeto a unas leyes tan estrictas que nos fuerza a pensar que no es casual ni, por supuesto, obra de un solo autor; por el contrario, es el producto de una larga tradición oral. No será inútil analizar, siguiendo a Kirk[6], las fases de esta tra-

---

[6] *Los poemas de Homero*, Buenos Aires, 1968 (trad. esp.).

dición, pues también nos pueden ayudar a comprender determinados desajustes dentro de la estructura de la *Odisea.*.

Prescindiendo de la que Kirk califica como fase originativa (que tiene que darse forzosamente en cualquier cultura, pero de la que no conservamos huellas en Grecia), la segunda fase, la creativa, es la que dio origen en Grecia a la *Ilíada* y *Odisea*. En ésta, el poeta ya cuenta con un *stock* abundante de fórmulas, aunque lógicamente el poeta aumenta el caudal de la tradición formular. La fase creativa es especialmente importante en Grecia, porque sólo allí se produjo la épica monumental de enormes proporciones.

Sigue una tercera fase reproductiva en la que el poeta ya no crea, sólo memoriza y transmite la épica anterior; ésta es la que se dio en Grecia en el siglo VII a.C.

Finalmente, se produce una fase degenerativa; el poeta pierde incluso su capacidad retentiva porque ya cuenta con la escritura. En Grecia es la época de los rapsodas o recitadores, cuya huella podemos detectar, como luego veremos, en algunas partes de la *Odisea* dotadas de un espíritu y un melodramatismo muy ajeno al espíritu del *epos* antiguo, o en algunos parches que sirven de introducción a la recitación independiente de algunas partes de la obra, que se prestaban a ello, como las Aventuras de Odiseo o la Telemaquia. Es también la época del *epos* historiado, de los poemas del Ciclo que tratan de llenar las lagunas dejadas por Homero.

La «Odisea»

I. *Resumen*

Esta es, pues, la técnica empleada en la composición de la *Odisea* y éstas las etapas por las que ha ido pasando el poema cuyo análisis voy a emprender a continuación.

La *Odisea* consta de 24 Cantos o Rapsodias, división que puede ser antigua, como prueban a menudo las junturas entre canto y canto (muchos finales de canto coinciden con unidades temporales, como demuestran frases como «se fueron a dormir» o «allí dormía», etc.), y éstos se reparten con una proporción perfectamente equilibrada entre la Telemaquia o Viaje de Telémaco (Cantos 1-4), las Aventuras de Odiseo narradas en tercera persona (Cantos 5-8), las Aventuras de Odiseo narradas en primera persona por Odiseo en Esqueria (Cantos 9-12), estancia de Odiseo con el Porquero (Cantos 13-16), Odiseo entre los Pretendientes (Cantos 17-20), Matanza de éstos y sus consecuencias (Cantos 21-24).

Así pues, se divide en seis bloques dramáticos, cada uno constituido por cuatro Cantos. Este mismo hecho demuestra el alto grado de elaboración formal y de madurez narrativa del poema en la que insistiremos luego.

Ofrezco ahora un resumen de la misma que será útil para tener una visión sinóptica de su estructura:

Los dioses deciden en Asamblea la vuelta de Odiseo a casa. Atenea pone en movimiento una doble acción que se desarrollará paralelamente hasta el Canto XV, en que se unen los dos hilos narrativos (aunque debido a la técnica épica parecen sucesivos)[7]: el viaje de Telémaco a Pilos y Esparta en busca de noticias de su padre y el retorno de Odiseo desde la isla de Ogigia, donde se encuentra en el momento de comenzar la historia. Atenea baja a Itaca disfrazada del forastero Mentes para aconsejar a Telémaco que realice el viaje aludido. Esto sirve al mismo tiempo para poner en evidencia la situación en Itaca: unos petendientes apremian a Penélope a que se case y al tiempo se comen las posesiones de Odiseo y Telémaco (Canto I).

Telémaco, instigado por Atenea-Mentes, reúne la asamblea del pueblo, donde expone su pretensión de viajar y trata de arrojar del palacio a los pretendientes. La situación es doblemente dramática: en la asamblea los pretendientes señalan que han descubierto los trucos de Penélope para retrasar la boda y que ésta debe casarse inmediatamente, pero al mismo tiempo el adivino Haliterses afirma que Odiseo vive y está cerca «sembrando la muerte contra los pretendientes». Telémaco pide a éstos una nave que le es negada, pero se la ofrece Méntor (realmente Atenea disfrazada) (Canto II).

---

[7] Sobre la ley de sucesión de acciones simultáneas, cfr. T. Zielinski en *Philologus*, supl. 8, 1901, págs. 407 y ss.

Con los compañeros y la nave que le ha proporcionado Atenea-Méntor, Telémaco marcha a Pilos. Allí Néstor le cuenta los regresos de los aqueos que él vio, pero no le puede dar detalle alguno del de Odiseo. Sin embargo, en sus parlamentos introduce el *leit-motiv* de la muerte de Egisto a manos de Orestes (probable incitación a Telémaco para que obre de forma semejante), y le da esperanzas de que Odiseo puede volver. Le aconseja que marche a Esparta a informarse, ya que Menelao es el último que ha regresado; al mismo tiempo le ofrece un hijo suyo como acompañante y un carro (Canto III).

En Esparta, Telémaco conversa con Menelao, quien le cuenta su propio regreso y las peripecias que le acompañaron. Otra vez se insiste en la muerte de Egisto y ya se le ofrece a Telémaco una primera noticia importante: Odiseo no ha muerto, vive en Ogigia, como le contó a Menelao el Viejo del Mar, Proteo.

En Itaca los pretendientes se inquietan cuando descubren la marcha de Telémaco y le preparan una emboscada para matarlo cuando regrese (Canto IV).

Nueva asamblea de los dioses. Atenea sugiere que Hermes sea enviado a Ogigia para que se cumpla la segunda decisión de la primera asamblea. Hermes ordena a Calipso que deje marchar a Odiseo. La Ninfa ayuda a éste a construir una balsa, le entrega provisiones y le despide. Poseidón (el dios que impedía el retorno de Odiseo porque éste había cegado a su hijo Polifemo) divisa la balsa y levanta una tempestad. Cuando Odiseo está a punto de perecer, Ino Leucotea le entrega un velo inmortal con el que podrá llegar sano y salvo a tierra en medio del oleaje. Odiseo divisa una isla, Esqueria de los feacios, y logra con dificultad llegar a la ribera; sube a un bosque cercano y allí se echa a dormir (Canto V).

Atenea incita en sueños a Nausícaa, hija de Alcínoo, rey de los feacios, que vaya por la mañana a lavar al río junto a la ribera del mar. Descubre a Odiseo dormido mientras juega a la pelota con sus esclavas; éste la implora como suplicante y Nausícaa le informa sobre la manera de llegar al palacio de su padre y hacerse bienquisto con Arete, su madre (Canto VI).

Atenea se transforma en niña y conduce a Odiseo, envuelto en una nube, al palacio de Alcínoo. Odiseo entra en el salón, donde están los príncipes de los feacios con Alcínoo y Arete, se dirige a ésta y entonces Atenea disipa la nube que le rodea; le suplica y ésta reconoce los vestidos que le había entregado Nausícaa. Hacen libación a Zeus, protector de los suplicantes, y Antínoo promete agasajar al forastero al día siguiente y prepararle una nave y escolta para que regrese. Se marchan los príncipes, Arete interroga a Odiseo y éste le cuenta su llegada a Ogigia y su partida de allí, así como la tempestad y llegada a Esqueria (Canto VII).

A la mañana siguiente los feacios establecen unos juegos atléticos en honor del héroe; Euríalo lo desafía con palabras injuriosas y Odiseo lanza el disco mucho más lejos que nadie. Luego establecen un concurso de danza. El aedo Demódoco canta los amores de Ares y Afrodita. Finalmente, Alcínoo ordena a los príncipes de los feacios que le hagan regalos a Odiseo, y Euríalo, el primero, le entrega, para desagraviarle, una espada de bronce, plata y marfil. Los feacios llevan sus regalos y Arete los pone dentro de un arca, regalo suyo; luego ordena a las esclavas que bañen a Odiseo.

Por fin comienza la cena en la que Demódoco canta, instigado por el héroe, la estratagema del Caballo de Troya y la destrucción de esta ciudad. Odiseo llora, Alcínoo lo advierte, detiene a Demódoco y finalmente le pregunta quién es y de dónde viene (Canto VIII).

Éste se da a conocer y cuenta las aventuras de su regreso: la lucha con los Cícones, su llegada y huida del país de los lotófagos, la isla de los Cíclopes y ceguera de Polifemo (Canto IX).

Llegada a la isla de Eolo y despedida; llegada a Telépilo de los lestrigones y huida; llegada a la isla de Eea y al palacio de Circe, quien convierte en cerdos a sus compañeros. Odiseo obliga a la hechicera que rompa el hechizo de éstos y permanecen en la isla un año entero. Al fin Circe despide a Odiseo y le ordena ir al Hades para preguntar al adivino Tiresias la forma de regresar a Itaca. Cuando van a partir cae Elpenor del techo y se desnuca (Canto X).

Odiseo llega a las puertas del Hades. Conversa con Elpenor y luego con Tiresias, quien le aconseja no tocar las vacas de Helios cuando lleguen a Trinaquia, le informa sobre los pretendientes y le ordena hacer un viaje de expiación a Poseidón una vez los haya matado.

Luego conversa con su madre y ve una larga lista de heroínas.

El héroe interrumpe su narración. Alcínoo y Arete le ruegan que continúe (olvidando, al parecer, que ya tenía preparado todo para volver aquella noche, con lo que retrasan el viaje para el día siguiente).

Odiseo continúa narrando su conversación, ahora dentro del Hades, con Agamenón y Aquiles. Luego cuenta su visión de Minos y de los condenados célebres —Ticiol, Tántalo y Sísifo— y de héroes célebres, como Orión y Heracles (Canto XI).

Continúa narrando su regreso a la isla de Circe, quien le previene contra Escila y Caribdis, las Sirenas y las vacas de Helios.

Paso por entre Escila y Caribdis y la isla de las Sirenas, llegada a la isla de Trinaquía, donde sus compañeros, agotados por el cansancio y el hambre, matan y se comen los rebaños de Helios. Destrucción de los compañeros por el rayo de Zeus. Odiseo, ya solo y sobre los restos de su nave, llega a los diez días a la isla de Ogigia, donde lo retiene Calipso, le ofrece la inmortalidad y quiere convertirlo en su esposo (Canto XII).

Acaba Odiseo el relato y se van a dormir. Por la mañana llegan a la nave todos los regalos, retornan al palacio y preparan un banquete. Durante éste, el héroe se muestra inquieto esperando que caiga el sol. Ya por la tarde van a la ribera del mar, ponen un lecho para el héroe en la cubierta de la nave y ésta zarpa.

Llegada de Odiseo a Itaca. Encuentro con Atenea disfrazada de joven pastor, quien le aconseja ocultar las riquezas y dirigirse a la majada del fiel porquero Eumeo. Atenea le convierte con su varita en un viejo mendigo y marcha a Esparta para inducir a Telémaco a que regrese (Canto XIII).

Eumeo recibe hospitalariamente a Odiseo mendigo. Éste le cuenta una historia falsa de sí mismo y le anuncia que Fidón, rey de los tesprotos, le ha asegurado que el héroe estaba a punto de regresar a Itaca. Eumeo se muestra escéptico. Por la noche, Odiseo pone a prueba a Eumeo, a ver si le presta un manto, contándole una extraña historia que, dice, le pasó con Odiseo en Troya (Canto XIV).

Entre tanto, Atenea incita a Telémaco en sueños a que regrese previniéndole contra la emboscada de los pretendientes. Al despedirse de Menelao y Helena presencian un presagio —un águila llevando entre sus garras a un ganso—, y Helena lo interpreta como Odiseo matando a los pretendientes. Telémaco y Pisístrato, su acompañante, llegan a Pilos, y al separarse se le acerca a Telémaco un adivino, Teoclímeno de Argos, quien le ruega le reciba en su nave, pues anda huyendo por haber matado a alguien de su tribu.

Entre tanto, en la majada, Odiseo —por probar de nuevo a Eumeo— manifiesta su intención de ir al palacio a mendigar entre los pretendientes y comunicar a Penélope la vuelta de su esposo. Eumeo se lo desaconseja y le cuenta su propia historia.

Telémaco y sus compañeros llegan a Itaca. Presencian un presagio —un gavilán desplumando a una paloma entre sus garras— y Teoclímeno lo interpreta diciendo que la estirpe de Odiseo siempre reinará en Itaca. Telémaco ordena a sus compañeros que acomoden a Teoclímeno en Itaca, y él marcha a la majada por instigación de Atenea (Canto XV).

Atenea prepara el reconocimiento de padre e hijo. Telémaco ordena a Eumeo que marche a la ciudad para comunicar a Penélope su regreso, y al quedarse solos Atenea convierte de nuevo a Odiseo en un hombre joven. Se reconocen por fin y traman un plan para matar a los pretendientes (Telémaco tiene que retirar del salón todas las armas excepto dos equipos completos para ellos).

Entre tanto, los pretendientes se enteran del regreso de Telémaco y el fracaso de su emboscada. Hablan vagamente de volver a intentar matarlo, aunque Eurímaco tranquiliza a Penélope (Canto XVI).

Telémaco regresa a la ciudad dando órdenes a Eumeo de que acompañe a Odiseo al palacio para que mendigue entre los pretendientes. Allí conversa con su madre. Teoclímeno vuelve a afirmar ante Penélope que el héroe ya está en Itaca y prepara la muerte contra los pretendientes.

Odiseo y Eumeo llegan al palacio y encuentran al cabrero

Melantio, quien insulta a su amo. También ve al perro Argos, que muere después de reconocer a su dueño.

Odiseo entra en el mégaron detrás de Eumeo. Antínoo le insulta. Odiseo comienza a pedir comida a todos por orden. Antínoo lo amenaza y le arroja un escabel. Penélope quiere hablar con el forastero, pero éste contesta, a través de Eumeo, que hablará con ella cuando todos se hayan ido (Canto XVII).

Pelea de Odiseo con el mendigo Iro. Anfímono se muestra amable con él y éste le aconseja que se marche a su casa para no tener que enfrentarse con Odiseo.

Atenea induce a Penélope a que se muestre ante los pretendientes y la dota de una belleza especial. Reprende a Telémaco por haber permitido a los pretendientes vejar al forastero y pide a éstos regalos de esponsales. Odiseo se alegra internamente por la astucia de su esposa.

Llega la noche y el héroe se queda en el mégaron para alumbrar a los pretendientes. Nuevos insultos de Eurímaco, quien le arroja un escabel que aquél esquiva (Canto XVIII).

Los pretendientes se van a dormir a sus casas. Odiseo y Telémaco se quedan solos y retiran todas las armas del salón (con lo que se anula el plan que habían tramado en la majada).

Converación de Odiseo con Penélope, en la que aquél le da detalles sobre el regreso del héroe.

Penélope le ofrece baño y cama. Odiseo acepta que le lave los pies la esclava más anciana, quien reconoce al héroe por una cicatriz; éste la amenaza para que no le descubra.

Finalmente, Penélope le cuenta un sueño que ha tenido —un águila matando a sus gansos—, que no necesita interpretación porque el águila misma se identifica como Odiseo (Canto XIX).

El héroe se acuesta, pero no puede dormir. Penélope tampoco duerme, y pide la muerte a los dioses. Odiseo pide a Zeus un portento y un presagio, que corroboren la voluntad de los dioses de que mate a los pretendientes, y Zeus se los concede.

Por la mañana Euriclea dispone el último banquete de los pretendientes. Mientras lo preparan, Odiseo es insultado de nuevo por Melantio —que lleva las cabras al banquete—, pero comprueba la fidelidad de Filetio —que lleva los toros.

Los pretendientes contemplan un presagio —un águila

apresando entre sus garras a una paloma— que los disuade de matar a Telémaco.

Comienza el banquete con nuevas vejaciones de los pretendientes a Odiseo: Ctesipo le tira una pata de buey que aquél evita. Los pretendientes apremian a Telémaco para que entregue su madre a un pretendiente, pero éste se niega con evasivas. Entonces ellos rompen a reír a carcajadas impulsados por Atenea, y Teoclímeno, en tono profético, les predice su muerte (Canto XX).

Atenea inspira a Penélope que establezca un certamen entre los pretendientes consistente en tender el arco de Odiseo y pasar una flecha por el ojo de doce hachas puestas en fila.

Comienza el certamen el adivino Leodes, que se esfuerza en vano en tender el arco. Antínoo ordena a Melantio calentar un pan de sebo para suavizar el arco, pero ni aun así puede tenderlo ninguno de los pretendientes.

Entre tanto, fuera del palacio Odiseo se da a conocer a Eumeo y Filetio y prepara un plan con ellos: que a una señal cierren el salón y cubran las salidas.

En el salón sólo quedan por probar el arco Antínoo y Eurímaco. Fracasa el primero y propone dejarlo para el día siguiente, pues se celebra en el pueblo la fiesta de Apolo.

Odiseo pide a los pretendiente que le dejen probar a él, y a pesar de las amenazas de los pretendientes, Eumeo se lo entrega a instancias de Penélope y Telémaco. El héroe palpa el arco, lo tiende y hace pasar la flecha por las doce hachas. A una señal suya se arma Telémaco y se pone a su lado (Canto XXI).

Odiseo salta al umbral del salón con el arco en sus manos y comienza a disparar. Cae Antínoo el primero. Los pretendientes lo reconocen; Eurímaco implora piedad en vano; los pretendientes sacan las espadas y se defienden con las mesas. Se le acaban al héroe las flechas, y Telémaco va a buscar equipos para ellos dos, para el porquero y para el boyero. Entre tanto, Melantio sube a una habitación de arriba y consigue doce equipos. Eumeo se ofrece para sorprender a Melantio cuando suba de nuevo y matarlo. Atenea-Méntor anima al héroe en la lucha. Caen todos los pretendientes menos el heraldo Medonte y el aedo Femio a quienes perdona la vida.

Acabada la matanza, Odiseo purifica el salón con azufre y ordena a Telémaco, boyero y porquero que limpien la sala y maten a las esclavas infieles (Canto XXII).

También da orden de que llamen a su esposa y se dispongan todos a danzar para que los del pueblo crean que se celebra ya la boda de Penélope.

Entre tanto, Odiseo se da a conocer a Penélope, quien acaba aceptándole como tal sólo después que éste ha superado la prueba del lecho. Finalmente, se van a acostar y se cuentan mutuamente sus sufrimientos y peripecias. El héroe.hace un resumen de todas sus aventuras, ya que Atenea alarga la noche (Canto XXIII).

Los pretendientes descienden al Hades acompañados por Hermes y encuentran al alma de Agamenón contando a la de Aquiles sus funerales. Luego Anfimedonte cuenta a Agamenón la muerte de los pretendientes (en una versión que difiere de la *Odisea*).

Entre tanto, Odiseo y los suyos van a la finca de Laertes, donde aquél se da a conocer a su padre y celebran un banquete.

En Itaca los familiares de los preendientes se enteran de la matanza, entierran sus cadáveres y, capitaneados por Eupites, padre de Antínoo, se dirigen en son de guerra a la hacienda de Laertes. Se traba combate, y éste, rejuvenecido por Atenea, mata a Eupites, pero la diosa, en connivencia con Zeus, detiene la lucha, los hace olvidarse de sus hijos y familiares muertos y establece una paz duradera entre el linaje de Odiseo y el pueblo de Itaca (Canto XXIV).

II. *Composición y estructura: análisis de la obra*

Esta es la *Odisea* en resumen. Un lector normal, sin los «prejuicios» profesionales de un filólogo clásico, encontrará el poema más o menos divertido, con mayor o menor viveza en la narración, lento en unos pasajes y fluido o excesivamente rápido en otros, pero de todas formas lo percibirá como un todo bien trabado.

Sin embargo, desde el pasado siglo, siguiendo los pasos de la crítica analítica, volcada desde el siglo XVIII hacia la *Ilíada*, se han levantado voces que pretenden ver en la *Odisea* un conglomerado mecánico, en ocasiones, débilmente ensamblado de diferentes poemas, obra de diferentes autores.

Kirchhoff[8] fue el primero en proponer la ya célebre teoría de la «compilación», según la cual la *Odisea* se compone de tres o más poemas independientes, y su idea ha sido desarrollada, pretendiendo incluso dilucidar con detalle la cronología del proceso mecánico de ensamblaje, por autores de la talla de Bethe, Wilamowitz, Schwartz, Von der Mühl, Merkelbach[9] y otros.

En general, las opiniones de estos autores analíticos son muy semejantes en lo fundamental, aunque varíen en el detalle. Otros autores están incondicionalmente del lado de la unidad de autor y composición[10], aunque, dada la naturaleza especial de la composición de la *Odisea*, es difícil hoy encontrar posturas unitarias a ultranza. Por otra parte, dado el avance tremendo de nuestro conocimiento actual sobre la épica en general y la griega en particular, las posiciones analíticas actuales con respecto a esta obra no se pueden comparar ni de lejos con las mucho más decididas y radicales con respecto a la *Ilíada*[11].

Las posiciones de un Kirchhoff, un Schwartz o la primera de Wilamowitz, que consideraban la *Odisea* como el resultado de una fusión mecánica de tres o cuatro poemas realizada por un pésimo poeta hacia el siglo VI a.C., son insostenibles y no las comparte hoy nadie. El mismo Wilamowitz rectificó su posición[12] primera admitiendo que la *Odisea* es obra en su mayor

[8] A. Kirchhoff, *Die Homerische Odyssee*, Berlín, 1879.

[9] E. Bethe, *Homer,* Leipzig, 1914-1922; U. von Wilamowitz, *Homerische Untersuchungen,* Berlín, 1884; E. Schwartz, *Die Odyssee,* Munich, 1924; P. von der Mühll, en *RE,* supl. VII, 696 y ss.; R. Merkelbach, *Untersuchungen zur Odyssee,* Munich, 1951.

[10] Así, por ejemplo. K. Reinhardt, «Die Abenteuer der Odyssee», en *Von Werken und Formen,* Godesberg, 1948, y especialmente W. B. Stanford, *Odyssey,* Londres, 1947-1948, quien mantiene una actitud monolítica.

[11] Sobre la Cuestión Homérica en general, cfr. F. R. Adrados, en *Introducción a Homero,* caps. I y II, Madrid, 1963, y A. Heubeck, «Homeric Studies today, en *Tradition and Invention,* ed. B. C. Fenik, Leiden, 1978.

[12] En su obra *Die Heimkehr des Odysseus,* Berlín, 1927.

parte de un único y genial poeta, que se sirvió, eso sí, de tres poemas preexistentes que desembocaban en el triunfo de Odiseo sobre los pretendientes, y que añadió toda la Telemaquia y el Canto XXIV.

Los analíticos del siglo xx, que constituyen la mayoría de los críticos de la *Odisea,* están de acuerdo en que el resultado, es decir, la *Odisea* que nos ha sido transmitida, es obra de un gran poeta (aunque inferior al poeta originario) refundidor de materiales anteriores a él y que añade determinados pasajes. Aquí es donde no están todos de acuerdo.

Para Focke[13], por ejemplo, solamente la Telemaquia y el final (desde XXIII.334 hasta el final) son añadidos.

Schaedewaldt[14] se inclina a considerar como interpolaciones de Telemaquia, parte de la Feacia, el Baño y el segundo plan de matanza contra los pretendientes (VII.148-232; XXIII.117-172), etc., con lo que asigna a Homero (el poeta A, como él dice) más de dos tercios de la *Odisea.*

Por su parte, Page[15] va espigando aquí y allá, y considera espúreos parte de —no toda— la Telemaquia, la segunda Asamblea (V. 1 ss.), toda la Nekya, ciertas partes de la Matanza y todo el final.

En cuanto a los autores unitarios, con las excepciones ya señaladas, han acercado sus posiciones a las de los analíticos, y hoy se puede decir que la diferencia entre unos y otros es cuestión de *voce:* lo que los analíticos llaman poemas preexistentes, los unitarios lo denominan fuentes, temas, motivos; en una palabra, material heredado de la tradición épica.

De esta forma un autor unitario como Kirk solamente difiere de Page en considerar propios del «poeta monumental» (Homero o como se le quiera llamar) también la Telemaquia y toda la Venganza; en cuanto a la segunda Asamblea, la Nekya y el final los considera agregados de la época rapsódica.

Ahora bien, ¿cuáles son las incongruencias, inconsistencias y fallos que han llevado a los analíticos a diseccionar la *Odisea*

---

[13] *Die Odyssee,* Stuttgart, 1943.

[14] En varios trabajos, así «Der Prolog der Odyssee», en *Harv. Stud.,* 63, 1958; Neue Kriterien zur Odyssee-Analyse, Heidelberg, 1959.

[15] *Homeric Odyssey,* Oxford, 1955.

y considerarla como un agregado mecánico de diferentes poemas? Vamos a estudiarlos a continuación prescindiendo de los detalles sin importancia —meros olvidos del poeta— que ocurren en todos los géneros y épocas. Me refiero a hechos como el que en el Canto I Atenea baje con una lanza que se queda en el portalanzas cuando ésta «se remontó como un ave». Detalles como éste, a los que hasta hace poco se daba mucha importancia, son —repito— meros olvidos de un poeta que tiene que recitar más de 12.000 versos.

Más importancia tienen, sin embargo, otros que han llevado a postular seriamente la presencia de varias manos.

Limitándonos a las más conspicuas, vamos a pasar revista, pues, a las incongruencias que aparecen en las diferentes partes de la obra, especialmente en la Telemaquia, las Aventuras, la Venganza y el Final del Poema.

Desde una posición unitaria, vamos a defender aquí la unidad de la casi totalidad de la obra, tratando de explicar la mayoría de estas inconsistencias por varias causas, entre las que destacan:

— el carácter oral de la épica que propicia los olvidos del poeta.
— la tremenda complejidad del material que sirvió al autor como materia poética para crear su Odisea.
— a veces, un cambio consciente del poeta en su estructura narrativa o una elección del mismo entre varias versiones anteriores a su obra.

Sin embargo, aun desde esta posición unitaria, hemos de reconocer las dificultades de explicar dos pasajes (la segunda Asamblea y el Canto XXIV) sin admitir la hipótesis de un refundidor posthomérico. Por ello vamos a distinguir en esta exposición las inconsistencias, etc., que se pueden explicar fácilmente sin recurrir a la hipótesis de varios autores y las que no.

A. *Inconsistencias que no exigen la hipótesis de un refundidor posthomérico.*

1. La «Telemaquia»

Hemos visto que todos los analíticos, sin excepción, la consideran un agregado. El hecho de que tenga un protagonista diferente de Odiseo, de que sea un bloque compacto de tres cantos y que III y IV sean relatos de *Nostoi* (regresos de los héroes que lucharon en Troya) ha hecho suponer a los analíticos que era un *epos* separado y que fue aprovechado por el refundidor de la *Odisea* como introducción a la misma.

Sin embargo, es obvio que la unión de los dos hilos narrativos (las Aventuras de Odiseo y el Viaje de Telémaco) en los Cantos XIV y —especialmente— XV es tan extraordinariamente habilidosa que no es suficiente explicarla como obra de un refundidor; es necesaria la visión amplia de un gran poeta que escribe una obra a gran escala en cuyo plan inicial entraba la fusión de los dos temas.

El último de los grandes analíticos de la *Odisea,* Page, no se atreve a desechar toda la Telemaquia, y concede que la mayor parte de ella pertenece a Homero, si bien el canto II fue ampliado hasta convertirse en una Introducción a la antigua Telemaquia, cuando los rapsodas decidieron recitarla por separado. Igualmente, según este autor, algunas partes del Canto I serían ampliadas y remodeladas basándose en los sucesos del Canto II, especialmente el confuso y contradictorio discurso de Atenea-Mentes a Telémaco. Esta remodelación explicaría para Page el que Atenea aconseje incomprensiblemente a éste que mande a Penélope a casa de su padre «si su deseo la impulsa a casarse» (algo que es obvio que ésta no desea) y que luego mate a los pretendientes (quienes ya no estarían allí porque Penélope se habría casado con uno de ellos y los demás habrían vuelto a sus casas).

También ha llamado la atención el que Telémaco no pida ayuda a Néstor o Menelao (cosa que, precisamente, suponen los pretendientes que va a hacer, ya que le niegan la nave). La explicación de este «problema» es bien sencilla: Homero *aprovecha* materiales prehoméricos sobre los *Nostoi,* y en ellos cabía difícilmente tal petición de ayuda.

En cualquier caso, creo que el principal defecto de la crítica analítica en este punto, como en muchos otros, estriba en querer exigir a un poeta una lógica cartesiana; defecto que han heredado, evidentemente, de sus colegas del siglo XVIII.

La postura de Kirk en este punto creo que es sumamente acertada: Homero es el autor de *Telemaquia* y *Odisea,* las cuales combina habilidosamente, aunque aprovecha materiales existentes, como no podía menos de hacer siendo un poeta épico oral. Por otra parte, este autor se muestra escéptico ante la hipótesis de Page sobre la existencia de dos versiones del viaje de Telémaco (una en la que los pretendientes le impiden el viaje y otra en que no), cuya fusión precisamente daría lugar a las incongruencias de los Cantos I y II.

2. Las Aventuras (Cantos IX al XII)

Aquí podemos establecer una ulterior división entre las Aventuras propiamente dichas y la Nekya, que presenta problemas peculiares y más graves.

a) *Las Aventuras propiamente dichas.*—También en esta parte del poema los analíticos han visto varias manos debido a diferentes razones.

Algunas de las aventuras, dicen, son excesivamente cortas y, por tanto, suponen resúmenes de materiales diversos (así, el episodio de los Cícones, que además de corto es insípido; el de los Lestrigones y Escila Caribdis). Por otra parte, desde el punto de vista geográfico, hay una mezcla de aventuras espacialmente localizables y otras imaginarias: la isla de los Cíclopes y la de Esqueria no tienen localización precisa porque son tierras paradisiacas, como tampoco la tiene la de Eolo, porque es flotante, pero en cambio los Cícones están en Asia Menor, y los Lotófagos, en África del Norte, si llegaron allí las naves de Odiseo después de nueve días de viajar hacia el Sur desde Malea. Con la excepción de Ogigia, que debe estar en el extremo Oeste, las demás aventuras de localización posible se desarrollan en el Nordeste lejano; así, los Lestrigones (donde «son cercanos los caminos del día y de la noche»), la isla de Eea (pues Circe es hermana de Eetes, rey de la Cólquide), las puertas de Hades (cerca de los Cimerios, que no ven el sol), la isla de Trinaquía (pues es la isla del Sol). En cuanto a las Sirenas y Escila y Caribdis, proceden de la saga argonáutica, cuyo escenario es el lejano Nordeste.

Nadie niega hoy que tenía razón Meuli[16] cuando afirmaba que gran parte de estas aventuras están tomadas del Viaje de los Argonautas, sumamente rico en aventuras y plenamente elaborado antes del siglo VIII, pero no es preciso ver dierentes manos ni agregados mecánicos. Nadie, si no es un poeta genial, ha podido hacer converger de una forma tan precisa y perfecta todo este material hacia la figura de Odiseo y su retorno.

Otras inconsistencias menores, como el que Atenea no aparece para nada en las aventuras, se deben a que en el material que aprovecha Homero no era relevante su figura. Sin embargo, el poeta mismo es consciente de ello, y trata de subsanarlo haciendo a Odiseo quejarse ante Atenea de que no la ha visto desde que partió de Troya hasta que llegó a Itaca (V. XIII. 316 y siguientes).

Finalmente, el que las aventuras tengan un tratamiento diferente respecto a su longitud o el que en el episodio del Cíclope haya una fusión del tema de la Edad de Oro con el del Gigante Malvado y el de Nadie, no implican diferentes manos ni la presencia de un refundidor; o, mejor, sí que requieren un refundidor, pero éste no es otro que Homero.

b) *La Nekya (Canto XI)*.—Este episodio presenta graves problemas e inconsistencias que han llevado a algunos autores a eliminarlo de la *Odisea* primitiva como espúreo, y a otros —menos decididos— a considerarlo como un breve poema prehomérico sobre un viaje de Odiseo a ultratumba expandido por la inclusión de Catálogos beocios.

En primer lugar, hay, evidentemente, una fusión o confusión entre una *Nekyomanteia* (o consulta oracular a los muertos) y una *Katábasis* (o descenso a los infiernos). En efecto,

---

[16] *Odyssee und Argonautika*, Basilea, 1921.

Odiseo va propiamente a consultar al alma del adivino Tiresias *a las puertas de Hades.* Sin embargo, sin transición ninguna lo vemos de repente *en medio del Hades* conversando animadamente con las almas de Agamenón y Aquiles o recorriéndolo para visitar a los condenados y otras figuras relevantes de la Mitología, de las que, curiosamente, una es Heracles, protagonista de la más célebre Katábasis.

En segundo lugar, todo el Canto tiene un sabor inconfundiblemente beocio —el mismo personaje de Tiresias, los Catálogos de heroínas y héroes—, por lo que se ha considerado una interpolación hecha a base de retazos de la épica beocia entre los viajes de Odiseo.

Sin embargo, contra todas estas razones se puede argumentar que el oráculo de Tiresias era lo suficientemente antiguo como para ser conocido fuera de los límites de Beocia; que la conversación de Odiseo con el adivino, aunque es bien cierto que aclara poco sobre el retorno de Odiseo, ofrece una información en parte esencial para el conjunto de la obra (así los problemas que va a encontrar Odiseo en Itaca) y en parte conveniente para cerrar del todo el poema; me refiero al viaje que tendrá que llevar a cabo Odiseo tierra adentro para aplacar a Poseidón, cuya ira, después de todo, es el motivo cardinal de casi toda la acción.

Y si bien es verdad que el llamado Interludio del Canto XI.333-384 presenta el problema de que ignora los preparativos del viaje de Odiseo y alarga un día más su estancia en Esqueria, también es cierto que sirve muy habilidosamente para insertar el episodio del Hades, que después de todo es necesario, como acabamos de ver, dentro de la parte de las aventuras.

Se puede concluir lícitamente, después de examinar los problemas que presenta la Nekya, que se trata una vez más de un material prehomérico que el poeta aprovecha habilidosamente para incardinarlo en la acción y que no hay nada que exija una mano diferente de la de Homero en la manipulación del mismo, a no ser —quizá— en los catálogos de heroínas y condenados. Pero no hay motivo alguno que justifique su total exclusión de la autoría de Homero, y sí las hay, en cambio, que justifiquen su inclusión. Después de todo, el Canto XI traza una vez más el paralelo entre el caso de Agamenón y el de Odiseo, y sirve para recoger motivos anteriores y adelantar otros que aparecerán después.

3. La Venganza (Cantos XVII a XXIII)

En estos cantos hay algunos detalles que han llevado a pensar en diferentes versiones que, al ser fundidas mecánicamente, producen ciertas incongruencias. Me refiero al disfraz de Odiseo y al plan (o planes) para retirar las armas.

Atenea cambia en viejo a Odiseo cuando éste llega a la majada de Eumeo; de nuevo lo convierte en joven para la anagnórisis de Telémaco; otra vez lo convierte en viejo cuando va al palacio para que no lo reconozcan los pretendientes. Lógicamente, se dice, debería haberle hecho joven de nuevo después de la matanza de los pretendientes para su reconocimiento final por Penélope; sin embargo, parece que al poeta se le olvidó este detalle.

No es esto cierto del todo, pues en el Canto XXIII.153 y ss. se describe el baño de Odiseo, y aunque no se dice expresamente que Atenea lo convirtiera de nuevo de viejo en joven, sí dice (y esto, evidentemente, era idéntico para el poeta y su auditorio) que le hizo más alto y grueso, que derramó una gracia sobre su cabeza, que de ésta colgaron cabellos negros y que salió del baño semejante a los inmortales.

Otro punto que nos hace pensar en una distracción del poeta, o quizá en un cambio de plan —pero nada más— es el siguiente: en el Canto XVI.281 forma Odiseo un plan con Telémaco para que éste retire las armas del mágaron dejando sólo dos equipos. Esto debe hacerlo estando los pretendientes dentro, pues Odiseo sugiere una excusa para éstos, que, lógicamente, deben extrañarse del comportamiento de Telémaco.

Sin embargo, en el Canto XIX.1 y ss. se van todos a dormir y quedan solos en el mégaron Odiseo y su hijo, quienes, lógicamente, retiran las armas. Ahora bien, las retiran todas y ni siquiera mencionan un cambio de plan para la matanza.

De este detalle los analíticos deducen la existencia de dos versiones yuxtapuestas, pero es obvio que no es necesario acudir a esta explicación. Es mucho más fácil pensar en un «olvido» más del poeta o incluso en un cambio del poeta en su plan narrativo al decidir incluir la conversación entre Odiseo y Penélope, que es —al menos— conveniente desde el punto de vista dramático, ya que pone de relieve una vez más la proximidad de la venganza, por un lado, y la aporía de la situación, por otro.

4. El personje de Teoclímeno

Es éste un personaje relativamente oscuro e incómodo de explicar. Su misma presentación a Telémaco en el Canto XV, que a algunos les ha parecido ridícula, sugería una mayor importancia de este personaje en la obra. Sin embargo, sólo aparece dos veces más en situaciones extrañas y con una actuación que a algunos ha parecido sospechosa.

En el Canto XV interpreta a Telémaco un presagio —un águila destrozando una paloma—, diciéndole que el linaje de Odiseo reinará siempre en Itaca; sin embargo, en el Canto XVII le dice a Penélope que él había interpretado a Telémaco un presagio —el del Canto XV— diciéndole que Odiseo ya estaba en Itaca. Esta contradicción puede ser considerada como un mero olvido del poeta. Pero es su tercera actuación la que más ha extrañado a todos los críticos. En el Canto XX los pretendientes, enloquecidos por Atenea, rompen a reír a carcajadas ante la —un tanto infantil— respuesta de Telémaco a la petición de Antímaco de que ordene por fin a su madre que se case. Es entonces cuando se levanta Teoclímeno (de quien no se ha dicho que estuviera presente) y les predice la muerte en tono profético. Este pasaje, todo él, es de una rara belleza, pero un tanto extraño, aparte del tono y el lenguaje, por el hecho de que es la única vez que en Homero un adivino está dotado de poderes proféticos. Los adivinos son siempre intérpretes de presagios, sueños, etc., pero carecen de visión profética respecto del futuro.

Con todo, por extraño que parezca este personaje, no hay nada serio que impida considerarlo creación homérica, y por ello habremos de admitirlo como tal, aunque sintamos cierta inclinación a aceptar la sugerencia de Page, en el sentido de que podría muy bien tratarse de un resto inorgánico de una versión distinta de la *Odisea* en la que el protagonisa podría regresar a casa disfrazado de adivino, para lo cual hay paralelos en otras literaturas.

B. *Inconsistencias que sólo se explican —o se explican mejor— con la hipótesis de un refundidor posthomérico.*

1. La segunda Asamblea (Canto V.1-42)

Aquí, evidentemente, nos encontramos con la mano de un refundidor. Esta segunda Asamblea, en efecto, contradice dos leyes de la épica, la de economía o no repetición de lo superfluo y la de sucesión de acciones simultáneas.

Ya al comienzo del Canto I hay otra similar en la que se decide: *a*) enviar a Hermes a Ogigia con la orden de que Calipso deje libre a Odiseo, y *b*) bajar Atenea en persona a Itaca para aconsejar a Telémaco, entre otras cosas, que haga el viaje a Pilos y Lacedemonia. Según la conocida ley de sucesión[17], dos acciones realmente simultáneas se describen en la épica como sucesivas. Ahora bien, del Canto I al IV se describe *b*); como *a*) era simultánea, bastaba con un verso que dijera algo como «Entonces Hermes se lanzó desde las cumbres del Olimpo y bajó a Ogigia», en vez de repetir la primera Asamblea.

Pero no es sólo esto; lingüísticamente el pasaje es un cosido de frases tomadas de cantos anteriores (concretamente, de Méntor, Proteo y Medonte). Creo que en este caso no sería imprudente admitir con Page que esta segunda Asamblea es obra de un rapsoda que necesitaba un prólogo más amplio que la frase antes citada para recitar por separado las Aventuras de Odiseo.

---

[17] Cfr. nota 7. Delebecque *(Télémaque et la structure de l'Odysée,* Aix-en-Provençe, 1958) se basa precisamente en esta ley para justificar la 2.ª Asamblea.

2. El final de la *Odisea* (XXIII. 296 hasta el final)

Mucho más graves son los problemas que plantea todo el final de la obra.

Según el escolio al verso XXIII.296, los filólogos alejandrinos Aristarco y Aristófanes consideraban este verso el final de la *Odisea* («Aristarco y Aristófanes ponen aquí el fin de la *Odisea*»). Se ha discutido si ellos encontraron alguna(s) rama(s) de la tradición del poema en que acababa aquí la obra o si su juicio es meramente valorativo e implica «aquí debería acabar» o «éste es el final lógico de la *Odisea*».

En cualquier caso, es evidente que el Canto XXIII, a partir de este verso, y todo el Canto XXIV presentan tal cúmulo de problemas, contradicciones con el resto de la obra e inconsistencias que, incluso unitarios a ultranza, han sentido aquí la necesidad de admitir la mano de un refundidor posthomérico. Vamos a analizarlos por partes.

Los versos 310-341 del Canto XXIII constituyen un resumen de todas las aventuras de Odiseo. En realidad, se los puede admitir como genuinos, ya que ni contradicen lingüísticamente al resto de la obra, ni desentonan abiertamente de su contexto como algo inorgánico. Odiseo y Penélope han ido al lecho, y es lógico que se cuenten sus peripecias. El suponer, como se ha hecho, que se trata de un resumen mnemotécnico para facilitar la labor de un recitador es improbable y, desde luego, no carente de fantasía.

Más difíciles de admitir como genuinos son los versos 344 hasta el final del Canto XXIII. Parecen compuestos meramente para justificar el encuentro (y *anagnórisis)* de Odiseo con Laertes. Es evidente que si la *Odisea* acabara en el Canto XXIII.296 quedarían algunos cabos sueltos —uno de ellos preocupante para un auditorio griego, como la necesidad de purificación de Odiseo tras el homicidio múltiple. Se ha dicho con razón que la *Odisea* no podía dejar sin resolver este problema. Lo que sucede es que probablemente se resolvía en un par de versos que han sido «hinchados» hasta 624. Ahora bien, otros cabos sueltos como la bajada al Hades de los pretendientes y el encuentro de Odiseo con Laertes —único de su familia que le quedaba por ver— no le importaban demasiado al autor de una epopeya de corte dramático, y sí, en cambio, a los autores de la epopeya cíclica cuyo único interés era narrar una historia hasta el final.

Con todo, esto sólo no sería razón suficiente para desechar el final de la *Odisea* si no fuera por otras razones que, aisladas, tampoco son concluyentes, pero que todas juntas aportan un peso definitivo. Estas razones se basan en incongruencias graves de lengua, estilo y argumento, así como en hechos que desentonan de la concepción religiosa de Homero.

Anomalías lingüísticas.—No voy a ofrecer aquí un examen detallado de las mismas, ya que esto ha sido realizado exhaustivamente por Page (ob. cit., págs. 102-111).

Este autor reúne no menos de cincuenta anomalías que se refieren tanto al uso de palabras sueltas (ya de aparición única, ya con un sentido que no tienen hasta tres o cuatro siglos más tarde, ya de aplicación incorrecta), como al de expresiones forzadas, mal empleadas o mal combinadas, como a quebrantamientos violentos de reglas métricas.

En algunos casos es evidente que el refundidor no entendió algunas fórmulas que aparecen en otros lugares de la *Odisea*, y las aplica incoherentemente, dando lugar a monstruos lingüísticos, tan extraños e irrepetidos como el φιλίων (comparativo de φίλος) en el Canto XXIV.267.

Anomalías estilísticas e incoherencias argumentales.—Empecemos por la llamada segunda Nekya o Bajada de los pretendientes al Hades. Es un pasaje singular por varias razones. Primero, porque desconoce por completo la forma en que un muerto baja al Hades *siempre* en Homero (baja sin acompañamiento y tiene que esperar a que entierren su cuerpo); por el epíteto Cilenio que se aplica a Hermes (es un epíteto local de Arcadia, y la épica rechaza las advocaciones locales de los dioses), y sobre todo por su papel de Psicopompo, que pertenece a su naturaleza esencial de dios prehelénico, pero que es desconocida completamente por el resto de la épica; por la alusión al Pueblo de los Sueños, la Roca Leúcade, las Puertas de Helios, desconocidas por completo de la épica griega; por la conversación entre Agamenón y Aquiles, que carece de relevancia para la *Odisea* y supone que no se habían encontrado en el Hades, ignorando la primera Nekya[18].

Todavía más extraña es la narración que hace Anfimedonte de la muerte de los pretendientes a manos de Odiseo. Es extraña porque narra una historia distinta de la que tenemos en el Canto XXII y, por tanto, supone una versión distinta de la Venganza, en la que Penélope reconoce a Odiseo antes y juntos planean la matanza de los pretendientes. La historia que cuenta Anfimedonte es la siguiente: Penélope engañaba a los pretendientes deshaciendo de noche la tela que tejía de día; por fin es descubierta, y *en ese momento,* cuando ya tiene que casarse, llega Odiseo, se da a conocer a su esposa y *juntos* planean la matanza. Esta es una versión más corta y quizá más dramática que la que sigue Homero. Al alargarla Homero, sin duda tuvo que introducir un *tempo* más lento, pero lo que pierde su versión en lógica dramática lo gana en intensidad y en suspense.

La escena con Laertes también es singular. Todo su espíritu es diferente del resto de la *Odisea,* debido, entre otras cosas, al ambiente bucólico y al tono melodramático del reconocimiento. En cuanto a inconsistencias con el resto, Laertes ya no es el anciano que duerme en el campo «donde los esclavos» y es cuidado por una anciana. Vive en una villa y tiene un grupo de criados. El padre de éstos se llama Dolio, tercer personaje con este nombre que aparece en la *Odisea* (uno es el padre de la esclava infiel Melanto y el otro un criado particular de Penélope que le «cuida su huerto abundante en árboles» a quien envía a avisar a Laertes (IV. 737) para que impida la muerte de Telémaco; sin duda, el poeta del Canto XXIV pensó que este Dolio era un criado de Laertes).

Para terminar, la lucha final entre la casa de Laertes y los familiares de los pretendientes es especialmente torpe y trata de crear un efectismo con su mezcolanza de transformaciones, rayos, campesinos y dioses que resulta ridícula y completamente inadecuada como final para una obra como la *Odisea.*

En general, desde el punto de vista estilístico, todo el Can-

---

[18] Page, en o. c., págs. 119 y ss., trata de demostrar, incluso gramaticalmente, la adición mecánica de la conversación entre ambos.

to XXIV es sorprendentemente distinto del resto de la épica griega conocida. Y una de las cosas que más han llamado la atención son los cambios bruscos de un escenario a otro, de Ítaca al campo, del campo al Olimpo y otra vez al campo. La transición al Olimpo es especialmente sorprendente, ya que en Homero *nunca* se produce un «salto» del plano humano al divino, sino una transición suave y cuidadosamente preparada.

Otro aspecto chocante es, en general, el tono melodramático tan extraño a la épica y el ambiente bucólico, que no encuentra paralelo hasta la época helenística; en efecto, el encuentro de Odiseo con Laertes más parece un epilio helenístico que un episodio de epopeya.

Resumiendo, pues, podemos concluir desde un punto de vista unitario:

a) Que la casi totalidad de la obra está compuesta por un solo poeta, y un poeta monumental que crea, a partir de elementos heredados, una gran epopeya dramática. La unidad de autor la demuestran en forma incontrovertible la uniformidad de la lengua, el estilo en general, el desarrollo argumental y especialmente la congruencia en el dibujo de los caracteres. Este último punto es importante, porque la multiplicidad de autores habría influido decisivamente en crear unos caracteres endebles e incoherentes. Sin embargo, el carácter de Odiseo se presenta a los ojos del lector como único a pesar de que el héroe de las aventuras y el matador de los pretendientes originariamente son dispares.

Especialmente bien logrado es el carácter de Telémaco, al que vemos en desarrollo a lo largo de toda la obra, desde el adolescente carente de recursos para actuar hasta el hombre decidido que colabora con su padre en la matanza de los pretendientes. En cuanto a éstos, auténticos protagonistas del drama, no carecen de los rasgos del héroe trágico. Son un héroe colectivo, dotados de la *hybris* y la determinación del héroe que acepta inflexible su destino. No es cierto, como afirma Kirk, que carecen de fuerza dramática, porque, salvo en cuatro o cinco casos, no conocemos ni siquiera su nombre; por el contrario, es precisamente su anonimato el que les presta ese carácter de héroe colectivo.

b) A pesar de la unidad general, existen algunas inconsistencias estructurales. Entre ellas, unas carecen de relieve y se explican fácilmente por la complejidad del material, por el carácter oral, etc. Otras, por el contrario, sólo se explican ya por la incorporación mecánica e inorgánica de resúmenes posthoméricos que servían al propósito de recitar algunas partes por separado (así la Segunda Asamblea) o sencillamente de alargar y completar el poema (así los catálogos de la *Nekya* y todo el final desde el Canto XXIII.296).

Salvo estos pasajes, el resto es de un solo autor, pero ¿quién fue ese autor y en qué época vivió?

III. *Autor y época*

En realidad, el problema de autoría de la *Odisea* se viene planteando en relación con la *Ilíada* desde los orígenes de la cuestión homérica en que se puso en duda la unidad interna de ambas obras y la existencia misma de Homero, el poeta a quien la Antigüedad asignó la paternidad de toda la épica griega conservada.

Por esto, la pregunta que se ha planteado siempre es doble:

a) ¿Pertenecen *Ilíada* y *Odisea* a un mismo autor?
b) En caso afirmativo, ¿es Homero este autor?

Generalmente, las respuestas suelen depender de la posición unitaria o analítica adoptada, aunque también se da el caso de quien, siendo unitario, niega una y otra cosa.

Quizá podríamos aportar aquí las dos opiniones extremas mantenidas por Page, por un lado, que niega *a*) y *b*), y F. R. Adrados, que afirma ambas; aunque hay que añadir que la postura analítica es siempre más radical, mientras que la unitaria pone menos énfasis en este problema que en el de la unidad interna de ambas.

Page[19] mantiene la opinión extrema y altamente improbable de que la *Odisea* fue escrita por un poeta que incluso desconocía la existencia de la *Ilíada;* que fue escrita en una región aislada, concretamente «en una de las islas (del Egeo oriental), en la que el arte épico pudo ser practicado en mayor o menor aislamiento durante la Edad Oscura».

Page llega a esta conclusión después de un estudio de la lengua en que aporta ejemplos de palabras y fórmulas que aparecen en *Ilíada,* pero no en *Odisea* (o viceversa) cuando el tema y las circunstancias lo habrían exigido. También se basa en ciertos detalles por los que el poeta de la *Odisea* parece ignorar los hechos fundamentales de la *Ilíada* (por ejemplo, que Odiseo nunca manejó el arco, que es un arma propia de los bárbaros) o en el hecho de que, cuando se menciona la guerra de Troya, el poeta de la *Odisea* «nunca repite o se refiere a ningún incidente relatado en la *Ilíada*»; también en las diferencias sociales y éticas, en la concepción de los dioses, etc., que reflejan una y otra obra.

Frente a esta postura merece resaltarse la opuesta mantenida por F. R. Adrados[20]:

> En realidad, no hay argumentos suficientes para probar que la *Odisea* sea más reciente que la *Ilíada.* No lo son los lingüísticos ni los de estilo... Tampoco es estrictamente demostrable que *Ilíada* y *Odisea* sean obras del mismo autor. El argumento más importante para creerlo así es que personajes como Ulises, Néstor, Helena, aparecen en ambos poemas con rasgos prácticamente idénticos... De otra parte, siempre se puede echar mano a la hipótesis de que Homero escribió la *Odisea* en su vejez. En un asunto como éste no es posible llegar a soluciones decisivas. Solamente conviene observar que la hipótesis del autor único es menos complicada que la otra, que admite el nacimiento de dos poetas geniales en fechas próximas y con tendencias semejantes. Parece que el *onus probandi* debe recaer sobre los hombros de los modernos corizontes o separatistas. Mientras éstos no demuestren su tesis mejor que hasta ahora, seguiremos teniendo derecho a considerar también la *Odisea* como obra de Homero.

---

[19] O. c., págs. 149-160.
[20] O. c., pág. 87.

Finalmente, hay otros autores que, siendo unitarios, sostienen (sin caer en el extremismo de Page) que factores como la lengua, tema e incluso otros detalles arriba citados son pruebas suficientes de que *Ilíada* y *Odísea* pertenecen a diferentes autores. Así, Kirk cree que el autor de la *Odisea* es posterior al de la *Ilíada* entre una y tres generaciones.

En todo caso, incluso los unitarios tienen serias dudas en atribuir ambas obras a Homero debido a la oscuridad en que este nombre está envuelto. Y digo nombre porque para muchos esto es lo que es Homero, un mero nombre. Ni la *Vita Homeri*, atribuida falsamente a Heródoto, ni el *Certamen* entre Homero y Hesíodo, que para algunos autores contienen ciertas dosis de verdad histórica, pueden quitarnos del todo la duda de si Homero no será una pura invención griega para llenar el hueco del *prõtos heuretés* (o «inventor») de la épica.

Pero haya existido Homero o no, lo cierto es que hubo un poeta genial que dio conformación monumental y dramática a una serie de materiales épicos por él heredados, creando lo que hoy conocemos como *Ilíada* y *Odisea*.

En cuanto a la fecha de creación de esta última, en gran medida depende de la posición adoptada en el punto anterior. Si el autor es Homero, evidentemente hay que fecharla junto con la *Ilíada*, entre los siglos ix y el vii a.C., aunque quizá en la vejez del poeta.

Kirk, después de analizar concienzudamente los criterios en que se puede basar la datación —internos (arqueológicos y lingüísticos) y externos (citas de Homero datables, escenas épicas pintadas en vasos, testimonios de cronologistas de la Antigüedad, etc.)— coloca a ambos poetas dentro de un amplio margen que va desde finales del siglo ix a principios del viii para la *Ilíada*, y mediados del siglo viii a principios del vii para la *Odisea*.

Ningún autor se atreve a precisar más, ya que los datos nunca son definitivos, y casi todos se inclinan a separar ambas obras entre una y tres generaciones.

IV. *La presente edición*

Finalmente, una aclaración sobre la presente traducción. Antes que nada he de hacer notar que está hecha sobre el texto de la *Odisea* establecido por T. W. Allen en *Homeri opera. Odyssea*, Oxford, 1967.

Entre los dos tipos posibles de traducción de la *Odisea* —poética en verso libre y en prosa suelta— he optado por el segundo, ya que puede servir a dos fines: primero, que al estar en prosa y ser literal es de más utilidad al erudito que quiera estudiar en la obra los elementos históricos y culturales, debido a la exactitud de la traducción; segundo, porque una versión poética limita automáticamente el número de lectores, y es mi intención —y la de esta colección— que llegue al mayor número posible.

Por otra parte, la *Odisea,* con ser poesía y poesía genial, es fundamentalmente narrativa; una de sus mayores virtudes es precisamente la agilidad de su movimiento narrativo. El verterla en verso, creo, conllevaría el cerrarla en un corsé demasiado estrecho y darle un paso lento de que carece en el original griego.

Por esta razón he tratado de darle en castellano un tinte de novela o cuento aprovechando al máximo los elementos lingüísticos de transición que suelen aparecer en el cuento en castellano («así que», «ello es que», «conque», etc.), traduciendo con ellos los elementos copulativos griegos, típicos del estilo paratáctico de la épica. Sin embargo, a veces los he traducido como meras cópulas, porque, a pesar de que pueden producir cierta monotonía, dan al texto un carácter arcaico que, después de todo, merecía la pena conservar.

BIBLIOGRAFÍA

Ofrecer una bibliografía completa de Homero es tarea poco menos que imposible. Pero además sería engorrosa para el lector común e innecesaria para el especialista que puede encontrarla en excelentes repertorios bibliográficos de los cuales el más reciente es W. Packard-T. Meyers, *A bibliography of Homeric scholarship 1930-1970,* Malibú, 1974. La lista que ofrezco a continuación es, por consiguiente, una selección de los libros que más han hecho progresar nuestro conocimiento sobre la *Odisea,* aunque no pocos de ellos, especialmente los de orientación analítica, hayan perdido la vigencia que tuvieron en su día y constituyan un monumento a los excesos de una filología metodológicamete equivocada.

1. Obras generales sobre Homero

Kirk, G. S., *Los poemas de Homero* (trad. esp.), Buenos Aires, 1968.
Gil, L., y otros, *Introducción a Homero,* Madrid, 1963.
Wace, A. J. B.-Stubbings, F. H., *A Companion to Homer,* Londres, 1967.

2. Ediciones de la «Odisea»

Allen, T. W., *Homeri Opera,* vols. III y IV, Oxford, 1965.
Stanford, *Homers Odyssey,* I y II, Londres, 1959[2] (con comentario).
West, S., *Omero Odissea,* cantos 1-4: Hainsworth, J. B., 5-8: Heubeck, A., 9-12; Hoekstra, A., 13-16 (en preparación, con traducción y comentario), Roma, 1981-84.

3. Estudios monográficos sobre la «Odisea»

Austin, N., *Archery of the dark of the moon,* Berkeley, 1975.
Besslich, S., *Schweigen, Verschweigen, Übergehen...,* Heidelberg, 1966.

Bethe, E., *Homer, Dichtung und Sage, II Odyssee,* Leipzig, 1929.

Carpenter, R., *Folk Tale, Fiction and Saga in the homeric epics,* Berkeley, 1946.

Delebecque, E., *Télémaque et la structure de l'Odyseée,* Aix en Provence, 1958.

Eisenberger, H., *Studien zur Odysee,* Wiesbaden, 1973.

Erbse, H., *Beiträge zum Verständniss der Odysee,* Berlín, 1972.

Fenik, B., *Studies in the Odyssey,* Wiesbaden, 1974.

Finley, M. I., *El mundo de Odiseo* (trad. esp.), Madrid, 1984.

Focke, F., *Die Odysee,* Stuttgart, 1943.

Germain, G., *Genèse de l'Odyssée,* París, 1954.

Heubeck, A., *Der Odysee Dichter und die Ilias,* Erlangen, 1954.

Hölscher, U., *Untersuchungen zur Form der Odyssee,* Leipzig, 1939.

Kirchhoff, A., *Die homerische Odyssee,* Berlín, 1879.

Mattes, W., *Odysseus bei den Phäaken,* Würzburg, 1958.

Merkelbach, R., *Untersuchungen zur Odyssee,* Munich, 1969.

Meuli, K., *Odysee und Argonautika,* Basilea, 1921.

Page, D. L., *The Homeric Odyssey,* Oxford, 1955.

Rothe, K., *Die Odyssee als Dichtung,* Paderborn, 1914.

Rüter, K., *Odysseeinterpretationen. Untersuchungen zum ersten Buch und zur Phaiakis, Göttingen,* 1969.

Schadewaldt, W., *Neue Kriterien zur Odyssee-Analyse,* Heidelberg, 1959.

Schwartz, E., *Die Odyssee,* Munich, 1924.

Stanford, W. B., *The Ulysses Theme,* Michigan, 1963.

Stella, L. A., *Il poema di Ulisse,* Florencia, 1955.

Thornton, A., *People and Themes in Homer's Odyssey,* Londres, 1970.

Von der Mühll, O., «Odyssee», en *RE,* supl. VII, 696 y ss.

Wilamowitz, U. von, *Die Heimkehr des Odysseus,* Berlín, 1927.

Woodhouse, W. J., *The Composition of Homer's Odyssey,* Oxford, 1969[2].

ODISEA

Polifemo, Ulises y sus compañeros

CANTO I

LOS DIOSES DECIDEN EN ASAMBLEA
EL RETORNO DE ODISEO

CUÉNTAME, *Musa, la historia del hombre de muchos senderos*[1],
que anduvo errante muy mucho después de Troya sagrada asolar;
vio muchas ciudades de hombres y conoció su talante,
y dolores sufrió sin cuento en el mar tratando
de asegurar su vida y el retorno de sus compañeros.
Mas no consiguió salvarlos, con mucho quererlo,
pues de su propia insensatez sucumbieron víctimas;
ilocos!, de Hiperión Helios[2] *las vacas comieron,*
y en tal punto acabó para ellos el día del retorno.
Diosa, hija de Zeus, también a nosotros,
cuéntanos algún pasaje de estos sucesos[3].   10

Ello es que todos los demás[4], cuantos habían escapado a la
amarga muerte, estaban en casa, dejando atrás la guerra y el

---

[1] En gr. *polýtropos*, puede significar «de muchos senderos» o bien «de muchas mañas», versátil. Es un epíteto de Odiseo que solamente recurre en X.330.

[2] Homero suele unir los nombres de Helios y de Hiperión como si éste fuera un epíteto de aquel («el que transcurre por encima»), cfr. también XII.133, 346, 374. Solamente en una ocasión (XII.176) Homero lo llama Hiperiónida, «hijo de Hiperión», lo que responde a la tradición hesiódica (cfr. *Teogonía,* 371-74) que hace de este Titán el padre de Helios, de Selene y de Eos. La alusión se refiere a los sucesos narrados en XII.353 y ss.

[3] Destaco los diez primeros versos, aunque están en hexámetro como el resto, porque constituyen un auténtico proemio, construido en composición anular, que contiene un programa de lo que va a ser la *Odisea.* No sucede así con la *Ilíada,* donde la invocación a la Musa va seguida casi inmediatamente del relato.

[4] Los demás héroes de la guerra de Troya, cuyas vicisitudes en sus viajes de

mar. Sólo él estaba privado de regreso y esposa, y lo retenía en su cóncava cueva la ninfa Calipso[5], divina entre las diosas, deseando que fuera su esposo.

Y el caso es que cuando transcurrieron los años y le llegó aquel en el que los dioses habían hilado[6] que regresara a su casa de Itaca, ni siquiera entonces estuvo libre de pruebas; ni cuando estuvo ya con los suyos. Todos los dioses se compadecían de él excepto Poseidón, quién se mantuvo siempre rencoroso[7] con el divino Odiseo hasta que llegó a su tierra. 20

Pero había acudido entonces junto a los Etíopes[8] que habitan lejos (los Etíopes que están divididos en dos grupos, unos donde se hunde Hiperión y otros donde se levanta), para asistir a una hecatombe de toros y carneros; en cambio, los demás dioses estaban reunidos en el palacio de Zeus Olímpico. Y comenzó a hablar el padre de hombres y dioses, pues se había acordado del irreprochable Egisto, a quien acababa de matar el afamado Orestes, hijo de Agamenón[9]. Acordóse, pues, de éste, 30 y dijo a los inmortales su palabra:

_____

regreso (Nostoi) son narradas sumariamente en la Telemaquia (III.130-312 y IV.351-584) y aludidos parcialmente en la Nekya —XI.405-34 en que Agamenón narra su propia muerte.

[5] Esta Calipso, cuya genealogía nos ofrece Atenea más adelante (vv. 51 y ss.) no tiene nada que ver con la Calipso hesiódica, hija de Tetis y de Océano (_Teogonía,_ 359). Es un personaje puramente odiseico, «La que esconde», y su función es retener a Odiseo para que su regreso dure diez años, tanto como la guerra de Troya.

[6] Sólo por extensión se puede decir que los dioses hilan el destino de un mortal. En realidad, al menos en la concepción homérica, las que hilan el Destino son la Aisa y las Hilanderas (_klôthes,_ cfr. VII.197). Los dioses no pueden hacer nada por evitarlo y están sujetos a aquél. Ver Dietrich, _Death, Fate and the Gods,_ Londres, 1965.

[7] El motivo de su rencor se explica más abajo, vv. 68-71.

[8] No es probable que se refiera exactamente a los habitantes de la actual Etiopía. La palabra griega _aithíops_ significa «de aspecto quemado» y es una denominación genérica de los negros. Se trata de una tribu mítica favorita de Poseidón.

[9] El mito de la muerte de Agamenón a manos de Egisto —a quien Clitemnestra se limita a _ayudar_ (o _instigar_) en la versión homérica— y la venganza de Orestes es un _leit-motiv_ en la _Odisea._ Aparte de que Orestes es ofrecido a Telémaco como paradigma, la muerte de Agamenón sirve de contraste al triunfo de Odiseo, y la figura de Penélope se opone moralmente a la de Clitemnestra (cfr. XXIV.192 y ss.). En realidad, una y otra historia reflejan, con diferentes resul-

«¡Ay, ay, cómo culpan los mortales a los dioses!, pues de nosotros, dicen, proceden los males. Pero también ellos por su estupidez soportan dolores más allá de lo que les corresponde. Así, ahora Egisto ha desposado —cosa que no le correspondía— a la esposa legítima del Atrida y ha matado a éste al regresar; y eso que sabía que moriría lamentablemente, pues le habíamos dicho, enviándole a Hermes, al vigilante Argifonte[10], que no le matara ni pretendiera a su esposa. "Que habrá una venganza por parte de Orestes cuando sea mozo y sienta nostalgia de su tierra." Así le dijo Hermes, mas con tener buenas intenciones no logró persuadir a Egisto. Y ahora las ha pagado todas juntas.» 40

Y le contestó luego la diosa de ojos brillantes[11], Atenea:

«Padre nuestro Cronida, supremo entre los que mandan, ¡claro que aquél yace víctima de una muerte justa!, así perezca cualquiera que cometa tales acciones. Pero es por el prudente Odiseo por quien se acongoja mi corazón, por el desdichado que lleva ya mucho tiempo lejos de los suyos y sufre en una isla rodeada de corriente donde está el ombligo del mar. La isla es boscosa y en ella tiene su morada una diosa, la hija de Atlante, de pensamientos perniciosos, el que conoce las profundidades de todo el mar y sostiene en su cuerpo las largas columnas que mantienen apartados Tierra y Cielo[12]. La hija de 50

---

tados, la situación de peligro en que se encontraban las monarquías aqueas al final de la era micénica.

[10] Me limito a transcribir la palabra griega *Argeiphóntēs*, epíteto de significación oscura como tantos otros epítetos arcaicos de los dioses olímpicos. Tradicionalmente se ha interpretado como «el que mató a Argos», pero, aparte de que esta leyenda es tardía, un epíteto se refiere *siempre* a una cualidad permanente y general, no a un hecho aislado.

[11] En gr. *glaukôpis*. Aunque este epíteto originariamente hiciera alusión a algún tipo de relación de Atenea con la lechuza *(glaúx)*, parece claro que nuestro poeta la desconoce, puesto que relaciona a Atenea *sistemáticamente* con otras aves: en I.320 la diosa se convierte en ave en general; en XXII.240 en golondrina, y en III.372 en buitre. En general se cree que Homero, más bien, piensa en el adjetivo *glaukós*, «brillante».

[12] Atlante, «El que soporta», según Hesíodo sostiene en sus hombros la bóveda del cielo «en el extremo de la tierra, cerca de las Hespérides de sonora voz» *(Teogonía,* vv. 517 y ss.). Según la concepción que representa este pasaje, se limitaría a vigilar las columnas que separan el cielo de la tierra o bien a sostenerlas *(échei)* en su cuerpo, como sin duda entendió Esquilo (cfr. *Prometeo,*

éste lo retiene entre dolores y lamentos y trata continuamente de hechizarlo con suaves y astutas razones para que se olvide de Ítaca; pero Odiseo, que anhela ver levantarse el humo de su tierra, prefiere morir. Y ni aun así se te conmueve el corazón, Olímpico. ¿Es que no te era grato Odiseo cuando en la amplia Troya te sacrificaba víctimas junto a las naves aqueas? ¿Por qué tienes tanto rencor, Zeus?» 60

Y le contestó el que reúne las nubes, Zeus:

«Hija mía, ¡qué palabra ha escapado del cerco de tus dientes! ¿Cómo podría olvidarme tan pronto del divino Odiseo, quien sobresale entre los hombres por su astucia y más que nadie ha ofrendado víctimas a los dioses inmortales que poseen el vasto cielo? Pero Poseidón, el que conduce su carro por la tierra[13], mantiene un rencor incesante y obstinado por causa del Cíclope a quien aquél privó del ojo, Polifemo, igual a los dioses, cuyo poder es el mayor entre los Cíclopes[14]. Lo parió la ninfa Toosa, hija de Forcis[15], el que se cuida del estéril mar, uniéndose a Poseidón en profunda cueva. Por esto, Poseidón, el que sacude la tierra, no mata a Odiseo, pero lo hace andar errante lejos de su tierra patria. Conque, vamos, pensemos todos los aquí presentes sobre su regreso, de forma que vuelva. Y Poseidón depondrá su cólera; que no podrá él solo rivalizar frente a todos los inmortales dioses contra la voluntad de éstos.» 70

Y le contestó luego la diosa de ojos brillantes, Atenea: 80

«Padre nuestro Cronida, supremo entre los que mandan, si por fin les cumple a los dioses felices que regrese a casa el muy astuto Odiseo, enviemos enseguida a Hermes, al vigilante Argifonte, para que anuncie inmediatamente a la Ninfa de lindas trenzas nuestra inflexible decisión: el regreso del sufridor Odi-

---

348-501). En todo caso, Atlante conoce las profundidades marinas porque dichas columnas hunden su base en el mar.

[13] Gr. *gaiéochos* se ha interpretado tradicionalmente como «el que abraza, o contiene, la tierra». Sin embargo, su sentido es «el que conduce su carro por la tierra», dado que la segunda parte del compuesto es *–wochos* (cfr. *Inscript. Graec.* 15.213). Poseidón es el dios de los terremotos además de soberano del mar.

[14] Cfr. IX.106 y ss.

[15] Forcis es uno de los «ancianos del mar, lo mismo que Nereo, su padre, y Proteo (cfr. también XIII.96 y 345). De Nereo dice Hesíodo *(Teogonía,* 234-6) «lo llaman anciano porque es veraz y sabio y no olvida la ley, sino que conoce justos y sabios designios».

seo. Que yo me presentaré en Itaca para empujar a su hijo —y ponerle valor en el pecho— a que convoque en asamblea a los aqueos de largo cabello a fin de que pongan coto a los preten- 90 dientes que siempre le andan sacrificando gordas ovejas y cuernitorcidos bueyes de rotátiles patas. Lo enviaré también a Esparta y a la arenosa Pilos para que indague sobre el regreso de su padre, por si oye algo, y para que cobre fama da valiente entre los hombres.»

Así diciendo, ató bajo sus pies las hermosas sandalias inmortales, doradas, que la suelen llevar sobre la húmeda superficie o sobre tierra firme a la par del soplo del viento. Y tomó una fuerte lanza con la punta guarnecida de agudo bronce, pe- 100 sada, grande, robusta, con la que domeña las filas de los héroes guerreros contra los que se encoleriza la hija del padre Todopoderoso. Luego descendió lanzándose de las cumbres del Olimpo y se detuvo en el pueblo de Itaca sobre el pórtico de Odiseo, en el umbral del patio. Tenía entre sus manos una lanza de bronce y se parecía a un forastero, a Mentes, caudillo de los tafios[16].

Y encontró a los pretendientes. Éstos complacían su ánimo con los dados delante de las puertas y se sentaban en pieles de bueyes que ellos mismos habían sacrificado. Sus heraldos y solícitos sirvientes se afanaban, unos en mezclar vino con agua 110 en las cráteras, y los otros en limpiar las mesas con agujereadas esponjas; se las ponían delante y ellos se distribuían carne en abundancia. El primero en ver a Atenea fue Telémaco, semejante a un dios; estaba sentado entre los pretendientes con corazón acongojado y pensaba en su noble padre: ¡ojalá viniera e hiciera dispersarse a los pretendientes por el palacio!, ¡ojalá tuviera él sus honores y reinara sobre sus posesiones! Mientras esto pensaba sentado entre los pretendientes, vio a Atenea. Se

---

[16] «Mentes, caudillo de los tafios» aparece ya citado en *Ilíada*, XVII.73, y de ahí sin duda ha sido tomado para este pasaje. Tafos pertenece probablemente a la geografía mítica de la *Odisea*. Desde luego, no es probable que sea la isla, del mismo nombre, en las cercanías de Léucade (cfr. Estrabón 10.2.4). Está demasiado cerca de Itaca, y Mentes habría sido un personaje conocido de Telémaco y los Pretendientes. En todo caso, en la *Odisea* los tafios son siempre la contrapartida folklórica de los sidonios —un pueblo de comerciantes con pocos escrúpulos (cfr. XIV.452, XV.427, XVI.426).

fue derecho al pórtico, y su ánimo rebosaba de ira por haber
dejado tanto tiempo al forastero a la puerta. Se puso cerca, 120
tomó su mano derecha, recibió su lanza de bronce y le dirigió
aladas palabras:

«Bienvenido, forastero, serás agasajado en mi casa. Luego
que hayas probado del banquete, dirás qué precisas.»

Así diciendo, la condujo y ella le siguió, Palas Atenea.
Cuando ya estaban dentro de la elevada morada, llevó la lanza
y la puso contra una larga columna, dentro del pulimentado
guardalanzas donde estaban muchas otras del sufridor Odiseo.
La condujo e hizo sentar en un sillón y extendió un hermoso 130
tapiz bordado; y bajo sus pies había un escabel. Al lado colocó
un canapé labrado lejos de los pretendientes, no fuera que el
huésped, molesto por el ruido, no se deleitara con el banquete
alcanzado por sus arrogancias y para preguntarle sobre su padre ausente. Y una esclava derramó sobre fuente de plata el
aguamanos que llevaba en hermosa jarra de oro, para que se lavara, y al lado extendió una mesa pulimentada. Luego la venerable ama de llaves puso comida sobre ella y añadió abundantes piezas escogidas, favoreciéndole entre los que estaban pre- 140
sentes. El trinchante les ofreció fuentes de toda clase de carnes
que habían sacado del trinchador y a su lado colocó copas de
oro. Y un heraldo se les acercaba a menudo y les escanciaba
vino.

Luego entraron los arrogantes pretendientes y enseguida
comenzaron a sentarse por orden en sillas y sillones. Los heraldos les derramaron agua sobre las manos, las esclavas
amontonaron pan en las canastas y los jóvenes coronaron de
vino las cráteras. Y ellos echaron mano de los alimentos que
tenían dispuestos delante. Después que habían echado de sí el 150
deseo de comer y beber, ocuparon su pensamiento el canto y
la danza, pues éstos son complementos de un banquete; así que
un heraldo puso hermosa cítara en manos de Femio[17], quien

---

[17] Dos son los aedos que aparecen en la *Odisea:* Femio, que canta a la fuerza
entre los pretendientes, y Demódoco, el poeta ciego de los Feacios (cfr. VIII.44,
etcétera). Homero, como es lógico, trata con especial afecto a estos personajes
de su propia profesión: aparte de aplicarles el epíteto «deseable», les atribuye todos los que reserva para los héroes como «divino», «honrado por el pueblo»,

cantaba a la fuerza entre los pretendientes, y éste rompió a cantar un bello canto acompañándose de la cítara.

Entonces Telémaco se dirigió a Atenea, de ojos brillantes, y mantenía cerca su cabeza para que no se enteraran los demás:

«Forastero amigo, ¿vas a enfadarte por lo que te diga? Éstos se ocupan de la cítara y el canto —¡y bien fácilmente!—, pues 160 se están comiendo sin pagar unos bienes ajenos, los de un hombre cuyos blancos huesos ya se están pudriendo bajo la acción de la lluvia, tirados sobre el litoral, o los voltean las olas en el mar. ¡Si al menos lo vieran de regreso a Ítaca...! Todos desearían ser más veloces de pies que ricos en oro y vestidos. Sin embargo, ahora ya está perdido de aciago destino, y ninguna esperanza nos queda por más que alguno de los terrenos hombres asegure que volverá. Se le ha acabado el día del regreso.

»Pero, vamos, dime esto —e infórmame con verdad—: ¿quién, de dónde eres entre los hombres?, ¿dónde están tu ciu- 170 dad y tus padres?, ¿en qué nave has llegado?, ¿cómo te han conducido los marineros hasta Ítaca y quiénes se precian de ser? Porque no creo en absoluto que hayas llegado aquí a pie. Dime también con verdad, para que yo lo sepa, si vienes por primera vez o eres huésped de mi padre; que muchos otros han venido a nuestro palacio, ya que también él hacía frecuentes visitas a los hombres.»

Y Atenea, de ojos brillantes, se dirigió a él:

«Claro que te voy a contestar sinceramente a todo esto. Afirmo con orgullo ser Mentes, hijo de Anquíalo, y reino so- 180 bre los tafios, amantes del remo. Ahora acabo de llegar aquí con mi nave y compañeros navegando sobre el ponto rojo

«ilustre», etc. Femio es, entre los que frecuentan el palacio del héroe, uno de los pocos que escaparán a la matanza, y Demódoco es tratado con especial deferencia en VIII.45 y ss. Pero además, los pasajes en que habla de los aedos y su canto son documentos importantes sobre la función y estatus del poeta épico en la época de Homero: según XVII.385 y ss. los aedos están en la lista de los «servidores del pueblo» a los que «se invita a venir». Y los cantos que entonan son los que, sin duda, estaban en boga en época de Homero: los Nostoi de los héroes de Troya (Femio en I.325 y ss.), o episodios de esta guerra (Demódoco en VIII.80 y ss.) o la propia destrucción de Troya (Demódoco en VIII.499 y ss.). A veces se trata de cantos de naturaleza más bien lírica, como el adulterio de Ares y Afrodita (VIII.266 y ss.), con acompañamiento de danza.

como el vino hacia hombres de otras tierras; voy a Temesa[18] en busca de bronce y llevo reluciente hierro. Mi nave está atracada lejos de la ciudad en el puerto Reitro, a los pies del boscoso monte Neyo. Tenemos el honor de ser huéspedes por parte de padre; puedes bajar a preguntárselo al viejo héroe Laertes, de quien afirman que ya no viene nunca a la ciudad y sufre penalidades en el campo en compañía de una anciana sierva que le pone comida y bebida cuando el cansancio se apodera de sus miembros, de recorrer penosamente la fructífera tierra de sus productivos viñedos[19].

»He venido ahora porque me han asegurado que tu padre estaba en el pueblo. Pero puede que los dioses lo hayan detenido en el camino, porque en modo alguno está muerto sobre la tierra el divino Odiseo, sino que estará retenido, vivo aún, en algún lugar del ancho mar, en alguna isla rodeada de corriente donde lo tienen hombres crueles y salvajes que lo sujetan contra su voluntad.

»Así que te voy a decir un presagio —porque los inmortales lo han puesto en mi pecho y porque creo que se va a cumplir, no porque yo sea adivino ni entienda una palabra de aves de agüero—: ya no estará mucho tiempo lejos de su tierra patria, ni aunque lo retengan ligaduras de hierro. Él pensará cómo volver, que es rico en recursos.

»Pero, vamos, dime —e infórmame con verdad— si tú, tan grande ya, eres hijo del mismo Odiseo. Te pareces a aquél asombrosamente en la cabeza y los lindos ojos; que muy a menudo nos reuníamos antes de embarcar él para Troya, donde otros argivos, los mejores, embarcaron en las cóncavas naves. Desde entonces no he visto a Odiseo, ni él a mí.»

Y Telémaco le contestó discretamente:

«Desde luego, huésped, te voy a hablar sinceramente. Mi madre asegura que soy hijo de él; yo, en cambio, no lo sé; que jamás conoció nadie por sí mismo su propia estirpe. ¡Ojalá fue-

---

[18] Tampoco se sabe si esta ciudad es real o ficticia, aunque se la ha identificado con una Tempsa de Italia y una Tamassos de Chipre.

[19] Esta descripción de Laertes no concuerda con la del Canto XXIV donde se dice que éste tenía una mansión en su finca y esclavos forzosos (vv. 205 y ss.). Es uno de los argumentos en que se apoyan los críticos analíticos para condenar el final de la *Odisea* como producto de una mano diferente y tardía.

Penélope con Telémaco

ra yo el hijo dichoso de un hombre al que alcanzara la vejez en medio de sus posesiones! Sin embargo, se ha convertido en el más desdichado de los mortales hombres aquél de quien dicen 220 que yo soy hijo, ya que me lo preguntas.»

Y Atenea, de ojos brillantes, se dirigió a él:

«Seguro que los dioses no te han dado linaje sin nombre, puesto que Penélope te ha engendrado tal como eres. Conque, vamos, dime esto —e infórmame con verdad—: ¿qué banquete, qué reunión es ésta y qué necesidad tienes de ella? ¿Se trata de un convite o de una boda?, porque seguro que no es una comida a escote: ¡tan irrespetuosos me parece que comen en el palacio, más de lo conveniente! Se irritaría viendo tantas torpezas cualquier hombre con sentido común que viniera.»

Y Telémaco le contestó discretamente: 230

«Huésped, puesto que me preguntas esto e inquieres, este palacio fue en otro tiempo seguramente rico e irreprochable mientras aquel hombre estaba todavía en casa. Pero ahora los dioses han decidido otra cosa maquinando desgracias; lo han hecho ilocalizable más que al resto de los hombres. No me lamentaría yo tanto por él aunque estuviera muerto, si hubiera sucumbido entre sus compañeros en el pueblo de los troyanos o entre los brazos de los suyos, una vez que hubo cumplido la odiosa tarea de la guerra. En este caso le habría construido una tumba el ejército panaqueo[20] y habría cosechado para el 240 futuro un gran renombre para su hijo. Sin embargo, las Harpías[21] se lo han llevado sin gloria; se ha marchado sin que nadie lo viera, sin que nadie le oyera, y a mí sólo me ha legado dolores y lágrimas.

»Pero no sólo lloro y me lamento por aquél; que los dioses me han proporcionado otras malas preocupaciones, pues cuantos nobles reinan sobre las islas —Duliquio, Same y la boscosa

---

[20] El conjunto del ejército griego. Este compuesto aparece en *Odisea* solamente dos veces, aquí y en XXIV.32-3, dentro de la misma fórmula.

[21] Por el juego etimológico que hay en el texto, parece claro que las Harpías son, para Homero, «las que arrebatan». No especifica su número y más adelante (cfr. XX.66 y 77) las identifica con las tempestades. Hesíodo habla ya de dos, a las que llama Aelló y Ocípete «las cuales siguen a los soplos del viento y a las aves con sus rápidas alas» *(Teogonía*, 265-66).

Zante[22]— y cuantos son poderosos en la escarpada Itaca pretenden a mi madre y arruinan mi casa. Ella ni se niega al odioso matrimonio ni es capaz de ponerles coto, y ellos arruinan mi hacienda comiéndosela. Luego acabarán incluso conmigo 250
mismo.»

Y le contestó, irritada, Palas Atenea:

«¡Ay, ay, mucha falta te hace ya el ausente Odiseo!; que pusiera él sus manos sobre los desvergonzados pretendientes. Pues si ahora, ya de regreso, estuviera en pie ante el pórtico del palacio sosteniendo su hacha, su escudo y sus dos lanzas tal como yo le vi por primera vez en nuestro palacio bebiendo y gozando del banquete recién llegado de Efira[23], del palacio de Ilo Mermérida... (había marchado allí Odiseo en rápida nave 260 para buscar veneno homicida con que untar sus broncíneas flechas. Aquél no se lo dio, pues veneraba a los dioses que viven siempre, pero se lo entregó mi padre, pues lo amaba en exceso). ¡Con tal atuendo se enfrentara Odiseo con los pretendientes! Corto el destino de todos sería y amargas sus nupcias. Pero está en las rodillas de los dioses[24] si tomará venganza en su palacio al volver o no.

»En cuanto a ti, te ordeno que pienses la manera de echar 270 del palacio a los pretendientes. Conque, vamos, escúchame y presta atención a mis palabras: convoca mañana en asamblea a los héroes aqueos y hazles a todos manifiesta tu palabra; y que los dioses sean testigos. Ordena a los pretendientes que se dis-

---

[22] La identidad y localización de estas islas —Itaca incluida— ha sido objeto de discusión desde la Antigüedad (cfr. Estrabón 10.2 y ss.) Hoy, con la excepción de los seguidores de Dörpfeld, se cree que tanto Itaca como la Zante homéricas son las actuales; y que Same y Duliquio son partes de la actual Cefalonia. Para una amplia discusión del tema, cfr. F. H. Stubbings, *Companion...*, páginas 398 y ss.

[23] Quizá la ciudad de Tesprotia, en la desembocadura del Aqueronte, que cita Tucídides en 1.46.4. De Ilo Mermérida no sabemos más de lo que aquí se dice.

[24] Expresión metafórica por «la voluntad de los dioses», posiblemente originada de la actitud del suplicante abrazando las rodillas de una persona o una estatua (cfr. VI.310). Atractiva, pero menos probable, es la sugerencia de R. B. Onians *(The Origins of european Thought,* Cambridge, 1954, págs. 303 y ss.), quien lo refiere al hecho de que los dioses hilan el destino y la posición para hilar es sedente.

persen a sus casas, y a tu madre... si su deseo la impulsa a casarse, que vuelva al palacio de su poderoso padre; le prepararán unas nupcias y le dispondrán una dote abundante, cuanta es natural que acompañe a una hija querida.

»A ti, sin embargo, te voy a aconsejar sagazmente, por si quieres obedecerme: bota una nave de veinte remos, la mejor, 280 y marcha para informarte sobre tu padre largo tiempo ausente, por si alguno de los mortales pudiera decirte algo o por si escucharas la Voz[25] que viene de Zeus, la que, sobre todas, lleva a los hombres las noticias.

»Primero dirígete a Pilos y pregunta al divino Néstor, y desde allí a Esparta al palacio del rubio Menelao, pues él ha llegado el postrero de los aqueos que visten bronce. Si oyes de tu padre que vive y está de vuelta, soporta todavía otro año, aunque tengas pesar; pero si oyes que ha muerto y que ya no vive, regresa enseguida a tu tierra patria, levanta una tumba en su 290 honor y ofréndale exequias en abundancia, cuantas están bien. Y entrega tu madre a un marido. Luego que esto hayas concluido, medita en tu mente y en tu corazón la manera de matar a los pretendientes en tu casa con engaño o a las claras[26].

Y es preciso que no juegues a cosas de niños, pues no eres de edad para hacerlo. ¿No has oído qué fama ha cobrado el divino Orestes entre todos los hombres por haber matado al asesino de su padre, a Egisto fecundo en ardides, porque había 300 quitado la vida a su ilustre padre? También tú, amigo —pues te veo vigoroso y bello—, sé valiente para que alguno de tus descendientes hable bien de ti. Yo me marcho ahora mismo a la rápida nave junto a mis compañeros, que deben estar cansados de tanto esperarme. Tú ocúpate de esto y presta oídos a mis palabras.»

---

[25] El rumor, cuyo origen es siempre desconocido, se atribuye en último término a Zeus. Cfr. también II.216 y XXIV.413.

[26] Este discurso es confuso y contradictorio, aparte de que el tono general («te ordeno», etc.) está mejor en boca de Atenea que de un extranjero desconocido. De hecho, los vv 269-80 contradicen a 287-96. Pero además los vv. 275-8 están en boca del pretendiente Eurímaco en II.195-7; y los vv. 280-92 están en boca del mismo Telémaco en II.214-23. Ello ha hecho que esta parte del canto primero sea considerada por los analíticos como una ampliación a base de retazos del canto segundo.

Y le contestó Telémaco discretamente:

«Huésped, en verdad dices esto con sentimientos amigos, como un padre a su hijo, y jamás los echaré a olvido. Mas, vamos, quédate ahora por muy deseoso que estés del camino, para que después de bañarte y gozar en tu pecho marches alegre a la nave portando un presente, un regalo estimable y hermoso que será para ti un tesoro de mí, como los que hospedan dan a sus huéspedes.» 310

Y contestó luego Atenea, de ojos brillantes:

«No me detengas más, que ya ansío el camino. El regalo que tu corazón te empuje a darme, entrégamelo cuando vuelva otra vez para llevarlo a casa. Escoge uno bueno de verdad y tendrás otro igual en recompensa.»

Así hablando, partió la de ojos brillantes, Atenea, y se remontó como un ave, e infundió audacia en el pecho de Telémaco y valentía. Pero después de reflexionar en su mente quedó estupefacto, pues pensó que era un dios. Y, mortal a los dioses igual, marchó enseguida junto a los pretendientes. 320

Entre éstos estaba cantando el ilustre aedo, y ellos escuchaban sentados en silencio. Cantaba el regreso de los aqueos que Palas Atenea les había deparado funesto desde Troya[27]. La hija de Icario, la prudente Penélope, acogió en su pecho el inspirado canto desde el piso de arriba y descendió por la elevada escalera de su palacio; mas no sola, que la acompañaban dos siervas. Cuando hubo llegado a los pretendientes la divina entre las mujeres, se detuvo junto al pilar central del techo labrado llevando ante sus mejillas un grueso velo, y a cada lado se puso una fiel sirvienta. Luego habló llorando al divino aedo: 330

«Femio, sabes otros muchos cantos, hechizo de los mortales, hazañas de hombres y dioses que los aedos hacen famosas. Cántales uno de éstos sentado a su lado y que ellos beban su vino en silencio; mas deja ya ese canto triste que me está da- 340

---

[27] Está claro que Femio no podía cantar otra cosa que los *Nostoi*. Ello sirve a varios fines: primero, potenciar el ambiente que reina en el palacio de Odiseo —la complacencia de los pretendientes y el dolor de los familiares—; en segundo lugar sirve para presentar dramáticamente, ya desde los primeros versos, la figura de Penélope; finalmente, es una referencia adelantada al contenido de los cantos siguientes (III y IV).

ñando el corazón dentro del pecho, puesto que a mí sobre todos me ha alcanzado un dolor inolvidable, pues añoro, acordándome continuamente, la cabeza de un hombre cuyo renombre es amplio en la Hélade y hasta el centro de Argos»[28].

Y Telémaco le dijo discretamente:

«Madre mía, ¿por qué reprochas al amable aedo que nos deleite como le impulse su voluntad? No son los aedos culpables, sino en cierto sentido Zeus, el que dota a los hombres que comen grano como quiere a cada uno.

»Para éste no habrá castigo porque cante el destino aciago 350 de los dánaos, pues éste es el canto que más celebran los hombres, el que llega más reciente a los oyentes.

»Que tu corazón y tu espíritu soporten escucharlo, pues no sólo Odiseo perdió en Troya el día de su regreso, que también perecieron otros muchos hombres. Conque marcha a tu habitación y cuídate de tu trabajo, el telar y la rueca, y ordena a las esclavas que se ocupen del suyo. La palabra debe ser cosa de hombres, de todos, y sobre todo de mí, de quien es el poder en este palacio.»

Admiróse ella y se encaminó de nuevo a su habitación, pues 360 puso en su interior la palabra discreta de su hijo. Subió al piso de arriba en compañía de las esclavas y luego rompió a llorar a Odiseo su esposo hasta que Atenea, de ojos brillantes, echó dulce sueño sobre sus párpados.

Los pretendientes rompieron a alborotar en el sombrío mégaron[29] y deseaban todos acostarse en su cama al lado de ella. Entonces comenzó a hablarles Telémaco discretamente:

---

[28] En Homero, *Hellás* designa habitualmente el norte de Grecia, especialmente la Tesalia superior (el reino de Peleo) y Argos designa todo el Peloponeso. La frase significa, por tanto, «en toda Grecia». Hasta Hesiodo *(Trabajos y Días*, 653) *Hellás* no designa a Grecia en su conjunto.

[29] El mégaron es la estancia principal de un palacio micénico. Conservo la palabra griega para no traducirla por «sala» o «salón» que no responde exactamente a las características y funciones del mégaron. Éste se suele encontrar a un lado del gran patio central y consta de tres partes: el pórtico *(aíthousa)*, el vestíbulo *(pródromos)* y el mégaron propiamente dicho, una gran estancia con un hogar en la que se centra la vida del palacio: allí se celebran sacrificios y banquetes y se recibe a los huéspedes. Además de la puerta principal, de dos batientes, que se encuentra debajo del pórtico, suele tener un portón de una sola hoja que da a un corredor por donde se accede a las habitaciones privadas *(thálamoi)*

«Pretendientes de mi madre que tenéis excesiva insolencia, gocemos ahora con el banquete y que no haya vocerío, puesto que lo mejor es escuchar a un aedo como éste, semejante en su voz a los dioses. 370

»Al amanecer marchemos a la plaza y sentémonos todos para que os diga sin empacho que salgáis de mi palacio, os preparéis otros banquetes y comáis vuestros propios bienes invitándoos mutuamente. Pero si os parece lo mejor y más acertado destruir sin pagar la hacienda de un solo hombre, consumidla. Yo clamaré a los dioses, que viven siempre, por si Zeus de algún modo me concede que vuestras obras sean castigadas: pereceréis al punto, sin nadie que os vengue, dentro de este palacio!» 380

Así habló, y todos clavaron los dientes en sus labios. Estaban admirados de Telémaco porque había hablado audazmente. Y Antínoo[30], hijo de Eupites, se dirigió a él:

«Telémaco, seguramente los dioses mismos te enseñan a ser ya arrogante en la palabra y a hablar audazmente. ¡Que el hijo de Crono no te haga rey de Itaca, rodeada de mar, cosa que por linaje te corrresponde como herencia paterna!»

Y Telémaco le contestó discretamente:

«Antínoo, aunque te enojes conmigo por lo que voy a decir, esto es precisamente lo que quisiera yo obtener si Zeus me lo concede. ¿O acaso crees que es lo peor entre los hombres? No es nada malo ser rey, no; rápidamente tu palacio se hace rico y tú mismo más respetado. Pero hay muchos otros personajes reales en Itaca, rodeada de mar; que uno de ellos ocupe el trono, muerto el divino Odiseo. Yo seré soberano de mi palacio y de los esclavos que el divino Odiseo tomó para mí como botín.» 390

Y Eurímaco, hijo de Pólibo, le dijo a su vez:

---

tanto de la planta baja como del piso de arriba. Cfr. Alan J. B. Wace, «Houses and Palaces», en *Companion...*, págs. 489-97.

[30] De los 108 pretendientes (cfr. XVI.247 y ss.) sólo catorce se destacan de la masa anónima con su nombre y patronímico, y aun entre éstos sólo tres o cuatro juegan un papel activo en la obra. Antínoo es precisamente el más insolente de todos y el que planea la muerte de Telémaco. Es el primero en ser presentado y será el primero en morir sin haber siquiera reconocido a Odiseo como su verdugo, cfr. XXII.8 y ss.

«Telémaco, en verdad está en las rodillas de los dioses quién 400
de los aqueos va a reinar en Itaca, rodeada de mar; tú harías
mejor en conservar tus posesiones y reinar sobre tus esclavos.
¡Cuidado no venga algún hombre que te prive de tus posesiones
por la fuerza, contra tu voluntad, mientras Itaca siga habitada!

»Pero quiero, excelente, preguntarte sobre el forastero de
dónde es, de qué tierra se precia de ser y dónde tiene ahora su
linaje y heredad paterna. ¿Acaso trae un mensaje de tu padre
ausente o ha llegado aquí por algún asunto propio? Cuán rápi- 410
do se levantó y marchó enseguida sin esperar a que lo conocié-
ramos. Desde luego no parecía en su aspecto un hombre del
pueblo.»

Y Telémaco le contestó discretamente:

«Eurímaco, con certeza se ha acabado el regreso de mi padre. No hago ya caso a noticia alguna, venga de donde viniere,
ni presto oídos al oráculo de procedencia divina que mi madre
pueda comunicarme llamándome al mégaron. Este hombre es
huésped paterno mío y afirma con orgullo que es Mentes, hijo
del prudente Anquíalo, y reina sobre los Tafios, amantes del
remo.»

Así dijo Telémaco, aunque había reconocido a la diosa in- 420
mortal en su mente.

Volvieron ellos al baile y al canto para deleitarse y aguarda-
ron al lucero de la tarde y cuando se estaban deleitando les sobrevino éste, así que se pusieron en camino cada uno a su casa
deseando acostarse.

Entonces Telémaco se dirigió cavilando hacia el lecho, hacia
donde tenía construido su suntuoso dormitorio en el muy hermoso patio[31], en lugar de amplia visión. Junto a él llevaba teas
ardientes la fiel Euriclea[32], hija de Ope Pisenórida, a la que había 430
comprado en otro tiempo Laertes, cuando todavía era adoles-

---

[31] El dormitorio de Telémaco era, sin duda, uno de los *thálamoi* que rodeaban el patio central, en el ala opuesta al mégaron.

[32] Euriclea, como todos los personajes que van a jugar un papel importante
en el relato (especialmente en el canto XIX), es presentada pronto y con todo
detalle. Esta es la razón por la que Homero se recrea en describir el momento
en que Telémaco se dirige al dormitorio.

cente, por el valor de veinte bueyes; la honraba en el palacio igual que a su casta esposa, pero nunca se unió a ella en la cama por evitar la cólera de su mujer. Ésta era quien llevaba a su lado las ardientes antorchas y lo amaba más que ninguna esclava, pues lo había criado cuando era pequeño.

Abrió Telémaco las puertas del dormitorio, suntuosamente construido, y se sentó en el lecho, se desnudó del suave manto y lo echó sobre las manos de la muy diligente anciana. Ésta estiró y dobló el manto y colgándolo de un clavo junto al techo agujereado[33] se puso en camino para salir del dormitorio. Tiró de la puerta con una anilla de plata y echó el cerrojo con la correa. 440

Durante toda la noche, cubierto por el vellón de una oveja, planeaba él en su mente el viaje que le había dispuesto Atenea.

---

[33] Las camas en esta época eran catres de madera con los tableros «agujereados» a fin de introducir cuerdas y tensarlas para que sirvieran de soporte al colchón, de cualquier clase que éste fuera (probablemente simples pieles). Cfr. *Etymologicum Magnum* s.v. *Tretòn léchos.*

Canto II

TELÉMACO REÚNE EN ASAMBLEA
AL PUEBLO DE ITACA

Y cuando se mostró Eos, la que nace de la mañana, la de dedos de rosa[34], al punto el amado hijo de Odiseo se levantó del lecho, vistió sus vestidos, colgó de su hombro la aguda espada y bajo sus pies, brillantes como el aceite, calzó hermosas sandalias.

Luego se puso en marcha, salió del dormitorio semejante a un dios en su porte y ordenó a los vocipotentes heraldos que convocaran en asamblea[35] a los aqueos de largo cabello; aquéllos dieron el bando y éstos comenzaron a reunirse con premura. Después, cuando hubieron sido reunidos y estaban ya congregados, se puso en camino hacia la plaza —en su mano una lanza de bronce—; mas no solo, que le seguían dos lebreles de veloces patas. Entonces derramó Atenea sobre él una gracia divina y lo contemplaban admirados todos los ciudadanos; se

10

---

[34] Es una fórmula que aparece veinte veces en la *Odisea* y una sola en la *Ilíada* (I.477). Eos es la aurora, hija de Hiperión y hermana de Helios y Selene. Cfr. Hesíodo, *Teogonía*, 371 y ss.

[35] Aquí tenemos un ejemplo de lo que podía ser una asamblea en la época arcaica, aunque, por razones obvias, no se deben deducir conclusiones tajantes como algunos historiadores han pretendido. Parece deducirse del texto que es el rey quien la convoca —pues ya hace veinte años que no la hay y la gente se pregunta quién puede ser el convocante; no hay orden fijo de intervención y ésta cuenta con la presencia de unos «ancianos» que podrían ser los representantes de las familias más importantes y cuya función no queda nada clara. Cfr. M. I. Finley, *El mundo de Odiseo*, págs. 95 y ss.

sentó en el trono de su padre y los ancianos le cedieron el sitio.

A continuación comenzó a hablar entre ellos el héroe Egiptio, quien estaba ya encorvado por la vejez y sabía miles de cosas, pues también su hijo, el lancero Antifo, había embarcado en las cóncavas naves en compañía del divino Odiseo hacia Ilión[36], de buenos potros; lo había matado el salvaje Cíclope en su profunda cueva y lo había preparado como último bocado de su cena. Aún le quedaban tres: uno estaba entre los pretendientes y los otros dos cuidaban sin descanso los bienes paternos. Pero ni aun así se había olvidado de aquél, siempre lamentándose y afligiéndose[37]. Derramando lágrimas por su hijo levantó la voz y dijo:

«Escuchadme ahora a mí, itacenses, lo que voy a deciros. Nunca hemos tenido asamblea ni sesión desde que el divino Odiseo marchó en las cóncavas naves. ¿Quién, entonces, nos convoca ahora de esta manera? ¿A quién ha asaltado tan grande necesidad ya sea de los jóvenes o de los ancianos? ¿Acaso ha oído alguna noticia de que llega el ejército, noticia que quiere revelarnos una vez que él se ha enterado?, ¿o nos va a manifestar alguna otra cosa de interés para el pueblo? A mí me parece que es noble, afortunado. ¡Así Zeus llevara a término lo bueno que él revuelve en su mente!»

Así habló, y el amado hijo de Odiseo se alegró por sus palabras. Con que ya no estuvo sentado por más tiempo y sintió un deseo repentino de hablar. Se puso en pie en mitad de la plaza y le colocó el cetro en la mano el heraldo Pisenor, conocedor de consejos discretos.

Entonces se dirigió primero al anciano y dijo:

«Anciano, no está lejos ese hombre, soy yo el que ha convocado al pueblo (y tú lo sabrás pronto), pues el dolor me ha alcanzado en demasía. No he escuchado noticia alguna de que llegue el ejército que os vaya a revelar después de enterarme

---

[36] Ilión es el nombre epicórico de Troya. Cfr. R. Carpenter, *Folk tale...*, página 63.

[37] Aquí hay una pequeña inconsistencia. Por muchas cosas que supiera Egiptio, una que no podía saber es que su hijo había sido devorado por el Cíclope. Quizá por ello el filólogo alejandrino Aristarco eliminó los vv. 19-20.

yo, ni voy a manifestaros ni a deciros nada de interés para el pueblo, sino un asunto mío privado que me ha caído sobre el palacio como una peste, o mejor como dos: uno es que he perdido a mi noble padre, que en otro tiempo reinaba sobre vosotros aquí presentes y era bueno como un padre. Pero ahora me ha sobrevenido otra peste aún mayor que está a punto de destruir rápidamente mi casa y me va a perder toda la hacienda: asedian a mi madre, aunque ella no lo quiere, unos pretendientes hijos de hombres que son aquí los más nobles. Éstos tienen miedo de ir a casa de su padre Icario para que éste dote a su hija y se la entregue a quien él quiera y encuentre el favor de ella. En cambio vienen todos los días a mi casa y sacrifican bueyes, ovejas y gordas cabras y se banquetean y beben a cántaros el rojo vino. Así que se están perdiendo muchos bienes, pues no hay un hombre como Odiseo que arroje esta maldición de mi casa. Yo todavía no soy para arrojarla, pero ¡seguro que más adelante voy a ser débil y desconocedor del valor! En verdad que yo la rechazaría si me acompañara la fuerza, pues ya no son soportables las acciones que se han cometido y mi casa está perdida de la peor manera. Indignaos también vosotros y avergonzaos de vuestros vecinos, los que viven a vuestro lado. Y temed la cólera de los dioses, no vaya a ser que cambien la situación irritados por sus malas acciones. Os lo ruego por Zeus Olímpico y por Temis, la que disuelve y reúne las asambleas de los hombres; conteneos, amigos, y dejad que me consuma en soledad, víctima de la triste pena —a no ser que mi noble padre Odiseo alguna vez hiciera mal a los aqueos de hermosas grebas, a cambio de lo cual me estáis dañando rencorosamente y animáis a los pretendientes. Para mí sería más ventajoso que fuerais vosotros quienes consumen mis propiedades y ganado. Si las comierais vosotros algún día obtendría la devolución, pues recorrería la ciudad con mi palabra demandándoos el dinero hasta que me fuera devuelto todo; ahora, sin embargo, arrojáis sobre mi corazón dolores incurables.»

Así habló indignado y arrojó el cetro a tierra con un repentino estallido de lágrimas. Y la lástima se apoderó de todo el pueblo. Quedaron todos en silencio y nadie se atrevió a replicar a Telémaco con palabras duras; sólo Antínoo le dijo en contestación:

«Telémaco, fanfarrón, incapaz de reprimir tu cólera; ¿qué cosa has dicho cubriéndonos de vergüenza? Desearías cubrirnos de baldón. Sabe que los culpables no son los pretendientes de entre los aqueos, sino tu madre, que sabe muy bien de astucias. Pues ya es éste el tercer año, y con rapidez se acerca el cuarto, desde que aflige el corazón en el pecho de los aqueos. A todos da esperanzas y hace promesas a cada pretendiente enviándole recados; pero su imaginación maquina otras cosas. 90

»Y ha meditado este otro engaño en su pecho: levantó un gran telar en el palacio y allí tejía, telar sutil e inacabable, y sin dilación nos dijo: "Jóvenes pretendientes míos, puesto que ha muerto el divno Odiseo, aguardad, por mucho que deseéis esta boda conmigo, a que acabe este manto —no sea que se me pierdan inútilmente los hilos—, este sudario para el héroe Laertes, para cuando lo arrebate el destructor destino de la 100 muerte de largos lamentos[38]. Que no quiero que ninguna de las aqueas del pueblo se irrite conmigo si yace sin sudario el que tanto poseyó."

»Así dijo, y nuestro noble ánimo la creyó. Así que durante el día tejía la gran tela y por la noche, colocadas antorchas a su lado, la destejía. Su engaño pasó inadvertido durante tres años y convenció a los aqueos, pero cuando llegó el cuarto año[39] y pasaron las estaciones, una de sus mujeres, que lo sabía todo, nos lo reveló y sorprendimos a ésta destejiendo la brillante tela. Así fue como la terminó, y no voluntariamente, sino por 110 la fuerza.

»Conque ésta es la respuesta que te dan los pretendientes,

_____

[38] En gr. _tanelegḗs_. Es un epíteto fijo con la palabra _thánatos_ en la Odisea. Puede significar «de largos o tensos (_tan-_) lamentos» (_elegḗs_) o bien, por falso corte, «que no se cuida, despiadada» (_anelegḗs_).

[39] Esta frase es incongruente con lo que se afirmó en los vv. 89-90 («este es el tercer año y con rapidez se acerca el cuarto»). Como por otra parte, XIII.377 coincide con 89-90, no han faltado intentos de acomodar los vv. 106-7 a 89-90 cambiando el texto (_tríetes_ y _tétarton_ por _díetes_ y _tríton_). En cualquier caso, confuso como es el pasaje, se puede deducir de él que los pretendientes llevan frecuentando el palacio de Odiseo algo más de tres años; que Penélope acaba de terminar la tela, y que sigue dando largas a los pretendientes. Sólo la llegada de Odiseo puede salvarla y, según las palabras de Anfimedonte en XXIV.147 y ss., Odiseo llegó exactamente cuando la había terminado, lavado y enseñado a los pretendientes.

para que la conozcas tú mismo y la conozcan todos los aqueos: envía por tu madre y ordénala que se case con quien la aconseje su padre y a ella misma agrade. Pero si todavía sigue atormentando mucho tiempo a los hijos de los aqueos ejercitando en su mente las cualidades que la ha concedido Atenea en exceso (ser entendida en trabajos femeninos muy bellos y tener pensamientos agudos y astutos como nunca hemos oído que tuvieran ninguna de las aqueas de lindas trenzas ni siquiera de las que vivieron antiguamente, como Tiro, Alcmena y Micena[40] de linda corona —ninguna de ellas pensó planes semejantes a los de Penélope—), entonces esto al menos no habrá sido lo más conveniente que haya planeado. Pues tu hacienda y propiedades te serán devoradas mientras ella mantenga semejante decisión que los dioses han puesto ahora en su pecho. Se está creando para sí una gran gloria[41], pero para ti sólo la añoranza de tu mucha hacienda.

»En cuanto a nosotros, no marcharemos a nuestros trabajos ni a parte alguna hasta que se case con el que quiera de los aqueos.»

Y le respondió Telémaco discretamente:

«Antínoo, no me es posible echar de mi casa contra su voluntad a la que me ha dado a luz, a la que me ha criado, mientras mi padre está en otra parte de la tierra —viva él o esté muerto. Y será terrible para mí devolver a Icario muchas cosas si envío a mi madre por propia iniciativa. Por parte de mi padre sufriré castigo y otros me darán la divinidad, puesto que mi madre conjurará a las diosas Erinias[42] si se marcha de

120

130

---

[40] No sabemos por qué Homero selecciona precisamente a estas tres heroínas para compararlas con Penélope. No parece, por lo que de ellas sabemos, que sobresalieran en el tejido o en la astucia. A las dos primeras se alude de nuevo en la Nekya: XI.235 y ss. (Tiro) y 265 y ss. (Alcmena). De Micena sólo sabemos que es la epónima de la ciudad de los Atridas y que, según Pausanias (2.16.4) «los poemas épicos que los griegos llaman *Grandes Eeas* dicen que era hija de Inaco y esposa de Aréstor».

[41] Efectivamente, la fama de Penélope se debe a la estratagema del telar. Y quizá a ésta se deba también su nombre, pues *pēne* significa «hilo de un tejido» y *-lópeia* bien pudiera estar relacionado con el verbo *lépō* que significa «pelar» o «cardar».

[42] Las Erinias (a veces la Erinia en singular) son divinidades que pertenecen a la generación anterior a los Olímpicos (cfr. Esquilo, *Euménides, passim*). Su

casa, y también por parte de los hombres tendré castigo. Por esto jamás diré yo esa palabra. Conque, si vuestro ánimo se irrita por esto, salid de mi palacio y preparaos otros banquetes comiendo vuestras posesiones e invitándoos en vuestras casas 140 recíprocamente, que yo clamaré a los dioses, que viven siempre, por si Zeus me concede que vuestras obras sean castigadas de algún modo: ¡pereceréis al punto, sin nadie que os vengue, dentro de este palacio!»

Así habló Telémaco, y Zeus que ve a lo ancho, le echó a volar dos águilas desde arriba, desde las cumbres de la montaña[43]. Éstas se dirigían volando a la par del soplo del viento cerca una de otra, extendidas las alas. Cuando llegaron al centro de la plaza, donde mucho se habla, comenzaron a dar vuel- 150 tas batiendo sus espesas alas y llegaron cerca de las cabezas de todos, y en sus ojos brillaba la muerte. Y desgarrándose con las uñas mejillas y cuellos se lanzaron por la derecha a través de las casas y la ciudad de los itacenses. Admiraron éstos aterrados a las aves cuando las vieron con sus ojos, y removían en su corazón qué era lo que iba a cumplirse. Y entre ellos habló el anciano héroe Haliterses Mastorida, pues sólo él aventajaba a los de su edad en conocer los pájaros y explicar presagios. Levantó la voz con buenas intenciones hacia ellos y comenzó a 160 hablar:

«Ahora, itacenses, escuchadme a mí lo que voy a deciros —y es sobre todo a los pretendientes a quienes voy a hacer esta revelación—: sobre ellos anda dando vueltas una gran

---

función es vengar los delitos intrafamiliares, especialmente el parricidio, con toda suerte de desgracias y enfermedades que culminan en la muerte del culpable. Esquilo las describe detalladamente en *Coéforas,* 275 y ss. Sin embargo, en la *Odisea* Homero les presta una función más amplia: en XV.234 Erinia es sinónimo de Ate, la obcecación culpable, y en XVII.475 se habla de una Erinia que venga a los mendigos.

[43] La presencia de Odiseo se va haciendo cada vez más cercana a través de presagios y sueños de carácter muy similar: generalmente hay un águila (símbolo de la realeza) que mata (o lleva muerto) a un animal inferior (paloma, ganso, etc.). Éste es el primer presagio y es el menos claro. Se trata de dos águilas en cuyos ojos «brilla la muerte», pero ninguna es vencedora. De todas formas, el que se dirijan por la derecha es un buen presagio para Telémaco, como interpreta Haliterses. Los presagios se van acumulando a partir del canto XV: cfr. XV.161, 525 y ss., XIX.536 y ss., XX.243 y ss.

desgracia, pues Odiseo ya no estará mucho tiempo lejos de los suyos, sino que ya está cerca, en alguna parte, y está sembrando la muerte y el destino para todos éstos. También para otros muchos de los que habitamos Itaca, hermosa al atardecer[44], habrá desgracias. Pensemos entonces cuanto antes cómo ponerles término o bien que se lo pongan ellos a sí mismos, pues esto será lo que más les conviene. Y yo no vaticino como un inexperto, sino como uno que sabe bien. Os aseguro que todo se está cumpliendo para él como se lo dije cuando los argivos embarcaron para Ilión y con ellos marchó el astuto Odiseo. Le dije que sufriría muchas calamidades, que perdería a todos sus compañeros y que volvería a casa a los veinte años desconocido de todos. Y ya se está cumpliendo todo.»

Y le contestó Eurímaco, hijo de Pólibo:

«Viejo, vete ya a casa a profetizar a tus hijos, no sea que sufran alguna desgracia en el futuro. Estas cosas las vaticino yo mucho mejor que tú. Numerosos son los pájaros que van y vienen bajo los rayos del Sol y no todos son de agüero. Está claro que Odiseo ha muerto lejos —¡ojalá que hubieras perecido tú también con él!; no habrías dicho tantos vaticinios ni habrías incitado al irritado Telémaco esperando ansiosamente un regalo[45] para tu casa, por si te lo daba. Conque voy a hablarte, y esto sí se va a cumplir: si tú, sabedor de muchas y antiguas cosas, incitas con tus palabras a un hombre más joven a que se irrite, para él mismo primero será más penoso —pues nada podrá conseguir con estas predicciones—, y a ti, viejo, te pondremos una multa que te será doloroso pagar. Y tu dolor será insoportable.

En cuanto a Telémaco, yo mismo voy a darle un consejo delante de todos: que ordene a su madre volver a casa de su padre. Ellos le prepararán unas nupcias y le dispondrán una muy abundante dote, cuanta es natural que acompañe a una

170

180

190

---

[44] Gr. *eudeíelon*, es un epíteto que se aplica en la *Odisea* a Itaca, pero también a las islas en general (cfr. XIII.234). Puede significar «bien visible» *(délos)* o, como aquí se traduce, «hermosa al atardecer» *(deílē)*. Los antiguos ya dudaban entre ambos significados, pero el primero es demasiado banal.

[45] Es la misma acusación de venalidad que Edipo lanza contra Tiresias (cfr. Sófocles, *Edipo Rey*, vv. 380 y ss.). Los pretendientes tienen, por su *hybris*, el carácter del tirano de una tragedia clásica.

hija querida. No creo yo que los hijos de los aqueos renuncien a su pretensión laboriosa, pues no tememos a nadie a pesar de todo y no, desde luego, a Telémaco por mucha palabrería que muestre. Tampoco hacemos caso del presagio sin cumplimiento que tú, viejo, nos revelas haciéndotenos todavía más odioso. Igualmente serán devorados tus bienes de mala manera y jamás te serán compensados, al menos mientras ella entretenga a los aqueos respecto de su boda. Pues nosotros nos mantenemos expectantes todos los días y rivalizamos por causa de su excelencia, y no marchamos tras otras con las que a cada uno nos convendría casar.»

Entonces le contestó Telémaco discretamente:

«Eurímaco y demás ilustres pretendientes: no voy a apelar más a vosotros ni tengo más que decir; ya lo saben los dioses y todos los aqueos. Pero dadme ahora una rápida nave y veinte compañeros que puedan llevar a término conmigo un viaje aquí y allá, pues me voy a Esparta y a la arenosa Pilos para enterarme del regreso de mi padre, largo tiempo ausente, por si alguno de los mortales me lo dice o escucho la Voz que viene de Zeus, la que, sobre todas, lleva a los hombres las noticias. Si oigo que mi padre vive y está de vuelta, soportaré todavía otro año; pero si oigo que ha muerto y que ya no vive, regresaré enseguida a mi tierra patria, levantaré una tumba en su honor y le ofrendaré exequias en abundancia, cuantas está bien, y entregaré mi madre a un marido.»

Así hablando se sentó, y entre ellos se levantó Méntor, que era compañero del irreprochable Odiseo y a quien éste al marchar en las naves había encomendado toda su casa —que obedecieran todos al anciano y que él conservara todo intacto[46]—. Éste levantó la voz con buenos sentimientos hacia ellos y dijo:

«Escuchadme ahora a mí, itacenses, lo que voy a deciros: ¡que de ahora en adelante ningún rey portador de cetro sea benévolo, ni amable, ni bondadoso, y no sea justo en su pensamiento, sino que siempre sea cruel y obre injustamente!, pues

200

210

220

230

---

[46] Méntor es, como su nombre indica, el «consejero» a quien Odiseo encomendó el cuidado de su hogar cuando marchó a Troya. También Agamenón había encomendado la misma misión a un aedo (cfr. III.267), pero el papel de ambos resultó ineficaz.

del divino Odiseo no se acuerda ninguno de los ciudadanos sobre los que reinó, aunque era tierno como un padre. Mas yo me lamento no de que los esforzados pretendientes cometan acciones violentas por la maldad de su espíritu, pues exponen sus propias cabezas al comerse con violencia la hacienda de Odiseo, asegurando que éste ya no volverá jamás. Me irrito más bien contra el resto del pueblo, de qué modo estáis todos sentados en silencio y, aun siendo muchos, no contenéis a los pretendientes, que son pocos, cercándoles con vuestras palabras.»

Y le contestó Leócrito, el hijo de Evenor:

«Obstinado Méntor, ayuno de sesos; ¿qué has dicho incitándolos a que nos contengan? Difícil sería incluso a hombres más numerosos luchar por un banquete. Pues aunque el itacense Odiseo viniera en persona y maquinara en su mente arrojar del palacio a los nobles pretendientes que se banquetean en su casa, no se alegraría su esposa de que viniera, por mucho que lo desee, sino que allí mismo atraería sobre sí vergonzosa muerte si luchara con hombres más numerosos. Y tú no has hablado como te corresponde. Vamos, ciudadanos, dispersaos cada uno a sus trabajos. A éste le ayudarán para el viaje Méntor y Haliterses, que son compañeros de su padre desde hace mucho tiempo. Aunque sentado por mucho tiempo, creo yo, escuchará las noticias en Itaca y jamás llevará a término tal viaje.»

Así habló y disolvió la asamblea rápidamente. Se dispersaron cada uno a su casa y los pretendientes marcharon al palacio del divino Odiseo.

Telémaco, en cambio, se alejó hacia la orilla del mar, lavó sus manos en el canoso mar y suplicó a Atenea:

«Préstame oídos tú, divinidad que llegaste ayer a mi palacio y me diste la orden de marchar en una nave sobre el brumoso ponto para informarme sobre el regreso de mi padre, largo tiempo ausente. Todo esto lo están retrasando los aqueos, sobre todo los pretendientes, funestamente arrogantes.»

Así habló suplicándola; Atenea se le acercó semejante a Méntor en la figura y voz y se dirigió a él con aladas palabras:

«Telémaco, no serás en adelante cobarde ni estúpido si has heredado el noble corazón de tu padre; ¿cómo era él para reali-

zar obras y palabras! Por esto tu viaje no va a ser infructuoso
ni baldío. Pero si no eres hijo de aquél y de Penélope, no tengo
esperanza alguna de que lleves a cabo lo que meditas. Pocos,
en efecto, son los hijos iguales a su padre; la mayoría son peo-
res y sólo unos pocos son mejores que su padre. Pero puesto
que en el futuro no vas a ser cobarde ni estúpido ni te ha abandonado del todo el talento de Odiseo, hay esperanza de que lle-   280
gues a realizar tal empresa.

»Deja, pues, ahora las intenciones y pensamientos de los enloquecidos pretendientes, pues no son sensatos ni justos; no
saben que la muerte y la negra Ker[47] están ya a su lado para
matar a todos en un día. El viaje que preparas ya no está tan
lejano para ti, y es que yo soy tan buen amigo de tu padre que
te voy a aparejar una rápida nave y acompañar en persona.

»Conque marcha ahora a tu casa a reunirte con los pretendientes; prepara provisiones y métlas todas en recipientes, el   290
vino en cántaros, y la harina, sustento de los hombres, en pe-
llejos espesos. Yo voy por el pueblo a reunir voluntarios. Existen numerosas naves en Itaca, rodeada de corriente, nuevas y
viejas; veré cuál es la mejor y aparejándola rápidamente la lanzaremos al ancho ponto.»

Así habló Atenea, hija de Zeus, y Telémaco ya no aguardó
más, pues había escuchado la voz de un dios. Así que se puso
en camino, su corazón acongojado, hacia el palacio y encontró
a los altivos pretendientes degollando cabras y asando cerdos   300
en el patio.

Antínoo se encaminó riendo hacia Telémaco, le tomó de la
mano, le dijo su palabra y le llamó por su nombre:

«Telémaco, fanfarrón, incapaz de contener tu cólera, que no
ocupe tu pecho ninguna acción o palabra mala, sino comer y
beber conmigo como antes. Los aqueos te prepararán una
nave y remeros elegidos para que llegues con más rapidez a la
agradable Pilos en busca de noticias de tu ilustre padre.»

Y le respondió Telémaco discretamente:

«Antínoo, no me es posible comer callado en vuestra arro-   310

---

[47] La Ker (o Keres en plural) es el destino mortal del hombre tanto en sentido individual como colectivo. De ahí que sea a menudo sinónimo de «muerte».
Otras veces, las menos, es pura y simplente sinónimo del destino o Moira.

gante compañía y gozar tranquilamente. ¿O es que no es bastante que me hayáis destruido hasta ahora muchas y buenas cosas de mi propiedad, pretendientes, mientras era todavía un niño? Mas ahora que ya soy grande y que, escuchando la palabra de los demás, comprendo todo y el arrojo me ha crecido en el pecho, intentaré enviaros las funestas Keres, ya sea marchando a Pilos o aquí mismo, en el pueblo.

»Me marcho —y el viaje que os anuncio no será infructuoso— como pasajero, pues no poseo naves ni remeros. Esto os parecía lo más ventajoso para vosotros!»

320

Así dijo y retiró con rapidez su mano de la mano de Antínoo.

Y los pretendientes se aplicaban al banquete dentro del palacio y se mofaban de él zahiriéndolo con sus palabras.

Así decía uno de los jóvenes arrogantes:

«Seguro que Telémaco nos está meditando la muerte; traerá alguien de la arenosa Pilos para que lo defienda o tal vez de Esparta, pues mucho lo desea. O quizá quiere ir a Efira, tierra fértil, a fin de traer de allí venenos que corrompen la vida y echarlos en la crátera para destruirnos a todos.»

330

Y otro de los jóvenes arrogantes decía:

«¡Quién sabe si, marchando en la cóncava nave, no perece también él vagando lejos de los suyos como Odiseo! Así nos acrecentaría el trabajo, pues repartiríamos todos sus bienes y la casa se la daríamos a su madre y al que con ella casara para que la conservaran.»

Mientras así hablaban descendió Telémaco a la despensa[48] de elevado techo de su padre, espaciosa, donde había oro amontonado en el suelo y bronce, y en arcones vestidos, y oloroso aceite en abundancia. También había allí dispuestas en fila, junto a la pared, tinajas de añejo vino sabroso que conte-

340

---

[48] Gr. *Thálamos.* Esta palabra designa en Homero (cfr. nota 29) cualquier estancia privada y reservada a los habitantes del palacio. Significa, por tanto, «dormitorio», pero también «despensa» y «almacén», como aquí. Es probable (contra la opinión de S. West, *Odissea...* pág. 270 y nota 337) que en este caso, como indica el verbo, estuviera situada en una especie de sótano. Con ello concuerdan los restos arqueológicos; cfr. Alan J. B. Wace, *loc. cit.*, pág. 491. Este almacén es, en todo caso, diferente al que es aludido en XXI.8 y ss., donde se guardaban el arco y las armas de Odiseo.

[72]

nían sin mezcla la divina bebida por si alguna vez volvía a casa Odiseo después de sufrir dolores sin cuento. Las puertas que allí había se podían cerrar fuertemente ensambladas, eran de dos hojas, y permanecía allí día y noche un ama de llaves que vigilaba todo con la agudeza de su mente, Euriclea, hija de Ope Pisenórida.

A ésta dirigió Telémaco su palabra llamándola a la despensa:

«Vamos, ama, sácame en ánforas sabroso vino, el más pre- 350
ciado después del que tú guardas pensando en aquel desdicha-
do, por si viene algún día Odiseo de linaje divino después de evitar la muerte y las Keres; llename doce hasta arriba y ajusta todas con tapas. Échame también harina en bien cosidos pelle-
jos, hasta veinte medidas de harina de trigo molido. Sólo tú de-
bes saberlo. Que esté todo preparado, pues lo recogeré por la tarde cuando ya mi madre haya subido al piso de arriba y esté ocupada en acostarse. Me marcho a Esparta y a la arenosa Pilos para enterarme del regreso de mi padre, por si oigo algo.» 360

Así habló; rompió en lamentos su nodriza Euriclea y dijo llorando aladas palabras:

«¿Por qué, hijo mío, tienes en tu interior este proyecto? ¿Por dónde quieres ir a una tierra tan grande siendo el bienamado hijo único? Ha sucumbido lejos de su patria Odiseo, de linaje divino, en un país desconocido, y éstos te andan meditando la muerte para el mismo momento en que te marches, para que mueras en emboscada. Ellos se lo repartirán todo. Anda, quédate aquí sentado sobre tus cosas; no tienes necesidad ninguna de sufrir penalidades en el estéril ponto ni de andar errante.» 370

Y Telémaco le contestó discretamente:

«Anímate, ama, puesto que esta decisión me ha venido no sin un dios. Ahora júrame que no dirás esto a mi madre antes de que llegue el día décimo o el duodécimo, o hasta que ella misma me eche de menos y oiga que he partido, para que no afee, desgarrándola, su hermosa piel.»

Así habló, y la anciana juró por los dioses con gran juramento que no lo haría. Cuando hubo jurado y llevado a térmi-
no este juramento vertió enseguida vino en las ánforas y echó harina en bien cosidos sacos. Y Telémaco se puso en camino 380
hacia las habitaciones de abajo para reunirse con los preten-
dientes.

Entonces la diosa de ojos brillantes, Atenea, concibió otra idea. Tomando la forma de Telémaco marchó por toda la ciudad y poniéndose cerca de cada hombre les decía su palabra; les ordenaba que se congregaran con el crepúsculo junto a la rápida nave. Después pidió una rápida nave a Noemón, esclarecido hijo de Fronio, y éste se la ofreció de buena gana. Y se sumergió Helios y todos los caminos se llenaron de sombras. Entonces empujó hacia el mar a la rápida nave, puso en ella todas las provisiones que suelen llevar las naves de buenos bancos y la detuvo al final del puerto.

Los valientes compañeros ya se habían congregado en grupo, pues la diosa había movido a cada uno en particular.

Entonces la diosa de ojos brillantes, Atenea, concibió otra idea: se puso en camino hacia el palacio del divino Odiseo y una vez allí derramó dulce sueño sobre los pretendientes, los hechizó cuando bebían e hizo caer las copas de sus manos. Y éstos se apresuraron por la ciudad para ir a dormir y ya no estuvieron sentados por más tiempo, pues el sueño se posaba sobre sus párpados.

Entonces Atenea, de ojos brillantes, se dirigió a Telémaco llamándolo desde fuera del palacio, agradable para vivir, asemejándose a Méntor en la figura y timbre de voz:

«Ya tienes sentados al remo a tus compañeros de hermosas grebas y esperan tu partida. Vamos, no retrasemos por más tiempo el viaje.»

Así habló, y lo condujo rápidamente Palas Atenea, y él marchaba en pos de las huellas de la diosa. Cuando llegaron a la nave y al mar encontraron sobre la ribera a los aqueos de largo cabello y entre ellos habló la sagrada fuerza[49] de Telémaco:

«Aquí, los míos, traigamos las provisiones; ya está todo junto en mi palacio. Mi madre no está enterada de nada ni las demás esclavas; sólo una ha oído mi palabra.»

---

[49] «La sagrada fuerza (*ís, ménos*) de Telémaco» es una pura perífrasis del nombre propio, aunque quizás originariamente intentara resaltar el carácter real de los personajes a quienes se aplica. La fuerza *es* su carácter real y sólo ella (no el personaje en sí) puede ser calificada de «sagrada». La misma expresión aparece referida a Alcínoo en VII.167, VIII.421, etc., con toda propiedad. Sin embargo, se aplica inadecuadamente al pretendiente Antínoo en XVIII.34 dentro de una fórmula en la que se ha cambiado mecánicamente el nombre de Alcínoo por el de Antínoo, equivalentes métricamente.

Así habló y los condujo, y ellos le seguían de cerca. Se llevaron todo y lo pusieron en la nave de buenos bancos como había ordenado el querido hijo de Odiseo.

Subió luego Telémaco a la nave; Atenea iba delante y se sentó en la popa, y a su lado se sentó Telémaco.

Los compañeros soltaron las amarras, subieron todos y se sentaron en los bancos. Y Atenea, de ojos brillantes, les envió 420 un viento favorable, el fresco Céfiro que silba sobre el ponto rojo como el vino.

Telémaco animó a sus compañeros, les ordenó que se asieran a las jarcias y éstos escucharon al que les urgía. Levantaron el mástil de abeto y lo colocaron dentro del hueco construido en medio, lo ataron con maromas y extendieron las blancas velas con bien retorcidas correas de piel de buey. El viento 430 hinchó la vela central y las purpúreas olas bramaron a los lados de la quilla de la nave en su marcha, y corría apresurando su camino sobre las olas.

Después ataron los aparejos a la rápida nave y levantaron las cráteras llenas de vino hasta los bordes haciendo libaciones a los inmortales dioses, que han nacido para siempre, y entre todos especialmente a la de ojos brillantes, a la hija de Zeus.

Y la nave continuó su camino toda la noche y durante el amanecer. 440

Canto III

TELÉMACO VIAJA A PILOS PARA INFORMARSE
SOBRE SU PADRE

HABÍASE levantado Helios, abandonando el hermosísimo estanque del mar, hacia el broncíneo cielo para alumbrar a los inmortales y a los mortales caducos sobre la Tierra donadora de vida, cuando llegaron a Pilos[50], la bien construida ciudadela de Neleo.

Los pilios estaban sacrificando sobre la ribera del mar toros totalmente negros en honor del de azuloscura cabellera, el que sacude la tierra[51]. Había nueve asientos[52] y en cada uno estaban sentados quinientos hombres y de cada uno hacían ofrenda de nueve toros. Mientras éstos gustaban las entrañas y quemaban los muslos en honor del dios, los itacenses entraban en el puerto; amainaron las velas de la equilibrada nave, las ataron, fondearon la nave y descendieron.

Entonces descendió Telémaco de la nave y Atenea iba de-

10

---

[50] Había en la Antigüedad tres ciudades del mismo nombre —en Mesenia, en Elide y en Trifilia. Los antiguos, sin duda, situaban la Pilos de Néstor en Mesenia (cfr. Píndaro, *Pítica* 6.35) y probablemente es en ésta en la que piensa Homero, pues la sitúa en la misma costa. Sin embargo, la verdadera Pilos micénica fue descubierta por Blegen a 17 kilómetros al norte de la anterior y hoy constituye una de las mejores muestras de un palacio micénico.

[51] Poseidón. En las tablillas descubiertas en Pilos, en linear B, es precisamente uno de los dioses que más aparecen.

[52] En realidad, «lugares o zonas de asiento». Es de notar que el número de ciudadanos pilios presentes (9 × 500) coincide exactamente con el número de los guerreros que van a Troya con Néstor (90 × 50); cfr. *Ilíada*, II.591 y ss.

lante. Y a él dirigió sus primeras palabras la diosa de ojos brillantes:

«Telémaco, ya no has de tener vergüenza, ni un poco siquiera, pues has navegado el mar para inquirir dónde oculta la tierra a tu padre y qué suerte ha corrido.

»Conque, vamos, marcha directamente a casa de Néstor, domador de caballos; sepamos qué pensamientos guarda en su pecho. Y suplícale para que te diga la verdad; mentira no te 20 dirá, es muy discreto.»

Y le contestó Telémaco discretamente:

«Méntor, ¿cómo voy a ir a abrazar sus rodillas? No tengo aún experiencia alguna en discursos ajustados. Y además a un hombre joven le da vergüenza preguntar a uno más viejo.»

Y la diosa de ojos brillantes, Atenea, se dirigió de nuevo a él:

«Telémaco, unas palabras las concebirás en tu propia mente y otras te las infundirá la divinidad. Estoy seguro de que tú has nacido y te has criado no sin la voluntad de los dioses.»

Así habló y lo condujo con rapidez Palas Atenea, y él siguió 30 en pos de la diosa. Llegaron a la asamblea y a los asientos de los hombres de Pilos, donde Néstor estaba sentado con sus hijos, y en torno a ellos los compañeros asaban la carne y la ensartaban preparando el banquete.

Cuando vieron a los forasteros se reunieron todos en grupo, les tomaron de las manos en señal de bienvenida y les ordenaron sentarse. Pisístrato, el hijo de Néstor, fue el primero que se les acercó: les tomó a ambos de la mano y los hizo sentarse en torno al banquete sobre blandas pieles de ovejas, en las arenas marinas, a la vera de su hermano Trasimedes y de su padre. Luego les dio parte de las entrañas, les vertió vino en copa de 40 oro y dirigió a Palas Atenea, la hija de Zeus, portador de égida[53], sus palabras de bienvenida:

---

[53] La égida es un atributo mágico de Zeus, único dios a quien se aplica el epíteto «portador de égida». Sin embargo, en la *Ilíada* la utilizan Atenea (II.447 y ss.) y Apolo (XV.318), y más tarde en época clásica se considera también atributo de Atenea (cfr. Esquilo, *Euménides*, 404). Homero la describe como un escudo (aunque no dice que lo sea) con cien franjas de oro y representaciones de la Gorgona y abstracciones como la Huida, la Discordia y la Fuerza *(Ilíada,*

«Forastero, eleva tus súplicas al soberano Poseidón, pues en su honor es el banquete con el que os habéis encontrado al llegar aquí. Luego que hayas hecho las libaciones y súplicas como está mandado, entrega también a éste la copa de agradable vino para que haga libación; que también él, creo yo, hace súplicas a los inmortales, pues todos los hombres necesitan a los dioses. Pero es más joven, de mi misma edad, por eso quiero 50 darte a ti primero la copa de oro.»

Así diciendo, puso en su mano la copa de agradable vino; Atenea dio las gracias al discreto, al cabal hombre, porque le había dado a ella primero la copa de oro y a continuación dirigió una larga plegaria al soberano Poseidón:

«Escúchame, Poseidón, que conduces tu carro por la tierra, y no te opongas por rencor a que los que te suplican llevemos a término esta empresa. Concede a Néstor antes que a nadie, y a sus hijos, honor, y después concede a los demás pilios una recompensa en reconocimiento por su espléndida hecatombe[54]. Concede también a Telémaco y a mí que volvamos después de 60 haber conseguido aquello por lo que hemos venido aquí en veloz, negra nave.»

Así orando, realizó (ritualmente) todo y entregó a Telémaco la hermosa copa doble. Y el querido hijo de Odiseo elevó su súplica de modo semejante.

Cuando habían asado la carne exterior de las víctimas, la sacaron del asador, repartieron las porciones y se aplicaron al magnífico festín. Y después que habían echado de sí el apetito de comer y beber, comenzó a hablarles el de Gerenia[55], el caballero Néstor:

---

vv. 738-42). Su epíteto más corriente es «terrible», pero su objeto es doble: producir terror en los enemigos *(Ilíada,* XV.308, *Odisea,* XXII.297 y ss.) y también vigorizar a los amigos *(Ilíada,* II.447 y ss.). Los griegos siempre la relacionaron con *aix,* «cabra» (sería una piel de este animal), pero puede que originariamente tenga que ver con el verbo *aísso,* «lanzarse», y estar en relación con los fenómenos atmosféricos más violentos, esfera de dominio de Zeus; cfr. *Ilíada,* XVII.593 y ss.

[54] Como tantas otras veces, hecatombe no significa literalmente «sacrificio de 100 bueyes». Aquí son 81.

[55] *Gerénios* es un epíteto fijo de Néstor, cuya etimología y significación son poco claras. De un lado tiene forma de patronímico eolio, pero no conocemos

«Ahora que se han saciado de comida, lo mejor es entablar conversación y preguntar a los forasteros quiénes son. Foras- 70 teros, ¿quiénes sois?, ¿de dónde habéis llegado navegando los húmedos senderos? ¿Andáis errantes por algún asunto o sin rumbo como los piratas por la mar, los que andan a la aventura exponiendo sus vidas y llevando la destrucción a los de otras tierras?»

Y Telémaco se llenó de valor y le contestó discretamente —pues la misma Atenea le infundió valor en su interior para que le preguntara sobre su padre ausente y para que cobrara fama de valiente entre los hombres:

«Néstor, hijo de Neleo, gran honra de los aqueos, preguntas 80 de dónde somos y yo te lo voy a exponer en detalle.

»Hemos venido de Itaca, a los pies del monte Neyo, y el asunto de que te voy a hablar es privado, no público. Ando a lo ancho en busca de noticias sobre mi padre —por si las oigo en algún sitio—, de Odiseo el divino, el sufridor, de quien dicen que en otro tiempo arrasó la ciudad de Troya luchando a tu lado. Ya me he enterado dónde alcanzó luctuosa muerte cada uno de cuantos lucharon contra los troyanos, pero su muerte la ha hecho desconocida el hijo de Crono, pues nadie es capaz de decirme claramente dónde está muerto, si ha sucumbido en tierra firme a manos de hombres enemigos o en el mar 90 entre las olas de Anfitrite[56]. Por esto me llego ahora a tus rodillas, por si quieres contarme su luctuosa muerte —la hayas visto con tus propios ojos o hayas escuchado el relato de algún caminante—; ¡digno de lástima lo parió su madre! Y no endulces tus palabras por respeto ni piedad, antes bien cuéntame detalladamente cómo llegaste a verlo. Te lo suplico si es que alguna vez mi padre, el noble Odiseo, te prometió algo y

ningún héroe llamado Geren, y Néstor es hijo de Neleo y nieto de Poseidón. Por otra parte, en las más antiguas fuentes del mito se habla de Gerenia como la ciudad donde Néstor se crió, pero ningún héroe homérico lleva por epíteto el nombre de una ciudad. Finalmente, se ha pensado que el adjetivo podría tener relación con *gérōn*, «anciano», dado que esta fórmula completa es intercambiable con otra que contiene dicho adjetivo.

[56] En la *Odisea*, Anfítrite siempre es metonimia del mar. Según el mito, es una de las 50 hijas de Nereo y Dóride y esposa de Poseidón. Cfr. Hesiodo, *Teogonía* 243.

te lo cumplió en el pueblo de los troyanos donde los aqueos 100
sufríais penalidades. Acuérdate de esto ahora y cuéntame la
verdad.»

Y le contestó luego el de Gerenia, el caballero Néstor:

«Hijo mío, puesto que me has recordado los infortunios que
tuvimos que soportar en aquel país los hijos de los aqueos de
incontenible furia: cuánto vagamos con las naves en el brumoso ponto, a la deriva en busca de botín por donde nos guiaba
Aquiles y cuánto combatimos en torno a la gran ciudad del soberano Príamo... Allí murieron los mejores: allí reposa Ayax,
hijo de Ares, y allí Aquiles, y allí Patroclo, consejero de la talla 110
de los dioses, y allí mi querido hijo, fuerte a la vez que irreprochable, Antíloco, que sobresalía en la carrera y en el combate.
Otros muchos males sufrimos además de éstos. ¿Quién de los
mortales hombres podría contar todas aquellas cosas? Nadie,
por más que te quedaras a su lado cinco o seis años para preguntarle cuántos males sufrieron allí los aqueos de linaje divino. Antes volverías apesadumbrado a tu tierra patria. Durante
nueve años tramamos desgracias contra ellos acechándoles con
toda clase de engaños y a duras penas puso término (a la guerra) el hijo de Cronos[57].

»Jamás quiso nadie igualársele en inteligencia, puesto que el 120
divino Odiseo era muy superior en toda clase de astucias, tu
padre, si es que verdaderamente eres descendencia suya. (Al
verte se apodera de mí el asombro. En verdad vuestras palabras son parecidas y no se puede decir que un hombre joven
hable tan discretamente.)

»Jamás, durante todo el tiempo que estuvimos allí, hablába-
mos de diferente modo yo y el divino Odiseo ni en la asamblea
ni en el consejo, sino que teníamos un solo pensamiento, y con
juicio y prudente consejo mostrábamos a los aqueos cómo sal-
dría todo mejor.

»Después, cuando habíamos saqueado la elevada ciudad de 130
Príamo y embarcamos en las naves y la divinidad dispersó a
los aqueos, Zeus concibió en su mente un regreso lamentable
para los argivos porque no todos eran prudentes ni justos. Así
que muchos de éstos fueron al encuentro de una desgraciada

---

[57] Zeus.

muerte por causa de la funesta cólera de la de poderoso padre, de la de ojos brillantes que asentó la Disensión entre ambos atridas. Convocaron éstos en asamblea a todos los aqueos, insensatamente, a destiempo, cuando Helios se sumerge, y los hijos de los aqueos se presentaron pesados por el vino, y les dijeron por qué habían reunido al ejército.

»Allí Menelao aconsejaba a todos los aqueos que pensaran en volver sobre el ancho lomo del mar. Pero no agradó en absoluto a Agamenón, pues quería retener al pueblo y ejecutar sagradas hecatombes para aplacar la tremenda cólera de Atenea. ¡Necio!, no sabía que no iba a persudirla, que no se doblega rápidamente la voluntad de los dioses que viven siempre. Así que los dos se pusieron en pie y se contestaban con palabras agrias. Y los hijos de los aqueos de hermosas grebas se levantaron con un vocerío sobrehumano: divididos en dos bandos les agradaba una u otra decisión.

»Pasamos la noche removiendo en nuestro interior maldades unos contra otros, pues ya Zeus nos preparaba el azote de la desgracia.

»Al amanecer algunos arrastramos las naves hasta el divino mar y metimos nuestros botines y las mujeres de profundas cinturas. La mitad del ejército permaneció allí, al lado del atrida Agamenón, pastor de su pueblo, pero la otra mitad embarcamos y partimos. Nuestras naves navegaban muy aprisa —una divinidad había calmado el ponto que encierra grandes monstruos— y llegados a Ténedos[58] realizamos sacrificios a los dioses con el deseo de volver a casa. Pero Zeus no se preocupó aún de nuestro regreso. ¡Cruel! Él, que levantó por segunda vez agria disensión: unos dieron la vuelta a sus bien curvadas naves[59] y retornaron con el prudente soberano Odiseo, el de pensamientos complicados, para dar satisfacción al atrida Agamenón, pero yo, con todas mis naves agrupadas, las que

140

150

160

---

[58] Pequeña isla cercana a la Tróade, donde, según Virgilio *(Eneida,* II, 21 y ss.), los griegos se retiraron dolosamente antes de la toma de Troya. Constituye una primera etapa muy corta.

[59] El epíteto *amphielíssas* es convencional para las naves y siempre ocupa los dos últimos metros del hexámetro. Puede significar «que giran de uno y otro lado», es decir, «manejables» o bien «curvadas por ambos lados». Me inclino por el último, que es el significado que se le atribuye tradicionalmente.

me seguían, marché de allí porque barruntaba que la divinidad nos preparaba desgracias.

»También marchó el belicoso hijo de Tideo[60] y arrastró consigo a sus compañeros y más tarde navegó a nuestro lado el rubio Menelao —nos encontró en Lesbos cuando planeábamos el largo regreso[61]: o navegar por encima de la escabrosa Quios en dirección de la isla Psiría dejándola a la izquierda o bien por debajo de Quios junto al ventiscoso Mimante. Pedimos a la divinidad que nos mostrara un prodigio y enseguida ésta nos lo mostró y nos aconsejó cortar por la mitad del mar en dirección a Eubea, para poder escapar rápidamente de la desgracia. Así que levantó, para que soplara, un sonoro viento y las naves recorrieron con suma rapidez los pecillenos caminos. Durante la noche arribaron a Geresto[62] y ofrecimos a Poseidón muchos muslos de toros por haber recorrido el gran mar. Era el cuarto día cuando los compañeros del tidida Diomedes, el domador de caballos, fondearon sus equilibradas naves en Argos. Después yo me dirigí a Pilos y ya nunca se extinguió el viento desde que al principio una divinidad lo envió para que soplara. Así llegué, hijo mío, sin enterarme, sin saber quiénes se salvaron de los aqueos y quiénes perecieron, pero cuanto he oído sentado en mi palacio lo sabrás —como es justo— y nada te ocultaré. Dicen que han llegado bien los mirmidones[63] famosos por sus lanzas, a los que conducía el ilustre hijo del valeroso Aquiles y que llegó bien Filoctetes, el brillante hijo de Poyante. Idomeneo condujo hasta Creta a todos sus compañeros, los que habían sobrevivido a la guerra, y el mar no se le engulló a ninguno. En cuanto al Atrida, ya habéis oído vosotros mismos, aunque estáis lejos, cómo llegó y cómo Egisto le había preparado una miserable muerte, aunque ya ha pagado lamentablemente. ¡Qué bueno es que a un hombre

---

60 Diomedes.
61 Es el regreso atravesando el Egeo desde Troya hasta la Grecia continental. La alternativa es o cruzar directamente a Eubea desde Lesbos dejando a la izquierda Psiría (hoy Psará) y Quios, o bien ir costeando entre Quíos y el continente asiático y cruzar desde el sur de esta isla pasando por Andros, etc.
62 Promontorio al sureste de Eubea.
63 Pueblo de Tesalia cuyo jefe era Aquiles.

muerto le quede un hijo! Pues aquél[64] se ha vengado del asesino de su padre, del tramposo Egisto, porque le había asesinado a su ilustre padre. También tú, hijo —pues te veo vigoroso y bello—, sé fuerte para que cualquiera de tus descendientes hable bien de ti.»   200

Y le contestó Telémaco discretamente:

«Néstor, hijo de Neleo, gran honra de los aqueos, así es, por cierto; aquél se vengó y los aqueos llevarán a lo largo y a lo ancho su fama, motivo de canto para los venideros.

»¡Ojalá los dioses me dotaran de igual fuerza para hacer pagar a los pretendientes por su dolorosa insolencia!, pues ensoberbecidos me preparan acciones malvadas. Pero los dioses no han tejido para mí tal dicha; ni para mi padre ni para mí. Y ahora no hay más remedio que aguantar.»

Y le contestó luego el de Gerenia, el caballero Néstor: 210

«Amigo —puesto que me has recordado y dicho esto—, dicen que muchos pretendientes de tu madre están cometiendo muchas injusticias en el palacio contra tu voluntad. Dime si cedes de buen gusto o te odia la gente en el pueblo siguiendo una inspiración de la divinidad. ¡Quién sabe si llegará Odiseo algún día y los hará pagar sus acciones violentas, él solo o todos los aqueos juntos! Pues si la de ojos brillantes, Atenea, quiere amarte del mismo modo que protegía al ilustre Odiseo en aquel entonces en el pueblo de los troyanos donde los   220 aqueos pasamos penalidades (pues nunca he visto que los dioses amen tan a las claras como Palas Atenea le asistía a él), si quiere amarte a ti así y preocuparte de ti en su ánimo, cualquiera de aquéllos se olvidaría del matrimonio.»

Y le contestó Telémaco discretamente:

«Anciano, no creo que esas palabras lleguen a realizarse nunca. Has dicho algo excesivamente grande. El estupor me tiene sujeto. Esas cosas no podrían sucederme por más que lo espere ni aunque los dioses lo quisieran así.»

Y de pronto la diosa de ojos brillantes, Atenea, se dirigió a él:

«¡Telémaco, qué palabra ha escapado del cerco de tus dientes! Es fácil para un dios, si quiere, salvar a un hombre aun   230

---

[64] Orestes.

desde lejos. Preferiría yo volver a casa aun después de sufrir mucho y ver el día de mi regreso, antes que morir al llegar, en mi propio hogar, como ha perecido Agamenón víctima de una trampa de Egisto y de su esposa. Pero, en verdad, ni siquiera los dioses pueden apartar la muerte, común a todos, de un hombre, por muy querido que les sea, cuando ya lo ha alcanzado el funesto Destino de la muerte de largos lamentos.»

Y le contestó discretamente Telémaco:

«Méntor, no hablemos más de esto aun a pesar de nuestra preocupación. En verdad ya no hay para él regreso alguno, que los dioses le han pensado la muerte y la negra Ker. Ahora quiero hacer otra indagación y preguntarle a Néstor, puesto que él sobresale por encima de los demás en justicia e inteligencia. Pues dicen que ha sido soberano de tres generaciones de hombres, y así me parece inmortal al mirarlo. Néstor, hijo de Neleo —y dime la verdad—, ¿cómo murió el poderoso atrida Agamenón?, ¿dónde estaba Menelao?, ¿qué muerte le preparó el tramposo Egisto, puesto que mató a uno mucho mejor que él? ¿O es que no estaba en Argos de Acaya, sino que andaba errante, en cualquier otro sitio, y Egisto lo mató cobrando valor?»

Y le contestó a continuación el de Gerenia, el caballero Néstor:

«Hijo, te voy a decir toda la verdad. Tú mismo puedes imaginarte qué habría pasado si al volver de Troya el Atrida, el rubio Menelao, hubiera encontrado vivo a Egisto en el palacio. Con seguridad no habrían echado tierra sobre su cadáver, sino que los perros y las aves, tirado en la llanura lejos de la ciudad, lo habrían despedazado sin que lo llorara ninguna de las aqueas: ¡tan gran crimen cometió! Mientras nosotros realizábamos en Troya innumerables pruebas, él estaba tranquilamente en el centro de Argos, criadora de caballos, y trataba de seducir poco a poco a la esposa de Agamenón con sus palabras.

»Ésta, al principio, se negaba al vergonzoso hecho[65], la divi-

---

[65] El que Clitemnestra se negara en un principio al adulterio es un dato que añade aquí Homero. De los diversos pasajes donde se alude al asesinato de Agamenón se puede deducir que Homero probablemente confunde dos versiones diferentes, una de origen jonio y otra doria. Según la primera, Agamenón reina

na Clitemnestra, pues poseía un noble corazón, y a su lado estaba también el aedo, a quien el Atrida al marchar a Troya había encomendado encarecidamente que protegiera a su esposa. Pero cuando el Destino de los dioses la forzó a sucumbir se llevó al aedo a una isla desierta y lo dejó como presa y botín de las aves. Y Egisto la llevó a su casa de buen grado sin que se opusiera. Luego quemó muchos muslos sobre los sagrados altares de los dioses y colgó muchas ofrendas —vestidos y oro— —por haber realizado la gran hazaña que jamás esperó en su ánimo llevar a cabo. 270

»Nosotros navegábamos juntos desde Troya, el Atrida y yo, con sentimientos comunes de amistad. Pero cuando llegamos al sagrado Sunio, el promontorio de Atenas[66], Febo Apolo mató al piloto de Menelao alcanzándole con sus suaves flechas[67] cuando tenía entre sus manos el timón de la nave, a Frontis, hijo de Onetor, que superaba a la mayoría de los hombres en gobernar la nave cuando se desencadenaban las tempestades. Así que se detuvo allí, aunque anhelaba el camino, para enterrar a su compañero y hacerle las honras fúnebres. 280

»Cuando ya de camino sobre el ponto rojo como el vino alcanzó con sus cóncavas naves la escarpada montaña de Maleas[68] en su carrera, en ese momento el que ve a lo ancho, Zeus, concibió para él un viaje luctuoso y derramó un huracán de silbantes vientos y monstruosas bien nutridas olas semejantes a montes. Allí dividió parte de las naves e impulsó a unas hacia Creta, donde viven los Cidones en torno a la corriente del Jardano. Hay una pelada y elevada roca que se mete en el 290

en Micenas (cfr. III.304) y el único responsable del asesinato es Egisto (cfr. IV.524 y ss.) a quien mataría Orestes. Según la versión doria, Agamenón reina en Laconia (cfr. IV.514) y Clitemnestra sería la instigadora del crimen, aunque el ejecutor material fuera Egisto. En este caso, Orestes mataría a ambos. En cualquier caso, hasta la Tragedia no aparecería Clitemnestra como ejecutora del crimen. Cfr. P. Mazon, *Eschyle*, II, París, 1925, págs. V y ss.

[66] Atenas designa a toda el Ática sistemáticamente en Homero.

[67] Es frase formular para referirse a la muerte repentina de los varones (cfr. también VII.64, etc.); la de las mujeres la produce Artemis por los mismos medios (salvo en el caso de Orión en V.123), cfr. XI.172, 324, XV.478, etc.

[68] El cabo más oriental del sur del Peloponeso. Es habitual en la literatura griega aludir a las dificultades para remontarlo debido al fuerte viento. Cfr. también IX.80, donde Odiseo es alejado de allí «por el oleaje y el Bóreas».

agua, en el extremo de Górtina, en el nebuloso ponto, donde Noto impulsa las grandes olas hacia el lado izquierdo del saliente, en dirección a Festos, y una pequeña piedra detiene las grandes olas. Allí llegaron las naves y los hombres consiguieron evitar la muerte a duras penas, pero las olas quebraron las naves contra los escollos. Sin embargo, a otras cinco naves de azuloscuras proas el viento y el agua las impulsaron hacia Egipto. Allí reunió éste abundantes bienes y oro, y se dirigió con sus naves en busca de gentes de lengua extraña.

»Y, entre tanto, Egisto planeó estas malvadas acciones en casa, y después de asesinar al Atrida, el pueblo le estaba sometido. Siete años reinó sobre la dorada Micenas, pero al octavo llegó de vuelta de Atenas el divino Orestes para su mal y mató al asesino de su padre, a Egisto, al inventor de engaños, porque había asesinado a su ilustre padre. Y después de matarlo dio a los argivos un banquete fúnebre por su odiada madre y por el cobarde Egisto.

»Ese mismo día llegó Menelao, de recia voz guerrera, trayendo muchas riquezas, cuantas podían soportar sus naves en peso.

»En cuanto a ti, amigo, no andes errante mucho tiempo lejos de tu casa, dejando tus posesiones y hombres tan arrogantes en tu palacio, no sea que se te repartan todos tus bienes y se los coman y camines un viaje baldío. Antes bien, te aconsejo y exhorto a que vayas junto a Menelao, pues él está recién llegado de otras regiones, de entre tales hombres de los que nunca soñaría poder regresar aquel a quien los huracanes lo impulsen desde el principio hacia un mar tan grande que ni las aves son capaces de recorrerlo en un año entero, puesto que es grande y terrorífico. Vamos, márchate con la nave y los compañeros, pero si quieres ir por tierra tienes a tu disposición un carro y caballos y a tu disposición están mis hijos que te servirán de escolta hasta la divina Lacedemonia, donde está el rubio Menelao. Ruégale para que te diga la verdad; mentira no te dirá, es muy discreto.»

Así habló, y Helios se sumergió y sobrevino la oscuridad.

Y les dijo la diosa de ojos brillantes, Atenea:

«Anciano, has hablado como te corresponde. Pero, vamos, cortad las lenguas y mezclad el vino para que hagamos libaciones a Poseidón y a los demás inmortales y nos ocupemos de dormir, pues ya es hora. Ya ha descendido la luz a la región de las sombras y no es bueno estar sentado mucho tiempo en un banquete en honor de los dioses, sino regresar.»

Así habló la hija de Zeus y ellos prestaron atención a la que hablaba.

Y los heraldos derramaron agua sobre sus manos y los jóvenes coronaron de vino las cráteras y lo repartieron entre todos haciendo una primera ofrenda, por orden, en las copas. Luego arrojaron las lenguas al fuego y se pusieron en pie para hacer la libación.

Cuando hubieron libado y bebido cuanto su apetito les pedía, Atenea y Telémaco, semejante a un dios, se pusieron en camino para volver a la cóncava nave. Pero Néstor todavía los retuvo tocándolos con sus palabras:

«No permitirán Zeus y los demás dioses inmortales que volváis de mi casa a la rápida nave como de casa de uno que carece por completo de ropas, o de un indigente que no tiene mantas ni abundantes sábanas en casa ni un dormir blando para sí y para sus huéspedes. Que en mi casa hay mantas y sábanas hermosas. No dormirá sobre los maderos de su nave el querido hijo de Odiseo mientras yo viva y aún me queden hijos en el palacio para hospedar a mis huéspedes, quienquiera que sea el que arribe a mi palacio.»

Y la diosa de ojos brillantes, Atenea, le dijo:

«Has hablado bien, anciano amigo. Sería conveniente que Telémaco te hiciera caso. Así, pues, él te seguirá para dormir en tu palacio, pero yo marcharé a la negra nave para animar a los compañeros y darles órdenes, pues me precio de ser el más anciano entre ellos. Y los demás nos siguen por amistad, hombres jóvenes todos, de la misma edad que el valiente Telémaco. Yo dormiré en la cóncava, negra nave, y al amanecer iré junto a los impetuosos caucones[69], donde se me debe una deuda no de ahora ni pequeña, desde luego.

»Tú, envíalo con un carro y un hijo tuyo, pues ha llegado a

340

350

360

---

[69] Tribu predoria que probablemente estaba bajo el dominio de Pilos (Heródoto, 1.147, los llama caucones pilios). Estrabón los sitúa en Trifilia y Elide (cfr. 7.7.1 y 8.3.11 y ss.).

tu casa como huésped. Y dale caballos, los que sean más veloces en la carrera y más excelentes en vigor.»

Así hablando partió la de ojos brillantes, Atenea, tomando la forma del buitre barbado.

Y la admiración atenazó a todos los aqueos. Admiróse el anciano cuando lo vio con sus ojos y tomando la mano de Telémaco le dirigió su palabra y le llamó por su nombre[70]:

«Amigo, no creo que llegues a ser débil ni cobarde si ya, tan joven, te siguen los dioses como escolta. Pues éste no era otro de entre los que ocupan las mansiones del Olimpo que la hija de Zeus, la rapaz Tritogenia[71], la que honraba también a tu noble padre entre los argivos. Soberana, séme propicia, dame fama de nobleza a mí mismo, a mis hijos y a mi venerable esposa y a cambio yo te sacificaré una cariancha novilla de un año, no domada, a la que jamás un hombre haya llevado bajo el yugo. Te la sacrificaré rodeando de oro sus cuernos.»

Así dirigió sus súplicas y Palas Atenea le escuchó. Y el de Gerenia, el caballero Néstor, condujo a sus hijos y yernos hacia sus hermosas mansiones.

Cuando llegaron al palacio de este soberano se sentaron por orden en sillas y sillones y, una vez llegados, el anciano les mezcló una crátera de vino dulce al paladar que el ama de lla- ves abrió —a los once años de estar cerrada— desatando la cubierta. El anciano mezcló una crátera de este vino y oró a Atenea al hacer la libación, a la hija de Zeus el que lleva la égida.

Después, cuando hubieron hecho la libación y bebido cuanto les pedía su apetito, los parientes marcharon cada uno a su casa para dormir. Pero a Telémaco, el querido hijo del divino Odiseo, lo hizo acostarse allí mismo el de Gerenia, el caballero

---

[70] Frase formular a la que debería seguir un nombre propio y quizá creada en un contexto en el que realmente seguía. Cuando no sucede así, como en este caso, resulta extraña.

[71] Dos epítetos exclusivos de Atenea variamente interpretados desde la Antigüedad. *Ageleíe* puede ser «la que se lleva el botín» o «la que conduce al ejército». *Tritogéneia* se entendía como «nacida junto a la laguna Tritón (Libia), el río Tritón (Arcadia) o nacida de la cabeza» (de Zeus): *tritó* en eolio significa cabeza. P. Kretschmer *(Glotta* X, 1919, 38 y ss.) lo relaciona con la palabra *Tritopátores*, «los padres legítimos».

Néstor, en un lecho taladrado bajo el sonoro pórtico. Y a su lado hizo acostarse a Pisístrato de buena lanza de fresno, caudillo de guerreros, el que de sus hijos permanecía todavía soltero en el palacio.

Néstor durmió en el centro de la elevada mansión y su señora esposa le preparó el lecho y la cama.

Y cuando se mostró Eos, la que nace de la mañana, la de dedos de rosa, se levantó del lecho el de Gerenia, el caballero Néstor. Salió y se sentó sobre las pulimentadas piedras que tenía, blancas, resplandecientes de aceite, delante de las elevadas puertas, sobre las que solía sentarse antes Neleo, consejero de la talla de los dioses. Pero éste había ya marchado a Hades sometido por Ker, y entonces se sentaba Néstor, el de Gerenia, el guardián de los aqueos, el que tenía el cetro.

Y sus hijos se congregaron en torno suyo cuando salieron de sus dormitorios, Equefrón y Estratio, Perseo y Trasímedes semejante a un dios. A continuación llegó a ellos en sexto lugar el héroe Pisístrato, y a su lado sentaron a Telémaco semejante a los dioses.

Y entre ellos comenzó a hablar el de Gerenia, el caballero Néstor:

«Hijos míos, llevad a cabo rápidamente mi deseo para que antes que a los demás dioses propicie a Atenea, la que vino manifiestamente al abundante banquete en honor del dios. Vamos, que uno marche a la llanura a por una novilla de modo que llegue lo antes posible: que la conduzca el boyero; que otro marche a la negra nave del valiente Telémaco y traiga a todos los compañeros dejando sólo dos; que otro ordene que se presente aquí Laerques, el que derrama el oro, para que derrame oro en torno a los cuernos de la novilla. Los demás quedaos aquí reunidos y decid a las esclavas que dispongan un banquete dentro del ilustre palacio; que traigan asientos y leña alrededor y brillante agua.»

Así habló, y al punto todos se apresuraron. Y llegó enseguida la novilla de la llanura y llegaron los compañeros del valiente Telémaco de junto a la equilibrada nave; y llegó el broncero llevando en sus manos las herramientas de bronce, perfección del arte: el yunque y el martillo y las bien labradas tenazas con las que trabajaba el oro. Y llegó Atenea para asistir a los sacrificios.

El anciano, el cabalgador de caballos, Néstor, le entregó oro a Laerques, y éste lo trabajó y derramó por los cuernos de la novilla para que la diosa se alegrara al ver la ofrenda. Y llevaron a la novilla por los cuernos Estratio y el divino Equefrón; y Areto salió de su dormitorio llevándoles el agua-manos en una vasija adornada con flores y en la otra llevaba la cebada tostada dentro de una cesta. Y Trasímedes, el fuerte en la lucha, se presentó con una afilada hacha en la mano para herir a la novilla, y Perseo sostenía el vaso para la sangre.

El anciano, el cabalgador de caballos, Néstor, comenzó las abluciones y la esparsión de la cebada sobre el altar suplicando insitentemente a Atenea mientras realizaba el rito preliminar de arrojar al fuego cabellos de su testuz.

Cuando acabaron de hacer las súplicas y la esparsión de la cebada, el hijo de Néstor, el muy valiente Trasímedes, condujo a la novilla, se colocó cerca, y el hacha segó los tendones del cuello y debilitó la fuerza de la novilla. Y lanzaron el grito ritual[72] las hijas y nueras y la venerable esposa de Néstor, Eurídice, la mayor de las hijas de Climeno.

Luego levantaron a la novilla de la tierra de anchos caminos, la sostuvieron y al punto la degolló Pisístrato, caudillo de guerreros.

Después que la oscura sangre le salió a chorros y el aliento abandonó sus huesos, la descuartizaron enseguida, le cortaron las piernas según el rito, las cubrieron con grasa por ambos lados, haciéndolo en dos capas y pusieron sobre ellas la carne cruda. Entonces el anciano las quemó sobre la leña y por encima vertió rojo vino mientras los jóvenes cerca de él sostenían en sus manos tenedores de cinco puntas.

Después que las piernas se habían consumido por completo y que habían gustado las entrañas cortaron el resto en pequeños trozos, lo ensartaron y lo asaron sosteniendo los puntiagudos tenedores en sus manos.

Entre tanto, la linda Policasta lavaba a Telémaco, la más joven hija de Néstor, el hijo de Neleo. Después que lo hubo lavado y ungido con aceite le rodeó el cuerpo con una túnica y un

---

[72] En gr. *ololygé*. Es palabra onomatopéyica y designa el grito ritual, de júbilo o de duelo según el contexto, lanzado por las mujeres.

manto. Salió Telémaco del baño, su cuerpo semejante a los inmortales, y fue a sentarse al lado de Néstor, pastor de su pueblo. Luego que la parte superior de la carne estuvo asada, la 470 sacaron y se sentaron a comer, y unos jóvenes nobles se levantaron para escanciar el vino en copas de oro.

Después que arrojaron de sí el deseo de comida y bebida, comenzó a hablarles el de Gerenia, el caballero Néstor:

«Hijos míos, vamos, traed a Telémaco caballos de hermosas crines y enganchadlos al carro para que prosiga con rapidez su viaje.»

Así habló, y ellos le escucharon y le hicieron caso, y con diligencia engancharon al carro ligeros corceles. Y la mujer, la ama de llaves, le preparó vino y provisiones como las que co- 480 men los reyes a los que alimenta Zeus.

Enseguida ascendió Telémaco al hermoso carro, y a su lado subió el hijo de Néstor, Pisístrato, el caudillo de guerreros. Empuñó las riendas y restalló el látigo para que partieran, y los dos caballos se lanzaron de buena gana a la llanura abandonando la elevada ciudad de Pilos. Durante todo el día agitaron el yugo sosteniéndolo por ambos lados.

Y Helios se sumergió y todos los caminos se llenaron de sombras cuando llegaron a Feras[73], al palacio de Diocles, el hijo de Ortíloco a quien Alfeo había engendrado. Allí durmie- 490 ron aquella noche, pues él les ofreció hospitalidad.

Y se mostró Eos, la que nace de la mañana, la de dedos de rosa; engancharon los caballos, subieron al bien trabajado carro y salieron del pórtico y de la resonante galería.

Restalló Pisístrato el látigo para que partieran, y los dos caballos se lanzaron de buena gana, y llegaron a la llanura, a la que produce trigo, poniendo término a su viaje: ¡de tal manera lo llevaban los veloces caballos!

Y se sumergió Helios y todos los caminos se llenaron de sombras.

---

[73] Feras es la actual Kalamata y se encuentra exactamente a medio camino entre Pilos y Esparta. Se ha discutido cómo es posible recorrer ese camino en un solo día, de pie sobre un carro y atravesando el Taigeto. Ello es, sin embargo, irrelevante y no significa, desde luego, que nuestro poeta desconociera la geografía del Peloponeso (cfr. Schmidt-Stählin, *Griechische Literatur...*, pág. 122 y nota 3.

Canto IV

TELÉMACO VIAJA A ESPARTA
PARA INFORMASE SOBRE SU PADRE

L LEGARON éstos a la cóncava y cavernosa Lacedemonia y se encaminaron al palacio del ilustre Menelao. Lo encontraron con numerosos allegados, celebrando con un banquete la boda de su hijo e ilustre hija. A su hija iba a enviarla al hijo de Aquiles, el que rompe las filas enemigas; que en Troya se la ofreció por vez primera y prometió entregarla, y los dioses iban a llevarles a término las bodas. Mandábala ir con caballos y carros a la muy ilustre ciudad de los mirmidones, sobre los cuales reinaba aquél. A su hijo le entregaba 10 como esposa la hija de Alector, procedente de Esparta. El vigoroso Megapentes, su hijo, le había nacido muy querido de una esclava, que los dioses ya no dieron un hijo a Helena luego que le hubo nacido el primer hijo, la deseada Hermione, que poseía la hermosura de la dorada Afrodita.

Conque se deleitaban y celebraban banquetes en el gran palacio de techo elevado los vecinos y parientes del ilustre Menelao; un divino aedo les cantaba tocando la cítara, y dos volatineros giraban en medio de ellos, dando comienzo a la danza.

Y los dos jóvenes, el héroe Telémaco y el ilustre hijo de 20 Néstor se detuvieron y detuvieron los caballos a la puerta del palacio. Violos el noble Eteoneo cuando salía, ágil servidor del ilustre Menelao, y echó a andar por el palacio para comunicárselo al pastor de su pueblo. Y poniéndose junto a él le dijo aladas palabras:

«Hay dos forasteros, Menelao, vástago de Zeus, dos mozos

semejantes al linaje del gran Zeus. Dime si desenganchamos sus rápidos caballos o les mandamos que vayan a casa de otro que los reciba amistosamente.»

Y el rubio Menelao le dijo muy irritado: 30

«Antes no eras tan simple, Eteoneo, hijo de Boeto, mas ahora dices sandeces como un niño. También nosotros llegamos aquí, los dos, después de comer muchas veces por mor de la hospitalidad de otros hombres. ¡Ojalá Zeus nos quite de la pobreza para el futuro! Desengancha los caballos de los forasteros y hazlos entrar para que se les agasaje en la mesa»[74].

Así dijo; salió aquél del palacio y llamó a otros diligentes servidores para que lo acompañaran. Desengancharon los caballos sudorosos bajo el yugo y los ataron a los pesebres, al 40 lado pusieron escanda y mezclaron blanca cebada; arrimaron los carros al muro resplandeciente e introdujeron a los forasteros en la divina morada. Éstos, al observarlo, admirábanse del palacio del rey, vástago de Zeus; que había un resplandor como del sol o de la luna en el palacio de elevado techo del glorioso Menelao. Luego que se hubieron saciado de verlo con sus ojos, marcharon a unas bañeras bien pulidas y se lavaron. Y luego que las esclavas los hubieron ungido con aceite, les pusieron ropas de lana y mantos y fueron a sentarse en sillas 50 junto al Atrida Menelao. Y una esclava virtió agua de lavamanos que traía en bello jarro de oro sobre fuente de plata y colocó al lado una pulida mesa. Y la venerable ama de llaves trajo pan y sirvió la mesa colocando abundantes alimentos, favoreciéndoles entre los que estaban presentes. Y el trinchador les sacó platos de carnes de todas clases y puso a su lado copas de oro. Y mostrándoselos, decía el prudente Menelao:

«Comed y alegraos, que luego que os hayáis alimentado con 60 estos manjares os preguntaremos quiénes sois de los hombres. Pues sin duda el linaje de vuestros padres no se ha perdido,

---

[74] Es notable, pero típicamente homérico, el que a partir de aquí se olvide por completo el doble banquete de esponsales que Menelao está ofreciendo a sus familiares y amigos. Tan pronto como Telémaco y Pisístrato entran en el palacio, ellos son los únicos huéspedes y acaparan toda la atención de Menelao y Helena. Algo parecido sucede con Odiseo cuando entra en el palacio de Alcínoo, aunque allí éste tiene la precaución de despedir a sus invitados (cfr. VII.226 y ss.).

sino que sois vástagos de reyes que llevan cetro de linaje divino, que los plebeyos no engendran mozos así.»

Así diciendo puso junto a ellos, asiéndolo con la mano, un grueso lomo asado de buey que le habían ofrecido a él mismo como presente de honor. Echaron luego mano a los alimentos colocados delante, y después que arrojaron el deseo de comida y bebida, Telémaco habló al hijo de Néstor acercando su cabeza para que los demás no se enteraran: 70

«Observa, Nestórida grato a mi corazón, el resplandor de bronce en el resonante palacio, y el del oro, el electro[75], la plata y el marfil. Seguro que es así por dentro el palacio de Zeus Olímpico. ¡Cuántas cosas inefables!, el asombro me atenaza al verlas.»

El rubio Menelao se percató de lo que decía y habló aladas palabras:

«Hijos míos, ninguno de los mortales podría competir con Zeus, pues son inmortales su casa y posesiones; pero de los hombres quizá alguno podría competir conmigo —o quizá 80 no— en riquezas; las he traído en mis naves —y llegué al octavo año— después de hacer padecido mucho y andar errante mucho tiempo. Errante anduve por Chipre, Fenicia y Egipto; llegué a los etíopes, a los sidonios, a los erembos[76] y a Libia, donde los corderos enseguida crían cuernos, pues las ovejas paren tres veces en un solo año. Ni amo ni pastor andan allí faltos de queso ni de carne, ni de dulce leche, pues siempre están dispuestas para dar abundante leche. Mientras andaba yo errante por allí, reuniendo muchas riquezas, otro mató a mi 90 hermano a escondidas, sin que se percatara, con el engaño de su funesta esposa. Así que reino sin alegría sobre estas riquezas. Ya habréis oído esto de vuestros padres, quienes quiera que sean, pues sufrí muy mucho y destruí un palacio muy agradable para vivir que contenía muchos y valiosos bienes. ¡Ojalá habitara yo mi palacio aún con un tercio de éstos, pero estu-

---

[75] *Eléktron* en griego significa habitualmente «ámbar», pero también designa una aleación de oro y plata que, dado el contexto inmediato, es lo que aquí debe ser.

[76] Es el único pasaje donde se alude a este curioso pueblo que, por la semejanza del nombre, muy bien podrían ser los árabes, como conjetura Estrabón (cfr. 1.2.31 y ss.), quizá basándose en una corrección de Zenón el alejandrino.

vieran sanos y salvos los hombres que murieron en la ancha Troya lejos de Argos, criadora de caballos. Y aunque lloro y me aflijo a menudo por todos en mi palacio, unas veces deleito 100 mi ánimo con el llanto y otras descanso, que pronto trae cansancio el frío[77] llanto. Mas no me lamento tanto por ninguno, aunque me aflija, como por uno que me amarga el sueño y la comida al recordarlo, pues ninguno de los aqueos sufrió tanto como Odiseo sufrió y emprendió. Para él habían de ser las preocupaciones, para mí el dolor siempre insoportable por aquél, pues está lejos desde hace tiempo y no sabemos si vive o ha muerto. Sin duda lo lloran el anciano Laertes y la discreta 110 Penélope y Telémaco, a quien dejó en casa recién nacido.»

Así dijo y provocó en Telémaco el deseo de llorar por su padre. Cayó a tierra una lágrima de sus párpados al oír hablar de éste, y sujetó ante sus ojos el purpúreo manto con las manos.

Menelao se percató de ello, y dudaba en su mente y en su corazón si dejarle que recordara a su padre o indagar él primero y probarlo en cada cosa en particular. En tanto que agitaba 120 esto en su mente y en su corazón, salió Helena de su perfumada estancia de elevado techo semejante a Afrodita, la de rueca de oro.

Colocó Adrastra junto a ella un sillón bien trabajado, y Alcipe trajo un tapete de suave lana. También trajo Filo la canastilla de plata que le había dado Alcandra, mujer de Pólibo, quien habitaba en Tebas la de Egipto, donde las casas guardan muchos tesoros. (Dio Pólibo a Menelao dos bañeras de plata, dos trípodes y diez talentos de oro. Y aparte, su esposa hizo a He- 130 lena bellos obsequios: le regaló una rueca de oro y una canastilla sostenida por ruedas de plata, sus bordes terminados con oro.) Ofreciósela, pues, Filo, llena de hilo trabajado, y sobre él se extendía un huso con lana de color violeta. Y se sentó en la silla y a sus pies tenía un escabel. Y luego preguntó a su esposo, con su palabra, cada detalle:

«¿Sabemos ya, Menelao, vástago de Zeus, quiénes de los hombres se precian de ser éstos que han llegado a nuestra

---

[77] Homero llama «frío» (quizá «que hiela») al llanto con gemidos *(góos)*, cfr. también XI.212. Sin embargo, a las lágrimas suele calificarlas como «calientes», cfr. IV.533, XIX.362, XXIV.46.

casa? ¿Me engañaré o será cierto lo que voy a decir? El ánimo 140
me lo manda. Y es que creo que nunca vi a nadie tan semejante, hombre o mujer (¡el asombro me atenaza al contemplarlo!),
como éste se parece al magnífico hijo de Odiseo, a Telémaco, a
quien aquel hombre dejó recién nacido en casa cuando los
aqueos marchasteis a Troya por causa de mí, ¡desvergonzada!,
para llevar la guerra.»

Y el rubio Menelao le contestó diciendo:

«También pienso yo ahora, mujer, tal como lo imaginas,
pues tales eran los pies y las manos de aquél, y las miradas de 150
sus ojos, y la cabeza y por encima los largos cabellos. Así que,
al recordarme a Odiseo, he referido ahora cuánto sufrió y se
fatigó aquél por mí. Y él vertía espeso llanto de debajo de sus
cejas sujetando con las manos el purpúreo manto ante sus
ojos.»

Y luego Pisístrato, el hijo de Néstor, le dijo:

«Atrida Menelao, vástago de Zeus, caudillo de tu pueblo, en
verdad éste es el hijo de aquél, tal como dices, pero es prudente y se avergüenza en su ánimo de decir palabras descaradas al
venir por primera vez ante ti, cuya voz nos cumple como la de 160
un dios.

»Néstor me ha enviado, el caballero de Gerenia, para seguir-
lo como acompañante, pues deseaba verte a fin de que le sugi-
rieras una palabra o una obra. Pues muchos pesares tiene en
palacio el hijo de un padre ausente si no tiene otros defensores
como le sucede a Telémaco. Ausentóse su padre y no hay
otros defensores entre el pueblo que lo aparten de la desgracia.»

Y el rubio Menelao contestó y dijo a éste:

«¡Ay!, ha venido a mi casa el hijo del querido hombre que
por mí padeció muchas pruebas. Pensaba estimarlo por encima 170
de los demás argivos cuando volviera, si es que Zeus Olímpico, el que ve a lo ancho, nos concedía a los dos regresar en las
veloces naves. Le habría dado como residencia una ciudad en
Argos y le habría edificado un palacio trayéndolo desde Itaca
con sus bienes, su hijo y todo el pueblo, después de despoblar
una sola ciudad de las que se encuentran en las cercanías y son
ahora gobernadas por mí. Sin duda nos habríamos reunido con
frecuencia estando aquí y nada nos habría separado en siendo

amigos y estando contentos, hasta que la negra nube de la 180
muerte nos hubiera envuelto. Pero debía envidiarlo el dios que
ha hecho a aquel desdichado el único que no puede regresar.»

Así dijo y despertó en todos el deseo de llorar. Lloraba la argiva Helena, nacida de Zeus, y lloraba Telémaco y el Atrida
Menelao. Tampoco el hijo de Néstor tenía sus ojos sin llanto,
pues recordaba en su interior al irreprochable Antíloco, a
quien mató el ilustre hijo de la resplandeciente Eos. Y acor-
dándose de él dijo aladas palabras:

«Atrida, decía el anciano Néstor cuando te mentábamos en 190
su palacio, y conversábamos entre nosotros, que eres muy sensato entre los mortales. Conque ahora, si es posible, préstame
atención. A mí no me cumple lamentarme después de la cena,
pero va a llegar Eos, la que nace de la mañana. No me impor-
tará entonces llorar a quien de los mortales haya perecido y
arrastrado su destino. Esta es la única honra para los miserables mortales, que se corten el cabello y dejen caer las lágrimas
por sus mejillas. Pues también murió un mi hermano que no
era el peor de los argivos —tú debes saberlo, pues yo ni fui ni 200
lo vi—, y dicen que era Antíloco superior a los demás, rápido
en la carrera y luchador.»

Y le contestó y dijo el rubio Menelao:

«Amigo, has hablado como hablaría y obraría un hombre
sensato y que tuviera más edad que tú. Eres hijo de tal padre
porque también tú hablas prudentemente. Es fácil de reconocer la descendencia del hombre a quien el Cronida concede felicidad cuando se casa o cuando nace, como ahora ha concedido a Néstor envejecer cada día tranquilamente en su palacio y 210
que sus hijos sean prudentes y los mejores con la lanza. Mas
dejemos el llanto que se nos ha venido antes y pensemos de
nuevo en la cena; y que viertan agua para las manos. Que Telémaco y yo tendremos unas palabras al amanecer para conversar entre nosotros.»

Así dijo, y Asfalión vertió agua sobre sus manos, rápido servidor del ilusre Menelao; y ellos echaron mano de los alimentos que tenían preparados delante.

Entonces Helena, nacida de Zeus, pensó otra cosa: al pronto echó en el vino del que bebían una droga para disipar el do- 220
lor y aplacadora de la cólera que hacía echar a olvido todos los

males. Quien la tomara después de mezclada en la crátera, no derramaría lágrimas por las mejillas durante un día, ni aunque hubieran muerto su padre y su madre o mataran ante sus ojos con el bronce a su hermano o a su hijo. Tales drogas ingeniosas tenía la hija de Zeus, y excelentes, las que le había dado Polidamna, esposa de Ton, la egipcia, cuya fértil tierra produce muchísimas drogas[78], y después de mezclarlas muchas son 230 buenas y muchas perniciosas; y allí cada uno es médico que sobresale sobre todos los hombres, pues es vástago de Peón. Así pues, luego que echó la droga ordenó que se escanciara vino de nuevo; y contestó y dijo su palabra:

«Atrida Menelao, vástago de Zeus, y vosotros, hijos de hombres nobles. En verdad el dios Zeus nos concede unas veces bienes y otras males, pues lo puede todo. Comed ahora sentados en el palacio y deleitaos con palabras, que yo voy a haceros un relato oportuno. Yo no podría contar ni enumerar 240 todos los trabajos de Odiseo el sufridor, pero sí esto que realizó y soportó el animoso varón en el pueblo de los troyanos donde los aqueos padecisteis penalidades: infligiéndose a sí mismo vergonzosas heridas y echándose por los hombros ropas miserables, se introdujo como un siervo en la ciudad de anchas calles de sus enemigos. Así que ocultándose, se parecía a otro varón, a un mendigo[79], quien no era tal en las naves de los aqueos. Y como tal se introdujo en la ciudad de los troyanos, pero ninguno de ellos le hizo caso; sólo yo lo reconocí e 250 interrogué, y él me evitaba con astucia. Sólo cuando lo hube lavado y arreglado con aceite, puesto un vestido y jurado con firme juramento que no lo descubriría entre los troyanos hasta que llegara a las rápidas naves y a las tiendas, me manifestó Odiseo todo el plan de los aqueos. Y después de matar a mu-

---

[78] Una vez más se revela el impacto que produjeron en la Grecia arcaica los primeros contactos con el Egipto de Psamético I. Aquí alude a un hecho que, por fuerza, tuvieron que observar los griegos desde el primer momento: el predominio de la Magia en aquel misterioso país.

[79] En gr. *déktēi*. Hay editores que lo interpretan como nombre propio, Dektes, siguiendo al poeta de la Ilias Parva. Sin embargo, Aristarco lo interpretaba como nombre común, sinónimo de *epaitēi* (mendigo). Parece probable que todo este punto sea un doblete del anterior, por lo que *déktēi* es el paralelo de *oikēi* en la frase anterior.

chos troyanos con afilado bronce, marchó junto a los argivos llevándose abundante información. Entonces las troyanas rompieron a llorar con fuerza, mas mi corazón se alegraba, porque ya ansiaba regresar rápidamente a mi casa y lamentaba la obcecación que me otorgó Afrodita cuando me condujo allí lejos de mi patria, alejándome de mi hija, de mi cama y de mi marido, que no es inferior a nadie ni en juicio ni en porte.»

Y el rubio Menelao le contestó y dijo:

«Sí, mujer, todo lo has dicho como te corresponde. Yo conocí el parecer y la inteligencia de muchos héroes y he visitado muchas tierras. Pero nunca vi con mis ojos un corazón tal como era el del sufridor Odiseo. ¡Como esto que hizo y aguantó el recio varón en el pulido caballo donde estábamos los mejores de los argivos para llevar muerte y desgracia a los troyanos! Después llegaste tú —debió impulsarte un dios que quería conceder gloria a los troyanos— y te seguía Deífobo[80] semejante a los dioses. Tres veces te acercaste a palpar la cóncava trampa y llamaste a los mejores dánaos, designando a cada uno por su nombre, imitando la voz de las esposas de cada uno de los argivos. También yo y el hijo de Tideo y el divino Odiseo, sentados en el centro, te oímos cuando nos llamaste. Nosotros dos tratamos de echar a andar para salir o responder luego desde dentro. Pero Odiseo lo impidió y nos contuvo, aunque mucho lo deseábamos. Así que los demás hijos de los aqueos quedaron en silencio, y sólo Anticlo[81] deseaba contestarte con su palabra. Pero Odiseo apretó su fuerte mano reciamente sobre la boca y salvó a todos los aqueos. Y mientras lo retenía, te llevó lejos Palas Atenea.»

Y le contestó Telémaco discretamente:

«Atrida Menelao, vástago de Zeus, caudillo de hombres, ello es más doloroso, pues esto no lo apartó de la funesta muerte ni aunque tenía dentro un corazón de hierro. Pero, vamos, envíanos a la cama para que nos deleitemos ya con el dulce sueño.»

---

[80] En la tradición épica posterior, Deífobo se casa con Helena después de la muerte de Paris.

[81] Este personaje no aparece citado nunca en la *Ilíada* y sí en el Ciclo épico. Aristarco ya lo atetizaba y algunos filólogos actuales se inclinan por la hipótesis de que todo el pasaje está tomado del Ciclo. Cfr. S. West, ob. cit., págs. 344-5.

Así dijo, y la argiva Helena ordenó a las esclavas colocar camas bajo el pórtico y disponer hermosas mantas de púrpura, extender por encima colchas y sobre ellas ropas de lana para cubrirse. Así que salieron de la sala sosteniendo antorchas en sus manos y prepararon las camas. Y un heraldo condujo a los huéspedes. Acostáronse allí mismo, en el vestíbulo de la casa[82], el héroe Telémaco y el ilustre hijo de Néstor. El Atrida durmió en el interior del magnífico palacio y Helena, de largo peplo, se acostó junto a él, la divina entre las mujeres. 300

Y cuando se mostró Eos, la que nace de la mañana, la de dedos de rosa, Menelao, el de recia voz guerrera, se levantó del lecho, vistió sus vestidos, colgó de su hombro la aguda espada y bajo sus pies brillantes como el aceite calzó hermosas sandalias. Luego se puso en marcha, salió del dormitorio semejante de frente a un dios y se sentó junto a Telémaco, le dijo su palabra y le llamó por su nombre: 310

«¿Qué necesidad te trajo aquí, héroe Telémaco, a la divina Lacedemonia, sobre el ancho lomo del mar? ¿Es un asunto público o privado? Dímelo sinceramente.»

Y Telémaco le contestó discretamente:

«Atrida Menelao, vástago de Zeus, caudillo de hombre, he venido por si podías darme alguna noticia sobre mi padre. Se consume mi casa y mis ricos campos se pierden; el palacio está lleno de hombres malvados que continuamente degüellan gordas ovejas y cuernitorcidos bueyes de rotátiles patas, los pretendientes de mi madre, que tienen una arrogancia insolente. Por esto me llego ahora a tus rodillas, por si quieres contarme su luctuosa muerte, la hayas visto con tus propios ojos o hayas escuchado el relato de algún caminante; digno de lástima más que nadie lo parió su madre. Y no endulces tus palabras por respeto ni piedad; antes bien, cuéntame detalladamente cómo llegaste a verlo. Te lo suplico, si es que alguna vez mi padre, el 320

---

[82] Se refiere aquí no al vestíbulo del palacio en general, sino al del mégaron (cfr. nota 29), donde duerme, por ejemplo, Odiseo en XX.1 y ss. Otras veces se extiende para los huéspedes un lecho en el pórtico *(aithousa)* como en III.399. Aunque son dos partes diferentes del mégaron, aquí parece confundirlas el poeta, ya que un poco mas arriba (v. 297) Helena ordenaba poner camas «bajo el pórtico».

noble Odiseo, te prometió y cumplió alguna palabra o alguna obra en el pueblo de los troyanos, donde los aqueos sufristeis 330 penalidades. Acuérdate de esto ahora y cuéntame la verdad»[83].

Y le contestó irritado el rubio Menelao:

«¡Ay, ay, conque quieren dormir en el lecho de un hombre intrépido quienes son cobardes! Como una cierva acuesta a sus dos recién nacidos cervatillos en la cueva de un fuerte león y mientras sale a buscar pasto en las laderas y los herbosos valles, aquél regresa a su guarida y da vergonzosa muerte a ambos, así Odiseo dará vergonzosa muerte a aquéllos[84]. ¡Padre 340 Zeus, Atenea y Apolo, ojalá que fuera como cuando en la bien construida Lesbos se levantó para disputar y luchó con Filomeleides[85], lo derribó violentamente y todos los aqueos se alegraron! Ojalá que con tal talante se enfrentara Odiseo con los pretendientes: corto el destino de todos sería y amargas sus nupcias[86]. En cuanto a lo que me preguntas y suplicas, no querría apartarme de la verdad y engañarte. Conque no te ocultaré ni guardaré secreto sobre lo que me dijo el veraz anciano 350 del mar[87].

»Los dioses me retuvieron en Egipto, aunque ansiaba regresar aquí, por no realizar hecatombes perfectas; que siempre quieren los dioses que nos acordemos de sus órdenes. Hay una isla en el ponto de agitadas olas delante de Egipto —la llaman Faro[88]—, tan lejos cuanto una cóncava nave puede recorrer en

---

[83] Los vv. 322-31 son repetición de III.92-101.

[84] Sobre las comparaciones homéricas en general, es ya clásico el libro de H. Fränkel, *Die homerischen Geichnisse*, Göttingen, 1921. Más recientes son R. Hamp, *Die Gleichnisse Homers und die Bildkunst seiner Zeit*, Tübingen, 1952, y D. J. N. Lee, *The Similes of the Iliad and the Odyssey compared*, Melbourne, 1964.

[85] Filomeleides era un rey de Lesbos que, según la leyenda, retaba a todos los extranjeros. De acuerdo con una noticia de Helánico *(Fragm. Gr. Hist.* 4 F 150), Odiseo y Diomedes lo mataron con engaño. Ignoramos si se basa en este pasaje o no.

[86] Cfr. I.255-66. En ambos casos se expresa el deseo de que Odiseo se enfrente con los pretendientes, pero mientras en el canto I se alude sólo al atuendo del héroe, aquí se recuerda más concretamente un hecho victorioso del mismo.

[87] Proteo, cfr. nota 90.

[88] Es el islote, a una milla de Alejandría, donde se construyó el célebre Faro, convertido desde entonces en nombre común en todas las lenguas cultas. Hoy se piensa que el nombre es una adaptación al griego del egipcio *Pr-Hr*, «casa de

un día si sopla por detrás sonoro viento, y un puerto de buen fondeadero de donde echan al mar las equilibradas naves, luego de sacar negra agua. Retuviéronme allí los dioses veinte 360 días, y no aparecían los vientos que soplan favorables, los que conducen a la naves sobre el ancho lomo del mar. Todos los víveres y el vigor de mis hombres se habría acabado a no ser que una de las diosas se hubiera compadecido y sentido piedad de mí, Idotea[89], la hija del valiente Proteo, el anciano de los mares, pues la conmovió el ánimo. Encontróse conmigo cuando vagaba solo lejos de mis compañeros (continuamente vagaban éstos por la isla pescando con curvos anzuelos, pues el hambre retorcía sus estómagos), y acercándose me dijo estas 370 palabras: "¿Eres así de simple y atontado, forastero, o te abandonas de buen grado y gozas padeciendo males?, puesto que permaneces en la isla desde hace tiempo sin poder hallar remedio y se consume el ánimo de tus compañeros." Así dijo, y yo le contesté: "Te diré, quienquiera que seas de las diosas, que no estoy detenido de buen grado; que debo haber faltado a los inmortales que poseen el ancho cielo. Pero dime tú, pues los dioses lo saben todos, quién de ellos me detiene y aparta de mi ca- 380 mino, y cómo llevaré a cabo el regreso a través del ponto rico en peces." Así dije, y ella, la divina entre las diosas, me respondió luego: "Forastero, te voy a informar muy sinceramente. Viene aquí con frecuencia el veraz anciano del mar, el inmortal Proteo[90] egipcio, que conoce las profundidades de todo el

---

Horus», cfr. H. Gauthier, *Dictionaire des noms géographiques,* II, El Cairo, 1925. La localización de este islote a gran distancia de Egipto demuestra que las ideas del poeta de la *Odisea* sobre este país son más bien vagas. Sin embargo, R. Carpenter, ob. cit., págs. 98 y ss., lo explica diciendo que hasta finales del siglo VII los griegos desconocían la rama canópica del delta del Nilo y entraban en Egipto por la bolbinítica que desemboca en Rosetta.

[89] Sobre esta diosa «que toma formas» (como su padre), no sabemos más que lo que aquí se dice. El que para ayudar a un extranjero, del que se enamora, una hija traicione a su padre es un motivo muy común de folklore. Homero elimina como siempre el motivo erótico.

[90] Proteo no aparece en las genealogías de Hesiodo, donde los dioses marinos son Nereo y Forcis. Probablemente pertenece al folklore mediterráneo, aunque se le hace entrar en el círculo de estas divinidades como «siervo de Poseidón». La primera noticia que de él tenemos es ésta. Después Heródoto lo convertirá en un rey egipcio, antecesor de Rampsinito, que recibió a Paris y Helena (cfr. 3.112-19). Heródoto a su vez se basó probablemente en Estesícoro

mar, siervo de Poseidón —dicen que él me engendró y es mi
padre. Si tú pudieras apresarlo de alguna manera, poniéndote
al acecho, él te diría el camino, la extensión de la ruta y cómo
llevarás a cabo el regreso a través del ponto rico en peces.   390
Y también te diría, vástago de Zeus, si es que lo deseas, lo bueno
y lo malo que ha sucedido en tu palacio después que empren-
diste este viaje largo y difícil." Así dijo, y yo le contesté y dije:
"Sugiéreme tú misma una emboscada contra el divino anciano
a fin de que no me rehúya si me conoce y se da cuenta de ante-
mano, pues es difícil para un hombre mortal sujetar a un dios."
Así dije, y ella, la divina entre las diosas, me respondió luego:
"Yo te diré esto muy sinceramente. Cuando el sol va por el   400
centro del cielo, el veraz anciano marino sale del mar con el
soplo de Céfiro, oculto por el negro encrestamiento de las olas.
Una vez fuera, se acuesta en honda gruta y a su alrededor
duermen apiñadas las focas, descendientes de la hermosa Ha-
losidne[91], que salen del canoso mar exhalando el amargo olor
de las profundidades marinas. Yo te conduciré allí al despuntar la aurora, te acostaré enseguida y escogerás a tres compañeros, a los mejores de tus naves de buenos bancos. Te diré todas las argucias de este anciano: primero contará y pasará re-   410
vista a las focas y cuando las haya contado y visto todas, se
acostará en medio de ellas como el pastor de un rebaño de
ovejas. Tan pronto como lo veáis durmiendo, poned a prueba
vuestra fuerza y vigor y retenedlo allí mismo, aunque trate de
huir ansioso y precipitado. Intentará tornarse en todos los rep-
tiles que hay sobre la tierra, así como en agua y en violento
fuego. Pero vosotros retenedlo con firmeza y apretad más
fuerte. Y cuando él te pregunte, volviendo a mostrarse tal   420
como lo visteis durmiendo, abstente de la violencia y suelta al
anciano. Y pregúntale cuál de los dioses te maltrata y cómo
llevarás a cabo el regreso a través del ponto rico en peces."

(cfr. *Fr.* 193.16 Page) para el cual Proteo era ya el rey de Egipto con quien permaneció Helena durante toda la guerra de Troya, mientras que a esta ciudad
marchaba una imagen de ella.
[91] Es propiamente un epíteto de Anfítrite (cfr. nota 56), aunque en *Ilíada*,
XX.207 aparece junto al nombre de Tetis, otra diosa marina. En su etimología,
no muy clara, podrían estar las raíces de las palabras que significan «mar» y
«agua».

Habiendo hablado así, se sumergió en el ponto alborotado y yo marché hacia las naves que se encontraban en la arena. Y mientras caminaba, mi corazón agitaba muchos pensamientos. Pero una vez que llegué a las naves y al mar, preparamos la cena y se nos vino la divina noche. Entonces nos acostamos en la ribera del mar. 430

»Tan pronto como apuntó la que nace de la mañana, la de dedos de rosa, me marché luego a la orilla del mar, el de anchos caminos, suplicando mucho a los dioses. Y llevé tres compañeros en los que más fiaba para empresas de toda suerte.

»Entre tanto, Idotea, que se había sumergido en el ancho seno del mar, sacó cuatro pieles de foca del ponto, todas ellas recién desolladas, pues había ideado un engaño contra su padre: había cavado hoyos en la arena del mar y se sentó para esperar. Nosotros llegamos muy cerca de ella, nos acostó en fila 440 y echó sobre cada uno una piel. La emboscada era angustiosa, pues nos atormentaba terriblemente el mortífero olor de las focas criadas en el mar. Pues ¿quién se acostaría junto a un monstruo marino? Pero ella nos salvó y nos dio un gran remedio: colocó a cada uno debajo de la nariz ambrosía que despedía un muy agradable olor y acabó con la fetidez del monstruo. Esperamos toda la mañana con ánimo resignado y las focas salieron del mar apiñadas y se tendieron en fila sobre la ribera. El anciano salió del mar al mediodía y encontró a las rollizas 450 focas, pasó revista a todas y contó el número. Nos contó los primeros entre los monstruos, pero no se percató su ánimo de que había engaño. A continuación se acostó también él. Conque nos lanzamos gritando y le echamos mano. El anciano no se olvidó de sus engañosas artes, y primero se convirtió en melenudo león, en dragón, en pantera, en gran jabalí; también se convirtió en fluida agua y en árbol de frondosa copa, mas nosotros lo reteníamos con fuerte coraje. Y cuando el artero 460 anciano estaba ya fastidiado me preguntó y me dijo: "Quién de los dioses, hijo de Atreo, te aconsejó para que me apresaras contra mi voluntad tendiéndome emboscada? ¿Qué necesitas de mí?" Así dijo, y yo le contesté y dije: "Sabes anciano (¿por qué me dices esto intentando engañarme?) que tiempo ha que estoy retenido en esta isla sin poder hallar remedio y mi corazón se me consume dentro. Pero dime —puesto que los dioses lo saben todo— quién de los inmortales me detiene y aparta de mi camino y cómo llevaré a cabo el regreso a través del ponto rico en peces." Así dije, y al punto me contestó y dijo: "Debieras haber hecho al embarcar hermosos sacrificios a Zeus y a los demás dioses que poseen el ancho cielo para llegar a tu patria navegando sobre el ponto rojo como el vino. No creo que tu destino sea ver a los tuyos y llegar a tu bien edificada casa y a tu patria hasta que vuelvas a recorrer las aguas del Egipto, río nacido de Zeus[92] y sacrifiques sagradas hecatombes a los dioses inmortales que poseen el ancho cielo. Entonces los dioses te concederán el camino que tanto deseas." Así dijo y se me conmovió el corazón, pues me mandaba ir de nuevo a Egipto a través del ponto, sombrío camino, largo y difícil. Pero aun así le contesté y le dije: "Anciano, haré como mandas. Pero, vamos, dime e infórmame con verdad si llegaron sanos y salvos todos los aqueos que Néstor y yo dejamos cuando partimos de Troya o murió alguno de cruel muerte en su nave o a manos de los suyos después de soportar la guerra laboriosa." Así dije, y él me contestó y dijo: "¡Atrida!, ¿por qué me preguntas esto? No te es necesario saberlo ni conocer mi pensamiento. Te aseguro que no estarás mucho tiempo sin llanto luego que te enteres de todo, pues muchos de ellos murieron y muchos han sobrevivido. Sólo dos jefes de los aqueos que visten bronce murieron en el regreso (pues tú mismo asististe a la guerra); y uno que vive aún está retenido en el vasto ponto. Ayante[93] pereció junto con sus naves de largos remos: primero lo arrimó Poseidón a las grandes rocas de Girea[94] y lo salvó del mar, y habría escapado de la muerte, aunque odiado de Atenea, si no hubiera pronunciado una palabra orgullosa y se hubiera obcecado grandemente. Dijo que escaparía al gran abis-

470

480

490

500

---

[92] Es decir, «nacido de la lluvia». En Homero, Egipto es primariamente el río Nilo (nombre desconocido para él) y sólo secundariamente el país.

[93] Es Ayante hijo de Oileo, que intentó violar a Casandra en el templo de Atenea tras la toma de Troya. Este sacrilegio es la causa última, nunca aludida en *Odisea* por conocida, del regreso accidentado de los griegos.

[94] Según los escoliastas, estas rocas se sitúan entre Míconos y Tenos, lo que indica que el itinerario de Ayante es, a diferencia del resto, a través de las Cícladas.

mo del mar contra la voluntad de los dioses[95]. Poseidón le oyó hablar orgullosamente y a continuación, cogiendo con sus manos el tridente, golpeó la roca Gírea y la dividió: una parte quedó allí, pero se desplomó en el ponto el trozo sobre el que Ayante, sentado desde el principio, había incurrido en gran cegazón; y lo arrastró hacia el inmenso y alborotado ponto. Así 510 pereció después de beber la salobre agua.

»"También tu hermano escapó a la maldición de Zeus y huyó en las cóncavas naves, pues lo salvó la venerable Hera. Mas cuando estaba a punto de llegar al escarpado monte de Malea, arrebatólo una tempestad que lo llevó gimiendo penosamente por el ponto rico en peces hasta un extremo del campo donde en otro tiempo habitó Tiestes; mas entonces la habitaba Egisto, el hijo de Tiestes. Así que cuando, una vez allí, le parecía feliz el regreso y los dioses cambiaron el viento y llega- 520 ron a sus casas, entonces tu hermano pisó alegre su tierra patria: tocaba y besaba la tierra y le caían muchas ardientes lágrimas cuando contemplaba con júbilo su tierra. Pero lo vio desde una atalaya el vigilante que había puesto allí el tramposo Egisto (le había ofrecido en recompensa dos talentos de oro). Vigilaba éste desde hacía un año, para que no le pasara inadvertido si llegaba y recordara su impetuosa fuerza. Y marchó a palacio para dar la noticia al pastor de su pueblo. Y enseguida Egisto tramó una engañosa trampa: eligiendo los veinte mejo- 530 res hombres entre el pueblo, los puso en emboscada y luego mandó preparar un banquete en otra parte, y marchó a llamar a Agamenón, pastor de su pueblo, con caballos y carros meditando obras indignas. Condújolo, desconocedor de su muerte, y mientras lo agasajaba lo mató como se mata a un buey en el pesebre. No quedó vivo ninguno de los compañeros del Atrida que lo acompañaban, ni ninguno de Egisto, que todos fueron muertos en el palacio."

»Así dijo, y se me conmovió el corazón; lloraba sentado en la arena, y mi corazón no quería vivir ya ni ver la luz del sol. 540 Y después que me harté de llorar y agitarme me dijo el veraz anciano del mar: "No llores, hijo de Atreo, mucho tiempo y

---

[95] Ayante vuelve a incurrir en *hýbris* (insolencia sacrílega) por segunda vez retando a los dioses. Ello explica su obcecación *(átē)*.

sin cesar, puesto que así no hallaremos ningún remedio. Conque trata de volver a tu patria rápidamente, pues o lo encontrarás aún vivo o bien Orestes lo habrá matado adelantándose y tú puedes estar presente a sus funerales." Así dijo, y mi corazón y ánimo valeroso se caldearon de nuevo en mi pecho, aunque estaba afligido. Y le hablé y le dije aladas palabras: "De éstos ya sé ahora. Nómbrame, pues, al tercer hombre, el que, aún vivo, está retenido en el vasto ponto o está ya muerto. Pues aunque afligido quiero oírlo." Así le dije, y él al punto me contestó y me dijo: "El hijo de Laertes que habita en Itaca. Lo vi en una isla derramando abundante llanto, en el palacio de la ninfa Calipso, que lo retiene por la fuerza. No puede regresar a su tierra, pues no tiene naves provistas de remos ni compañeros que lo acompañen por el ancho lomo del mar. Respecto a ti, Menelao, vástago de Zeus, no está determinado por los dioses que mueras en Argos, criadora de caballos, enfrentándote con tu destino, sino que los inmortales te enviarán a la llanura Elisia[96], al extremo de la tierra, donde está el rubio Radamanto. Allí la vida de los hombres es más cómoda, no hay nevadas y el invierno no es largo; tampoco hay lluvias, sino que Océano[97] deja siempre paso a los soplos de Céfiro que sopla sonoramente para refrescar a los hombres. Porque tienes por esposa a Helena y para ellos[98] eres yerno de Zeus."

»Y hablando así, se sumergió en el alborotado ponto. Yo enfilé hacia las naves con mis divinos compañeros, y mientras caminaba, mi corazón agitaba muchas cosas; y luego que llegamos a la nave y al mar, preparamos la cena y se nos echó encima la divina noche; así que nos acostamos en la ribera del mar.

550

560

570

---

[96] *Elýsion* es una palabra formada, por falso corte, del adjetivo *enelýsios* que significa «golpeado por el rayo» y, por tanto, sacralizado como todo lo que toca el rayo de Zeus. A partir de aquí se convierte en un lugar semejante a las «Islas de los Bienaventurados» (cfr. Hesiodo, *Trabajos...*, 167 y ss.), donde van todos los héroes de la cuarta generación. El Elíseo, en cambio, es más restrictivo: Homero sólo registra la presencia de Radamante y la futura de Menelao. La descripción de este paraíso es muy similar a la del Olimpo, cfr. VI.43-5.

[97] Océano es, en la concepción geográfica arcaica, un río circular que rodea la tierra. En la concepción mítica es, junto con Tetis su esposa, el padre de todos los ríos.

[98] Se entiende, «para los inmortales» —palabra que aparece al comienzo de la descripción del Elisio (v. 564).

»Y cuando apareció Eos, la que nace de la mañana, la de dedos de rosa, en primer lugar lanzamos al mar divino las naves y colocamos los mástiles y velas en las proporcionadas naves y todos se fueron a sentar en los bancos; y sentados en fila, batían el canoso mar con los remos.

»Detuve las naves en el Egipto, río nacido de Zeus, e hice perfectas hecatombes. Y cuando había puesto fin a la cólera de los dioses que existen siempre, levanté un túmulo a Agamenón para que su gloria sea inextinguible.

»Acabado esto, partí, y los inmortales me concedieron viento favorable y rápidamente me devolvieron a mi tierra. Pero, vamos, permanece ahora en mi palacio, hasta que llegue el undécimo o el duodécimo día. Entonces te despediré y te daré como espléndidos regalos tres caballos y un carro bien trabajado; también te daré una hermosa copa para que hagas libaciones a los dioses inmortales y te acuerdes de mí todos los días.»

Y a su vez, Telémaco le contestó discretamente:

«¡Atrida!, no me retengas aquí durante mucho tiempo, pues yo permanecería un año junto a ti sin que me atenazara la nostalgia de mi casa ni de mis padres, que me cumple sobremanera escuchar tus relatos y palabras. Pero ya mis compañeros estarán disgustados en la divina Pilos y tú me retienes aquí hace tiempo. Que el regalo que me des sea un objeto que se pueda conservar. Los caballos no los llevaré a Itaca, te los dejaré aquí como ornato, pues tú reinas en una llanura vasta en la que hay mucho loto, juncia, trigo, espelta y blanca cebada que cría el campo. En Itaca no hay recorridos extensos ni prado; es tierra criadora de cabras y más encantadora que la criadora de caballos. Pues ninguna de las islas que se reclinan sobre el mar es apta para el paso de caballos ni rica en prados, e Itaca menos que ninguna.»

Así dijo, y Menelao, de recia voz guerrera, sonrió y lo acarició con la mano; le llamó por su nombre y le dijo su palabra:

«Hijo querido, eres de sangre noble, según hablas. Te cambiaré el regalo, pues puedo. Y de cuantos objetos hay en mi palacio que se pueden conservar, te daré el más hermoso y el de más precio. Te daré una crátera bien trabajada, de plata toda ella y con los bordes pulidos en oro. Es obra de Hefesto;

me la dio el héroe Fedimo, rey de los sidonios, cuando me alojó en su casa al regresar. Esto es lo que quiero regalarte.»

Mientras departían entre sí iban llegando los invitados al 620 palacio del divino rey. Unos traían ovejas, otros llevaban confortante vino, y las esposas de lindos velos les enviaban el pan. Así preparaban comida en el palacio[99].

Entre tanto, los pretendientes se complacían arrojando discos y venablos ante el palacio de Odiseo, en el sólido pavimento donde acostumbraban, llenos de arrogancia.

Hallábanse sentados Antínoo y Eurímaco, semejantes a los dioses, los jefes de los pretendientes y los mejores con preferencia por su valor. Y acercándoseles el hijo de Fronio, Noe- 630 món, le preguntó y dijo a Antínoo su palabra:

«Antínoo, ¿sabemos cuándo vendrá Telémaco de la arenosa Pilos o no? Se fue llevándose mi nave y preciso de ella para pasar a la espaciosa Elide, donde tengo doce yeguas y mulos no domados, buenos para el laboreo; si traigo alguno de estos podría domarlo.»

Así dijo, y ellos quedaron atónitos, pues no pensaban que Telémaco hubiera marchado a Pilos de Neleo, sino que se encontraba en el campo con las ovejas o con el porquerizo. 640

Mas, al fin, Antínoo, hijo de Eupites, contestóle diciendo:

«Háblame sinceramente. ¿Cuándo se fue y qué mozos lo acompañaban? ¿Los mejores de Itaca o sus obreros y criados? Que también pudo hacerlo así. Dime también con verdad, para que yo lo sepa, si te quitó la negra nave por la fuerza y contra tu voluntad o se la diste de buen grado, luego de suplicarte una y otra vez.»

Y Noemón, el hijo de Fronio, le contestó:

«Yo mismo se la di de buen grado. ¿Qué se podría hacer si te la pide un hombre como él, con el ánimo lleno de preocupa- 650 ciones? Sería difícil negársela. Los jóvenes que le acompaña-

---

[99] Los vv. 621-24 que describen un *éranos*, «comida a escote», es probablemente un intento tardío de conectar esta parte con el comienzo del Canto en que Menelao está ofreciendo un banquete de esponsales. Intento torpe e inadecuado, por lo que dichos versos se consideran espúreos.

ban son los que sobresalen entre nosotros en el pueblo. También vi embarcando como jefe a Méntor, o a un dios, pues así parecía en todo. Lo que me extraña es que vi ayer por la mañana al divino Méntor aquí, y eso que entonces se embarcó para Pilos.»

Cuando así hubo hablado marchó hacia la casa de su padre, y a éstos se les irritó su noble ánimo. Hicieron sentar a los pretendientes todos juntos y detuvieron sus juegos. Y entre ellos habló irritado Antínoo, hijo de Eupites; su corazón rebosaba negra cólera y sus ojos se asemejaban al resplandeciente fuego: 660

«¡Ay, ay, buen trabajo ha realizado Telémaco arrogantemente con este viaje; y decíamos que no lo llevaría a cabo! Contra la voluntad de tantos hombres un crío se ha marchado sin más, después de botar una nave y elegir los mejores entre el pueblo. Enseguida comenzará a ser un azote. ¡Así Zeus le destruya el vigor antes de que llegue a la plenitud de la juventud! Conque, ea, dadme una rápida nave y veinte compañeros para ponerle emboscada y esperarle cuando vuelva en el estrecho 670 entre Itaca y la escarpada Same. Para que el viaje que ha emprendido por causa de su padre le resulte funesto.»

Así dijo, y todos aprobaron sus palabras y lo apremiaban.

Así que se levantaron y se pusieron en camino hacia el palacio de Odiseo.

Penélope no tardó mucho en enterarse de los planes que los prentendientes meditaban en secreto. Pues se los comunicó el heraldo Medonte, que escuchó sus decisiones aunque estaba fuera del patio cuando éstos las urdían dentro. Y se puso en camino por el palacio para comunicárselo a Penélope. Cuando atravesaba el umbral le dijo ésta: 680

«Heraldo, ¿a qué te mandan los ilustres pretendientes? ¿Acaso para que ordenes a las esclavas del divino Odiseo que dejen sus labores y les preparen comida? ¡Ojalá dejaran de cortejarme y de reunirse y cenaran su última y definitiva cena! Con tanto reuniros aquí estáis acabando con muchos bienes, con las posesiones del prudente Telémaco. ¿No habéis oído contar a vuestros padres cuando erais niños cómo era Odiseo con ellos, que ni hizo ni dijo nada injusto en el pueblo? Este es 690 el proceder habitual de los divinos reyes: a un hombre le odian mientras que a otro le aman. Pero aquél jamás hizo injusticia a hombre alguno. Así que han quedado al descubierto vuestro ánimo e injustas obras, y no tenéis agradecimiento por sus beneficios.»

Y a su vez le dijo Medonte, de pensamientos prudentes:

«Reina, ¡ojalá fuera ésta el mayor mal! Pero los pretendientes meditan otro mucho mayor y más penoso que ojalá no cumpla el Cronida! Desean ardientemente matar a Telémaco 700 con el agudo bronce cuando vuelva a casa, pues partió a la augusta Pilos y a la divina Lacedemonia en busca de noticias de su padre.»

Así dijo. Flaqueáronle a Penélope las rodillas y el corazón, el estupor le arrebató las palabras por largo tiempo, y los ojos se le llenaron de lágrimas, y la vigorosa voz se le quedó detenida. Más tarde le contestó y dijo:

«¡Heraldo! ¿Por qué se ha marchado mi hijo? No precisaba embarcar en las naves que navegan veloces, que son para los hombres caballos en la mar y atraviesan la abundante humedad. ¿Acaso lo hizo para que no quede ni siquiera su nombre 710 entre los hombres?»

Y le contestó a continuación Medonte, conocedor de prudencia:

«No sé si lo impulsó algún dios o su propio ánimo a ir a Pilos para indagar acerca del regreso de su padre o del destino con el que se ha enfrentado.»

Cuando hubo hablado así, se fue por el palacio de Odiseo. Envolvió a Penélope una pena mortal y no soportó estar sentada en la silla, de las que había abundancia en la casa, sino que se sentó en el muy trabajado umbral de su aposento, quejándose de manera lamentable. Y a su alrededor gemían todas las criadas, cuantas había en el palacio, jóvenes y viejas. Y Penélo- 720 pe les dijo, llorando agudamente:

«Escuchadme, amigas, pues el Olímpico me ha concedido dolores por encima de las que nacieron o se criaron conmigo: perdí primero a un esposo noble de corazón de león y que se distinguía entre los dánaos por excelencias de todas clases, un noble varón cuya vasta gloria se extiende por la Hélade y hasta el centro de Argos.

»Y ahora las tempestades han arrebatado sin gloria del palacio a mi amado hijo. No me enteré cuándo marchó. Desdicha-

das, tampoco a vosotras se os ocurrió levantarme de la cama, 730
aunque bien sabíais cuándo partió aquél en la cóncava y negra
nave; pues si hubiera barruntado que pensaba en este viaje, se
habría quedado aquí por más que lo ansiara o me habría tenido
que dejar muerta en el palacio. Vamos, que llame alguna al anciano Dolio, mi esclavo, el que me dio mi padre cuando vine
aquí y cuida mi huerto abundante en árboles, para que vaya
cerca de Laertes lo antes posible a contarle todo esto, por si
urdiendo alguna astucia en su mente sale a quejarse a los ciudadanos que desean destruir el linaje de Odiseo, semejante a 740
un dios.»

Y a su vez le dijo su nodriza Euriclea:

«¡Hija mía!, mátame con implacable bronce o déjame en palacio, mas no te ocultaré mi palabra; yo sabía todo esto y le di
cuanto ordenó, pan y dulce vino, y me tomó un solemne juramento: que no te lo dijera antes de que llegara el duodécimo
día o tú misma lo echaras de menos y escucharas que se había
marchado, para que no afearas llorando tu hermosa piel.

»Vamos, báñate, toma vestidos limpios para tu cuerpo y 750
sube al piso superior con las esclavas. Y suplica a Atenea, hija
de Zeus, portador de égida, pues ella, en efecto, lo salvará de la
muerte. No hagas desgraciado a un pobre anciano, pues no
creo en absoluto que el linaje del hijo de Arcisio[100] sea odiado
por los bienaventurados dioses; que alguno sobrevivirá que
ocupe el palacio de elevado techo y posea en la lejanía los fértiles campos.»

Así diciendo, calmóse y cerró sus ojos al llanto.

Y luego de bañarse y coger vestidos limpios para su cuerpo,
subió al piso superior con las criadas y colocó en una cesta 760
granos de cebada[101]. E imploró a Atenea:

«Escúchame, hija de Zeus, portador de égida, Atritona[102]; si

---

[100] El hijo de Arcisio es Laertes. R. Carpenter (ob. cit., págs. 128 y ss.) quiere relacionar este nombre con la palabra *arktos,* «oso», y hacer de Odiseo "el hijo
del Oso" *(The Bearson)* —personaje mítico que aparece en otras culturas.

[101] Normalmente, la aspersión de la cebada sobre el altar y la víctima es parte de la compleja ceremonia del sacrificio cruento (cfr. III.445 y ss., XII.351
y ss.). En el caso presente, bastante insólito, debe tratarse de una simple ofrenda vegetal previa a la súplica de Penélope.

[102] Epíteto fijo de Atenea. Su etimología, como en otros casos, es bastante

alguna vez el muy hábil Odiseo quemó en el palacio gordos muslos de buey o de oveja, acuérdate de ellos ahora, salva a mi hijo y aleja a los muy orgullosos pretendientes.»

Cuando hubo hablado así lanzó el grito ritual y la diosa escuchó su oración. Los pretendientes alborotaban en la sombría sala, y uno de los jóvenes orgullosos decía así:

«La reina muy solicitada por nosotros prepara sus nupcias 770 sin saber que ha sido fabricada la muerte para su hijo.»

Así decía uno, ignorando lo que había ocurrido. Y entre ellos habló Antínoo y dijo:

«Desgraciados, evitad toda palabra arrogante, no sea que alguien se la vaya a comunicar. Mas, vamos, levantémonos y ejecutemos en silencio ese plan que a todos nos cumple.»

Cuando hubo dicho así, escogió a los veinte mejores y se dirigió hacia la rápida nave y a la orilla del mar. Arrastráronla 780 primero al profundo mar y colocaron el mástil y las velas a la negra nave. Prepararon luego los remos con estrobos de cuero, todo como corresponde, desplegaron las blancas velas y los audaces sirvientes les trajeron las armas. Anclaron la nave en aguas profundas y luego que hubieron desembarcado comieron allí y esperaron a que cayera la tarde.

Entre tanto, la discreta Penélope yacía en ayunas en el piso superior sin tomar comida ni bebida, cavilando si su ilustre hijo escaparía a la muerte o sucumbiría a manos de los sober- 790 bios pretendientes. Y le sobrevino el dulce sueño mientras meditaba lo que suele meditar un león entre una muchedumbre de hombres cuando lo llevan acorralado en engañoso círculo. Dormía reclinada y todos sus miembros se aflojaron.

En esto, tramó otro plan la diosa de ojos brillantes, Atenea: construyó una figura semejante al cuerpo de una mujer, de Iftima, hija del magnánimo Icario, a la que había desposado Eumelo, que tenía su casa en Feras, y envióla al palacio del divino 800 Odiseo para que aliviara del llanto y los gemidos a Penélope, que se lamentaba entre sollozos. Entró en el dormitorio por la correa del pasador, se colocó sobre la cabeza de Penélope y le dijo su palabra:

---

oscura, aunque los antiguos la relacionaron probablemente con el adjetivo *átry-tos*, «infatigable» (cfr. Esquilo, *Euménides,* 403).

«Penélope, ¿duermes afligida en tu corazón? No, los dioses que viven fácilmente no van a permitir que llores ni te aflijas, pues tu hijo ya está en su camino de vuelta, que en nada es culpable a los ojos de los dioses.»

Y le contestó luego la discreta Penélope, durmiendo plácidamente en las mismas puertas del sueño:

«Hermana, ¿por qué has venido? No sueles venir con fre- 810 cuencia, al menos hasta ahora, ya que vives muy lejos.

»Así que me mandas dejar los lamentos y los numerosos dolores que se agitan en mi interior, a mí que ya he perdido mi marido noble y valiente como un león, dotado de toda clase de virtudes entre los dánaos, cuya fama de nobleza es extensa en la Hélade y hasta el centro de Argos. Ahora de nuevo mi hijo amado ha partido en cóncava nave, mi hijo inocente desconocedor de obras y palabras. Es por éste por quien me lamento 820 más que por aquél. Por éste tiemblo y temo no le vaya a pasar algo, sea por obra de los del pueblo a donde ha marchado o sea en el mar. Pues muchos enemigos traman contra él deseando matarlo antes de que llegue a su tierra patria.»

Y le contestó la imagen invisible:

«Ánimo, no temas ya nada en absoluto. Ésta es quien le acompaña como guía, Palas Atenea —pues puede—, a quien cualquier hombre desearía tener a su lado. Se ha compadecido de tus lamentos y me ha enviado ahora para que te comunique esto.»

Y le contestó a su vez la prudente Penélope: 830

«Si de verdad eres una diosa y has oído la voz de un dios, vamos, háblame también de aquel desdichado, si vive aún y contempla la luz del sol o ya ha muerto y está en el Hades.»

Y le contestó y dijo la imagen invisible:

«De aquél no te voy a decir de fijo si vive o ha muerto, que es malo hablar cosas vanas.»

Así diciendo, desapareció en el viento por la cerradura de la puerta. Y ella se desperezó del sueño, la hija de Icario. Y su co- 840 razón se calmó, porque en lo más profundo de la noche se le había presentado un claro sueño.

Conque los pretendientes embarcaron y navegaban los húmedos caminos removiendo en su interior la muerte para Telémaco.

Hay una isla pedregosa en mitad del mar entre Itaca y la escarpada Same, la isla de Asteris[103]. No es grande, pero tiene puertos de doble entrada que acogen a las naves. Así que allí se emboscaron los aqueos y esperaban a Telémaco.

[103] Si la Itaca de Homero es la actual, Asteris debe ser un islote, hoy llamado Daskalion, que se encuentra situado al noroeste de la isla, en el canal que la separa de Cefalonia. Cfr. F. H. Stubbings, ob. cit., pág. 398 y ss.

Canto V

ODISEO LLEGA A ESQUERIA
DE LOS FEACIOS

En esto, Eos se levantó del lecho, de junto al noble Titono[104], para llevar la luz a los inmortales y a los mortales. Los dioses se reunieron en asamblea, y entre ellos Zeus, que truena en lo alto del cielo, cuyo poder es el mayor. Y Atenea les recordaba y relataba las muchas penalidades de Odiseo. Pues se interesaba por éste, que se encontraba en el palacio de la ninfa:

«Padre Zeus y demás bienaventurados dioses inmortales, que ningún rey portador de cetro sea benévolo ni amable ni bondadoso y no sea justo en su pensamiento, sino que siempre sea cruel y obre injustamente, ya que no se acuerda del divino Odiseo ninguno de los ciudadanos entre los que reinaba y era tierno como un padre. Ahora éste se encuentra en una isla soportando fuertes penas en el palacio de la ninfa Calipso y no tiene naves provistas de remos ni compañeros que lo acompañen por el ancho lomo del mar. Y, encima, ahora desean matar a su querido hijo cuando regrese a casa, pues ha marchado a la sagrada Pilos y a la divina Lacedemonia en busa de noticias de su padre»[105].

10

20

---

[104] Titono es hijo de Laomedonte y hermano de Príamo. Fue raptado por Eos, que se enamoró de su belleza y lo convirtió en su esposo. Eos pidió a Zeus la inmortalidad para Titono, pero se le olvidó pedir también la juventud, por lo que envejecía eternamente. Al final lo encerró en una habitación «y desde allí fluye incesante su voz» convertido en cigarra, cfr. *Himno a Afrodita*, V.218-38.

[105] Este discurso de Atenea es un cosido de II.230-4 (palabras de Méntor),

Y le contestó y dijo Zeus, el que amontona las nubes:

«Hija mía, ¡qué palabra ha escapado del cerco de tus dientes! ¿Pues no concebiste tú misma la idea de que Odiseo se vengara de aquéllos cuando llegara? Tú acompaña a Telémaco diestramente, ya que puedes, para que regrese a su patria sano y salvo, y que los pretendientes regresen en la nave.»

Y luego se dirigió a Hermes, su hijo, y le dijo:

«Hermes, puesto que tú eres el mensajero en lo demás, ve a comunicar a la ninfa de lindas trenzas nuestra firme decisión: 30 la vuelta de Odiseo el sufridor, que regrese sin acompañamiento de dioses ni de hombres mortales. A los veinte días llegará en una balsa de buena trabazón a la fértil Esqueria, después de padecer desgracias, a la tierra de los feacios, que son semejantes a los dioses, quienes lo honrarán como a un dios de todo corazón y lo enviarán a su tierra en una nave dándole bronce, oro en abundancia y ropas, tanto como nunca Odiseo hubiera sacado de Troya si hubiera llegado indemne habiendo obteni- 40 do parte del botín. Pues su destino es que vea a los suyos, llegue a su casa de alto techo y a su patria.»

Así dijo, y el mensajero Argifonte no desobedeció. Conque ató luego a sus pies hermosas sandalias, divinas, de oro, que suelen llevarlo igual por el mar que por la ilimitada tierra a la par del soplo del viento. Y cogió la varita[106] con la que hechiza los ojos de los hombres que quiere y los despierta cuando duermen. Con ésta en las manos echó a volar el poderoso Argifonte y llegado a Pieria cayó desde el éter en el ponto, y se movía 50 sobre el oleaje semejante a una gaviota que, pescando sobre los terribles senos del estéril ponto, empapa sus espesas alas en el agua del mar. Semejante a ésta se dirigía Hermes sobre las numerosas olas.

Pero cuando llegó a la isla lejana salió del ponto color violeta y marchó tierra adentro hasta que llegó a la gran cueva en la que habitaba la ninfa de lindas trenzas. Y la encontró dentro.

III:556-60 (palabras de Proteo) y IV.700-2 (palabras de Medonte). Ello ha llevado a los analíticos a considerar esta segunda Asamblea como una interpolación rapsódica para recitar las Aventuras por separado, cfr. Introducción.

[106] Estos versos se repiten en XXIV-2-4, donde la presencia del caduceo o varita está más justificada que aquí.

Un gran fuego ardía en el hogar y un olor de quebradizo cedro
y de incienso se extendía al arder a lo largo de la isla. Calipso
tejía dentro con lanzadera de oro y cantaba con hermosa voz
mientras trabajaba en el telar. En torno a la cueva había nacido un florido bosque de alisos, de chopos negros y olorosos ci-
preses, donde anidaban las aves de largas alas, los búhos y hal-
cones y las cornejas marinas de afilada lengua que se ocupan
de las cosas del mar.

Había cabe a la cóncava cueva una viña tupida que abundaba en uvas, y cuatro fuentes de agua clara que corrían cercanas
unas de otras, cada una hacia un lado, y alrededor, suaves y
frescos prados de violetas y apios. Incluso un inmortal que allí
llegara se admiraría y alegraría en su corazón[107].

El mensajero Argifonte se detuvo allí a contemplarlo, y luego que hubo admirado todo en su ánimo, se puso en camino
hacia la ancha cueva. Al verlo lo reconoció Calipso, divina en-
tre las diosas, pues los dioses no se desconocen entre sí por
más que uno habite lejos. Pero no encontró dentro al magnánimo Odiseo, pues éste, sentado en la orilla, lloraba donde
muchas veces, desgarrando su ánimo con lágrimas, gemidos y
pesares, solía contemplar el estéril mar. Y Calipso, la divina
entre las diosas, preguntó a Hermes haciéndolo sentar en una
silla brillante, resplandeciente:

«¿Por qué has venido, Hermes, el de vara de oro, venerable
y querido? Pues antes no venías con frecuencia. Di lo que
piensas, mi ánimo me empuja a cumplirlo si puedo y es posible
realizarlo. Pero antes sígueme para que te ofrezca los dones de
hospitalidad.»

Habiendo hablado así, la diosa colocó delante una mesa llena de ambrosía y mezcló rojo néctar. El mensajero bebió y comió, y después que hubo cenado y repuesto su ánimo con la
comida, le dijo su palabra:

«Me preguntas tú, una diosa, por qué he venido yo, un dios.

---

[107] Tanto en esta descripción tópica de un *locus amoenus*, como en la del palacio de Alcínoo (cfr. VII.12-32) se incluyen árboles de sombra o frutales, una
viña y una o varias fuentes. En todo caso, es notable una descripción de este
género, porque la apreciación sensible de la Naturaleza es ajena a la Literatura
griega en general.

Pues bien, voy a decir con sinceridad mi palabra, pues lo mandas. Zeus me ordenó que viniera aquí sin yo quererlo. ¿Quién atravesaría de buen grado tanta agua salada, indecible? Además, no hay ninguna ciudad de mortales en la que hagan sacrificios a los dioses y perfectas hecatombes. 100

»Pero no le es posible a ningún dios rebasar o dejar sin cumplir la voluntad de Zeus, el que lleva la égida. Dice que se encuentra contigo un varón, el más desgraciado de cuantos lucharon durante nueve años en derredor de la ciudad de Príamo. Al décimo regresaron a sus casas, después de destruir la ciudad, pero en el regreso faltaron contra Atenea[108], y ésta les levantó un viento contrario. Allí perecieron todos sus fieles 110 compañeros, pero a él el viento y grandes olas lo acercaron aquí. Ahora te ordena que lo devuelvas lo antes posible, que su destino no es morir lejos de los suyos, sino ver a los suyos y regresar a su casa de elevado techo y a su patria.»

Así dijo, y Calipso, divina entre las diosas, se estremeció, habló y le dijo palabras aladas:

«Sois crueles, dioses, y envidiosos más que nadie, ya que os irritáis contra las diosas que duermen abiertamente con un hombre si lo han hecho su amante. Así, cuando Eos, de rosados dedos, arrebató a Orión[109], os irritasteis los dioses que vi- 120 vís con facilidad, hasta que la casta Artemis de trono de oro lo mató en Ortigia, atacándole con dulces dardos. Así, cuando Demeter, de hermosas trenzas, cediendo a su impulso, se unió en amor y lecho con Jasión[110] en campo tres veces labrado.

---

[108] Se refiere, sin citarlo expresamente, al sacrilegio de Ayante, hijo de Oileo (cfr. nota 93). En esta breve y confusa narración se mezclan los regresos de los aqueos en general con el de Odiseo. En todo caso, se trata de un resumen, demasiado sumario e impreciso, de los *Nostoi*. E inexacto: los compañeros de Odiseo perecieron por faltar a Helios, no a Atenea (cfr. XII.375-419). La propia Calipso demuestra más abajo (vv. 130 y ss.) conocer mejor los hechos.

[109] Orión, el cazador, es uno de los amantes de Eos. Otras versiones atribuyen su muerte a la picadura de un escorpión que le envió Artemis. Ambos fueron convertidos en astros y Orión huye eternamente de Escorpio —en términos astronómicos, cuando uno tiene su orto el otro tiene su ocaso. En la Nekya (XI.572-5) Orión aparece, como los demás, realizando las mismas actividades que en vida, lo que indica que su catasterismo es posterior.

[110] Héroe civilizador de Creta relacionado con la Agricultura. Según Hesiodo *(Teogonía,* 969 y ss.), Deméter se unió con él «en campo tres veces labrado»

No tardó mucho Zeus en enterarse, y lo mató alcanzándolo con el resplandeciente rayo. Así ahora os irritáis contra mí, dioses, porque está conmigo un mortal. Yo lo salvé, que Zeus le destrozó la rápida nave arrojándole el brillante rayo en medio del ponto rojo como el vino. Allí murieron todos sus nobles compañeros, pero a él el viento y las olas lo acercaron aquí. Yo lo traté como amigo y lo alimenté y le prometía hacerlo inmortal y sin vejez para siempre. Pero puesto que no es posible a ningún dios rebasar ni dejar sin cumplir la voluntad de Zeus, el que lleva la égida, que se vaya por el mar estéril si aquél lo impulsa y se lo manda. Mas yo no lo despediré de cualquier manera, pues no tiene naves provistas de remos ni compañeros que lo acompañen sobre el ancho lomo del mar. Sin embargo, le aconsejaré benévola y nada le ocultaré para que llegue a su tierra sano y salvo.»

Y el mensajero, el Argifonte, le dijo a su vez:

«Entonces despídele ahora y respeta la cólera de Zeus, no sea que se irrite contigo y sea duro en el futuro.»

Cuando hubo hablado así partió el poderoso Argifonte.

Y la soberana ninfa acercóse al magnánimo Odiseo luego que hubo escuchado el mensaje de Zeus. Lo encontró sentado en la orilla. No se habían secado sus ojos del llanto, y su dulce vida se consumía añorando el regreso, puesto que ya no le agradaba la ninfa, aunque pasaba las noches por la fuerza en la cóncava cueva junto a la que lo amaba sin que él la amara. Durante el día se sentaba en las piedras de la orilla desgarrando su ánimo con lágrimas, gemidos y dolores, y miraba al estéril mar derramando lágrimas.

Y deteniéndose junto a él le dijo la divina entre las diosas:

«Desdichado, no te me lamentes más ni consumas tu existencia, que te voy a despedir no sin darte antes buenos consejos. ¡Hala!, corta unos largos maderos y ensambla una amplia balsa con el bronce. Y luego adapta a ésta un elevado tablazón para que te lleve sobre el brumoso ponto, que yo te pondré en

---

(la misma frase que aquí) y alumbró a Pluto «quien camina sobre la tierra toda y el ancho lomo del mar» otorgando riqueza a quien lo alcanza con sus manos. Otras versiones (cfr. Diodoro Sículo 5.48) lo ponen en relación con Samotracia.

ella pan y agua y rojo vino en abundancia que alejen de ti el hambre. También te daré ropas y te enviaré por detrás un viento favorable de modo que llegues a tu patria sano y salvo, si es que lo permiten los dioses que poseen el ancho cielo, quienes son mejores que yo para hacer proyectos y cum- 170 plirlos.»

Así habló; estremecióse el sufridor, el divino Odiseo, y hablando le dirigió aladas palabras:

«Diosa, creo que andas cavilando algo distinto de mi marcha, tú que me apremias a atravesar el gran abismo del mar en una balsa, cosa difícil y peligrosa; que ni siquiera las bien equilibradas naves de veloz proa lo atraviesan animadas por el favorable viento de Zeus. No, yo no subiría a una balsa mal que te pese, si no aceptas jurarme con gran juramento, diosa, que no maquinarás contra mí desgracia alguna.»

Así habló; sonrió Calipso, divina entre las diosas, le acarició 180 la mano y le dijo su palabra, llamándole por su nombre:

«Eres malvado a pesar de que no piensas cosas vanas, pues te has atrevido a decir tales palabras. Sépalo ahora la Tierra, y desde arriba el ancho Cielo y el agua que fluye de la Estige[111] —éste es el mayor y el más terrible juramento para los bienaventurados dioses— que no maquinaré contra ti desgracia alguna. Esto es lo que yo pienso y te voy a aconsejar, cuanto para mí misma pensaría cuando me acuciara tal necesidad. Mi proyecto es justo, y no hay en mi pecho un ánimo de hierro, 190 sino compasivo.»

Hablando así la divina entre las diosas marchó luego delante y él marchó tras las huellas de la diosa. Y llegaron a la profunda cueva la diosa y el varón. Éste se sentó en el sillón de donde se había levantado Hermes, y la ninfa le ofreció toda clase de comida para comer y beber, cuantas cosas suelen yantar los mortales hombres. Sentóse ella frente al divino Odiseo y las siervas le colocaron néctar y ambrosía. Echaron mano a los 200 alimentos preparados que tenían delante y después que se saciaron de comida y bebida empezó a hablar Calipso, divina entre las diosas:

«Hijo de Laertes, de linaje divino, Odiseo, rico en ardides,

---

[111] En el río del Hades por el que juran los dioses, cfr. Hesiodo, *Teogonía* 400.

¿así que quieres marcharte enseguida a tu casa y a tu tierra patria? Vete enhorabuena. Pero si supieras cuántas tristezas te deparará el destino antes de que arribes a tu patria, te quedarías aquí conmigo para guardar esta morada y serías inmortal por más deseoso que estuvieras de ver a tu esposa, a la que 210 continuamente deseas todos los días. Yo en verdad me precio de no ser inferior a aquélla ni en el porte ni en el natural, que no conviene a las mortales jamás competir con las inmortales ni en porte ni en figura.»

Y le dijo el muy astuto Odiseo:

«Venerable diosa, no te enfades conmigo, que sé muy bien cuánto te es inferior la discreta Penélope en figura y en estatura al verla de frente, pues ella es mortal y tú inmortal sin vejez. Pero aun así quiero y deseo todos los días marcharme a mi 220 casa y ver el día del regreso. Si alguno de los dioses me maltratara en el ponto rojo como el vino, lo soportaré en mi pecho con ánimo paciente; pues ya soporté muy mucho sufriendo en el mar y en la guerra. Que venga esto después de aquello.»

Así dijo. El sol se puso y llegó el crepúsculo. Así que se dirigieron al interior de la cóncava cueva a deleitarse con el amor en mutua compañía.

Y cuando se mostró Eos, la que nace de la mañana, la de dedos de rosa, Odiseo se vistió de túnica y manto, y ella, la ninfa, vistió una gran túnica blanca, fina y graciosa, colocó al- 230 rededor de su talle hermoso cinturón de oro y un velo sobre la cabeza, y a continuación se ocupó de la partida del magnánimo Odiseo. Le dio una gran hacha de bronce bien manejable, aguzada por ambos lados y con un hermoso mango de madera de olivo bien ajustado. A continuación le dio una azuela bien pulimentada, y emprendió el camino hacia un extremo de la isla donde habían crecido grandes árboles, alisos y álamos negros y abetos que suben hasta el cielo, secos desde hace tiempo, rese- 240 cos, que podían flotar ligeros. Luego que le hubo mostrado dónde crecían los árboles, marchó hacia el palacio Calipso, divina entre las diosas, y él empezó a cortar troncos y llevó a cabo rápidamente su trabajo. Derribó veinte en total y los cortó con el bronce, los pulió diestramente y los enderezó con una plomada mientras Calipso, divina entre las diosas, le llevaba un berbiquí. Después perforó todos, los unió unos con

otros y los ajustó con clavos y junturas. Cuanto un hombre
buen conocedor del arte de construir redondearía el fondo de   250
una amplia nave de carga, así de grande hizo Odiseo la balsa.
Plantó luego postes, los ajustó con vigas apiñadas y construyó
una cubierta rematándola con grandes tablas. Hizo un mástil y
una antena adaptada a él y construyó el timón para gobernarla.
Cubrióla después con cañizos de mimbre a uno y otro lado
para que fuera defensa contra el oleaje y puso encima mucha
madera. Entre tanto, le trajo Calipso, divina entre las diosas,
tela para hacer las velas, y él las fabricó con habilidad. Ató en
ellas cuerdas, cables y bolinas y con estacas la echó al divi-   260
no mar.

Era el cuarto día y ya tenía todo preparado. Y al quinto lo
dejó marchar de la isla la divina Calipso después de lavarlo y
ponerle ropas perfumadas. Entrególe la diosa un odre de negro vino, otro grande de agua y un saco de víveres, y le añadió
abundantes golosinas. Y le envió un viento próspero y cálido.

Así que el divino Odiseo desplegó gozoso las velas al viento
y sentado gobernaba el timón con habilidad. No caía el sueño   270
sobre sus párpados contemplando las Pléyades y el Bootes, que
se pone tarde, y la Osa, que llaman carro por sobrenombre,
que gira allí y acecha a Orión y es la única privada de los baños
de Océano[112]. Pues le había ordenado Calipso, divina entre las
diosas, que navegase teniéndola a la mano izquierda. Navegó
durante diecisiete días atravesando el mar, y al decimoctavo

---

[112] Las constelaciones eran el único punto de referencia para la navegación
nocturna en la Grecia arcaica. Las Pléyades (también llamadas *Peleiades* o palomas) son un *cluster* de la constelación Taurus (M45 en el NGC). Bootes, el
boyero, tiene como estrella principal a Arturo (Alpha Bootis), y a ésta probablemente se refiere el pasaje, pues no se conoció como constelación hasta más tarde. La Osa debe ser la Mayor (hasta después de Tales de Mileto los marinos no
se guiaron por la Osa Menor) y «está privada de los baños de Océano» porque
nunca se pone. Con estos datos es difícil imaginar el tiempo y rumbo de la navegación de Odiseo —si es que hay algún intento por parte de Homero de ofrecer algo coherente. Si se viaja en dirección Este, la Osa Mayor queda a la izquierda *solamente en invierno*, pero en este caso, a la derecha (Sur), sólo son visibles las Pléyades y Orión (no Bootes). En otoño, en cambio, quedan en línea
Bootes, Osa y Pléyades, por lo que quedan todas a la izquierda. En todo caso, *la
dirección siempre tiene que ser Este* para que la Osa quede «a la izquierda». Cfr.
P. Moore, *Guide to the Stars and Planets*, Londres, 1983.

aparecieron los sombríos montes del país de los feacios, por donde éste le quedaba más cerca y parecía un escudo sobre el brumoso ponto. 280

El poderoso, el que sacude la tierra, que volvía de junto a los etíopes, lo vio de lejos, desde los montes Sólymos, pues se le apareció surcando el mar. Irritóse mucho en su corazón, y moviendo la cabeza habló a su ánimo:

«¡Ay!, seguro que los dioses han cambiado de resolución respecto a Odiseo mientras yo estaba entre los etíopes, que ya está cerca de la tierra de los feacios, donde es su destino escapar del extremo de las calamidades que le llegan. Pero creo que aún le han de alcanzar bastantes desgracias.» 290

Cuando hubo hablado así, amontonó las nubes y agitó el mar, sosteniendo el tridente entre sus manos, e hizo levantarse grandes tempestades de vientos de todas clases, y ocultó con las nubes al mismo tiempo la tierra y el ponto. Y la noche surgió del cielo. Cayeron Euro y Noto, Céfiro de soplo violento y Bóreas que nace en cielo despejado levantando grandes olas. Entonces las rodillas y el corazón de Odiseo desfallecieron, e irritado dijo a su magnánimo espíritu:

«Ay de mí, desgraciado, ¿qué me sucederá por fin ahora? Mucho temo que todo lo que dijo la diosa sea verdad; me aseguró que sufriría desgracias en el ponto antes de regresar a mi patria, y ahora todo se está cumpliendo. ¡Con qué nubes ha cerrado Zeus el vasto cielo y agitado el ponto, y las tempestades de vientos de todas clases se lanzan con ímpetu! 300

»Seguro que ahora tendré una terrible muerte. ¡Felices tres y cuatro veces los dánaos que murieron en la vasta Troya por dar satisfacción a los Atridas! Ojalá hubiera muerto yo y me hubiera enfrentado con mi destino el día en que tantos troyanos lanzaban contra mí broncíneas lanzas alrededor del Pelida muerto! Allí habría obtenido honores fúnebres y los aqueos celebrarían mi gloria, pero ahora está determinado que sea sorprendido por una triste muerte.» 310

Cuando hubo dicho así, le alcanzó en lo más alto una gran ola que cayó terriblemente y sacudió la balsa. Odiseo se precipitó fuera de la balsa soltando las manos del timón, y un terrible huracán de mezclados vientos le rompió el mástil por la mitad. Cayeron al mar, lejos, la vela y la antena, y a él lo tuvo

largo tiempo sumergido sin poder salir con presteza por el ímpetu de la ingente ola, pues le pesaban los vestidos que le había
dado la divina Calipso.

Al fin emergió mucho después y escupió de su boca la
amarga agua del mar que le caía en abundancia, con ruido,
desde la cabeza. Pero ni aun así se olvidó de la balsa, aunque
estaba agotado, sino que lanzándose entre las olas se apoderó
de ella. El gran oleaje la arrastraba con la corriente aquí y allá.
Como cuando el otoñal Bóreas arrastra por la llanura los espinos y se enganchan espesos unos con otros, así los vientos la
llevaban por el mar por aquí y por allá. Unas veces Noto la
lanzaba a Bóreas para que se la llevase, y otras Euro la cedía a
Céfiro para perseguirla.

Pero lo vio Ino Leucotea[113], la de hermosos tobillos, la hija
de Cadmo que antes era mortal dotada de voz, mas ahora par-
ticipaba del honor de los dioses en el fondo del mar. Compa-
decióse de Odiseo, que sufría pesares a la deriva, y emergió volando del mar semejante a una gaviota; se sentó sobre la balsa
y le dijo:

«¡Desgraciado! ¿Por qué tan acerbamente se ha encolerizado
contigo Poseidón, el que sacude la tierra, para sembrarte tantos males? No te destruirá por mucho que lo desee. Conque
obra del modo siguiente, pues paréceme que eres discreto: quí-
tate esos vestidos, deja que la balsa sea arrastrada por los vientos, y trata de alcanzar nadando la tierra de los feacios, donde
es tu destino que te salves. Toma, extiende este velo inmortal
bajo tu pecho, y no temas padecer ni morir. Mas cuando alcan-
ces con tus manos tierra firme, suéltalo enseguida y arrójalo al
ponto rojo como el vino, muy lejos de tierra, y apártate lejos.»

Cuando hubo hablado así la diosa, le dio el velo, y con presteza se sumergió en el alborotado ponto, semejante a una gaviota, y una negra ola la ocultó. El divino Odiseo, el sufridor,
dio en cavilar y habló irritado a su magnánimo corazón:

---

[113] Ino era hija de Cadmo y hermana de Semele y Agave, todas de materni-
dad trágica. Ino fue transformada en divinidad marina recibiendo el nombre de
Leucótea («diosa blanca», de la neblina o del mar) cuando se arrojó a éste con el
cadáver de su hijo Melicertes después que, enloquecida por Hera, lo hirviera en
un caldero. Su papel en la *Odisea* es similar al de Idotea, cfr. IV.365 y ss.

«¡Ay de mí! ¡No vaya a ser que alguno de los inmortales urde contra mí una trampa, cuando me ordena abandonar la balsa! Mas no obedeceré, que yo vi a lo lejos con mis propios ojos la tierra donde me dijo que tendría asilo. Más bien, pues me parece mejor, obraré así: mientras los maderos sigan unidos por las ligazones permaneceré aquí y aguantaré sufriendo males, pero una vez que las olas desencajen la balsa me pondré a nadar, pues no se me alcanza previsión mejor.»

Mientras esto agitaba en su mente, y en su corazón, Poseidón, el que sacude la tierra, levantó una gran ola, terrible y penosa, abovedada, y lo arrastró. Como el impetuoso viento agita un montón de pajas secas que dispersa acá y allá, así dispersó los grandes maderos de la balsa. Pero Odiseo montó en un madero como si cabalgase sobre potro de carrera y se quitó los vestidos que le había dado la divina Calipso. Y al punto extendió el velo por su pecho y púsose boca abajo en el mar, extendidos los brazos, ansioso de nadar.

Y el poderoso, el que sacude la tierra, lo vio, y moviendo la cabeza, habló a su ánimo:

«Ahora que has padecido muchas calamidades vaga por el ponto hasta que llegues a esos hombres vástagos de Zeus. Pero ni aun así creo que estimarás pequeña tu desgracia.»

Cuando hubo hablado así, fustigó a los caballos de hermosas crines y enfiló hacia Egas, donde tiene ilustre morada.

Pero Atenea, la hija de Zeus decidió otra cosa: cerró el camino a todos los vientos y mandó que todos cesaran y se calmaran; levantó al rápido Bóreas y quebró las olas hasta que Odiseo, movido por Zeus, llegara a los feacios, amantes del remo, escapando a la muerte y al destino.

Así que anduvo éste a la deriva durante dos noches y dos días por las sólidas olas, y muchas veces su corazón presintió la muerte. Pero cuando Eos, de lindas trenzas, completó el tercer día, cesó el viento y se hizo la calma, y Odiseo vio cerca la tierra oteando agudamente desde lo alto de una gran ola. Como cuando parece agradable a los hijos la vida de un padre que yace enfermo entre grandes dolores, consumiéndose durante mucho tiempo, pues le acomete un horrible demón y los dioses le libran felizmente del mal, así de agradable le parecieron a Odiseo la tierra y el bosque, y nadaba apresurándose por poner los pies en tierra firme. Pero cuando estaba a tal distancia que se le habría oído al gritar, sintió el estrépito del mar en las rocas. Grandes olas rugían estrepitosamente al romperse con estruendo contra tierra firme, y todo se cubría de espuma marina, pues no había puertos, refugios de las naves, ni ensenadas, sino acantilados, rocas y escollos. Entonces se aflojaron las rodillas y el corazón de Odiseo y decía afligido a su magnánimo corazón:

«¡Ay de mí! Después que Zeus me ha concedido inesperadamente ver tierra y he terminado de surcar este abismo, no encuentro por dónde salir del canoso mar. Afuera las rocas son 410 puntiagudas, y alrededor las olas se levantan estrepitosamente, y la roca se yergue lisa y el mar es profundo en la orilla, sin que sea posible poner allí los pies y escapar del mal. Temo que al salir me arrebate una gran ola y me lance contra pétrea roca, y mi esfuerzo sería inútil. Y si sigo nadando más allá por si encuentro una playa donde rompe el mar oblicuamente o un puerto marino, temo que la tempestad me arrebate de nuevo y me lleve al ponto rico en peces mientras yo gimo profundamente, 420 o una divinidad lance contra mí un gran monstruo marino de los que cría a miles la ilustre Anfítrite. Pues sé que el ilustre, el que sacude la tierra, está irritado conmigo.»

Mientras meditaba esto en su mente y en su corazón, lo arrastró una gran ola contra la escarpada orilla, y allí se habría desgarrado la piel y roto los huesos si Atenea, la diosa de ojos brillantes, no le hubiese inspirado a su ánimo lo siguiente: lanzóse, asió la roca con ambas manos y se mantuvo en ella gimiendo hasta que pasó una gran ola. De este modo consiguió 430 evitarla, pero al refluir ésta lo golpeó cuando se apresuraba y lo lanzó a lo lejos en el ponto. Como cuando al sacar a un pulpo de su escondrijo se pegan infinitas piedrecitas a sus tentáculos, así se desgarró en la roca la piel de sus robustas manos.

Luego lo cubrió una gran ola, y allí habría muerto el desgraciado Odiseo contra lo dispuesto por el destino si Atenea, la diosa de ojos brillantes, no le hubiera inspirado sensatez. Así que emergiendo del oleaje que rugía en dirección a la costa, nadó dando cara a la tierra por si encontraba orillas batidas por las olas o puertos de mar. Y cuando llegó nadando a la 440 boca de un río de hermosa corriente, aquél le pareció el mejor lugar, libre de piedras y al abrigo del viento. Y al advertir que fluía le suplicó en su ánimo:

«Escucha, soberano, quienquiera que seas; llego a ti, muy deseado, huyendo del ponto y de las amenazas de Poseidón. Incluso los dioses inmortales respetan al hombre que llega errante como yo llego ahora a tu corriente y a tus rodillas después de sufrir mucho. Compadécete, soberano, puesto que me precio de ser tu suplicante.» 450

Así dijo; hizo éste cesar al punto su corriente, retirando las olas, e hizo la calma delante de él, llevándolo salvo a la misma desembocadura. Y dobló Odiseo ambas rodillas y los robustos brazos, pues su corazón estaba sometido por el mar. Tenía todo el cuerpo hinchado, y de su boca y nariz fluía mucha agua salada: así que cayó sin aliento y sin voz y le sobrevino un terrible cansancio. Mas cuando respiró y se recuperó su ánimo, desató el velo de la diosa y lo echó al río que fluye hacia el 460 mar, y al punto se lo llevó una gran ola con la corriente y luego la recibió Ino en sus manos. Alejóse del río, se echó delante de una junquera y besó la fértil tierra. Y, afligido, decía a su magnánimo corazón:

«¡Ay de mí! ¿Qué me va a suceder? ¿Qué me sobrevendrá por fin? Si velo junto al río durante la noche inspiradora de preocupaciones, quizá la dañina escarcha y el suave rocío venzan al tiempo mi agonizante ánimo a causa de mi debilidad, pues una brisa fría sopla antes del alba desde el río. Pero si subo a la colina y umbría selva y duermo entre las espesas ma- 470 tas, si me dejan el frío y el cansancio y me viene el dulce sueño, temo convertirme en botín y presa de las fieras.»

Después de pensarlo, le pareció que era mejor así, y echó a andar hacia la selva y la encontró cerca del agua en lugar bien visible; y se deslizó debajo de dos matas que habían nacido del mismo lugar, una de aladierma y otra de olivo. No llegaba a ellos el húmedo soplo de los vientos ni el resplandeciente sol los hería con sus rayos, ni la lluvia los atravesaba de un extre- 480 mo a otro (tan apretados crecían entrelazados uno con el otro). Bajo ellos se introdujo Odiseo, y luego preparó ancha cama con sus manos, pues había un gran montón de hojarasca como para acoger a dos o tres hombres en el invierno por riguroso que fuera. Al verla se alegró el divino Odiseo, el sufridor, y se acostó en medio y se echó encima un montón de hojas. Como el que esconde un tizón en negra ceniza en el extremo de un campo (y no tiene vecinos) para conservar un germen de fuego y no tener que ir a encenderlo a otra parte, así se cubrió Odiseo con las hojas y Atenea vertió sobre sus ojos el sueño para que se le calmara rápidamente el penoso cansancio, cerrándole los párpados.

Canto VI

ODISEO Y NAUSÍCAA

A sí es como dormía allí el sufridor, el divino Odiseo, agotado por el sueño y el cansancio.

En tanto marchó Atenea al país y a la ciudad de los hombres feacios que antes habitaban la espaciosa Hiperea[114] cerca de los Cíclopes, hombres soberbios que los dañaban continuamente, pues eran superiores en fuerza. Sacándolos de allí los condujo Nausítoo, semejante a un dios, y los asentó en Esqueria[115], lejos de los hombres industriosos; rodeó la ciudad con un muro, construyó casas e hizo los templos de los dioses y repartió los campos. Pero éste, vencido ya por Ker, había marchado a Hades, y entonces gobernaba Alcínoo, inspirado en sus designios por los dioses.

Al palacio de éste se encaminó Atenea, la de ojos brillantes, planeando el regreso para el magnánimo Odiseo. Llegó a la muy adornada estancia en la que dormía una joven igual a las diosas en su porte y figura, Nausícaa, hija del magnánimo Alcí-

---

[114] Nombre mítico que significa «Tierra alta». En la *Ilíada* (II.734) es el nombre de una fuente.

[115] Nombre perteneciente también a la geografía mítica de la *Odisea,* aunque los antiguos la identificaran con la actual Corfú (cfr. Tucídides, 3.70, y Estrabón, 7.3.6). Todo lo que aquí se dice sobre su fundación y características urbanísticas se ajusta a las *poleis* fundadas en las colonizaciones de la época arcaica. Es una ciudad planificada urbanísticamente con su muralla, ágora, calles, templos y puerto (cfr. vv. 262 y ss.). Sin embargo, su sistema político y social tiene claras reminiscencias de la época micénica: Alcínoo, que vive en un palacio «micénico» es el *anax* y tiene preeminencia (aunque no se precisa de qué tipo) sobre los jefes *(basileis)* de los feacios. Cfr. F. R. Adrados, *Introducción a Homero,* págs. 321 y siguientes.

noo. Y dos sirvientas que poseían la belleza de las Gracias estaban a uno y otro lado de la entrada, y las suntuosas puertas estaban cerradas. Apresuróse Atenea como un soplo de viento 20 hacia la cama de la joven, y se puso sobre su cabeza y le dirigió su palabra tomando la apariencia de la hija de Dimante, famoso por sus naves, pues era de su misma edad y muy grata a su ánimo.

Asemejándose a ésta, le dijo Atenea, la de ojos brillantes:

«Nausícaa, ¿por qué tan indolente te parió tu madre? Tienes descuidados los espléndidos vestidos, y eso que está cercana tu boda, en que es preciso que vistas tus mejores galas y se las proporciones también a aquellos que te acompañen[116]. Pues de cosas así resulta buena fama a los hombres y se complacen el 30 padre y la venerable madre.

Conque marchemos a lavar tan pronto como despunte la aurora; también yo iré contigo como compañera para que dispongas todo enseguida, porque ya no vas a estar soltera mucho tiempo, que te pretenden los mejores de los feacios en el pueblo donde también tú tienes tu linaje. Así que, anda, pide a tu ilustre padre que prepare antes de la aurora mulas y un carro que lleve los cinturones, las túnicas y tu espléndida ropa. Es para ti mucho mejor ir así que a pie, pues los lavaderos están muy lejos de la ciudad.» 40

Cuando hubo hablado así se marchó Atenea, la de los brillantes, al Olimpo, donde dicen que está la morada siempre segura de los dioses, pues no es azotada por los vientos ni mojada por las lluvias, ni tampoco la cubre la nieve. Permanece siempre un cielo sin nubes y una resplandeciente claridad la envuelve. Allí se divierten durante todo el día los felices dioses[117]. Hacia allá marchó la de ojos brillantes cuando hubo aconsejado a la joven.

Al punto llegó Eos, la de hermoso trono, que despertó a Nausícaa, de lindo peplo, y asombrada del sueño echó a correr 50 por el palacio para contárselo a sus progenitores, a su padre y a su madre. Y encontró dentro a los dos; ella estaba sentada

---

[116] Se refiere a los amigos y amigas de la novia que la «conducen» a casa del novio en la boda.

[117] Cfr. la descripción del Elísio en IV.566-8.

junto al hogar con sus siervas hilando copos de lana teñidos con púrpura marina; a él lo encontró a las puertas cuando marchaba con los ilustres reyes al Consejo, donde lo reclamaban los nobles feacios.

Así que se acercó a su padre y le dijo:

«Querido papá, ¿no podrías aparejarme un alto carro de buenas ruedas para que lleve a lavar al río los vestidos que tengo sucios? Que también a ti conviene, cuando estás entre los principales, participar en el Consejo llevando sobre tu cuerpo vestidos limpios. Además, tienes cinco hijos en el palacio, dos casados ya, pero tres solteros en la flor de la edad, y éstos siempre quieren ir al baile con los vestidos bien limpios, y todo esto está a mi cargo.» 60

Así dijo, pues se avergonzaba de mentar el floreciente matrimonio a su padre. Pero él comprendió todo y le respondió con estas palabras:

«No te voy a negar las mulas, hija, ni ninguna otra cosa. Ve; al momento los criados te prepararán un alto carro de buenas ruedas con una cesta ajustada a él.» 70

Cuando hubo dicho así, daba órdenes a sus criados y éstos al momento le obedecieron. Prepararon fuera el carro mulero de buenas ruedas, trajeron mulas y las uncieron al yugo. La joven sacó de la habitación un lujoso vestido y lo colocó en el bien pulido carro, y la madre puso en un capacho abundante y rica comida, así como golosinas, y en un odre de cuero de cabra vertió vino. La joven subió al carro, y todavía le dio en un recipiente de oro aceite húmedo[118] para que se ungiera con sus sirvientas. Tomó Nausícaa el látigo y las resplandecientes riendas y lo restalló para que partieran. Y se dejó sentir el batir de las mulas, y mantenían una tensión incesante llevando los vestidos y a ella misma; mas no sola, que con ella marchaban sus esclavas. Así que hubieron llegado a la hermosísima corriente del río donde estaban los lavaderos perennes (manaba un caudal de agua muy hermosa para lavar incluso la ropa más sucia), 80

---

[118] En gr. *hygrón*. En Homero se aplica sistemáticamente a los líquidos, especialmente en dos fórmulas: una referida al mar «los húmedos senderos», cfr. III.71, IX.252, etc.) y otra al aceite, ocupando siempre los dos últimos metros del hexámetro (cfr. VI.215 y VII.107).

soltaron las mulas del carro y las arrearon hacia el río de hermosos torbellinos para que comieran la fresca hierba suave como la miel. Tomaron ellas en sus manos los vestidos, los llevaron a la oscura agua y los pisoteaban con presteza en las pilas, emulándose unas a otras.

Una vez que limpiaron y lavaron toda la suciedad, extendieron la ropa ordenadamente a la orilla del mar precisamente donde el agua devuelve a la tierra los guijarros más limpios.

Y después de bañarse y ungirse con el grasiento aceite, tomaron el almuerzo junto a la orilla del río y aguardaban a que la ropa se secara con el resplandor del sol.

Apenas habían terminado de disfrutar el almuerzo, las criadas y ella misma se pusieron a jugar con una pelota, despojándose de sus velos. Y Nausícaa, de blancos brazos, dio comienzo a la danza[119]. Como Artemis va por los montes, la Flechadora, ya sea por el Taigeto muy espacioso o por el Erimanto, mientras disfruta con los jabalíes y ligeros ciervos, y con ella las ninfas agrestes, hijas de Zeus portador de la égida, participan en los juegos y disfruta en su pecho Leto... (de todas ellas tiene por encima la cabeza y el rostro, así que es fácilmente reconocible, aunque todas son bellas), así se distinguía entre todas sus sirvientas la joven doncella.

Pero cuando ya se disponían a regresar de nuevo a casa, después de haber uncido las mulas y doblado los bellos vestidos, la diosa de ojos brillantes, Atenea, dispuso otro plan: que Odiseo se despertara y viera a la joven de hermosos ojos que lo conduciría a la ciudad de los feacios. Conque la princesa tiró la pelota a una sirvienta y no la acertó; arrojóla en un profundo remolino y ellas gritaron con fuerza. Despertó el divino Odiseo, y sentado meditaba en su mente y en su corazón:

«¡Ay de mí! ¿De qué clase de hombres es la tierra a la que he llegado? ¿Son soberbios, salvajes y carentes de justicia o amigos de los forasteros y con sentimientos de piedad hacia los dioses?[120]. Y es el caso que me rodea un griterío femenino

---

[119] Es probable que no se trate de un simple juego de pelota, sino de una danza ritual, por la alusión a Artemis, semejante a la de los jóvenes feacios en VIII.370 y ss. Cfr. F. R. Adrados, *Orígenes de la Lírica griega*, Madrid, 1976, pág. 51.

[120] Fórmula que se repite en IX.175 y ss. (referida a los Cíclopes) y en

como de doncellas, de ninfas que poseen las elevadas cimas de los montes, las fuentes de los ríos y los prados cubiertos de hierba. ¿O es que estoy cerca de hombres dotados de voz articulada? Pero, ea, yo mismo voy a comprobarlo e intentaré verlo.»

Cuando hubo dicho así, salió de entre los matorrales el divino Odiseo, y de la cerrada selva cortó con su robusta mano una rama frondosa para cubrirse alrededor las vergüenzas. Y se puso en camino como un león montaraz que, confiado en su 130 fuerza, marcha empapado de lluvia y contra el viento y le arden los ojos; entonces persigue a bueyes o a ovejas o anda tras los salvajes ciervos; pues su vientre lo apremia a entrar en un recinto bien cerrado para atacar a los ganados. Así iba a mezclarse Odiseo entre las doncellas de lindas trenzas, aun estando desnudo, pues la necesidad lo alcanzaba. Y apareció ante ellas terriblemente afeado por la salmuera.

Temblorosas se dispersan cada una por un lado hacia las salientes riberas. Sola la hija de Alcínoo se quedó, pues Atenea le infundió valor en su pecho y arrojó el miedo de sus miembros. 140 Y permaneció a pie firme frente a Odiseo. Éste dudó entre suplicar a la muchacha de lindos ojos abrazado a sus rodillas o pedirle desde lejos, con dulces palabras, que le señalara su ciudad y le entregara ropas. Y mientras esto cavilaba, le pareció mejor suplicar desde lejos con dulces palabras, no fuera que la doncella se irritara con él al abrazarle las rodillas. Así que pronunció estas dulces y astutas palabras:

«A ti suplico, soberana. ¿Eres diosa o mortal? Si eres una divinidad de las que poseen el espacioso cielo, yo te comparo a 150 Artemis, la hija del gran Zeus, en belleza, talle y distinción, y si eres uno de los mortales que habitan la tierra, tres veces felices tu padre y tu venerable madre; tres veces felices también tus hermanos, pues bien seguro que el ánimo se les ensancha por tu causa viendo entrar en el baile a tal retoño; y con mucho el más feliz de todos en su corazón aquel que venciendo con sus presentes te lleve a su casa. Que jamás he visto con mis ojos 160 semejante mortal, hombre o mujer. Al mirarte me atenaza el

---

XIII.201 y ss. (a Itaca cuando llega Odiseo) y en VIII.575 y ss. (en general a los pueblos que ha conocido Odiseo).

Ulises y Nausícaa (cuadro de P. Pieterez Lastman)

asombro. Una vez en Delos vi que crecía junto al altar de Apolo un retoño semejante de palmera (pues también he ido allí y me seguía un numeroso ejército en expedición en que me iban a suceder funestos males.) Así es que contemplando aquello quedé entusiasmado largo tiempo, pues nunca árbol tal había crecido de la tierra.

»Del mismo modo te admiro a ti, mujer, y te contemplo absorto al tiempo que temo profundamente abrazar tus rodillas. Pero me alcanza un terrible pesar. Ayer escapé del ponto, rojo como el vino, después de veinte días. Entretanto me han zarandeado sin cesar el oleaje y turbulentas tempestades desde la isla Ogigia, y ahora por fin me ha arrojado aquí algún demón, sin duda para que sufra algún contratiempo; pues no creo que éstos vayan a cesar, sino que todavía los dioses me preparan muchas desventuras.

»Pero tú, sobrerana, ten compasión, pues es a ti a quien primero encuentro después de haber soportado muchas desgracias, que no conozco a ninguno de los hombres que poseen esta tierra y ciudad. Muéstrame la ciudad y dame algo de ropa para cubrirme si al venir trajiste alguna para envoltura de tus vestidos. ¡Que los dioses te concedan cuantas cosas anhelas en tu corazón: un marido, una casa, y te otorguen también una feliz armonía! Seguro que no hay nada más bello y mejor que cuando un hombre y una mujer gobiernan la casa con el mismo parecer; pesar es para el enemigo y alegría para el amigo, y, sobre todo, ellos consiguen buena fama.»

Y le respondió luego Nausícaa, la de blancos brazos:

«Forastero, no pareces hombre plebeyo ni insensato. El mismo Zeus Olímpico reparte la felicidad entre los hombres tanto a nobles como a plebeyos, según quiere a cada uno. Sin duda también a ti te ha concedido esto, y es preciso que lo soportes con firmeza hasta el fin.

»Ahora que has llegado a nuestra ciudad y a nuestra tierra, no te verás privado de vestidos ni de ninguna otra cosa de las que son propias del desdichado suplicante que nos sale al encuentro. Te mostraré la ciudad y te diré los nombres de sus gentes. Los feacios poseen esta ciudad y esta tierra; yo soy la hija del magnánimo Alcínoo, en quien descansa el poder y la fuerza de los feacios.»

Así dijo, y ordenó a las doncellas de lindas trenzas:

«Deteneos, siervas. ¿A dónde huís por ver a este hombre? ¿Acaso creéis que es un enemigo? No existe viviente ni puede nacer hombre que llegue con ánimo hostil al país de los feacios, pues somos muy queridos de los dioses y habitamos lejos en el agitado ponto, los más apartados, y ningún otro mortal tiene trato con nosotros.

»Pero éste ha llegado aquí como un desdichado después de andar errante, y ahora es preciso atenderle. Que todos los huéspedes y mendigos proceden de Zeus, y para ellos una dádiva pequeña es querida. ¡Vamos!, dadle de comer y de beber y lavadlo en el río donde haya un abrigo contra el viento.»

Así dijo; ellas se detuvieron y se animaron unas a otras, hicieron sentar a Odiseo en lugar resguardado, según lo había ordenado Nausícaa, hija del magnánimo Alcínoo, le proporcionaron un manto y una túnica como vestido, le entregaron aceite húmedo en una ampolla de oro y lo apremiaban para que se bañara en las corrientes del río.

Entonces, por fin, dijo el divino Odiseo a las siervas:

«Siervas, deteneos ahí lejos mientras me quito de los hombros la salmuera y me unjo con aceite, pues ya hace tiempo que no hay grasa sobre mi cuerpo; que no me lavaré yo frente a vosotras, pues me avergüenzo de permanecer desnudo entre doncellas de lindas trenzas.»

Así dijo y ellas se alejaron y se lo contaron a la muchacha. Conque el divino Odiseo púsose a lavar su cuerpo en las aguas del río y a quitarse la salmuera que cubría sus anchas espaldas y sus hombros, y limpió de su cabeza la espuma de la mar infatigable. Después que se hubo lavado y ungido con aceite, se vistió las ropas que le proporcionara la no sometida[121] doncella. Entonces le concedió Atenea, la hija de Zeus, aparecer más apuesto y robusto e hizo caer de su cabeza espesa cabellera, semejante a la flor del jacinto. Así como derrama oro sobre plata un diestro orfebre a quien Hefesto y Palas Atenea han enseñado toda clase de artes y termina graciosos trabajos, así Atenea vertió su gracia sobre la cabeza y hombros de Odiseo. Fuese

---

[121] Simplemente «soltera».

entonces a sentar a lo lejos junto a la orilla del mar, resplandeciente de belleza y de gracia, y la muchacha lo contemplaba.

Por fin dijo a las siervas de lindas trenzas:

«Escuchadme, siervas de blancos brazos, mientras os hablo;
no en contra de la voluntad de todos los dioses, los que poseen   240
el Olimpo, tiene trato este hombre con los feacios semejantes a
los dioses. Es verdad que antes me pareció desagradable, pero
ahora es semejante a los dioses, los que poseen el amplio cielo.
¡Ojalá semejante varón fuera llamado esposo mío habitando
aquí y le cumpliera permanecer con nosotros! Vamos, siervas,
dad al huésped comida y bebida.»

Así dijo; ellas la escucharon y al punto realizaron sus deseos:
pusieron comida y bebida junto a Odiseo y verdad es que comía y bebía con voracidad el sufridor, el divino Odiseo, pues
durante largo tiempo estuvo ayuno de comida.   250

De pronto Nausícaa, de blancos brazos, cambió de parecer.
Después de haber plegado sus vestidos los colocó en el hermoso carro, unció las mulas de fuertes cascos y ascendió ella misma. Animó a Odiseo, le llamó por su nombre y le dirigió su
palabra:

«Forastero, levántate ahora para ir a la ciudad y para que yo
te acompañe a casa de mi prudente padre, donde te aseguro
que verás a los más excelentes de todos los feacios. Pero ahora
cuídate de obrar así —ya que no me pareces insensato—:
mientras vayamos por los campos y las labores de los hombres, marcha presto con las sirvientas tras las mulas y el carro   260
y yo seré guía. Pero cuando subamos a la ciudad... a ésta la rodea una elevada muralla; hay un hermoso puerto a ambos lados de la ciudad y es estrecha la entrada, y las curvadas naves
son arrastradas por el camino, pues todos ellos tienen refugios
para sus naves. También tienen en torno al hermoso templo
de Poseidón el ágora construida con piedras gigantescas que
hunden sus raíces en la tierra. Aquí se ocupan los hombres de
los aparejos de sus negras naves, cables y velas, y aquí afilan
sus remos. Pues los feacios no se ocupan de arco y carcaj, sino   270
de mástiles y remos, y de proporcionadas naves con las que recorren orgullosos el canoso mar. De éstos quiero evitar el
amargo comentario, no sea que alguno murmure por detrás,
pues muchos son los soberbios en el pueblo, y quizá alguno, el

más vil, diga al salirnos al encuentro: "¿Quién es este hermoso y apuesto forastero que sigue a Nausícaa?, ¿dónde lo encontró? Quizá llegue a ser su esposo, o quizá es algún navegante al que, errante en su nave, le dio hospitalidad, de los hombres que viven lejos, ya que nadie vive cerca de aquí. O quizá un dios le ha bajado del cielo tras invocarlo y lo va a tener con ella para siempre. Mejor si ha encontrado por ahí un esposo de fuera, pues desdeña a los demás feacios en el pueblo, aunque son muchos y nobles los que la pretenden." Así dirán, y para mí estas palabras serán odiosas. Pero yo también me indignaría con otra que hiciera cosas semejantes contra la voluntad de su padre y de su madre y se uniera con hombres antes que celebre público matrimonio.

»Conque, forastero, haz caso de mi palabra para que consigas pronto de mi padre escolta y regreso.

»Encontrarás un espléndido bosque de Atenea junto al camino, de álamos negros; allí mana una fuente y alrededor hay un prado; allí está el cercado de mi padre y la florida viña, tan cerca de la ciudad que se oye al gritar. Espera un poco allí sentado para que nosotras alcancemos la ciudad y lleguemos a casa de mi padre, y cuando supongas que hemos llegado al palacio, dispone entonces a marchar a la ciudad de los feacios y pregunta por la casa de mi padre, el magnánimo Alcínoo. Es fácilmente reconocible y hasta un niño pequeño te puede conducir, pues no es nada semejante a las casas de los demás feacios: ¡tal es el palacio del héroe Alcínoo! Y una vez que te cobijen la casa y el patio, cruza rápidamente el mégaron para llegar hasta mi madre; ella está sentada en el hogar a la luz del fuego, hilando copos purpúreos —¡una maravilla para verlos!— apoyada en la columna. Y sus esclavas se sientan detrás de ella. Allí también está el trono de mi padre apoyado contra la columna, en el que se sienta a beber su vino como un dios inmortal. Pásalo de largo y arrójate a abrazar con tus manos las rodillas de mi madre, a fin de que consigas pronto el día del regreso, para tu felicidad, aunque seas de lejana tierra. Pues si ella te guarda sentimientos amigos en su corazón, podrás cumplir el deseo de ver a los tuyos, tu bien construida casa y tu tierra patria.»

Hablando así golpeó con su brillante látigo a las mulas y éstas abandonaron veloces las corrientes del río: trotaban muy bien y cruzaban bien las patas. Y ella llevaba las riendas para que pudieran seguirle a pie las sirvientas y Odiseo; así es que manejaba el látigo con tiento. 320

Y se sumergió Helios y al punto llegaron al famoso bosquecillo sagrado de Atenea, donde se sentó el divino Odiseo.

Y se puso a invocar a la hija del gran Zeus:

«Escúchame, hija de Zeus, portador de égida, Atritona, escúchame en este momento, ya que antes no me escuchaste cuando sufrí naufragio, cuando me golpeó el famoso, el que sacude la tierra. Concédeme llegar a la tierra de los feacios como amigo y digno de lástima.»

Así dijo suplicando y le escuchó Palas Atenea.

Pero no le salió al encuentro, pues respetaba al hermano de su padre que mantenía su cólera violenta contra Odiseo, semejante a un dios, hasta que llegara a su patria. 330

CANTO VII

ODISEO EN EL PALACIO DE ALCÍNOO

Y mientras así rogaba el sufridor, el divino Odiseo, el vigor de las mulas llevaba a la doncella a la ciudad. Cuando al fin llegó a la famosa morada de su padre, se detuvo ante las puertas y la rodearon sus hermanos, semejantes a los inmortales, quienes desuncieron las mulas del carro y llevaron adentro las ropas. Ella se dirigió a su habitación y le encendió fuego una anciana de Apira[122], la camarera Eurimedusa, a la que trajeron desde Apira las curvadas naves. Se la habían elegido a Alcínoo como recompensa, porque reinaba 10 sobre todos los feacios y el pueblo lo escuchaba como a un dios. Ella fue quien crió a Nausícaa, la de blancos brazos, en el mégaron; ella le avivaba el fuego y le preparaba la cena[123].

Entonces Odiseo se dispuso a marchar a la ciudad, y Atenea, siempre preocupada por Odiseo, derramó en torno suyo una gran nube, no fuera que alguno de los magnánimos feacios, saliéndole al encuentro, le molestara de palabra y le preguntara quién era. Conque cuando estaba ya a punto de penetrar en la agradable ciudad, le salió al encuentro la diosa Atenea, de ojos brillantes, tomando la apariencia de una niña pe-

---

[122] Nombre mítico que significa «Tierra ilimitada».

[123] Eurimedusa tiene en el palacio de Alcínoo un papel semejante al de Eurínome (sus nombres significan lo mismo) en el de Odiseo (cfr. XXIII.295 y ss.). Son *thalamepóloi*, es decir, se cuidan de las habitaciones privadas del palacio (sea la despensa o los dormitorios). La presentación de Eurimedusa es muy semejante a la de Euriclea (cfr. I.430 y ss.), aunque no se justifica por su insignificante papel en el relato.

queña con un cántaro, y se detuvo delante de él, y le preguntó 20
luego el divino Odiseo:

«Pequeña, ¿querrías llevarme a casa de Alcínoo, el que gobierna entre estos hombres? Pues yo soy forastero y después
de muchas desventuras he llegado aquí desde lejos, de una tierra apartada; por esto no conozco a ninguno de los hombres
que poseen esta ciudad y estas tierras de labor.»

Y le respondió luego Atenea, la diosa de ojos brillantes:

«Yo te mostraré, padre forastero, la casa que me pides, ya
que vive cerca de mi irreprochable padre. Anda, ven en silencio y te mostraré el camino, pero no mires ni preguntes a nin- 30
guno de los hombres, pues no soportan con agrado a los forasteros ni agasajan con gusto al que llega de otra parte. Confia-
dos en sus rápidas naves surcan el gran abismo del mar, pues
así se lo ha encomendado el que sacude la tierra, y sus naves
son tan ligeras como las alas o como el pensamiento.»

Hablando así le condujo rápidamente Palas Atenea y él marchaba tras las huellas de la diosa. Pero no lo vieron los feacios,
famosos por sus naves, mientras marchaba entre ellos por su
ciudad, ya que no lo permitía Atenea, de lindas trenzas, la te- 40
rrible diosa que preocupándose por él en su ánimo le había cubierto con una nube divina.

Odiseo iba contemplando con admiración los puertos y las
proporcionadas naves, las ágoras de ellos, de los héroes y las
grandes murallas elevadas, ajustadas con piedras, maravilla de
ver. Y cuando al fin llegó a la famosa morada del rey, Atenea,
de ojos brillantes, comenzó a hablar:

«Ese es, padre forastero, el palacio que me pedías que te
mostrara; encontrarás a los reyes, vástagos de Zeus, celebrando un banquete. Tú pasa adentro y no te turbes en tu ánimo, 50
pues un hombre con arrojo resulta ser el mejor en toda acción,
aunque llegue de otra tierra. Primero encontrarás a la reina en
el mégaron; su nombre es Arete y desciende de los mismos padres que engendraron a Alcínoo. A Nausítoo lo engendraron
primero Poseidón, el que sacude la tierra, y Peribea, la más excelente de las mujeres en su porte, hija menor del magnánimo
Eurimedonte, que entonces gobernaba sobre los soberbios Gigantes —éste hizo perecer a su arrogante pueblo, pereciendo 60
también él—; con ella se unió Poseidón y engendró a su hijo,

el magnánimo Nausítoo, que reinó entre los feacios. Nausítoo fue el padre de Rexenor y Alcínoo. A aquél lo alcanzó Apolo[124], el del arco de plata, recién casado y sin hijos varones y en la casa dejó a una niña sola, a Arete, a la que Alcínoo hizo su esposa y honró como jamás ninguna otra ha sido honrada de cuantas mujeres gobiernan una casa sometidas a su esposo. Así ella ha sido honrada en su corazón y lo sigue siendo por sus hijos y el mismo Alcínoo y por su pueblo que la contempla   70
como a una diosa, y la saludan con agradables palabras cuando pasea por la ciudad, que no carece tampoco ella de buen juicio y resuelve los litigios, incluso a los hombres por los que siente amistad. Si ella te recibe con sentimientos amigos puedes tener la esperanza de ver a los tuyos, regresar a tu casa de alto techo y a tu tierra patria.»

Cuando hubo hablado así marchó Atenea, de ojos brillantes, por el estéril ponto y abandonó la agradable Esqueria. Llegó así a Maratón y a Atenas, de anchas calles, y penetró en la sóli-   80
da morada de Erecteo.

Entretanto, Odiseo caminaba hacia la famosa morada de Alcínoo, y su corazón removía diversos pensamientos cuando se detuvo antes de alcanzar el broncíneo umbral. Pues hay un resplandor como de sol o de luna en el elevado palacio del magnánimo Alcínoo[125]; a ambos lados se extienden muros de bronce desde el umbral hasta el fondo y en su torno un azulado friso; puertas de oro cierran por dentro la sólida estancia; las jambas sobre el umbral son de plata y de plata el dintel, y el tirador, de oro. A uno y otro lado de la puerta había perros de   90
oro y plata que había esculpido Hefesto con la habilidad de su mente para custodiar la morada del magnánimo Alcínoo —perros que son inmortales y no envejecen nunca. A lo largo de la pared y a ambos lados, desde el umbral hasta el fondo, había tronos cubiertos por ropajes hábilmente tejidos, obra de mujeres. En ellos se sentaban los señores feacios mientras bebían y comían; y los ocupaban constantemente. Había también

---

[124] Cfr. nota 67.
[125] Este verso aparece también en IV.45, referido al palacio de Menelao. Pero allí se interrumpe, mientras que aquí es el de una descripción muy detallada del palacio de Alcínoo.

[143]

unos jovenes de oro en pie sobre pedestales perfectamente 100
construidos, portando en sus manos antorchas encendidas, los
cuales alumbraban los banquetes nocturnos del palacio. Tiene
cincuenta esclavas en su mansión: unas muelen el dorado fruto, otras tejen telas y sentadas hacen funcionar los husos, semejantes a las hojas de un esbelto álamo negro, y del lino tejido gotea el húmedo aceite. Tanto como los feacios son más
expertos que los demás hombres en gobernar su rápida nave
sobre el ponto, así son sus mujeres en el telar. Pues Atenea les
ha concedido en grado sumo el saber realizar brillantes labores 110
y buena cabeza.

Fuera del patio, cerca de las puertas, hay un gran huerto de
cuatro yugadas y alrededor se extiende un cerco a ambos lados. Allí han nacido y florecen árboles: perales y granados,
manzanos de espléndidos frutos, dulces higueras y verdes olivos; de ellos no se pierde el fruto ni falta nunca en invierno ni
en verano: son perennes. Siempre que sopla Céfiro, unos nacen y otros maduran. La pera envejece sobre la pera, la manzana sobre la manzana, la uva sobre la uva y también el higo so- 120
bre el higo. Allí tiene plantada una viña muy fructífera, en la
que unas uvas se secan al sol en lugar abrigado, otras las ven-
dimian y otras las pisan: delante están las vides que dejan salir
la flor y otras hay también que apenas negrean. Allí también,
en el fondo del huerto, crecen liños de verduras de todas clases
siempre lozanas. También hay allí dos fuentes, la una que corre por todo el huerto, la otra que va de una parte a otra bajo
el umbral del patio hasta la elevada morada a donde van por 130
agua los ciudadanos. Tales eran las brillantes dádivas de los
dioses en la mansión de Alcínoo.

Allí estaba el divino Odiseo, el sufridor, y lo contemplaba
con admiración. Conque una vez que hubo contemplado todo
boquiabierto cruzó el umbral con rapidez para entrar en la
casa. Y encontró a los jefes y señores de los feacios que hacían
libación con sus copas al vigilante Argifonte, a quien solían
ofrecer libación en último lugar, cuando ya sentían necesidad
del lecho. Así que el sufridor, el divino Odiseo, echó a andar
por la casa envuelto en la espesa niebla que le había derramado 140
Atenea, hasta que llegó ante Arete y el rey Alcínoo.

Abrazó Odiseo las rodillas de Arete y entonces, por fin, se

disipó la divina nube. Quedaron todos en silencio al ver a un hombre en el palacio y se llenaron de asombro al contemplarle. Y Odiseo suplicaba de esta guisa:

«Arete, hija de Rexenor, semejante a un inmortal, me he llegado a tu esposo, a tus rodillas y ante éstos tus invitados, después de sufrir muchas desventuras. ¡Ojalá los dioses concedan a éstos vivir en la abundancia; que cada uno pueda legar a sus hijos los bienes de su hacienda y las prerrogativas que les ha concedido el pueblo. En cuanto a mí, proporcionadme escolta para llegar rápidamente a mi patria. Pues ya hace tiempo que padezco pesares lejos de los míos.» 150

Así diciendo se sentó entre las cenizas junto al fuego del hogar. Todos ellos permanecían inmóviles en silencio. Al fin tomó la palabra un anciano héroe, Equeneo, que era el más anciano entre los feacios y sobresalía por su palabra, pues era conocedor de muchas y antiguas cosas. Éste les habló y dijo con sentimientos de amistad:

«Alcínoo, no me parece lo mejor, ni está bien, que el huésped permanezca sentado en el suelo entre las cenizas del hogar. Éstos permanecen callados esperando únicamente tu palabra. Anda, haz que se levante y siéntalo en un trono de clavos de plata. Ordena también a los heraldos que mezclen vino para que hagamos libaciones a Zeus, el que goza con el rayo, el que asiste a los venerables suplicantes. En fin, que el ama de llaves proporcione al forastero alguna vianda de las que hay dentro.» 160

Cuando hubo escuchado esto, la sagrada fuerza de Alcínoo[126] asiendo de la mano a Odiseo, prudente y hábil en astucias, lo hizo levantar del hogar y lo asentó en su brillante trono, después de haber levantado a su hijo, al valeroso Laodamante, que solía sentarse a su lado y al que sobre todos quería. Una sirvienta trajo aguamanos en hermoso jarro de oro y la vertió sobre una jofaina de plata para que se lavara. A su lado extendió una pulimentada mesa. La venerable ama de llaves le proporcionó pan y le dejó allí toda clase de manjares, favoreciéndole gustosa entre los presentes. En tanto que comía y bebía el sufridor, divino Odiseo, la fuerza de Alcínoo dijo a un heraldo: 170

---

[126] Cfr. nota 49.

«Pontónoo, mezcla vino en la crátera y repártelo a todos en la casa para que ofrezcamos libaciones a Zeus, el que goza con el rayo, el que asiste siempre a los venerables suplicantes.» 180

Así dijo; Pontónoo mezcló el dulce vino y lo repartió entre todos, haciendo una primera ofrenda, por orden, en las copas. Una vez que hicieron las libaciones y bebieron cuanto quiso su ánimo, habló entre ellos Alcínoo y dijo:

«Escuchadme, jefes y señores de los feacios, para que os diga lo que mi corazón me ordena en el pecho. Dad ahora fin al banquete y marchad a acostaros a vuestra casa. Y a la aurora, después de convocar al mayor número de ancianos, ofreceremos hospitalidad al forastero, haremos hermosos sacrificios 190 a los dioses y después trataremos de su escolta para que el forastero alcance su tierra patria sin fatiga ni esfuerzo con nuestra escolta —de la que recibirá contento— por muy lejana que sea, y para que no sufra ningún daño antes de desembarcar en su tierra. Una vez allí sufrirá cuantas desventuras le tejieron con el hilo en su nacimiento, cuando lo parió su madre, la Aisa y las graves Hilanderas[127]. Pero si fuera uno de los inmortales que ha venido desde el cielo, alguna otra cosa nos preparan los 200 dioses, pues hasta ahora siempre se nos han mostrado a las claras, cuando les ofrecemos magníficas hecatombes y participan con nosotros del banquete sentados allí donde nos sentamos nosotros. Y si algún caminante solitario se topa con ellos, no se le ocultan, y es que somos semejantes a ellos tanto como los Cíclopes y la salvaje raza de los Gigantes.»

Y le respondió y dijo el muy astuto Odiseo:

«Alcínoo, deja de preocuparte por esto, que yo en verdad en nada me asemejo a los inmortales que poseen el ancho cielo, ni 210 en continente ni en porte, sino a los mortales hombres; quien vosotros sepáis que ha soportado más desventuras entre los hombres mortales, a éste podría yo igualarme en pesares. Y todavía podría contar desgracias mucho mayores, todas

---

[127] Aisa es, junto con Moira, una personificación del Destino. Aquí va unida a las *Klothes*, las Hilanderas, a las que Hesiodo (cfr. *Teogonía*, 217) llama Moiras en general sin especificar su número. Posteriormente, como demuestran los versos interpolados 218-9, se convirtieron en tres, cuyos nombres eran Kloto («la que hila»), Láquesis («la que echa suertes») y Atropo («la inflexible»).

cuantas soporté por la voluntad de los dioses. Pero dejadme cenar, por más angustiado que yo esté, pues no hay cosa más inoportuna que el maldito estómago que nos incita por fuerza a acordarnos de él, y aun al que está muy afligido y con un gran pesar en las mientes, como yo ahora tengo el mío, lo fuerza a comer y beber. También a mí me hace olvidar todos los males que he padecido; y me ordena llenarlo.

»Vosotros, en cuanto apunte la aurora, apresuraos a dejarme a mí, desgraciado, en mi tierra patria, a pesar de lo que he sufrido. Que me abandone la vida una vez que haya visto mi hacienda, mis siervos y mi gran morada de elevado techo.»

Así dijo; todos aprobaron sus palabras y aconsejaban dar escolta al forastero, ya que había hablado como le correspondía.

Una vez que hicieron las libaciones y bebieron cuanto su ánimo quiso, cada uno marchó a su casa para acostarse. Así que quedó sólo en el mégaron el divino Odiseo y a su lado se sentaron Arete y Alcínoo, semejante a un dios. Las siervas se llevaron los útiles del banquete.

Y Arete, de blancos brazos, comenzó a hablar, pues, al verlos, reconoció el manto, la túnica y los hermosos ropajes que ella misma había tejido con sus siervas. Y le habló y le dijo aladas palabras:

«Huésped, seré yo la primera en preguntarte: ¿quién eres?, ¿de dónde vienes?, ¿quién te dio esos vestidos?, ¿no dices que has llegado aquí después de andar errante por el ponto?»

Y le respondió y dijo el muy astuto Odiseo:

«Es doloroso, reina, que enumere uno a uno mis padecimientos[128], que los dioses celestes me han otorgado muchos. Pero con todo te contestaré a lo que me preguntas e inquieres. Lejos, en el mar, está la isla de Ogigia, donde vive la hija de Atlante, la engañosa Calipso de lindas trenzas, terrible diosa; ninguno de los dioses ni de los hombres mortales tienen trato con ella. Sólo a mí, desventurado, me llevó como huésped un demón después que Zeus, empujando mi rápida nave, la incendió con un brillante rayo en medio del ponto rojo como el

220

230

240

250

---

[128]. Este es el célebre verso que imita Virgilio en *Eneida* II.3: *infandum regina iubes renovare dolorem.*

vino. Todos mis demás valientes compañeros perecieron, pero yo, abrazado a la quilla de mi curvada nave, aguanté durante nueve días; y al décimo, en negra noche, los dioses me echaron a la isla Ogigia, donde habita Calipso de lindas trenzas, la terrible diosa que acogiéndome gentilmente me alimentaba y no dejaba de decir que me haría inmortal y libre de vejez para siempre; pero no logró convencer a mi corazón dentro del pecho. Allí permanecí, no obstante, siete años regando sin cesar con mis lágrimas las inmortales ropas que me había dado Calipso. Pero cuando por fin cumplió su curso el año octavo, me apremió e incitó a que partiera ya sea por mensaje de Zeus o quizá porque ella misma cambió de opinión. Despidióme en una bien trabada balsa y me proporcionó abundante pan y dulce vino, me vistió inmortales ropas y me envió un viento próspero y cálido.

Diecisiete días navegué por el ponto, hasta que el decimoctavo aparecieron las sombrías montañas de vuestras tierras. Conque se me alegró el corazón, ¡desdichado de mí!, pues aún había de verme envuelto en la incesante aflicción que me proporcionó Poseidón, el que sacude la tierra, quien impulsando los vientos me cerró el camino, sacudió el mar infinito y el oleaje no permitía que yo, mientras gemía incesamente, avanzara en mi balsa; después la destruyó la tempestad. Fue entonces cuando surqué nadando el abismo hasta que el viento y el agua me acercaron a vuestra tierra; y cuando trataba de alcanzar la orilla, habríame arrojado violentamente el oleaje contra las grandes rocas, en lugar funesto; pero retrocedí de nuevo nadando, hasta que llegué al río, allí donde me pareció el mejor lugar, limpio de piedras y al abrigo del viento. Me dejé caer allí para recobrar el aliento y se me echó encima la noche divina. Alejéme del río nacido de Zeus y entre los matorrales acomodé mi lecho amontonando alrededor muchas hojas; y un dios me vertió profundo sueño. Allí, entre las hojas, dormí con el corazón afligido toda la noche, la aurora y hasta el mediodía. Se ponía el Sol cuando me abandonó el dulce sueño. Vi jugando en la orilla a las siervas de tu hija; y ella era semejante a las diosas. Le supliqué y no estuvo ayuna de buen juicio, como no se podría esperar que obrara una joven que se encuentra con alguien. Pues con frecuencia los jóvenes son sandios. Me entregó pan suficiente y oscuro vino, me lavó[129] en el río y me proporcionó esta ropa. Aun estando apesadumbrado te he contado toda la verdad.»

Y le respondió Alcínoo y dijo:

«Huésped, en verdad mi hija no tomó un acuerdo sensato al no traerte a nuestra casa con sus siervas. Y sin embargo fue   300
ella la primera a quien dirigiste tus súplicas.»

Y le respondió y dijo el muy astuto Odiseo:

«¡Héroe! No reprendas por esto a tu irreprochable hija; ella me aconsejó seguirla con sus siervas, pero yo no quise por vergüenza, y temiendo que al verme pudieras disgustarte. Que la raza de los hombres sobre la tierra es suspicaz.»

Y le respondió Alcínoo y dijo:

«¡Huésped! El corazón que alberga mi pecho no es tal como para irritarse sin motivo, pero todo es mejor si es ajustado.   310
¡Zeus padre, Atenea y Apolo, ojalá que siendo como eres y pensando las mismas cosas que yo pienso, tomases a mi hija por esposa y permaneciendo aquí pudiese llamarte mi yerno!; que yo te daría casa y hacienda si permanecieras aquí de buen grado. Pero ninguno de los feacios te retendrá contra tu voluntad, no sea que esto no fuera grato a Zeus. Yo te anuncio, para que lo sepas bien, tu viaje para mañana. Mientras tú descansas sometido por el sueño, ellos remarán por el mar encalmado hasta que llegues a tu patria y a tu casa, o a donde quiera   320
que te sea grato, por distante que esté (aunque más lejos que Eubea, la más lejana según dicen los que la vieron de nuestros soldados cuando llevaron allí al rubio Radamanto para que visitara a Ticio[130], hijo de la Tierra. Allí llegaron y, sin cansancio, en un solo día, llevaron a cabo el viaje y regresaron a casa). Tú mismo podrás observar qué excelentes son mis navíos y mis jóvenes en golpear el mar con el remo.»

Así dijo y se alegró el divino Odiseo, el sufridor, y suplicando dijo su palabra y lo llamó por su nombre: 330

«Padre Zeus, ¡ojalá cumpla Alcínoo cuanto ha prometido!

---

[129] En realidad, Odiseo no permitió *a las siervas* de Nausícaa que lo lavaran. Lo hizo solo. Cfr. 215 y ss.

[130] Fuera de este pasaje, en ninguna parte se relaciona a Radamante con Ticio. Sobre el castigo de éste en el Hades, cfr. XI.576 y ss.

Que su fama jamás se extinga sobre la nutricia tierra y que yo llegue a mi tierra patria.»

Mientras ellos cambiaban estas palabras, Arete, de blancos brazos, ordenó a las mujeres colocar lechos bajo el pórtico y disponer las más bellas mantas de púrpura y extender encima las colchas y sobre ellas ropas de lana para cubrirse.

Así que salieron las siervas de la sala con hachas ardiendo, y una vez que terminaron de hacer diligentemente la cama, diri- 340 giéronse a Odiseo y lo invitaron con estas palabras:

«Huésped, levántate y ven a dormir, tienes hecha la cama.»

Así hablaron y a él le plugo marchar a acostarse. Así que allí durmió debajo del sonoro pórtico el sufridor, el divino Odiseo, en lecho taladrado. Luego se acostó Alcínoo en el interior de la alta morada; le había dispuesto su esposa y señora el lecho y la cama.

Canto VIII

ODISEO AGASAJADO POR LOS FEACIOS

Y cuando se mostró Eos, la que nace de la mañana, la de
dedos de rosa, se levantó del lecho la sagrada fuerza de
Alcínoo y se levantó Odiseo del linaje de Zeus, el destructor de ciudades. La sagrada fuerza de Alcínoo los conducía
al ágora que los feacios tenían construida cerca de las naves.
Y cuando llegaron se sentaron en piedras pulimentadas, cerca
unos de otros.

Y recorría la ciudad Palas Atenea, que tomó el aspecto del
heraldo del prudente Alcínoo, preparando el regreso a su patria para el valeroso Odiseo. La diosa se colocaba cerca de   10
cada hombre y le decía su palabra:

«¡Vamos, caudillos y señores de los feacios! Id al ágora para
que os informéis sobre el forastero que ha llegado reciente-
mente a casa del prudente Alcínoo después de recorrer el ponto, semejante en su cuerpo a los inmortales.»

Así diciendo movía la fuerza y el ánimo de cada uno. Bien
pronto el ágora y los asientos se llenaron de hombres que se
iban congregando y muchos se admiraron al ver al prudente
hijo de Laertes; que Atenea derramaba una gracia divina por
su cabeza y hombros e hizo que pareciese más alto y más grue-   20
so: así sería grato a todos los feacios y temible y venerable, y
llevaría a término muchas pruebas, las que los feacios iban a
poner a Odiseo. Cuando se habían reunido y estaban ya congregados, habló entre ellos Alcínoo y dijo:

«Oídme, caudillos y señores de los feacios, para que os diga
lo que mi ánimo me ordena dentro del pecho. Este forastero

—y no sé quién es— ha llegado errante a mi palacio bien de los hombres de Oriente o de los de Occidente; nos pide una escolta y suplica que le sea asegurada. Apresuremos nosotros su escolta como otras veces, que nadie que llega a mi casa está suspirando mucho tiempo por ella.

»Vamos, echemos al mar divino una negra nave que navegue por primera vez, y que sean escogidos entre el pueblo cincuenta y dos jóvenes, cuantos son siempre los mejores. Atad bien los remos a los bancos y salid. Preparad a continuación un convite al volver a mi palacio, que a todos se lo ofreceré en abundancia. Esto es lo que ordeno a los jóvenes. Y los demás, los reyes que lleváis cetro, venid a mi hermosa mansión para que honremos en el palacio al forastero. Que nadie se niegue. Y llamad al divino aedo Demódoco, a quien la divinidad ha otorgado el canto para deleitar siempre que su ánimo lo empuja a cantar.»

Así habló y los condujo y ellos le siguieron, los reyes que llevan cetro. El heraldo fue a llamar al divino aedo y los cincuenta y dos jóvenes se dirigieron, como les había ordenado, a la ribera del mar estéril. Cuando llegaron a la negra nave y al mar echaron la nave al abismo del mar y pusieron el mástil y las velas y ataron los remos con correas, todo según correspondía. Extendieron hacia arriba las blancas velas, anclaron la nave en aguas profundas y se pusieron en camino para ir a la gran casa del prudente Alcínoo. Y los pórticos, el recinto de los patios y las habitaciones se llenaron de hombres que se congregaban, pues eran muchos, jóvenes y ancianos. Para ellos sacrificó Alcínoo doce ovejas y ocho cerdos albidentes y dos bueyes de rotátiles patas. Los desollaron y prepararon e hicieron un agradable banquete.

Y se acercó el heraldo con el deseable aedo a quien Musa amó mucho y le había dado lo bueno y lo malo: le privó de los ojos, pero le concedió el dulce canto. Pontónoo le puso un sillón de clavos de plata en medio de los comensales, apoyándolo a una elevada columna, y el heraldo le colgó de un clavo la sonora cítara sobre su cabeza y le mostró cómo tomarla con las manos. También le puso al lado un canastillo y una linda mesa y una copa de vino para beber siempre que su ánimo le impulsara.

Y ellos echaron mano de las viandas que tenían delante. Y cuando hubieron arrojado el deseo de comida y bebida, Musa empujó al aedo a que cantara la gloria de los guerreros con un canto cuya fama llegaba entonces al ancho cielo: la disputa de Odiseo y del Pelida Aquiles, cómo en cierta ocasión discutieron en el suntuoso banquete de los dioses con horribles palabras. Y el soberano de hombres, Agamenón, se alegraba en su ánimo de que riñeran los mejores de los aqueos. Así se lo había dicho con su oráculo Febo Apolo en la divina Pitó cuan- 80
do sobrepasó el umbral de piedra para ir a consultarle; en aquel momento comenzó a desarrollarse el principio de la cala-midad para teucros y dánaos por los designios del gran Zeus. Esto cantaba el muy ilustre aedo. Entonces Odiseo tomó con sus pesadas manos su grande, purpúreo manto, se lo echó por encima de la cabeza y cubrió su hermoso rostro; le daba ver-güenza dejar caer lágrimas bajo sus párpados delante de los feacios. Siempre que el divino aedo dejaba de cantar se enjuga- 90
ba las lágrimas y retiraba el manto de su cabeza y, tomando una copa doble, hacía libaciones a los dioses.

Pero cuando comenzaba otra vez —lo impulsaban a cantar los más nobles de los feacios porque gozaban con sus ver-sos—, Odiseo se cubría nuevamente la cabeza y lloraba. A los demás les pasó inadvertido que derramaba lágrimas. Sólo Alcí-noo lo advirtió y observó, pues estaba sentado al lado y le oía gemir gravemente. Entonces dijo el soberano a los feacios amantes del remo:

«¡Oídme, caudillos y señores de los feacios! Ya hemos goza-do del bien distribuido banquete y de la cítara que es compañe-ra del festín espléndido; salgamos y probemos toda clase de 100
juegos. Así también el huésped contará a los suyos al volver a casa cuánto superamos a los demás en el pugilato, en la lucha, en el salto y en la carrera.»

Así habló y los condujo y ellos les siguieron. El heraldo col-gó del clavo la sonora cítara y tomó de la mano a Demódoco; lo sacó del mégaron y lo conducía por el mismo camino que llevaban los mejores de los feacios para admirar los juegos. Se pusieron en camino para ir al ágora y los seguía una gran mul-titud, miles. Y se pusieron en pie muchos y vigorosos jóvenes, se levantó Acroneo, y Ocíalo, y Elatreo, y Nauteo, y Primneo, 110

[153]

y Anquíalo, y Eretmeo, y Ponteo, y Poreo, y Toón, y Anabesineo, y Anfíalo, hijo de Polineo Tectónida[131]. Se levantó también Euríalo, semejante a Ares, funesto para los mortales, el que más sobresalía en cuerpo y hermosura de todos los feacios después del irreprochable Laodamante. También se pusieron en pie tres hijos del egregio Alcínoo: Laodamante, Halio y Clitoneo, parecido a un dios. Éstos hicieron la primera prueba con los pies. Desde la línea de salida se les extendía la pista y volaban velozmente por la llanura levantando polvo. Entre ellos fue con mucho el mejor en el correr el irreprochable Clitoneo; cuanto en un campo noval es el alcance de dos mulas[132], tanto se les adelantó llegando a la gente mientras los otros se quedaron atrás. Luego hicieron la prueba de la fatigosa lucha y en ésta venció Euríalo a todos los mejores. Y en el salto fue Anfíalo el mejor, y en el disco fue Elatreo el mejor de todos con mucho, y en el pugilato Laodamante, el noble hijo de Alcínoo. Y cuando todos hubieron deleitado su ánimo con los juegos, entre ellos habló Laodamante, el hijo de Alcínoo:

120

130

«Aquí, amigos, preguntemos al huésped si conoce y ha aprendido algún juego. Que no es vulgar en su natural: en sus músculos y piernas, en sus dos brazos, en su robusto cuello y en su gran vigor. Y no carece de vigor juvenil, sino que está quebrantado por numerosos males; que no creo yo que haya cosa peor que el mar para abatir a un hombre por fuerte que sea.»

Y Euríalo le contestó y dijo:

140

«Has hablado como te corresponde. Ve tú mismo a desafiarlo y manifiéstale tu palabra.»

Cuando le oyó se adelantó el noble hijo de Alcínoo, se puso en medio y dijo a Odiseo:

«Ven aquí, padre huésped, y prueba tú también los juegos si es que has aprendido alguno. Es natural que los conozcas, pues

---

[131] Todos los nombres propios de los feacios (excepto Alcínoo y Arete) hacen alusión al mar (Ponteo, Halio y terminados en -alo), a las naves (Nausícaa y terminados en -neo) o a una parte de éstas (Primneo); a su velocidad (Tóon, Ocíalo), a su capacidad de navegar (Nauteo) o de construir naves (Tectónida).

[132] Se refiere a la extensión que dos mulas pueden arar en un día, comparada *implícitamente* con la que aran dos bueyes. Cfr. *Ilíada* X.351, donde la comparación es más explícita y de donde esta frase ha sido tomada y abreviada.

no hay gloria mayor para el hombre mientras vive que lo que hace con sus pies o con sus manos. Vamos, pues, haz la prueba y arroja de tu ánimo las penas, pues tu viaje no se diferirá por más tiempo; ya la nave te ha sido botada y tienes preparados unos acompañantes.»

Y le respondió y dijo el muy astuto Odiseo:

«¡Laodamante! ¿Por qué me ordenáis tal cosa por burlaros de mí? Las penas ocupan mi interior más que los juegos. Yo he sufrido antes mucho y mucho he soportado. Y ahora estoy sentado en vuestra asamblea necesitando el regreso, suplicando al rey y a todo el pueblo.»

Entonces, Euríalo le contestó y le echó en cara:

«No, huésped, no te asemejas a un hombre entendido en juegos, cuantos hay en abundancia entre los hombres, sino al que está siempre en una nave de muchos bancos, a un comandante de marinos mercantes que cuida de la carga y vigila las mercancías y las ganancias debidas al pillaje. No tienes traza de atleta.»

Y lo miró torvamente y le contestó el muy astuto Odiseo:

«¡Huésped! No has hablado bien y me pareces un insensato. Los dioses no han repartido de igual modo a todos sus amables dones de hermosura, inteligencia y elocuencia. Un hombre es inferior por su aspecto, pero la divinidad lo corona con la hermosura de la palabra y todos miran hacia él complacidos. Les habla con firmeza y con suavidad respetuosa y sobresale entre los congregados, y lo contemplan como a un dios cuando anda por la ciudad.

»Otro, por el contrario, se parece a los inmortales en su porte, pero no lo corona la gracia cuando habla.

»Así tu aspecto es distinguido y ni un dios te habría formado de otra guisa, mas de inteligencia eres necio. Me has movido el ánimo dentro del pecho al hablar inconvenientemente. No soy desconocedor de los juegos como tú aseguras, antes bien, creo que estaba entre los primeros mientras confiaba en mi juventud y mis brazos. Pero ahora estoy poseído por la adversidad y los dolores, pues he soportado mucho guerreando con los hombres y atravesando las dolorosas olas. Pero aun así, aunque haya padecido muchos males, probaré en los juegos: tu palabra ha mordido mi corazón y me has provocado al hablar.»

Dijo, y con su mismo vestido se levantó, tomó un disco mayor y más ancho y no poco más pesado que con el que solían competir entre sí los feacios. Le dio vueltas, lo lanzó de su pesada mano y la piedra resonó. Echáronse a tierra los feacios 190 de largos remos, hombres ilustres por sus naves, por el ímpetu de la piedra, y ésta sobrevoló todas las señales al salir velozmente de su mano. Atenea le puso la señal tomando la forma de un hombre, le dijo su palabra y lo llamó por su nombre:

«Incluso un ciego, forastero, distinguiría a tientas la señal, pues no está mezclada entre la multitud sino mucho más adelante; confía en esta prueba; ninguno de los feacios la alcanzará ni sobrepasará.»

Así habló, y se alegró el sufridor, el divino Odiseo gozoso porque había visto en la competición un compañero a su fa- 200 vor. Y entonces habló más suavemente a los feacios:

«Alcanzad esta señal, jóvenes; en breve lanzaré, creo yo, otra piedra tan lejos o aún más. Y aquél entre los demás feacios, salvo Laodamante, a quien su corazón y su ánimo le impulse, que venga acá, que haga la prueba —puesto que me habéis irritado en exceso— en el pugilato o en la lucha o en la carrera; a nada me niego. Pues Laodamante es mi huésped: ¿Quién lucharía con el que lo honra como huésped? Es hombre loco y de poco precio el que propone rivalizar en los juegos a quien le da hospitalidad en tierra extranjera, pues se cierra a 210 sí mismo la puerta. Pero de los demás no rechazo a ninguno ni lo desprecio, sino que quiero verlo y ejecutar las pruebas frente a él. Que no soy malo en todas las competiciones cuantas hay entre los hombres. Sé muy bien tender el arco bien pulimentado; sería el primero en tocar a un hombre enviando mi dardo entre una multitud de enemigos aunque lo rodearan muchos compañeros y lanzaran flechas contra los hombres. Sólo Filoctetes me superaba en el arco en el pueblo de los troyanos cuando disparábamos los aqueos[133]. De los demás os aseguro que 220 yo soy el mejor con mucho, de cuantos mortales hay sobre la

---

[133] Es la segunda vez que se alude a la destreza de Odiseo con el arco (la primera en I.255 y ss.). En la *Ilíada*, Odiseo nunca maneja el arco, por lo que su comparación con Filoctetes, etc., resulta extraña. Es una de las razones que llevan a Page, *Homeric...*, a afirmar que el autor de la *Odisea* no conocía la *Ilíada*.

tierra que comen pan. Aunque no pretendo rivalizar con hombres antepasados como Heracles[134] y Eurito Ecaliense[135], los que incluso con los inmortales rivalizaban en el arco. Por eso murió el gran Eurito y no llegó a la vejez en su palacio, pues Apolo lo mató irritado porque le había desafiado a tirar con el arco.

»También lanzo la jabalina a donde nadie llegaría con una flecha. Sólo temo a la carrera, no sea que uno de los feacios me sobrepase; que fui excesivamente quebrantado en medio del abundante oleaje, puesto que no había siempre provisiones en la nave y por esto mis miembros están flojos.»

Así habló, y todos enmudecieron en silencio. Sólo Alcínoo contestó y dijo:

«Huésped, puesto que esto que dices entre nosotros no es desagradable, sino que quieres mostrar la valía que te acompaña, irritado porque este hombre se ha acercado a injuriarte en el certamen —pues no pondría en duda tu valía cualquier mortal que supiera en su interior decir cosas apropiadas—. ...Pero, vamos, atiende a mi palabra para que a tu vez se lo comuniques a cualquiera de los héroes, cuando comas en tu palacio junto a tu esposa y tus hijos, acordándote de nuestra valía: qué obras nos concede Zeus también a nosotros continuamente ya desde nuestros antepasados. No somos irreprochables púgiles ni luchadores, pero corremos velozmente con los pies y somos los mejores en la navegación; continuamente tenemos agradables banquetes y cítara y bailes y vestidos mudables y baños calientes y camas.

»Conque, vamos, bailarines de los feacios, cuantos sois los mejores, danzad; así podrá también decir el huésped a los suyos cuando regrese a casa cuánto superamos a los demás en

230

240

250

---

[134] En Homero, Heracles es un héroe importante, pero está en el mismo plano que los demás. Es mortal (cfr. también *Ilíada*, XVIII.117-9) y, por tanto, se encuentra en el Hades (cfr. XI.605). Sin embargo, en este pasaje se añade que goza de los banquetes de los inmortales y que está casado con Hebe, lo que indica, a menos que se trate de una interpolación, que ya había comenzado el proceso de divinización de Heracles. Cfr. W. K. C. Guthrie, *The Greeks and their Gods*, Londres, 1950, págs. 235 y ss.

[135] Este Eurito es el padre de Ifito, que regaló a Odiseo el arco con el que mató a los pretendientes, cfr. XXI.14 y ss.

la náutica y en la carrera y en el baile y en el canto. Que alguien vaya a llevar a Demódoco la sonora cítara que yace en algún lugar de nuestro palacio.»

Así habló Alcínoo semejante a un dios, y se levantó un heraldo para llevar la curvada cítara de la habitación del rey. También se levantaron árbitros elegidos, nueve en total —los que organizaban bien cada cosa en los concursos—, allanaron el piso y ensancharon la hermosa pista. Se acercó el heraldo 260 trayendo la sonora cítara a Demódoco y éste enseguida salió al centro. A su alrededor se colocaron unos jóvenes adolescentes conocedores de la danza y batían la divina pista con los pies. Odiseo contemplaba el brillo de sus pies y quedó admirado en su ánimo.

Y Demódoco, acompañándose de la cítara, rompió a cantar bellamente sobre los amores de Ares y de la de linda corona, Afrodita: cómo se unieron por primera vez a ocultas en el palacio de Hefesto. Ares le hizo muchos regalos y deshonró el lecho y la cama de Hefesto, el soberano. Entonces se lo fue a co- 270 municar Helios, que los había visto unirse en amor. Cuando oyó Hefesto la triste noticia, se puso en camino hacia su fragua meditando males en su interior; colocó sobre el tajo el enorme yunque y se puso a forjar unos hilos irrompibles, indisolubles, para que se quedaran allí firmemente.

Y cuando había construido su trampa irritado contra Ares, se puso en camino hacia su dormitorio, donde tenía la cama, y extendió los hilos en círculo por todas partes en torno a las patas de la cama; muchos estaban tendidos desde arriba, desde el techo, como suaves hilos de araña, hilos que no podría ver na- 280 die, ni siquiera los dioses felices, pues estaban fabricados con mucho engaño. Y cuando toda su trampa estuvo extendida alrededor de la cama, simuló marcharse a Lemnos, bien edificada ciudad, la que le era más querida de todas las tierras.

Ares, el que usa riendas de oro, no tuvo un espionaje ciego, pues vio marcharse lejos a Hefesto, al ilustre herrero, y se puso en camino hacia el palacio del muy ilustre Hefesto deseando el amor de la diosa de linda corona, de la de Citera. Estaba ella sentada, recién venida de junto a su padre, el poderoso hijo de 290 Cronos. Y él entró en el palacio y la tomó de la mano y la llamó por su nombre:

«Ven acá, querida, vayamos al lecho y acostémonos, pues Hefesto ya no está entre nosotros, sino que se ha marchado a Lemnos, junto a los sintias, de salvaje lengua.»

Así habló, y a ella le pareció deseable acostarse. Y los dos marcharon a la cama y se acostaron. A su alrededor se extendían los hilos fabricados del prudente Hefesto y no les era posible mover los miembros ni levantarse. Entonces se dieron cuenta que no había escape posible. Y llegó a su lado el muy ilustre cojo de ambos pies, pues había vuelto antes de llegar a tierra de Lemnos; Helios mantenía la vigilancia y le dio la noticia y se puso en camino hacia su palacio, acongojado su corazón. Se detuvo en el pórtico y una rabia salvaje se apoderó de él, y gritó estrepitosamente haciéndose oír de todos los dioses:

«Padre Zeus y los demás dioses felices que vivís siempre, venid aquí para que veáis un acto ridículo y vergonzoso: cómo Afrodita, la hija de Zeus, me deshonra continuamente porque soy cojo y se entrega amorosamente al pernicioso Ares; que él es hermoso y con los dos pies, mientras que yo soy lisiado. Pero ningún otro es responsable, sino mis dos padres: ¡no me debían haber engendrado! Pero mirad dónde duermen estos dos en amor; se han metido en mi propia cama. Los estoy viendo y me lleno de dolor, pues nunca esperé ni por un instante que iban a dormir así por mucho que se amaran. Pero no van a desear ambos seguir durmiendo, que los sujetará mi trampa y las ligaduras hasta que mi padre me devuelva todos mis regalos de esponsales, cuantos le entregué por la muchacha de cara de perra. Porque su hija era bella, pero incapaz de contener sus deseos.»

Así habló, y los dioses se congregaron junto a la casa de piso de bronce. Llegó Poseidón, el que conduce su carro por la tierra; llegó el subastador, Hermes, y llegó el soberano que dispara desde lejos, Apolo. Pero las hembras, las diosas, se quedaban por vergüenza en casa cada una de ellas.

Se apostaron los dioses junto a los pórticos, los dadores de bienes, y se les levantó inextinguible la risa al ver las artes del prudente Hefesto. Y al verlo, decía así uno al que tenía más cerca:

«No prosperan las malas acciones; el lento alcanza al veloz. Así, ahora, Hefesto, que es lento, ha cogido con sus artes a

300

310

320

330

Ares, aunque es el más veloz de los dioses que ocupan el Olimpo, cojo como es. Y debe la multa por adulterio.»

Así decían unos a otros. Y el soberano, hijo de Zeus, Apolo, se dirigió a Hermes:

«Hermes, hijo de Zeus, Mensajero, dador de bienes, ¿te gustaría dormir en la cama junto a la dorada Afrodita sujeto por fuertes ligaduras?»

Y le contestó el mensajero, el Argifonte:

«¡Así sucediera esto, soberano disparador de lejos, Apolo! ¡Que me sujetaran interminables ligaduras tres veces más que ésas y que vosotros me mirarais, los dioses y todas las diosas!»

Así dijo y se les levantó la risa a los inmortales dioses. Pero a Poseidón no le sujetaba la risa y no dejaba de rogar a Hefesto, al insigne artesano, que liberara a Ares. Y le habló y le dirigió aladas palabras:

«Suéltalo y te prometo, como ordenas, que te pagaré todo lo que es justo entre los inmortales dioses.»

Y le contestó el insigne cojo de ambos pies:

«No, Poseidón, que conduces tu carro por la tierra, no me ordenes eso; sin valor son las fianzas que se toman por gente sin valor. ¿Cómo iba yo a requerirte entre los inmortales dioses si Ares se escapa evitando la deuda y las ligaduras?

Y le respondió Poseidón, el que sacude la tierra:

«Hefesto, si Ares se escapa huyendo sin pagar la deuda, yo mismo te la pagaré.»

Y le contestó el muy insigne cojo de ambos pies:

«No es posible ni está bien negarme a tu palabra.»

Así hablando los liberó de las ligaduras la fuerza de Hefesto. Y cuando se vieron libres de las ligaduras, aunque eran muy fuertes, se levantaron enseguida: él marchó a Tracia y ella se llegó a Chipre, Afrodita, la que ama la risa. Allí la lavaron las Gracias y la ungieron con aceite inmortal, cosas que aumentan el esplendor de los dioses que viven siempre y la vistieron deseables vestidos, una maravilla para verlos.

Esto cantaba el muy insigne aedo. Odiseo gozaba en su interior al oírlo y también los demás feacios que usan largos remos, hombres insignes por sus naves.

Alcínoo ordenó a Halio y Laodamante que danzaran solos, pues nadie rivalizaba con ellos. Así que tomaron en sus manos una hermosa pelota de púrpura (se la había hecho el sabio Pólibo); el uno la lanzaba hacia las sombrías nubes doblándose hacia atrás y el otro saltando hacia arriba la recibía con facilidad antes de tocar el suelo con sus pies.

Después, cuando habían hecho la prueba de lanzar la pelota en línea recta, danzaban sobre la tierra nutricia cambiando a menudo sus posiciones; los demás jóvenes aplaudían en pie entre la concurrencia y gradualmente se levantaba un gran murmullo. 380

Fue entonces cuando el divino Odiseo se dirigió a Alcínoo:

«Alcínoo, poderoso, el más insigne de todo tu pueblo, con razón me asegurabas que erais los mejores bailarines. Se ha presentado esto como un hecho cumplido, la admiración se apodera de mí al verlo.»

Así habló, y se alegró la sagrada fuerza de Alcínoo. Y enseguida dijo a los feacios amantes del remo:

«Escuchad, caudillos y señores de los feacios. El huésped me parece muy discreto. Vamos, démosle un regalo de hospitalidad, como es natural. Puesto que gobiernan en el pueblo 390 doce esclarecidos reyes —yo soy el decimotercero—, cada uno de éstos entregadle un vestido bien lavado y un manto y un talento de estimable oro. Traigámoslo enseguida todos juntos para que el huésped, con ello en sus manos, se acerque al banquete con ánimo gozoso. Y que Euríalo lo aplaque con sus palabras y con un regalo, que no dijo su palabra como le correspondía.»

Así dijo, y todos aprobaron sus palabras y se lo aconsejaron a Euríalo. Y cada uno envió un heraldo para que trajera los regalos.

Entonces, Euríalo le contestó y dijo: 400

«Alcínoo poderoso, el más señalado de todo el pueblo, aplacaré al huésped como tú ordenas. Le regalaré esta espada toda de bronce, cuya empuñadura es de plata y cuya vaina está rodeada de marfil recién cortado. Y le será de mucho valor.»

Así dijo, y puso en manos de Odiseo la espada de clavos de plata; le habló y le dirigió aladas palabras:

«Salud, padre huésped, si alguna palabra desagradable ha sido dicha, que la arrebaten los vendavales y se la lleven. Y a ti, que los dioses te concedan ver a tu esposa y llegar a tu pa- 410

[161]

tria, pues sufres penalidades largo tiempo ya lejos de los tuyos.»

Y le contestó y dijo el muy astuto Odiseo:

«También a ti, amigo, salud y que los dioses te concedan felicidad, y que después no sientas nostalgia de la espada ésta que ya me has dado aplacándome con tus palabras.»

Así dijo, y colocó la espada de clavos de plata en torno a sus hombros.

Cuando se sumergió Helios ya tenía él a su lado los insignes regalos; los ilustres heraldos los llevaban al palacio de Alcínoo y los hijos del irreprochable Alcínoo los recibieron y colocaron 420 los muy hermosos regalos junto a su venerable madre.

Ante ellos marchaba la sagrada fuerza de Alcínoo y al llegar se sentaron en elevados sillones.

Entonces se dirigió a Arete la fuerza de Alcínoo:

«Trae acá, mujer, un arcón insigne, el que sea mejor. Y en él coloca un vestido bien lavado y un manto. Calentadle un caldero de bronce con fuego alrededor y templad el agua para que se lave y vea bien puestos todos los regalos que le han traído aquí los irreprochables feacios, y goce con el banquete escuchando también la música de una tonada. También yo le entregaré esta copa mía hermosísima, de oro, para que se acuerde 430 de mí todos los días al hacer libaciones en su palacio a Zeus y a los demás dioses.»

Así dijo, y Arete ordenó a sus esclavas que colocaran al fuego un gran trípode lo antes posible. Ellas colocaron al fuego ardiente una bañera de tres patas, echaron agua, pusieron leña y la encendieron debajo. Y el fuego lamía el vientre de la bañera y se calentaba el agua.

Entretanto Arete traía de su tálamo un arcón hermosísimo para el huésped —en él había colocado los lindos regalos, vestidos y oro, que los feacios le habían dado. También había co- 440 locado en el arcón un hermoso vestido y un manto y le habló y le dirigió aladas palabras:

«Mira tú mismo esta tapa y échale enseguida un nudo, no sea que alguien la fuerce en el viaje cuando duermas dulce sueño al marchar en la negra nave.»

Cuando escuchó esto el sufridor, el divino Odiseo, adaptó la tapa y le echó enseguida un bien trabado nudo, el que le había enseñado en otro tiempo la soberana Circe.

Acto seguido el ama de llaves ordenó que lo lavaran una vez metido en la bañera, y él vio con gusto el baño caliente, pues no se había cuidado a menudo de él desde que había abandonado la morada de Calipso, la de lindas trenzas. En aquella época le estaba siempre dispuesto el baño como para un dios.

Cuando las esclavas lo habían lavado y ungido con aceite y le habían puesto túnica y manto, salió de la bañera y fue hacia los hombres que bebían vino. Y Nausícaa[136], que tenía una hermosura dada por los dioses, se detuvo junto a un pilar del bien fabricado techo. Y admiraba a Odiseo al verlo en sus ojos, y le habló y le dijo aladas palabras:

«Salud, huésped, acuérdate de mí cuando estés en tu patria, pues es a mí la primera a quien debes la vida.»

Y le contestó y le dijo el muy astuto Odiseo:

«Nausícaa, hija del valeroso Alcínoo, que me conceda Zeus, el que truena fuerte, el esposo de Hera, volver a mi casa y ver el día del regreso. Y a ti, incluso allí te haré súplicas como a una diosa, pues tú, muchacha, me has devuelto la vida.»

Dijo, y se sentó en su sillón junto al rey Alcínoo.

Y ellos ya estaban repartiendo las porciones y mezclando el vino.

Y un heraldo se acercó conduciendo al deseable aedo, a Demódoco, honrado en el pueblo, y le hizo sentar en medio de los comensales apoyándolo junto a una enorme columna.

Entonces se dirigió al heraldo el muy inteligente Odiseo, mientras cortaba el lomo —pues aún sobraba mucho— de un albidente cerdo (y alrededor había abundante grasa):

«Heraldo, ven acá, entrega esta carne a Demódoco para que lo coma, que yo le mostraré cordialidad por triste que esté. Pues entre todos los hombres terrenos los aedos participan de la honra y del respeto, porque Musa les ha enseñado el canto y ama a la raza de los aedos.»

Así dijo, el heraldo lo llevó y se lo puso en las manos del hé-

---

[136] Nausícaa desapareció bruscamente al final del canto VI y reaparece brevemente para despedirse de Odiseo. Es todo lo que puede hacer Homero (quien suele eliminar el elemento erótico) con un personaje cuya función en el foklore es conquistar al extranjero desconocido que llega a su patria, cfr. W. J. Woodhouse, *The composition*, págs. 58 y ss.

roe Demódoco, y éste lo recibió y se alegró en su ánimo. Y ellos echaban mano de las viandas que tenían delante.

Cuando hubieron arrojado lejos de sí el deseo de bebida y de comida, ya entonces se dirigió a Demódoco el muy inteligente Odiseo:

«Demódoco, muy por encima de todos los mortales te alabo: seguro que te han enseñado Musa, la hija de Zeus, o Apolo. Pues con mucha belleza cantas el destino de los aqueos —cuánto hicieron y sufrieron y cuánto soportaron— como si 490 tú mismo lo hubieras presenciado o lo hubieras escuchado de otro allí presente.

»Pero, vamos, pasa a otro tema y canta la estratagema del caballo de madera que fabricó Epeo con la ayuda de Atenea, la emboscada que en otro tiempo condujo el divino Odiseo hasta la Acrópolis, llenándola de los hombres que destruyeron Ilión.

»Si me narras esto como te corresponde, yo diré bien alto a todos los hombres que la divinidad te ha concedido benigna el divino canto.»

Así habló, y Demódoco, movido por la divinidad, inició y mostró su canto desde el momento en que los argivos se em- 500 barcaron en las naves de buenos bancos y se dieron a la mar después de incendiar las tiendas de campaña. Ya estaban los emboscados con el insigne Odiseo en el ágora de los troyanos, ocultos dentro del caballo, pues los mismos troyanos lo habían arrastrado hasta la Acrópolis.

Así estaba el caballo, y los troyanos deliberaban en medio de una gran incertidumbre sentados alrededor de éste. Y les agradaban tres decisiones: rajar la cóncava madera con el mortal bronce, arrojarlo por las rocas empujándolo desde lo alto, o dejar que la gran estatua sirviera para aplacar a los dioses. Esta última decisión es la que iba a cumplirse. Pues era su Destino 510 que perecieran una vez que la ciudad encerrara el gran caballo de madera donde estaban sentados todos los mejores de los argivos portando la muerte y Ker para los troyanos. Y cantaba cómo los hijos de los aqueos asolaron la ciudad una vez que salieron del caballo y abandonaron la cóncava emboscada. Y cantaba que unos por un lado y otros por otro iban devastando la elevada ciudad, pero que Odiseo marchó semejante a Ares en compañía del divino Menelao hacia el palacio de Deífobo.

Y dijo que, una vez allí, sostuvo el más terrible combate y que al fin venció con la ayuda de la valerosa Atenea. 520

Esto es lo que cantaba el insigne aedo, y Odiseo se derretía: el llanto empapaba sus mejillas deslizándose de sus párpados.

Como una mujer llora a su marido arrojándose sobre él caído ante su ciudad y su pueblo por apartar de ésta y de sus hijos el día de la muerte —ella lo contempla moribundo y palpitante, y tendida sobre él llora a voces; los enemigos cortan con sus lanzas la espalda y los hombros de los ciudadanos y se los llevan prisioneros para soportar el trabajo y la pena, y las mejillas de ésta se consumen en un dolor digno de lástima—, así 530 Odiseo destilaba bajo sus párpados un llanto digno de lástima[137].

A los demás les pasó desapercibido que derramaba lágrimas, y sólo Alcínoo lo advirtió y observó sentado como estaba cerca de él y le oyó gemir pesadamente.

Entonces dijo al punto a los feacios amantes del remo:

«Escuchad, caudillos y señores de los feacios. Que Demódoco detenga su cítara sonora, pues no agrada a todos al cantar esto. Desde que estamos cenando y comenzó el divino aedo, no ha dejado el huésped un momento el lamentable llanto. El 540 dolor le rodea el ánimo.

»Vamos, que se detenga para que gocemos todos por igual, los que le damos hospitalidad y el huésped, pues así será mucho mejor. Que por causa del venerable huésped se han preparado estas cosas, la escolta y amables regalos, cosas que le entregamos como muestra de afecto. Como un hermano es el huésped y el suplicante para el hombre que goce de sensatez por poca que sea. Por ello, tampoco tú escondas en tu pensamiento astuto lo que voy a preguntarte, pues lo mejor es hablar. Dime tu nombre, el que te llamaban allí tu madre y tu pa- 550 dre y los demás, los que viven cerca de ti. Pues ninguno de los hombres carece completamente de nombre, ni el hombre del pueblo ni el noble, una vez que han nacido. Antes bien, a todos se lo ponen sus padres una vez que lo han dado a luz.

---

[137] Se trata de una comparación, nada exacta en los detalles y muy poco en sus líneas generales. Pero sin duda viene traída por asociación de ideas con la Iliupersis que acaba de cantar Demódoco.

Dime también tu tierra, tu pueblo y tu ciudad para que te acompañen allí las naves dotadas de inteligencia. Pues entre los feacios no hay pilotos ni timones en sus naves, cosas que otras naves tienen. Ellas conocen las intenciones y los pensamientos de los hombres y conocen las ciudades y los fértiles 560 campos de todos los hombres. Recorren velozmente el abismo del mar aunque estén cubiertas por la oscuridad y la niebla, y nunca tienen miedo de sufrir daño ni de ser destruidas. Pero yo he oído decir en otro tiempo a mi padre Nausítoo que Poseidón estaba celoso de nosotros porque acompañamos a todos sin daño. Y decía que algún día destruiría en el nebuloso ponto a una bien fabricada nave de los feacios al volver de una escolta y nos bloquearía la ciudad con un gran monte. Así decía el anciano; que la divinidad cumpla esto o lo deje sin cumplir, 570 como sea agradable a su ánimo.

»Pero, vamos, dime —e infórmame en verdad— por dónde has andado errante y a qué regiones de hombres has llegado. Háblame de ellos y de sus bien habitadas ciudades, los que son duros y salvajes y no justos, y los que son amigos de los forasteros y tienen sentimientos de veneración hacia los dioses. Dime también por qué lloras y te lamentas en tu ánimo al oír el destino de los argivos, de los dánaos y de Ilión. Esto lo han hecho los dioses y han urdido la perdición para esos hombres, para que también sea motivo de canto para los venideros. ¿Es 580 que ha perecido ante Ilión algún pariente tuyo..., un noble yerno o suegro, los que son más objeto de preocupación después de nuestra propia sangre y linaje? ¿O un noble amigo de sentimientos agradables? Pues no es inferior a un hermano el amigo que tiene pensamientos discretos.»

Canto IX

ODISEO CUENTA SUS AVENTURAS:
LOS CICONES, LOS LOTÓFAGOS, LOS CÍCLOPES

Y le contestó y dijo el muy astuto Odiseo:

«Poderoso Alcínoo, el más noble de todo tu pueblo, en verdad es agradable escuchar al aedo, tal como es, semejante a los dioses en su voz. No creo yo que haya un cumplimiento más delicioso que cuando el bienestar perdura en todo el pueblo y los convidados escuchan a lo largo del palacio al aedo sentados en orden, y junto a ellos hay mesas cargadas de pan y carne y un escanciador trae y lleva vino que ha sacado de las cráteras y lo escancia en las copas. Esto me parece lo más bello.   10

»Tu ánimo se ha decidido a preguntar mis penalidades a fin de que me lamente todavía más en mi dolor. Porque, ¿qué voy a narrarte lo primero y qué en último lugar?, pues son innumerables los dolores que los dioses, los hijos de Urano, me han proporcionado. Conque lo primero que voy a decir es mi nombre para que lo conozcáis y para que yo después de escapar del día cruel continúe manteniendo con vosotros relaciones de hospitalidad, aunque el palacio en que habito esté lejos.

»Soy Odiseo, el hijo de Laertes, el que está en boca de todos los hombres por toda clase de trampas[138], y mi fama llega hasta el cielo. Habito en Itaca, hermosa al atardecer. Hay en ella   20

---

[138] Esta frase está mejor en boca del aedo Homero que de Odiseo mismo. En XII.70 hay una expresión similar referida a la nave Argo, y es evidente que significa que es objeto de canto *para los aedos.*

un monte, el Nérito de agitado follaje, muy sobresaliente, y a su alrededor hay muchas islas habitadas cercanas unas de otras, Duliquio y Same, y la poblada de bosques Zante. Itaca se recuesta sobre el mar con poca altura, la más remota hacia el Occidente, y las otras están más lejos hacia Eos y Helios. Es áspera, pero buena criadora de mozos.

»Yo en verdad no soy capaz de ver cosa alguna más dulce que la tierra de uno. Y eso que me retuvo Calipso, divina entre las diosas, en profunda cueva deseando que fuera su esposo, e igualmente me retuvo en su palacio Circe, la hija de Eeo, la engañosa, deseando que fuera su esposo. 30

»Pero no persuadió a mi ánimo dentro de mi pecho, que no hay nada más dulce que la tierra de uno y de sus padres, por muy rica que sea la casa donde uno habita en tierra extranjera y lejos de los suyos.

»Y ahora os voy a narrar mi atormentado regreso, el que Zeus me ha dado al venir de Troya. El viento que me traía de Ilión me empujó hacia los Cícones[139], hacia Ismaro. Allí asolé la ciudad, a sus habitantes los pasé a cuchillo, tomamos de la ciudad a las esposas y abundante botín y lo repartimos de manera que nadie se me fuera sin su parte correspondiente. Entonces ordené a los míos que huyeran con rápidos pies, pero ellos, los muy estúpidos, no me hicieron caso. Así que bebieron mucho vino y degollaron muchas ovejas junto a la ribera y cuernitorcidos bueyes de rotátiles patas. 40

»Entre tanto, los Cícones, que se habían marchado, lanzaron sus gritos de ayuda a otros Cícones que, vecinos suyos, eran a la vez más numerosos y mejores, los que habitaban tierra adentro, bien entrenados en luchar con hombres desde el carro y a pie, donde sea preciso. Y enseguida llegaron tan numerosos como nacen en primavera las hojas y las flores, veloces. 50

---

[139] Los cícones son el único pueblo que aparece en las Aventuras de Odiseo cuya realidad geográfica e histórica es incontestable. Y es significativo que sea *el primero:* desde aquí se pasa a la pura ficción. En *Ilíada,* II.846, aparecen como aliados de los troyanos, y aunque el Catálogo los sitúa entre los tracios del Helesponto y los peonios, no tienen una localización precisa. Sin embargo, Heródoto (7.59 y 108) dice que antiguamente les pertenecía la región de Tracia entre Abdera y el Hebro con las localidades de Sale, Zona y el cabo Serreo. Su capital era Ismaro y era región vinícola (cfr. más adelante, vv. 196-200).

»Entonces la funesta Aisa de Zeus se colocó junto a nosotros, de maldito destino, para que sufriéramos dolores en abundancia; lucharon pie a tierra junto a las veloces naves, y se herían unos a otros con sus lanzas de bronce. Mientras Eos duró y crecía el sagrado día, los aguantamos rechazándoles aunque eran más numerosos. Pero cuando Helios se dirigió al momento de desuncir los bueyes[140], los Cicones nos hicieron retroceder venciendo a los aqueos y sucumbieron seis compañeros de buenas grebas de cada nave. Los demás escapamos de la muerte y de nuestro destino, y desde allí proseguimos navegando hacia adelante con el corazón apesadumbrado, escapando gustosos de la muerte aunque habíamos perdido a los compañeros. Pero no prosiguieron mis curvadas naves, que cada uno llamamos por tres veces a nuestros desdichados compañeros, los que habían muerto en la llanura a manos de los Cicones.

»Entonces el que reúne las nubes, Zeus, levantó el viento Bóreas junto con una inmensa tempestad, y con las nubes ocultó la tierra y a la vez el ponto. Y la noche surgió del cielo. Las naves eran arrastradas transversalmente y el ímpetu del viento rasgó sus velas en tres y cuatro trozos. Las colocamos sobre cubierta por temor a la muerte, y haciendo grandes esfuerzos nos dirigimos a remo hacia tierra.

»Allí estuvimos dos noches y dos días completos, consumiendo nuestro ánimo por el cansancio y el dolor.

»Pero cuando Eos, de lindas trenzas, completó el tercer día, levantamos los mástiles, extendimos las blancas velas y nos sentamos en las naves, y el viento y los pilotos las conducían. En ese momento habría llegado ileso a mi tiera patria, pero el oleaje, la corriente y Bóreas me apartaron al doblar las Maleas y me hicieron vagar lejos de Citera. Así que desde allí fuimos arrastrados por fuertes vientos durante nueve días sobre el ponto abundante en peces, y al décimo arribamos a la tierra de los Lotófagos[141], los que comen flores de alimento. Descendi-

---

[140] A la caída del sol.

[141] Los lotófagos son un pueblo mítico, de localización irrelevante —aunque lógicamente deben estar al sur si Odiseo llega allí vagando desde Citera. Los historiadores posteriores los identificaron con un pueblo del norte de África, en

mos a tierra, hicimos provisión de agua y al punto mis compañeros tomaron su comida junto a las veloces naves. Cuando nos habíamos hartado de comida y bebida, yo envié delante a unos compañeros para que fueran a indagar qué clase de hombres, de los que se alimentan de trigo, había en esa región; escogí a dos, y como tercer hombre les envié a un heraldo. 90
Y marcharon enseguida y se encontraron con los Lotófagos. Éstos no decidieron matar a nuestros compañeros, sino que les dieron a comer loto, y el que de ellos comía el dulce fruto del loto ya no quería volver a informarnos ni regresar, sino que preferían quedarse allí con los Lotófagos, arrancando loto, y olvidándose del regreso. Pero yo los conduje a la fuerza, aunque lloraban, y en las cóncavas naves los arrastré y até bajo los bancos. Después ordené a mis demás leales compañeros que se 100
apresuraran a embarcar en las rápidas naves, no fuera que alguno comiera del loto y se olvidara del regreso. Y rápidamente embarcaron y se sentaron sobre los bancos, y, sentados en fila, batían el canoso mar con los remos.

»Desde allí proseguimos navegando con el corazón acongojado, y llegamos a la tierra de los Cíclopes[142], los soberbios, los sin ley; los que, obedientes a los inmortales, no plantan con sus manos frutos ni labran la tierra, sino que todo les nace sin sembrar y sin arar: trigo y cebada y viñas que producen vino 110
de gordos racimos; la lluvia de Zeus se los hace crecer. No tienen ni ágoras donde se emite consejo ni leyes; habitan las

---

las Sirtes o en la misma isla de Djerba (cfr. Heródoto, 4.177, y Polibio, 1.39). Sobre el loto, los autores antiguos no se ponen de acuerdo: Heródoto dice *(loc. cit.)* que por su tamaño se parece al lentisco y por su dulzor al dátil y que con él hacen vino. Polibio hace una descripción muy detallada en 12.2 que, según F. W. Walbank, *A historical Commentary on Polibius,* Oxford, 1957 y 1967 *(ad. loc.),* corresponde al *zizyphus lotus,* de la familia de las ramnacias, cuyo nombre vulgar en español es azufaifo.

[142] Los Cíclopes, que en Hesíodo (cfr. *Teogonía,* 139 y ss., 501 y ss.) pertenecen a la cateogría de los Titanes y descienden directamente de Urano y Gea, están aquí plenamente humanizados. Solamente Polifemo tiene ascendencia divina y su ceguera por Odiseo es la causa última de las aventuras y desventuras del héroe (cfr. I.68 y ss.). Los demás constituyen el prototipo de una tribu bárbara carente de leyes, de religión y de civilización. Homero combina en este pasaje el tema folklórico universal del Gigante malvado y el de Nadie, cfr. D. L. Page, ob. cit., cap. I.

cumbres de elevadas montañas en profundas cuevas y cada uno es legislador de sus hijos y esposas, y no se preocupan unos de otros.

»Más allá del puerto se extiende una isla llana[143], no cerca ni lejos de la tierra de los Cíclopes, llena de bosques. En ella se crían innumerables cabras salvajes, pues no pasan por allí hombres que se lo impidan ni las persiguen los cazadores, los que sufren dificultades en el bosque persiguiendo las crestas de los montes. La isla tampoco está ocupada por ganados ni sembrados, sino que, no sembrada ni arada, carece de cultivadores todo el año y alimenta a las baladoras cabras. No disponen los Cíclopes de naves de rojas proas, ni hay allí armadores que pudieran trabajar en construir bien entabladas naves; éstas tendrían como término cada una de las ciudades de mortales a las que suelen llegar los hombres atravesando con sus naves el mar, unos en busca de otros, y los Cíclopes se habrían hecho una isla bien fundada. Pues no es mala y produciría todos los frutos estacionales; tiene prados junto a las riberas del canoso mar, húmedos, blandos. Las viñas sobre todo producirían constantemente, y las tierras de pan llevar son llanas. Recogerían siempre las profundas mieses en su tiempo oportuno, ya que el subsuelo es fértil. También hay en ella un puerto fácil para atracar, donde no hay necesidad de cable ni de arrojar las anclas ni de atar las amarras. Se puede permanecer allí, una vez arribados, hasta el día en que el ánimo de los marineros les impulse y soplen los vientos.

»En la parte alta del puerto corre un agua resplandeciente, una fuente que surge de la profundidad de una cueva, y en torno crecen álamos. Hacia allí navegamos y un demón nos conducía a través de la oscura noche. No teníamos luz para verlo, pues la bruma era espesa en torno a las naves y Selene no irradiaba su luz desde el cielo y era retenida por las nubes; así que nadie vio la isla con sus ojos ni vimos las enormes olas que rodaban hacia tierra hasta que arrastramos las naves de buenos bancos. Una vez arrastradas, recogimos todas las velas y des-

120

130

140

---

[143] No es la tierra de los Cíclopes, sino una isla cercana donde Odiseo amarra su escuadra y desde donde, con una sola nave, se dirige a la tierra de los Cíclopes. Cfr. los vv. 543 y ss.

cendimos sobre la orilla del mar y esperamos a la divina Eos   150
durmiendo allí.

»Y cuando se mostró Eos, la que nace de la mañana, la de
dedos de rosa, deambulamos llenos de admiración por la isla.

»Entonces las ninfas, las hijas de Zeus, portador de égida,
agitaron a las cabras montaraces para que comieran mis compañeros. Así que enseguida sacamos de las naves los curvados
arcos y las lanzas de largas puntas, y ordenados en tres grupos
comenzamos a disparar, y pronto un dios nos proporcionó
abundante caza. Me seguían doce naves, y a cada una de ellas
tocaron en suerte nueve cabras, y para mí solo tomé diez. Así   160
estuvimos todo el día hasta el sumergirse de Helios, comiendo
innumerables trozos de carne y dulce vino; que todavía no se
había agotado en las naves el dulce vino, sino que aún quedaba, pues cada uno había guardado mucho en las ánforas cuando tomamos la sagrada ciudad de los Cicones.

»Echamos un vistazo a la tierra de los Cíclopes que estaban
cerca y vimos el humo de sus fogatas y escuchamos el vagido
de sus ovejas y cabras. Y cuando Helios se sumergió y sobrevino la oscuridad, nos echamos a dormir sobre la ribera del mar.

»Cuando se mostró Eos, la que nace de la mañana, la de de-   170
dos de rosa, convoqué asamblea y les dije a todos:

»"Quedaos ahora los demás, mis fieles compañeros, que yo
con mi nave y los que me acompañan voy a llegarme a esos
hombres para saber quiénes son, si soberbios, salvajes y carentes de justicia o amigos de los forasteros y con sentimientos de
piedad para con los dioses."

»Así dije, y me embarqué y ordené a mis compañeros que
embarcaran también ellos y soltaran amarras. Embarcaron éstos sin tardanza y se sentaron en los bancos, y sentados batían
el canoso mar con los remos. Y cuando llegamos a un lugar   180
cercano, vimos una cueva cerca del mar, elevada, techada de
laurel. Allí pasaba la noche abundante ganado —ovejas y cabras—, y alrededor había una alta cerca construida con piedras
hundidas en tierra y con enormes pinos y encinas de elevada
copa. Allí habitaba un hombre monstruoso que apacentaba sus
rebaños, solo, apartado, y no frecuentaba a los demás, sino que
vivía alejado y tenía pensamientos impíos. Era un monstruo
digno de admiración: no se parecía a un hombre, a uno que   190

come trigo, sino a una cima cubierta de bosque de las elevadas montañas que aparece sola, destacada de las otras. Entonces ordené al resto de mis fieles compañeros que se quedaran allí junto a la nave y que la botaran.

»Yo escogí a mis doce mejores compañeros y me puse en camino. Llevaba un pellejo de cabra con negro, agradable vino que me había dado Marón, el hijo de Evanto, el sacerdote de Apolo protector de Ismaro, porque lo había yo salvado junto con su hijo y esposa respetando su techo. Habitaba en el bosque arbolado de Febo Apolo y me había donado regalos excelentes: me dio siete talentos de oro bien trabajados y una cráter toda de plata, y, además, vino en doce ánforas que llenó, vino agradable, no mezclado, bebida divina. Ninguna de las esclavas ni de los esclavos de palacio conocían su existencia, sino sólo él y su esposa y solamente la despensera. Siempre que bebían el rojo, agradable vino llenaba una copa y vertía veinte medidas de agua, y desde la cráter se esparcía un olor delicioso, admirable; en ese momento no era agradable alejarse de allí. De este vino me llevé un gran pellejo lleno y también provisiones en un saco de cuero, porque mi noble ánimo barruntó que marchaba en busca de un hombre dotado de gran fuerza, salvaje, desconocedor de la justicia y de las leyes.

»Llegamos enseguida a su cueva y no lo encontramos dentro, sino que guardaba sus gordos rebaños en el pasto. Conque entramos en la cueva y echamos un vistazo a cada cosa: los canastos se inclinaban bajo el peso de los quesos, y los establos estaban llenos de corderos y cabritillos. Todos estaban cerrados por separado: a un lado los lechales, a otro los medianos y a otro los recentales.

»Y todos los recipientes rebosaban de suero —colodras y jarros bien construidos, con los que ordeñaba.

»Entonces mis compañeros me rogaron que nos apoderásemos primero de los quesos y regresáramos, y que sacáramos luego de los establos cabritillos y corderos y, conduciéndolos a la rápida nave, diéramos velas sobre el agua salada. Pero yo no les hice caso —aunque hubiera sido más ventajoso—, para poder ver al monstruo y por si me daba los dones de hospitalidad. Pero su aparición no iba a ser deseable para mis compañeros.

200

210

220

230

»Así que, encendiendo una fogata, hicimos un sacrificio, repartimos quesos, los comimos y aguardamos sentados dentro de la cueva hasta que llegó conduciendo el rebaño. Traía el Cíclope una pesada carga de leña seca para su comida y la tiró dentro con gran ruido. Nosotros nos arrojamos atemorizados al fondo de la cueva, y él a continuación introdujo sus gordos rebaños, todos cuantos solía ordeñar, y a los machos —a los carneros y cabrones— los dejó a la puerta, fuera del profundo establo. Después levantó una gran roca y la colocó arriba, tan pesada que no la habrían levantado del suelo ni veintidós buenos carros de cuatro ruedas: ¡tan enorme piedra colocó sobre la puerta! Sentóse luego a ordeñar las ovejas y las baladoras cabras, cada una en su momento, y debajo de cada una colocó un recental. Enseguida puso a cuajar la mitad de la blanca leche en cestas bien entretejidas y la otra mitad la colocó en cubos, para beber cuando comiera y le sirviera de adición al banquete.

Cuando hubo realizado todo su trabajo prendió fuego, y al vernos nos preguntó:

»"Forasteros, ¿quiénes sois? ¿De dónde venís navegando los húmedos senderos? ¿Andáis errantes por algún asunto, o sin rumbo como los piratas por la mar, los que andan a la aventura exponiendo sus vidas y llevando la destrucción a los de otras tierras?"[144].

»Así habló, y nuestro corazón se estremeció por miedo a su voz insoportable y a él mismo, al gigante. Pero le contesté con mi palabra y le dije:

»"Somos aqueos y hemos venido errantes desde Troya, zarandeados por toda clase de vientos sobre el gran abismo del mar, desviados por otro rumbo, por otros caminos, aunque nos dirigimos de vuelta a casa. Así quiso Zeus proyectarlo. Nos preciamos de pertenecer al ejército del Atrida Agamenón, cuya fama es la más grande bajo el cielo: ¡tan gran ciudad ha devastado y tantos hombres ha hecho sucumbir! Conque hemos dado contigo y nos hemos llegado a tus rodillas por si nos ofreces hospitalidad y nos das un regalo, como es costumbre entre los huéspedes. Ten respeto, excelente, a los dioses; so-

---

[144] La misma pregunta de III.71-4, en boca de Néstor. En todo caso, la piratería era una actividad normal en época arcaica.

mos tus suplicantes, y Zeus es el vengador de los suplicantes y   270
de los huéspedes, Zeus Hospitalario, quien acompaña a los
huéspedes, a quienes se debe respeto."

»Así hablé, y él me contestó con corazón cruel:

»"Eres estúpido, forastero, o vienes de lejos, tú que me ordenas temer o respetar a los dioses, pues los Cíclopes no se
cuidan de Zeus, portador de égida, ni de los dioses felices[145].
Pues somos mucho más fuertes. No te perdonaría ni a ti ni a
tus compañeros, si el ánimo no me lo ordenara, por evitar la
enemistad de Zeus.

»"Pero dime dónde has detenido tu bien fabricada nave al
venir, si al final de la playa o aquí cerca, para que lo sepa."   280

»Así habló para probarme, y a mí, que sé mucho, no me
pasó esto desapercibido. Así que me dirigí a él con palabras
engañosas:

»"La nave me la ha destrozado Poseidón, el que conmueve
la tierra; la ha lanzado contra los escollos en los confines de
vuestro país, conduciéndola hasta un promontorio, y el viento
la arrastró del ponto. Por ello he escapado junto con éstos de
la dolorosa muerte."

»Así hablé, y él no me contestó nada con corazón cruel, mas
lanzóse y echó mano a mis compañeros. Agarró a dos a la vez
y los golpeó contra el suelo como a cachorrillos, y sus sesos se   290
esparcieron por el suelo empapando la tierra. Cortó en trozos
sus miembros, se los preparó como cena y se los comió, como
un león montaraz, sin dejar ni sus entrañas ni sus carnes ni sus
huesos llenos de meollo.

»Nosotros elevamos llorando nuestras manos a Zeus, pues
veíamos acciones malvadas, y la desesperación se apoderó de
nuestro ánimo.

»Cuando el Cíclope había llenado su enorme vientre de carne humana y leche no mezclada, se tumbó dentro de la cueva,
tendiéndose entre los rebaños. Entonces yo tomé la decisión
en mi magnánimo corazón de acercarme a éste, sacar la aguda
espada de junto a mi muslo y atravesarle el pecho por donde el   300

---

[145] Esta frase contradice abiertamente al v. 107, donde dice que son «obedientes a los inmortales». Pero allí se estaba describiendo su tierra como un lugar paradisiaco y aquí a ellos mismos como una tribu salvaje.

diafragma contiene el hígado y la tenté con mi mano. Pero me contuvo otra decisión, pues allí hubiéramos perecido también nosotros con muerte cruel: no habríamos sido capaces de retirar de la elevada entrada la piedra que había colocado. Así que llorando esperamos a Eos divina. Y cuando se mostró Eos, la que nace de la mañana, la de dedos de rosa, se puso a encender fuego y a ordeñar a sus insignes rebaños, todo por orden, y bajo cada una colocó un recental. Luego que hubo realizado sus trabajos, agarró a dos compañeros a la vez y se los preparó como desayuno. Y cuando había desayunado, condujo fuera de la cueva a sus gordos rebaños retirando con facilidad la gran piedra de la entrada. Y la volvió a poner como si colocara la tapa a una aljaba. Y mientras el Cíclope encaminaba con gran estrépito sus rebaños hacia el monte, yo me quedé meditando males en lo profundo de mi pecho: ¡si pudiera vengarme y Atenea me concediera esto que la suplico...! 310

»Y ésta fue la decisión que me pareció mejor. Junto al establo yacía la enorme clava del Cíclope, verde, de olivo; la había cortado para llevarla cuando estuviera seca. Al mirarla la comparábamos con el mástil de una negra nave de veinte bancos de remeros, de una nave de transporte amplia, de las que recorren el negro abismo: así era su longitud, así era su anchura al mirarla. Me acerqué y corté de ella como una braza, la coloqué junto a mis compañeros y les ordené que la afilaran. Éstos la alisaron y luego me acerqué yo, le agucé el extremo y después la puse al fuego para endurecerla. La coloqué bien cubriéndola bajo el estiércol que estaba extendido en abundancia por la cueva. Después ordené que sortearan quién se atrevería a levantar la estaca conmigo y a retorcerla en su ojo cuando le llegara el dulce sueño, y eligieron entre ellos a cuatro, a los que yo mismo habría deseado escoger. Y yo me conté entre ellos como quinto. 320

330

Llegó el Cíclope por la tarde conduciendo sus ganados de hermosos vellones e introdujo en la amplia cueva a sus gordos rebaños, a todos, y no dejó nada fuera del profundo establo, ya porque sospechara algo o porque un dios así se lo aconsejó. Después colocó la gran piedra que hacía de puerta, levantándola muy alta, y se sentó a ordeñar las ovejas y las baladoras cabras, todas por orden, y bajo cada una colocó un recental. 340

Ulises escapa de Polifemo asido a un carnero

»El Cíclope gemía y se retorcía de dolor, y palpando con las manos retiró la piedra de la entrada. Y se sentó a la puerta, las manos extendidas, por si pillaba a alguien saliendo afuera entre las ovejas. ¡Tan estúpido pensaba en su mente que era yo! Entonces me puse a deliberar cómo saldrían mejor las cosas 420 —¡si encontrara el medio de liberar a mis compañeros y a mí mismo de la muerte...! Y me puse a entretejer toda clase de engaños y planes, ya que se trataba de mi propia vida . Pues un gran mal estaba cercano. Y me pareció la mejor esta decisión: los carneros estaban bien alimentados, con densos vellones, hermosos y grandes, y tenían una lana color violeta. Conque los até en silencio, juntándolos de tres en tres, con mimbres bien trenzadas sobre las que dormía el Cíclope, el monstruo de pensamientos impíos; el carnero del medio llevaba a un hombre, y los otros dos marchaban a cada lado, salvando a mis 430 compañeros. Tres carneros llevaban a cada hombre.

»Entonces yo... había un carnero, el mejor con mucho de todo su rebaño. Me apoderé de éste por el lomo y me coloqué bajo su velludo vientre hecho un ovillo, y me mantenía con ánimo paciente agarrado con mis manos a su divino vellón. Así aguardamos gimiendo a Eos divina, y cuando se mostró la que nace de la mañana, la de dedos de rosa, sacó a pastar a los machos de su ganado. Y las hembras balaban por los corrales sin ordeñar, pues sus ubres rebosaban. Su dueño, abatido por 440 funestos dolores, tentaba el lomo de todos sus carneros, que se mantenían rectos. El inocente no se daba cuenta de que mis compañeros estaban sujetos bajo el pecho de las lanudas ovejas. El último del rebaño en salir fue el carnero cargado con su lana y conmigo, que pensaba muchas cosas. El poderoso Polifemo lo palpó y se dirigió a él:

»"Carnero amigo, ¿por qué me sales de la cueva el último del rebaño? Antes jamás marchabas detrás de las ovejas, sino que, a grandes pasos, llegabas el primero a pastar las tiernas 450 flores del prado y llegabas el primero a las corrientes de los ríos y el primero deseabas llegar al establo por la tarde. Ahora, en cambio, eres el último de todos. Sin duda echas de menos el ojo de tu soberano, el que me ha cegado un hombre villano con la ayuda de sus miserables compañeros, sujetando mi mente con vino, Nadie, quien todavía no ha escapado —te lo aseguro— de la muerte. ¡Ojalá tuvieras sentimientos iguales a los míos y estuvieras dotado de voz para decirme dónde se ha escondido aquél de mi furia! Entonce sus sesos, cada uno por un lado, reventarían contra el suelo por la cueva, herido de muerte, y mi corazón se repondría de los males que me ha causado el vil Nadie." 460

»Así diciendo alejó de sí al carnero. Y cuando llegamos un poco lejos de la cueva y del corral, yo me desaté el primero de debajo del carnero y liberé a mis compañeros. Entonces hicimos volver rápidamente al ganado de finas patas, gordo por la grasa, abundante ganado, y lo condujimos hasta llegar a la nave.

»Nuestros compañeros dieron la bienvenida a los que habíamos escapado de la muerte, y a los otros los lloraron entre gemidos. Pero yo no permití que lloraran, haciéndoles señas negativas con mis cejas, antes bien, les di órdenes de embarcar al abundante ganado de hermosos vellones y de navegar el salino mar. 470

»Embarcáronlo enseguida y se sentaron sobre los bancos, y, sentados, batían el canoso mar con los remos.

»Conque cuando estaba tan lejos como para hacerme oír si gritaba, me dirigí al Cíclope con mordaces palabras:

»"Cíclope, no estaba privado de fuerza el hombre cuyos compañeros ibas a comerte en la cóncava cueva con tu poderosa fuerza. Con razón te tenían que salir al encuentro tus malvadas acciones, cruel, pues no tuviste miedo de comerte a tus huéspedes en tu propia casa. Por ello te han castigado Zeus y los demás dioses."

»Así hablé, y él se irritó más en su corazón. Arrancó la cresta de un gran monte, nos la arrojó y dio detrás de la nave de azuloscura proa, tan cerca que faltó poco para que alcanzara lo alto del timón. El mar se levantó por la caída de la piedra, y el oleaje arrastró en su reflujo la nave hacia el litoral y la impulsó hacia tierra. Entonces tomé con mis manos un largo botador y la empujé hacia fuera, y di órdenes a mis compañeros de que se lanzaran sobre los remos para escapar del peligro, haciéndoles señas con mi cabeza. Así que se inclinaron hacia adelante y remaban. Cuando en nuestro recorrido estábamos alejados dos veces la distancia de antes, me dirigí al Cíclope, aunque mis 480 490 compañeros intentaban impedírmelo con dulces palabras a uno y otro lado:

»"Desdichado, ¿por qué quieres irritar a un hombre salvaje?, un hombre que acaba de arrojar un proyectil que ha hecho volver a tierra nuestra nave y pensábamos que íbamos a morir en el sitio. Si nos oyera gritar o hablar machacaría nuestras cabezas y el madero del navío, tirándonos una roca de aristas resplandecientes, ¡tal es la longitud de su tiro!"

»Así hablaron, pero no doblegaron mi gran ánimo y me dirigí de nuevo a él airado:

»"Cíclope, si alguno de los mortales hombres te pregunta por la vergonzosa ceguera de tu ojo, dile que te ha dejado ciego Odiseo, el destructor de ciudades, el hijo de Laertes que tiene su casa en Itaca."

»Así hablé, y él dio un alarido y me contestó con su palabra:

»"¡Ay, ay, ya me ha alcanzado el antiguo oráculo! Había aquí un adivino noble y grande, Telemo Eurímida, que sobresalía por sus dotes de adivino y envejeció entre los Cíclopes vaticinando. Éste me dijo que todo esto se cumpliría en el futuro, que me vería privado de la vista a manos de Odiseo. Pero siempre esperé que llegara aquí un hombre grande y bello, dotado de un gran vigor; sin embargo, uno que es pequeño, de poca valía y débil me ha cegado el ojo después de sujetarme con vino. Pero ven acá, Odiseo, para que te ofrezca los dones de hospitalidad y exhorte al ínclito, al que conduce su carro por la tierra, a que te dé escolta, pues soy hijo suyo y él se gloría\de ser mi padre. Sólo él, si quiere, me sanará, y ningún otro de los dioses felices ni de los mortales hombres."

»Así habló, y yo le contesté diciendo:

»"¡Ojalá pudiera privarte también de la vida y de la existencia y enviarte a la mansión de Hades! Así no te curaría el ojo ni el que sacude la tierra."

»Así dije, y luego hizo él una súplica a Poseidón soberano, tendiendo su mano hacia el cielo estrellado:

»"Escúchame tú, Poseidón, el que abrazas la tierra, el de cabellera azuloscura. Si de verdad soy hijo tuyo —y tú te precias de ser mi padre—, concédeme que Odiseo, el destructor de ciudades, no llegue a casa, el hijo de Laertes que tiene su morada en Itaca. Pero si su destino es que vea a los suyos y llegue a

500

510

520

530

su bien edificada morada y a su tierra patria, que regrese de mala manera: sin sus compañeros, en nave ajena, y que encuentre calamidades en casa."

»Así dijo suplicando, y le escuchó el de azuloscura cabellera. A continuación levantó de nuevo una piedra mucho mayor y la lanzó dando vueltas. Hizo un esfuerzo inmenso y dio detrás de la nave de azuloscura proa, tan cerca que faltó poco para que alcanzara lo alto del timón. Y el mar se levantó por la caída de la piedra, y el oleaje arrastró en su reflujo la nave hacia el litoral y la impulsó hacia tierra. 540

»Conque por fin llegamos a la isla donde las demás naves de buenos bancos nos aguardaban reunidas. Nuestros compañeros estaban sentados llorando alrededor, anhelando continuamente nuestro regreso. Al llegar allí, arrastramos la nave sobre la arena y desembarcamos sobre la ribera del mar. Sacamos de la cóncava nave los ganados del Cíclope y los repartimos de modo que nadie se fuera sin su parte correspondiente.

»Mis compañeros, de hermosas grebas, me dieron a mí solo, 550 al repartir el ganado, un carnero de más, y lo sacrifiqué sobre la playa en honor de Zeus, el que reúne las nubes, el hijo de Crono, el que es soberano de todos, y quemé los muslos. Pero no hizo caso de mi sacrificio, sino que meditaba el modo de que se perdieran todas mis naves de buenos bancos y mis fieles compañeros.

»Estuvimos sentados todo el día comiendo carne sin parar y bebiendo dulce vino, hasta el sumergirse de Helios. Y cuando Helios se sumergió y cayó la oscuridad, nos echamos a dormir sobre la ribera del mar.

»Cuando se mostró Eos, la que nace de la mañana, la de de- 560 dos de rosa, di orden a mis compañeros de que embarcaran y soltaran amarras, y ellos embarcaron, se sentaron sobre los bancos y, sentados, batían el canoso mar con los remos.

»Así que proseguimos navegando desde allí, nuestro corazón acongojado, huyendo con gusto de la muerte, aunque habíamos perdido a nuestros compañeros.»

Canto X

LA ISLA DE EOLO.
EL PALACIO DE CIRCE LA HECHICERA

«**A**RRIBAMOS a la isla Eolia, isla flotante donde habita Eolo Hipótada[147], amado de los dioses inmortales. Un muro indestructible de bronce la rodea, y se yergue como roca pelada.

»Tiene Eolo doce hijos nacidos en su palacio, seis hijas y seis hijos mozos, y ha entregado sus hijas a sus hijos como esposas. Siempre están ellos de banquete en casa de su padre y su venerable madre, y tienen a su alcance alimentos sin cuento. Durante el día resuena la casa, que huele a carne asada, con el sonido de la flauta, y por la noche duermen entre colchas y sobre lechos taladrados junto a sus respetables esposas. Conque llegamos a la ciudad y mansiones de éstos. Durante un mes me agasajó y me preguntaba detalladamente por Ilión, por las naves de los argivos y por el regreso de los aqueos, y yo le relaté todo como me correspondía. Y cuando por fin le hablé de volver y le pedí que me despidiera, no se negó y me proporcionó

10

---

[147] No sabemos mucho más de este Eolo, señor de los vientos, a quien a veces se identifica erróneamente con el hijo de Helen y fundador de la estirpe eolia. Los mitógrafos, sin embargo, se esfuerzan en distinguirlos y hacen a éste hijo de Poseidón pese a que Homero le llama hijo de Hipotes, personaje por lo demás desconocido. Un detalle llamativo es la endogamia incestuosa de su familia, aunque tiene paralelos en el mismo Olimpo (Zeus y Hera, etc.). La isla donde vive es flotante y, por tanto, ilocalizable. Pese a todo, R. Carpenter, que supone esta parte de las aventuras en el Occidente, sugiere que podría ser la isla de Pantellería, entre Túnez y Sicilia, ob. cit., pág. 105).

escolta. Me entregó un pellejo de buey de nueve años que él había desollado, y en él ató las sendas de mugidores vientos, 20 pues el Cronida le había hecho despensero de vientos, para que amainara o impulsara al que quisiera. Sujetó el odre a la curvada nave con un brillante hilo de plata para que no escaparan ni un poco siquiera, y me envió a Céfiro para que soplara y condujera a las naves y a nosotros con ellas. Pero no iba a cumplirlo, pues nos vimos perdidos por nuestra estupidez.

»Navegamos tanto de día como de noche durante nueve días, y al décimo se nos mostró por fin la tierra patria y pudimos ver muy cerca gente calentándose al fuego. Pero en ese 30 momento me sobrevino un dulce sueño, cansado como estaba, pues continuamente gobernaba yo el timón de la nave —que no se lo encomendé nunca a ningún compañero, a fin de llegar más rápidamente a la tierra patria.

»Mis compañeros conversaban entre sí y creían que yo llevaba a casa oro y plata, regalo del magnánimo Eolo Hipótada. Y decía así uno al que tenía al lado:

»"¡Ay, ay, cómo quieren y honran a éste todos los hombres a cuya ciudad y tierra llega! De Troya se trae muchos y buenos 40 tesoros como botín; en cambio, nosotros, después de llevar a cabo la misma expedición, volvemos a casa con las manos vacías. También ahora Eolo le ha entregado esto correspondiendo a su amistad. Conque, vamos, examinemos qué es, veamos cuánto oro y plata se encierra en este odre."

»Así hablaban, y prevaleció la decisión funesta de mis compañeros: desataron el odre y todos los vientos se precipitaron fuera, mientras que a mis compañeros los arrebataba un huracán y los llevó llorando de nuevo al ponto lejos de la patria. Entonces desperté yo y me puse a cavilar en mi irreprochable 50 ánimo si me arrojaría de la nave para perecer en el mar o soportaría en silencio y permanecería todavía entre los vivientes. Conque aguanté y quedéme y me eché sobre la nave cubriendo mi cuerpo. Y las naves eran arrastradas de nuevo hacia la isla Eolia por una terrible tempestad de vientos, mientras mis compañeros se lamentaban.

»Por fin pusimos pie en tierra, hicimos provisión de agua y enseguida comenzaron mis compañeros a comer junto a las rápidas naves. Cuando nos habíamos hartado de comida y bebida tomé como acompañantes al heraldo y a un compañero y me encaminé a la ínclita morada de Eolo, y lo encontré banqueteando en compañía de su esposa e hijos. Cuando llegamos a la casa nos sentamos sobre el umbral junto a las puertas, y ellos se levantaron admirados y me preguntaron:

»"¿Cómo es que has vuelto, Odiseo? ¿Qué demón maligno ha caído sobre ti? Pues nosotros te despedimos gentilmente para que llegaras a tu patria y hogar a donde quiera que te fuera grato."

»Así dijeron, y yo les contesté con el corazón acongojado:

»"Me han perdido mis malvados compañeros y, además, el maldito sueño. Así que remediadlo, amigos, pues está en vuestras manos."

»Así dije, tratando de calmarlos con mis suaves palabras, pero ellos quedaron en silencio, y por fin su padre me contestó:

»"Márchate enseguida de esta isla, tú, el más reprobable de los vivientes, que no me es lícito acoger ni despedir a un hombre que resulta odioso a los dioses felices. ¡Fuera!, ya que has llegado aquí odiado por los inmortales."

»Así diciendo, me arrojó de su casa entre profundos lamentos. Así que continuamos nagevando con el corazón acongojado, y el vigor de mis hombres se gastaba con el doloroso remar, pues debido a nuestra insensatez ya no se nos presentaba medio de volver.

»Navegamos tanto de día como de noche durante seis días, y al séptimo arribamos a la escarpada ciudadela de Lamo, a Telépilo de Lestrigonia[148], donde el pastor que entra llama a voces al que sale y éste le contesta; donde un hombre que no duerma puede cobrar dos jornales, uno por apacentar vacas y otro por conducir blancas ovejas, pues los caminos del día y de la noche son cercanos.

---

[148] Lugar mítico —significa «de lejanas puertas»— al que se supone, por lo general, en el nordeste: su fuente se llama Artacia, como la de Cízico, y la expresión «los caminos del día y de la noche son cercanos» podría aludir a un país donde las noches son largas (cfr. G. S. Kirk, *Los poemas*..., pág. 218). R. Carpenter, por el contrario, cree que se trata de Bonifacio en la isla de Córcega (ob. cit., págs. 107-8).

»Cuando llegamos a su excelente puerto —lo rodea por todas partes roca escarpada, y en su boca sobresalen dos acantilados, uno frente a otro, por lo que la entrada es estrecha—, 90
todos mis compañeros amarraron dentro sus curvadas naves, y
éstas quedaron atadas, muy juntas, dentro del puerto, pues no
se hinchaban allí las olas ni mucho ni poco, antes bien había
en torno una blanca bonanza. Sólo yo detuve mi negra nave
fuera del puerto, en el extremo mismo, sujeté el cable a la roca
y subiendo a un elevado puesto de observación me quedé allí:
no se veía labor de bueyes ni de hombres, sólo humo que se levantaba del suelo.

»Entonces envié a mis compañeros para que indagaran qué 100
hombres eran de los que comen pan sobre la tierra, eligiendo a
dos hombres y dándoles como tercer compañero a un heraldo.
Partieron éstos y se encaminaron por una senda llana por donde los carros llevaban leña a la ciudad desde los altos montes.
Y se toparon con una moza que tomaba agua delante de la ciudad, con la robusta hija de Antífates Lestrigón. Había bajado
hasta la fuente Artacia de bella corriente, de donde solían llevar agua a la ciudad. Acercándose mis compañeros se dirigieron a ella y le preguntaron quién era el rey y sobre quiénes reinaba. Y enseguida les mostró el elevado palacio de su padre. 110
Apenas habían entrado, encontraron a la mujer del rey, grande
como la cima de un monte, y se atemorizaron ante ella. Hizo
ésta venir enseguida del ágora al ínclito Antífates, su esposo,
quien tramó la triste muerte para aquéllos. Así que agarró a
uno de mis compañeros y se lo preparó como almuerzo, pero
los otros dos se dieron a la fuga y llegaron a las naves. Entonces el rey comenzó a dar grandes voces por la ciudad, y los gigantescos Lestrígones que lo oyeron empezaron a venir cada
uno de un sitio, a miles, y se parecían no a hombres, sino a gigantes. Y desde las rocas comenzaron a arrojarnos peñascos 120
grandes como hombres, así que junto a las naves se elevó un
estruendo de hombres que morían y de navíos que se quebraban. Además, ensartábanlos como si fueran peces y se los llevaban como nauseabundo festín.

»Conque mientras mataban a éstos dentro del profundo
puerto, saqué mi aguda espada de junto al muslo y corté las
amarras de mi nave de azuloscura proa. Y, apremiando a mis

compañeros, les ordené que se inclinaran sobre los remos para poder escapar de la desgracia. Y todos a un tiempo saltaron sobre ellos, pues temían morir.

»Así que mi nave evitó de buena gana las elevadas rocas en dirección al ponto, mientras que las demás se perdían allí todas juntas. Continuamos navegando con el corazón acongojado, huyendo de la muerte gozosos, aunque habíamos perdido a los compañeros.

»Y llegamos a la isla de Eea[149], donde habita Circe, la de lindas trenzas, la terrible diosa dotada de voz, hermana carnal del sagaz Eetes: ambos habían nacido de Helios, el que lleva la luz a los mortales, y de Perses, la hija de Océano.

»Allí nos dejamos llevar silenciosamente por la nave a lo largo de la ribera hasta un puerto acogedor de naves —y es que nos conducía un dios. Desembarcamos y nos echamos a dormir durante dos días y dos noches, consumiendo nuestro ánimo por mor del cansancio y el dolor. Pero cuando Eos, de lindas trenzas, completó el tercer día, tomé ya mi lanza y aguda espada y, levantándome de junto a la nave, subí a un puesto de observación por si conseguía divisar labor de hombres y oír voces. Cuando hube subido a un puesto de observación, me detuve y ante mis ojos ascendía humo de la tierra de anchos caminos a través de unos encinares y espeso bosque, en el palacio de Circe. Así que me puse a cavilar en mi interior si bajaría a indagar, pues había visto humo enrojecido.

»Mientras así cavilaba me pareció lo mejor dirigirme primero a la rápida nave y a la ribera del mar para distribuir alimentos a mis compañeros y enviarlos a que indagaran ellos. Y cuando ya estaba cerca de la curvada nave, algún dios se compadeció de mí —solo como estaba—, pues puso en mi camino un enorme ciervo de elevada cornamenta. Bajaba éste desde el pasto del bosque a beber al río, pues ya lo tenía agobiado la

130

140

150

160

---

[149] No hay que confundir esta isla con la ciudad de Eea en la Cólquide, donde reina Eetes. En la intención de Homero, la isla, que toma su nombre de la ciudad, debe encontrarse en el lejano Este, pues pertenece a la familia de Helios (cfr. XII.1-5) y no en Italia, como pensaron los romanos. Tanto Eetes como sus hermanas Pasífae y Circe poseen poderes mágicos. En este canto tenemos una notable acumulación de elementos mágicos conservados a través del folklore.

fuerza del sol. Así que en el momento en que salía lo alcancé en medio de la espalda, junto al espinazo. Atravesólo mi lanza de bronce de lado a lado y se desplomó sobre el polvo chillando —y su vida se le escapó volando. Me puse sobre él, saqué de la herida la lanza de bronce y lo dejé tirado en el suelo. Entre tanto, corté mimbres y varillas y, trenzando una soga como de una braza, bien torneada por todas partes, até los pies del terrible monstruo. Me dirigí a la negra nave con el animal colgando de mi cuello y apoyado en mi lanza, pues no era posible 170 llevarlo sobre el hombro con una sola mano —y es que la bestia era descomunal. Arrojéla por fin junto a la nave y desperté a mis compañeros, dirigiéndome a cada uno en particular con dulces palabras:

»"Amigos, no descenderemos a la morada de Hades —por muy afligidos que estemos—, hasta que nos llegue el día señalado. Conque, vamos, mientras tenemos en la rápida nave comida y bebida, pensemos en comer y no nos dejemos consumir por el hambre."

»Así dije, y pronto se dejaron persuadir por mis palabras. Se quitaron de encima las ropas, junto a la ribera del estéril mar, y contemplaron con admiración al ciervo —y es que la bestia era 180 descomunal. Así que cuando se hartaron de verlo con sus ojos, lavaron sus manos y se prepararon espléndido festín.

»Así pasamos todo el día, hasta que se puso el sol, dándonos a comer abundante carne y delicioso vino. Y cuando se puso el sol y cayó la oscuridad nos echamos a dormir junto a la ribera del mar.

»Cuando se mostró Eos, la que nace de la mañana, la de dedos de rosa, los reuní en asamblea y les comuniqué mi palabra:

»"Escuchad mis palabras, compañeros, por muchas calamidades que hayáis soportado. Amigos, no sabemos dónde cae el 190 Poniente ni dónde el Saliente, dónde se oculta bajo la tierra Helios, que alumbra a los mortales, ni dónde se levanta. Conque tomemos pronto una resolución, si es que todavía es posible, que yo no lo creo. Al subir a un elevado puesto de observación he visto una isla a la que rodea, como corona, el ilimitado mar. Es isla de poca altura, y he podido ver con mis ojos, en su mismo centro, humo a través de unos encinares y espeso bosque."

»Así dije, y a mis compañeros se les quebró el corazón cuando recordaron las acciones de Antífates Lestrigón y la violencia del magnánimo Cíclope, el comedor de hombres. Lloraban a gritos y derramaban abundante llanto; pero nada conseguían con lamentarse. Entonces dividí en dos grupos a todos mis compañeros de buenas grebas y di un jefe a cada grupo. A unos los mandaba yo y a los otros el divino Euríloco. Enseguida agitamos unos guijarros en un casco de bronce y saltó el guijarro del magnánimo Euríloco. Conque se puso en camino y con él veintidós compañeros que lloraban, y nos dejaron atrás a nosotros gimiendo también.

»Encontraron en un valle la morada de Circe, edificada con piedras talladas, en lugar abierto. La rodeaban lobos montaraces y leones, a los que había hechizado dándoles brebajes maléficos, pero no atacaron a mis hombres, sino que se levantaron y jugueteaban alrededor moviendo sus largas colas. Como cuando un rey sale del banquete y le rodean sus perros moviendo la cola —pues siempre lleva algo que calme sus impulsos—, así los lobos de poderosas uñas y los leones rodearon a mis compañeros, moviendo la cola. Pero éstos se echaron a temblar cuando vieron las terribles bestias. Detuviéronse en el pórtico de la diosa de lindas trenzas y oyeron a Circe que cantaba dentro con hermosa voz, mientras se aplicaba a su enorme e inmortal telar —¡y qué suaves, agradables y brillantes son las labores de las diosas! Entonces comenzó a hablar Polites, caudillo de hombres, mi más preciado y valioso compañero:

»"Amigos, alguien —no sé si diosa o mujer— está dentro cantando algo hermoso mientras se aplica a su gran telar —que todo el piso se estremece con el sonido—. Conque hablémosle enseguida."

»Así dijo, y ellos comenzaron a llamar a voces. Salió la diosa enseguida, abrió las brillantes puertas y los invitó a entrar. Y todos la siguieron en su ignorancia, pero Euríloco se quedó allí barruntando que se trataba de una trampa. Los introdujo, los hizo sentar en sillas y sillones, y en su presencia mezcló queso, harina y rubia miel con vino de Pramnio. Y echó en esta pócima brebajes maléficos para que se olvidaran por completo de su tierra patria.

»Después que se lo hubo ofrecido y lo bebieron, golpeólos con su varita y los encerró en las pocilgas. Quedaron éstos con cabeza, voz, pelambre y figura de cerdos, pero su mente permaneció invariable, la misma de antes. Así quedaron encerrados mientras lloraban; y Circe les echó de comer bellotas, fabucos y el fruto del cornejo, todo lo que comen los cerdos que se acuestan en el suelo.

»Conque Euríloco volvió a la rápida, negra nave para informarme sobre los compañeros y su amarga suerte, pero no podía decir palabra —con desearlo mucho—, porque tenía atravesado el corazón por un gran dolor: sus ojos se llenaron de lágrimas y su ánimo barruntaba el llanto. Cuando por fin le interrogamos todos llenos de admiración, comenzó a contarnos la pérdida de los demás compañeros:

»"Atravesamos los encinares como ordenaste, ilustre Odiseo, y encontramos en un valle una hermosa mansión edificada con piedras talladas, en lugar abierto. Allí cantaba una diosa o mujer mientras se aplicaba a su enorme telar; los compañeros comenzaron a llamar a voces; salió ella, abrió las brillantes puertas y nos invitó a entrar. Y todos la siguieron en su ignorancia, pero yo no me quedé por barruntar que se trataba de una trampa. Así que desaparecieron todos juntos y no volvió a aparecer ninguno de ellos, y eso que los esperé largo tiempo sentado."

»Así habló; entonces me eché al hombro la espada de clavos de plata, grande, de bronce, y el arco en bandolera, y le ordené que me condujera por el mismo camino, pero él se abrazó a mis rodillas y me suplicaba, y, lamentándose, me dirigía aladas palabras:

»"No me lleves allí a la fuerza, Odiseo de linaje divino; déjame aquí, pues sé que ni volverás tú ni traerás a ninguno de tus compañeros. Huyamos rápidamente con éstos, pues quizá podamos todavía evitar el día funesto"150.

»Así habló, pero yo lo contesté diciendo:

»"Euríloco, quédate tú aquí comiendo y bebiendo junto a la negra nave, que yo me voy. Me ha venido una necesidad imperiosa."

---

150 Eufemismo por «muerte».

»Así diciendo, me alejé de la nave y del mar. Y cuando en mi marcha por el valle iba ya a llegar a la mansión de Circe, la de muchos brebajes, me salió al encuentro Hermes, el de la varita de oro, semejante a un adolescente, con el bozo apuntándole ya y radiante de juventud. Me tomó de la mano y, llamándome por mi nombre, dijo:

»"Desdichado, ¿cómo es que marchas solo por estas lomas, desconocedor como eres del terreno? Tus compañeros están encerrados en casa de Circe, como cerdos, ocupando bien construidas pocilgas. ¿Es que vienes a rescatarlos? No creo que regreses ni siquiera tú mismo, sino que te quedarás donde los demás. Así que, vamos, te voy a librar del mal y a salvarte. Mira, toma este brebaje benéfico, cuyo poder te protegerá del día funesto, y marcha a casa de Circe. Te voy a manifestar todos los malvados propósitos de Circe: te preparará una poción y echará en la comida brebajes, pero no podrá hechizarte, ya que no lo permitirá este brebaje benéfico que te voy a dar. Te aconsejaré con detalle: cuando Circe trate de conducirte con su larga varita, saca de junto a tu muslo la aguda espada y lánzate contra ella como queriendo matarla. Entonces te invitará, por miedo, a acostarte con ella. No rechaces por un momento el lecho de la diosa, a fin de que suelte a tus compañeros y te acoja bien a ti. Pero debes ordenarla que jure con el gran juramento de los dioses felices que no va a meditar contra ti maldad alguna ni te va a hacer cobarde y poco hombre cuando te hayas desnudado"[151].

»Así diciendo, me entregó el Argifonte una planta que había arrancado de la tierra y me mostró su propiedades: de raíz era negra, pero su flor se asemejaba a la leche. Los dioses la llaman *moly*, y es difícil a los hombres mortales extraerla del suelo, pero los dioses lo pueden todo.

»Luego marchó Hermes al lejano Olimpo a través de la isla boscosa y yo me dirigí a la mansión de Circe. Y mientras marchaba, mi corazón revolvía muchos pensamientos. Me detuve ante las puertas de la diosa de lindas trenzas, me puse a gritar y la diosa oyó mi voz. Salió ésta, abrió las brillantes puertas y me invitó a entrar. Entonces yo la seguí con el corazón acongoja-

---

[151] Es el juramento por la Estige, cfr. nota 111.

Ulises y Circe (de Annibale Carracci – Palacio Farnesio)

do. Me introdujo e hizo sentar en un sillón de clavos de plata, hermoso, bien trabajado, y bajo mis pies había un escabel. Preparóme una pócima en copa de oro, para que la bebiera, y echó en ella un brebaje, planeando maldades en su corazón.

»Conque cuando me lo hubo ofrecido y lo bebí —aunque no me había hechizado—, tocóme con su varita y, llamándome por mi nombre, dijo:

»"Marcha ahora a la pocilga, a tumbarte en compañía de tus amigos." 320

»Así dijo, pero yo, sacando mi aguda espada de junto al muslo, me lancé sobre Circe, como deseando matarla. Ella dio un fuerte grito y corriendo se abrazó a mis rodillas y, lamentándose, me dirigió aladas palabras:

»"¿Quién y de dónde eres? ¿Dónde tienes tu ciudad y tus padres? Estoy sobrecogida de admiración, porque no has quedado hechizado a pesar de haber bebido estos brebajes. Nadie, ningún otro hombre ha podido soportarlos una vez que los ha bebido y han pasado el cerco de sus dientes. Pero tú tienes en el pecho un corazón imposible de hechizar. Así que seguro que 330 eres el asendereado Odiseo, de quien me dijo el de la varita de oro, el Argifonte que vendría al volver de Troya en su rápida, negra nave. Conque, vamos, vuelve tu espada a la vaina y subamos los dos a mi cama, para que nos entreguemos mutuamente unidos en amor y lecho."

»Así dijo, pero yo me dirigí a ella y le contesté:

»"Circe, ¿cómo quieres que sea amoroso contigo? A mis compañeros los has convertido en cerdos en tu palacio, y a mí me retienes aquí y, con intenciones perversas, me invitas a subir a tu aposento y a tu cama para hacerme cobarde y poco 340 hombre cuando esté desnudo. No desearía ascender a tu cama si no aceptaras al menos, diosa, jurarme con gran juramento que no vas a meditar contra mí maldad alguna."

»Así dije, y ella al punto juró como yo le había dicho. Conque, una vez que había jurado y terminado su promesa, subí a la hermosa cama de Circe.

»Entre tanto, cuatro siervas faenaban en el palacio, las que tiene como asistentas en su morada. Son de las que han nacido de fuentes, de bosques y de los sagrados ríos que fluyen al mar. Una colocaba sobre los sillones cobertores hermosos y alfombras debajo; otra extendía mesas de plata ante los sillones, y sobre ellas colocaba canastillas de oro; la tercera mezclaba delicioso vino en una crátera de plata y distribuía copas de oro, y la cuarta traía agua y encendía abundante fuego bajo un gran trípode —y así se calentaba el agua. Cuando el agua comenzó a hervir en el brillante bronce, me sentó en la bañera y me lavaba con el agua del gran trípode, vertiéndola agradable sobre mi cabeza y hombros, a fin de quitar de mis miembros el cansancio que come el vigor. Cuando me hubo lavado, ungido con aceite y vestido hermosa túnica y manto, me condujo e hizo sentar sobre un sillón de clavos de plata, hermoso, bien trabajado —y bajo mis pies había un escabel. Una sierva derramó sobre fuente de plata el aguamanos que llevaba en hermosa jarra de oro, para que me lavara, y al lado extendió una mesa pulimentada. La venerable ama de llaves puso comida sobre ella y añadió abundantes piezas escogidas, favoreciéndome entre los presentes[152]. Y me invitaba a que comiera, pero esto no placía a mi ánimo y estaba sentado con el pensamiento en otra parte, pues mi ánimo presentía la desgracia. Cuando Circe me vio sentado sin echar mano a la comida y con fuerte pesar, colocóse a mi lado y me dirigió aladas palabras:

»"¿Por qué, Odiseo, permaneces sentado como un mudo consumiendo tu ánimo y no tocas siquiera la comida y la bebida? Seguro que andas barruntando alguna otra desgracia, pero no tienes nada que temer, pues ya te he jurado un poderoso juramento."

»Así habló, y entonces le contesté diciendo:

»"Circe, ¿qué hombre como es debido probaría comida o bebida antes de que sus compañeros quedaran libres y él los viera con sus ojos? Conque, si me invitas con buena voluntad a beber y comer, suelta a mis fieles compañeros para que pueda verlos con mis ojos."

»Así dije; Circe atravesó el mégaron con su varita en las ma-

360

370

380

---

[152] Resulta extraña la aparición de otra sierva y de un ama de llaves, cuando más arriba (vv. 348 y ss.) se dice que hay cuatro siervas y se describe su actividad. La razón es que los vv. 368-72 son fórmulas de aplicación mecánica en escenas típicas de banquete, cfr. también I.136 y ss., IV.52 y ss., VII.172 y ss., XV.135 y ss., y XVII.91 y ss.

nos, abrió las puertas de las pocilgas y sacó de allí a los que parecían cerdos de nueve años. Después se colocaron enfrente, y 39
Circe, pasando entre ellos, untaba a cada uno con otro brebaje.
Se les cayó la pelambre que había producido el maléfico brebaje que les diera la soberana Circe y se convirtieron de nuevo en
hombres aún más jóvenes que antes y más bellos y robustos de
aspecto. Y me reconocieron y cada uno me tomaba de la
mano. A todos les entró un llanto conmovedor —toda la casa
resonaba que daba pena—, y hasta la misma diosa se compadeció de ellos. Así que se vino a mi lado y me dijo la divina entre 40(
las diosas:

»"Hijo de Laertes, de linaje divino, Odiseo rico en ardides,
marcha ya a tu rápida nave junto a la ribera del mar. Antes que
nada, arrastrad la nave hacia tierra, llevad vuestras posesiones
y armas todas a una gruta y vuelve aquí después con tus fieles
compañeros."

»Así dijo, mi valeroso ánimo se dejó persuadir y me puse en
camino hacia la rápida nave junto a la ribera del mar. Conque
encontré junto a la rápida nave a mis fieles compañeros que
lloraban lamentablemente derramando abundante llanto.
Como las terneras que viven en el campo salen todas al encuentro y retozan en torno a las vacas del rebaño que vuelven 41(
al establo después de hartarse de pastar (pues ni los cercados
pueden ya retenerlas y, mugiendo sin cesar corretean en torno
a sus madres), así me rodearon aquéllos, llorando cuando me
vieron con sus ojos. Su ánimo se imaginaba que era como si
hubieran vuelto a su patria y a la misma ciudad de Itaca, donde
se habían criado y nacido. Y, lamentándose, me decían aladas
palabras:

»"Con tu vuelta, hijo de los dioses, nos hemos alegrado lo
mismo que si hubiéramos llegado a nuestra patria Itaca. Vamos, cuéntanos la pérdida de los demás compañeros." 42

»Así dijeron, y yo les hablé con suaves palabras:

»"Antes que nada, empujaremos la rápida nave a tierra y llevaremos hasta una gruta nuestras posesiones y armas todas.
Luego, apresuraos a seguirme todos, para que veáis a vuestros
compañeros comer y beber en casa de Circe, pues tienen comida sin cuento."

»Así dije, y enseguida obedecieron mis órdenes. Sólo Euríloco trataba de retenerme a todos los compañeros y, hablándoles, decía aladas palabras:

»"Desgraciados, ¿a dónde vamos a ir? ¿Por qué deseáis vuestro daño bajando a casa de Circe, que os convertirá a todos en cerdos, lobos o leones para que custodiéis por la fuerza su gran morada, como ya hizo el Cíclope cuando nuestros compañeros llegaron a su establo y con ellos el audaz Odiseo? También aquéllos perecieron por la insensatez de éste."

»Así habló; entonces dudé si sacar la larga espada de junto a mi robusto muslo y, cortándole la cabeza, arrojarla contra el suelo, aunque era pariente mío cercano. Pero mis compañeros me lo impidieron, cada uno de un lado, con suaves palabras:

»"Hijo de los dioses, dejaremos aquí a éste, si tú así lo ordenas, para que se quede junto a la nave y la custodie. Y a nosotros llévanos a la sagrada mansión de Circe."

»Así diciendo, se alejaron de la nave y del mar. Pero Euríloco no se quedó atrás, junto a la cóncava nave, sino que nos siguió, pues temía mis terribles amenazas.

»Entre tanto, Circe lavó gentilmente a mis otros compañeros que estaban en su morada, los ungió con brillante aceite y los vistió con túnicas y mantos. Y los encontramos cuando se estaban banqueteando en el palacio. Cuando se vieron unos a otros y se contaron todo, rompieron a llorar entre lamentos, y la casa toda resonaba. Así que la divina entre las diosas se vino a mi lado y dijo:

»"Hijo de Laertes, de linaje divino, Odiseo rico en ardides, no excitéis más el abundante llanto, pues también yo conozco los trabajos que habéis sufrido en el ponto lleno de peces y los daños que os han causado en tierra firme hombres enemigos. Conque, vamos, comed vuestra comida y bebed vuestro vino hasta que recobréis las fuerzas que teníais el día que abandonasteis la tierra patria de la escarpada Itaca; que ahora estáis agotados y sin fuerzas, con el duro vagar siempre en vuestras mientes. Y vuestro ánimo no se llena de pensamientos alegres, pues ya habéis sufrido mucho."

»Así dijo, y nuestro valeroso ánimo se dejó persuadir. Allí nos quedamos un año entero —día tras día—, dándonos a comer carne en abundancia y delicioso vino. Pero cuando se cumplió el año y volvieron las estaciones con el transcurrir de

los meses —ya habían pasado largos días—, me llamaron mis 470
fieles compañeros y me dijeron:

»"Amigo, piensa ya en la tierra patria, si es que tu destino es
que te salves y llegues a tu bien edificada morada y a tu tierra
patria."

»Así dijeron, y mi valeroso ánimo se dejó persuadir. Estuvimos todo un día, hasta la puesta del sol, comiendo carne en
abundancia y delicioso vino. Y cuando se puso el sol y cayó la
oscuridad, mis compañeros se acostaron en el sombrío palacio.
Pero yo subí a la hermosa cama de Circe y, abrazándome a sus 480
rodillas, la supliqué, y la diosa escuchó mi voz. Y hablándole,
decía aladas palabras:

»"Circe, cúmpleme la promesa que me hiciste de enviarme a
casa, que mi ánimo ya está impaciente y el de mis compañeros,
quienes, cuando tú estás lejos, me consumen el corazón llorando a mi alrededor."

»Así dije, y al punto contestó la divina entre las diosas:

»"Hijo de Laertes, de linaje divino, Odiseo rico en ardides,
no permanezcáis más tiempo en mi palacio contra vuestra voluntad. Pero antes tienes que llevar a cabo otro viaje; tienes 490
que llegarte a la mansión de Hades y la terrible Perséfone para
pedir oráculo al alma del tebano Tiresias, el adivino ciego,
cuya mente todavía está inalterada. Pues sólo a éste, incluso
muerto, ha concedido Perséfone tener conciencia[153]; que los
demás revolotean como sombras."

»Así dijo, y a mí se me quebró el corazón. Rompí a llorar
sobre el lecho, y mi corazón ya no quería vivir ni volver a contemplar la luz del sol.

---

153 No sabemos a qué responde este don de Perséfone a Tiresias o si es,
simplemente, una invención de Homero para que el célebre adivino pueda pre-
decir el futuro a Odiseo. Porque, según la concepción homérica del más allá, el
alma *(psyché)* es como una sombra que se desprende del cuerpo al morir el hombre y que posee la forma de éste, pero ninguna de sus cualidades (cfr. los versos 218 y ss.). Las demás almas se reaniman con la sangre del sacrificio, pero
sólo hablan de su pasado, ignoran el presente y el futuro: Anticlea desconoce la
presencia de los pretendientes en el palacio de Itaca (cfr. vv. 184-6). Sobre la
concepción homérica del más allá, son ya clásicas las obras de E. Rohde *Psique*,
Barcelona, 1973 (trad. esp.), y L. Radermacher, *Das Jenseits im Mythos der Helle-
nen,* Bonn, 1903.

»Cuando me había hartado de llorar y de agitarme, le dije, contestándole: 500

»"Circe, ¿y quién iba a conducirme en este viaje? Porque a la mansión de Hades nunca ha llegado nadie en negra nave."

»Así dije, y al punto me contestó la divina entre las diosas:

»"Hijo de Laertes, de linaje divino, Odiseo rico en ardides, no sientas necesidad de guía en tu nave. Coloca el mástil, extiende las blancas velas y siéntate. El soplo de Bóreas[154] la llevará, y cuando hayas atravesado el Océano y llegues a las planas riberas y al bosque de Perséfone —esbeltos álamos negros y estériles cañaverales—, amarra la nave allí mismo, sobre el   510 Océano de profundas corrientes, y dirígete a la espaciosa morada de Hades. Hay un lugar donde desembocan en el Aqueronte el Piriflegetón y el Kotyto[155], difluente de la laguna Estigia, y una roca en la confluencia de los dos sonoros ríos. Acércate allí, héroe —así te lo aconsejo—, y, cavando un hoyo como de un codo por cada lado, haz una libación en honor de todos los muertos, primero con leche y miel, luego con delicioso vino, y en, tercer lugar, con agua. Y esparce por encima   520 blanca harina. Suplica insistentemente a las inertes cabezas de los muertos[156] y promete que, cuando vuelvas a Itaca, sacrificarás una vaca que no haya parido, la mejor, y llenarás una pira de obsequios y que, aparte de esto, sólo a Tiresias le sacrificarás una oveja negra por completo, la que sobresalga entre vuestro rebaño. Cuando hayas suplicado a la famosa raza de los difuntos, sacrifica allí mismo un carnero y una borrega negra, de cara hacia el Erebo[157]; y vuélvete para dirigirte a las corrientes del río, donde se acercarán muchas almas de difun-   530

---

[154] Aquí hay una inconsecuencia, aunque de poca monta. De hecho, según la detallada descripción que se hace de la llegada a las puertas del Hades, éste debe situarse en el lejano Norte, cfr. XI.13 y ss., por lo que es imposible que sea el viento Bóreas el que impulsa la nave.

[155] Los tres nombres son parlantes y significan «río del llanto», «del fuego ardiente» y «de las lamentaciones».

[156] Fórmula exclusivamente odiseica de sentido no muy claro (cfr. también en v. 536 y XI.29 y 49). El adjetivo *amenená* puede significar «carente de fuerza *(menos)*», pero ya en la Antigüedad se dudaba de su sentido (cfr. Aristófanes, *Frg.* 222).

[157] Paso tenebroso entre la tierra y el Hades. Contiene una raíz indoeuropea que significa «oscuridad».

tos. Entonces ordena a tus compañeros que desuellen las víctimas que yacen en tierra atravesadas por el agudo bronce, que las quemen después de desollarlas y que supliquen a los dioses, al tremendo Hades y a la terrible Perséfone. Y tú saca de junto al muslo la aguda espada y siéntate sin permitir que las inertes cabezas de los muertos se acerquen a la sangre antes de que hayas preguntado a Tiresias. Entonces llegará el adivino, caudillo de hombres, que te señalará el viaje, la longitud del camino y el regreso, para que marches sobre el ponto lleno de peces."

»Así dijo, y enseguida apareció Eos, la del trono de oro. Me vistió de túnica y manto, y ella, la ninfa, se puso una túnica grande, sutil y agradable, echó un hermoso ceñidor de oro a su cintura y sobre su cabeza puso un velo. Entonces recorrí el palacio apremiando a mis compañeros con suaves palabras, poniéndome al lado de cada hombre:

»"Ya no durmáis más tiempo con dulce sueño; marchémonos, que la soberana Circe me ha revelado todo."

»Así dije, y su valeroso ánimo se dejó persuadir. Pero ni siquiera de allí pude llevarme sanos y salvos a mis compañeros. Había un tal Elpenor, el más joven de todos, no muy brillante en la guerra ni muy dotado de mientes, que, por buscar la fresca, borracho como estaba, se había echado a dormir en el sagrado palacio de Circe, lejos de los compañeros. Cuando oyó el ruido y el tumulto, levantóse de repente y no reparó en volver para bajar la larga escalera, sino que cayó justo desde el techo. Y se le quebraron las vértebras del cuello y su alma bajó al Hades. 560

»Cuando se acercaron los demás les dije mi palabra:

»"Seguro que pensáis que ya marchamos a casa, a la querida patria, pero Circe me ha indicado otro viaje a las mansiones de Hades y la terrible Perséfone para pedir oráculo al tebano Tiresias."

»Así dije, y el corazón se les quebró; sentáronse de nuevo a llorar y se mesaban los cabellos. Pero nada consiguieron con lamentarse.

»Y cuando ya partíamos acongojados hacia la nave y la ribera del mar derramando abundante llanto, acercóse Circe a la negra nave y ató un carnero y una borrega negra, marchando inadvertida. ¡Con facilidad!, pues ¿quién podría ver con sus ojos a un dios comiendo aquí o allá si éste no quiere?»

Canto XI

DESCENSUS AD INFEROS[158]

«Y cuando habíamos llegado a la nave y al mar, antes que nada empujamos la nave hacia el mar divino y colocamos el mástil y las velas a la negra nave. Embarcamos también ganados que habíamos tomado, y luego ascendimos nosotros llenos de dolor, derramando gruesas lágrimas. Y Circe, la de lindas trenzas, la terrible diosa dotada de voz, nos envió un viento que llenaba las velas, buen compañero detrás de nuestra nave de azuloscura proa. Colocamos luego el aparejo, nos sentamos a lo largo de la nave y a ésta la dirigían el viento y el piloto. Durante todo el día estuvieron extendidas las velas en su viaje a través del ponto.

»Y Helios se sumergió, y todos los caminos se llenaron de sombras. Entonces llegó nuestra nave a los confines de Océano de profundas corrientes, donde está el pueblo y la ciudad de los hombres Cimerios[159] cubiertos por la oscuridad y la niebla. Nunca Helios, el brillante, los mira desde arriba con sus rayos, ni cuando va al cielo estrellado ni cuando de nuevo se vuelve a la tierra desde el cielo, sino que la noche se extiende sombría

10

---

[158] Sobre los problemas que plantea este canto, llamado habitualmente Nekya, cfr. Introducción y W. Büchner, «Probleme der homerischen Nekya», *Hermes* 72, 1937, págs. 104-22.

[159] La tradición manuscrita no se pone de acuerdo sobre el nombre de este pueblo. Quizá la lectura «cimerios» sea un intento de darle nombre real a un pueblo que para Homero era simplemente mítico. Los cimerios históricos habitaban en el sur de Rusia (cfr. el nombre de Crimea) y allí ciertamente no hay noche perpetua.

sobre estos desgraciados mortales. Llegados allí, arrastramos 20
nuestra nave, sacamos los ganados y nos pusimos en camino
cerca de la corriente de Océano, hasta que llegamos al lugar
que nos había indicado Circe. Allí Perimedes y Euríloco sostuvieron las víctimas y yo saqué la aguda espada de junto a mi
muslo e hice una fosa como de un codo por uno y otro lado.
Y alrededor de ella derramaba las libaciones para todos los difuntos, primero con leche y miel, después con delicioso vino y,
en tercer lugar, con agua. Y esparcí por encima blanca harina.

»Y hacía abundantes súplicas a las inertes cabezas de los
muertos, jurando que, al volver a Itaca, sacrificaría en mi pala- 30
cio una vaca que no hubiera parido, la que fuera la mejor, y
que llenaría una pira de obsequios y que, aparte de esto, sacrificaría a sólo Tiresias una oveja negra por completo, la que so-
bresaliera entre nuestros rebaños.

»Luego que hube suplicado al linaje de los difuntos con promesas y súplicas, yugulé los ganados que había llevado junto a
la fosa y fluía su negra sangre. Entonces se empezaron a congregar desde el Erebo las almas de los difuntos, esposas y sol-
teras; y los ancianos que tienen mucho que soportar; y tiernas
doncellas con el ánimo afectado por un dolor reciente; y muchos alcanzados por lanzas de bronce, hombres muertos en la 40
guerra con las armas ensangrentadas. Andaban en grupos aquí
y allá, a uno y otro lado de la fosa, con un clamor sobrenatural, y a mí me atenazó el pálido terror.

»A continuación di órdenes a mis compañeros, apremiándo-
los a que desollaran y asaran las víctimas que yacían en el suelo
atravesadas por el cruel bronce, y que hicieran súplicas a los
dioses, al tremendo Hades y a la terrible Perséfone. Entonces
saqué la aguda espada de junto a mi muslo, me senté y no dejaba que las inertes cabezas de los muertos se acercaran a la sangre antes de que hubiera preguntado a Tiresias. 50

»La primera en llegar fue el alma de mi compañero Elpenor[160]. Todavía no estaba sepultado bajo la tierra, la de anchos

---

[160] Cfr. X.552 y ss. El hecho de que la primera en aparecer sea el alma de
Elpenor enlaza más directamente la problemática bajada al Hades con las demás
aventuras de Odiseo. El que Elpenor pueda hablar con Odiseo sin beber la sangre se debe a que está a las puertas del Hades; todavía no está enterrado.

caminos, pues habíamos abandonado su cadáver, no llorado y no sepulto, en casa de Circe, que nos urgía otro trabajo. Contemplándolo entonces, lo lloré y compadecí en mi ánimo, y, hablándole, decía aladas palabras:

»"Elpenor, ¿cómo has bajado a la nebulosa oscuridad? ¿Has llegado antes a pie que yo en mi negra nave?"

»Así le dije, y él, gimiendo, me respondió con su palabra:

»"Hijo de Laertes, de linaje divino, Odiseo rico en ardides, me enloqueció el Destino funesto de la divinidad y el vino abundante. Acostado en el palacio de Circe, no pensé en descender por la larga escalera, sino que caí justo desde el techo y mi cuello se quebró por la nuca. Y mi alma descendió a Hades.

»Ahora te suplico por aquellos a quienes dejaste detrás de ti, por quienes no están presentes; te suplico por tu esposa y por tu padre, el que te nutrió de pequeño, y por Telémaco, el hijo único a quien dejaste en tu palacio: sé que cuando marches de aquí, del palacio de Hades, fondearás tu bien fabricada nave en la isla de Eea. Te pido, soberano, que te acuerdes de mí allí, que no te alejes dejándome sin llorar ni sepultar, no sea que me convierta para ti en una maldición de los dioses. Antes bien, entiérrame con mis armas, todas cuantas tenga, y acumula para mí un túmulo sobre la ribera del canoso mar —¡desgraciado de mí!— para que lo sepan también los venideros. Cúmpleme esto y clava en mi tumba el remo con el que yo remaba cuando estaba vivo, cuando estaba entre mis compañeros."

»Así habló, y yo, respondiéndole, dije:

»"Esto te cumpliré, desdichado, y realizaré."

»Así permanecíamos sentados, contestándonos con palabras tristes; yo sostenía mi espada sobre la sangre y, enfrente, hablaba largamente el simulacro de mi compañero.

»También llegó el alma de mi difunta madre, la hija del magnánimo Autólico, Anticlea[161], a quien había dejado viva cuando marché a la sagrada Ilión. Mirándola la compadecí en

---

[161] Anticlea es hija de Autólico y madre de Odiseo. Según una rama importante de la tradición, que recoge la tragedia ática, antes de casarse con Laertes tuvo relaciones con Sísifo, por lo que realmente Odiseo es hijo de este héroe.

mi ánimo, pero ni aun así la permití, aunque mucho me dolía, acercarse a la sangre antes de interrogar a Tiresias.

»Y llegó el alma del Tebano Tiresias —en la mano su cetro de oro[162]—, y me reconoció, y dijo: 90

»"Hijo de Laertes, de linaje divino, Odiseo rico en ardides, ¿por qué has venido, desgraciado, abandonando la luz de Helios, para ver a los muertos y este lugar carente de goces? Apártate de la fosa y retira tu aguda espada para que beba de la sangre y te diga la verdad."

»Así dijo; yo entonces volví a guardar mi espada de clavos de plata, la metí en la vaina, y sólo cuando hubo bebido la negra sangre se dirigió a mí con palabras el irreprochable adivino:

»"Tratas de conseguir un dulce regreso, brillante Odiseo; sin 100 embargo, la divinidad te lo hará difícil, pues no creo que pases desapercibido al que sacude la tierra. Él ha puesto en su ánimo el resentimiento contra ti, airado porque le cegaste a su hijo. Sin embargo, llegaréis, aun sufriendo muchos males, si es que quieres contener tus impulsos y los de tus compañeros cuando acerques tu bien construida nave a la isla de Trinaquía, escapando del ponto de color violeta, y encontréis unas novillas paciendo y unos gordos ganados, los de Helios, el que ve todo y todo lo oye. Si dejas a éstas sin tocarlas y piensas en el regre- 110 so, llegaréis todavía a Itaca, aunque después de sufrir mucho; pero si les haces daño, entonces te predigo la destrucción para la nave y para tus compañeros. Y tú mismo, aunque escapes, volverás tarde y mal, en nave ajena, después de perder a todos tus compañeros. Y encontrarás desgracias en tu casa: a unos hombres insolentes que te comen tu comida, que pretenden a tu divina esposa y le entregan regalos de esponsales.

»"Pero, con todo, vengarás al volver las violencias de aquéllos. Después de que hayas matado a los pretendientes en tu palacio con engaño o bien abiertamente con el agudo bronce, 120 toma un bien fabricado remo y ponte en camino hasta que llegues a los hombres que no conocen el mar ni comen la comida

---

[162] El cetro es, por lo general, símbolo del poder *real*. El que aquí aparezca en manos de un *mantis* puede reflejar la primitiva indistinción entre rey y profeta o sacerdote.

sazonada con sal; tampoco conocen éstos naves de rojas proas
ni remos fabricados a mano, que son alas para las naves. Conque te voy a dar una señal manifiesta y no te pasará desaperci-
bida: cuando un caminante te salga al encuentro y te diga que
llevas un bieldo sobre tu espléndido hombro, clava en tierra el
remo fabricado a mano y, realizando hermosos sacrificios al   130
soberano Poseidón —un carnero, un toro y un verraco semental de cerdas— vuelve a casa y realiza sagradas hecatombes a
los dioses inmortales, los que ocupan el ancho cielo, a todos
por orden. Y entonces te llegará la muerte fuera del mar, una
muerte muy suave que te consuma agotado bajo la suave vejez[163]. Y los ciudadanos serán felices a tu alrededor. Esto que
te digo es verdad."

»Así habló, y yo le contesté diciendo:

»"Tiresias, esto lo han hilado los mismos dioses. Pero, vamos, dime esto e infórmame con verdad: veo aquí el alma de   140
mi madre muerta; permanece en silencio cerca de la sangre y
no se atreve a mirar a su hijo ni hablarle. Dime, soberano, de
qué modo reconocería que soy su hijo."

»Así hablé y él me respondió diciendo:

»"Te voy a decir una palabra fácil y la voy a poner en tu
mente. Cualquiera de los difuntos a quien permitas que se
acerque a la sangre te dirá la verdad, pero al que se lo impidas
se retirará."

»Así habló, y marchó a la mansión de Hades el alma del so-   150
berano Tiresias después de decir sus vaticinios.

»En cambio, yo permanecí allí constante hasta que llegó mi
madre y bebió la negra sangre. Al pronto me reconoció y, llorando, me dirigió aladas palabras:

»"Hijo mío, ¿cómo has bajado a la nebulosa oscuridad si estás vivo? Les es difícil a los vivos contemplar esto, pues hay en
medio grandes ríos y terribles corrientes, y, antes que nada,
Océano, al que no es posible atravesar a pie si no se tiene una
fabricada nave. ¿Has llegado aquí errante desde Troya con la   160

---

[163] Esta profecía dio lugar a un poema épico tardío que narra nuevas aventuras de Odiseo tras la muerte de los pretendientes, la *Telegonía* de Eugammon de
Cirene. Sin embargo, en este poema, Odiseo no moría «bajo la suave vejez»,
sino a manos de su hijo Telégono, habido de sus relaciones con Circe.

nave y los compañeros después de largo tiempo? ¿Es que no has llegado todavía a Itaca y no has visto en el palacio a tu esposa?"

»Así habló, y yo le respondí diciendo:

»"Madre mía, la necesidad me ha traído a Hades para pedir oráculo al alma del tebano Tiresias. Todavía no he llegado cerca de Acaya ni he tocado nuestra tierra en modo alguno, sino que ando errante en continuas dificultades desde al día en que seguí al divino Agamenón a Ilión, la de buenos potros, para luchar con los troyanos.

»"Pero, vamos, dime esto e infórmame con verdad: ¿Qué ¹⁷⁰ Ker de la terrible muerte te dominó? ¿Te sometió una larga enfermedad o te mató Artemis[164], la que goza con sus saetas, atacándote con sus suaves dardos? Háblame de mi padre y de mi hijo, a quien dejé; dime si mi autoridad real sigue en su poder o la posee otro hombre, pensando que ya no volveré más. Dime también la resolución y las intenciones de mi esposa legítima, si todavía permanece junto al niño y conserva todo a salvo o si ya la ha desposado el mejor de los aqueos."

»Así dije, y al pronto me respondió mi venerable madre: 180

»"Ella permanece todavía en tu palacio con ánimo afligido, pues las noches se le consumen entre dolores y los días entre lágrimas. Nadie tiene todavía tu hermosa autoridad, sino que Telémaco cultiva tranquilamente tus campos y asiste a banquetes equitativos de los que está bien que se ocupe un administrador de justicia, pues todos le invitan[165].

»"Tu padre permanece en el campo, y nunca va a la ciudad, y no tiene sábanas en la cama ni cobertores ni colchas espléndidas, sino que en invierno duerme como los siervos en el sue- 190 lo, cerca del hogar —y visten su cuerpo ropas de mala calidad—, mas cuando llega el verano y el otoño... tiene por todas partes humildes lechos, formados por hojas caídas, en la parte alta de su huerto fecundo en vides. Ahí yace doliéndose, y crece en su interior una gran aflicción añorando tu regreso, pues ya ha llegado a la molesta vejez.

---

¹⁶⁴ Cfr. nota 67.
¹⁶⁵ Cfr. nota 153.

»"En cuanto a mí, así he muerto y cumplido mi destino: no me mató Artemis, la certera cazadora, en mi palacio, acercándose con sus suaves dardos, ni me invadió enfermedad alguna de las que suelen consumir el ánimo con la odiosa podredumbre de los miembros, sino que mi nostalgia y mi preocupación por ti, brillante Odiseo, y tu bondad me privaron de mi dulce vida." 200

»Así dijo, y yo, cavilando en mi mente, quería abrazar el alma de mi difunta madre. Tres veces me acerqué —mi ánimo me impulsaba a abrazarla—, y tres veces voló de mis brazos semejante a una sombra o a un sueño.

»En mi corazón nacía un dolor cada vez más agudo, y, hablándole, le dirigí aladas palabras:

»"Madre mía, ¿por qué no te quedas cuando deseo tomarte para que, rodeándonos con nuestros brazos, ambos gocemos del frío llanto, aunque sea en Hades? ¿Acaso la ínclita Perséfone me ha enviado este simulacro para que me lamente y llore más todavía?" 210

»Así dije, y al pronto me contestó mi soberana madre:

»"¡Ay de mí, hijo mío, el más infeliz de todos los hombres! De ningún modo te engaña Perséfone, la hija de Zeus, sino que ésta es la condición de los mortales cuando uno muere: los nervios ya no sujetan la carne ni los huesos, que la fuerza poderosa del fuego ardiente los consume tan pronto como el ánimo ha abandonado los blancos huesos, y el alma anda revoloteando como un sueño. Conque dirígete rápidamente a la luz del día y sabe todo esto para que se lo digas a tu esposa después." 220

»Así nos contestábamos con palabras. Y se acercaron —pues las impulsaba la ínclita Perséfone— cuantas mujeres eran esposas e hijas de nobles. Se congregaban amontonándose alrededor de la negra sangre y yo cavilaba de qué modo preguntaría a cada una. Y ésta me pareció la mejor determinación: saqué la aguda espada de junto a mi vigoroso muslo y no permitía que bebieran la negra sangre todas a la vez. Así que se iban acercando una tras otra y cada una de ellas contaba su estirpe. 230

»A la primera que vi fue a Tiro, nacida de noble padre, la cual dijo ser hija del eximio Salmoneo y esposa de Creteo el

Eólida, la que deseó al divino Enipeo[166] que se desliza sobre la tierra como el más hermoso de los ríos.

»Andaba ella paseando junto a la hermosa corriente de Enipeo, cuando el que conduce su carro por la tierra tomó la figura de éste y se acostó junto a ella en los orígenes del voraginoso río. Y los cubrió una ola de púrpura semejante a un monte, encorvada, y escondió al dios y a la mujer mortal. Desató el dios su virginal ceñidor y le infundió sueño y, después que hubo llevado a cabo las obras de amor, la tomó de la mano, le dijo su palabra y la llamó por su nombre: "Alégrate, mujer, por este amor, pues cuando pase un año parirás hermosos hijos, que no son estériles los concúbitos de los inmortales. Por tu parte, cuídate de ellos y nútrelos. Ahora marcha a casa, contente y no me nombres. Yo soy Poseidón, el que sacude la tierra." Así habló y se sumergió en el ponto lleno de olas. Y ella, grávida, acabó pariendo a Pelias y Neleo, los cuales fueron poderosos servidores de Zeus. Pelias habitaba en Jolcos, rico en ganado, y el otro en la arenosa Pilos. A sus demás hijos los parió de Creteo esta reina entre las mujeres: a Esón, Feres y Mitaón, guerrero ecuestre.

»Después de ésta vi a Antíope, hija de Asopo, que también se gloriaba de haber dormido entre los brazos de Zeus y parió a dos hijos, Anfión y Zeto, quienes fueron los fundadores del reino de Tebas, la de siete puertas, y la dotaron de torres, que sin torres no podían habitar la espaciosa Tebas por muy poderosos que fueran.

»Después de ésta vi a Alcmena, la mujer de Anfitrión, la que parió al invencible Heracles, feroz como león, uniéndose al gran Zeus, entre sus brazos.

»Y a Mégara, la hija del valeroso Creonte, a la que tuvo como esposa el hijo de Anfitrión[167], indomable siempre en su valor.

»También vi a la madre de Edipo, la hermosa Epicasta[168], la que cometió una acción descomedida, por ignorancia de su mente, al casarse con su hijo, quien, después de dar muerte a

---

[166] Río de Tesalia.
[167] Heracles. Aquí se acentúa su filiación humana. Cfr. XXI.26 y nota.
[168] En época clásica se la conoce con el nombre de Yocasta.

su padre, se casó con ella (los dioses han divulgado esto rápidamente entre los hombres). Entonces reinaba él sobre los cadmeos sufriendo dolores por la funesta decisión de los dioses en la muy deseable Tebas, pero ella había descendido al Hades, el de puertas poderosamente trabadas, después de atar una alta soga al techo de su elevado palacio, poseída de su furor. Y dejó a Edipo numerosos dolores para el futuro, cuantos llevan a cumplimiento las Erinias de una madre. 280

»También vi a la hermosísima Cloris, a quien desposó Neleo en otro tiempo por causa de su hermosura, dándole innumerables regalos de esponsales; era la hija menor de Anfión Jásida, el que en otro tiempo imperaba con fuerza en Orcómenos de los Minios. Ella imperaba en Pilos y le dio a luz hijos ínclitos, Néstor y Cromio y el arrogante Periclimeno. Y después de éstos parió a la hermosa Peró, objeto de admiración para los mortales, a quien todos los vecinos pretendían, mas Neleo no se la daba a quien no hubiera robado de Fílace[169] los cuernitorcidos bueyes carianchos de Íficlo, difíciles de robar. Sólo un irreprochable adivino[170] prometió robarlas, pero lo trabó el pesado Destino de la divinidad y las crueles ligaduras y los boyeros del campo. Cuando ya habían pasado los meses y los días, por dar la vuelta el año, y habían pasado de largo las estaciones, sólo entonces lo desató de nuevo la fuerza de Íficlo cuando le comunicó la palabra de los dioses[171]. Y se cumplía la decisión de Zeus. 290

»También vi a Leda, esposa de Tíndaro, la cual dio a luz dos hijos de poderosos sentimientos, Cástor, domador de caballos, y Polideuces, bueno en el pugilato, a quienes mantiene vivos la tierra nutricia; que incluso bajo tierra son honrados por Zeus y un día viven y otro están muertos, alternativamente, pues tienen por suerte este honor, igual que los dioses[172]. 300

---

[169] Ciudad de Tesalia.

[170] Melampo. En XV.225 y ss. se dan más detalles de este mito, pero ni aquí ni allí se relata completo. Es habitual en Homero contar muy episódicamente historias que su auditorio conocía bien.

[171] Le reveló cómo podría tener hijos, pues era impotente.

[172] Según Píndaro (*Pítica*, XI.63 y ss., y *Nemea*, X.112), un día habitaban en el Olimpo y otro en Terapne. Aunque hermanos de madre, Cástor era hijo de

»Después de ésta vi a Ifimedea, esposa de Alceo, la cual dijo que se había unido a Poseidón y parido dos hijos[173] —aunque de breve vida—, Otón, semejante a los dioses y el ínclito Efialtes. La tierra nutricia los crió los más altos y los más bellos, aunque menos que el ínclito Orión. Éstos vivieron nueve años, su anchura era de nueve codos y su longitud de nueve brazas; amenazaron a los inmortales con establecer en el Olimpo la discordia de una impetuosa guerra; intentaron colocar a Osa sobre Olimpo y sobre Osa al boscoso Pelión, para que el cielo les fuera escalable, y tal vez lo habrían conseguido si hubieran alcanzado la medida de la juventud. Pero los aniquiló el hijo de Zeus[174], a quien parió Leto, de lindas trenzas, antes de que les floreciera el vello bajo las sienes y su mentón se espesara con bien florecida barba.

»También vi a Fedra, y a Procris[175], y a la hermosa Ariadna[176], hija del funesto Minos, a quien en otro tiempo llevó Teseo de Creta al elevado suelo de la sagrada Atenas, pero no la disfrutó, que antes la mató Artemis en Dia, rodeada de corriente, ante la presencia de Dioniso.

»También vi a Mera[177], y a Climena[178], y a la odiosa Erifile[179], la que recibió estimable oro a cambio de su marido.

310

320

Tíndaro y Polideuces de Zeus. Este último, a quien correspondía la inmortalidad, prefirió compartirla con su hermano.

[173] Son los Alóadas, niños gigantescos que crecían un codo de anchura y una braza de altura por año. También hicieron prisionero a Ares durante un año, hasta que Hermes lo liberó con trampa, cfr. *Ilíada* V.385.

[174] Apolo. Según otras versiones sería Zeus quien los fulminó con el rayo o Artemis con sus flechas.

[175] Son dos heroínas unidas por un mismo rasgo: la infidelidad a su marido. Fedra es la esposa de Teseo y se enamora de Hipólito, su hijastro (tema de la tragedia *Hipólito* de Eurípides). Procris es ateniense, hija de Erecteo y esposa de Céfalo, a quien engañaba con Pteleón.

[176] Ariadna es una antigua diosa mediterránea incorporada, como heroína, al mito cretense. Hija de Minos y Pasífase, ayuda a Teseo a escapar del Laberinto. Huye con él, pero lo abandona en Naxos (antes Dia). Este momento de su biografía es oscuro, aunque en todas las versiones aparece Díoniso. Según este pasaje, murió repentinamente ante la presencia de Díoniso. Según otras versiones, el dios se casó con ella y tuvieron cuatro hijos: Toante, Estáfilo, Enopión y Pepareto.

[177] Todo lo que sabemos de Mera, por el escolio a este pasaje, es que es una de las hijas de Preto y madre de Locro. Compañera de la diosa Artemis, ésta la mató por sus relaciones con Zeus.

»No podría enumerar a todas, ni podría nombrar a cuántas esposas vi de héroes y a cuántas hijas. Antes se acabaría la noche inmortal. También es hora de dormir o bien marchando junto a la rápida nave con mis compañeros, o bien aquí. La escolta será cosa vuestra y de los dioses.»

Así dijo Odiseo[180], todos enmudecieron en medio del silencio, y estaban poseídos como por un hechizo en el sombrío palacio. Y entre ellos comenzó a hablar Arete, de blancos brazos:

«Feacios, ¿cómo os parece este hombre en hermosura y grandeza y en pensamientos bien equilibrados en su interior? Huésped mío es, pero todos vosotros participáis del mismo honor. No os apresuréis a despedirlo ni le privéis de regalos, ya que lo necesita. Muchas cosas buenas tenéis en vuestros palacios por la benignidad de los dioses.»

Y entre ellos habló el anciano héroe Equeneo —él era el más anciano de los feacios—:

«Amigos, las palabras de la prudente reina no han dado lejos del blanco ni de nuestra opinión. Obedecedla, pues. De Alcínoo, aquí presente, depende el obrar y el decir.»

Y Alcínoo le respondió a su vez y dijo:

«Cierto, esta palabra se mantendrá mientras yo viva para mandar sobre los feacios amantes del remo: que el huésped acepte, por mucho que ansíe el regreso, esperar hasta el atardecer, hasta que complete todo mi regalo, y la escolta será cuestión de todos los hombres, y sobre todo de mí, de quien es el poder sobre el pueblo.»

Y respondiendo dijo el magnánimo Odiseo:

330

340

350

[178] Climena es una de las hijas de Minias, rey de Orcómeno, y madre de Ificlo.

[179] Es una de las heroínas más denostadas del mito. Esposa de Anfiarao, lo traicionó a cambio del collar de Harmonía. Su hijo Alcmeón lo mató para vengar a su padre en un gesto que acerca su leyenda a la de los Atridas.

[180] Este pasaje, llamado Interludio por los comentaristas, nos devuelve a Feacia por un momento. Funcionalmente, sirve para dividir la Nekya en dos partes con notable paralelismo: en la primera, Odiseo ha *conversado* con personajes conocidos (Elpenor, Anticlea) y luego *contempla* a una serie de heroínas del pasado; en la segunda parte, va a *conversar* con los grandes héroes de Troya y después va a *contemplar* una galería de héroes, especialmente los célebres condenados del Hades. Sobre el paralelismo como técnica estructural en la *Odisea,* cfr. B. Fenik, *Studies...* (Sobre la Nekya, págs. 144 y ss.)

«Poderoso Alcínoo, señalado entre todo tu pueblo, si me rogarais permanecer hasta un año incluso, y me dispusierais una escolta y me entregarais espléndidos dones, lo aceptaría y, desde luego, me sería más ventajoso llegar a mi querida patria con las manos más llenas. Así, también sería más honrado y querido de cuantos hombres me vieran de vuelta en Itaca.»

Y de nuevo le respondió Alcínoo diciendo:

«Odiseo, al mirarte de ningún modo sospechamos que seas impostor y mentiroso como muchos hombres dispersos por todas partes, a quienes alimenta la negra tierra, ensambladores de tales embustes que nadie podría comprobarlos. Por el contrario, hay en ti una como belleza de palabras y buen juicio, y nos has narrado sabiamente tu historia, como un aedo: todos los tristes dolores de los argivos y los tuyos propios. Pero, vamos, dime —e infórmame con verdad— si viste a alguno de los eximios compañeros que te acompañaron a Ilión y recibieron la muerte allí. La noche esta es larga, interminable, y no es tiempo ya de dormir en el palacio. Sigue contándome estas hazañas dignas de admiración. Aún aguantaría hasta la divina Eos si tú aceptaras contar tus dolores en mi palacio.»

Y respondiéndole habló el muy astuto Odiseo:

«Poderoso Alcínoo, señalado entre todo tu pueblo, hay un tiempo para los largos relatos y un tiempo también para el sueño. Si aún quieres escuchar, no sería yo quien se negara a narrarte otros dolores todavía más luctuosos: las desgracias de mis compañeros, los cuales perecieron después; habían escapado a la luctuosa guerra de los troyanos, pero sucumbieron en el regreso por causa de una mala mujer.

»Después que la casta Perséfone había dispersado aquí y allá las almas de las mujeres, llegó apesadumbrada el alma del Atrida Agamenón y a su alrededor se congregaron otras, cuantas junto con él habían perecido y recibido su destino en casa de Egisto. Reconocióme al pronto, luego que hubo bebido la negra sangre, y lloraba agudamente dejando caer gruesas lágrimas. Y extendía hacía mí sus brazos, deseoso de tocarme, pero ya no tenía una fuerza firme, ni en absoluto fuerza, cual antes había en sus ágiles miembros. Al verlo lloré y lo compadecí en mi ánimo y, dirigiéndome a él, le dije aladas palabras:

»"Noble Atrida, soberano de tu pueblo, Agamenón, ¿qué

Ker de la triste muerte te ha domeñado? ¿Es que te sometió en las naves Poseidón levantando inmenso soplo de crueles vientos?, ¿o te hirieron en tierra hombres enemigos por robar bueyes y hermosos rebaños de ovejas o por luchar por tu ciudad y tus mujeres?"

»Así dije, y él, respondiéndome, habló enseguida:

»"Hijo de Laertes, de linaje divino, Odiseo rico en ardides, no me ha sometido Poseidón en las naves levantando inmenso soplo de crueles vientos ni me hirieron en tierra hombres enemigos, sino que Egisto me urdió la muerte y el destino, y me asesinó en compañía de mi funesta esposa, invitándome a entrar en casa, recibiéndome al banquete, como el que mata a un novillo junto al pesebre. Así perecí con la muerte más miserable, y en torno mío eran asesinados cruelmente otros compañeros, como los jabalíes albidentes que son sacrificados en las nupcias de un poderoso o en un banquete a escote o en un abundante festín. Tú has intervenido en la matanza de muchos hombres muertos en combate individual o en la poderosa batalla, pero te habrías compadecido mucho más si hubieras visto cómo estábamos tirados en torno a la crátera y las mesas repletas en nuestro palacio, y todo el pavimento humeaba con la sangre. También puede oír la voz desgraciada de la hija de Príamo, de Casandra, a la que estaba matando la tramposa Clitemnestra a mi lado. Yo elevaba mis manos y las batía sobre el suelo, muriendo con la espada clavada, y ella, la de cara de perra, se apartó de mí y no esperó siquiera, aunque ya bajaba a Hades, a cerrarme los ojos ni juntar mis labios con sus manos. Que no hay nada más terrible ni que se parezca más a un perro que una mujer que haya puesto tal crimen en su mente, como ella concibió el asesinato para su inocente marido. ¡Y yo que creía que iba a ser bien recibido por mis hijos y esclavos al llegar a casa! Pero ella, al concebir tamaña maldad, se bañó en la infamia y la ha derramado sobre todas las hembras venideras, incluso sobre las que sean de buen obrar."

»Así habló, y yo me dirigí a él contestándole:

»"¡Ay, ay, mucho odia Zeus, el que ve a lo ancho, a la raza de Atreo por causa de las decisiones de sus mujeres, desde el principio! Por causa de Helena perecimos muchos, y a ti, Clitemnestra te ha peparado una trampa mientras estabas lejos."

»Así dije, y él, respondiéndome, se dirigió a mí:

»"Por eso ya nunca seas ingenuo con una mujer, ni le reveles todas tus intenciones, las que tú te sepas bien, mas dile una cosa y que la otra permanezca oculta. Aunque tú no, Odiseo, tú no tendrás la perdición por causa de una mujer. Muy prudente es y concibe en su mente buenas decisiones la hija de Icario, la prudente Penélope. Era una joven recién casada cuando la dejamos al marchar a la guerra y tenía en su seno un hijo inocente que debe sentarse ya entre el número de los hombres; ¡feliz él! Su padre lo verá al llegar y él abrazará a su padre —ésta es la costumbre—, pero mi esposa no me permitió siquiera saturar mis ojos con la vista de mi hijo, pues me mató antes. Te voy a decir otra cosa que has de poner en tu pecho: dirige la nave a tu tierra patria a ocultas y no abiertamente, pues ya no puede haber fe en las mujeres.

»"Pero vamos, dime —e infórmame con verdad— si has oído que aún vive mi hijo en Orcómenos o en la arenosa Pilos, o junto a Menelao en la ancha Esparta, pues seguro que toda- vía no está muerto sobre la tierra el divino Orestes."

Así dijo, y yo, respondiendo, me dirigí a él:

»"Atrida, ¿por qué me preguntas esto? Yo no sé si vive él o está muerto, y es cosa mala hablar inútilmente."

»Así nos contestábamos con palabras tristes y estábamos en pie acongojados, derramando gruesas lágrimas. Llegó después el alma del Pelida Aquiles y la de Patroclo, y la del irreprochable Antíloco y la de Áyax, el más hermoso de aspecto y cuerpo entre los dánaos después del irreprochable hijo de Peleo. Reco- nocióme el alma del Eácida[181] de pies veloces y, lamentándose, me dijo aladas palabras:

»"Hijo de Laertes, de linaje divino, Odiseo rico en ardides, desdichado, ¿qué acción todavía más grande preparas en tu mente? ¿Cómo te has atrevido a descender a Hades, donde habitan los muertos, los que carecen de sentidos, los fantasmas de los mortales que han perecido?"

»Así habló, y yo, respondiéndole, dije:

---

[181] Aquiles. Eaco era su abuelo. El patronímico es adecuado a la situación, pues Eaco, aunque no aparezca luego en el Hades, es uno de los jueces de los muertos.

»"Aquiles, hijo de Peleo, el más excelente de los aqueos, he venido en busca de un vaticinio de Tiresias, por si me revelaba algún plan para poder llegar a la escarpada Itaca; que aún no he llegado cerca de Acaya ni he desembarcado en mi tierra, sino que tengo desgracias continuamente. En cambio, Aquiles, ningún hombre es más feliz que tú, ni de los de antes ni de los que vengan; pues antes, cuando vivo, te honrábamos los argivos igual que a los dioses, y ahora de nuevo imperas poderosamente sobre los muertos aquí abajo. Conque no te entristezcas de haber muerto, Aquiles."

»Así hablé, y él, respondiéndome, dijo:

»"No intentes consolarme de la muerte, noble Odiseo. Preferiría estar sobre la tierra y servir en casa de un hombre pobre, aunque no tuviera gran hacienda, que ser el soberano de todos los cadáveres, de los muertos. Pero, vamos, dime si mi hijo ha marchado a la guerra para ser el primer guerrero o no. Dime también si sabes algo del irreprochable Peleo, si aún conserva sus prerrogativas entre los numerosos mirmidones, o lo desprecian en la Hélade y en Ptía porque la vejez le sujeta las manos y los pies, pues ya no puedo servirle de ayuda bajo los rayos del sol, aunque tuviera el mismo vigor que en otro tiempo, cuando en la amplia Troya mataba a los mejores del ejército defendiendo a los argivos. Si me presentara de tal guisa, aunque fuera por poco tiempo, en casa de mi padre, haría odiosas mis poderosas e invencibles manos a cualquiera de aquellos que le hacen violencia y lo excluyen de sus honores."

»Así habló, y yo, respondiendo, me dirigí a él:

»"En verdad, no he oído nada del ilustre Peleo, pero te voy a decir toda la verdad sobre tu hijo Neoptólemo —ya que me lo mandas—, pues yo mismo lo conduje en mi cóncava y equilibrada nave desde Esciro en busca de los aqueos de hermosas grebas. Desde luego, cuando meditábamos nuestras decisiones en torno a la ciudad de Troya, siempre hablaba el primero y no se equivocaba en sus palabras. Sólo Néstor, igual a un dios, y yo lo superábamos. Y cuando luchábamos los aqueos en la llanura de los troyanos, nunca permanecía entre la muchedumbre de los guerreros ni en las filas, sino que se adelantaba un buen trecho, no cediendo a ninguno en valor. Mató a muchos guerreros en duro combate, pero no te podría decir todos ni

nombrar a cuántos del ejército mató defendiendo a los argivos;
pero sí cómo mató con el bronce al hijo de Telefo, al héroe
Euripilo, mientras muchos de sus compañeros sucumbían a su   520
alrededor por causa de regalos femeninos. Siempre lo vi el más
hermoso, después del divino Memnón. Y cuando ascendíamos
al caballo que fabricó Epeo los mejores entre los argivos (a mí
se me había enconmendado todo: el abrir la bien trabada emboscada o cerrarla), en ese momento los demás jefes de los dánaos y los consejeros se secaban las lágrimas y temblaban los
miembros de cada uno, pero a él nunca vi con mis ojos ni que
le palideciera la hermosa piel, ni que secara las lágrimas de sus   530
mejillas. Y me suplicaba insistentemente que saliéramos del caballo, y apretaba la empuñadura de la espada y la lanza pesada
por el bronce, meditando males contra los troyanos. Después,
cuando ya habíamos devastado la escarpada ciudad de Príamo,
con una buena parte y un buen botín, ascendió a la nave incólume y no herido desde lejos por el agudo bronce, ni de cerca
en el cuerpo a cuerpo, como suele suceder a menudo en la
guerra, cuando Ares enloquece indistintamente."

»Así hablé, y el alma del Eácida de pies veloces marchó a
grandes pasos a través del prado de asfódelo, alegre porque le   540
había dicho que su hijo era insigne.

»Las demás almas de los difuntos estaban entristecidas y
cada una preguntaba por sus cuitas. Sólo el alma de Áyax, el
hijo de Telamón, se mantenía apartada a lo lejos, airada por
causa de la victoria en la que lo vencí contendiendo en el juicio
sobre las armas de Aquiles, junto a las naves. Lo estableció la
venerable madre y fueron jueces los hijos de los troyanos y Palas Atenea. ¡Ojalá no hubiera vencido yo en tal certamen!
Pues por causa de estas armas la tierra ocultó a un hombre
como Áyax, el más excelente de los dánaos en hermosura y   550
gestas después del irreprochable hijo de Peleo.

»A él me dirigí con dulces palabras:

»"Áyax, hijo del irreprochable Telamón. ¿Ni siquiera muerto
vas a olvidar tu cólera contra mí por causa de las armas nefas-
tas? Los dioses proporcionaron a los argivos aquella ceguera,
pues pereciste siendo tamaño baluarte para los aqueos. Los
aqueos nos dolemos por tu muerte igual que por la vida del
hijo de Peleo. Y ningún otro es responsable, sino Zeus, que

odiaba al ejército de los belicosos dánaos y a ti te impuso la   560
muerte. Ven aquí, soberano, para escuchar nuestra palabra y
nuestras explicaciones. Y domina tu ira y tu generoso ánimo."

»Así dije, pero no me respondió, sino que se dirigió tras las
otras almas al Erebo de los muertos. Con todo, me hubiera hablado entonces, aunque airado —o yo a él—, pero mi ánimo
deseaba dentro de mi pecho ver las almas de los demás difuntos.

»Allí vi[182] sentado a Minos[183], el brillante hijo de Zeus, con
el cetro de oro impartiendo justicia a los muertos. Ellos expo-
nían sus causas a él, al soberano, sentados o en pie, a lo largo   570
de la mansión de Hades de anchas puertas.

»Y después de éste vi al gigante Orión[184] persiguiendo por
el prado de asfódelo a las fieras que había matado en los montes desiertos, sosteniendo en sus manos la clava toda de bronce, eternamente irrompible.

»Y vi a Ticio[185], al hijo de la Tierra augusta, yaciendo en el
suelo. Estaba tendido a lo largo de nueve yugadas, y dos águilas posadas a sus costados le roían el hígado, penetrando en
sus entrañas. Pero él no conseguía apartarlas con sus manos,   580
pues había violado a Leto, esposa augusta de Zeus, cuando ésta
se dirigía a Pito a través del hermoso Panopeo.

»También vi a Tántalo[186], que soportaba pesados dolores,

---

[182] Desde este verso hasta el 607, Odiseo se encuentra *en medio* del Hades. Se
ha pensado que hay una confusión entre una *nekyomenteia* (consulta oracular a
los muertos) y una *Katábasis* o descenso al Hades, que se basaría en la de Heracles o en la órfica. Cfr. Ganschinietz, «Katábasis», en *RE*, X 2, págs. 2395-6.

[183] Minos es un héroe civilizador, especialmente legislador, de Creta y da
nombre a la era de esplendor que reinó en esta isla durante el segundo milenio.
Según *Ilíada* XIV.322 y ss., es hijo de Zeus y de Europa. También es hermano
de Radamante, con quien comparte en el Hades la prerrogativa de juzgar a los
muertos.

[184] Cfr. nota 109.

[185] Lo que inspiró a Ticio su pasión amorosa por Letó fueron los celos de
Hera. Según Píndaro *(Pítica*, IV.90 y ss.), Ticio es un ejemplo para que el hombre busque lo que está a su alcance.

[186] Tántalo, «el que soporta» (cfr. Platón, *Crátilo*, 395d y ss.), debe sin duda
su nombre al castigo que padece en el Hades. Sobre la forma de este castigo hay
dos versiones: Homero lo sitúa aquí en un lago eternamente sediento y ham-
briento; Píndaro *(Olímpica*, I.55 y ss.) afirma que Zeus puso sobre su cabeza una
gran piedra. Sobre su culpa ni Homero ni Píndaro nos informan, pero según la

en pie dentro del lago; éste llegaba a su mentón, pero se le veía siempre sediento y no podía tomar agua para beber, pues cuantas veces se inclinaba el anciano para hacerlo, otras tantas desaparecía el agua absorbida y a sus pies aparecía negra la tierra, pues una divinidad la secaba. También había altos árboles que dejaban caer su fruto desde lo alto —perales, manzanos de hermoso fruto, dulces higueras y verdeantes olivos—, pero 590 cuando el anciano intentaba asirlas con sus manos, el viento las impulsaba hacia las oscuras nubes.

»Y vi a Sísifo[187], que soportaba pesados dolores, llevando una enorme piedra entre sus brazos. Hacía fuerza apoyándose con manos y pies y empujaba la piedra hacia arriba, hacia la cumbre, pero cuando iba a trasponer la cresta, una poderosa fuerza le hacía volver una y otra vez y rodaba hacia la llanura la desvergonzada piedra. Sin embargo, él la empujaba de nuevo con los músculos en tensión y el sudor se deslizaba por sus miembros y el polvo caía de su cabeza. 600

»Después de éste vi a la fuerza de Héracles[188], a su imagen. Éste goza de los banquetes entre los dioses inmortales y tiene como esposa a Hebe de hermosos tobillos, la hija del gran Zeus y de Hera, la de sandalias de oro.

»En torno suyo había un estrépito de cadáveres, como de pájaros, que huían asustados en todas direcciones. Y él estaba allí, semejante a la oscura noche, su arco sosteniendo desnudo y sobre el nervio una flecha, mirando alrededor que daba miedo y como el que está siempre a punto de disparar. Y rodeando su pecho estaba el terrible tahalí, el cinturón de oro en el 610 que había cincelados admirables trabajos —osos, salvajes jabalíes, leones de mirada torcida, combates, luchas, matanzas, homicidios. Ni siquiera el artista que puso en este cinturón todo su arte podría realizar otra cosa parecida. Me reconoció al

---

variada tradición mitográfica, que recogen los escolios, sería algún tipo de traición a la confianza que los dioses habían depositado en él, ya sea porque revelara sus secretos o porque les robara el néctar y la ambrosía.

[187] Tampoco nos informa Homero sobre la causa del tormento de Sísifo. Y también hay varias versiones aunque la mayoría coinciden en señalar como causa última el haber revelado al río Asopo que el raptor de su hija había sido Zeus.

[188] Cfr. nota 134.

pronto cuando me vio con sus ojos y, llorando, dijo aladas palabras:

»"Hijo de Laertes, de linaje divino, Odiseo rico en ardides, ¡también tú andas arrastrando una existencia desgraciada, como la que yo soportaba bajo los rayos del sol! Hijo de Zeus 620 Cronida era yo y, sin embargo, tenía una pesadumbre inacabable. Pues estaba sujeto a un hombre muy inferior a mí que me imponía pesados trabajos. También me envió aquí en cierta ocasión para sacar al Perro[189], pues pensaba que ninguna otra prueba me sería más difícil. Pero yo me llevé al Perro a la luz y lo saqué de Hades. Y me escoltó Hermes y la de ojos brillantes, Atenea."

»Así habló y se volvió de nuevo a la mansión de Hades. Yo, sin embargo, me quedé allí por si venía alguno de los otros héroes guerreros, los que ya habían perecido. También habría 630 visto a hombres todavía más antiguos a quienes mucho deseaba ver, a Teseo y Pirítoo, hijos gloriosos de los dioses, pero se empezaron a congregar multitudes incontables de muertos con un vocerío sobrenatural y se apoderó de mí el pálido terror, no fuera que la ilustre Perséfone me enviara desde Hades la cabeza de la Gorgona, del terrible monstruo.

»Entonces marché a la nave y ordené a mis compañeros que embarcaran enseguida y soltaran amarras. Y ellos embarcaron rápidamente y se sentaron sobre los remos.

»Y el oleaje llevaba a la nave por el río Océano, primero al impulso de los remos y después se levantó una brisa favora- 640 ble.»

---

[189] Cerbero, como nombre para el Perro del infierno aparece por primera vez en Hesiodo, *Teogonía*, 311.

Canto XII

LAS SIRENAS. ESCILA Y CARIBDIS.
LA ISLA DEL SOL. OGIGIA

«C UANDO la nave abandonó la corriente del río Océano y
arribó al oleaje del ponto de vastos caminos y a la isla
de Eea, donde se encuentran la mansión y los lugares
de danza de Eos y donde sale Helios, la arrastramos por la arena, una vez llegados. Desembarcamos sobre la ribera del mar,
y dormidos esperamos a la divina Eos.

»Y cuando se mostró Eos, la que nace de la mañana, la de
dedos de rosa, envié a unos compañeros al palacio de Circe
para que se trajeran el cadáver del difunto Elpenor. Cortamos   10
enseguida unos leños y lo enterramos apenados, derramando
abundante llanto, en el lugar donde la costa sobresalía más.
Cuando habían ardido el cadáver y las armas del difunto, erigi-
mos un túmulo y, levantando un mojón, clavamos en lo más
alto de la tumba su manejable remo. Y luego nos pusimos a
discutir los detalles del regreso.

»Pero no dejó Circe de percatarse que habíamos llegado de
Hades y se presentó enseguida para proveernos. Y con ella sus
siervas llevaban pan y carne en abundancia y rojo vino. Y colocándose entre nosotros dijo la divina entre las diosas: 20

»"Desdichados vosotros que habéis descendido vivos a la
morada de Hades; seréis dos veces mortales, mientras que los
demás hombres mueren sólo una vez. Pero, vamos, comed
esta comida y bebed este vino durante todo el día de hoy y al
despuntar la aurora os pondréis a navegar; que yo os mostraré
el camino y os aclararé las incidencias para que no tengáis que

lamentaros de sufrir desgracias por trampa dolorosa del mar o sobre tierra firme."

»Así dijo, y nuestro valeroso ánimo se dejó persuadir. Así que pasamos todo el día, hasta la puesta del sol, comiendo carne en abundancia y delicioso vino. Y cuando se puso el sol y cayó la oscuridad, mis compañeros se echaron a dormir junto a las amarras de la nave. Pero Circe me tomó de la mano y me hizo sentar lejos de mis compañeros y, echándose a mi lado, me preguntó detalladamente. Yo le conté todo como correspondía y entonces me dijo la soberana Circe:

»"Así es que se ha cumplido todo de esta forma. Escucha ahora tú lo que voy a decirte y te recordará después el dios mismo.

»"Primero llegarás a las Sirenas[190], las que hechizan a todos los hombres que se acercan a ellas. Quien acerca su nave sin saberlo y escucha la voz de las Sirenas ya nunca se verá rodeado de su esposa y tiernos hijos, llenos de alegría porque ha vuelto a casa; antes bien, lo hechizan éstas con su sonoro canto sentadas en un prado donde las rodea un gran montón de huesos humanos putrefactos, cubiertos de piel seca. Haz pasar de largo a tu nave y, derritiendo cera agradable como la miel, unta los oídos de tus compañeros para que ninguno de ellos las escuche. En cambio, tú, si quieres oírlas, haz que te amarren de pies y manos, firme junto al mástil —que sujeten a éste las amarras—, para que escuches complacido la voz de las dos Sirenas; y si suplicas a tus compañeros o los ordenas que te desaten, que ellos te sujeten todavía con más cuerdas.

»"Cuando tus compañeros las hayan pasado de largo, ya no te diré cuál de dos caminos será el tuyo; decídelo tú mismo en el ánimo. Pero te voy a decir los dos: a un lado hay unas rocas

---

[190] Son divinidades marinas hijas del río Aqueloo y una Musa (Melpómene o Terpsícore). Homero no se refiere aquí a su aspecto externo (mitad ave, mitad mujer o solamente mujer) y entre sus características destaca solamente: que son dos (utiliza el dual); que sus *cantos* ofrecen el conocimiento de todo cuanto sucede (v. 109) y que este canto es letal para quien lo escucha. En la interpretación alegórica posterior, de orgen estoico, representan una de las tentaciones que el hombre debe soportar en su peregrinar por la tierra, interpretación llevada a su extremo por el Cristianismo, para el cual simbolizan concretamente la lujuria. Cfr. J. Pepin, *Mythe et Allégorie*, París, 1953.

altísimas, contra las que se estrella el oleaje de la oscura Anfi- 60
trite. Los dioses felices las llaman Rocas Errantes[191]. No se les
acerca ningún ave, ni siquiera las temblorosas palomas que llevan ambrosía al padre Zeus; que, incluso de éstas, siempre
arrebata alguna la lisa piedra, aunque el Padre (Zeus) envía
otra para que el número sea completo. Nunca las ha conseguido evitar nave alguna de hombres que haya llegado allí, sino
que el oleaje del mar, junto con huracanes de funesto fuego,
arrastran maderos de naves y cuerpos de hombres. Sólo consiguió pasar de largo por allí una nave surcadora del ponto, la
célebre Argo, cuando navegaba desde el país de Eetes. Incluso 70
entonces la habría arrojado el oleaje contra las gigantescas piedras, pero la hizo pasar de largo Hera, pues Jasón le era querido.

»"En cuanto a los dos escollos, uno llega al vasto cielo con
su aguda cresta y le rodea oscura nube. Ésta nunca le abandona, y jamás, ni en invierno ni en verano, rodea su cresta un
cielo despejado. No podría escalarlo mortal alguno, ni ponerse
sobre él, aunque tuviera veinte manos y veinte pies, pues es
piedra lisa, igual que la pulimentada. En medio del escollo hay 80
una oscura gruta vuelta hacia Poniente, que llega hasta el Erebo, por donde vosotros podéis hacer pasar la cóncava nave,
ilustre Odiseo. Ni un hombre vigoroso, disparando su flecha
desde la cóncava nave, podría alcanzar la hueca gruta. Allí habita Escila, que aúlla que da miedo: su voz es en verdad tan
aguda como la de un cachorro recién nacido[192], y es un monstruo maligno. Nadie se alegraría de verla, ni un dios que le diera cara. Doce son sus pies, todos deformes, y seis sus largos 90
cuellos; en cada uno hay una espantosa cabeza y en ella tres filas de dientes apiñados y espesos, llenos de negra muerte. De

---

[191] Son las Simplégades («las que entrechocan») del viaje de los Argonautas
que Apolonio de Rodas sitúa a la salida del Bósforo (II.528-647). Según la narración de Apolonio, éstas quedaron fijas una vez que las cruzó la nave Argo.
Odiseo no pasa por ellas, toma la ruta alternativa de Escila y Caribdis. Según
Meuli, *Odyssee...*, esta parte de las aventuras de Odiseo procede del ciclo de las
Argonáuticas.
[192] Esta descripción de los aullidos de Escila, inapropiada y hasta ridícula, se
debe a la afición etimológica de Homero: Escila *(Skýllē)* es una palabra similar a
la que en griego significa cachorrillo *(skýllax)*. Cfr. también con las Harpías en
I.241 y XIV.371.

la mitad para abajo está escondida en la hueca gruta, pero tiene sus cabezas sobresaliendo fuera del terrible abismo, y allí pesca —explorándolo todo alrededor del escollo—, por si consigue apresar delfines o perros marinos, o incluso algún monstruo mayor de los que cría a miles la gemidora Anfitrite. Nunca se precian los marineros de haberlo pasado de largo incólumes con la nave, pues arrebata con cada cabeza a un hombre de la nave de oscura proa y se lo lleva. 100

»"También verás, Odiseo, otro escollo más llano —cerca uno de otro—. Harías bien en pasar por él como una flecha. En éste hay un gran cabrahigo cubierto de follaje y debajo de él la divina Caribdis[193] sorbe ruidosamente la negra agua. Tres veces durante el día la suelta y otras tres vuelve a sorberla que da miedo. ¡Ojalá no te encuentres allí cuando la está sorbiendo, pues no te libraría de la muerte ni el que sacude la tierra! Conque acércate, más bien, con rapidez al escollo de Escila y haz pasar de largo la nave, porque mejor es echar en falta a seis 110 compañeros que no a todos juntos."

»Así dijo, y yo le contesté y dije:

»"Diosa, vamos, dime con verdad si podré escapar de la funesta Caribdis y rechazar también a Escila cuando trate de dañar a mis compañeros."

»Así dije, y ella al punto me contestó, la divina entre las diosas:

»"Desdichado, en verdad te placen las obras de la guerra y el esfuerzo. ¿Es que no quieres ceder ni siquiera a los dioses inmortales? Porque ella no es mortal, sino un azote inmortal, terrible, doloroso, salvaje e invencible. Y no hay defensa alguna, 120 lo mejor es huir de ella, porque si te entretienes junto a la piedra y vistes tus armas contra ella, mucho me temo que se lance por segunda vez y te arrebate tantos compañeros como cabezas tiene. Conque conduce tu nave con fuerza e invoca a gritos a Cratais, madre de Escila, que la parió para daño de los mortales. Ésta la impedirá que se lance de nuevo.

»"Luego llegarás a la isla de Trinaquía[194], donde pastan las

---

[193] Caribdis es una palabra formada por dos raíces que significan «grieta» y «sorber».

[194] Nada tiene que ver esta isla de *Thrinakia* con la de Sicilia, también llama-

muchas vacas y pingües rebaños de ovejas de Helios: siete rebaños de vacas y otros tantos hermosos apriscos de ovejas con cincuenta animales cada uno. No les nacen crías, pero tampoco mueren nunca. Sus pastoras son diosas, ninfas de lindas trenzas, Faetusa y Lampetía[195], a las que parió para Helios Hiperiónida la diosa Neera. Nada más de parirlas y criarlas su soberana madre, las llevó a la isla de Trinaquía para que vivieran lejos y pastorearan los apriscos de su padre y las vacas de rotátiles patas.

»"Si dejas incólumes estos rebaños y te ocupas del regreso, aun con mucho sufrir podréis llegar a Itaca, pero si les haces daño, predigo la perdición para la nave y para tus compañeros. Y tú, aunque evites la muerte, llegarás tarde y mal, después de perder a todos tus compañeros."

»Así dijo y, al pronto, llegó Eos, la de trono de oro.

»Ella regresó a través de la isla, la divina entre las diosas, y yo partí hacia la nave y apremié a mis compañeros para que embarcaran y soltaran amarras. Así que embarcaron con presteza y se sentaron sobre los bancos y, sentados en fila, batían el canoso mar con los remos. Y Circe de lindas trenzas, la terrible diosa dotada de voz, envió por detrás de nuestra nave de azuloscura proa, muy cerca, un viento favorable, buen compañero, que hinchaba las velas. Después de disponer todos los aparejos, nos sentamos en la nave y la conducían el viento y el piloto.

»Entonces dije a mis compañeros con corazón acongojado:

»"Amigos, es preciso que todos —y no sólo uno o dos— conozcáis las predicciones que me ha hecho Circe, la divina entre las diosas. Así que os las voy a decir para que, después de conocerlas, perezcamos o consigamos escapar evitando la muerte y el destino.

»"Antes que nada me ordenó que evitáramos a las divinas Sirenas y su florido prado. Ordenó que sólo yo escuchara su

130

140

150

160

---

da *Trinakía*. Homero conoce la isla de Sicilia a la que denomina Sicania (cfr. XXIV.307). Parece deducirse del v. 380 que la isla del Sol se sitúa en el lejano Este.

[195] Son dos nombres muy adecuados para las hijas del Sol: «la que arde» y «la que brilla».

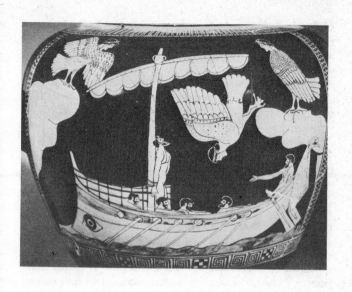

Ulises y las sirenas (vaso griego)

voz; mas atadme con dolorosas ligaduras para que permanezca firme allí, junto al mástil; que sujeten a éste las amarras, y si os suplico o doy órdenes de que me desatéis, apretadme todavía con más cuerdas."

»Así es como yo explicaba cada detalle a mis compañeros.

»Entretanto la bien fabricada nave llegó velozmente a la isla de las dos Sirenas —pues la impulsaba próspero viento—. Pero enseguida cesó éste y se hizo una bonanza apacible, pues un dios había calmado el oleaje.

»Levantáronse mis compañeros para plegar las velas y las pusieron sobre la cóncava nave y, sentándose al remo, blanqueaban el agua con los pulimentados remos.

»Entonces yo partí en trocitos, con el agudo bronce, un gran pan de cera y lo apreté con mis pesadas manos. Enseguida se calentó la cera —pues la oprimían mi gran fuerza y el brillo del soberano Helios Hiperiónida— y la unté por orden en los oídos de todos mis compañeros. Éstos, a su vez, me ataron igual de manos que de pies, firme junto al mástil —sujetaron a éste las amarras— y, sentándose, batían el canoso mar con los remos.

»Conque, cuando la nave estaba a una distancia en que se oye a un hombre al gritar —en nuestra veloz marcha—, no se les ocultó a las Sirenas que se acercaba y entonaron su sonoro canto:

»"Vamos, famoso Odiseo, gran honra de los aqueos, ven aquí y haz detener tu nave para que puedas oír nuestra voz. Que nadie ha pasado de largo con su negra nave sin escuchar la dulce voz de nuestras bocas, sino que ha regresado después de gozar con ella y saber más cosas. Pues sabemos todo cuanto los argivos y troyanos trajinaron en la vasta Troya por voluntad de los dioses. Sabemos cuanto sucede sobre la tierra fecunda."

»Así decían lanzando su hermosa voz. Entonces mi corazón deseó escucharlas y ordené a mis compañeros que me soltaran haciéndoles señas con mis cejas, pero ellos se echaron hacia adelante y remaban, y luego se levantaron Perimedes y Euríloco y me ataron con más cuerdas, apretándome todavía más.

»Cuando por fin las habían pasado de largo y ya no se oía más la voz de las Sirenas ni su canto, se quitaron la cera mis

fieles compañeros, la que yo había untado en sus oídos, y a mí   200
me soltaron de las amarras.

»Conque, cuando ya abandonábamos su isla, al pronto comencé a ver vapor y gran oleaje y a oír un estruendo. Como a
mis compañeros les entrara el terror, volaron los remos de sus
manos y éstos cayeron todos estrepitosamente en la corriente.
Así que la nave se detuvo allí mismo, puesto que ya no movían
los largos remos con sus manos.

»Entonces iba yo por la nave apremiando a mis compañeros
con suaves palabras, poniéndome al lado de cada uno:

»"Amigos, ya no somos inexpertos en desgracias. Este mal
que nos acecha no es peor que cuando el Cíclope nos encerró   210
con poderosa fuerza en su cóncava cueva. Pero por mis artes,
mi decisión y mi inteligencia logramos escapar de allí —y creo
que os acordaréis de ello. Así que también ahora, vamos,
obedezcamos todos según yo os indique. Vosotros sentaos en
los bancos y batid con los remos la profunda orilla del mar,
por si Zeus nos concede huir y evitar esta perdición; y a ti, piloto, esto es lo que te ordeno —ponlo en tu interior, ya que
gobiernas el timón de la cóncava nave—: mantén a la nave
alejada de ese vapor y oleaje y pégate con cuidado a la roca no   220
sea que se te lance sin darte cuanta hacia el otro lado y nos
pongas en medio del peligro."

»Así dije y enseguida obedecieron mis palabras. Todavía no
les hablé de Escila, desgracia imposible de combatir, no fuera
que por temor dejaran de remar y se me escondieran todos
dentro[196].

»Entonces no hice caso de la penosa recomendación de Circe, pues me ordenó que en ningún caso vistiera mis armas
contra ella. Así que vestí mis ínclitas armas y con dos lanzas
en mis manos subí a la cubierta de proa, pues esperaba que allí   230
se me apareciera primero la rocosa Escila, la que iba a llevar
dolor a mis compañeros. Pero no pude verla por lado alguno y
se me cansaron los ojos de otear por todas partes la brumosa
roca.

»Así que comenzamos a sortear el estrecho entre lamentos,
pues de un lado estaba Escila, y del otro la divina Caribdis sor-

---

[196] Se entiende en la bodega o sentina.

bía que daba miedo la salada agua del mar. Y es que cuando vomitaba, todo ella borbollaba como un caldero que se agita sobre un gran fuego —la espuma caía desde arriba sobre lo alto de los dos escollos—, y cuando sorbía de nuevo la salada agua del mar, aparecía toda arremolinada por dentro, la roca resonaba espantosamente alrededor y al fondo se veía la tierra con azuloscura arena.

»El terror se apoderó de mis compañeros y, mientras la mirábamos temiendo morir, Escila me arrebató de la cóncava nave seis compañeros, los que eran mejores de brazos y fuerza. Mirando a la rápida nave y siguiendo con los ojos a mis compañeros, logré ver arriba sus pies y manos cuando se elevaban hacia lo alto. Daban voces llamándome por mi nombre, ya por última vez, acongojados en su corazón. Como el pescador en un promontorio, sirviéndose de larga caña, echa comida como cebo a los pececillos (arroja al mar el cuerno de un toro montaraz) y luego tira hacia fuera y los coge palpitantes, así mis compañeros se elevaban palpitantes hacia la roca.

»Escila los devoró en la misma puerta mientras gritaban y tendían sus manos hacia mí en terrible forcejeo. Aquello fue lo más triste que he visto con mis ojos de todo cuanto he sufrido recorriendo los caminos del mar. Cuando conseguimos escapar de la terrible Caribdis y de Escila, llegamos enseguida a la irreprochable isla del dios donde estaban las hermosas carianchas vacas y los numerosos rebaños de ovejas de Helios Hiperión.

»Cuando todavía me encontraba en la negra nave pude oír el mugido de las vacas en sus establos y el balar de las ovejas. Entonces se me vino a las mientes la palabra del adivino ciego, el tebano Tiresias, y de Circe de Eea, quienes me encomendaron encarecidamente evitar la isla de Helios, el que alegra a los mortales.

»Así que dije a mis compañeros acongojado en mi corazón:

»"Escuchad mis palabras, compañeros que tantas desgracias habéis sufrido, para que os manifieste las predicciones de Tiresias y de Circe de Eea, quienes me encomendaron encarecidamente evitar la isla de Helios, el que alegra a los mortales, pues me dijeron que aquí tendríamos el más terrible mal. Conque conducid la negra nave lejos de la isla."

»Así dije y a ellos se les quebró el corazón.

»Entonces Euríloco me contestó con odiosa palabra:

»"Eres terrible, Odiseo, y no se cansa tu vigor ni tus miembros. En verdad todo lo tienes de hierro si no permites a tus compañeros agotados por el cansancio y por el sueño poner pie a tierra en una isla rodeada de corriente, donde podríamos prepararnos sabrosa comida. Por el contrario, les ordenas que anden errantes por la rápida noche en el brumoso ponto, alejándose de la isla. De la noche surgen crueles vientos, azote de las naves. ¿Cómo se podría huir del total exterminio si por casualidad se nos viene de repente un huracán de Noto o de Céfiro de soplo violento, que son quienes, sobre todo, destruyen las naves por voluntad de los soberanos dioses? Cedamos, pues, a la negra noche y preparémonos una comida quedándonos junto a la rápida nave. Y al amanecer embarcaremos y lanzaremos la nave al vasto ponto." 280 290

»Así dijo Euríloco y los demás compañeros aprobaron sus palabras. Entonces me di cuenta de que un demón nos preparaba desgracia y, hablándoles, dije aladas palabras:

»"Euríloco, mucho me forzáis, solo como estoy. Pero, vamos, juradme al menos con fuerte juramento que si encontramos una vacada o un gran rebaño de ovejas, nadie, llevado de funesta insensatez, matará vaca u oveja alguna. Antes bien, comed tranquilos el alimento que nos dio la inmortal Circe." 300

»Así dije y todos juraron al punto tal como les había dicho. Así que cuando habían jurado y completado su juramento, detuvimos en el cóncavo puerto nuestra bien construida nave, cerca de agua dulce; desembarcaron mi compañeros y se prepararon con habilidad la comida.

»Luego que habían arrojado de sí el deseo de comida y bebida, comenzaron a llorar —pues se acordaron enseguida— por los compañeros a quienes había devorado Escila, arrebatándolos de la cóncava nave; y mientras lloraban, les sobrevino un profundo sueño. 310

»Cuando terciaba la noche y declinaban los astros, Zeus, el que amontona las nubes, levantó un viento para que soplara en terrible huracán y cubrió de nubes tierra y mar. Y se levantó del cielo la noche.

»Cuando se mostró Eos, la que nace de la mañana, la de dedos de rosa, anclamos la nave arrastrándola hasta una gruta, donde estaba el hermoso lugar de danza de las Ninfas y sus asientos.

»Entonces los convoqué en asamblea y les dije:

»"Amigos, en la rápida nave tenemos comida y bebida; 320 apartémonos de las vacas no sea que nos pase algo malo, que estas vacas y gordas ovejas pertenecen a un dios terrible, a Helios, el que lo ve todo y todo lo oye."

»Así dije y su valeroso ánimo se dejó persuadir.

»Durante todo un mes sopló Noto sin parar y no había ningún otro viento, salvo Euro y Noto. Así que, mientras mis compañeros tuvieron comida y rojo vino, se mantuvieron alejados de las vacas por deseo de vivir; pero cuando se consumieron todos los víveres de la nave, pusiéronse por necesidad 330 a la caza de peces y aves, todo lo que llegaba a sus manos, con curvos anzuelos, pues el hambre retorcía sus estómagos.

»Yo me eché entonces a recorrer la isla para suplicar a los dioses, por si alguno me manifestaba algún camino de vuelta; y, cuando caminando por la isla ya estaba lejos de mis compañeros, lavé mis manos al abrigo del viento y supliqué a todos los dioses que poseen el Olimpo. Y ellos derramaron el dulce sueño sobre mis párpados.

»Entonces Euríloco comenzó a manifestar a mis compañeros esta funesta decisión:

»"Escuchad mis palabras, compañeros que tantos males ha- 340 béis sufrido. Todas las clases de muerte son odiosas para los desgraciados mortales, pero lo más lamentable es morir de hambre y arrastrar el destino. Conque, vamos, llevémonos las mejores vacas de Helios y sacrifiquémoslas a los inmortales que poseen el vasto cielo. Si llegamos a Itaca, nuestra patria, edificaremos a Helios Hiperión un espléndido templo donde podríamos erigir muchas y excelentes estatuas.

»"Pero si, irritado por sus vacas de alta cornamenta, quiere destruir nuestra nave —y los demás dioses les acompañan— prefiero perder la vida de una vez, de bruces contra una ola, 350 antes que irme consumiendo poco a poco en una isla desierta."

»Así dijo Euríloco y los demás compañeros aprobaron sus palabras. Así que se llevaron enseguida las mejores vacas de Helios, de por allí cerca —pues las hermosas vacas carianchas de rotátiles patas pastaban no lejos de la nave de azuloscura proa. Pusiéronse a su alrededor e hicieron súplica a los dioses, cortando ramas tiernas de una encina de elevada copa —pues no tenían blanca cebada en la nave de buenos bancos. Cuando habían hecho la súplica, degollado y desollado las vacas, cortaron los muslos y los cubrieron de grasa a uno y otro lado y colocaron carne sobre ellos. No tenían vino para libar sobre las víctimas mientras se asaban, pero libaron con agua mientras se quemaban las entrañas. Cuando ya se habían quemado los muslos y probaron las entrañas, cortaron en trozos lo demás y lo ensartaron en pinchos. 360

»Entonces el profundo sueño desapareció de mis párpados y me puse en camino hacia la rápida nave y la ribera del mar. Y, cuando me hallaba cerca de la curvada nave, me rodeó un agradable olor a grasa. Rompí en lamentos e invoqué a gritos a los dioses inmortales: 370

»"Padre Zeus y demás dioses felices que vivís siempre; para mi perdición me habéis hecho acostar con funesto sueño, pues mis compañeros han resuelto un tremendo acto mientras estaban aquí."

»En esto llegó Lampetía, de luengo peplo, rápida mensajera a Helios Hiperión, para anunciarle que habíamos matado a sus vacas. Y éste se dirigió al punto a los inmortales acongojado en su corazón:

»"Padre Zeus y los demás dioses felices que vivís siempre, castigad ya a los compañeros de Odiseo Laertíada que me han matado las vacas —¡obra impía!—, con las que yo me complacía al dirigirme hacia el cielo estrellado y al volver de nuevo hacia la tierra desde el cielo. Porque si no me pagan una recompensa equitativa por las vacas, me hundiré en el Hades y brillaré para los muertos." 380

»Y contestándole dijo Zeus, el que reúne las nubes:

»"Helios, sigue brillando entre los inmortales y los mortales hombres sobre la tierra nutricia, que yo lanzaré mi brillante rayo y quebraré enseguida su nave en el ponto rojo como el vino."

»Esto es lo que yo oí decir a Calipso, de hermoso peplo, y ella decía que se lo había oído a su vez a Hermes. 390

»Conque, cuando bajé hasta la nave y el mar, los reprendí a unos y otros poniéndome a su lado, pero no podíamos encontrar remedio —las vacas estaban ya muertas. Entonces los dioses comenzaron a manifestarles prodigios: las pieles caminaban, la carne mugía en el asador, tanto la cruda como la asada. Así es como las vacas cobraron voz.

»Durante seis días mis fieles compañeros prosiguieron banqueteándose y llevándose las mejores vacas de Helios, pero cuando Zeus Cronida nos trajo el séptimo, dejó el viento de lanzarse huracanado y nosotros embarcamos y empujamos la nave al vasto ponto no sin colocar el mástil y extender las blancas velas.

»Cuando abandonamos la isla y ya no se divisaba tierra alguna sino sólo cielo y mar, el Cronida puso una negra nube sobre la cóncava nave y el mar se oscureció bajo ella. La nave no pudo avanzar mucho tiempo, porque enseguida se presentó el silbante Céfiro lanzándose en huracán y la tempestad de viento quebró los dos cables del mástil. Cayó éste hacia atrás y todos los aparejos se desparramaron bodega abajo. En la misma proa de la nave golpeó el mástil al piloto en la cabeza, rompiendo todos los huesos de su cráneo y, como un volatinero, se precipitó de cabeza contra la cubierta —y su valeroso ánimo abandonó los huesos.

»Zeus comenzó a tronar al tiempo que lanzaba un rayo contra la nave, y ésta se revolvió toda, sacudida por el rayo de Zeus, y se llenó de azufre. Mis compañeros cayeron fuera y, semejantes a las cornejas marinas, eran arrastrados por el oleaje en torno a la negra nave. Dios les había arrebatado el regreso.

»Entonces yo iba de un lado a otro de la nave, hasta que el huracán desencajó las paredes de la quilla y el oleaje la arrastraba desnuda. El mástil se partió contra ésta, pero, como había sobre aquél un cable de piel de buey, até juntos quilla y mástil y, sentándome sobre ambos, me dejé llevar de los funestos vientos.

»Entonces Céfiro dejó de lanzarse huracanado y llegó enseguida Noto trayendo dolores a mi ánimo, haciendo que volviera a recorrer de nuevo la funesta Caribdis.

»Dejéme llevar por el oleaje durante toda la noche y al salir el sol llegué al escollo de Escila y a la terrible Caribdis. Ésta comenzó a sorber la salada agua del mar, pero entonces yo me lancé hacia arriba, hacia el elevado cabrahigo y quedé adherido a él como un murciélago. No podía apoyarme en él con los pies para trepar, pues sus raíces estaban muy lejos y sus ramas muy altas —ramas largas y grandes que daban sombra a Caribdis. Así que me mantuve firme hasta que ésta volviera a vomitar el mástil y la quilla, y un rato más tarde me llegaron mientras estaba a la expectativa. Mis maderos aparecieron fuera de Caribdis a la hora en que un hombre se levanta del ágora para ir a comer, después de juzgar numerosas causas de jóvenes litigantes. Dejéme caer desde arriba de pies y manos y me desplomé ruidosamente sobre el oleaje junto a mis largos maderos, y sentado sobre ellos, comencé a remar con mis brazos. El padre de hombres y dioses no permitió que volviera a ver a Escila, pues no habría conseguido escapar de la ruina total. 440

»Desde allí me dejé llevar durante nueve días, y en la décima noche los dioses me impulsaron hasta la isla de Ogigia, donde habitaba Calipso de lindas trenzas, la terrible diosa dotada de voz que me entregó su amor y sus cuidados.

»Pero, ¿para qué te voy a contar esto? Ya os lo he narrado ayer[197] a ti y a tu fuerte esposa en el palacio, y me resulta odioso volver a relatar lo que he expuesto detalladamente.» 450

---

[197] Cfr. VII.241-97.

Canto XIII

LOS FEACIOS DESPIDEN A ODISEO.
LLEGADA A ITACA

Así habló, y todos enmudecieron en el silencio; estaban poseídos como por un hechizo en el sombrío palacio. Entonces Alcínoo le contestó y dijo:

«Odiseo, ya que has llegado a mi palacio de piso de bronce, de elevado techo, creo que no vas a volver a casa errabundo otra vez por mucho que hayas sufrido. En cuanto a vosotros, cuantos acostumbráis a beber en mi palacio el rojo vino de los ancianos escuchando al aedo, os voy a hacer este encargo: el forastero ya tiene, en un arca bien pulimentada, oro bien tra- 10 bajado y cuantos regalos le han traído los consejeros de los fea- cios. Démosle también un gran trípode y una caldera cada hombre, que nosotros después os recompensaremos recogién- dolo por el pueblo, pues es doloroso que uno haga dones gratis.»

Así habló Alcínoo y les agradó su palabra. Y se marchó cada uno a su casa con ganas de dormir.

Y cuando se mostró Eos, la que nace de la mañana, la de dedos de rosa, se apresuraron hacia la nave llevando el bronce propio de los guerreros.

Y la sagrada fuerza de Alcínoo, marchando en persona, co- 20 locó todo bien bajo los bancos de la nave, no fuera que causa- ran daño a alguno de los compañeros durante el viaje cuando se apresuraran moviendo los remos.

Luego marcharon al palacio de Alcínoo y dispusieron el al- muerzo. La sagrada fuerza de Alcínoo sacrificó entre ellos un buey en honor de Cronida Zeus, el que oscurece las nubes, el que gobierna a todos. Quemaron los muslos y se repartieron gustosos un magnífico banquete; y entre ellos cantaba el divino aedo, Demódoco, venerado por su pueblo. Pero Odiseo volvía una y otra vez su cabeza hacia el resplandeciente sol, deseando que se pusiera, pues ya pensaba en el regreso. Como cuando un hombre desea vivamente cenar cuando su pareja de bueyes ha estado todo el día arrastrando el bien construido arado por el campo —la luz del sol se pone para él con agrado, ya que se va a cenar, y sus rodillas le duelen al caminar—, así se puso el sol con agrado para Odiseo.

Y volvió a dirigirse a los feacios amantes del remo y, dirigiéndose sobre todo a Alcínoo, dijo su palabra:

«Poderoso Alcínoo, el más ilustre de tu pueblo, haced una libación y devolvedme a casa sin daño. Y a vosotros, ¡salud! Ya se me ha proporcionado lo que mi ánimo deseaba, una escolta y amables regalos que ojalá los dioses, hijos de Urano, hagan prosperar. ¡Que encuentre en casa, al volver, a mi irreprochable esposa junto con los míos sanos y salvos! Vosotros quedaos aquí y seguid llenando de gozo a vuestras esposas legítimas y a vuestros hijos; que los dioses os repartan bienes de todas clases y que ningún mal se instale entre vosotros.»

Así habló y todos aprobaron sus palabras y aconsejaban dar escolta al forastero, porque había hablado como le correspondía. Entonces Alcínoo se dirigió a un heraldo:

«Pontónoo, mezcla una crátera y reparte vino a todos en el palacio, para que demos escolta al forastero hasta su tierra patria después de orar al padre Zeus.»

Así habló, y Pontónoo mezcló el vino que alegra el corazón y se lo repartió a todos, uno tras otro. Y libaron desde sus mismos asientos en honor de los dioses felices, los que poseen el ancho cielo.

El divino Odiseo se puso en pie, colocó una copa de doble asa en manos de Arete y le dijo aladas palabras:

«Sé siempre feliz, reina, hasta que te lleguen la vejez y la muerte que andan rondando a los hombres. Yo vuelvo a casa, goza tú en este palacio entre tus hijos, tu pueblo y el rey Alcínoo.»

Así hablando el divino Odiseo traspasó el umbral. Y la fuerza de Alcínoo le envió un heraldo para que le condujera hasta la rápida nave y la ribera del mar. También le envió Arete a sus esclavas, a una con un manto bien lavado y una túnica, a otra le dio un arca adornada para que la llevara y otra portaba trigo y rojo vino.

Cuando arribaron a la nave y al mar, sus ilustres acompañantes colocaron todo en la cóncava nave, la bebida y la comida toda, y para Odiseo extendieron una manta y una sábana en la cubierta de proa, para que durmiera sin despertar. Subió él y se acostó en silencio, y ellos se sentaron en los bancos, cada uno en su sitio, y soltaron el cable de una piedra perforada. Después se inclinaron y batían el mar con el remo.

A Odiseo se le vino un sueño profundo a los párpados, sueño sosegado, delicioso, semejante en todo a la muerte. Y la nave... como los cuadrúpedos caballos se arrancan todos a la vez en la llanura a los golpes del látigo y elevándose velozmente apresuran su marcha, así se elevaba su proa y un gran oleaje de púrpura rompía en el resonante mar. Corría ésta con firmeza, sin estorbos; ni un halcón la habría alcanzado, la más rápida de las aves. Y en su carrera cortaba veloz las olas del mar portando a un hombre de pensamientos semejantes a los de los dioses que había sufrido muchos dolores en su ánimo al probar batallas y dolorosas olas, pero que ya dormía imperturbable, olvidado de todas sus penas.

Y cuando despuntó el más brillante astro, el que avanza anunciando la luz de Eos que nace de la mañana, la nave se acercó para fondear en la isla.

En el pueblo de Itaca hay un puerto, el de Forcis[198], el viejo del mar, y en él hay dos salientes escarpados que se inclinan hacia el puerto y que dejan fuera el oleaje producido por silbantes vientos[199]; dentro, las naves de buenos bancos permanecen sin amarras cuando llegan al término del fondeadero. Al extremo del puerto hay un olivo de anchas hojas y cerca de éste una gruta sombría y amable consagrada a las ninfas que

---

[198] Cfr. I.72 y nota.
[199] Descripción convencional de un puerto. Cfr. también el puerto de Telépilo de Lestrigonia en X.90 y ss.

llaman Náyades[200]. Hay dentro cráteras y ánforas de piedra y también dentro fabrican las abejas sus panales. Hay dentro grandes telares de piedra donde las ninfas tejen sus túnicas con púrpura marina —¡una maravilla para velas!— y también dentro corren las aguas sin cesar. Tiene dos puertas, la una del lado de Bóreas accesible a los hombres; la otra, del lado de Noto, es en cambio sólo para dioses y no entran por ella los hombres, que es camino de inmortales. Hacia allí remaron, pues ya lo conocían de antes, y la nave se apresuró a fondear en tierra firme, como a media altura —¡tales eran las manos de los remeros que la impulsaban! Éstos descendieron de la nave de buenos bancos y levantando primero a Odiseo de la cóncava nave, le colocaron sobre la arena, rendido por el sueño, junto con su manta y resplandeciente sábana. También sacaron las riquezas que los ilustres feacios le habían donado cuando volvía a casa por voluntad de la magnánima Atenea.

Conque colocaron todo junto, cerca del tronco de olivo, lejos del camino —no fuera que algún caminante cayera sobre ello y lo robara antes de que Odiseo despertase—, y se volvieron a casa.

Pero el que sacude la tierra no se había olvidado de las amenazas que había hecho al divino Odiseo al principio y preguntó la decisión de Zeus:

«Padre Zeus, ya no tendré nunca honores entre los dioses inmortales si los mortales no me honran, los feacios que, además, son de mi propia estirpe. Yo pensaba que Odiseo regresaría a casa después de mucho sufrir —el regreso no se lo había quitado del todo porque tú se lo prometiste desde el principio—, pero los feacios lo han traído durmiendo en rápida nave sobre el ponto y lo han dejado en Ítaca. Le han entregado además innumerables regalos, bronce y oro en abundancia y ropa tejida, tantos como jamás habría sacado de Troya si hubiera vuelto incólume con su parte sorteada del botín.»

Y le contestó y dijo el que reúne las nubes, Zeus:

110

120

130

140

---

[200] Su nombre se deriva de una raíz que significa «fluir», por tanto son las ninfas del elemento líquido, generalmente un manantial o una fuente a los que suelen dar nombre. En el v. 356, Odiseo las llama «hijas de Zeus», pero hay muchas que son hijas de los diferentes ríos de la zona donde habitan.

«¡Ay, ay, poderoso dios que sacudes la tierra, qué cosas has dicho! Nunca te deshonrarán los dioses. Sería difícil despachar sin honores al más antiguo y excelente. Si alguno de los hombres, cediendo a su violencia y poder, no te honra, tienes y tendrás siempre tu compensación. Obra como desees y sea agradable a tu ánimo.»

Y le contestó Poseidón, el que sacude la tierra:

«Enseguida actuaría, oh tú que oscureces las nubes, como dices, pero estoy siempre acechando tu cólera y procurando evitarla. Con todo, quiero ahora destruir en el brumoso ponto la hermosa nave de los feacios en su viaje de vuelta, para que se contengan y dejen de escoltar a los hombres. Quiero también ocultar su ciudad toda bajo un monte»[201].

Y le contestó y dijo el que reúne las nubes, Zeus:

«Amigo mío, creo que lo mejor será que, cuando todo el pueblo esté contemplando desde la ciudad a la nave acercándose, coloques cerca de tierra un peñasco semejante a una rápida nave, para que todos se asombren y puedas ocultar su ciudad bajo un gran monte.»

Luego que oyó esto Poseidón, el que sacude la tierra, se puso en camino hacia Esqueria, donde los feacios nacen, y allí se detuvo. Y la nave surcadora del ponto se acercó en su veloz carrera. El que sacude la tierra se acercó, la convirtió en piedra y la estableció firmemente, como si tuviera raíces, golpeándola con la palma de su mano. Y se alejó de allí. Los feacios de largos remos se dirigían mutuamente aladas palabras, hombres célebres por sus naves, y decía uno así mirando al que tenía al lado:

«Ay de mí, ¿quién ha encadenado en el ponto a la rápida nave en su regreso a casa? Ya se la veía del todo.»

Así decía uno —pues no sabían cómo había sucedido. Entonces Alcínoo habló entre ellos y dijo:

«¡Ay, ay, en verdad ya me ha alcanzado el antiguo presagio de mi padre, quien aseguraba que Poseidón se irritaría con nosotros por ser prósperos acompañantes de todo el mundo! Decía que algún día destruiría en el brumoso ponto una hermosa nave de los feacios al volver de una expedición, y que ocultaría

---

[201] Se refiere a la profecía ya anunciada por Alcínoo en VIII.569.

nuestra ciudad bajo un monte. Así decía el anciano y todo se está cumpliendo ahora. Conque, vamos, obedeced todos lo que yo os señale: dejad de acompañar a los mortales cuando alguien llegue a nuestra ciudad. Sacrificaremos a Poseidón doce toros escogidos, por si se compadece y no nos oculta la ciudad bajo un enorme monte.»

Así habló y ellos sintieron miedo y prepararon los toros. Así es que suplicaban al soberano Poseidón los jefes y consejeros de los feacios, en pie, rodeando el altar.

En esto se despertó el divino Odiseo acostado en su tierra patria, pero no la reconoció pues ya llevaba mucho tiempo ausente. La diosa Palas Atenea esparció en torno suyo una nube, la hija de Zeus, para hacerlo irreconocible y contarle todo, no fuera que su esposa, ciudadanos y amigos le reconocieran antes de que los pretendientes pagaran todos sus excesos. Por esto, todo le parecía distinto al soberano, los largos caminos, los puertos de cómodo anclaje, las elevadas rocas y los verdeantes árboles.

Así que se puso en pie de un salto y comenzó a mirar su tierra patria. Dio un grito lastimero, golpeó sus muslos con las palmas de las manos y entre lamentos decía su palabra:

«Ay de mí, ¿a qué tierra de mortales he llegado? ¿Son acaso soberbios, salvajes y carentes de justicia, o amigos de los forasteros y con sentimientos de piedad hacia los dioses?[202]. ¿A dónde llevo tantas riquezas?, ¿por dónde voy a marchar? ¡Ojalá me hubiera quedado junto a los feacios! También podría haberme llegado a otro rey de los muy poderosos y quizá éste me habría recibido como amigo y escoltado de vuelta a casa, porque ahora no sé dónde dejar esto ni voy a dejarlo aquí, no sea que se me convierta en botín de otro. ¡Ay!, ¡ay!, en verdad no eran del todo prudentes ni justos los jefes y consejeros de los feacios, quienes me han traído a otra tierra. Decían que me iban a llevar a Itaca, hermosa al atardecer, pero no lo han cumplido. Que Zeus los castigue, el dios de los suplicantes, el que vigila a todos los hombres y castiga a quien yerra.

»Pero, ea, voy a contar mis riquezas y a contemplarlas, no sea que se marchen llevándose algo en la cóncava nave.»

---

[202] Cfr. también IX.175 y ss.

Así diciendo, se puso a contar los hermosos trípodes y calderos y el oro y la hermosa ropa tejida. Pero no echó nada de menos. Y sentía dolor por su tierra patria caminando por la ribera del resonante mar, en medio de lamentos.

Conque se le acercó Atenea, semejante en su aspecto a un hombre joven, un pastor de rebaños delicado como suelen ser los hijos de los reyes, portando sobre sus hombros un manto doble, bien trabajado. Bajo sus brillantes pies llevaba sandalias y en sus manos un venablo.

Alegróse al verla Odiseo y fue a su encuentro; y hablándole dirigió aladas palabras:

«Amigo, puesto que eres el primero a quien encuentro en este país, ¡salud! No te me acerques con aviesas intenciones, salva esto y sálvame a mí, pues te lo pido como a un dios y me he acercado a tus rodillas. Dime esto en verdad para que yo lo sepa: ¿qué tierra es ésta, qué pueblo, qué hombres viven aquí? ¿Es una isla hermosa al atardecer o la ribera de un continente de fecunda tierra que se inclina hacia el mar?

Y la diosa de ojos brillantes, Atenea, se dirigió a él a su vez:

«Eres tonto, forastero, o vienes de lejos si me preguntas por esta tierra. No carece de nombre, no. La conocen muy muchos, tanto los que habitan hacia la aurora y el sol como los que se orientan hacia la brumosa oscuridad. Cierto que es escarpada y difícil para cabalgar, pero tampoco es excesivamente pobre, aunque no extensa: en ella se produce trigo sin medida y también vino. Siempre tiene lluvia y floreciente rocío; alimenta buenas cabras y buenos toros; hay madera de todas clases y abrevaderos inagotables. Por eso, forastero, el nombre de Ítaca ha llegado incluso hasta Troya, que aseguran se encuentra muy lejos de la tierra aquea.»

Así habló, y el sufridor, el divino Odiseo, sintió gozo y alegría por su tierra patria: así se lo había dicho Palas Atenea, la hija de Zeus, el que lleva égida.

Y hablándole le dijo aladas palabras (aunque no la verdad) y, de nuevo, tomó la palabra, controlando continuamente en el pecho su astuto pensamiento:

«He oído sobre Ítaca incluso en la extensa Creta, lejos, más allá del Ponto. Y ahora he llegado yo con estas riquezas. He dejado otro tanto a mis hijos y ando huyendo, pues he matado

a Ortíloco[203], hijo de Idomeneo, el que vencía en la extensa   260
Creta a los hombres comerciantes con sus rápidos pies. Quería
éste privarme de todo mi botín conseguido en Troya, por el
que sufrí dolores probando guerras y dolorosas olas, porque no
servía complaciente a su padre en el pueblo de los troyanos,
sino que mandaba yo sobre otros compañeros. Y lo alcancé
con mi lanza guarnecida de bronce cuando volvía del campo,
emboscándome cerca del camino con un amigo. La oscura noche cubría el cielo —nadie nos vio—, y le arranqué la vida a   270
escondidas. Así que, luego de matarlo con el agudo bronce,
me dirigí a una nave de ilustres fenicios[204] y les supliqué, en-
tregándoles abundante botín, que me dejaran en Pilos o en la
divina Elide, donde dominan los epeos, pero la fuerza del
viento los alejó de allí muy contra su voluntad, pues no querían engañarme.

»Así que hemos llegado por la noche después de andar a la
deriva. Remamos con vigor hasta el puerto y ninguno de nosotros se acordó de almorzar por más que lo ansiábamos. Con-   280
que descendimos todos de la nave y nos acostamos. A mí se
me vino un dulce sueño, cansado como estaba, y ellos, sacando mis riquezas de la cóncava nave, las dejaron cerca de donde
yo yacía sobre la arena.

»Y embarcando se marcharon a la bien habitada Sidón. Así
que yo me quedé atrás con el corazón acongojado.»

Así dijo y sonrió la diosa de ojos brillantes, Atenea, y lo acarició con su mano. Tomó entonces el aspecto de una mujer
hermosa y grande, conocedora de labores brillantes, y le habló
y dijo aladas palabras: 290

«Astuto sería y trapacero el que te aventajara en toda clase

---

[203] No consta en ninguna parte que Idomeneo tuviera un hijo con este nombre, pero sí que todos sus hijos murieron de muerte violenta. Era práctica normal en la Grecia arcaica que el asesino se exiliara para evitar la venganza de la
familia del muerto a quien por derecho correspondía; ello sin olvidar las razones
de tipo religioso. Cfr. también Teoclímeno en XV.230 y las palabras de Odiseo
en XXIII.115 y ss.

[204] Las frecuentes alusiones a los fenicios (a quienes también se llama «sidonios» con más propiedad en IV.84 y XV.118) son prueba de su presencia en el
Egeo durante los siglos VIII y VII a.C. De ellos tomaron los griegos el alfabeto y
aprendieron el comercio. Básicamente eran comerciantes, pero es probable que
mezclaran esta actividad con la piratería, como vemos aquí.

de engaños, por más que fuera un dios el que tuvieras delante. Desdichado, astuto, que no te hartas de mentir, ¿es que ni siquiera en tu propia tierra vas a poner fin a los engaños y las palabras mentirosas que te son tan queridas? Vamos, no hablemos ya más, pues los dos conocemos la astucia: tú eres el mejor de los mortales todos en el consejo y con la palabra, y yo tengo fama entre los dioses por mi previsión y mis astucias. Pero ¡aun así, no has reconocido a Palas Atenea, la hija de 300 Zeus, la que te asiste y protege en todos tus trabajos, la que te ha hecho querido a todos los feacios! De nuevo he venido a ti para que juntos tramemos un plan para ocultar cuantas riquezas te donaron los ilustres feacios al volver a casa por mi decisión, y para decirte cuántas penas estás destinado a soportar en tu bien edificada morada. Tú has de aguantar por fuerza y no decir a hombre ni mujer, a nadie, que has llegado después de vagar; soporta en silencio numerosos dolores aguantando las 310 violencias de los hombres.»

Y contestándole dijo el muy astuto Odiseo:

«Es difícil, diosa, que un mortal te reconozca si contigo topa, por muy experimentado que sea, pues tomas toda clase de apariencias. Ya sabía yo que siempre me has sido amiga mientras los hijos de los aqueos combatíamos en Troya, pero desde que saqueamos la elevada ciudad de Príamo y nos embarcamos —y un dios dispersó a los aqueos— no te había vuelto a ver, hija de Zeus. No te vi embarcar en mi nave para protegerme de desgracia alguna, sino que he vagado siempre 320 con el corazón acongojado hasta que los dioses me han librado del mal, hasta que en el rico pueblo de los feacios me animaste con tus palabras y me condujiste en persona hasta la ciudad[205]. Ahora te pido abrazado a tus rodillas (pues no creo que haya llegado a Itaca hermosa al atardecer sino que ando dando vueltas por alguna otra tierra y creo que tú me has dicho esto para burlarte y confundirme), dime si de verdad he llegado a mi patria.»

Y le contestó la diosa de ojos brillantes, Atenea:

«En tu pecho siempre hay la misma cordura. Por esto no 330 puedo abandonarte en el dolor, porque eres discreto, sagaz y

---

[205] Tomando la apariencia de niña. Cfr. VII.15 y ss.

sensato. Cualquier otro que llegara después de andar errante, marcharía gustosamente a ver a sus hijos y esposa en el palacio; sólo tú no deseas conocer ni enterarte hasta que hayas puesto a prueba a tu mujer, quien permanece inconmovible en el palacio mientras las noches se le consumen entre dolores y los días entre lágrimas. En verdad, yo jamás desconfié, pues sabía que volverías después de haber perdido a todos sus compañeros, pero no quise enfrentarme con Poseidón, hermano de mi padre, quien había puesto el rencor en su corazón irritado porque le habías cegado a su hijo.

»Pero, vamos, te voy a mostrar el suelo de Itaca para que te convenzas. Este es el puerto de Forcis, el viejo del mar, y éste el olivo de anchas hojas, al extremo del puerto. Cerca de él, la gruta sombría, amable, consagrada a las ninfas que llaman Náyades. Es la cueva amplia y sombría donde tú solías sacrificar a las Ninfas numerosas hecatombes perfectas. Y éste es el monte Nérito, revestido de bosque.»

Así diciendo, la diosa dispersó la nube y apareció el país ante sus ojos. Alegróse entonces el sufridor, el divino Odiseo, y se llenó de gozo por su patria y besó la tierra donadora de grano. Luego suplicó a las Ninfas levantando sus manos:

«Ninfas Náyades, hijas de Zeus, nunca creí que volvería a veros. Alegraos con mi suave súplica, volveré a haceros dones como antes si la hija de Zeus, la diosa Rapaz, me permite benévola que viva y hace crecer a mi hijo.»

Y se dirigió a él la diosa de ojos brillantes, Atenea:

«Cobra ánimo, no te preocupes ahora de esto; coloquemos ahora mismo tus riquezas en lo profundo de la divina gruta a fin de que se conserven intactas y pensemos para que todo salga lo mejor posible.»

Así hablando, la diosa se introdujo en la sombría gruta buscando un escondrijo por ella, mientras Odiseo la seguía de cerca llevando todo, el oro y el sólido bronce y los bien fabricados vestidos que le habían donado los feacios. Conque colocó todo bien y arrimó un peñasco a la entrada Palas Atenea, la hija de Zeus, el que lleva égida. Y sentándose los dos junto al tronco del olivo sagrado, meditaban la muerte para los soberbios pretendientes. La diosa de ojos brillantes, Palas Atenea, comenzó a hablar:

«Hijo de Laertes, de linaje divino, Odiseo, rico en ardides, piensa cómo vas a poner tus manos sobre los desvergonzados pretendientes que llevan ya tres años mandando en tu palacio, cortejando a tu divina esposa y haciéndole regalos de esponsales, aunque ella se lamenta continuamente por tu regreso y da esperanzas a todos y hace promesas a cada uno enviándoles recados[206], si bien su mente revuelve otros planes.» 380

Y le contestó y dijo el muy astuto Odiseo:

«¡Ay, ay! ¡Conque he estado a punto de perecer en mi palacio con la vergonzosa muerte del Atrida Agamenón si tú, diosa, no me hubieras revelado todo, como es debido! Vamos, trama un plan para que los haga pagar y asísteme tú misma poniendo dentro de mí el mismo vigor y valentía que cuando destruimos las espesas almenas de Troya. Si tú me socorrieras con el mismo interés, diosa de ojos brillantes, sería capaz de luchar junto a ti contra trescientos hombres, diosa soberana, 390 siempre que me socorrieras benevolente.»

Y la diosa de ojos brillantes, Palas Atenea, le contestó:

«En verdad, estaré a tu lado y no me pasarás desapercibido cuando tengamos que arrostrar este peligro. Conque creo que mancharán con su sangre y sus sesos el maravilloso pavimento los pretendientes que consumen tu hacienda.

»Vamos, te voy a hacer irreconocible para todos: arrugaré la hermosa piel de tus ágiles miembros y haré desaparecer de tu cabeza los rubios cabellos[207]; te cubriré de harapos que te harán odioso a la vista de cualquier hombre y llenaré de legañas 400 tus antes hermosos ojos, de forma que parezcas desastroso a los pretendientes, a tu esposa y a tu hijo, a quienes dejaste en palacio.

»Llégate en primer lugar al porquero, el que vigila tus cerdos, quien se mantiene fiel y sigue amando a tu hijo y a la prudente Penélope. Lo encontrarás sentado junto a los cerdos; éstos están paciendo junto a la Roca del Cuervo, cerca de la

---

[206] Estas palabras, repetición de las de Antínoo en II.91, contradicen lo que se dice sobre la tela en varios pasajes. De ahí que se haya querido ver una inconsistencia estructural, cfr. G. S. Kirk, *Los poemas...*, pág. 216.

[207] Es extraño que se le atribuya a Odiseo cabello rubio. Aunque varios héroes de la *Ilíada*, como Aquiles y Menelao, son rubios, a Odiseo siempre se alude como moreno, XVI.175, VI.225 y XXIII.156 y ss.

fuente Aretusa, comiendo innumerables bellotas y bebiendo agua negra, cosas que crían en los cerdos abundante grasa. Detente allí, siéntate a su lado y pregúntale por todo, mientras yo voy a Esparta de hermosas mujeres a buscar a tu hijo Telémaco, Odiseo, pues ha marchado a la extensa Lacedemonia junto a Menelao para preguntar noticias sobre ti, por si aún vives.»

Y le contestó y dijo el muy astuto Odiseo:

«¿Por qué no se lo dijiste, si conoces todo en tu interior? ¿Acaso para que también él sufriera penalidades vagando por el estéril ponto mientras los demás consumen mi hacienda?»

Y le contestó la diosa de ojos brillantes, Palas Atenea:

«No te preocupes demasiado por él. Yo misma lo escolté para que cosechara fama de valiente marchando allí. En verdad, no sufre penalidad alguna, está en el palacio del Atrida y tiene de todo a su disposición. Cierto que unos jóvenes le acechan en negra nave con intención de matarlo antes de que regrese a tu tierra, pero no creo que esto suceda antes de que la tierra abrace a alguno de los pretendientes que consumen tu hacienda.»

Hablando así, lo tocó Atenea con su varita[208]: arrugó la hermosa piel de sus ágiles miembros e hizo desaparecer de su cabeza los rubios cabellos; colocó sobre sus miembros la piel de un anciano y llenó de legañas sus antes hermosos ojos. Le cubrió de andrajos miserables y una túnica desgarrada, sucia, ennegrecida por el humo, y le vistió con una gran piel, ya sin pelo, de veloz ciervo; le dio un cayado y un feo zurrón rasgado por muchos sitios y con la correa retorcida.

Así deliberaron y se separaron los dos; y ella marchó luego a la divina Lacedemonia en busca del hijo de Odiseo.

410

420

430

440

---

[208] Es la única vez que Atenea aparece con una varita mágica, más propia de Hermes. En los demás casos realiza sus transformaciones sin necesidad de ella, cfr. II.12 y ss., etc.

Canto XIV

ODISEO EN LA MAJADA DE EUMEO

Entonces él se puso en camino desde el puerto a través de un sendero escarpado en lugar boscoso, por las cumbres, hacia donde Atenea le había manifestado que encontraría al divino porquero, el que cuidaba de su hacienda más que los demás siervos que el divino Odiseo había adquirido. Y lo encontró sentado en el pórtico, donde tenía edificada una elevada cuadra, hermosa y grande, aislada, en lugar abierto. El porquero mismo la había edificado para los cerdos de su soberano ausente, lejos de su dueña y del anciano Laertes, con piedras de cantera, y lo había coronado de espino; tendió fuera   10
una empalizada completa, espesa y cerrada, sacando estacas de lo negro de una encina.

Dentro de la cuadra había construido doce pocilgas, unas junto a otras, para encamar a las cerdas, y en cada una se encerraban cincuenta cerdas, todas hembras que habían ya parido. Los cerdos dormían fuera y eran muy inferiores en número, pues los habían diezmado los divinos pretendientes con sus banquetes: el porquero les enviaba cada vez el mejor de sus robustos cebones, trescientos sesenta en total.   20

También dormían a su lado cuatro perros, semejantes a fieras, que alimentaba el porquero, caudillo de hombres[209].

Este andaba entonces sujetando a sus pies unas sandalias después de cortar una moteada piel de buey. Los demás porqueros, tres en total, habían marchado cada uno por su lado

---

[209] Se trata de una frase formular de aplicación poco afortunada en este caso.

con los cerdos en manada; al cuarto lo había enviado Eumeo a la fuerza a la ciudad para que llevara un cebón a los soberbios pretendientes a fin de que lo sacrificaran y saciaran con la carne su apetito.

De pronto los perros de incesantes ladridos vieron a Odiseo y corrieron hacia él ladrando. Entonces Odiseo se sentó astutamente y el cayado se le escapó de las manos.

Allí, sin duda, en su propia cuadra habría sufrido un dolor vergonzoso, pero el porquero, siguiéndolos con veloces pies, se lanzó a través del pórtico —la piel cayó de sus manos— y a grandes voces dispersó a los perros en varias direcciones con una espesa pedrea. Y se dirigió al soberano:

«Anciano, por poco te han despedazado los perros en un instante y quizá me habrías culpado a mí. También a mí me han dado los dioses dolores y lamentos, pues sentado lloro a mi divino soberano y cebo cerdos para que se los coman otros. En cambio, él andará errante por pueblos y ciudades extranjeras mendigando comida —si es que vive aún y contempla la luz del sol.

»Pero sígueme, vayamos a mi cabaña, anciano, para que también tú sacies el apetito de comer y beber y me digas de dónde eres y cuántas penas has tenido que sufrir.»

Así diciendo, lo condujo a su cabaña el divino porquero; le hizo entrar y sentarse, extendió maleza espesa y encima tendió la piel de una hirsuta cabra salvaje, su propia yacija, grande y peluda. Alegróse Odiseo porque lo había recibido así y le dijo su palabra llamándolo por su nombre:

«Forastero, ¡que Zeus y los demás dioses inmortales te concedan lo que más vivamente deseas, ya que me has acogido con bondad!»

Y tú le contestaste, porquero Eumeo, diciendo:

«Forastero, no es santo deshonrar a un extraño, ni aunque viniera uno más miserable que tú, que de Zeus son los forasteros y mendigos todos. Nuestros dones son pequeños, pero amistosos, pues la naturaleza de los siervos es tener siempre miedo cuando dominan nuevos soberanos. En verdad, los dioses han impedido el regreso de quien me habría estimado gentilmente y otorgado cuanto un dueño bondadoso suele conceder a su siervo —una casa, un lote de tierra y una esposa solicitada—, cuando éste se esfuerza por él y un dios hace prosperar sus labores, como está haciendo prosperar el trabajo en el que yo me mantengo activo. Por esto me habría beneficiado mucho mi soberano si hubiera envejecido aquí, pero ha muerto —¡así pereciera por completo la raza de Helena, pues aflojó las rodillas de muchos hombres!—, pues también mi soberano marchó por causa del honor de Agamenón a Ilión, de buenos potros, para combatir a los troyanos.»

Hablando así, sujetó enseguida su túnica con el ceñidor y se puso en camino de las pocilgas donde tenía encerradas las manadas de cochinillos. Tomó dos de allí y los sacrificó, quemó, troceó y atravesó con asadores. Y, después de asar todos, se los ofreció a Odiseo calientes en sus mismos asadores —y extendió blanca harina. Después mezcló vino agradable como la miel en su cuenco y se sentó enfrente, y animándole decía:

«Come ahora, forastero, lo que es dado comer a los siervos, cochinillo[210], que de los cebones se encargan los pretendientes, sin miedo a la venganza divina ni compasión. No aman los dioses felices las acciones impías, sino que honran la justicia y las obras discretas de los hombres. Es cierto que son enemigos y hostiles quienes invaden una tierra ajena, por más que Zeus les conceda el botín, pero cuando vuelven repletos a las naves para regresar a su patria, incluso a éstos les sobreviene un pesado temor a la venganza divina. Sin duda, los pretendientes deben conocer —porque quizá hayan oído la palabra de algún dios— la triste muerte de Odiseo, pues no quieren cortejar[211] con justicia ni volver a sus posesiones, y con gusto devoran entre excesos la hacienda, despreocupadamente. Todas las noches y días que nos manda Zeus sacrifican víctimas, no sólo una ni sólo dos ovejas; y el vino... lo consumen a cántaros, sin mesura. Y es que la fortuna de Odiseo era inmensa; ninguno de los héroes del oscuro continente ni de la misma Itaca poseía tanta. Ni veinte hombres juntos tienen tanta abundancia. Te voy a echar la cuenta: doce rebaños en el continente, otros tantos de ovejas, otros tantos de cerdos y cabras apacientan

---

[210] Sin embargo, en vv. 419 y ss. sacrifican un «cerdo bien gordo de cinco años».
[211] A Penélope.

para él pastores asalariados y sus propios pastores. Aquí se alimentan en total once numerosos rebaños de cabras en el extremo de la isla, pues se las vigilan hombres de bien. Todos los días, sin excepción, cada uno de éstos lleva a los pretendientes un animal, la mejor de sus gordas cabras. Y yo vigilo y protejo estos cerdos y les hago llegar el mejor de ellos, eligiéndolo bien.»

Así habló mientras Odiseo comía la carne y bebía el vino con voracidad, en silencio. Y estaba sembrando la desgracia para los pretendientes. 110

Cuando acabó de almorzar y saciar su apetito con la comida, le entregó Eumeo un cuenco repleto de vino en el que solía él beber. Aquél lo recibió y se alegró en su interior y, hablando, le dijo aladas palabras:

«Amigo, ¿quién te compró con sus bienes, tan rico y poderoso como dices? Aseguras que ha perecido por causa del honor de Agamenón; dime su nombre por si lo conozco ¡siendo como es! Seguro que Zeus y los demás dioses inmortales saben si te puedo hablar de él porque lo haya visto, pues he vagado 120 mucho.»

Y le contestó el porquero, caudillo de hombres:

«Anciano, ningún caminante que viniera con noticias de él lograría persuadir a su esposa y querido hijo, que los vagabundos suelen mentir por mor del sustento y no gustan de decir verdad. Todo caminante que llega al pueblo de Itaca se llega a mi dueña para decirle mentiras. Claro que ella lo acoge con amor y le pregunta detalladamente, y las lágrimas se deslizan de sus mejillas lamentándose por él, como es propio de mujer 130 que ha perdido a su marido en tierra extraña.

»Puede que tú también, anciano, inventes cualquier cuento con tal de que alguien te regale una túnica y un manto. Pero seguro que los perros y las veloces aves están tratando de arrancar la piel de sus huesos y su alma le ha abandonado, o puede que lo hayan devorado los peces en el mar y sus huesos anden tirados por tierra, revueltos entre la arena. Así es como ha muerto él, y a todos los suyos, y sobre todo a mí, sólo nos queda tristeza para el futuro. Que no podré nunca encontrar a un soberano tan bueno adonde quiera que vaya, ni aunque vuelva a casa de mi padre y mi madre, donde un día nací y 140

ellos me criaron. Y es que no es tan grande mi dolor por ellos
—aunque mucho deseo verlos en mi tierra patria— como es la
añoranza que me ha invadido por Odiseo ausente. No me atre-
vo, forastero, a nombrarlo incluso ausente —¡tanto me estimaba y se preocupaba por mí!—, pero lo llamo amigo aunque se
encuentre lejos.»

Y le contestó el sufridor, el divino Odiseo:

«Amigo, puesto que te niegas por completo y crees que
nunca volverá, tu corazón anda ya sin esperanza. Pero yo te   150
voy a decir —y no a tontas, sino con jurameto— que Odiseo
viene de camino hacia acá. Este será el don por mi buena nueva cuando haya llegado él: vestidme con un manto y una túnica hermosas; no antes, pues no lo aceptaría por más necesitado
que estuviera. Que para mí es más odioso que las puertas de
Hades el que por ceder a su pobreza cuenta mentiras[212]. Sea
testigo Zeus antes que ningún otro dios y la mesa de hospitalidad y el hogar del irreprochable Odiseo al que acabo de llegar.
En verdad todo esto se cumplirá tal como anuncio: dentro de   160
este mismo año llegará Odiseo; cuando acabe este mes y entre
otro, volverá a casa y hará pagar a cuantos deshonran a su esposa e ilustre hijo.»

Y contestando le dijiste, porquero Eumeo:

«Anciano, no te voy a conceder ese don por tu buena nueva
ni va a regresar ya Odiseo a casa, pero bebe gustoso y volvamos nuestros recuerdos a otro lado; no me traigas esto a la
memoria, que mi ánimo se llena de dolor cada vez que alguien
me recuerda a mi fiel soberano.   170

»Dejemos, pues, el juramento, aunque ¡ojalá vuelva Odiseo!
como quiero yo y quieren Penélope, el anciano Laertes y Telémaco, semejante a los dioses. También ahora me lamento sin
consuelo por el hijo que engendró Odiseo, por Telémaco.
Cuando los dioses lo criaron semejante a un retoño, ya decía
yo que no sería en nada inferior, entre los hombres, a su querido padre, admirable en cuerpo y aspecto; pero alguno de los
inmortales —o quizá de los hombres— debe haberle dañado la
bien equilibrada mente, pues ha marchado a la divina Pilos en

---

[212] Es una expresión modelada a partir de *Ilíada*, IX.312-3, donde Aquiles
está contestando precisamente al discurso de Odiseo en la Embajada.

.busca de noticias de su padre, y los ilustres pretendientes lo 180
acechan al volver a casa para que desaparezca sin gloria de Itaca la progenie del divino Arcisio. Pero dejemos a éste, ya sea sorprendido, ya escape porque el Cronida tienda su mano sobre él.

»Vamos, cuéntame ahora, anciano, tus propias desgracias y dime con verdad para que yo lo sepa: ¿quién y de dónde eres entre los hombres? ¿Dónde se encuentran tu ciudad y tus padres? ¿En qué barco has llegado? ¿Cómo te han traído hasta Itaca los marineros y quiénes se preciaban de ser? Porque no creo que hayas llegado aquí a pie»[213]. 190

Y contestándole dijo el muy astuto Odiseo:

«En verdad, te voy a contestar con exactitud. Ni aunque tuviéramos por mucho tiempo comida y dulce bebida para celebrar un festín dentro de tu cabaña —mientras los demás continúan su labor— podría yo fácilmente, ni siquiera en un año entero, acabar la narración de cuantas penalidades ha soportado mi ánimo por voluntad de los dioses. Mi raza procede de Creta —lo digo bien alto— y soy hijo de un hombre rico. Nu- 200
merosos hijos legítimos nacieron de su esposa en el palacio y fueron criados, pero a mí me parió una madre comprada, una concubina, aunque mi padre, Cástor Hilácida, de cuya raza me precio de ser, me estimaba igual que a sus legítimos. Como un dios era venerado éste en el pueblo de Creta por su abundancia, riqueza y vigorosos hijos. Pero las Keres de la muerte se lo llevaron a las moradas de Hades y sus magnánimos hijos sortearon la hacienda y se la repartieron, entregándome a mí una 210
nonada y una casa. Caséme con mujer de casa rica por mis muchas virtudes, que no era yo inútil ni temeroso de luchar. Pero ya se ha acabado todo, aunque viendo la caña seca[214] te darás cuenta, pues un gran infortunio me abruma.

»En verdad, Ares y Atenea me concedieron audacia y hom-

---

[213] Fórmula que se dirige habitualmente a un forastero. Aquí la tenemos completa, igual que en I.170 y ss., o en XXIV.298 y ss., donde aparece más elaborada. En los demás casos sólo se hacen las dos primeras preguntas, cfr. X.325, XV.264 y XIX.105.

[214] A este pasaje se refiere Aristóteles en la *Retórica* (1410b14): «cuando se llama caña seca a la vejez, (la metáfora) proporciona un conocimiento y noción a través del género; pues ambos han perdido la flor».

bría. Cada vez que elegía para el combate a hombres sobresalientes, sembrando desgracias para el enemigo, jamás mi valeroso corazón puso los ojos en la muerte, sino que, saltando el primero, solía matar con mi lanza a cuantos enemigos no se igualaran a mis pies. Así era yo en el combate.

»En cambio, no me agradaba la labor ni el cuidado de la hacienda que suele criar hijos brillantes: siempre me gustaron las naves remeras, los combates, los bien torneados venablos y las flechas, cosas funestas que suelen causar espanto en los demás. Sin embargo, la divinidad puso en mi alma estos intereses, que cada hombre se complace en un trabajo. Antes de que los hijos de los aqueos desembarcaran en Troya, ya me había puesto nueve veces al frente de hombres y naves de veloces proas contra gentes de otras tierras. Y conseguía mucho botín, del que elegía lo mejor, y también me tocaba mucho en suerte. Así que rápidamente prosperó mi casa y me convertí en un hombre temido y respetado en Creta.

»Pero cuando Zeus, que ve a lo ancho, dispuso la luctuosa expedición que iba a aflojar las rodillas de muchos hombres, nos dieron órdenes a mí y al ilustre Idomeneo de capitanear las naves que marchaban a Ilión. No había medio de negarse, nos lo impedían las duras habladurías del pueblo. Allí combatimos nueve años los hijos de los aqueos, pero al décimo destruimos la ciudad de Príamo y volvimos a casa en las naves; y un dios dispersó a los aqueos. Entonces fue cuando el providente Zeus meditó desgracias contra mí, miserable. Había permanecido sólo un mes complaciéndome con mis hijos y legítima esposa, cuando mi ánimo me impulsó a hacer una expedición a Egipto[215] después de equipar bien mis naves en compañía de mis divinos compañeros.

»Equipé nueve naves y enseguida se congregó la dotación. Durante seis días comieron en mi casa mis leales compañeros; les ofrecí numerosas víctimas para que las sacrificaran en ho-

---

[215] Esta historia fingida de Odiseo es muy similar a la descripción que hace Heródoto (cfr. 2.152 y ss.) de la llegada a Egipto de los jonios en el reinado de Psamético. Es difícil dilucidar si Heródoto está siguiendo insconscientemente a Homero o si ambos, por el contrario, registran independientemente el mismo hecho histórico. Cfr. R. Carpenter, ob. cit., págs. 93 y ss.

nor de los dioses y prepararan comida para sí. Conque el séptimo día zarpamos tranquilamente de la extensa Creta impulsados por un Bóreas fresco, agradable, como si navegáramos por una corriente. Ninguna nave se me dañó, nosotros estábamos sanos y salvos, y a las naves las dirigían el viento y los pilotos.

»A los cinco días llegamos al Egipto de buena corriente y atraqué mis bien equilibradas naves en este río. Entonces ordené a mis leales compañeros que se quedaran junto a ellas 260 para vigilarlas y envié espías a lugares de observación con orden de que regresaran, pero éstos, cediendo a su ambición y dejándose arrastrar por sus impulsos, saquearon los hermosos campos de los egipcios, se llevaron a las mujeres y niños y mataron a los hombres. Pronto llegó el griterío a la ciudad, así que al escucharlo se presentaron al despuntar la aurora. Llenóse la llanura toda de gentes de pie y a caballo y del estruendo del bronce. Zeus, el que goza con el rayo, indujo a mis compañeros a huir cobardemente y ninguno se atrevió a dar el pecho. Por todas partes nos rodeaba la destrucción; allí mataron 270 con agudo bronce a muchos de mis compañeros y a otros se los llevaron vivos para forzarlos a trabajar sus campos.

»Entonces Zeus puso en mi mente el siguiente plan (¡ojalá hubiera muerto saliendo al encuentro de mi destino allí en Egipto, pues todavía me tenía que tender sus brazos la desgracia!): al punto quité de mi cabeza el bien trabajado yelmo y de mis hombros el escudo y arrojé de mi brazo la lanza. Lleguéme frente al carro del rey y besé sus rodillas. Él me protegió y se compadeció de mí y, sentándome en su carro, me condujo a su 280 palacio con lágrimas en mis ojos. Cierto que muchos trataron de acosarme con sus lanzas deseando matarme —pues estaban muy enfurecidos—, pero el rey me protegió por temor a la cólera de Zeus Hospitalario, el que se irrita sobremanera por las obras malvadas.

»Allí me quedé siete años y conseguí reunir mucha riqueza entre los egipcios —pues todos me regalaban. Pero cuando se acercó el octavo año cumpliendo su ciclo llegó un hombre fenicio conocedor de mentiras, un laña que ya había causado perjuicios a muchos hombres. Éste me convenció para mar- 290 char a Fenicia, donde tenía su casa y posesiones. Allí permanecí durante un año completo junto a él, pero cuando pasaron meses y días en el ciclo del año y pasaron las estaciones me envió a Libia en una nave surcadora del ponto, tramando falacias para que llevara con él una mercancía, pero en realidad con intención de venderme y cobrar inmensa fortuna. Le seguía en la nave a la fuerza —pues ya barruntaba yo algo. Ésta corría impulsada por un Bóreas fresco, agradable, a la altura del centro de Creta. Y Zeus nos preparaba la perdición.   300

»Cuando por fin dejamos atrás Creta y no se veía tierra alguna, sino sólo cielo y mar, el Cronida puso una oscura nube sobre la cóncava nave y bajo ella se oscureció el ponto. Y Zeus comenzó a tronar al tiempo que lanzaba un rayo contra la nave. Y esta se revolvió toda sacudida por el rayo de Zeus y se llenó de azufre. Todos cayeron fuera de la nave y, semejantes a las cornejas marinas eran arrastrados por las olas en torno a la nave[216]. Dios les había arrebatado el regreso. En cuanto a mí..., afligido como estaba, el mismo Zeus puso entre mis manos   310 el mástil gigantesco de la nave de azuloscura proa para que escapara una vez más de la perdición. Así que, trabado al mástil, me dejaba llevar de los funestos vientos. Durante nueve días me dejé llevar y al décimo una gran ola rodante me acercó —era noche cerrada— a la tierra de los tesprotos, donde me acogió sin pagar precio el héroe Fidón, el rey de los tesprotos.

»Acercóseme su hijo cuando ya estaba yo agotado por la intemperie y el cansancio y me llevó a casa sosteniéndome en su brazo hasta que llegó al palacio de su padre, donde me vistió   320 de manto y túnica.

»Allí fue donde supe de Odiseo, pues el rey me dijo que estaba hospedándolo y agasajándolo a punto de volver a su tierra patria. Además, me mostró cuantas riquezas había conseguido Odiseo reunir —bronce y oro y bien trabajado hierro. En verdad, podrían éstas alimentar a otro hombre hasta la décima generación: ¡tantos tesoros tenía depositados en el palacio del rey! Me dijo que Odiseo había marchado a Dodona[217] para es-

---

[216] Versos tomados de la narración por Odiseo de la perdición de sus propios compañeros, después de salir de la isla de Helios, cfr. XII.415-19.

[217] Dodona es uno de los más antiguos oráculos griegos. Se encuentra en el Epiro (la Tesprotia homérica) y pertenecía a Zeus Naios. Homero, que habla dos veces de este oráculo (aquí y en *Ilíada* XVI.235-7), nos informa que la mán-

cuchar la voluntad de Zeus, el que habla desde la divina encina de elevada copa, para enterarse si debía volver a las claras u ocultamente al próspero pueblo de Itaca, después de tantos años de ausencia. Y juró ante mí, mientras hacía una libación en su palacio, que ya tenía dispuesta una nave y compañeros que lo escoltarían hasta su tierra patria. Pero a mí me despidió antes, pues resultó que una nave de tesprotos estaba a punto de zarpar hacia Duliquia, rica en grano. Les ordenó que me enviaran gentilmente al rey Acasto, pero les agradó más una malvada decisión sobre mi persona, para que aún estuviera más cerca de la perdición. Así que cuando la nave surcadora del ponto se había alejado bastante de tierra urdieron contra mí la esclavitud; me despojaron de túnica y manto y echaron sobre mí miserables andrajos y una mala túnica rasgada, lo que estás viendo ahora con tus ojos.

»Llegaron al atardecer a los campos de Itaca, hermosa al atardecer. Una vez allí, me ataron fuertemente a la nave de buenos bancos con un bien torneado cable y descendiendo precipitadamente a la ribera del mar se dispusieron a cenar. Pero los mismos dioses, sin duda, aflojaron mis ligaduras fácilmente. Cubrí mi cabeza con los andrajos y, deslizándome por el pulido timón hasta dar de pechos en el mar, comencé a nadar con ambos brazos como si fueran remos, y pronto estuve fuera de su alcance. Salí del agua por donde hay un bosque de verdeantes encinas y caí desplomado. Los tesprotos me buscaron aquí y allá, dando grandes gritos, pero como no les interesara molestarse más, embarcaron de nuevo en su cóncava nave. Conque han sido los dioses mismos los que me han ocultado fácilmente y me han hecho llegar al establo de un hombre prudente, pues mi destino es que viva aún.»

Y tú le contestaste, porquero Eumeo, diciendo:

«Ay, desdichado forastero, de verdad que has conmovido mi ánimo al contarme detalladamente tus sufrimientos y vagabundeos, pero no creo que sean razonables tus palabras y no vas a convencerme de cuanto has dicho sobre Odiseo. ¿Por qué tie-

330

340

350

360

---

tica se ejercía a través de una encina sagrada y que lo regentaban los Selloi «intérpretes de pies no lavados, que duermen en el suelo» *(Ilíada, loc. cit.)*. Probablemente se refiere a un cuerpo sacerdotal que llevaba una vida de austeridad.

nes que mentir en vano siendo como eres? Yo mismo reconozco el regreso de mi soberano; muy odioso debió de hacerse a los ojos de todos los dioses cuando no lo dejaron morir entre los troyanos ni en brazos de los suyos, una vez que hubo concluido la guerra. Entonces le habría construido una tumba el ejército panaqueo y habría él cobrado gran fama para su hijo, pero ahora se lo han llevado las Harpías sin gloria alguna. Así que yo ando solitartio entre mis cerdos y no me acerco a la ciudad, si no me ordena ir la prudente Penélope cuando llega alguna noticia. Entonces todos se sientan a preguntar detalles, tanto los que sienten dolor por la larga ausencia de su soberano como los que se alegran consumiendo su hacienda sin pagar. Pero a mí no me agrada ir allá a preguntar desde que me engañó con sus palabras un etolio que llegó a mi casa, vagamundo de muchas tierras, tras haber dado muerte a un hombre. Yo le agasajé y él me aseguró que lo había visto en casa de Idomeneo, en Creta, reparando las naves que le habían quebrado los vendavales. También me aseguró que volvería para el verano o el otoño con muchas riquezas en compañía de sus divinos compañeros. 370 380

»Conque no me halagues con mentiras ni trates de encantarme también tú, anciano sufridor, una vez que la divinidad te ha traído junto a mí. Si te respeto y agasajo no es por eso, sino por veneración a Zeus Hospitalario y por compasión hacia ti.»

Y le contestó y dijo el muy astuto Odiseo: 390

«De verdad que tienes un ánimo desconfiado cuando no consigo persuadirte y no logro convencerte ni siquiera con juramento.

»Pero, vamos, hagamos un pacto y que sean testigos los dioses que poseen el Olimpo: si vuelve tu soberano a esta casa, vísteme con manto y túnica y envíame a Duliquio, donde place a mi ánimo; pero si no vuelve tu soberano, como afirmo, ordena a las esclavas que me despeñen desde una gran roca para que todo mendigo se guarde de mentir.» 400

Y le contestó y dijo el divino porquero:

«Forastero, ¡había yo de tener a los ojos de los hombres buena fama y virtud ahora y para siempre, si después de introducirte en mi cabaña y darte dones de hospitalidad te matara y arrebatara la vida! ¡Con buenos sentimientos iba yo después a dirigir mis plegarias a Zeus Cronida!

»Pero ya es hora de cenar; pronto tendré dentro a mis compañeros para preparar en la cabaña sabrosa comida.»

Esto se decían uno a otro, cuando se acercaron cerdos y 410 porqueros. Los encerraron para que se acostaran por grupos y se levantó un inenarrable estruendo de cerdas acomodándose en las pocilgas.

Después, el divino porquero daba estas órdenes a sus compañeros:

«Traed el mejor cerdo para que se lo sacrifique al forastero de lejanas tierras, que también nosotros tendremos parte, los que ya llevamos tiempo soportando miserias por culpa de los cerdos de blancos dientes, pues otros se comen nuestro esfuerzo sin pagarlo.»

Así diciendo, partió leña con su implacable bronce y ellos metieron un cerdo bien gordo de cinco años, poniéndole junto 420 al hogar. Y el porquero no se olvidó de los inmortales, pues estaba dotado de noble corazón. Así que arrojó al fuego, como primicias, unos pelos de la cabeza del cerdo de blancos dientes y oró a todos los dioses para que volviera el prudente Odiseo a casa.

Luego levantó el cerdo y lo golpeó con una rama de encina que había dejado al hacer leña. Y el alma abandonó a éste. Así que lo degollaron, chamuscaron y trocearon, y el porquero envolvió los trozos en gorda grasa, miembro por miembro, y arrojó algunos al fuego rebozándolos en harina de cebada; después los partieron y atravesaron con pinchos, los asaron con 430 cuidado y sacaron y pusieron sobre la mesa de trinchar. Levantóse el porquero para distribuirlos —pues su corazón conocía la equidad— y dividió todo en siete partes: una la ofreció, al tiempo que oraba, a las Ninfas y a Hermes, el hijo de Maya, y las demás las distribuyó a cada uno. Odiseo recibió contento con el alargado lomo del cerdo de blancos dientes, pues éste fortaleció el ánimo del soberano, y dirigiéndose a Eumeo dijo el prudente Odiseo:

«¡Ojalá, Eumeo, seas tan querido al padre Zeus como lo eres 440 de mí, pues, siendo como soy, me has distinguido con tus bienes.»

Y tú le contestaste, porquero Eumeo, diciendo:

«Come, desdichado forastero, y alégrate con todo lo que tienes a tu alcance, que dios te dará unas cosas y otras las dejará pasar, según le cumpla a su ánimo, pues lo puede todo.»

Así diciendo, ofreció las primicias a los dioses que han nacido para siempre y, luego de libar, puso rojo vino en manos de Odiseo, el destructor de ciudades, que se hallaba sentado junto a su porción.

También les repartió pan Mesaulio, a quien había adquirido el porquero mismo, una vez que se hubo ausentado su soberano y se quedó sólo, lejos de su dueña y del anciano Laertes. Se lo había comprado a los tafios con su propio dinero[218].

Y ellos echaron mano de los alimentos que tenían delante y, cuando hubieron arrojado de sí el deseo de comer y beber, les retiró Mesaulio el pan y se dispusieron a ir al lecho, saciados de pan y carne.

Y llegó una noche desapacible, noche sin luna, que Zeus estuvo lloviendo toda ella, pues soplaba un fuerte Céfiro que siempre trae lluvia. Entonces se dirigió Odiseo a ellos para poner a prueba al porquero, por ver si se quitaba el manto y se lo entregaba o incitaba a uno de sus compañeros, ya que tanto se preocupaba de él:

«Escuchadme ahora, Eumeo y todos vosotros, compañeros; os voy a decir mi palabra con una súplica, pues me ha impulsado el perturbador vino, el que hace cantar y reír suavemente incluso al más prudente, el que induce a danzar y hace soltar palabras que estarían mejor no dichas. Pero ya que he empezado a hablar, no voy a ocultároslo. ¡Ojalá fuera yo joven y mi vigor no estuviera trabado como cuando marchamos a poner una emboscada junto a Troya! Iban como jefes Odiseo y el Atrida Menelao y junto a ellos mandaba yo como tercero, pues ellos me lo ordenaron. Cuando ya habíamos llegado a la empinada muralla de la ciudad nos apostamos entre espesos espinos, en un cañaveral bajo nuestras armas y se nos vino una noche desapacible, glacial, pues caía el Bóreas. Así que se nos vino de arriba una nieve helada, como escarcha, y el hielo se condensaba en nuestros escudos. Todos tenían mantos y tú-

450

460

470

---

218 Los esclavos que aparecen en la *Odisea* no solamente gozan de una cierta libertad de acción, sino incluso, al parecer, del derecho a la propiedad privada. Cfr. L. Gil, Introducción..., 372 y ss.

nicas y dormían apaciblemente cubriendo sus hombros con los escudos, pero yo había dejado al marchar mi manto a unos 480 compañeros por imprevisión, pues no creía que iría a tener frío en absoluto; así que había partido sólo con mi escudo y una escarcela brillante. Cuando ya estaba terciada la noche y los astros declinaban, me dirigí a Odiseo, que estaba a mi lado, tocándolo con mi codo —y él enseguida prestó oídos— "Laertiada de linaje divino, Odiseo rico en ardides, ya no me contaré más entre los vivos pues me está doblegando el temporal, que no tengo manto. Un dios me ha engañado para que viniera con una sola túnica y ahora ya no hay escape posible."

»Así dije y él enseguida echó mano a esta treta —¡cómo era 490 el hombre para decidir y combatir!— y hablando en voz baja me dijo su palabra: "Calla, no te oiga alguno de los aqueos." Así diciendo se apoyó sobre el codo y levantando la cabeza dijo su palabra: "Escuchadme, los míos: acaba de venirme un sueño divino mientas dormía. Nos hemos alejado demasiado de las naves, que vaya alguien a decir al Atrida Agamenón, pastor de su pueblo, si ordena que vengan más hombres desde las naves." Así dijo y enseguida se levantó Toante, hijo de Andremón, y dejando su rojo manto echó a correr hacia las naves. 500 Así que yo me acosté con alegría envuelto en su manto y se mostró Eos de trono de oro. ¡Ojalá fuera yo joven y mi vigor no estuviera trabado, pues quizá alguno de los porqueros me daría un manto en esta cuadra tanto por amor como por respeto a un hombre valeroso!, que ahora me desprecian por tener mala ropa sobre mi cuerpo.»

Y tú le contestaste, porquero Eumeo, diciendo:

«Anciano es una irreprochable historia la que has contado y no creo que hayas dicho palabra inútil, fuera de lugar. Por eso no vas a carecer de vestido ni de cosa alguna de la que está 510 bien que tengan los desdichados suplicantes que nos salen al encuentro; pero cuando amanezca sacudirás tus andrajos, pues no hay aquí muchos mantos ni túnicas de recambio para cubrirse, que cada hombre tiene sólo uno. Mas cuando venga el querido hijo de Odiseo, él te dará un manto y una túnica y te enviará a donde tu corazón te empuje.»

Así diciendo, se levantó y le tendió un camastro cerca del fuego y le puso encima pieles de ovejas y cabras.

Echóse allí Odiseo y sobre él arrojó Eumeo un manto grue- 520
so y grande que tenía de repuesto para cuando se levantara terrible temporal.

Así que allí se acostó Odiseo, y los jóvenes a su lado. Pero al
porquero no le gustaba dormir lejos de la piara, por lo que se
aprestó a salir —y Odiseo se alegró por lo mucho que se cuidaba de su hacienda, aunque él estaba lejos. Primero se echó a
los fuertes hombros la aguda espada y luego se vistió un grueso manto que le protegiera del viento; tomó la piel de un ca- 530
brón bien gordo y un agudo venablo que le protegiera de perros y hombres; y se puso en camino, deseando dormir, hacia
el lugar donde dormían los machos, bajo una cóncava roca, al
abrigo del Bóreas.

Canto XV

TELÉMACO REGRESA A ITACA

Entre tanto había marchado Palas Atenea hacia la extensa Lacedemonia para sugerir el regreso al ilustre hijo del magnánimo Odiseo y ordenarle que regresara.

Y encontró a Telémaco y al brillante hijo de Néstor durmiendo en el pórtico del glorioso Menelao[219], aunque en verdad sólo al hijo de Néstor dominaba el dulce sueño, que a Telémaco no lo sujetaba el blando sueño y en la noche inmortal agitaba en su interior la angustia por su padre. Se acercó Atenea, la de ojos brillantes y le dijo:

«Telémaco, no está bien vagar más tiempo lejos de casa dejando allí tus bienes y a hombres tan soberbios. ¡Cuidado, no vayan a repartirse y devorarlo todo mientras tú haces un viaje baldío! Vamos, apremia a Menelao, de recia voz guerrera, para que te despida, a fin de que encuentres a tu ilustre madre todavía en casa, que ya su padre y hermanos andan empujándola a que se case con Eurímaco, pues éste aventaja a todos los pretendientes en regalarla y en aumentar su dote. Guárdate de que no se lleve de casa, contra tu voluntad, algún bien. Pues ya sabes cómo es el alma de una mujer: está dispuesta a acrecentar la casa de quien la despose olvidando y despreocupándose de sus primeros hijos y de su esposo, una vez que ha muerto.

---

[219] En este canto se unen los dos hilos del relato. Para ello éste vuelve a Telémaco, que se encuentra todavía en el palacio de Menelao. En IV.590 y ss., se encuentra cenando en compañía de su huésped. La economía del relato hace que nos lo encontremos ahora unos momentos antes del alba del día siguiente.

»Conque ponte en camino y deja todo en manos de la esclava que te parezca la mejor, hasta que los dioses te den una esposa ilustre.

»Te voy a decir algo más, ponlo en tu interior: los más nobles de los pretendientes te han puesto emboscada en el paso entre Itaca y la escarpada Same, deliberadamente, pues desean matarte antes de que llegues a tu tierra patria. Pero no creo que esto suceda antes de que la tierra abrace a alguno de los pretendientes que se comen tu hacienda. Así que aleja de las islas tu bien construida nave y navega por la noche, pues te enviará viento favorable aquel de los inmortales que te custodia y protege. Tan pronto como hayas llegado a la ribera de Itaca, envía la nave y a tus compañeros a la ciudad y tú marcha primero junto al porquero, el que vigila los cerdos y te es fiel. Pasa allí la noche y envíale a la ciudad para que anuncie a la prudente Penélope que estás a salvo y has llegado de Pilos.»

Hablando así marchó hacia el lejano Olimpo. Despertó Telémaco al hijo de Néstor de su dulce sueño empujándole con el pie y le dijo su palabra:

«Despierta, Pisístrato, hijo de Néstor, unce al carro los caballos de una sola pezuña a fin de apresurar nuestro viaje.»

Y le contestó Pisístrato, el hijo de Néstor:

«Telémaco, no es posible conducir en la oscura noche, aunque estemos ansiosos de ponernos en camino. Pronto despuntará la aurora. Esperemos a que el héroe Atrida Menelao, ilustre por su lanza, nos traiga sus dones, los ponga en el carro y nos despida con palabras amables; que un huésped se acuerda cada día del hombre que lo ha acogido si éste le ha ofrecido su amistad.»

Así habló y al punto apareció Eos de trono de oro.

Y se les acercó Menelao, de recia voz guerrera, levantándose del lecho de junto a Helena de lindas trenzas.

Cuando lo vio el hijo de Odiseo vistió apresuradamente sobre su cuerpo la brillante túnica, echó sobre sus resplandecientes hombros un gran manto y se dirigió a la puerta. Y colocándose a su lado le dijo el querido hijo de Odiseo:

«Atrida Menelao, vástago de Zeus, pastor de tu pueblo, despídeme ya a mi querida patria, pues mi ánimo desea regresar.»

Y le contestó Menelao, de recia voz guerrera:

«Telémaco, no te detendré más tiempo si deseas volver, que también a mí me irrita quien recibe a un huésped y lo ama en exceso o en exceso lo aborrece. Todo es mejor si es moderado. 70 La misma bajeza comete quien anima a su huésped a que se vaya, cuando éste no quiere hacerlo, que quien se lo impide cuando lo desea. Hay que agasajar al huésped cuando está en tu casa, pero también despedirlo si lo desea. Mas espera a que te traiga mis hermosos dones y los ponga en el carro, dones hermosos —lo verás con tus propios ojos—, y a que diga a las mujeres que preparen en palacio un almuerzo de cuanto aquí abunda. Que es honor y gloria, al tiempo que provecho, el que os marchéis por la tierra inmensa después de almorzar. Si deseas volver por la Hélade y el centro de Argos, para que yo 80 mismo te acompañe, unciré mis caballos y te conduciré por las ciudades de los hombres. Nadie nos despedirá con las manos vacías, sino que nos darán algo para llevarnos —un trípode de buen bronce, un jarrón o dos mulos o una copa de oro.»

Y Telémaco le contestó con sensatez:

«Atrida Menelao, vástago de Zeus, caudillo de tu pueblo, quiero volver ya a mis cosas, pues no he dejado al venir ningún vigilante de mis posesiones; no quiero que por buscar a mi padre vaya a perderme yo, o que me desaparezca del palacio al- 90 gún tesoro de valor.»

Luego que le oyó Menelao, de recia voz guerrera, ordenó a su esposa y esclavas que preparasen en palacio un almuerzo de cuanto allí abundaba. Acercósele después Eteoneo, hijo de Boeto, tras levantarse de la cama —pues no habitaba lejos—, y le ordenó Menelao, de recia voz guerrera, que encendiera fuego y asara carne. Y aquél no desobedeció.

Menelao ascendió a su perfumado dormitorio, pero no sólo, que junto a él marchaban Helena y Megapentes[220]. Cuando ha- 100 bían llegado adonde tenía sus tesoros el Atrida Menelao, tomó una copa de doble asa y ordenó a su hijo Megapentes que llevara una crátera de plata. Helena habíase detenido junto a sus arcas donde tenía peplos multicolores que ella misma había bordado. Tomó uno de éstos y se lo llevó Helena, divina entre

---

[220] Hijo de Menelao con una esclava, cfr. IV.10 y ss.

las mujeres, el más hermoso por sus adornos y el más grande
—brillaba como una estrella y estaba encima de los demás.

Conque atravesaron el palacio hasta que llegaron junto a Telémaco. Y le dijo el rubio Menelao: 110

«Telémaco, ¡ojalá Zeus, el tronador esposo de Hera, te lleve
a término el regreso tal como tú lo pretendes! En cuanto a los
dones..., te voy a entregar el más hermoso y estimable de
cuantos tesoros tengo en casa. Te voy a dar una crátera trabajada, toda ella de plata, con los bordes fundidos con oro, obra
de Hefesto —me la dio el héroe Fédimo, rey de los sidonios,
cuando su palacio me cobijó al regresar yo allí. Esto quiero
regalarte a ti.»

Hablando así, puso en sus manos la copa de doble asa el hé- 120
roe Atrida; luego el vigoroso Megapentes le acercó una crátera
de plata. También se le acercó Helena, de lindas mejillas, con el
peplo en sus manos, le dijo su palabra y le llamó por su nombre:

«También yo, hijo mío, te entrego este regalo, recuerdo de
las manos de Helena, para que se lo lleves a tu esposa en el
momento de la deseada boda, y que permanezca junto a tu madre en palacio hasta entonces. Que llegues feliz a tu bien edificada morada y a tu tierra patria.»

Así diciendo lo puso en sus manos y él lo recibió gozoso. Lo 130
tomó después el héroe Pisístrato y lo puso en la caja del carro,
no sin admirarlo con toda su alma.

Después el rubio Menelao los condujo hasta el salón y ambos se sentaron en sillas y sillones. Y una esclava derramó sobre fuente de plata el aguamanos que llevaba en hermosa jarra
de oro para que se lavaran y a su lado extendió una mesa pulimentada. Y la venerable ama de llaves puso comida sobre ella
y añadió abundantes piezas escogidas favoreciéndoles entre los
que estaban presentes. El hijo de Boeto repartía la carne y dis- 140
tribuía las porciones, y el hijo del ilustre Menelao escanciaba el
vino. Echaron ellos mano de los alimentos que tenían delante
y, cuando habían arrojado de sí el deseo de comer y beber, Telémaco y el brillante hijo de Néstor uncieron los caballos, subieron al carro de variados colores y lo condujeron fuera del
pórtico y de la resonante galería. Y el rubio Menelao salió tras
ellos llevando en su mano derecha rojo vino en copa de oro,
para que marcharan después de hacer libación.

Se colocó delante de los caballos y dijo como despedida: 150

«¡Salud, muchachos!, y transmitid mis saludos a Néstor, pastor de su pueblo, pues fue conmigo tierno como un padre mientras los hijos de los aqueos combatíamos en Troya.»

Y Telémaco le contestó discretamente:

«Vástago de Zeus, de verdad que al llegar comunicaremos a aquél todo, según nos lo has dicho. ¡Ojalá al volver yo a Itaca encontrara a Odiseo en casa y pudiera decirle que vengo de junto a ti y he ganado toda tu amistad!, pues llevo regalos hermosos y buenos.»

Mientras así hablaba le voló un pájaro por la derecha, un   160
halcón que llevaba entre sus garras a un enorme ganso blanco, doméstico, de algún corral —pues le seguían gritando hombres y mujeres—; y el halcón se acercó a aquéllos y se lanzó por la derecha, frente a los caballos. Al verlo se llenaron de contento y alegróseles a todos el ánimo.

Y entre ellos comenzó a hablar Pisístrato, el hijo de Néstor:

«Piensa, Menelao, vástago de Zeus, caudillo de tu pueblo, si es para nosotros o para ti para quien ha mostrado el dios este presagio.»

Así dijo, y Menelao, amado de Ares, se puso a cavilar para   170
poder contestarle oportunamente después de pensarlo.

Pero Helena, de largo peplo, tomándole delantera dijo su palabra:

«Escuchadme, voy a hacer una predicción tal como los inmortales me lo están poniendo en el pecho y como creo que se va a cumplir. Del mismo modo que este halcón ha venido del monte y arrebatado al ganso mientras se alimentaba en la casa donde está su progenie y sus padres, así Odiseo, después de mucho sufrir y mucho vagar, llegará a casa y los hará pagar, o quizá ya está en casa sembrando la muerte para todos los pretendientes.»

Y Telémaco le contestó discretamente:

«¡Ojalá lo disponga así Zeus, el tronante esposo de Hera! En   180
este caso te invocaría también allí como a una diosa.»

Así dijo y sacudió con el látigo a los caballos. Y éstos se lanzaron velozmente hacia la llanura precipitándose por la ciudad.

Y arrastraron el yugo por ambos lados durante todo el día. Se puso el sol y todos los caminos se llenaron de sombra cuando llegaron a Feras, a casa de Diocles, hijo de Ortíloco[221], a quien Alfeo engendró. Allí pasaron la noche y éste les entregó dones de hospitalidad.

Cuando se mostró Eos, la que nace de la mañana, la de dedos de rosa, uncieron sus caballos y ascendieron al carro de variados colores y lo condujeron fuera del pórtico y de la resonante galería. Restalló el látigo para que partieran y los caballos se lanzaron muy a gusto. Por fin llegaron a la elevada ciudad de Pilos y Telémaco se dirigió al hijo de Néstor:

«Hijo de Néstor, ¿podrías cumplir mi palabra si me haces una promesa?, ya que nos preciamos de tener viejos lazos de hospitalidad por el amor de nuestros padres, además de ser de la misma edad, y este viaje nos habrá de unir más. No me lleves más allá de la nave, déjame aquí mismo, no sea que el anciano me retenga contra mi voluntad en su palacio por mor de agasajarme. Y tengo que llegar pronto.»

Así habló y el hijo de Néstor deliberó en su interior cómo cumpliría su palabra, como le correspondía. Mientras así pensaba, parecióle mejor volver sus caballos hacia la rápida nave y la ribera del mar. Así que puso en la popa los hermosísimos dones, vestidos y oro, que Menelao le había dado y apremiándole decía aladas palabras:

«Embarca enseguida y ordénaselo a tus compañeros antes que llegue yo a casa y se lo anuncie al anciano; tal como tiene de irritable el ánimo no te dejará ir, antes bien vendrá él en persona a buscarte y te aseguro que no volvería de baldío, y se irritaría sobremanera.»

Así hablando torció sus caballos de hermosas crines hacia la ciudad de los Pilios y arribó enseguida a casa.

Entretanto, Telémaco apremiaba a sus compañeros con estas órdenes:

«Poned en orden los aparejos, compañeros, en la negra nave, y embarquemos para acelerar el viaje.»

Así habló y ellos le escucharon y obedecieron. Conque embarcaron y se sentaron sobre los bancos.

---

[221] Personajes ya citados en III.490. Se trata de la dinastía de Feras, que Homero cita en *Ilíada*, V.541-60, cuando los dos hijos de Diocles, Creton y Ortíloco, mueren a manos de Eneas.

Ocupábase él en esto, así como en orar y hacer sacrificio a Atenea junto a la proa, cuando se le acercó un forastero, uno que había huido de Argos por haber dado muerte a alguien, un adivino[222]. Por linaje era descendiente de Melampo, quien en otro tiempo vivió en Pilos, criadora de ganados, habitando con extrema prosperidad un palacio entre los pilios. Luego marchó a otras tierras huyendo de su patria y del magnánimo Neleo, el más noble de los vivientes, quien le retuvo por la fuerza muchos bienes durante un año completo. Todo este tiempo estuvo en el palacio de Fílaco encadenado con dolorosas ligaduras, padeciendo grandes sufrimientos por causa de la hija de Neleo[223] y la pesada ceguera que puso en su mente Erinis, la diosa horrenda.

Pero consiguió escapar de la muerte y terminó llevándose a Pilos, desde Filace, sus mugidores bueyes. Así que castigó al divino Neleo por su acción indigna y llevó a casa mujer para su hermano. Y marchó luego a otras tierras, a Argos, criadora de caballos, pues su destino era que habitara allí reinando sobre numerosos argivos. Allí tomó mujer y construyó un palacio de elevado techo. Y engendró a Antífates y Mantio, robustos hijos. Antífates engendró al magnánimo Oicleo, y Oicleo a su vez a Anfiarao, salvador de su pueblo, a quien amó de corazón Zeus, portador de égida, y Apolo dispensó numerosas pruebas de amistad. Pero no llegó al umbral de la vejez, sino que pereció en Tebas por la traición de una mujer. Y sus hijos fueron Alcmeón y Anfíloco. Mantio, por su parte, engendró a Polífides y a Clito. Pero, ¡ay!, que a Clito se lo llevó Eos, de hermoso trono, por ser tan bello, así que Apolo hizo adivino al magnánimo Polífides, el mejor de los hombres, una vez que hubo muerto Anfiarao. Pero, irritado con su padre, emigró a Hiperesia y, poniendo allí su morada, profetizaba para todos los hombres.

---

[222] Cfr. XIII.260 y nota.

[223] La hija de Neleo es Peró (cfr. XI.290). Ni aquí ni en el pasaje citado se relata la historia completa, que es como sigue: Neleo tenía una hija, Peró, de quien estaba enamorado Biante, hermano de Melampo. Neleo no entregaba su hija si el pretendiente no le traía el rebaño de Ificlo (o de su padre Fílaco). Melampo, que era adivino, se prestó a ayudar a su hermano, pero fue sorprendido en el acto de robarlo y pasó un año encerrado. Después de este periodo, curó la impotencia de Ificlo, y Fílaco le donó el rebaño.

De éste era hijo el que se acercó entonces a Telémaco y su nombre era Teoclímeno. Lo encontró haciendo libación y súplicas sobre la rápida, negra nave, y le dirigió aladas palabras:

«Amigo, ya que te encuentro sacrificando en este lugar, te 260 ruego por las ofrendas y el dios, e incluso por tu propia cabeza y la de los compañeros que te siguen, me digas la verdad y nada ocultes a mis preguntas: ¿de dónde eres? ¿Dónde se encuentran tu ciudad y tus padres?»

Y Telémaco le contestó discretamente:

«En verdad, forastero, te voy a hablar sinceramente. De origen soy itacense y mi padre es Odiseo —si es que alguna vez ha existido; ahora, desde luego, ha perecido con triste muerte. Por esto he tomado compañeros y una negra nave para preguntar por mi padre, largo tiempo ausente.» 270

Y Teoclímeno, semejante a los dioses, le dijo a su vez:

«Así estoy también yo, huido de mi patria por matar a un hombre de mi propia tribu. Muchos son mis hermanos y parientes en Argos, criadora de caballos, y mucho es su poder sobre los aqueos. Por evitar la muerte y la negra Ker ando huyendo de éstos, que mi destino es vagar entre los hombres. Conque admíteme en tu nave, ya que he llegado a ti como suplicante; cuidado no me maten, pues creo que me andan persiguiendo.»

Y Telémaco a su vez le contestó discretamente:

«No, no te rechazaré de mi equilibrada nave si tanto lo de- 280 seas. Conque sígueme, te agasajaremos con lo que tengamos.»

Así hablando, tomó de sus manos la lanza de bronce y la tendió sobre la cubierta de la curvada nave, y también él ascendió a la nave surcadora del ponto. Luego que se hubo sentado en la proa, puso a Teoclímeno a su lado y soltaron amarras. Telémaco ordenó a sus compañeros que se aplicaran a los aparejos y éstos le obedecieron con prontitud. Así que levantaron el mástil de abeto y lo encajaron en el hueco travesaño, lo amarraron con cables y extendieron las blancas velas con correas bien trenzadas de piel de buey. Y la de ojos brillantes, 290 Atenea, les envió un viento favorable, que se abalanzó impetuoso por el éter, para que la nave recorriera rápidamente en su carrera la salada agua del mar.

Pasaron bordeando Crunos y el río Calcis, de hermosa corriente. Se puso el sol y todos los caminos se llenaron de sombra, y la nave dio proa a Feas[224] impulsada por el viento favorable de Zeus y pasó junto a la divina Elide, donde dominan los epeos. Desde allí enfiló Telémaco hacia las Islas Puntiagudas[225] cavilando si conseguiría escapar o sería sorprendido.   300

Entre tanto, Odiseo y el divino porquero se daban a comer en la cabaña y junto a ellos comían otros hombres. Cuando habían echado de sí el deseo de comer y beber, se dirigió a ellos Odiseo tratando de probar si el porquero aún le seguiría agasajando gentilmente y le ordenaba quedarse en la majada o si le despachaba a la ciudad:

«Escúchame, Eumeo, y también vosotros, todos sus compañeros. Al amanecer deseo ponerme en camino hasta la ciudad para mendigar. No quiero ser ya un peso para ti y los compañeros. Pero dame indicaciones y un buen compañero que me   310 guíe, que me lleve hasta allí. En la ciudad vagaré por mi cuenta, por si alguien me larga un vaso de vino y un mendrugo. También me presentaré en el palacio del divino Odiseo para dar noticias a la prudente Penélope y quizás me acerque a los soberbios pretendientes por si me dan de comer, que tienen alimentos en abundancia. Con diligencia haría yo cuanto quisieran, porque te voy a decir una cosa —y tú ponla en tu mente y escúchame—: por la gracia de Hermes, el mensajero, el que da gracia y honor a las obras de los hombres, ningún hom-   320 bre podría competir conmigo en habilidad para remejer el fuego y quemar leña seca, para trinchar, asar y escanciar; en fin, para cuanto los plebeyos sirven a los nobles.»

Y tú, porquero Eumeo, le dijiste irritado:

«Ay, forastero, ¿por qué te ha venido a la mente ese proyecto? Lo que tú deseas en verdad es morir allí si pretendes mezclarte con el grupo de los pretendientes, cuya soberbia y violencia han llegado al férreo cielo. No son como tú los que sir-   330 ven a aquéllos; son jóvenes bien vestidos de manto y túnica, siempre brillantes de cabeza y rostro quienes les sirven. Y las bien pulimentadas mesas están repletas de pan y carne y de

---

[224] De ninguno de estos lugares se puede afirmar otra cosa que pertenecen a la Elide.

[225] Estrabón las identifica con las Equínades en el mar Jónico (cfr. 8.3.26).

vino. Conque quédate aquí. Nadie te va a molestar mientras estés conmigo, ni yo ni los compañeros que tengo. Y cuando llegue el querido hijo de Odiseo te vestirá de manto y túnica y te despedirá a donde tu corazón te empuje.»

Y le contestó a continuación el sufridor, el divino Odiseo: 340

«¡Ojalá, Eumeo, llegues a ser tan amado del padre Zeus como lo eres de mí por librarme del vagabundeo y de la miseria! Que no hay nada peor para el hombre que ser vagamundo; por culpa del maldito estómago sufren pesares los hombres a quienes les llega el vagar, la desgracia y el dolor. Pero ya que me retienes y aconsejas que aguarde a aquél, háblame de la madre del divino Odiseo y de su padre, a quien aquél abandonó cuando se acercaba al umbral de la vejez; dime si viven aún bajo los rayos del sol o ya han muerto y están en la morada de Hades.»   350

Y le contestó el porquero, caudillo de hombres:

«En verdad, huésped, te voy a hablar con toda sinceridad. Laertes vive todavía, aunque todos los días le pide a Zeus morir en su palacio, pues se lamenta terriblemente por su ausente hijo y por su prudente esposa que le dejó afligido al morir y le puso en la más cruel vejez. Ella murió de dolor por su ilustre hijo, de muerte cruel —¡que nadie muera así de quienes viviendo aquí conmigo me son amigos y obran como amigos! Mientras ella vivió, aunque entre dolores, me agradaba hablarle y preguntarle, ya que ella me había criado junto con Ctimena de luengo peplo, ilustre hija suya, a quien parió la última de sus hijos. Junto con ésta me crié y poco menos que a ésta me quería su madre. Pero cuando llegamos ambos a la amable juventud, entregaron a Ctimena como esposa a alguien de Same, recibiendo una buena dote, y a mí me vistió de hermosos túnica y manto y, dándome calzado para mis pies, me envió al campo. Y me amaba de corazón. Ahora echo en falta todo aquello, pero con todo, los dioses felices están haciendo prosperar la labor de la que me ocupo. De aquí como y bebo e incluso doy a los necesitados, pero no me es dado oír las palabras ni las obras de mi dueña desde que ha caído sobre el palacio esa peste de hombres soberbios. Y eso que los siervos necesitamos mucho hablar con la dueña y conocer todas las órdenes y comer y beber e, incluso, llevarnos algo al campo; cosas, en fin, que alegran siempre el corazón de los siervos.»

Y contestándole dijo el muy astuto Odiseo:

«¡Ay, ay!, así que ya de pequeño, porquero Eumeo, anduviste errante lejos de tu patria y de tus padres. Vamos, dime —y cuéntame con verdad— si fue devastada la ciudad de amplias calles en que habitaban tu padre y tu venerable madre, o si te capturaron hombres enemigos cuando te hallabas solo junto a tus ovejas o bueyes y te trajeron en sus naves a venderte en casa de este hombre, quien seguro que entregó un precio digno de ti.»

Y a su vez le contestó el porquero, caudillo de hombres:

«Forastero, ya que me preguntas esto e inquieres, escucha en silencio, goza y recuéstate a beber vino. Interminables son estas noches: hay para dormir y para escuchar complacido. No tienes por qué acostarte antes de tiempo, que el mucho dormir es dañino. De los demás, si a alguien le impulsa el corazón, que salga a acostarse y al despuntar la aurora desayúnese y conduzca los cerdos del dueño. Pero nosotros gocemos con nuestras tristes penas, recordándolas mientras bebemos y comemos en mi cabaña, que también un hombre goza con sus penas cuando ya tiene mucho sufrido y mucho trajinado. Así que te voy a contar lo que me preguntas.

»Hay una isla llamada Siría[226] —no sé si la conoces de oídas— por cima de Ortigia, donde el sol da la vuelta; no es excesivamente populosa, pero es buena, cría buenos pastos y buenos animales, abunda en vino y en trigo. La pobreza jamás se acerca al pueblo y las odiosas enfermedades tampoco rondan a los mortales. Sólo cuando envejecen sus habitantes en la ciudad se acerca Apolo, el del arco de plata, junto con Artemis, y los matan acechándolos con sus suaves dardos. Allí hay dos ciudades y todo está repartido entre ellas. Sobre las dos reinaba mi padre, Ktesio Ormenida, semejante a los inmortales.

»Conque un día llegaron allí unos fenicios, célebres por sus naves, unos lañas, llevando en su negra nave muchas maravillas. Mi padre tenía en palacio una mujer fenicia, hermosa y

[226] Podría tratarse de Syros, isla cercana a Renea, que era la antigua Ortigia (cfr. Estrabón, 10.5.5), pero la descripción que de ella se hace la convierte en un lugar paradisiaco, similar a la tierra de los Cíclopes, etc.

grande, conocedora de labores brillantes. Entonces los muy
taimados fenicios la sedujeron. Cuando estaba lavando, un fenicio se unió con ella en amor y lecho junto a la cóncava nave,   420
cosa que trastorna la mente de las hembras, incluso de la que
es laboriosa. Luego la preguntó quién era y de dónde procedía,
y ella le habló enseguida del palacio de elevado techo de su padre: "Me precio de ser de Sidón, abundante en bronce, y soy
hija del poderoso y rico Arybante, pero me raptaron unos piratas de Tafos cuando volvía del campo y me trajeron a casa de
este hombre para venderme, y él pagó un precio digno
de mí."

»Y le contestó el hombre que se había unido a hurtadillas   430
con ella: "Bien podrías volver con nosotros a casa para que
puedas ver el palacio de elevado techo de tu padre y madre y a
ellos mismos, que todavía viven y se los llama ricos." Y la mujer se dirigió a él y le contestó con su palabra: "Bien podría ser
así, marineros, pero sólo si me queréis asegurar con juramento
que me llevaréis intacta a casa." Así dijo y todos juraron como
ella les pidió.

»Conque cuando habían concluido su juramento, de nuevo
les dijo y contestó con su palabra: "Chitón ahora, que ninguno   440
de vuestros compañeros me dirija la palabra si me encuentra
en la calle o junto a la fuente, no sea que alguien vaya a casa y
se lo cuente al viejo y éste lo barrunte y me sujete con dolorosas ligaduras y a vosotros os prepare la muerte. Así que rete-
ned mis palabras en vuestra mente y apresurad la compra de lo
necesario para el viaje. Y cuando la nave se encuentre llena de
alimentos, que alguien venga al palacio con rapidez para co-
municármelo. Os traeré oro, cuanto halle a mano, y estoy dispuesta a daros otras cosas como pasaje: en efecto, yo cuido en   450
palacio del hijo de este hombre, un crío ya muy despierto, pues
corretea conmigo hasta la puerta. Podría llevármelo a la nave y
os produciría un buen precio si vais a venderlo a cualquier parte en el extranjero." Así diciendo, marchó al hermoso palacio.

»Los fenicios permanecieron todo el año con nosotros y llenaron su negra nave con bienes mercados. Y cuando su cóncava nave ya estaba cargada para volver, enviaron un mensajero a la mujer para que les diera el recado. Llegó al palacio de
mi padre un hombre muy astuto con un collar de oro engasta-   460

do con electro. Las esclavas del palacio y mi venerable madre lo palpaban con sus manos y lo contemplaban con sus ojos, prometiendo un buen precio. Y él hizo una seña a la mujer sin decir palabra y luego marchó a la cóncava nave. Ella me tomó de la mano y me sacó fuera. Encontró en el pórtico copas y mesas de unos convidados que frecuentaban la casa de mi padre. Habíanse marchado éstos a la asamblea y al lugar de reunión del pueblo, así que escondió tres copas en su regazo y se las llevó y yo en mi inocencia la seguía. Se puso el sol y todos 470 los caminos se llenaron de sombra, cuando, marchando a buen paso, llegamos al ilustre puerto donde estaba la veloz nave de los fenicios.

»Embarcaron haciéndonos subir a los dos y navegaban los húmedos caminos. Y Zeus envió viento favorable.

»Durante seis días navegamos sin parar, día y noche, y cuando el Cronida Zeus nos trajo el séptimo día, Artemis Flechadora alcanzó a la mujer y ésta se desplomó con ruido sobre la sentina como una gaviota del mar. Así que la arrojaron por la borda para que fuera pasto de focas y peces y yo quedé solo 480 acongojado en mi corazón.

»El viento que los llevaba y el agua los impulsaron a Itaca, donde Laertes me compró con su dinero. Así es como llegué a ver con mis ojos esta tierra.»

Y Odiseo, de linaje divino, le contestó con su palabra:

«Eumeo, mucho en verdad has conmovido mi corazón dentro del pecho al contar detalladamente cuánto has sufrido, pero también Zeus te ha puesto un bien al lado de un mal, ya que llegaste —sufriendo mucho— al palacio de un hombre bueno que te proporciona gentilmente comida y bebida, y lle- 490 vas una existencia agradable.

»En cambio, yo he llegado aquí después de recorrer sin rumbo muchas ciudades de mortales.»

Esto es lo que se contaban mutuamente y se echaron a dormir, pero no mucho tiempo, un poquito sólo, porque enseguida se presentó Eos, de trono de oro.

En esto los compañeros de Telémaco, ya en tierra, desataron las velas, quitaron el mástil rápidamente y se dirigieron luego remando hacia el fondeadero. Arrojaron el ancla y amarraron el cable; luego desembarcaron sobre la ribera del mar, se prepararon el almuerzo y mezclaron rojo vino. Y cuando había echado de sí el deseo de comer y beber, comenzó Telémaco a hablarles con discreción:

«Llevad vosotros la negra nave a la ciudad, que yo voy a inspeccionar los campos y los pastores. Por la tarde bajaré a la ciudad después de ver mis labores. Y al amanecer os voy a ofrecer un buen banquete de carnes y agradable vino como recompensa por el viaje.»

Y Teoclímeno, semejante a los dioses, se dirigió a él:

«¿Adónde iré yo, hijo mío? ¿A qué palacio voy a ir de los que dominan en la pedregosa Itaca? ¿Acaso marcharé directamente a tu palacio y al de tu madre?»

Y Telémaco le contestó discretamente:

«En otras circunstancias te pediría que fueras a nuestro palacio —y no echarías en falta dones de hospitalidad—, pero será peor para ti, pues yo voy a estar ausente y mi madre no podrá verte, que no se deja ver a menudo en la casa ante los pretendientes, sino que trabaja su telar lejos de éstos en el piso de arriba. Así que te diré de un hombre a cuya casa podrías ir: Eurímaco[227], hijo brillante del prudente Pólibo, a quien los itacenses miran como a un dios, pues es con mucho el más excelente y quien más ambiciona casar con mi madre y conseguir la dignidad de Odiseo. Pero sólo Zeus Olímpico, el que habita en el éter, sabe si les va a proporcionar antes de las nupcias el día de la destrucción.»

Cuando así hablaba le sobrevoló un pájaro por la derecha, un halcón, veloz mensajero de Apolo. Desplumaba entre sus patas una paloma y las plumas cayeron a tierra entre la nave y el mismo Telémaco.

Conque Teoclímeno, llamándolo aparte, lejos de sus compañeros, le tomó de la mano, le dijo su palabra y le llamó por su nombre:

«Telémaco, este pájaro te ha volado por la derecha no sin la

---

[227] Resulta extraña y abiertamente inadecuada esta propuesta de Telémaco. Más abajo (vv. 540 y ss.) se lo encomienda a Pireo Clítida como si no hubiera dicho antes nada.

voluntad del dios, pues al verlo de frente me he percatado que era un ave agüeral. Así que no existe otra estirpe más regia que la vuestra en el pueblo de Itaca. Siempre seréis dominadores.»

Y Telémaco le contestó a su vez discretamente:

«Forastero, ¡ojalá se cumpliera esa palabra! Pronto sabrías de mi afecto y mis muchos dones, de forma que cualquiera que te encontrara te llamaría dichoso.»

Dijo, y se dirigió a Pireo, fiel compañero:

«Pireo Clitida, tú eres quien más me has obedecido de estos 540 compañeros en lo demás; lleva también ahora al forastero a tu casa y agasájale gentilmente y respétalo hasta que yo llegue.»

Y Pireo, famoso por su lanza, le contestó:

«Telémaco, aunque te quedes aquí mucho tiempo yo me llevaré a éste y no echará en falta dones de hospitalidad.»

Así diciendo, subió a la nave y apremió a los compañeros para que embarcaran también ellos y soltaran amarras. Conque subieron y se sentaron sobre los bancos. Telémaco ató bajo sus pies hermosas sandalias y tomó su ilustre lanza, aguzada con 550 agudo bronce, de la cubierta del navío. Los compañeros soltaron amarras y echando la nave al mar enfilaron hacia la ciudad como se lo había ordenado Telémaco, el querido hijo del divino Odiseo.

Y sus pies lo llevaban veloz, dando grandes zancadas, hasta que llegó a la majada donde tenía las innumerables cerdas, con las que pasaba la noche el porquero, que era noble, que conocía la bondad hacia sus dueños.

Canto XVI

TELÉMACO RECONOCE A ODISEO

EN esto Odiseo y el divino porquero se preparaban el desayuno al despuntar la aurora dentro de la cabaña, encendiendo fuego —habían despedido a los pastores junto con las manadas de cerdos. Cuando se acercaba Telémaco, no ladraron los perros de incesantes ladridos, sino que meneaban la cola.

Percatóse el divino Odiseo de que los perros meneaban la cola, le vino un ruido de pasos y enseguida dijo a Eumeo aladas palabras:

«Eumeo, sin duda se acerca un compañero o conocido, pues los perros no ladran, sino que menean la cola. Y oigo ruido de pasos.»   10

No había acabado de decir toda su palabra, cuando su querido hijo puso pie en el umbral. Levantóse sorprendido el porquero y de sus manos cayeron los cuencos con los que se ocupaba de mezclar rojo vino. Salió al encuentro de su señor y besó su rostro, sus dos hermosos ojos y sus manos; y le cayó un llanto abundante. Como un padre acoge con amor a su hijo que vuelve de lejanas tierras después de diez años, a su único hijo amado por quien sufriera indecibles pesares, así el divino porquero besó a Telémaco, semejante a los inmortales, abra-   20
zando todo su cuerpo como si hubiera escapado de la muerte. Y, entre lamentos, decía aladas palabras:

«Has venido, Telémaco, como dulce luz. Creía que ya no volvería a verte más cuando marchaste a Pilos con tu nave. Vamos, entra, hijo mío, para que goce mi corazón contemplándote recién llegado de otras tierras. Que no vienes a menudo al campo ni junto a los pastores, sino que te quedas en la ciudad, pues es grato a tu ánimo contemplar el odioso grupo de los pretendientes.»

Y Telémaco le contestó a su vez discretamente: 30

«Así se hará, abuelo, que yo he venido aquí por ti, para verte con mis ojos y oír de tus labios si mi madre está todavía en palacio o ya la ha desposado algún hombre; que la cama de Odiseo está llena de telarañas por falta de quien se acueste en ella.»

Y se dirigió a él el porquero, caudillo de hombres:

«¡Claro que permanece ella en tu palacio con ánimo paciente! Las noches se le consumen entre dolores y los días entre lágrimas.»

Así diciendo, tomó de sus manos la lanza de bronce. Enton-   40
ces Telémaco se puso en camino y traspasó el umbral de piedra, y cuando entraba, su padre le cedió el asiento. Pero Telémaco le contuvo y dijo:

«Siéntate, forastero, que ya encontraremos asiento en otra parte de nuestra majada. Aquí está el hombre que nos lo proporcionará.»

Así diciendo, volvió a sentarse. El porquero le extendió ramas verdes y por encima unas pieles, donde fue a sentarse el querido hijo de Odiseo. También les acercó el porquero fuentes de carne asada que habían dejado de la comida del día ante-   50
rior, amontonó rápidamente pan en canastas y mezcló en un jarro vino agradable. Y luego fue a sentarse frente al divino Odiseo.

Conque echaron mano de los alimentos que tenían delante y cuando habían arrojado de sí el deseo de comer y beber, Telémaco se dirigió al divino porquero:

«Abuelo, ¿de dónde ha llegado este forastero? ¿Cómo le han traído hasta Itaca los marineros? ¿Quiénes se preciaban de ser? Porque no creo que haya llegado a pie hasta aquí.»

Y tú le contestaste, porquero Eumeo, diciendo: 60

«En verdad, hijo, te voy a contar toda la verdad. De origen se precia de ser de la vasta Creta y asegura que ha recorrido errante muchas ciudades de mortales. Que así se lo ha hilado el destino. Ahora ha llegado a mi majada huyendo de la nave de unos tesprotos y yo te lo encomiendo a ti; obra como gustes, se precia de ser tu suplicante.»

Y Telémaco le contestó discretamente:

«Eumeo, en verdad has dicho una palabra dolorosa. ¿Cómo voy a recibir en mi casa a este huésped? En cuanto a mí, soy joven y no confío en mis brazos para rechazar a un hombre si alguien lo maltrata. Y en cuanto a mi madre, su ánimo anda cavilando en su interior si permanecerá junto a mí y cuidará de su casa por vergüenza del lecho de su esposo y de las habladurías del pueblo, o si se marchará ya en pos del más excelente de los aqueos que la pretenda y le ofrezca más riquezas.

»Pero ya que ha llegado a tu casa, vestiré al forastero con manto y túnica, hermosos vestidos, y le daré afilada espada y sandalias para sus pies y le enviaré a donde su ánimo y su corazón lo empujen. Pero si quieres, retenlo en la majada y cuídate de él, que yo enviaré ropas y toda clase de comida para que no sea gravoso ni a ti ni a tus compañeros. Sin embargo, yo no la dejaría ir adonde están los pretendientes —pues tienen una insolencia en exceso insensata—, no sea que le ultrajen y a mí me cause una pena terrible; es difícil que un hombre, aunque fuerte, tenga éxito cuando está entre muchos, pues éstos son, en verdad, más poderosos.»

Y le dijo el sufridor, el divino Odiseo:

«Amigo —puesto que me es permitido contestarte—, mucho se me ha desgarrado el corazón al escuchar de vuestros labios cuántas obras insolentes realizan los pretendientes en el palacio contra tu voluntad, siendo como eres. Dime si te dejas dominar de buen grado o es que te odia la gente del pueblo, siguiendo una inspiración de la divinidad[228]; o si tienes algo que reprochar a tus hermanos, en los que un hombre suele confiar cuando surge una disputa por grande que sea. ¡Ojalá fuera yo así de joven —con los impulsos que siento— o fuera hijo del irreprochable Odiseo u Odiseo en persona que vuelve después de andar errante! —pues aún hay una parte de esperanza—. ¡Que me corte la cabeza un extranjero si no me convertía en azote de todos ellos, presentándome en el megaron de Odiseo Laertíada! Pero si me dominaran por su número, solo como

---

[228] Cfr. III.214-5.

estoy, preferiría morir en mi palacio asesinado antes que ver continuamente estas acciones vergonzosas: maltratar a forasteros y arrastrar por el palacio a las esclavas, sacar vino continuamente y comer el pan sin motivo, en vano, para un acto que no va a tener cumplimiento»[229].

Y Telémaco le contestó discretamente:

«Forastero, te voy a hablar sinceramente. No me es hostil todo el pueblo porque me odie, ni tengo nada que reprochar a mis hermanos, en los que un hombre suele confiar cuando surge una disputa, por grande que sea. Que el Cronida siempre dio hijos únicos a nuestra familia: Arcisio engendró a Laertes, hijo único, y a Odiseo lo engendró único su padre; a su vez Odiseo, después de engendrarme sólo a mí, me dejó en el palacio sin poder disfrutarme.

»Ello es que cuantos nobles dominan en las islas, Duliquio, Same y la Boscosa Zante, y cuantos mandan en la escarpada Itaca pretenden a mi madre y arruinan mi hacienda. Ella no se niega a este odioso matrimonio ni es capaz de poner un término, así que los pretendientes consumen mi casa y creo que pronto acabarán incluso conmigo mismo[230]. Pero en verdad esto está en las rodillas de los dioses.

»Abuelo, tú marcha rápido y di a la prudente Penélope que estoy a salvo y he llegado de Pilos. Entre tanto, yo permaneceré aquí y tú vuelve después de darle a ella sola la noticia; que no se entere ninguno de los demás aqueos, pues son muchos los que maquinan la muerte contra mí.»

Y tú le contestaste, porquero Eumeo, diciendo:

«Lo sé, me doy cuenta, se lo ordenas a quien lo comprende. Pero, vamos, vamos, dime —y contéstame con verdad— si hago el mismo camino para anunciárselo al desdichado Laertes, quien mientras tanto ha estado vigilando entre lamentos la labor de Odiseo y comía y bebía con los esclavos cuando su ánimo le empujaba a ello. En cambio, ahora desde que tú marchaste a Pilos con la nave, dicen que ya ni come ni bebe ni vigila la labor, sino que permanece sentado entre llantos y se le seca la piel pegada a los huesos.»

---

[229] Se entiende, la boda con Penélope.
[230] Cfr. I.246-51.

Y Telémaco le contestó discretamente:

«Es triste, pero lo dejaremos aunque nos duela, que si todo dependiera de los mortales, primero elegiríamos el día del regreso del padre. Conque marcha con la noticia y no andes por los campos en busca de Laertes. Ahora bien, dirás a mi madre que envíe a escondidas a la despensera y pronto, pues ésta se lo puede comunicar al anciano.»

Así dijo y apremió al porquero. Tomó éste las sandalias y atándolas a sus pies se dirigió hacia la ciudad. No se le ocultó a Atenea que el porquero Eumeo había salido de la majada y se acercó allí asemejándose a una mujer hermosa y grande, conocedora de labores brillantes.

Se detuvo a la puerta de la cabaña y se le apareció a Odiseo. Telémaco no la vio ni se percató —pues los dioses no se hacen visibles a todos los mortales—, pero la vieron Odiseo y los perros, aunque no ladraron, sino que huyeron espantados entre gruñidos a otra parte de la majada.

Atenea hizo señas con sus cejas, diose cuenta el divino Odiseo y salió de la habitación junto a la larga pared del patio. Se puso cerca de ella y Atenea le dijo:

«Hijo de Laertes, de linaje divino, Odiseo rico en ardides; manifiesta ya tu palabra a tu hijo y no se la ocultes más, a fin de que preparéis la muerte y Ker para los pretendientes y marchéis a la ínclita ciudad. Tampoco yo estaré mucho tiempo lejos de ellos, pues estoy ansiosa de luchar.»

Así dijo Atenea y lo tocó con su varita de oro. Primero puso en su cuerpo un manto bien limpio y una túnica, y aumentó su estatura y juventud. Luego volvió a tornarse moreno, sus mandíbulas se extendieron y de su mentón nació negra barba.

Cuando hubo realizado esto, marchó Atenea y Odiseo se encaminó a la cabaña. Su hijo se asombró al verlo y volvió la vista a otro lado no fuera un dios, y hablándole dijo aladas palabras:

«Forastero, ahora me pareces distinto de antes; tienes otros vestidos y tu piel no es la misma. En verdad eres un dios de los que poseen el vasto Olimpo. Sé benevolente para que te entregue en agradecimiento objetos sagrados y dones de oro bien trabajado. Cuídate de nosotros.»

Y le contestó el sufridor, el divino Odiseo:

«No soy un dios —¿por qué me comparas con los inmortales?— sino tu padre por quien sufres dolores sin cuento soportando entre lamentos las acciones violentas de esos hombres.»

Así hablando besó a su hijo y dejó que el llanto cayera a tierra de sus mejillas, pues antes lo estaba conteniendo, siempre inconmovible. 190

Y Telémaco —aún no podía creer que era su padre—, le dijo de nuevo contestándole:

«Tú no eres Odiseo, mi padre, sino un demón que me hechiza para que me lamente con más dolores todavía, pues un hombre no sería capaz con su propia mente de maquinar esto si un dios en persona no viene y le hace a su gusto y fácilmente joven o viejo. Que tú hace poco eras viejo y vestías ropas desastrosas, en cambio ahora pareces un dios de los que poseen 200 el vasto cielo.»

Y contestándole dijo Odiseo rico en ardides:

«Telémaco, no está bien que no te admires muy mucho ni te alegres de que tu padre esté en casa. Ningún otro Odiseo te vendrá ya aquí, sino éste que soy yo, tal cual soy, sufridor de males, muy asendereado, y he llegado a los veinte años a mi patria. En verdad esto es obra de Atenea la Rapaz que me convierte en el hombre que ella quiere —pues puede—: unas veces semejante a un mendigo y otras a un hombre joven ves- 210 tido de hermosas ropas, que es fácil para los dioses que poseen el vasto cielo exaltar a un mortal o arruinarlo.»

Así hablando se sentó, y Telémaco, abrazado a su padre, sollozaba derramando lágrimas. A los dos les entró el deseo de llorar y lloraban agudamente, con más intensidad que los pájaros —pigargos o águilas de curvadas garras—, a quienes los campesinos han arrebatado las crías antes de que puedan volar. Así derramaban ellos bajo sus párpados un llanto que daba lástima. Y se hubiera puesto el sol mientras sollozaban, si Te- 220 lémaco no se hubiera dirigido enseguida a su padre:

«Padre mío, ¿en qué nave te han traído a Itaca los marineros?, ¿quiénes se preciaban de ser?, pues no creo que hayas llegado aquí a pie.»

Y le contestó el sufridor, el divino Odiseo:

«Desde luego, hijo, te voy a decir la verdad. Me han traído los feacios, célebres por sus naves, quienes escoltan también a otros hombres que llegan hasta ellos. Me han traído dormido sobre el ponto en rápida nave y me han depositado en Itaca, 230 no sin entregarme brillantes regalos —bronce, oro en abundancia y ropa tejida—. Todo está en una gruta por la voluntad de los dioses. Así que por fin he llegado aquí por consejo de Atenea, para que decidamos sobre la muerte de mis enemigos. Conque, vamos, enumérame a los pretendientes para que yo vea cuántos y quiénes son, que después de reflexionar en mi irreprochable ánimo te diré si podemos enfrentarnos a ellos nosotros dos sin ayuda, o buscamos a otros.»

Y Telémaco le contestó discretamente: 240

«Padre, siempre he oído la fama que tienes de ser buen luchador con las manos y prudente en tus resoluciones, pero has dicho algo excesivamente grande —¡me atenaza la admiración!—, pues no sería posible que dos hombres lucharan contra muchos y aguerridos.

»Respecto a los pretendientes no son una decena ni sólo dos, sino muchas más. Enseguida sabrás su número: de Duliquio son cincuenta y dos jóvenes selectos —y le siguen seis escuderos—; de Same proceden veinticuatro hombres, de Zante veinte hijos de aqueos y de Itaca misma doce, todos excelentes, 250 con quienes están el heraldo Medonte, el divino aedo y dos siervos conocedores de los servicios del banquete. Si nos enfrentáramos a todos ellos mientras están dentro, temo que no podrías castigar —aunque hayas vuelto— sus violencias en forma amarga y terrible.

»Pero si puedes pensar en alguien que nos defienda, dímelo, alguien que con ánimo amigo nos sirva de ayuda.»

Y le contestó el sufridor, el divino Odiseo:

«Te lo diré; ponlo en tu pecho y escúchame. Piensa si Atenea —en unión del padre Zeus— nos pueden defender o tengo 260 que pensar en otro aliado.»

Y Telémaco le contestó discretamente:

«Excelentes en verdad son los dos aliados de que me hablas, pues se apuestan arriba, entre las nubes, y ambos dominan a los hombres y a los dioses inmortales.»

Y le contestó el sufridor, el divino Odiseo:

«Sí, en verdad no estarán mucho tiempo lejos de la fuerte lucha cuando la fuerza de Ares juzgue en mi palacio entre los

pretendientes y nosotros. Pero tú marcha a casa al despuntar 270
la aurora y reúnete con los soberbios pretendientes, que a mí
me conducirá después el porquero bajo el aspecto de un mendigo miserable y viejo.

»Si me deshonran en el palacio, que tu corazón soporte el
que yo reciba malos tratos, aunque me arrastren por los pies
hasta la puerta o incluso me arrojen sus dardos. Tú mira y
aguanta, pero ordénales, eso sí, que repriman sus insensateces
dirigiéndote a ellos con palabras dulces. Aunque no te harán
caso, pues ya tienen a su lado el día de su destino. Te voy a de- 280
cir otra cosa que has de poner en tus mientes: cuando Atenea,
de muchos pensamientos, lo ponga en mi interior, te haré señas con la cabeza; tú entonces calcula cuántas armas guerreras
hay en el mégaron y sube a depositarlas en lo más profundo de
la habitación del piso de arriba. Cuando te pregunten los pretendientes ansiosamente, contéstales con suaves palabras: "Las
he retirado del fuego, pues ya no se parecen a las que dejó Odiseo cuando marchó a Troya, que están manchadas hasta donde
las llega el aliento del fuego. Además el Cronida ha puesto en 290
mi pecho una razón más importante: no sea que os llenéis de
vino y levantando una disputa entre vosotros, lleguéis a heriros mutuamente y a llenar de vergüenza el banquete y vuestras
pretensiones de matrimonio; que el hierro por sí sólo arrastra
al hombre." Luego deja sólo para nosotros dos un par de espadas y otro de lanzas y dos escudos para nuestros brazos, a fin
de que los sorprendamos echándonos sobre ellos[231]. Te voy a
decir otra cosa —y tú ponla en tu interior—: si de verdad eres
mío y de mi propia sangre, que nadie se entere de que Odiseo 300
está en casa; que no lo sepa Laertes ni el porquero, ni ninguno
de los siervos ni siquiera la misma Penélope, sino solos tú y
yo. Conozcamos la actitud de las mujeres y pongamos a prueba

---

[231] Este plan supone que ambos van a estar en el mégaron con todos los pretendientes e incluye dejar un par de escudos y lanzas. Sin embargo, en XIX.4
y ss. Telémaco y Odiseo se quedan solos en el mégaron y Odiseo recomienda a su
hijo que retire *todas* las armas. Esta incongruencia ha llevado a pensar en la existencia de dos versiones, la primera de las cuales *excluiría* la conversación
posterior con Penélope y el reconocimiento por Euriclea. También se ha pensado que la Matanza excluía la utilización del arco, cfr. Schmidt-Stählin,
op. cit., I, pág. 118.

a los siervos, a ver quién nos honra y quién no se cuida y te deshonra, siendo quien eres.»

Y contestándole dijo su ilustre hijo:

«Padre, creo que de verdad vas a conocer mi coraje —y enseguida—, pues no es precisamente la irreflexión lo que me domina. Pero, con todo, no creo que vayamos a sacar ganancia ninguno de los dos. Te insto a que reflexiones, pues vas a recorrer en vano durante un tiempo los campos para probar a cada hombre, mientras ellos devoran tranquilamente en palacio nuestros bienes, insolentemente y sin cuidarse de nada. Te aconsejo, por el contrario, que trates de conocer a las siervas, las que te deshonran y las que te son inocentes. No me agradaría que fuéramos por las majadas poniendo a prueba a los hombres; ocupémonos después de esto, si es que en verdad conoces algún presagio de Zeus, portador de égida.» 320

Mientras así hablaban, arribó a Itaca la bien trabajada nave que había traído de Pilos a Telémaco y compañeros.

Cuando éstos entraron en el profundo puerto, empujaron a la negra nave hacia el litoral y sus valientes servidores les llevaron las armas. Luego llevaron a casa de Clitio los hermosos dones y enviaron un heraldo al palacio de Odiseo para comunicar a Penélope que Telémaco estaba en el campo y había ordenado llevar la nave a la ciudad para que la ilustre reina no 330 sintiera temor ni derramara tiernas lágrimas.

Encontráronse el heraldo[232] y el divino porquero para comunicar a la mujer el mismo recado y, cuando ya habían llegado al palacio del divino rey, fue el heraldo quien habló en medio de las esclavas.

«Reina, tu hijo ha llegado.»

Luego el porquero se acercó a Penélope y le dijo lo que su hijo le había ordenado decir. Cuando hubo acabado todo su 340 encargo, se puso en camino hacia los cerdos abandonando los patios y el palacio.

---

[232] El heraldo es Medonte y juega un doble papel de espía. Por un lado, comunica a Penélope la decisión de los pretendientes de matar a Telémaco (cfr. IV.677 y XVI.412). Por otro lado, es amigo de los pretendientes (cfr. XVI.252 y XVII.172 y ss). Al final Odiseo le perdonará la vida a ruegos de Telémaco (cfr. XXII.357 y ss.).

Los pretendientes estaban afligidos y abatidos en su corazón; salieron del mégaron a lo largo de la pared del patio y se sentaron allí mismo, cerca de las puertas. Y Eurímaco, hijo de Pólibo, comenzó a hablar entre ellos:

«Amigos, gran trabajo ha realizado Telémaco con este viaje; ¡y decíamos que no lo llevaría a término! Vamos, botemos una negra nave, la mejor, y reunamos remeros que vayan enseguida a anunciar a aquéllos que ya está de vuelta en casa.»   350

No había terminado de hablar, cuando Anfínomo volviéndose desde su sitio, vio a la nave dentro del puerto y a los hombres amainando velas o sentados al remo. Y sonriendo suavemente dijo a sus compañeros:

«No enviemos embajada alguna; ya están aquí. O se lo ha manifestado un dios o ellos mismos han visto pasar de largo a la nave y no han podido alcanzarla.»

Así dijo, y ellos se levantaron para encaminarse a la ribera del mar. Enseguida empujaron la negra nave hacia el litoral y sus valientes servidores les llevaron las armas. Marcharon to-   360 dos juntos a la plaza y no permitieron que nadie, joven o viejo, se sentara a su lado. Y comenzó a hablar entre ellos Antínoo, hijo de Eupites:

«¡Ay, ay, cómo han librado del mal los dioses a este hombre! Durante días nos hemos apostado vigilantes sobre las ventosas cumbres, turnándonos continuamente. Al ponerse el sol, nunca pasábamos la noche en tierra sino en el mar, esperando en la rápida nave a la divina Eos, acechando a Telémaco para sorprenderlo y matarlo. Pero entre tanto un dios le ha conducido   370 a casa.

Con que meditemos una triste muerte para Telémaco aquí mismo y que no se nos escape, pues no creo que mientras él viva consigamos cumplir nuestro propósito, que él es hábil en sus resoluciones y el pueblo no nos apoya del todo.

»Vamos, antes de que reúna a los aqueos en asamblea..., pues no creo que se desentienda, sino que, rebosante de cólera, se pondrá en pie para decir a todo el mundo que le hemos trenzado la muerte y no le hemos alcanzado. Y el pueblo no aprobará estas malas acciones cuando le escuche. ¡Cuidado, no   380 vayan a causarnos daño y nos arrojen de nuestra tierra —y tengamos que marchar a país ajeno—! Conque apresurémonos a matarlo en el campo lejos de la ciudad, o en el camino. Podríamos quedarnos con su bienes y posesiones repartiéndolas a partes iguales entre nosotros y entregar el palacio a su madre y a quien case con ella, para que se lo queden. Pero si estas palabras no os agradan, sino que preferís que él viva y posea todos sus bienes patrios, no volvamos desde ahora a reunirnos aquí para comer sus posesiones; que cada uno pretenda a Penélope asediándola con regalos desde su palacio, y quizá luego case ella con quien le entregue más y le venga destinado.»

Así habló y todos quedaron en silencio. Entonces se levantó y les dijo Anfínomo, ilustre hijo de Niso, el soberano hijo de Aretes (éste era de Duliquio, rica en trigo y pastos, y capitaneaba a los pretendientes; era quien más agradaba a Penélope por sus palabras, pues estaba dotado de buenas mientes)... Con sentimientos de amistad hacia ellos se levantó y dijo:

«Amigos, yo al menos no desearía acabar con Telémaco, pues la raza de los reyes es terrible de matar. Así que conozcamos primero la decisión de los dioses. Si la voluntad del gran Zeus lo aprueba, yo seré el primero en matarlo y os incitaré a los demás, pero si los dioses tratan de impedirlo, os aconsejo que pongáis término.»

Así dijo Anfínomo y les agradó su palabra. Se levantaron al punto y se encaminaron a casa de Odiseo y llegados allí se sentaron en pulidos sillones.

Entonces Penélope decidió mostrarse ante los pretendientes, poseedores de orgullosa insolencia, pues se había enterado de que pretendían matar a su hijo en palacio —se lo había dicho el heraldo Medonte, que conocía su decisión. Se puso en camino hacia el mégaron junto con sus siervas y cuando hubo llegado junto a los pretendientes, la divina entre las mujeres, se detuvo junto a una columna del bien labrado techo, sosteniendo delante de sus mejillas un grueso velo. Censuró a Antínoo, le dijo su palabra y le llamó por su nombre:

«Antínoo[233], insolente, malvado; dicen en Itaca que eres el

---

[233] Antínoo es el más insolente de los pretendientes y el único de quien se ofrecen detalles de su vida familiar. El favor que Odiseo hizo a su padre creó un vínculo entre sus familias que hace menos justificable todavía su insolencia.

mejor entre tus compañeros en pensamiento y palabra, pero no eres tal. ¡Ambicioso!, ¿por qué tramas la muerte y el destino para Telémaco y no prestas atención a los suplicantes, cuyo testigo es Zeus? No es justo tramar la muerte uno contra otro. ¿Es que no recuerdas cuando tu padre vino aquí huyendo por temor al pueblo, pues éste rebosaba de ira porque tu padre, siguiendo a unos piratas de Tafos, había causado daño a los tesprotos que eran nuestros aliados? Querían matarlo y romperle el corazón y comerse su mucha hacienda, pero Odiseo se lo impidió y los contuvo, deseosos como estaban. Ahora tú te comes sin pagar la hacienda de Odiseo, pretendes a su mujer y tratas de matar a su hijo, produciéndome un gran dolor. Te ordeno que pongas fin a esto y se lo aconsejes a los demás.»

Y Eurímaco, hijo de Pólibo, le contestó:

«Hija de Icario, prudente Penélope, cobra ánimos. No te preocupes por esto. No existe ni existirá ni va a nacer hombre que ponga sus manos sobre tu hijo Telémaco, al menos mientras yo viva y vean mis ojos sobre la tierra. Además, te voy a decir otra cosa que se cumplirá: pronto correría la sangre de ése por mi lanza, pues también a mí Odiseo, el destructor de ciudades, sentándome muchas veces sobre sus rodillas me ponía en las manos carne asada y me ofrecía rojo vino. Por esto Telémaco es para mí el más querido de los hombres y te ruego que no temas su muerte al menos a manos de los pretendientes; en cuanto a la que procede de los dioses, ésa es imposible evitarla.»

Así habló para animarla, aunque también él tramaba la muerte contra Telémaco.

Entonces Penélope subió al brillante piso de arriba y lloraba a Odiseo, su esposo, hasta que Atenea de ojos brillantes le puso dulce sueño sobre los párpados.

El divino porquero llegó al atardecer junto a Odiseo y su hijo cuando éstos se preparaban la cena, después de sacrificar un cerdo de un año. Entonces Atenea se acercó a Odiseo Laertíada y tocándole con su varita le hizo viejo de nuevo y vistió su cuerpo de tristes ropas, para que el porquero no lo reconociera al verlo de frente y fuera a comunicárselo a la prudente Penélope sin poder guardarlo para sí.

Telémaco fue el primero en dirigirle su palabra:

«Ya has llegado, Eumeo: ¿qué se dice por la ciudad? ¿Han vuelto ya los arrogantes pretendientes de su emboscada, o todavía esperan a que yo vuelva a casa?»

Y tú le contestaste, porquero Eumeo, diciendo:

«No tenía yo que inquirir ni preguntar eso al bajar a la ciudad. Mi ánimo me empujó a comunicar mi recado y volver aquí de nuevo. Pero se encontró conmigo un veloz enviado de tus compañeros, un heraldo que habló a tu madre antes que yo. También sé otra cosa, pues la he visto con mis ojos: al volver para acá había ya atravesado la ciudad —en el lugar donde está el cerro de Hermes— cuando vi entrar en nuestro puerto una veloz nave; había en ella numerosos hombres y estaba cargada de escudos y lanzas de doble punta. Pensé que eran ellos, pero no lo sé con certeza.» 470

Así habló, y sonrió la sagrada fuerza de Telémaco dirigiendo los ojos a su padre, evitando al porquero. Cuando habían acabado del trajín de preparar la comida, cenaron y su ánimo no se vio privado de un alimento proporcional. Y una vez que habían arrojado de sí el deseo de comer y beber, volvieron su 480 pensamiento al dormir y recibieron el don del sueño.

Canto XVII

ODISEO MENDIGA ENTRE
LOS PRETENDIENTES

Y cuando se mostró Eos, la que nace de la mañana, la de los dedos de rosa, calzó Telémaco bajo sus pies hermosas sandalias, el querido hijo del divino Odiseo, tomó la fuerte lanza que se adaptaba bien a sus manos deseando marchar a la ciudad y dijo a su porquero:

«Abuelo, yo me voy a la ciudad para que me vea mi madre, pues no creo que abandone los tristes lamentos y los sollozos acompañados de lágrimas, hasta que me vea en persona. Así que te voy a encomendar esto: lleva a la ciudad a este desdichado forastero para que mendigue allí su pan —el que quiera le dará un mendrugo y un vaso de vino—, pues yo no puedo hacerme cargo de todos los hombres, afligido como estoy en mi corazón. Y si el forastero se encoleriza, peor para él, que a mí me place decir verdad.»

Y contestándole dijo el astuto Odiseo:

«Amigo, tampoco yo quiero que me retengan. Para un pobre es mejor mendigar por la ciudad que por los campos —y me dará el que quiera—, pues ya no soy de edad para quedarme en las majadas y obedecer en todo a quien da las órdenes y los encargos. Conque, marcha, que a mí me llevará este hombre, a quien has ordenado, una vez que me haya calentado al fuego y haya solana. Tengo unas ropas que son terriblemente malas y temo que me haga daño la escarcha mañanera, pues decís que la ciudad está lejos.»

Así dijo, y Telémaco cruzó la majada dando largas zancadas; iba sembrando la muerte para los pretendientes.

Cuando llegó al palacio, agradable para vivir, dejó la lanza que llevaba junto a una elevada columna y entró en el interior, traspasando el umbral de piedra.

La primera en verlo fue la nodriza Euriclea, que extendía cobertores sobre los bien trabajados sillones y se dirigió llorando hacia él. A su alrededor se congregaron las demás siervas del sufridor Odiseo y acariciándolo besaban su cabeza y hombros.

Salió del dormitorio la prudente Penélope, semejante a Artemis o a la dorada Afrodita, y echó llorando sus brazos a su querido hijo, le besó la cabeza y los dos hermosos ojos y, entre lamentos, decía aladas palabras:

«Has llegado, Telémaco, como dulce luz. Ya no creía que volvería a verte desde que marchaste en la nave a Pilos, a ocultas y contra mi voluntad, en busca de noticias de tu padre. Vamos, cuéntame cómo has conseguido verlo.»

Y Telémaco le contestó discretamente:

«Madre mía, no despiertes mi llanto ni conmuevas mi corazón dentro del pecho, ya que he escapado de una muerte terrible. Conque, báñate, viste tu cuerpo con ropa limpia, sube al piso de arriba con tus esclavas y promete a todos los dioses realizar hecatombes perfectas, por si Zeus quiere llevar a cabo obras de represalia.

»Yo marcharé al ágora para invitar a un forastero que me ha acompañado cuando volvía de allí. Lo he enviado por delante con mis divinos compañeros y he ordenado a Pireo que lo lleve a su casa y lo agasaje gentilmente y honre hasta que yo llegue.»

Así habló, y a Penélope se le quedaron sin alas las palabras[234]. Así que se bañó, vistió su cuerpo con ropa limpia y prometió a todos los dioses realizar hecatombes perfectas por si Zeus quería llevar a cabo obras de represalia.

---

[234] E.d. «se quedó sin habla». Esta fórmula, que aparece sólo en *Odisea*, está modelada —y es negación— de «le dirigió aladas palabras», muy común también en *Ilíada*. En ambos casos la idea subyacente es que las palabras vuelan del emisor al receptor. Cfr. También XIX.29, XXI.386, XXII.398.

Entonces Telémaco atravesó el mégaron portando su lanza y le acompañaban dos veloces lebreles. Atenea derramó sobre él la gracia y todo el pueblo se admiraba al verlo marchar. Y los arrogantes pretendientes le rodearon diciéndole buenas palabras, pero en su interior meditaban secretas maldades. Telémaco entonces evitó a la muchedumbre de éstos y fue a sentarse donde se sentaban Méntor, Antifo y Haliterses, quienes desde el principio eran compañeros de su padre. Y éstos le preguntaban por todo. Se les acercó Pireo, célebre por su lanza, llevando al forastero a través de la ciudad hasta la plaza. Entonces Telémaco ya no estuvo mucho tiempo lejos de su huésped, sino que se puso a su lado. Y Pireo le dirigió primero aladas palabras: 70

«Telémaco, envía pronto unas mujeres a mi casa para que te devuelva los regalos que te hizo Menelao.»

Y Telémaco le contestó discretamente:

«Pireo, en verdad no sabemos cómo resultará todo esto. Si los pretendientes me matan ocultamente en palacio y se reparten todos los bienes de mi padre, prefiero que tú te quedes con los regalos y los goces antes que alguno de ellos. Pero si consigo sembrar para éstos la muerte y Ker, llévalos alegre a mi casa, que yo estaré alegre.» 80

Así diciendo condujo a casa a su asendereado huésped. Cuando llegaron al palacio agradable para vivir, dejaron sus mantos sobre sillas y sillones y se bañaron en bien pulimentadas bañeras. Después que las esclavas les hubieron bañado, ungido con aceite y puesto mantos de lana y túnicas, salieron de las bañeras y fueron a sentarse en sillas. Y una esclava derramó sobre fuente de plata el aguamanos que llevaba en hermosa jarra de oro para que se lavaran, y a su lado extendió una mesa pulimentada. Y la venerable ama de llaves puso comida sobre ella y añadió abundantes piezas, favoreciéndolas entre los que estaban presentes. Entonces la madre se sentó frente a él, junto a una columna del mégaron, se reclinó en un asiento y revolvía entre sus manos suaves copos de lana. Y ellos echaron mano de los alimentos que tenían delante. 90

Cuando habían arrojado de sí el deseo de comer y beber, comenzó a hablar entre ellos la prudente Penélope: 100

«Telémaco, en verdad voy a subir al piso de arriba y acostarme en el lecho que tengo regado de lágrimas desde que Odiseo partió a Ilión con los Atridas. Y es que no has sido capaz, antes de que los arrogantes pretendientes llegaran a esta casa, de hablarme claramente del regreso de tu padre, si es que has oído algo.»

Y Telémaco le contestó discretamente:

«Madre, te voy a contar la verdad. Marchamos a Pilos junto a Néstor, pastor de su pueblo, quien me recibió en su elevado palacio y me agasajó gentilmente, como un padre a su hijo recién llegado de otras tierras después de largo tiempo. Así de amable me recibió junto con sus ilustres hijos. Me dijo que no había oído nunca a ningún humano hablar sobre Odiseo, vivo o muerto, pero me envió junto al Atrida Menelao, famoso por su lanza, con caballos y un carro bien ajustado. Allí vi a la argiva Helena, por quien troyanos y argivos sufrieron mucho por voluntad de los dioses. Enseguida me preguntó Menelao, de recia voz guerrera, qué necesidad me había llevado a la divina Lacedemonia y yo le conté toda la verdad.

»Entonces, contestándome con su palabra, dijo: "¡Ay, ay! ¡Conque querían dormir en el lecho de un hombre intrépido quienes son cobardes! Como una cierva acuesta a sus dos recién nacidos cervatillos en la cueva de un fuerte león y mientras sale a pastar en los hermosos valles, aquél regresa a su guarida y da vergonzosa muerte a ambos, así Odiseo dará vergonzosa muerte a aquéllos. ¡Padre Zeus, Atenea y Apolo, ojalá que siendo como cuando en la bien construida Lesbos se levantó para disputar y luchó con Filomeleides, lo derribó violentamente y todos los aqueos se alegraron! Ojalá que con tal talante se enfrentara Odiseo con los pretendientes: corto el destino de todos sería y amargas sus nupcias. En cuanto a lo que me preguntas y suplicas, no querría apartarme de la verdad y engañarte. Conque no te ocultaré ni guardaré secreto sobre lo que me dijo el veraz anciano del mar. Este dijo que lo había visto sufriendo fuertes dolores en el palacio de la ninfa Calipso, quien lo retenía por la fuerza, y que no podía regresar a su tierra patria porque no tenía naves provistas de remos ni compañeros que le acompañaran por el ancho lomo del mar"[235]. Así me dijo el Atrida Menelao, famoso por su lanza, y

---

[235] Son las palabras que pronuncia Menelao en IV.333-50 y 556-60.

[292]

luego de acabar su relato regresamos. Los inmortales me concedieron un viento favorable y me escoltaron velozmente hasta mi patria.»

Así habló y conmovió el ánimo de Penélope. 150

Entonces Teoclímeno, semejante a los dioses, comenzó a hablar entre ellos:

«Esposa venerable de Odiseo Laertíada, en verdad él no sabe nada; escucha mi palabra, pues te voy a profetizar con veracidad y no voy a ocultarte nada. ¡Sea testigo Zeus, antes que los demás dioses, y la mesa de hospitalidad y el hogar del irreprochable Odiseo, al que he llegado, de que en verdad Odiseo ya está en su tierra patria, sentado o caminando, sabedor de estas malas acciones y sembrando la muerte para todos los pretendientes. Este es el augurio que yo observé, y me hice oír de 160 Telémaco mientras estaba en la nave de buenos bancos»[236].

Y le contestó la prudente Penélope:

«Forastero, ¡ojalá se cumpliera esta tu palabra! Entonces conocerías mi amistad enseguida y numerosos regalos de mí, hasta el punto de que cualquiera que contigo topara te llamaría dichoso.»

Así hablaban unos con otros.

Los pretendientes, por su parte, se complacían arrojando discos y venablos ante el palacio de Odiseo, en el sólido pavimento donde acostumbraban, llenos de arrogancia. Pero cuando fue la hora de comer y les llegaron de todas partes del cam- 170 po los animales que les traían los de siempre, se dirigió a ellos Medonte (éste era quien más les agradaba de los heraldos y solía acompañarlos al banquete):

«Mozos, una vez que todos habéis complacido vuestro ánimo con los juegos, dirigíos al palacio para preparar el almuerzo, que no es cosa mala yantar a su tiempo.»

Así habló y ellos se pusieron en pie y marcharon obedeciendo su palabra. Cuando llegaron a la bien edificada morada de-

---

[236] Se refiere a XV.525 y ss. No es cierto, sin embargo, que ésta fuera la interpretación que dio allí del augurio. Lo que dijo allí Teoclímeno era mucho más vago: «no hay una estirpe más regia que la vuestra en Itaca». ¿Olvido del poeta o intento de Teoclímeno por congraciarse con la reina? Sobre este desconcertante personaje, cfr. Introducción.

jaron sus mantos en sillas y sillones y sacrificaron grandes ovejas y gordas cabras; sacrificaron cebones y un toro del rebaño
para preparar su almuerzo.

Entre tanto Odiseo y el divino porquero se disponían a
marchar del campo a la ciudad y comenzó a hablar el porquero, caudillo de hombres:

«Forastero, puesto que deseas marchar hoy mismo a la ciudad, como recomendó mi soberano (que yo, desde luego, preferiría dejarte para vigilar la majada, pero tengo respeto por mi
amo y temo que me reprenda después y en verdad son duras
las reprimendas de los amos), marchemos ya, pues el día está
avanzado y quizá sea peor esperar a la tarde.»

Y contestándole dijo el muy astuto Odiseo:

«Lo sé, me doy cuenta, se lo dices a quien lo comprende.
Conque marchemos y tú sé mi guía. Dame un bastón —si es
que tienes uno cortado— para que me apoye, pues decís que el
camino es muy resbaladizo.»

Así dijo y echó a sus hombros el sucio zurrón desgarrado
por muchas partes, en el que había una correa retorcida. Entonces Eumeo le dio el deseado bastón y se pusieron los dos
en camino, quedando perros y pastores para guardar la majada.

Eumeo condujo hacia la ciudad a su soberano, que se asemejaba a un miserable y viejo mendigo, que se apoyaba en su
bastón y cubría su cuerpo con vestidos que daban pena. Cuando en su marcha por el empinado sendero se encontraban cerca de la ciudad y llegaron a una fuente labrada de hermosa corriente, a donde iban por agua los ciudadanos (la habían construido Itaco, Nérito y Políctor en el centro de un bosque de
álamos negros que crecían con su agua; era completamente re-
donda y de lo alto de una piedra caía agua fría, y encima de
ella había un altar de las Ninfas, donde solían sacrificar todos
los ciudadanos), allí se topó con ellos Melantio, hijo de Dolio[237], que conducía las cabras, las que sobresalían entre todo
el ganado, para festín de los pretendientes; y con él marchaban
dos pastores.

---

[237] Este Dolio es distinto del esclavo del mismo nombre que está al servicio
de Laertes en XXIV.220 y ss. Y distinto también del esclavo de Penélope que
se cita en IV.737.

Cuando los vio les reprendió de palabra y llamándolos por su nombre les dijo algo atroz e inconveniente que hizo saltar el corazón de Odiseo:

«Vaya, vaya, un desgraciado conduce a otro desgraciado; es claro que dios siempre lleva a la gente hacia los de su calaña. ¿Adónde, miserable porquero, llevas a ese gorrón, a ese mendigo pegajoso, a ese aguafiestas? Arrimará los hombros a muchas puertas para rascarse mientras pide mendrugos, que no espadas ni calderos. Si me lo dieras a mí para vigilante de mi majada, para mozo de cuadra y para llevar brezos a mis chivos, quizá bebiendo leche de cabra echaría gordos muslos. Pero ahora que ha aprendido esas malas artes no querrá ponerse a trabajar, que preferirá mendigar por el pueblo y alimentar su insaciable estómago. Conque te voy a decir algo que se va a cumplir: si se acerca a la casa del divino Odiseo, sus costillas van a romper muchas banquetas que lloverán sobre su cabeza desde las manos de esos hombres, pues va a ser su blanco por la casa.»

Así habló, y al pasar a su lado, el insensato dio una patada a Odiseo en la cadera, aunque no consiguió echarlo fuera del camino, sino que éste se mantuvo firme. Entonces Odiseo dudaba entre arrancarle la vida saltando tras él con el palo o levantarle y tirarle de cabeza contra el suelo, pero se aguantó y se contuvo. El porquero, en cambio, se encaró con él y le reprendió, y levantando las manos suplicó así:

«Ninfas de la fuente, hijas de Zeus, si alguna vez Odiseo quemó en vuestro honor muslos de corderos o cabritos cubriéndolos con gorda grasa, cumplidme este deseo: que vuelva este hombre conducido por un dios. Seguro que él acabaría con toda la insolencia que ahora paseas por la ciudad, mientras malos pastores acaban con los ganados.»

Y le contestó Melantio, el cabrero:

«¡Ay, ay, qué cosa ha dicho este perro urdidor de intrigas! Me lo voy a llevar algún día lejos de Ítaca en negra nave de buenos bancos para que me entreguen por él un buen precio, porque ¡ojalá Apolo, el de arco de plata, alcance hoy mismo a Telémaco dentro del palacio o sucumba a manos de los pretendientes, lo mismo que Odiseo ha perdido en tierras lejanas el día de su regreso!»

Así diciendo, los dejó caminando lentamente; en cambio, él se puso en camino y llegó enseguida a la morada del rey. Entró y sentó entre los pretendientes, frente a Eurímaco, pues a éste era a quien más estimaba. Pusieron junto a él una porción de carne los que servían y la venerable ama de llaves le llevó pan y se lo dejó al lado para que lo comiera.

Odiseo y el divino porquero se detuvieron en su caminar; 260 les llegaba el sonido de la sonora lira, pues Femio se había puesto a cantar para ellos. Entonces Odiseo tomó de la mano al porquero y le dijo:

«Eumeo, a lo que parece ésta es la hermosa morada de Odiseo, pues se destaca tanto que se la puede ver fácilmente entre otras muchas. Una estancia sigue a la otra, su patio está cercado con muro y cornisa y sus puertas bien firmes son de doble hoja. Ningún hombre podría rendirla por la fuerza. Me parece que muchos hombres se están banqueteando dentro, pues se levanta un olor a grasa y resuena la lira, a la que los dioses han 270 hecho compañera del banquete.»

Y contestando le dijiste, porquero Eumeo:

«Con facilidad te has percatado, que no eres sandio tampoco en lo demás. Pero, vamos, pensemos cómo actuar. Entra tú primero en la agradable morada y mézclate con los pretendientes, que yo me quedaré aquí; o, si quieres, quédate tú y entraré yo primero. Pero no te quedes parado mucho tiempo, no sea que te vea alguien fuera y te tire algo o te eche. Esto es lo que te aconsejo que consideres.»

Y le contestó luego el sufridor, el divino Odiseo: 280

«Lo sé, me doy cuenta, se lo dices a quien comprende. Conque marcha tú primero y yo me quedaré aquí, que ya sé lo que son golpes y pedradas. Mi ánimo es paciente, pues he sufrido muchos males en el mar y la guerra; que venga esto después de aquello. Cuando tiene apetito, no es posible acallar al maldito estómago que tantas desgracias suele acarrear a los hombres; por culpa suya incluso las bien entabladas naves se preparan para surcar el estéril mar portando la desgracia a hombres enemigos.»

Así hablaban entre sí. Entonces un perro que estaba tumba- 290 do enderezó la cabeza y las orejas, el perro Argos, a quien el sufridor Odiseo había criado, aunque no pudo disfrutar de él, pues antes se marchó a la divina Ilión. Al principio le solían llevar los jóvenes a perseguir cabras montaraces, ciervos y liebres, pero ahora yacía despreciado —una vez que se hubo ausentado Odiseo— entre el estiércol de mulos y vacas que estaba amontonado ante la puerta a fin de que los siervos de Odiseo se lo llevaran para abonar sus extensos campos. Allí estaba tumbado el perro Argos, lleno de pulgas. Cuando vio a Odiseo 300 cerca, entonces sí que movió la cola y dejó caer sus orejas, pero ya no podía acercarse a su amo. Entonces Odiseo, que le vio desde lejos, se enjugó una lágrima sin que se percatara Eumeo y le preguntó:

«Eumeo, es extraño que este perro esté tumbado entre el estiércol. Su cuerpo es hermoso, aunque ignoro si, además de hermoso, era rápido en la carrera o, por el contrario, era como esos perros falderos que crían los señores por lujo.» 310

Y contestándole dijiste, porquero Eumeo:

«Este perro era de un hombre que ha muerto lejos de aquí. Si su cuerpo y obras fueron como cuando lo dejó Odiseo al marchar a Troya, pronto te admirarías al contemplar su rapidez y vigor, que nunca salía huyendo de ninguna bestia en la profundidad del espeso bosque cuando la perseguía —pues también era muy diestro en seguir el rastro. Pero ahora lo tiene vencido la desgracia, pues su amo ha perecido lejos de su patria y las mujeres no se cuidan de él; que los siervos, cuando los amos ya no mandan, no quieren hacer los trabajos que les 320 corresponden, pues Zeus, que ve a lo ancho, quita a un hombre la mitad de su valía cuando le alcanza el día de la esclavitud.»

Así diciendo entró en la morada, agradable para vivir, y se fue derecho por el mégaron en busca de los ilustres pretendientes. Y a Argos le arrebató el destino de la negra muerte al ver a Odiseo después de veinte años.

Telémaco, semejante a los dioses, fue el primero en ver al porquero avanzar por la casa y enseguida le hizo señas invitándole a ponerse a su lado. Eumeo echó una ojeada, tomó una 330 banqueta que estaba cerca (donde se solía sentar el trinchante para repartir abundante carne entre los pretendientes cuando se banqueteaban en el palacio) y llevándoselo lo puso junto a la mesa de Telémaco y se sentó. Entonces el heraldo tomó una porción, sacó pan del canasto y se lo ofreció.

Enseguida, detrás de Eumeo, entró en el patio Odiseo semejante a un miserable y viejo mendigo que se apoyaba en su bastón y cubría su cuerpo con ropas que daban pena, sentóse sobre el umbral de madera de fresno dentro de las puertas y se 340 apoyó en la jamba de madera de ciprés que un artesano había pulimentado hábilmente y enderezado con la plomada. Telémaco llamó junto a sí al porquero y le dijo mientras cogía un pan entero del hermoso canasto y cuanta carne le cupo en las manos:

«Lleva esto al forastero y ofréceselo, y aconséjale que vaya recorriendo todos los pretendientes y les pida, que no es buena la vergüenza para el hombre necesitado.»

Así dijo; echó a andar el porquero cuando hubo oído su palabra y, poniéndose cerca, le dijo aladas palabras:

«Forastero, Telémaco te entrega esto y te aconseja que vayas 350 recorriendo todos los pretendientes y les pidas, que dice que no es buena la vergüenza para un hombre necesitado.»

Y contestándole dijo el astuto Odiseo:

«Soberano Zeus, ¡que Telémaco sea próspero entre los hombres y obtenga todo cuanto anhela en su corazón!»

Así dijo; tomólo en sus dos manos y lo puso a sus pies, sobre el sucio zurrón; y lo comió mientras cantaba el aedo en el palacio.

Cuando lo había comido terminó el divino aedo y los pretendientes comenzaron a alborotar en el palacio. 360

Entonces Atenea se puso cerca de Odiseo Laertíada y lo apremió a que recogiera mendrugos entre los pretendientes y pudiera conocer quiénes eran rectos y quiénes injustos, aunque ni aun así iba a librar a ninguno de la muerte. Así que se puso en marcha para mendigar de izquierda a derecha a cada uno de ellos, extendiendo sus manos a todas partes como si fuera un mendigo de siempre. Los pretendientes le daban compadecidos, se admiraban de él y se preguntaban unos a otros quién podría ser y de dónde vendría. Entonces habló entre ellos Melantio, el cabrero:

«Escuchadme, pretendientes de la ilustre reina, sobre este 370 forastero, pues yo lo he visto ya antes. En realidad lo ha traído aquí el porquero, aunque no sé de cierto de dónde se precia de ser su linaje.»

Así dijo, y Antínoo reprendió al porquero:

«Porquero ilustre, ¿por qué lo has traído a la ciudad? ¿Es que no tenemos suficientes vagabundos, mendigos pegajosos, aguafiestas? ¿O es que te parecen pocos los que se reúnen aquí para comer la hacienda de tu señor y has invitado también a éste?»

Y contestándole dijiste, porquero Eumeo:

«Antínoo, con ser noble no dices palabras justas. Pues ¿quién sale a traer de fuera un forastero como no sea uno de los servidores del pueblo, un adivino, un curador de enfermedades o un trabajador de la madera, o incluso un aedo inspirado que complazca con sus cantos? Estos sí, éstos son los hombres a quienes se invita a venir sobre la extensa tierra, pero nadie invitaría a un vagabundo a que le importune.

»Y es que tú has sido siempre entre todos los pretendientes el más duro para con los siervos de Odiseo, y en especial para conmigo. Ahora que a mí no me importa mientras me viva en el palacio la prudente Penélope y Telémaco, semejante a los dioses.»

Y Telémaco le contestó discretamente:

«Calla, no me contestes a éste con tantas palabras. Antínoo acostumbra a provocar continuamente con palabras duras e incluso incita a los demás.»

Así dijo, y dirigió a Antínoo aladas palabras:

«Antínoo, en verdad te cuidas de mí como un padre de su hijo al aconsejarme que arroje del palacio al forastero con palabra tajante; que no cumpla dios esto. Toma algo y dáselo; no lo veo con malos ojos, sino que te ordeno que lo hagas. Y no tengas temor por causa de mi madre ni de ninguno de los siervos que hay en la casa del divino Odiseo. Aunque creo que es otro pensamiento el que albergas en tu pecho, pues prefieres comer tú a destajo antes que dárselo a otro.»

Y Antínoo le contestó y dijo:

«¡Telémaco fanfarrón, incapaz de reprimir tu ira, qué cosa has dicho! Si todos los pretendientes le dieran tanto como yo, su casa lo retendría durante tres meses lejos de aquí.»

Así dijo, y tomándolo de debajo de la mesa, le enseñó el escabel sobre el que apoyaba sus brillantes pies mientras se daba al banquete. Pero todos los demás le dieron y llenaron su zurrón de pan y carne. Iba ya Odiseo por el pavimento a probar los regalos de los aqueos, cuando se detuvo junto a Antínoo y le dijo su palabra:

«Dame, amigo, que no me pareces el menos noble de los aqueos, sino el más excelente, pues te asemejas a un rey. Por ello tienes que darme incluso más comida que los demás y yo diré tu nombre por la infinita tierra. También yo habité en otro tiempo en casa rica y daba a menudo a un vagabundo así, 420 de cualquier ralea que fuera y cualquier cosa que llegara precisando. Tenía miles de esclavos y otras muchas cosas con las que los hombres viven bien y se les llama ricos. Pero Zeus Cronida me arruinó —pues debió de quererlo así— enviándome con unos errantes piratas a Egipto, camino largo, para que pereciera. Atraqué mis cuvadas naves en el río Egipto. Entonces ordené a mis leales compañeros que se quedaran junto a ellas para vigilarlas y envié espías a puestos de observación 430 con orden de que regresaran, pero éstos, cediendo a su ambición, saquearon los hermosos campos de los egipcios, se llevaron a las mujeres y tiernos niños y mataron a los hombres. Pronto llegó el griterío a la ciudad, así que, al escucharlo, se presentaron al despuntar la aurora: llenóse la llanura toda de gente de a pie y a caballo y del estruendo del bronce. Zeus, el que goza con el rayo, indujo a mis compañeros a huir cobardemente y ninguno se atrevió a dar el pecho. Por todas partes nos rodeaba la destrucción. Allí mataron con agudo bronce a 440 muchos de mis compañeros y a otros se los llevaron vivos para forzarlos a trabajar sus campos, pero a mí me llevaron a Chipre y me entregaron a un forastero que dio con nosotros, a Dmator Jasida, quien gobernaba con fuerza en Chipre. Desde allí he llegado aquí después de sufrir desgracias»[238].

Y Antínoo le contestó y dijo:

«¿Qué dios nos ha traído aquí esta peste, esta ruina del banquete? Quédate ahí en medio, lejos de mi mesa, no sea que tengas que volver enseguida al amargo Egipto y a Chipre, que eres un mendigo audaz y desvergonzado. Te pones ante éstos, 450

---

[238] La parte central de este relato es repetición literal de la falsa historia que contó a Eumeo en XIV.258 y ss. El final es diferente: allí llega con unos fenicios al país de los tesprotos.

uno tras otro, y todos te dan atolondradamente, pues no tienen moderación ni sienten compasión al regalar cosas ajenas que tienen en abundancia a su disposición.»

Y le contestó retirándose el astuto Odiseo:

«¡Ay, ay, que a tu gallardía no se añade también la cordura! En verdad, no darías ni siquiera sal de tu propia hacienda a quien se te acercara si, estando en casa ajena, no has podido tomar un poco de pan para darme, y eso que tienes en abundancia a tu disposición.»

Así habló; Antínoo se irritó más aún en su corazón y mirándole torvamente le dirigió aladas palabras:

«Ahora es cuando creo que no vas a retirarte con bien atra-   460
vesando el mégaron, ya que estás injuriándome.»

Así habló, y, tomando el escabel, se lo tiró al hombro derecho, acertándole en el extremo de la espalda. Odiseo se mantuvo en pie, firme como una roca, y el golpe de Antínoo no le hizo perder pie, pero movió la cabeza en silencio meditando secretos males.

Se retiró para sentarse en el umbral, dejó el bien lleno zurrón y comenzó a hablar a los pretendientes:

«Escuchadme, pretendientes de la ilustre reina, para que os diga lo que mi ánimo me ordena dentro del pecho. No es grande el dolor en las entrañas ni la pena cuando un hombre es   470
golpeado luchando por sus posesiones, sus toros o sus blancas ovejas. Pero Antínoo me ha golpeado por causa del miserable estómago, el maldito estómago que proporciona males sin cuento a los hombres. Conque, si en verdad existen dioses y Erinis de los mendigos[239], que el término de la muerte alcance a Antínoo antes de su matrimonio.»

Y Antínoo hijo de Eupites, le replicó:

«Siéntate a comer tranquilo, forastero, o lárgate a otra parte, no sea que los jóvenes te arrastren por el palacio, por lo que dices, asiéndote del pie o del brazo y te llenen todo de ara-   480
ñazos.»

Así habló, y todos ellos se indignaron sobremanera. Y uno de los jóvenes orgullosos decía así:

«Antínoo, cruel, no has hecho bien en golpear al pobre va-

---

[239] Cfr. nota 42.

gabundo, si es que existe un dios en el cielo. Que los dioses andan recorriendo las ciudades bajo la forma de forasteros de otras tierras y con otros mil aspectos, y vigilan la soberbia de los hombres o su rectitud.»

Así le dijeron los pretendientes, pero él no prestaba atención a sus palabras.

Telémaco hacía crecer en su corazón un gran dolor por su padre golpeado, pero no dejó caer a tierra lágrima alguna de sus párpados, sino que movió la cabeza en silencio, meditando secretos males. 490

Cuando la prudente Penélope oyó que el forastero había sido golpeado en el palacio dijo a sus siervas:

«¡Ojalá Apolo, de ilustre arco, te alcance también a ti de esta forma!»

Y la despensera Eurínome dijo:

«¡Ojalá se diera cumplimiento a nuestras maldiciones! Ninguno de éstos llegaría vivo hasta la aurora de hermoso trono.»

Y la prudente Penélope le dijo:

«Tata, todos son enemigos, pues maquinan maldades, pero Antínoo sobre todos se asemeja a una negra Ker. Ese pobre 500 forastero vaga por la casa pidiendo a los hombres, pues le obliga la pobreza; todos han llenado su zurrón y le han dado, pero éste le ha alcanzado con un escabel en el hombro derecho.»

Así hablaba ella con sus esclavas, sentada en el dormitorio, mientras comía el divino Odiseo. Entonces llamó junto a sí al divino porquero y le dijo:

«Ve, divino Eumeo, y ordena al forastero que venga para saludarlo y preguntarle si ha oído hablar sobre el sufridor Odiseo o lo ha visto con sus ojos pues parece un hombre muy 510 asendereado.»

Y tú le contestaste, porquero Eumeo, diciendo:

«Reina, ojalá se callaran los aqueos; este sí que hechizaría tu corazón con lo que cuenta. Yo lo he tenido tres noches y tres días en mi cabaña (pues fue a mí a quien llegó primero después de huir de una nave), pero todavía no ha terminado de contarme sus desgracias. Como cuando un hombre contempla embelesado a un aedo que canta inspirado por los dioses y conoce versos deseables para los hombres —y éstos desean escucharle 520 sin cesar siempre que se pone a cantar—, así me ha hechizado éste sentado en mi morada. Asegura que es huésped de Odiseo por parte de padre y que habitaba en Creta, donde está el linaje de Minos[240]. Ha llegado de allí sufriendo penalidades, después de mucho rodar, y afirma haber oído sobre Odiseo vivo y cercano, en el rico pueblo de los tesprotos; y trae a casa numerosos tesoros.»

Y le dijo la prudente Penélope:

«Marcha, invítalo a venir aquí para que me lo cuente en persona. Que se diviertan éstos fuera o aquí en la casa, puesto que 530 su ánimo está alegre: y es que sus bienes están intactos en su palacio; se los comen los siervos, en cambio ellos vienen todos los días a nuestro palacio y, sacrificando toros y ovejas y gordas cabras, se banquetean y beben el rojo vino sin mesura. Todo se está perdiendo, pues no hay un hombre como Odiseo para apartar de su casa esta peste. Si Odiseo llegara a su tierra patria haría pagar enseguida, junto con su hijo, las violencias de estos hombres.» 540

Así habló, y Telémaco lanzó un gran esturnudo[241] y toda la casa resonó espantosamente. Rióse Penélope y dirigió a Eumeo aladas palabras:

«Marcha y haz venir frente a mí al forastero. ¿No ves que mi hijo ha estornudado ante mis palabras? Por esto no puede dejar de cumplirse la muerte para todos los pretendientes; nadie podrá alejar de ellos la muerte y las Keres. Voy a decirte otra cosa que has de poner en tu interior: si reconozco que todo lo que dice es cierto, le vestiré de túnica y manto, hermo- 550 sos vestidos.»

Así habló; marchó el porquero luego que hubo escuchado su palabra y, poniéndose cerca, le dijo aladas palabras:

«Padre forastero, te llama la prudente Penélope, la madre de Telémaco. Su ánimo la impulsa a preguntarte por su esposo, ya que ha sufrido muchas penas. Y si reconoce que todo lo

---

[240] En XIV.200 y ss. no se dice exactamente que fuera del linaje de Minos. Odiseo se confiesa hijo de Cástor Hilacida. En cambio, sí le cuenta después a Penélope (cfr. XIX.165 y ss.) que es descendiente de Minos y hermano de Idomeneo.

[241] En Homero, el estornudo es considerado como un buen augurio (cfr. también Aristófanes, *Ranas*, 647), sin embargo en la época helenística aparece como un signo de mal agüero, cfr. Menandro 536.9, etc.

que le dices es cierto, te vestirá de túnica y manto, cosas que más necesitas. También podrás alimentar tu vientre pidiendo comida por el pueblo, y te dará quien lo desee.»

Y le contestó el sufridor, el divino Odiseo: 560

«Eumeo, contaría enseguida toda la verdad a la hija de Icario, a la prudente Penélope —pues sé muy bien sobre aquél y hemos recibido un infortunio semejante—, pero temo a la multitud de los terribles pretendientes, cuya soberbia y violencia ha llegado al férreo cielo. Además, cuando ese hombre me hizo daño golpeándome al cruzar el salón —y sin hacer yo nada malo—, ni Telémaco ni ningún otro me protegió. Por esto aconsejo a Penélope que se quede en sus habitaciones —por mucho que desee salir— hasta la puesta del sol. Pregúnteme entonces sobre el día del regreso de su esposo, sentada   570
muy cerca del fuego, pues tengo unos vestidos que dan pena y bien lo sabes tú, que ya te supliqué antes que a nadie.»

Así habló, y marchó el porquero cuando hubo escuchado su palabra. Cuando atravesaba el umbral le dijo Penélope:

«¿No me lo traes, Eumeo? ¿Qué es lo que ha pensado el vagabundo? ¿Es que tiene mucho miedo de alguien o se avergüenza por otros motivos de cruzar la casa? Malo es un vagabundo vergonzoso.»

Y tú le contestaste, porquero Eumeo, diciendo:

«Ha hablado como le corresponde y dice lo que pensaría   580
cualquier otro que quiere evitar la soberbia de esos hombres altivos. Conque te aconseja que esperes hasta la puesta del sol. Y es que será para ti mucho mejor, reina, que estés sola cuando dirijas tu palabra al forastero o le escuches.»

Y le contestó la prudente Penélope:

«No piensa como insensato el forastero, sea como fuere, pues entre los mortales hombres no hay quienes maquinen semejantes maldades, llenos de arrogancia.»

Así habló ella, y el divino porquero marchó hacia la multitud de los pretendientes, una vez que le hubo manifestado   590
todo. Luego dirigió a Telémaco aladas palabras, manteniendo cerca su cabeza para que no se enteraran los demás:

«Amigo, yo me marcho a vigilar los cerdos y todo aquello, tu sustento y el mío. Ocúpate tú aquí de todo. Antes que nada mira por tu seguridad y piensa la forma de que no te pase nada, que muchos de los aqueos andan meditando males. ¡Ojalá los destruya Zeus antes de que nos llegue la desgracia!»

Y Telémaco le contestó discretamente:

«Así será, abuelo. Márchate después de merendar pero vuelve al amanecer y trae hermosas víctimas, que yo y los inmortales nos cuidaremos de todo esto.»   600

Así habló; el porquero se sentó de nuevo sobre la bien pulida banqueta y después de saciar su apetito con comida y bebida se puso en marcha hacia los cerdos, abandonando el patio y el mégaron lleno de comensales.

Y éstos gozaban con la danza y el canto, pues ya había caído la tarde.

Canto XVIII

LOS PRETENDIENTES VEJAN A ODISEO

E N esto llegó un mendigo del pueblo que solía pedir por la
ciudad de Itaca y sobresalía por su vientre insaciable,
por comer y beber sin parar. No tenía vigor ni fortaleza,
pero su cuerpo era grande al mirarlo. Su nombre era Arneo,
que se lo puso su soberana[242] madre el día de su nacimiento,
pero todos los jóvenes[243] le llamaban Iro[244], porque solía ir de
correveidile cuando alguien se lo mandaba. Cuando llegó, empezó a perseguir a Odiseo por su casa y le insultaba diciendo
aladas palabras:

«Viejo, sal del pórtico, no sea que te arrastre por el pie. ¿No 10
has oído que todos me hacen guiños incitándome a que te
arrastre? Yo, sin embargo, siento vergüenza. Conque levántate, no sea que nuestra disputa llegue a las manos.»

Y mirándole torvamente dijo el muy astuto Odiseo:

«Desgraciado, ni te hago daño alguno ni te dirijo la palabra,
y no siento envidia de que alguien te dé, aunque recojas muchas cosas. Este umbral tiene cabida para los dos y no tienes
por qué envidiar lo ajeno. Me pareces un vagabundo como yo
y son los dioses los que dan fortuna. Pero no me provoques a
luchar, no sea que me irrites y, con ser viejo, te empape de 20

---

[242] Este es uno de los ejemplos más llamativos del epíteto fijo cuando está
mal aplicado. Cfr. también XXI.6.
[243] Los pretendientes.
[244] Iro es el masculino de Iris, la mensajera de los dioses en la *Ilíada* (en la
Odisea es siempre Hermes).

sangre el pecho y los labios. Así tendría más tranquilidad para mañana, pues no creo que volvieras por segunda vez al palacio de Odiseo Laertíada.»

Y el vagabundo Iro le contestó airado:

«¡Ay, ay, qué deprisa habla este gorrón que se parece a una vieja ennegrecida por el hollín! Y eso que podría yo pensar en dañarle golpeándolo con las dos manos y arrancar todos los dientes de sus mandíbulas, como los de un cerdo devorador de mieses, y tirarlos al suelo. Ponte el ceñidor para que todos vean que luchamos; aunque ¿cómo podrías luchar con un hombre más joven?»   30

Así es como se iban encolerizando sobre el pulimentado pavimento, delante de las elevadas puertas. La sagrada fuerza de Antínoo oyó a los dos y sonriendo dulcemente dijo a los pretendientes:

«Amigos, nunca hasta ahora nos había tocado en suerte una diversión como la que dios nos ha traído a esta casa. El forastero e Iro están incitándose mutuamente a llegar a las manos. Así que empujémosles enseguida.»

Así dijo y todos comenzaron a reírse; rodearon a los andra-   40
josos mendigos y les dijo Antínoo, hijo de Eupites:

«Escuchadme, ilustres pretendientes, mientras os hablo. Hay en el fuego unos vientres de cabra, éstos que hemos dejado para la cena llenándolos de grasa y de sangre. El que venza de los dos y resulte más fuerte podrá levantarse él mismo y coger el que quiera. Además, podrá participar siempre de nuestro banquete y no permitiremos que ningún otro mendigo se nos acerque a pedir.»

Así dijo Antínoo y les agradó su palabra. Entonces el astuto   50
Odiseo les dijo con intenciones engañosas:

«Amigos, no es posible que un viejo luche con un hombre más joven, sobre todo si está abrumado por el infortunio, pero el perverso vientre me empuja a que sucumba ante sus golpes. Conque, vamos, juradme todos con firme juramento que nadie prestará ayuda a Iro y me golpeará con mano pesada injustamente, haciéndome sucumbir ante éste por la fuerza.»

Así dijo, y todos juraron como les había pedido. Así que cuando habían completado su juramento dijo entre ellos la sa-   60
grada fuerza de Telémaco:

«Forastero, si tu corazón y tu valeroso ánimo te empujan a defenderte de éste, no temas a ninguno de los aqueos, pues tendrá que luchar contra muchos más quien te mate. Yo soy quien te hospeda y los dos reyes Antínoo y Eurímaco, ambos discretos, aprueban mis palabras.»

Así dijo, y todos asintieron. Así que Odiseo ciñó sus miembros con los andrajos y dejó al descubierto unos muslos grandes y hermosos y al descubierto quedaron sus anchos hombros, su torso y sus pesados brazos.

Entonces Atenea se puso a su lado y fortaleció los miembros del pastor de su pueblo. Todos los pretendientes se asombraron muy mucho y uno decía así al que tenía al lado:

«Pronto este Iro va a dejar de ser Iro y tener la desgracia que se ha buscado; ¡menudos muslos deja ver el viejo a través de sus andrajos!»

Así decían, y el corazón le dio un vuelco a Iro de mala manera. Pero aun así los escuderos le ciñeron y arrastraron a la fuerza atemorizado. Y sus carnes le temblaban en todo el cuerpo. Entonces Antínoo le dijo su palabra y le llamó por su nombre:

«¡Ojalá no existieras, fanfarrón, ni hubieras nacido si tanto tiemblas y temes a éste, a un viejo abrumado por el infortunio que le ha alcanzado! Pero te voy a decir algo que se va a cumplir: Si éste te vence y resulta más fuerte, te meteré en negra nave y te enviaré al continente, al rey Equeto[245], azote de todos los mortales, para que te corte la nariz y las orejas con cruel bronce y arrancando tus miembros se los arroje a los perros para que se los coman crudos.»

Así dijo, el temblor se apoderó todavía más de sus miembros y lo arrastraron hacia el medio. Y los dos extendieron sus brazos.

Entonces, el sufridor, el divino Odiseo, dudó entre derribarlo de forma que su alma le abandonara al caer o derribarlo suavemente y extenderlo en el suelo. Y mientras así dudaba le pareció más ventajoso derribarlo suavemente para que los

70

80

90

---

[245] Sólo aparece en *Odisea* (cfr. también 116 y XXI.308). Parece un nombre parlante, «el que retiene», y bien podría ser una especie de «coco» para personas mayores de carácter simplón.

aqueos no sospecharan nada. Así que levantando ambos los brazos, Iro golpeó a Odiseo en el hombro derecho y Odiseo golpeó el cuello de Iro bajo la oreja y rompió por dentro sus huesos. Al punto bajó por su boca la negra sangre y cayó al suelo gritando. Pateaba contra el suelo y hacía rechinar sus dientes, y los ilustres pretendientes levantaron sus manos y se morían de risa. Entonces Odiseo le asió por el pie y lo arrastró 100 a lo largo del pórtico hasta llegar al patio y las puertas de la galería. Lo dejó sentado contra la cerca del patio, le puso el bastón entre las manos y le dirigió aladas palabras:

«Quédate ahí sentado para espantar a cerdos y perros, y no pretendas ser jefe de forasteros y mendigos, miserable como eres, no sea que te busques un mal todavía mayor.»

Así diciendo echó a sus hombros el sucio zurrón rasgado por muchas partes, en el que había una correa retorcida, volvió al umbral y se sentó. Los pretendientes entraron riéndose sua- 110 vemente y le felicitaban con sus palabras, y uno de los jóvenes arrogantes decía así:

«Forastero, que Zeus y los demás dioses inmortales te concedan lo que más desees y sea caro a tu corazón, pues has hecho que este insaciable deje de vagabundear por el pueblo. Pronto lo llevaremos al continente, al rey Equeto, azote de todos los mortales.»

Así decían y el divino Odiseo se alegró con el presagio[246]. Entonces Antínoo le puso al lado un gran vientre lleno de grasa y sangre. También Anfínomo puso a su lado dos panes que 120 tomó de la cesta, le ofreció vino en copa de oro y dijo:

«Salud, padre forastero; que seas rico y feliz en el futuro, pues ahora estás envuelto en numerosas desgracias.»

Y contestándole dijo el muy astuto Odiseo:

«Anfínomo, de verdad que me pareces discreto, siendo hijo de tal padre, pues he oído la fama que tiene Niso de Duliquia de ser gallardo y rico. Dicen que eres hijo de éste y pareces hombre discreto. Por eso te voy a decir algo —préstame atención y escúchame—: nada cría la tierra más endeble que el 130 hombre de cuantos seres respiran y caminan por ella. Mientras

---

[246] También se considera buen presagio una frase inesperada y dicha al azar, cfr. también XX.112 y ss.

los dioses le prestan virtud y sus rodillas son ágiles, cree que nunca en el futuro va a recibir desgracias; pero cuando los dioses felices le otorgan miserias, incluso éstas tiene que soportarlas con ánimo paciente contra su voluntad. Pues el pensamiento de los hombres terrenos cambia con cada día que nos trae el padre de hombres y dioses. También en otro tiempo yo estuve a punto de ser rico y feliz entre los hombres, pero cometí numerosas violencias cediendo a mi fuerza y poder por confiar 140 en mi padre y mis hermanos. Por esto ningún hombre debe ser nunca injusto, sino retener en silencio los dones que los dioses le hagan.

»Estoy viendo a los pretendientes maquinar acciones semejantes, trasquilando los bienes y deshonrando a la esposa de un hombre que, te aseguro, no estará ya mucho tiempo lejos de los suyos y su patria, por el contrario, está cerca. Conque ¡ojalá un dios te saque de aquí y lleve a casa para no tener que enfrentarte con aquél el día que regrese a su tierra patria!; que creo no va a ser sin sangre la contienda entre él y los pretendientes, cuando haya entrado en su hogar.» 150

Así habló, después de hacer libación bebió el delicioso vino y volvió a depositar la copa en manos del conductor de su pueblo. Éste marchó por el palacio acongojado en su corazón moviendo la cabeza, pues ya veía en su interior la perdición. Pero ni aun así consiguió escapar a la muerte, que también a éste sujetó Atenea bajo los brazos de Telémaco para que sucumbiera con fuerza a su lanza.

Y volvió a sentarse en el sillón de donde se había levantado.

Entonces la diosa de ojos brillantes, Atenea, puso en la mente de la hija de Icario, la prudente Penélope, la idea de aparecer ante los pretendientes, a fin de que ensanchara aún 160 más el corazón de éstos y resultara aún más respetable que antes a los ojos de su esposo e hijo. Sonrió sin motivo, dijo su palabra a la despensera y la llamó por su nombre:

«Eurínome, mi ánimo desea, aunque nunca antes lo deseó, mostrarme ante los pretendientes por odiosos que me sigan siendo. Voy a decir a mi hijo una palabra que quizá le resulte provechosa: que no se mezcle con los pretendientes, quienes le hablan bien, pero por detrás le piensan mal.»

Y Eurínome, la despensera, le dirigió su palabra:

«Sí, todo esto lo dices como te corresponde, hija. Conque ve y di a tu hijo tu palabra y nada le ocultes, pero antes lava tu cuerpo y pinta tus mejillas. No vayas con el rostro tan empapado de llanto, que es cosa mala andar siempre entre penas. Tu hijo es ya tan grande como pedías a los inmortales verlo, cubierto de barba.»

Y le contestó la prudente Penélope:

«Eurínome, no digas, por más que te cuides de mí, que lave mi cuerpo y unja mis mejillas con aceite, que los dioses que ocupan el Olimpo me arrebataron la belleza el día que aquél se marchó en las cóncavas naves. Pero dile a Autónoe e Hipodamia que vengan, a fin de que me acompañen por el palacio. No quiero presentarme sola ante hombres, pues siento vergüenza.»

Así dijo, y la anciana atravesó el mégaron para dar el recado a las mujeres y apremiarlas a que marcharan.

Entonces Atenea, la diosa de ojos brillantes, concibió otra idea: derramó sobre la hija de Icario dulce sueño y ésta echóse a dormir en la misma silla y todos los miembros se le aflojaron. Entretanto, la divina entre las diosas le otorgó dones inmortales para que los aqueos se admiraran al verla. En primer lugar limpió su hermoso rostro con la belleza inmortal con que suele adornarse Citerea[247], de linda corona, cuando comparte el deseable coro de las Gracias. También la hizo más alta y más fuerte a la vista y la hizo más blanca que el marfil tallado. Realizado esto, se alejó la divina entre las diosas y llegaron del mégaron las siervas de blancos brazos, acercándose con vocerío.

Entonces abandonó el sueño a Penélope, frotóse las mejillas con sus manos y dijo:

«¡Qué blando letargo ha cubierto mis sufrimientos! Ojalá la casta Artemis me proporcionara una muerte así de blanda ahora mismo, para no seguir consumiendo mi vida con corazón acongojado en la nostalgia de las muchas virtudes de mi marido, pues era el más excelente de los aqueos.»

---

[247] Afrodita. Según el mito, inmediatamente después de nacer de los órganos sexuales de Urano cortados por Crono, se dirigió a Citera primero y luego a Chipre (cfr. Hesiodo, *Teogonía*, 188-93). De ahí que sus epítetos más habituales sean Cipris y Citerea.

Así diciendo, abandonó el brillante piso de arriba, pero no sola, que la acompañaban dos siervas. Cuando llegó junto a los pretendientes la divina entre las mujeres se detuvo junto a una columna del ricamente labrado techo, sosteniendo ante sus mejillas un grueso velo. Y una diligente sierva se colocó a cada lado. Las rodillas de los pretendientes se debilitaron allí mismo —pues había hechizado su corazón con el deseo— y todos desearon acostarse junto a ella en la cama.

Entonces se dirigió a Telémaco, su querido hijo:

«Telémaco, ya no tienes voluntad ni juicio firmes. Cuando eras niño regías tus intereses aún mejor que ahora; en cambio, ahora que eres grande y has alcanzado la medida de la juventud —y eso que cualquiera pensaría que eres hijo de un hombre rico mirando tu talla y hermosura, un ser de otro sitio—, y no tienes voluntad ni juicio como es debido. ¡Qué acción es esta que se ha producido en el palacio...!, y tú que has permitido que se ultrajara a este forastero... ¿Qué pasaría si un huésped alojado en nuestro palacio recibiera este doloroso trato? Seguro que la vergüenza y el escarnio de las gentes serían para ti.»

Y Telémaco le contestó discretamente:

«Madre mía, no me voy a indignar porque te irrites conmigo, que pienso en mi interior y sé muy bien cada cosa, lo bueno y lo malo, aunque hasta ahora he sido todavía un niño. Pero no puedo pensar en todo con discreción, pues me asustan éstos que se sientan a mi lado maquinando maldades y yo no tengo quien me ayude. El altercado entre el forastero e Iro se ha producido no por voluntad de los pretendientes, sino porque aquél era más vigoroso.

»¡Ojalá —por Zeus padre, Atenea y Apolo— que los pretendientes inclinaran su cabeza vencidos, en el patio los unos, dentro de la casa los otros, y se les aflojaran los miembros de la misma forma que el desdichado Iro está ahora sentado con la cabeza gacha, semejante a un borracho, sin poder tenerse en pie ni volver a casa, pues sus miembros están flojos.»

Así se decían uno a otro. Y Eurímaco se dirigió a Penélope con palabras:

«Hija de Icario, prudente Penélope, si te contemplaran todos los aqueos de Argos de Yaso[248], serían muchos más los pretendientes que se banquetearan desde el amanecer en vuestro palacio, pues sobresales entre las mujeres por tu forma y talla y por el juicio que tienes dentro bien equilibrado.»

Y le contestó luego la prudente Penélope: 250

«Eurímaco, en verdad han destruido los inmortales mis cualidades —forma y cuerpo—, el día en que los aqueos se embarcaron para Ilión, y con ellos estaba mi esposo Odiseo. Si al menos viniera él y cuidara mi vida, mayor sería mi gloria y yo más bella, pero estoy afligida, pues son tantos los males que la divinidad ha agitado contra mí. Cuando marchó Odiseo abandonando su tierra patria, me tomó de la mano derecha por la muñeca y me dijo: "Mujer, no creo que vuelvan incólumes de Troya todos los aqueos de buenas grebas, que dicen que los 260 troyanos son buenos luchadores, tanto lanzando el venablo como las flechas o montando en veloces caballos, los cuales pueden decidir rápidamente una gran contienda cuando está equilibrada. Por esto, no sé si va a librarme dios o pereceré en la misma Troya. Cuida tú aquí de todo; presta atención a mis padres en el palacio como ahora, o todavía más, cuando yo esté lejos. Cuando veas que mi hijo ya tiene barba, cásate con quien desees y abandona tu casa." Así dijo aquél y todo se está 270 cumpliendo. Llegará la noche en que el odioso matrimonio salga al encuentro de esta desgraciada a quien Zeus ha quitado la felicidad. Pero me ha llegado al corazón esta terrible aflicción: no suele ser así —al menos antes no lo era— el comportamiento de los pretendientes que quieren cortejar a una mujer noble, hija de un hombre rico, rivalizando entre sí; suelen llevar vacas y rico ganado para festín de los amigos de la novia y entregar a ésta brillantes presentes, pero no comerse sin pagar 280 una hacienda ajena.»

Así habló, y se llenó de alegría el sufridor, el divino Odiseo porque trataba de arrancar regalos y hechizar sus corazones con blandas palabras, mientras su mente revolvía otras intenciones.

---

[248] Yaso, hijo de Tríopas, se repartió el Peloponeso con sus hermanos Pelasgo y Agenor. A él le tocó toda la parte occidental que incluía la Elide, a la cual, sin duda, se refiere Eurímaco.

Entonces Antínoo, hijo de Eupites, se dirigió a ella:

«Hija de Icario, prudente Penélope, recibe los dones que quieran traerte los aqueos —pues no es bueno rechazar un regalo—, que nosotros no iremos a trabajo ni a parte alguna hasta que te desposes con el mejor de los aqueos.»

Así habló Antínoo y les agradó su palabra. Así que cada uno envió a un heraldo para que trajera presentes. A Antínoo le trajo su heraldo un gran peplo hermoso, bordado y con doce broches todos de oro encajados en sus bien dobladas corchetas. A Eurímaco le trajo enseguida un collar adornado de oro, engarzado con ámbar, como un sol. Sus siervos le llevaron a Euridamante dos pendientes con tres perlas, grandes como moras, que despedían una gracia sin cuento. De casa de Pisandro, el soberano hijo de Polictor, trajo un siervo una gargantilla, hermoso adorno. Cada uno de los aqueos llevó su hermoso regalo. Entonces subió la divina entre las mujeres al piso superior y a su lado las siervas portaban los hermosísimos presentes.

Los pretendientes se entregaron a la danza y al deseable canto y esperaron a que llegara la tarde, y cuando estaban gozando se les echó encima la oscura tarde. Entonces colocaron tres parrillas en el palacio para que les alumbraran, y en ellas madera seca, muy seca, reseca, recién cortada con el bronce, y la mezclaron con teas. Y las siervas del sufridor Odiseo se alternaban para alumbrar. Entonces les dijo el mismo hijo de los dioses, el muy astuto Odiseo:

«Siervas de Odiseo, señor vuestro largo tiempo ausente, marchad a las habitaciones de la venerable reina y moved la rueca junto a ella y divertidla sentadas en su estancia, o cardad copos de lana en vuestras manos, que yo me quedaré aquí para ofrecer luz a todos éstos. Aunque quieran aguardar a Eos, de hermoso trono, no me rendirán, que tengo mucho aguante.»

Así dijo, y ellas se echaron a reír mirándose unas a otras. Entonces empezó a censurarle con palabras de reproche Melanto de lindas mejillas (la había engendrado Dolio, pero la crió Penélope y la cuidaba como a una hija y le daba juguetes, pero ni aun así sentía lástima en su corazón por Penélope, sino que solía acostarse y hacer el amor con Eurímaco). Ésta, pues, reprendió a Odiseo con palabras ultrajantes:

«Desgraciado forastero, estás tocado en tus mientes; no quieres ir a dormir a casa del herrero ni al albergue público[249], sino que te quedas aquí y hablas mucho con audacia, en medio de tantos hombres, sin sentir miedo en tu corazón. Seguro que el vino se ha apoderado de tus entrañas, o quizá siempre es así tu juicio y dices sandeces. ¿Acaso estás fuera de ti por vencer a Iro, el vagabundo? Cuidado, no se levante contra ti alguien más fuerte que Iro y, golpeándote en la cabeza con pesadas manos, te arrastre fuera del patio manchado de sangre.»

Y mirándola torvamente, le dijo el muy astuto Odiseo:

«Perra, voy a ir a contar a Telémaco lo que estás diciendo, para que te corte en pedazos.»

Así diciendo, espantó a las mujeres con sus palabras y se pusieron en camino por el palacio, y sus miembros estaban flojos por el temor, pues pensaban que había dicho la verdad. Entonces Odiseo se puso junto a las parrillas ardientes para alumbrarlos y dirigía su mirada a todos ellos, pero su corazón revolvía dentro del pecho lo que no iba a quedar sin cumplimiento.

Y Atenea no permitió que los esforzados pretendientes contuvieran del todo los escarnios que laceran el corazón, para que el dolor se hundiera todavía más en el ánimo de Odiseo Laertíada. Así que Eurímaco, hijo de Pólibo, comenzó a hablar ultrajando a Odiseo —y produjo risa a sus compañeros:

«Escuchadme, pretendientes de la famosa reina, mientras os digo lo que mi corazón me ordena dentro del pecho. Este hombre ha llegado a casa de Odiseo no sin la voluntad de los dioses, que me parece que la luz de las antorchas sale de su misma cabeza, pues no le queda ni un solo pelo.»

Así dijo, y luego se dirigió a Odiseo, destructor de ciudades:

«Forastero, ¿querrías servirme como jornalero, si te acepto, en el extremo del campo (y tu jornal será suficiente), para construir cercas y plantar elevados árboles? Te ofrecería comi-

---

[249] Al parecer, los ancianos y vagabundos solían ir en época arcaica a la fragua para calentarse. Igualmente había algún tipo de albergue público *(léschē)* para cobijarlos en las noches de invierno. Hesiodo confirma estas palabras de Homero cuando aconseja no ir «a la fragua ni al cálido albergue cuando el frío aparta a un hombre de la labor» *(Trabajos...,* 493). También sabemos que posteriormente había albergues públicos *(léschai)* en las ciudades dorias e incluso en Atenas.

da todo el año y te daría ropa y calzado para tus pies. Aunque ahora que has aprendido malas artes no querrás ponerte al trabajo, sino mendigar por el pueblo para alimentar tu insaciable estómago.»

Y le contestó diciendo el muy astuto Odiseo:

«Eurímaco, si tú y yo rivalizáramos en el trabajo durante el verano, cuando los días son largos, en la siega del heno y yo tuviera una bien curvada hoz y tú otra igual para ponernos al trabajo sin comer hasta el crepúsculo —y hubiera hierba—, o si hubiera dos bueyes que arrear, los mejores bueyes, rojizos y grandes, saciados ambos de heno, de igual edad y peso, nada endebles de fortaleza, y hubiera un campo de cuatro fanegas y cediera el terrón al arado..., entonces verías si soy capaz de tirar un surco bien derecho. 370

»Lo mismo digo si hoy mismo el Cronida moviera guerra en algún lado y tuviera yo escudo y un par de lanzas y un yelmo de bronce bien ajustado a mis sienes; ibas a verme enzarzado entre los primeros combatientes y no mentarías mi estómago para ultrajarme. Pero eres arrogante y tu corazón es duro. Te crees grande y poderoso porque frecuentas la compañía de gente pequeña y villana, pero si viniera Odiseo de vuelta a su tierra patria, pronto estas puertas, con ser sobremanera anchas, te iban a resultar estrechas cuando trataras de salir huyendo a través del pórtico.» 380

Así dijo, y Eurímaco se encolerizó más todavía, y mirándole torvamente le dirigió aladas palabras:

«Ah, desgraciado, pronto voy a producirte daño por lo que dices en presencia de tantos hombres sin sentir miedo en tu corazón. Seguro que el vino se ha apoderado de tus entrañas o quizá siempre es así tu juicio y dices sandeces. ¿Acaso estás fuera de ti por haber vencido a Iro, el vagabundo?» 390

Así diciendo, cogió el escabel, pero Odiseo fue a sentarse junto a las rodillas de Anfínomo de Duliquia por temor a Eurímaco, y éste alcanzó al escanciador en el brazo derecho. La jarra cayó al suelo con estrépito y el copero se desplomó boca arriba gritando.

Los pretendientes alborotaron en el sombrío palacio y uno decía así al que tenía cerca:

«¡Ojalá el forastero éste hubiera muerto en otra parte antes 400 de venir! Así no habría organizado tal alboroto. Ahora, en cambio, estamos peleándonos por culpa de unos mendigos y no habrá placer en el magnífico festín, pues está venciendo lo peor.»

Y la divina fuerza de Telémaco habló entre ellos:

«Desdichados, estáis enloquecidos y ya no podéis ocultar más tiempo los efectos de la comida y bebida. Sin duda os empuja un dios. Conque marchaos a casa a dormir ahora que os habéis banqueteado bien, cuando os lo ordene el ánimo, que yo no empujaré a nadie.»

Así dijo, y todos clavaron los dientes en sus labios y se admiraban de Telémaco porque había hablado audazmente. Entonces Anfínomo, ilustre hijo de Niso, el soberano hijo de Aretes, se levantó entre ellos y dijo: 410

«Amigos, que nadie se moleste por lo dicho tan justamente, tocándole con palabras contrarias. No maltratéis tampoco al forastero ni a ninguno de los esclavos del palacio del divino Odiseo. Conque, vamos, que el copero haga una primera libación, por orden, en las copas, para que una vez realizada marchemos a casa a dormir. En cuanto al forastero, dejémoslo en   420 el palacio de Odiseo al cuidado de Telémaco, ya que es a su casa donde ha llegado.»

Así dijo y a todos les agradó su palabra. El héroe Mulio, heraldo de Duliquio, mezcló vino en la crátera —era siervo de Anfínomo— y, puesto en pie, repartió vino a todos. Éstos libaron en honor de los dioses felices con delicioso vino y, cuando habían hecho la libación y bebido cuanto quiso su ánimo, se pusieron en camino, cada uno a su casa, para dormir.

Canto XIX

LA ESCLAVA EURICLEA RECONOCE A ODISEO

E N cambio, el divino Odiseo se quedó en el palacio ideando, con la ayuda de Atenea, la muerte contra los pretendientes, y de súbito dijo a Telémaco aladas palabras:

«Telémaco, es preciso que lleves adentro todas las armas y que, cuando los pretendientes las echen de menos y pregunten, los engañes con estas suaves palabras: "Las he retirado del fuego, pues ya no se parecen a las que dejó Odiseo cuando marchó a Troya, que están ennegrecidas hasta donde las ha alcanzado el aliento del fuego. Además, un demón ha puesto en mi 10 interior una razón más poderosa: no sea que os llenéis de vino y, levantando disputa entre vosotros, lleguéis a heriros unos a otros y a llenar de vergüenza el convite y vuestras pretensiones de matrimonio; que el hierro por sí solo arrastra al hombre"»[250].

Así dijo; Telémaco obedeció a su padre, y llamando a su no- 20 driza Euriclea le dijo:

«Tata, reténme a las mujeres dentro de las habitaciones del palacio mientras transporto a la despensa las magníficas armas de mi padre a las que el humo ennegrece, pues están descuidadas por la casa mientras mi padre está ausente; que yo era hasta hoy un niño pequeño, pero ahora quiero transportarlas para que no las llegue el aliento del fuego.»

Y le respondió su nodriza Euriclea:

---

[250] Cfr. XVI.285-94 y nota.

«Hijo, ¡ojalá hubieras adquirido ya prudencia para cuidarte de la casa y guardar todas tus posesiones! Pero ¿quién portará entonces la luz a tu lado?, pues no dejas salir a las esclavas, quienes podrían alumbrarte.»

Y Telémaco le contestó discretamente:

«El forastero, éste, pues no permitiré que esté ocioso el que toca mi vasija, aunque haya venido de lejos.»

Así dijo, y a ella se le quedaron sin alas las palabras. Así que cerró las puertas de las habitaciones, agradables para vivir.   30

Entonces se apresuraron Odiseo y su resplandeciente hijo a llevar adentro los cascos y los abollados escudos y las agudas lanzas, y por delante Palas Atenea hacía una luz hermosísima con una lámpara[251]. Y Telémaco dijo de pronto a su padre:

«Padre, es una gran maravilla esto que veo con mis ojos: las paredes del palacio y los hermosos intercolumnios y las vigas de abeto y las columnas que las soportan arriba se muestran a mis ojos como si fueran de fuego encendido. Seguro que algún dios de los que poseen el ancho cielo está dentro.»   40

Y le respondió y dijo el muy astuto Odiseo:

«Calla y reténlo en tu pensamiento, y no preguntes; ésta es la manera de obrar de los dioses que poseen el Olimpo. Pero acuéstate, que yo me quedaré aquí para provocar todavía más a las esclavas y a tu madre; ella me preguntará sobre cada cosa entre lamentos.»

Así dijo, y Telémaco, iluminado por las brillantes antorchas, se puso en camino a través del palacio hacia el dormitorio donde solía acostarse cuando le llegaba el dulce sueño. También entonces se acostó allí y aguardaba a Eos divina. En cambio el divino Odiseo se quedó en el mégaron ideando, con la ayuda de Atenea, la muerte contra los pretendientes.   50

Entonces salió de su dormitorio la prudente Penélope semejante a Artemis o a la dorada Afrodita. Le habían colocado

---

[251] Esta frase es repetición de vv. 1-3 y pone de manifiesto la técnica arcaica de la composición en anillo *(Ringkomposition)*, en virtud de la cual, dentro de una narración más amplia, se destaca una unidad cerrada por dos frases iguales o similares. Aquí es el plan de Matanza lo que queda destacado. Cfr. en este mismo canto los vv. 393-466 (herida de Odiseo) y en XXI.13-38 (historia del arco). Cfr. J. Gaisser, «A Structural analysis of the Digressions in the Iliad and the Odyssey», *Harvard Stud. in Class. Phil.*, 73, 1969, 1-43.

junto al hogar el sillón bien labrado con marfil y plata donde solía sentarse. Lo había fabricado en otro tiempo el artífice Icmalio y, unido a él, había puesto para los pies un escabel sobre el que se echaba una gran piel. Allí se sentó la discreta Penélope y llegaron del mégaron las esclavas de blancos brazos; retiraron el abundante pan y las mesas y copas donde bebían los arrogantes varones, y arrojaron al suelo el fuego de las parrillas amontonando sobre él mucha leña para que hubiera luz y para calentar. Entonces Melanto reprendió a Odiseo por segunda vez: 60

«Forastero, ¿es que incluso ahora, por la noche, vas a importunar dando vueltas por la casa y espiar a las mujeres? Vete afuera, desdichado, y contente con la comida, o vas a salir afuera enseguida, aunque sea alcanzado por un tizón.»

Y mirándola torvamente le dijo el muy astuto Odiseo: 70

«Desdichada, ¿por qué te diriges contra mí con ánimo irritado? ¿Acaso porque voy sucio y visto mi cuerpo con ropa miserable y pido limosna por el pueblo? La necesidad me empuja; así son los mendigos y los vagabundos. También yo en otro tiempo habitaba feliz mi próspera casa entre los hombres y muchas veces daba a un vagabundo, de cualquier ralea que fuese, cualquier cosa que precisara al llegar. Y eso que tenía innumerables esclavos y muchas otras cosas con las que la gente vive bien y se la llama rica. Pero Zeus Cronida me las arrebató, pues así lo quiso. Por esto, ¡cuidado, mujer!, no sea que algún día también tú pierdas toda la hermosura por la que ahora, desde luego, brillas entre las esclavas: no vaya a ser que tu señora se irrite y enfurezca contigo, o llegue Odiseo, pues aún hay una parte de esperanza. Y si éste ha perecido y no es posible que regrese, sin embargo ya tiene, por voluntad de Apolo[252], un hijo como Telémaco a quien ninguna de las mujeres del palacio le pasa inadvertida si es insensata, pues ya no es tan joven.» 80

---

[252] Las referencias a Apolo, tanto aquí como en XXI.269 y XXII.7, etc., no sugieren un cambio en el dios que protege a la familia de Odiseo ni implican dobletes estructurales en la composición de la obra. Atenea sigue siendo su máxima protectora, como se ve en los cantos XXIII y XXIV *passim*.

Así dijo: le escuchó la prudente Penélope y respondió a la esclava, le habló y la llamó por su nombre:

«¡Atrevida, perra desvergonzada!, no se me oculta que cometes una mala acción que pagarás con tu cabeza. Sabías —pues me lo has oído a mí misma— que iba a preguntar al forastero en mis habitaciones acerca de mi esposo, pues estoy afligida intensamente.»

Así dijo, y luego se dirigió a la despensera Eurínome:

«Eurínome, trae ya una silla y sobre ella una piel para que se siente y diga su palabra el forastero y escuche la mía. Quiero interrogarle.»

Así dijo; ésta llevó enseguida una pulimentada silla y sobre ella extendió una piel donde se sentó después el sufridor, el divino Odiseo. Y entre ellos comenzó a hablar la prudente Penélope:

«Forastero, esto es lo primero que quiero preguntarte: ¿quién de los hombres eres y de dónde? ¿Dónde están tu ciudad y tus padres?

Y le respondió y dijo el muy astuto Odiseo:

«Mujer, ninguno de los mortales sobre la inmensa tierra podría censurarte, pues en verdad tu gloria llega al ancho cielo como la de un irreprochable rey que, reinando con temor a los dioses sobre muchos y valerosos hombres, sustenta la justicia y produce la negra tierra trigo y cebada y se inclinan los árboles por el fruto, y las ovejas paren robustas y el mar proporciona peces por su buen gobierno, y el pueblo es próspero bajo su cetro[253]. Con todo, hazme cualquier otra pregunta en tu casa, pero no me preguntes por mi linaje y tierra patria, no sea que cargues más mi espíritu de penas con el recuerdo. En verdad soy muy desgraciado, pero no está bien sentarse en casa ajena a gemir y lamentarse —que es cosa mala sufrir siempre sin descanso—, no sea que alguna de las esclavas se enoje contra mí —o tú misma— y diga que derramo lágrimas por tener la mente pesada por el vino.»

---

[253] Este célebre pasaje está, como señala M. I. Finley (ob. cit., págs. 117-8), fuertemente moralizado y supone una relación entre justicia y fecundidad natural que está más en consonancia con el mundo de Hesíodo. Cfr. Hesíodo, *Trabajos*, 230 y ss., y Platón, *República*, 363b y ss., que, por cierto, lo refieren al hombre justo en general.

Y le respondió la prudente Penélope:

«Forastero, en verdad los inmortales destruyeron mis cualidades —figura y cuerpo— el día en que los argivos se embarcaron para Ilión y entre ellos estaba mi esposo, Odiseo. Si al menos volviera él y cuidara de mi vida, mayor sería mi gloria y yo más bella. Pero ahora estoy afligida, pues son tantos los males que la divinidad ha agitado contra mí; pues cuantos nobles dominan sobre las islas, en Duliquio y Same, y la boscosa Zante, y los que habitan en la misma Itaca, hermosa al atardecer, me pretenden contra mi voluntad y arruinan mi casa. Por esto no me cuido de los huéspedes ni de los suplicantes y tampoco de los heraldos, los ministros públicos, sino que en la nostalgia de Odiseo se consume mi corazón. Éstos tratan de apresurar la boda, pero yo tramo engaños. Un dios me inspiró al principio que me pusiera a tejer un velo, una tela sutil e inacabable, y entonces les dije: "Jóvenes pretendientes míos, puesto que ha muerto el divino Odiseo, aguardad mi boda hasta que acabe un velo —no sea que se me destruyan inútiles los hilos—, un sudario para el héroe Laertes, para cuando le alcance el destino fatal de la muerte de largos lamentos; no vaya a ser que alguna entre el pueblo de las aqueas se irrite contra mí si es enterrado sin sudario el que tanto poseyó." Así les dije, y su ánimo generoso se dejó persuadir. Entonces hilaba sin parar durante el día la gran tela y la deshacía durante la noche, poniendo antorchas a mi lado. Así engañé y persuadí a los aqueos durante tres años, pero cuando llegó el cuarto y se sucedieron las estaciones en el transcurrir de los meses —y pasaron muchos días—, por fin me sorprendieron por culpa de mis esclavas —¡perras, que no se cuidan de mí!— y me reprendieron con sus palabras. Así que tuve que terminar el velo y no voluntariamente, sino por la fuerza[254].

»Ahora no puedo evitar la boda ni encuentro ya otro ardid. Mis padres me impulsan a casarme y mi hijo se indigna cuando devoran nuestra riqueza, pues se da cuenta, que ya es un hombre muy capaz de guardar su casa y Zeus le da gloria. Pero, con todo, dime tu linaje y de dónde eres, pues seguro que no

130

140

150

160

---

[254] Este largo discurso de Penélope es un cosido de XVIII.251-6, I.245-8 y II.94-110.

has nacido de una encina de antigua historia ni de un peñasco.»

Y le respondió y dijo el muy astuto Odiseo:

«Venerable mujer de Odiseo Laertíada, ¿no vas a dejar de preguntarme sobre mi linaje? Te lo voy a contar aunque me vas a hacer un regalo de penas todavía más numerosas que las que me cercan —pues ésta es la costumbre cuando un hombre está ausente de su patria durante tanto tiempo como yo, errante por muchas ciudades de mortales soportando males, pero aun así te voy a contestar a lo que me preguntas e inquieres. Creta es una tierra en medio del ponto, rojo como el vino, hermosa y fértil, rodeada de mar. En ella hay numerosos hombres, innumerables, y noventa ciudades en las que se mezclan unas y otras lenguas. En ellas están los aqueos y los magnánimos eteocretenses, en ellas los cidones y los dorios divididos en tres tribus, y los divinos pelasgos[255]. Entre estas ciudades está Cnossós, una gran urbe donde reinó durante nueve años Minos, confidente del gran Zeus, padre de mi padre el magnánimo Deucalión. Éste nos engendró a mí y al soberano Idomeneo, quien, juntamente con los Atridas, marchó a Ilión en las corvas naves. Mi ilustre nombre es Etón y soy el más joven, que él es mayor y más valiente. Allí fue donde vi a Odiseo y le di los dones de hospitalidad, pues lo había llevado a Creta la fuerza del viento cuando se dirigía hacia Troya, después de apartarlo de las Maleas. Había atracado en Amniso[256], cerca de donde está la gruta de Ilitia[257], en un puerto difícil, escapando a duras penas a las tormentas. Enseguida subió a la ciudad y preguntó por Idomeneo, pues decía que era su huésped querido y respetado. Era la décima o la undécima aurora desde que había partido con sus cóncavas naves hacia Ilión. Yo lo llevé a

170

180

190

---

[255] Homero demuestra conocer con detalle la geografía de Creta (cfr. también III.292 y ss.). Lo que aquí afirma sobre los dorios es, naturalmente, un anacronismo y responde a la realidad contemporánea del poeta. De todos los pueblos que cita eran autóctonos los eteocretenses, los pelasgos y los cidones que, según Estrabón (10.4.6), habitaban al norte de la isla, en la actual Chania.

[256] Puerto de Cnossós en época minoica, junto a la desembocadura del río del mismo nombre. Se han hallado restos del culto a una diosa (luego Ilitia) desde el Neolítico hasta el siglo v d.C.

[257] Diosa que preside los nacimientos y ayuda a las parturientas. Es hija de Zeus y Hera y nació junto con Hebe y Ares, cfr. Hesiodo, *Teogonía*, 922.

palacio y le procuré digna hospitalidad; le honré gentilmente con la abundancia de cosas que había en la casa y tanto a él como a sus compañeros les di harina a expensas del pueblo[258] y rojo vino que reuní, y bueyes para sacrificar, a fin de que saciaran su apetito.

»Allí permanecieron doce días los divinos aqueos, pues soplaba Bóreas, el viento impetuoso, y no dejaba estar de pie sobre el suelo —algún funesto demón lo había levantado—, pero al decimotercero cayó el viento y se dieron a la mar.»

Amañaba muchas mentiras al hablar, semejantes a verdades, y mientras ellas le oía le corrían las lágrimas y se le consumía el cuerpo. Lo mismo que en las altas montañas se derrite la nieve a la que funde Euro después que Céfiro la hace caer —y cuando está fundida los ríos aumentan su curso—, así se fundían sus hermosas mejillas vertiendo lágrimas por su marido, que estaba a su lado.

Odiseo sentía piedad por su mujer cuando sollozaba, pero los ojos se le mantuvieron firmes como si fueran de cuerno o hierro, inmóviles en los párpados. Y ocultaba sus lágrimas con engaño. De nuevo le contestó con palabras y dijo:

«Forastero, ahora quiero probar si de verdad albergaste en tu palacio a mi esposo, como afirmas, junto con sus compañeros, semejantes a los dioses. Dime cómo eran los vestidos que cubrían su cuerpo y cómo era él mismo, y háblame de sus compañeros, los que le seguían.»

Y le respondió y dijo el muy astuto Odiseo:

«Mujer, es difícil decirlo después de tan larga separación, pues ya hace veinte años que marchó de allí y dejó mi patria, pero aun así te lo diré como mi corazón me lo pinta. El divino Odiseo tenía un manto purpúreo de lana, manto doble que sujetaba un broche de oro con agujeros dobles y estaba bordado por delante: un perro sujetaba entre las patas delanteras a un cervatillo moteado y lo miraba fijamente forcejear. Y esto es lo que asombraba a todos, que, siendo de oro, el uno miraba al cervatillo mientras lo ahogaba y el otro, deseando escapar, for-

200

210

220

230

---

[258] Los dones de hospitalidad a veces se presentan como prestaciones obligatorias por parte del pueblo, o la aristocracia, a la casa real, cfr. también XIII.13-5.

cejeara con los pies. También vi alrededor de su cuerpo una
túnica resplandeciente y como binza de cebolla seca; ¡tan suave
era y brillante como el sol! Muchas mujeres la contemplaban
con admiración. Pero te voy a decir una cosa que has de poner
en tu interior: no sé si Odiseo rodeaba su cuerpo con ellas ya
en casa o se las dio, al marchar sobre la veloz nave, alguno de
sus compañeros o tal vez incluso algún huésped (ya que Odiseo era amigo para muchos), pues pocos entre los aqueos eran   240
semejantes a él.

»También yo le di una broncínea espada y un manto doble,
hermoso, purpúreo, y una túnica orlada, y lo despedí respetuo-
samente sobre su nave de sólidos bancos. Le acompañaba un
heraldo un poco mayor que él, de quien también te voy a decir
cómo era exactamente: caído de hombros, negra la tez, rizado
el cabello y de nombre Euríbates. Odiseo le honraba por encima de sus otros compañeros porque le concebía pensamientos
ajustados.»

Así dijo, y a ella se le levantó aún más el deseo de llorar al
reconocer las señales que le había dicho Odiseo con exactitud.   250
Y luego que se hubo saciado del gemido de abundantes lágrimas, le respondió con palabras y dijo:

«Forastero, aunque ya antes eras digno de compasión, ahora
vas a ser querido y respetado en mi palacio, pues yo misma le
di esas vestiduras que dices —las traje dobladas de la despensa
y les puse un broche resplandeciente para que fuera un adorno
para él; pero ya no lo recibiré nunca de vuelta en casa, pues
con funesto destino marchó Odiseo en cóncava nave para ver
la maldita Ilión[259], que no hay que nombrar.»   260

Y la respondió y dijo el muy astuto Odiseo:

«Mujer venerada de Odiseo Laertíada, ya no desfigures más
tu hermoso cuerpo ni consumas tu espíritu lamentando a tu
esposo. Aunque en nada te he de reprender, pues cualquier
mujer se lamenta de haber perdido a su legítimo esposo con
quien ha engendrado hijos uniéndose en amor, aunque sea distinto de Odiseo, de quien dicen que era semejante a los dioses.
Pero deja de gemir y atiende a mi palabra, pues te voy a hablar

---

[259] Gr. *Kakoílion*. Este compuesto, de valor apotropaico, vuelve a aparecer
en 597 y XXIII.19 dentro de la misma fórmula.

sinceramente y no te voy a ocultar que ya he oído acerca del ²⁷⁰ regreso de Odiseo, que está cerca y vivo en el rico pueblo de los tesprotos. También trae muchos y maravillosos bienes que ha mendigado por el pueblo, pero ha perdido a sus leales compañeros y la cóncava nave en el ponto, rojo como el vino, cuando venía de la isla de Trinaquía, pues estaban airados contra él Zeus y Helios, porque sus compañeros había matado las vacas de éste. Así que todos ellos perecieron en el alborotado ponto, pero a él lo empujó el oleaje sobre la quilla de su nave hacia tierra firme, hacia la tierra de los feacios, que han nacido cercanos a los dioses. Éstos le honraron de corazón como a un ²⁸⁰ dios y le dieron muchas cosas, y querían llevarlo ellos mismos a su patria sano y salvo. Podría estar aquí Odiseo hace mucho tiempo, pero a su ánimo le pareció más ventajoso marchar por tierra para reunir mucha riqueza. Así es como sobresale Odiseo por su mucha astucia entre los mortales hombres y ningún otro mortal podría rivalizar con él. Así me lo decía Fidón, el rey de los tesprotos, y juró delante de mí mientras hacía libación en su casa, que había echado su nave al mar y estaban dispuestos los compañeros que iban a llevarlo a su tierra patria, ²⁹⁰ pero a mí me envió antes, pues marchaba casualmente una nave de Tesprotos a Duliquio, rica en trigo. Y me mostró cuantas riquezas había reunido Odiseo; podrían alimentar a otro hombre hasta la décima generación: ¡tantos tesoros tenía depositados en el palacio del rey! También me dijo que Odiseo había marchado a Dodona para escuchar la voluntad de Zeus, el que habla desde la divina encina de elevada copa, para enterarse si debía volver a las claras u ocultamente a su tierra patria, después de tantos años de ausencia[260]. Así pues, él está a ³⁰⁰ salvo y vendrá muy pronto, no permaneciendo ya largo tiempo lejos de los suyos y de su tierra patria.

»Sin embargo, te haré un juramento: sea testigo Zeus antes que nadie, el más excelso y poderoso de los dioses, y el Hogar del irreprochable Odiseo, al que he llegado, que todo esto se cumplirá como yo digo; durante este mismo año vendrá Odiseo, cuando se haya acabado este mes y comenzado el siguiente.»

---

[260] Repetición de XIV.323-30.

Y se dirigió a él la prudente Penélope:

«Forastero, ¡ojalá llegara a cumplirse esa palabra! Rápidamente conocerías mi amistad y muchos regalos de mi parte, 310 hasta el punto de que cualquiera que contigo topara te llamaría dichoso. Pero mis presentimientos son —y así sucederá precisamente— que ni Odiseo volverá ya a casa ni tú lograrás conseguir una escolta, puesto que no hay en la casa jefes como era Odiseo entre los hombres —si es que alguna vez existió—para dar escolta y recibir a sus venerables huéspedes. Vamos, siervas, lavadlo y ponedle un lecho, mantas y sábanas resplandecientes, y así, bien caliente, le llegue Eos de trono de oro. Al amanecer lavadle y ungidle y que se ocupe de comer sentado 320 en la sala junto a Telémaco. Será doloroso para aquel de los pretendientes que, por envidia, llegara a molestarlo. Ninguna otra acción llevará a cabo aquí dentro, aunque se irrite terriblemente. ¿Cómo podrías saber, forastero, que aventajo a las demás mujeres en inteligencia y consejo si comieras en el palacio sucio, vestido miserablemente? Los hombres son de corta vida; para quien es cruel y tiene sentimientos crueles piden todos los mortales tristezas en el futuro mientras viva, y una vez 330 que está muerto todos le insultan. En cambio, el que es irreprochable y tiene sentimientos irreprochables... la fama de éste la llevan sus huéspedes a todos los hombres. Y muchos lo llaman noble.»

Y le respondió y dijo el muy astuto Odiseo:

«Mujer venerable de Odiseo Laertíada, las mantas y las resplandecientes sábanas me disgustan desde el día en que dejé los nevados montes de Creta marchando sobre la nave de largos remos. Me voy a acostar como antes, cuando dormía noches 340 insomnes, pues ya he descansado muchas noches en lecho miserable aguardando a Eos, de hermoso trono. Tampoco son agradables a mi ánimo los baños de pies; ninguna mujer tocará mi pie de las que te son servidoras en el palacio, si no hay alguna muy anciana y de sentimientos fieles que haya soportado en su ánimo tantas cosas como yo. A ésa no la impediría tocar mis pies.»

Y se dirigió a él la prudente Penélope:

«Huésped, amigo, pues jamás ha llegado a mi casa ningún 350 hombre tan sensato de entre los huéspedes de lejanas tierras;

con qué sabiduría dices todo, con qué discreción. Tengo una anciana que alberga en su mente decisiones discretas, la que alimentó y crió a aquel desdichado recibiéndolo en sus brazos cuando lo parió su madre. Ésta te lavará los pies, aunque está muy débil. Conque, vamos, levántate enseguida, prudente Euriclea, y lava al compañero en edad de tu soberano. También estarán así los pies y manos de Odiseo, pues los mortales envejecen enseguida en medio de la desgracia.»

Así dijo; la anciana se ocultaba con las manos el rostro y derramaba calientes lágrimas, y dijo lastimera palabra:

«¡Ay, hijo mío, que no tenga yo remedios para ti...! Con tener el ánimo temeroso de los dioses, Zeus te ha odiado más que a los demás hombres, que jamás mortal alguno quemó tantos pingües muslos para Zeus, el que se alegra con el rayo, ni excelentes hecatombes como tú le has ofrecido con la súplica de poder llegar a una ancianidad feliz y poder alimentar a un hijo ilustre. En cambio sólo a ti te ha privado del brillante día del regreso. Tal vez se burlen también así de aquél las esclavas de hospedadores de lejanas tierras cuando llegue al magnífico palacio de alguno, como se burlan de ti todas estas perras a las que no permites que te laven para evitar el escarnio y numerosos oprobios. A mí, sin embargo, me lo ordena la hija de Icario, la prudente Penélope, aunque no contra mi voluntad. Por esto te lavaré los pies, por la propia Penélope y a la vez por ti mismo, pues se me conmueve dentro el ánimo con tus penas. Pero, vamos, atiende ahora a una palabra que te voy a decir: muchos forasteros infortunados han venido aquí, pero creo que jamás he visto a ninguno tan parecido a Odiseo en el cuerpo, voz y pies, como tú.»

Y le respondió y dijo el muy astuto Odiseo:

«Anciana, así dicen cuantos nos han visto con sus ojos, que somos parecidos el uno al otro, como tú misma dices dándote cuenta.»

Así dijo; la anciana tomó un caldero reluciente y le lavaba los pies; echó mucha agua fría y sobre ella derramó caliente. Entonces Odiseo se sentó junto al hogar y se volvió rápidamente hacia la oscuridad, pues sospechó enseguida que ésta, al cogerlo, podría reconocer la cicatriz y sus planes se harían manifiestos. La anciana se acercó a su soberano y lo lavaba. Y enseguida reconoció la cicatriz que en otro tiempo le hiciera un jabalí con su blanco colmillo cuando fue al Parnaso en compañía de Autólico[261] y sus hijos, el padre ilustre de su madre, que sobresalía entre los hombres por el hurto y el juramento. Se lo había concedido el dios Hermes, pues en su honor quemaba muslos de corderos y cabritos en agradecimiento y éste le asistía benévolo. Cuando Autólico fue a la opulenta población de Itaca, se encontró a un hijo recién nacido de su hija. Euriclea 400 lo puso sobre sus rodillas cuando había terminado de cenar y le habló y llamó por su nombre:

«Autólico busca tú mismo un nombre para el hijo de tu hija, pues muy deseado es para ti.»

Y a su vez respondió Autólico y dijo:

«Yerno e hija mía, ponedle el nombre que voy a decir. Ya que he llegado hasta aquí enfadado con muchos hombres y mujeres a través de la fértil tierra, que su nombre epónimo sea Odiseo[262]. Y cuando en la plenitud de la juventud llegue a la 410 gran casa materna, al Parnaso donde tengo las riquezas, yo le daré de ellas y lo despediré contento.»

Por esto había marchado Odiseo, para que le diera espléndidos regalos. Autólico y los hijos de Autólico le acogieron cariñosamente con las manos y con dulces palabras. Y la madre de su madre, Anfitea, abrazó a Odiseo y le besó la cabeza y hermosos ojos. Autólico ordenó a sus gloriosos hijos que dispusieran la comida y éstos escucharon al que se lo mandaba. Enseguida llevaron un toro de cinco años, lo desollaron, prepararon y dividieron todo; lo partieron habilidosamente, lo clavaron en asadores y después de asarlo cuidadosamente distribuyeron las partes. Así que comieron durante todo el día, hasta que se puso el sol, y nadie carecía de un bien distribuido alimento. Y cuando el sol se puso y cayó la noche, se acostaron y recibieron el don del sueño.

---

[261] Hijo de Hermes y padre de Anticlea, la madre de Odiseo. Según algunas versiones, fue el responsable de que ésta se uniera con Sísifo concibiendo a Odiseo. Poco más sabemos de él excepto lo que aquí se dice. Apolodoro *(Biblioteca.* 1.9.16) lo incluye en la nómina de los Argonautas, junto con su suegro Laertes. Sin embargo, Apolonio de Rodas no lo cita entre ellos.

[262] Nuevo juego de palabras que revela el gusto de Homero por la etimología. «Enfadarse» es en griego *odýssomai,* parecido fonéticamente a *Odysseus.*

Tan pronto como se mostró Eos, la hija de la mañana, la de dedos de rosa, salieron de cacería los perros y los mismos hijos de Autólico, y entre ellos iba el divino Odiseo. Ascendieron al 430 elevado monte Parnaso, vestido de selva, y enseguida llegaron a los ventosos valles. El sol caía sobre los campos cultivados recién salido de las plácidas y profundas corrientes de Océano, cuando llegaron los cazadores a un valle. Delante de ellos iban los perros buscando las huellas y detrás los hijos de Autólico, y entre ellos marchaba el divino Odiseo blandiendo, cerca de los perros, su lanza de larga sombra. Un enorme jabalí estaba tumbado en una densa espesura a la que no atravesaba el húmedo 440 soplo de los vientos al agitarse ni golpeaba con sus rayos el resplandeciente Helios ni penetraba la lluvia por completo —¡tan densa era!—[263], y una gran alfombra de hojas la cubría. Llegó al jabalí el ruido de los pies de hombres y perros cuando marchaban cazando y desde la espesura, erizada la crin y brillando fuego sus ojos, se detuvo frente a ellos. Odiseo fue el primero en acometerlo, levantando la lanza de larga sombra con su robusta mano deseando herirlo. El jabalí se le adelantó y le atacó sobre la rodilla y, lanzándose oblicuamente, desgarró con el colmillo mucha carne, pero no llegó al hueso del mor- 450 tal. En cambio Odiseo le hirió alcanzándole en la paletilla derecha y la punta de la resplandeciente lanza lo atravesó de parte a parte y cayó en el polvo dando chillidos, y escapó volando su ánimo. Enseguida le rodearon los hijos de Autólico, vendaron sabiamente la herida del irreprochable Odiseo semejante a un dios y con un conjuro retuvieron la negra sangre.

Pronto llegaron a casa de su padre y Autólico y los hijos de Autólico lo curaron bien, le dieron espléndidos regalos y, ale- 460 gres, lo enviaron contento a su patria Itaca.

Su padre y venerable madre se alegraron al verlo volver y le preguntaban detalladamente por la cicatriz, qué le había pasado. Y él les contó con detalle cómo mientras cazaba, le había herido un jabalí con su blanco colmillo al marchar al Parnaso con los hijos de Autólico.

La anciana tomó entre las palmas de sus manos esta cicatriz

---

[263] Es la misma descripción del matorral donde busca cobijo Odiseo cuando llega a Esqueria, cfr. V.478 y ss.

y la reconoció después de examinarla. Soltó el pie para que se le cayera y la pierna cayó en el caldero. Resonó el bronce, inclinóse él hacia atrás, hacia el lado opuesto, y el agua se derramó por el suelo. El gozo y el dolor invadieron al mismo tiempo el corazón de la anciana y sus dos ojos se llenaron de lágrimas, y su floreciente voz se le pegaba. Asió de la barba a Odiseo y dijo:

«Sin duda eres Odiseo, hijo mío: no te había reconocido antes de ahora, hasta tocar a todo mi señor.»

Así dijo e hizo señas a Penélope con los ojos queriendo indicar que su esposo estaba dentro. Pero ésta no pudo verla, aunque estaba enfrente, ni comprenderla, pues Atenea le había distraído la atención. Entonces Odiseo acercó sus manos, la asió de la garganta con la derecha y con la otra la atrajo hacia sí diciendo:

«Nodriza, ¿por qué quieres perderme? Tú misma me criaste sobre tus pechos. Ya he llegado a la tierra patria tras sufrir muchas penalidades, a los veinte años. Pero ya que te has dado cuenta y un dios lo ha puesto en tu interior, calla, no vaya a ser que se dé cuenta algún otro en el palacio; porque te voy a decir esto y ciertamente se va a cumplir: si con la ayuda de un dios hiciese sucumbir a los ilustres pretendientes, no te perdonaré ni a ti, con ser mi nodriza, cuando mate a las otras esclavas en mi palacio.»

Y le contestó la prudente Euriclea:

«Hijo mío, ¡qué palabra ha escapado del cerco de tus dientes! Sabes que mi ánimo es firme y no domable; me mantendré como una sólida piedra o como el hierro. Te voy a decir otra cosa que has de poner en tu interior: si por tu causa un dios hace sucumbir a los ilustres pretendientes, entonces te hablaré minuciosamenre respecto a las mujeres del palacio, quiénes te deshonran y quiénes son inocentes.»

Y le respondió y dijo el muy astuto Odiseo:

«Nodriza, ¿por qué me las vas a señalar tú? Yo mismo las observaré y conoceré a cada una, pero mantén en silencio tus palabras y confía en los dioses.»

Así dijo, y la anciana marchó a través del mégaron para traer agua de lavar los pies, pues la primera se había derramado toda. Y después que lo lavó y ungió con espeso aceite, de

470

480

490

500

nuevo arrastró Odiseo la silla cerca del fuego para calentarse, y ocultó la cicatriz con los andrajos.

Y la prudente Penélope comenzó a hablar entre ellos:

«Forastero, sólo esto te voy a preguntar, poco más, que va a ser pronto la hora de dormir para aquel de quien el sueño se apodere dulcemente, aun estando afligido. A mí me ha dado un dios una pena inmensa, pues durante el día, aunque me lamente y gima, me complace atender a mis labores y las de las esclavas en el palacio, pero luego que llega la noche y el sueño las invade a todas, yazco en el lecho mientras agudas angustias inquietan sin cesar mi agitado corazón. Como cuando la hija de Pandáreo, el amarillo Aedón, canta hermosamente recién entrada la primavera sobre el tupido follaje de los árboles —cambia a menudo de tono y vierte su voz de múltiples ecos llorando a su hijo Itilo, hijo del rey Zeto, a quien en otro tiempo mató con el bronce sin darse cuenta[264]—, así también mi ánimo vacila entre permanecer junto a mi hijo y guardar todo intacto, mis bienes y esclavas y la casa grande de elevada techumbre, por vergüenza al lecho conyugal y a las habladurías del pueblo, o seguir a aquel de los aqueos que sea el mejor y me pretenda en el palacio entregándome innumerables presentes de boda. Porque mientras mi hijo era todavía pequeño e irreflexivo no me permitía casarme y abandonar la casa de mi esposo, pero ahora que es mayor y ha llegado al límite de la edad juvenil, incluso desea que me marche del palacio, indignado por los bienes que le comen los aqueos.

»Conque, vamos, interprétame este sueño, escucha: veinte gansos comían en mi casa trigo remojado con agua y yo me alegraba contemplándolos, pero vino desde el monte una gran águila de corvo pico y a todos les rompió el cuello y los mató, y ellos quedaron esparcidos por el palacio, todos juntos, mientras el águila ascendía hacia el divino éter. Yo lloraba a gritos, aunque era un sueño, y se reunieron en torno a mí las aqueas de lindas trenzas, mientras me lamentaba quejumbrosamente

---

[264] Esta es la información más completa que tenemos sobre el mito de Aedón, el «ruiseñor». Hija de Pandáreo, mató a su propio hijo Itilo (o Itis, onomatopeya del gorgeo) por error, cuando, por envidiar la fecundidad de Níobe, quiso matar al hijo de ésta. Los dioses la convirtieron en ruiseñor.

de que el águila me hubiera matado a los gansos. Entonces volvió ésta y se posó sobre la parte superior del palacio y, llamando con voz humana, dijo: "Cobra ánimos, hija del muy celebrado Icario, que no es un sueño, sino visión real y feliz que habrá de cumplirse. Los gansos son los pretendientes y yo antes era el águila, pero ahora he regresado como esposo tuyo, yo que voy a dar a todos los pretendientes un destino ignominio- 550 so." Así dijo y luego me abandonó el dulce sueño. Cuando miré en derredor vi a los gansos en el palacio comiendo trigo junto a la gamella en el mismo sitio de costumbre.»

Y le contestó y dijo el muy astuto Odiseo:

«Mujer, no es posible en modo alguno interpretar el sueño dándole otra intención, después que el mismo Odiseo te ha manifestado cómo lo va a llevar a cabo. Clara parece la muerte para los pretendientes, para todos en verdad; ninguno escapará a la muerte y a las Keres.»

Y le contestó la prudente Penélope:

«Forastero, sin duda se producen sueños inescrutables y de 560 oscuro lenguaje y no todos se cumplen para los hombres. Porque dos son las puertas de los débiles sueños: una construida con cuerno, la otra con marfil. De éstos, unos llegan a través del bruñido marfil, los que engañan portando palabras irrealizables; otros llegan a través de la puerta de pulimentados cuernos, los que anuncian cosas verdaderas cuando llega a verlos uno de los mortales[265]. Y creo que a mí no me ha llegado de aquí el terrible sueño, por grato que fuera para mí y para mi hijo.

»Te voy a decir otra cosa que has de poner en tu interior: 570 esta aurora llegará infausta, pues me va a alejar de la casa de Odiseo. Voy a establecer un certamen, las hachas de combate que aquél colocaba en línea recta como si fueran escoras, doce en total. Él se colocaba muy lejos y hacía pasar el dardo una y otra vez a través de ellas[266]. Ahora voy a establecer este certa-

---

[265] Aquí hay otro juego etimológico. Los sueños que cruzan la puerta de marfil *(élephas)* son falsos *(elephaírontai)*; los que cruzan la de cuerno *(keráōn)* se cumplen *(kraínousi)*. R. Carpenter, (ob. cit., págs. 101 y ss.) ve aquí una segunda intención, porque, según él, en época de Homero el cuerno sustituía al marfil.

[266] Con esta descripción es difícil imaginar en qué consistía el certamen. Sin

men para los pretendientes y el que más fácilmente tienda el arco entre sus manos y haga pasar una flecha por todas las doce hachas, a ése seguiré inmediatamente dejando esta casa legítima, muy hermosa, llena de riquezas. Creo que algún día 580 me acordaré de ella incluso en sueños.»

Y le contestó y dijo el muy astuto Odiseo:

«Mujer venerable de Odiseo Laertíada, no difieras por más tiempo ese certamen en tu casa, pues el muy astuto Odiseo llegará antes de que ellos toquen ese pulido arco, tiendan la cuerda y atraviesen el hierro con la flecha.»

Y le dijo a su vez la prudente Penélope:

«Si quisieras deleitarme, forastero, sentado junto a mí en la sala, no se me vertería el sueño sobre los párpados, pero no es 590 posible que los hombres estén siempre sin dormir, que los inmortales han establecido una porción para cada uno de los mortales sobre la fértil tierra. Así que subiré al piso de arriba y me acostaré en el funesto lecho, siempre regado por mis lágrimas desde que Odiseo marchó a la maldita Ilión que no hay que nombrar. Allí me acostaré; tú acuéstate en esta estancia extendiendo algo por el suelo, o que te pongan una cama.»

Así diciendo, subió al resplandeciente piso superior; mas no 600 sola, que con ella marchaban también las otras esclavas.

Y cuando hubo subido al piso superior con las esclavas, se puso a llorar a Odiseo, su esposo, hasta que la de ojos brillantes le infundió sueño sobre los párpados, Atenea.

---

embargo, este pasaje se puede completar con XXI.120 y ss. y 419-23. Según la interpretación de F. H. Stubbings (*Companion...*, pág. 534), debe tratarse de hachas dobles (*pélekys*) sin mango: una hoja quedaría enterrada dejando al descubierto la otra y los agujeros (*steleié*) para el mango, y por ahí pasaría la flecha. Con esto concuerda la descripción de XXI.120 y ss. en que Telémaco coloca las hachas, y 419-23, donde vemos que Odiseo dispara *sentado* desde su *diphros*, que es, propiamente, una banqueta.

Canto XX

LA ÚLTIMA CENA DE LOS PRETENDIENTES

Entonces el divino Odiseo comenzó a acostarse en el vestíbulo; extendió la piel no curtida de un buey y sobre ella muchas pieles de ovejas que habían sacrificado los aqueos, y Eurínome echó sobre él un manto cuando se hubo acostado.

Y mientras Odiseo yacía allí desvelado, meditando males en su interior contra los pretendientes, salieron del palacio riendo y chanceando unas con otras las mujeres que solían acostarse con éstos. El ánimo de Odiseo se conmovía dentro del pecho y meditaba en su mente y en su corazón si se lanzaría detrás y causaría la muerte a cada una, o si todavía las iba a dejar unirse por última y postrera vez con los orgullosos pretendientes. Y su corazón le ladraba dentro. Como la perra que camina alrededor de sus tiernos cachorrillos ladra a un hombre y se lanza a luchar con él si no lo conoce, así también le ladraba dentro el corazón indignado por las malas acciones. Y se golpeó el pecho y reprendió a su corazón con estas razones:

«¡Aguanta, corazón!, que ya en otra ocasión tuviste que soportar algo más desvergonzado, el día en que el Cíclope de furia incontenible comía a mis valerosos compañeros. Tú lo soportaste hasta que, cuando creías morir, la astucia te sacó de la cueva.»

Así dijo increpando a su corazón y éste se mantuvo sufridor, pero él se revolvía aquí y allá. Como cuando un hombre revuelve sobre abundante fuego un vientre lleno de grasa y sangre[267], pues desea que se ase deprisa, así se revolvía él a uno y otro lado, meditando cómo pondría las manos sobre los desvergonzados pretendientes, siendo él solo contra muchos. Entonces Atenea bajó del cielo y se llegó a su lado —semejante en su cuerpo a una mujer— y colocándose sobre su cabeza le dijo esta palabra:

«¿Por qué estás desvelado todavía, desdichado, más que ningún mortal? Esta es tu casa y tu mujer está en ella y tu hijo es como cualquiera desearía que fuese su hijo.»

Y le respondió y dijo el muy astuto Odiseo:

«Sí, diosa, todo eso lo dices con razón, pero lo que medita mi espíritu dentro del pecho es cómo pondría mis manos sobre los desvergonzados pretendientes solo como estoy, mientras que ellos están siempre dentro en grupo. También medito esto dentro del pecho, lo más importante: si lograra matarlos por la voluntad de Zeus y de ti misma, ¿a dónde podría refugiarme? Esto es lo que te invito a considerar.»

Y a su vez le dijo la diosa de ojos brillantes, Atenea:

«Desdichado, cualquiera suele seguir el consejo de un compañero peor, aunque éste sea mortal y no conciba muchas ideas, pero yo soy una diosa, la que constantemente te protege en tus dificultades. Te voy a hablar claramente: aunque nos rodearan cincuenta compañías de hombres de voz articulada, deseosos de matar por causa de Ares, incluso a éstos podrías arrebatarles los bueyes y las pingües ovejas. Conque procura coger el sueño; es locura mantenerse en vela y vigilar durante toda la noche cuando ya vas a salir de tus desgracias.»

Así diciendo, le vertió sueño sobre los párpados y se volvió al Olimpo la divina entre las diosas.

Cuando ya comenzaba a vencerlo el sueño, el que desata las preocupaciones del espíritu y afloja los miembros, despertó su fiel esposa y rompió a llorar sentada en el blando lecho. Y luego que se hubo saciado de llorar la divina entre las mujeres, suplicó en primer lugar a Artemis:

«Artemis, diosa soberana hija de Zeus, ¡ojalá me quitaras la

---

[267] Una especie de morcilla. La comparación es vulgar y tomada del entorno inmediato del poeta como las demás, pero al menos es, en líneas generales, adecuada al *comparatum*, cosa que no sucede siempre.

vida ahora mismo arrojando a mi pecho una flecha, o que me arrebatara un huracán y me llevara sobre los brumosos caminos arrojándome en la desembocadura del refluente Océano —como cuando los huracanes se llevaron a las hijas de Pandáreo![268]. Los dioses aniquilaron a sus padres y ellas quedaron huérfanas en el palacio, pero la divina Afrodita las alimentó con queso y dulce miel y con delicioso vino; Hera les otorgó 70 una belleza y prudencia superior a todas las mujeres; la casta Artemis les concedió gran estatura, y Atenea les enseñó a realizar labores brillantes. Un día que Afrodita había subido al elevado Olimpo a fin de pedir para ellas el cumplimiento de un floreciente matrimonio a Zeus, que goza con el rayo (pues éste conoce todo, tanto la suerte como el infortunio de los mortales hombres), las Harpías arrebataron a las doncellas y se las entregaron a las odiosas Erinias para que fueran sus criadas. ¡Así me mataran los que poseen mansiones en el Olimpo, o me alcanzara con sus flechas Artemis, de lindas trenzas, para hundirme en la odiosa tierra y ver a Odiseo y no tener que satisfacer los designios de un hombre inferior a él! Que la desgracia es soportable cuando uno pasa los días llorando, acongojado en su corazón, si por la noche se apodera de él el sueño (pues éste hace olvidar lo bueno y lo malo cuando cubre los párpados), pero a mí la divinidad incluso me envía malos sueños, pues esta noche ha vuelto a dormir a mi lado un hombre igual a como era Odiseo cuando marchó con el ejército. Con que mi corazón se llenó de alegría, pues no creía que era un sueño, 90 sino realidad.»

Así dijo, y enseguida llegó Eos, de trono de oro. Mientras aquélla lloraba, escuchó su voz el divino Odiseo y, meditando después, se le hacía que ella ya le había reconocido y puesto a su cabecera. Así que recogió el manto y las pieles en que se había acostado y las puso sobre una silla dentro del mégaron, pero la piel de buey se la llevó afuera. Y suplicó a Zeus, levantando sus manos:

---

[268] Sobre las hijas de Pándaro, la tradición mitográfica no se pone de acuerdo en lo que se refiere a número y nombres. En todo caso, una de ellas debe ser Aedón (cfr. XIX.518 y ss.). La muerte de los padres se debe a un castigo de Zeus por haber robado un mágico perro de oro que custodiaba el templo del dios en Creta.

«Zeus padre, si por vuestra voluntad me habéis traído a mi patria sobre lo seco y lo húmedo, después de llenarme de males en exceso, que cualquiera de los hombres que se despiertan dentro muestre un presagio, y que fuera se muestre otro prodigio de Zeus.»

Así dijo suplicando y le escuchó Zeus, el que ve a lo ancho. Al punto tronó desde el resplandeciente Olimpo, desde lo alto de las nubes, y se alegró el divino Odiseo. El presagio lo envió una molinera desde la casa, cerca de donde el pastor de su pueblo tenía las muelas en las que se afanaban doce mujeres en total, fabricando harina de cebada y trigo, médula de los hombres. Las demás mujeres dormían ya, una vez que hubieron molido su trigo, pero ésta, que era la más débil, todavía no había terminado. Entonces se puso en pie y dijo su palabra, señal para su amo:

«Zeus padre, que reinas sobre dioses y hombres, has tronado fuertemente desde el cielo estrellado —y en ninguna parte hay nubes—. Como señal, sin duda, se lo muestras a alguien. Cúmpleme ahora también a mí, desdichada, la palabra que voy a decirte: que los pretendientes tomen su agradable comida hoy por última y postrera vez en el palacio de Odiseo. Ellos son quienes con el cansado trabajo han hecho flaquear mis rodillas mientras fabricaba harina; que cenen ahora por última vez.»

Así dijo, y se alegró con el presagio[269] el divino Odiseo y con el trueno de Zeus, pues pensaba que castigaría a los culpables.

Entonces se congregaron las esclavas en el hermoso palacio de Odiseo y encendían en el hogar el infatigable fuego. Telémaco se levantó del lecho, mortal igual a un dios, después de vestir sus vestidos, se echó a los hombros la aguda espada, ató a sus relucientes pies hermosas sandalias y, asiendo la fuerte lanza de punta de bronce, se puso sobre el umbral y dijo a Euriclea:

«Tata, ¿habéis honrado al huésped con lecho y comida, o yace descuidado?; pues así es mi madre, aun siendo prudente: honra inconsideradamente al peor de los hombres de voz articulada y, en cambio, al mejor lo despide sin haberlo honrado.»

---

[269] Se trata de nuevo, como en XVIII.117, de una frase dicha al azar.

[338]

Y a su vez le dijo la prudente Euriclea:

«Hijo, no vayas ahora a culpar a la inocente, pues mientras él quiso bebió vino y de comida aseguró que ya no le apetecía más, que ella se lo preguntaba. Cuando, finalmente, se acordó del lecho y del sueño, tu madre ordenó a las esclavas preparárselo, pero él no quiso dormir en lecho y colchas, sino en el vestíbulo sobre una piel no curtida de buey y pieles de ovejas, como alguien completamente mísero y desventurado. Y nosotras le cubrimos con un manto.» 140

Así dijo; Telémaco salió del mégaron sosteniendo la lanza —a su lado marchaban dos veloces lebreles[270]—, y echó a caminar hacia el ágora junto a los aqueos de hermosas grebas.

Entonces la divina entre las mujeres, Euriclea, hija de Ope Pisenórida, comenzó a dar órdenes a las mujeres:

«Vamos, unas barred diligentes y regad el palacio, y colocad en las labradas sillas tapetes purpúreos; otras fregad con esponjas todas las mesas y limpiad las cráteras y las labradas copas de doble asa; y otras marchad por agua a la fuente y volved enseguida con ella, pues los pretendientes no estarán mucho tiempo lejos del palacio, sino que volverán temprano, que hoy es para todos día de fiesta»[271]. 150

Así dijo, y ellas la escucharon y obedecieron. Unas veinte marcharon hacia la fuente de aguas profundas y otras trabajaban habilidosamente allí mismo, en la casa.

En esto entraron los nobles sirvientes, quienes luego cortaron leña bien y con habilidad. Las mujeres volvieron de la fuente y detrás llegó el porquero conduciendo tres cerdos —los mejores entre todos—; los dejó paciendo en el hermoso cercado y se dirigió a Odiseo con dulces palabras: 160

«Forastero, ¿te ven mejor los aqueos ahora, o te siguen ultrajando en el palacio, como antes?»

Y le respondió y dijo el muy astuto Odiseo:

«¡Ojalá, Eumeo, castigaran ya los dioses el ultraje que éstos

---

[270] Es el acompañamiento habitual de Telémaco, pero sólo cuando se dirige al ágora. Cfr. también II.11 y XVII.62.

[271] Es la fiesta de Apolo a la que se alude más abajo (v. 276) y luego en XXI.258. Pero probablemente también tiene doble sentido. Es un rasgo de ironía trágica.

infieren con insolencia ejecutando acciones inicuas en casa extraña y sin tener ni parte de vergüenza!»

Esto es lo que se decían uno a otro cuando se les acercó
Melantio, el cabrero, conduciendo junto con dos pastores las
cabras que sobresalían entre todo el rebaño para festín de los
pretendientes; las ató bajo el sonoro pórtico y se dirigió a Odiseo con mordaces palabras:

«Forastero, ¿vas a seguir importunando en el palacio pidiendo limosna a los hombres?; ¿es que no vas a salir fuera? Creo
que no nos vamos a separar sin que pruebes mis brazos, pues
tú no pides como se debe. También hay otros convites entre
los aqueos.»

Así dijo, pero a éste no le contestó el muy astuto Odiseo,
sino que movió la cabeza en silencio, meditando males. Después de éstos llegó tercero Filetio el caudillo de hombres, llevando una vaca no paridera y pingües cabras para los pretendientes (los habían pasado los barqueros, quienes también
transportan a los demás hombres, a cualquiera que les llegue):
las ató bajo el sonoro pórtico e interrogaba al porquero poniéndose a su lado:

«Porquero, ¿quién es este forastero recién llegado a nuestra
casa?, ¿de qué hombres se precia de ser?, ¿dónde están su familia y su tierra patria? ¡Infeliz!, desde luego parece por su cuerpo
un rey soberano. En verdad los dioses abruman con desgracia
a los hombres que vagan mucho, cuando incluso a los reyes
otorgan infortunio.»

Así dijo y poniéndose a su lado le saludó con la diestra y,
hablándole, dijo aladas palabras:

«Bienvenido, padre huésped, ¡ojalá tengas felicidad en el futuro, que lo que es ahora estás sujeto por numerosos males!
Padre Zeus, ningún otro de los dioses es más cruel que tú; una
vez que creas a los hombres no te compadeces de que caigan
en el infortunio y los tristes dolores. ¡Cosa singular!, según te
vi los ojos me lloraban, pues me acordé de Odiseo; que también aquél, creo yo, vaga entre los hombres con tales andrajos,
si es que de alguna manera vive aún y ve la luz del sol. Porque
si ya está muerto y en las mansiones de Hades... ¡ay de mí,
irreprochable Odiseo, el que me puso al frente de las vacas,
siendo niño aún en el país de los cefalenios! Ahora éstas son

innumerables; de ninguna manera le podría crecer más a un hombre la raza de vacunos de anchas frentes. Pero otros me ordenan traerlas para comérselas ellos y no se cuidan de su hijo en el palacio ni temen la venganza de los dioses, pues desean ya repartirse las posesiones del señor, largo tiempo ausente. Y mi corazón revuelve esto dentro del pecho: es cosa mala marchar mientras vive su hijo al pueblo de otros, emigrando con estas vacas hacia hombres de un país extraño, pero todavía lo es más quedarme aquí guardando las vacas para otros y soportar tristezas. Hace tiempo me habría marchado huyendo junto a otros reyes poderosos, pues esto ya es insoportable, pero aún espero que ese desdichado vuelva de algún sitio y haga dispersarse a los pretendientes en el palacio.»

Y le respondió y dijo el muy astuto Odiseo:

«Boyero, puesto que no pareces cobarde ni insensato —sé bien que la prudencia te ha llegado a la mente—, te diré y juraré un gran juramento: ¡sea testigo Zeus antes que los demás dioses y la hospitalaria mesa y el Hogar de Odiseo al que he llegado!; mientras estés tú mismo aquí dentro, vendrá a casa Odiseo y con tus ojos podrás ver muertos, si quieres, a los pretendientes que aquí mandan.»

Y el boyero le dijo:

«Forastero, ¡ojalá el Cronida cumpliera de verdad esta tu palabra! Conocerías entonces cuál es mi fuerza y qué brazos me acompañan.»

También Eumeo suplicaba a todos los dioses que el prudente Odiseo volviera a casa. Y esto es lo que se decían uno al otro.

Entre tanto los pretendientes preparaban la muerte contra Telémaco[272]. Se les acercó por el lado izquierdo un pájaro, el águila que vuela alto, reteniendo a una temblorosa paloma, y Anfínomo comenzó a hablar entre ellos y dijo:

«Amigos, no nos saldrá bien la decisión de dar muerte a Telémaco, conque pensemos en la comida.»

220

230

240

---

[272] Resulta extemporáneo introducir aquí de repente una nueva propuesta de matar a Telémaco. Después de la emboscada fallida en el islote de Asteris (cfr. IV.844 y ss.), Antínoo propone en XVI.363 y ss. acabar con Telémaco, pero Anfínomo se opone dando largas. Esta nueva propuesta es un doblete desangelado de aquélla y parece introducida para insertar un nuevo presagio.

Así dijo Anfínomo y a ellos les agradó su palabra. Entraron en el palacio del divino Odiseo, pusieron sus mantos sobre sillas y sillones y comenzaron a sacrificar grandes ovejas y pingües cabras, así como gordos cerdos y una vaca del rebaño. 250 Luego asaron las entrañas, las repartieron, mezclaron el vino en las cráteras y el porquero distribuía las copas; Filetio, caudillo de hombres, les distribuía el pan en hermosos canastos y Melantio vertía el vino. Y ellos echaron mano de los alimentos que tenían delante.

Telémaco, pensando astutamente, hizo sentar a Odiseo dentro del bien construido palacio, junto al umbral de piedra, le puso una pobre silla y una mesa pequeña y le colocaba parte de las asaduras y le vertía vino en copa de oro. Y le dijo estas pa- 260 labras:

«Siéntate aquí con los hombres y bebe vino; yo mismo te libraré de las injurias y de las manos de todos los pretendientes, pues esta casa no es del pueblo[273], sino de Odiseo, y la adquirió para mí. En cuanto a vosotros, pretendientes, contened vuestras manos para que nadie suscite disputa ni altercado.»

Así habló; todos ellos clavaron los dientes en sus labios y admiraban a Telémaco, porque había hablado audazmente. Y entre ellos habló Antínoo, hijo de Eupites: 270

«Por más dura que sea, aceptemos, aqueos, la palabra de Telémaco quien mucho nos ha amenazado. No lo quiso Zeus Cronida, si no ya le habríamos parado los pies en el palacio, aunque sea sonoro hablador.»

Así dijo Antínoo, pero Telémaco no hizo caso de sus palabras.

Los heraldos iban conduciendo a través de la ciudad la sagrada hecatombe de los dioses, mientras los melenudos aqueos se congregaban bajo el sombrío bosque de Apolo, el que hiere de lejos. Y después que hubieron asado la carne de las partes externas, las retiraron, repartieron y celebraban un gran ban- 280 quete. Y los que servían pusieron junto a Odiseo una porción igual a las que había tocado en suerte a ellos; así lo había ordenado Telémaco, el hijo del divino Odiseo.

---

[273] Esto confirma la existencia de los albergues públicos que aparecían citados en XVIII.328 y ss.

Y Atenea no dejaba que los arrogantes pretendientes contuvieran del todo los escarnios que laceran el corazón, para que el dolor se hundiera todavía más en el ánimo de Odiseo Laertíada. Había entre los pretendientes un hombre de pensamientos impíos. Ctesipo era su nombre y en Same habitaba su casa. Éste pretendía a la esposa de Odiseo, largo tiempo ausente, 290 confiado en sus muchas posesiones. Y decía entonces a los soberbios pretendientes:

«Escuchadme, ilustres pretendientes, lo que voy a deciros. El forastero tiene una parte igual, como es razonable, pues no es decoroso ni justo privar del festín a los huéspedes de Telémaco, cualquiera que llegue a este palacio. Pero también yo voy a darle un regalo de hospitalidad para que él mismo se lo entregue al bañero o a otro de los esclavos que habitan el palacio del divino Odiseo.»

Así diciendo, cogió de una bandeja una pata de buey y se la arrojó con robusta mano. Odiseo inclinó la cabeza ligeramen- 300 te, la esquivó y sonrió en su ánimo con sonrisa sardónica[274]. La pata dio en el bien construido muro y Telémaco reprendió a Ctesipo con su palabra:

«Ctesipo, lo mejor para tu vida ha sido no alcanzar al forastero, pues él ha evitado el golpe; en caso contrario, yo te habría alcanzado de lleno con la aguda lanza, y en vez de boda, tu padre se habría cuidado de tu funeral. Por esto, que ninguno muestre sus insolencias en mi casa, pues ya comprendo y sé cada cosa, las buenas y las malas. Hace poco aún era niño y to- 310 leraba, aun viéndolo, el degüello de ovejas así como el vino que se bebía y la comida, pues es difícil que uno solo contenga a muchos. Conque, vamos, no me causéis ya más daños como si fuerais enemigos, aunque si me queréis matar con el bronce, sería mejor morir que ver continuamente estas obras inicuas: a los huéspedes maltratados y a las esclavas indignamente forzadas en mi hermoso palacio.»

---

[274] Gr. *sardánion*, sonrisa entre amarga y desdeñosa. La palabra está quizá relacionada con *saírō*, que significa «sonreír» o simplemente «separar los labios y enseñar los dientes». Posteriormente fue relacionada con una planta de Cerdeña (*Sardó*), cuya deglución producía tal efecto, la *Ranunculus Sardous*, con lo que el adjetivo cambió a *sardónion* y ha pasado a todas las lenguas cultas con el mismo sentido que tiene en este pasaje.

Así dijo y todos ellos enmudecieron en el silencio. Y más 320
tarde dijo Agelao Damastórida:

«Amigos, ninguno vaya a irritarse contestando con razones
contrarias a lo dicho con justicia. No maltratéis al forastero ni
a ningún otro de los esclavos que hay en la casa de Odiseo,
aunque yo diría una palabra dulce a Telémaco y a su madre, si
ésta fuera agradable a su corazón: mientras vuestro ánimo
confiaba en que regresaría a casa el prudente Odiseo, no os in-
dignabais porque permanecieran los pretendientes ni por rete- 330
nerlos en la casa; incluso habría sido lo mejor si Odiseo hubiese regresado a casa. Pero ya es evidente que no ha de volver de
ningún modo; conque, vamos, siéntate junto a tu madre y dile
que case con quien sea el mejor y le entregue más cosas, para
que tú sigas poseyendo con alegría todo lo de tu padre, comiendo y bebiendo, y ella cuide la casa de otro.»

Y le contestó Telémaco discretamente:

«¡No, por Zeus, Agelao, y por las triztezas de mi padre
quien puede que haya muerto o ande errante lejos de Itaca! De 340
ninguna manera trato de retrasar el casamiento de mi madre;
por el contrario, la exhorto a casarse con el que quiera e incluso le doy regalos innumerables. Pero me avergüenzo de arrojarla del palacio contra su voluntad, con palabra forzosa. ¡No
permita la divinidad que esto suceda!»

Así dijo Telémaco, y Palas Atenea levantó una risa inextinguible entre los pretendientes y les trastornó la razón. Reían
con mandíbulas ajenas y comían carne sanguinolenta; sus ojos
se llenaban de lágrimas y su ánimo presagiaba el llanto. En- 350
tonces les habló Teoclímeno, semejante a un dios[275]:

«¡Ah, desdichados!, ¿qué mal es éste que padecéis? En noche
están envueltas vuestras cabezas y rostros y de vuestras rodillas abajo. Se enciende el gemido y vuestras mejillas están llenas de lágrimas. Con sangre están rociados los muros y los
hermosos intercolumnios y de fantasmas lleno el vestíbulo y
lleno está el patio de los que marchan a Erebo bajo la oscuri-

---

[275] Esta es la tercera intervención, inesperada y extraña como siempre, de
Teoclímeno; inesperada, porque no se había mencionado su presencia en el
banquete; extraña, porque habla no como un *mantis,* sino como un vidente
—cosa completamente ajena a Homero.

dad. El sol ha desaparecido del cielo y se ha extendido funesta niebla.»

Así dijo, y todos se rieron de él dulcemente. Y Eurímaco, hijo de Pólibo, comenzó a hablar entre ellos:

«Está loco el forastero recién llegado de tierra extraña. Vamos, jóvenes, llevadlo rápidamente fuera de la casa; que marche al ágora, ya que piensa que aquí es de noche.»

Y le contestó Teoclímeno, semejante a un dios:

«Eurímaco, no te he pedido que me des acompañamiento, que tengo ojos, oídos y ambos pies y una razón bien construida en mi pecho, en absoluto incongruente. Con éstos me voy afuera, pues veo claro que la destrucción se os acerca, de la que no va a poder huir ninguno de los pretendientes, los que en la casa de Odiseo, semejante a un dios, insultáis a los hombres y ejecutáis acciones inicuas.»

Así diciendo salió del palacio, agradable vivienda, y marchó a casa de Pireo, quien lo recibió benévolo. Y los pretendientes se miraban unos a otros e irritaban a Telémaco, burlándose de sus huéspedes. Así decía uno de los arrogantes jóvenes:

«Telémaco, nadie es más desafortunado con los huéspedes que tú. Tienes uno como ese mendigo vagabundo necesitado de comida y vino, en absoluto conocedor de hazañas ni de vigor, sino un peso muerto de la tierra, y ese otro que se levantó a vaticinar; si me hicieras caso, lo mejor sería que metiéramos a los forasteros en una nave de muchos bancos y los enviáramos a Sicilia, donde te darían un precio conveniente.»

Así dijeron los pretendientes, pero Telémaco no hacía caso de sus palabras, sino que miraba a su padre en silencio, aguardando siempre cuándo pondría las manos sobre los desvergonzados pretendientes.

Y la hermosa hija de Icario, la prudente Penélope, poniendo su sillón enfrente escuchaba las palabras de cada uno de los hombres en el palacio. Así es como se prepararon, entre risas, un almuerzo dulce y agradable, pues habían sacrificado en abundancia. Pero ninguna otra cena podría ser más desgraciada como la que iban a prepararles más tarde la diosa y el fuerte hombre, pues ellos fueron los primeros en ejecutar acciones indignas.

Canto XXI

EL CERTAMEN DEL ARCO

ENTONCES Atenea, la diosa de ojos brillantes, inspiró en la mente de la hija de Icario, la prudente Penélope, que dispusiera el arco y el ceniciento hierro en el palacio de Odiseo para los pretendientes, como competición y para comienzo de la matanza. Subió a la alta escalera de su casa y tomando en su vigorosa[276] mano una bien curvada llave, hermosa, de bronce y con mango de marfil, echó a andar con sus esclavas hacia la última habitación donde se hallaban los objetos preciosos del señor —bronce, oro y labrado hierro. Allí estaba también el flexible arco y el carcaj de las flechas con muchos y dolorosos dardos que le había dado como regalo un huésped, Ifito Eurítida, semejante a los inmortales, cuando lo encontró en Lacedemonia. Se encontraron los dos en Mesenia, en casa del prudente Ortíloco. Odiseo había ido por una deuda que le debía todo el pueblo: en efecto, unos mesenios se le habían llevado de Itaca trescientas ovejas, con sus pastores, en naves de muchos bancos. A causa de éstas, Odiseo caminó mucho camino seguido, aunque era joven, pues le habían mandado su padre y otros ancianos. Ifito, por su parte, buscaba unos animales que le habían desaparecido, doce yeguas y mulos pacientes en el trabajo. Éstas serían después muerte y destrucción para él, cuando llegó junto al hijo de Zeus de ánimo esforzado, junto al mortal Heracles concebidor de grandes empresas, quien,

---

[276] Es un epíteto fijo, más adecuado a la mano de un guerrero que a la de una reina.

aun siendo su huésped, lo mató en su casa. ¡Desdichado!, no temió la venganza de los dioses ni respetó la mesa que le había puesto; y, después de matarlo, retuvo a las yeguas de fuertes 30 pezuñas en el palacio. Cuando buscaba a éstas, se encontró con Odiseo y le dio el arco que usaba el gran Eurito y que había legado a su hijo al morir en su elevado palacio.

Odiseo, por su parte, le entregó aguda espada y fuerte lanza como inicio de una afectuosa amistad, pero no llegaron a sentarse uno a la mesa del otro, pues antes el hijo de Zeus mató a Ifito Eurítida, semejante a los inmortales, quien había dado el arco a Odiseo[277]. Éste lo llevaba en su patria, pero no lo tomó 40 al marchar al combate sobre las negras naves, sino que estaba en el palacio como recuerdo de su huésped.

Cuando hubo llegado a la habitación la divina entre las mujeres y puso el pie sobre el umbral de roble (en otro tiempo lo había pulido sabiamente el artífice, había enderezado con la plomada y levantado las jambas colocando sobre ella las resplandecientes puertas) desató la correa del tirador, introdujo la llave apuntando de frente y corrió los cerrojos de las puertas. Éstas resonaron como el toro que pace en la pradera[278] —¡tanto resonó la hermosa puerta empujada por la llave!— y 50 se le abrieron inmediatamente. Luego ascendió a la hermosa tarima donde estaban las arcas en que yacían los perfumados vestidos. Extendió el brazo, tomó del clavo el arco con su misma funda, el cual resplandecía, y sentada con él sobre sus rodi-

---

[277] Las digresiones (generalmente en composición anular, cfr. nota 251) son características de Homero cuando trata de explicar un objeto o un hecho relevante (cfr. cetro de Agamenón en *Ilíada*, II.101 y ss., o armas de Aquiles en *íd.*, XVIII.468 y ss., etc.). Aquí se trata del arco con el que Odiseo mata a los pretendientes. La historia que cuenta es incompleta como siempre, aunque su audiencia conocía los detalles. En todo caso, se enmarca en el ciclo de Heracles: Eurito murió por obra de Apolo al desafiarlo con su arco (cfr. VIII.224-5). Éste pasó a manos de su hijo Ifito, quien a su vez se lo regaló a Odiseo. Lateralmente se alude a la muerte de Ifito a manos de Heracles (que le había robado ganado) a pesar de estar hospedado en su casa. No sabemos por qué lo mató, aunque los mitógrafos aducen que no había sido él el ladrón o que cayó en un acceso de locura. Sea como fuere, Heracles aparece de nuevo como un varón esforzado, pero mortal y lleno de *hybris*.
[278] Nueva comparación poco afortunada.

llas, rompió a llorar ruidosamente sin soltar el arco del rey. Luego que se hubo saciado del gemido de muchas lágrimas, echó a andar hacia el mégaron en busca de los ilustres pretendientes con el flexible arco entre sus manos y la aljaba portadora de dardos con muchas y dolorosas saetas; y junto a ella 60 las siervas llevaban un arcón en que había mucho hierro y bronce, ¡los trofeos de un soberano como él!

Cuando llegó a los pretendientes, se detuvo junto a una columna del techo, sólidamente construido, sosteniendo un grueso velo ante sus mejillas; y a uno y a otro lado de ella estaba en pie una fiel doncella.

Al punto se dirigió a los pretendientes y dijo:

«Escuchadme, ilustres pretendientes que hacéis uso de esta casa para comer y beber sin cesar un instante, la de un hombre que lleva ausente largo tiempo. Ningún otro pretexto podéis 70 poner sino que estáis deseosos de casaros conmigo y tomarme por mujer. Conque, vamos, pretendientes, esto es lo que se os muestra como certamen: colocaré el gran arco del divino Odiseo y aquel que lo tense más fácilmente y haga pasar el dardo por las doce hachas, a éste seguiré inmediatamente abandonando esta casa querida, muy hermosa, llena de riqueza, de la que un día, creo, me acordaré incluso en sueños.»

Así dijo y ordenó a Eumeo, el divino porquero, que ofrecie- 80 ra a los pretendientes el arco y el ceniciento hierro. Eumeo lo recibió llorando y lo puso en tierra; y al otro lado lloraba el boyero cuando vio el arco del soberano. Y Antínoo les increpó, les habló y llamó por su nombre:

«Necios campesinos, que sólo pensáis en las cosas del día; cobardes, ¿por qué derramáis lágrimas y conmovéis el ánimo de esta mujer? Dolorido está ya por otras razones, desde que perdió a su esposo. Conque, vamos, sentaos a comer en silencio o marchaos afuera a llorar y dejad ahí mismo el arco, certa- 90 men inofensivo para los pretendientes. No creo que se tense fácilmente este bien pulido arco, pues no hay entre todos éstos un hombre como era Odiseo. Le vi —me acuerdo— siendo yo niño pequeño.»

Así dijo, y es que en su interior esperaba tensar el arco y hacer pasar la flecha por el hierro. Pero en verdad el irreprochable Odiseo, a quien entonces deshonraba en el palacio —e in-

citaba a sus compañeros—, iba a darle a probar, antes que a 100
nadie, el dardo despedido de sus manos.

Y entre ellos habló la sagrada fuerza de Telémaco:

«No, no me ha hecho muy prudente Zeus, el hijo de Crono;
mi madre, prudente como es, me dice que va a seguir a otro
dejando esta casa y yo me río y alegro con ánimo insensato.
Conque apresuraos, pretendientes, que esta competición os la
pone una mujer cual no hay ya en la tierra aquea ni en la sagrada Pilos ni en Argos ni en Micenas ni en la misma Itaca ni en
el oscuro continente. Pero también vosotros lo sabéis, ¿qué 110
necesidad tengo de alabar a mi madre? Así que, vamos, no lo
retraséis con pretextos ni esperéis más tiempo a tender el arco
para que os veamos. También yo probaré este arco y, si logro
tenderlo y traspasar el hierro con la flecha, no dejaría, para dolor mío, esta casa mi venerable madre por seguir a otro, ni me
quedaría yo atrás cuando soy capaz de llevarme el hermoso
trofeo de mi padre.»

Así dijo, y quitándose el manto purpúreo de los hombros, se
puso en pie y descolgó de su hombro la aguda espada. En primer lugar colocó las hachas abriendo para todas un largo sur- 120
co, las alineó a cuerda y puso tierra alrededor.

El asombro se apoderó de todos los que veían cuán ordenadamente las había colocado —nunca antes lo habían visto. Entonces fue a ponerse sobre el umbral y probar el arco. Tres veces lo movió deseando tenderlo y tres veces desistió de su ímpetu esperando en su interior tender la cuerda y atravesar el
hierro con una flecha. Y quizá lo habría tendido, tirando con
fuerza por cuarta vez, pero Odiseo le hizo señas de que no,
aunque mucho lo deseaba. Y habló de nuevo entre ellos la sagrada fuerza de Telémaco: 130

«¡Ay, ay, creo que voy a ser en adelante cobarde y débil!, o
quizá es que soy demasiado joven y no puedo confiar en mis
brazos para rechazar a un hombre cuando alguien me ataca
primero. Pero, vamos, vosotros que sois superiores a mí en
fuerzas, probad el arco y acabemos el certamen.»

Así diciendo, dejó el arco en el suelo, lejos de sí, lo apoyó contra las bien ajustadas, bien pulidas puertas y colgó la aguda flecha
de una hermosa anilla y volvió a sentarse en la silla de donde
se había levantado. Y entre ellos habló Antínoo, hijo de Eupites: 140

«Compañeros, levantaos todos, uno tras otro, comenzando por la derecha del lugar donde se escancia el vino.»

Así dijo Antínoo, y les agradó su palabra.

Levantóse el primero Leodes, hijo de Enopo, el cual era su arúspice y se sentaba junto a una hermosa crátera, siempre en el rincón más escondido; sólo a él eran odiosas las iniquidades y estaba indignado contra todos los pretendientes[279]. Entonces fue el primero en tomar el arco y el agudo dardo y marchó a ponerse sobre el umbral. Probó el arco y no pudo tenderlo, pues antes se cansó de tirar hacia atrás con sus blandas, no encallecidas manos. Y dijo entre los pretendientes: 150

«Amigos[280], yo no puedo tenderlo, que lo coja otro. Este arco privará de la vida y del alma a muchos nobles. Aunque es preferible morir que no conseguir aquello por lo que estamos reunidos siempre aquí, esperando todos los días. Ahora cualquiera espera y desea en su ánimo casarse con Penélope, la esposa de Odiseo, pero una vez que pruebe el arco y lo vea, que pretenda, buscando con regalos de boda, a alguna otra de las aqueas   160 de hermoso peplo, y aquélla rápidamente se casará con quien más cosas le regale y le venga designado por el destino.»

Así diciendo, dejó el arco en el suelo, lejos de sí, lo apoyó contra las bien ajustadas, bien pulidas puertas y colgó la aguda flecha de una hermosa anilla, y volvió a sentarse en la silla de donde se había levantado.

Entonces le increpó Antínoo, le habló y le llamó por su nombre:

«Leodes, ¡qué palabra terrible e inaguantable —me he irritado al escucharla— ha escapado del cerco de tus dientes!; que   170 este arco privará a los pretendientes de la vida y el alma porque tú no puedes tenderlo. No, sólo a ti no te parió tu venerable madre para ser tirador de arco y flechas, pero otros ilustres pretendientes lo tenderán enseguida.»

Así dijo y ordenó a Melantio el cabrero:

«Apresúrate a encender fuego en el palacio, Melantio, y co-

---

[279] A pesar de todo, como se ve más abajo (v. 155), también él era un pretendiente y por eso no se salvó de la muerte. Es el primero que intenta tender el arco y será el último en morir (cfr. XXII.310 y ss.).

[280] Cfr. nota 70.

loca al lado un sillón grande con pieles encima; y trae un gran pan de sebo que hay dentro para que calentemos el arco, le untemos con grasa y lo probemos, para terminar de una vez el certamen.» 180

Así dijo; Melantio encendió enseguida un fuego infatigable, acercóle un sillón, con pieles encima y llevó un gran pan de sebo que había dentro. Los jóvenes calentaron el arco y trataron de tenderlo, pero no podían, pues estaban muy faltos de fuerzas. Pero todavía Antínoo estaba a la expectativa y Eurímaco semejante a un dios, jefes de los pretendientes y señaladamente los mejores por su valor. Habían salido del palacio, en mutua compañía, el boyero y el porquero del divino Odiseo. Y les siguió él mismo, el divino Odiseo, desde la casa; y 190 cuando ya estaban fuera de las puertas y del patio les habló con suaves palabras:

«Boyero y tú, porquero, ¿os diré alguna palabra o mejor la mantendré oculta? El ánimo me ordena decirla. ¿Cómo seríais para defender a Odiseo si llegara de alguna parte, así de repente, y alguna divinidad lo enviara? ¿Defenderíais a los pretendientes o a Odiseo? Contestad como el corazón y el ánimo os lo ordenen.»

Y el boyero dijo:

«Zeus padre, ¡ojalá cumplieras este deseo mío de que llegue 200 aquel hombre conducido por alguna divinidad! Conocerías cuál es mi fuerza y qué brazos me acompañan.»

Eumeo suplicaba a todos los dioses de la misma manera que regresara a casa el prudente Odiseo.

Y una vez que éste conoció su verdadero pensamiento, de nuevo les contestó con sus palabras y dijo:

«Ya está él dentro; soy yo mismo, que después de pasar muchas calamidades he llegado a los veinte años a la tierra patria. También me doy cuenta que sólo vosotros dos entre los esclavos deseabais mi llegada, que de los otros, a ninguno he oído 210 que suplicara para que yo regresara a casa. Así que a vosotros dos os diré la verdad de lo que va a suceder: si por mi mano la divinidad hace sucumbir a los ilustres pretendientes, os daré a ambos esposa y posesiones, y casas edificadas cerca de la mía; y seréis, además, compañeros y hermanos de mi Telémaco. Vamos, os voy a mostrar otra señal manifiesta para que me re-

conozcáis bien y confiéis en vuestro ánimo, la cicatriz que en
otro tiempo me infirió un jabalí con su blanco colmillo cuando
marché al Parnaso con los hijos de Autólico.»   220

Así diciendo, apartó los andrajos de la gran cicatriz y luego
que éstos la vieron y examinaron bien cada parte rompieron
en llanto, echaron los brazos alrededor del prudente Odiseo y
le besaban y acariciaban la cabeza y los hombros. También él
besaba sus cabezas y manos y se les habría puesto la luz del sol
mientras lloraban, si no los hubieran calmado y hablado Odiseo mismo:

«Contened el llanto y el gemido, no sea que alguien os vea si
sale del palacio y vaya adentro a decirlo. Entrad uno tras otro,
no juntos; primero yo y después vosotros. La señal será la si- 230
guiente: todos los demás, cuantos son ilustres pretendientes no
dejarán que me sean entregados el arco y el carcaj, pero tú, divino Eumeo, llévalo a través de la habitación para ponerlo en
mi mano y di a las mujeres que cierren las puertas del palacio
ajustándolas fuertemente. En el caso de que alguna oiga gemido o golpe de hombres entre nuestras paredes que no acuda a
la puerta, que se quede en silencio junto a su labor. En cuanto
a ti, divino Filetio, te encargo cerrar con llave las puertas del 240
patio y poner enseguida una cadena.»

Así diciendo, entró en la bien construida casa y se fue a sentar en la silla de donde se había levantado; y después entraron
los dos siervos del divino Odiseo.

Eurímaco ya estaba moviendo el arco con las manos hacia
uno y otro lado, calentándolo con el brillo del fuego, pero ni
aun así podía tenderlo y se afligía grandemente en su noble corazón. Así que suspiró, dijo su palabra, habló y llamó por su
nombre:

«¡Ay, ay, en verdad siento pesar por mí mismo y por todos!
Y no es que me lamente tanto por la boda, aunque me duela 250
—pues hay muchas otras aqueas, unas en la misma Itaca rodeada de mar y otras en las restantes ciudades—, como porque
seamos tan débiles de fuerza comparados con el divino Odiseo, que no podemos tender el arco. ¡Será una vergüenza que
se enteren los venideros!»

Y Antínoo, hijo de Eupites, se dirigió luego a él:

«Eurímaco, no será así —y lo sabes también tú—. Ahora se celebra en el pueblo la sagrada fiesta del dios. ¿Quién podría tender el arco? Dejadle tranquilamente en el suelo y las hachas de doble filo dejémoslas ahí puestas, pues no creo que se las 260 lleve nadie que venga al palacio de Odiseo Laertíada. Conque vamos, que el copero haga una primera ofrenda, por orden, en las copas para que una vez realizada dejemos el curvado arco. Ordenad a Melantio que traiga cabras al amanecer, las que sobresalgan entre todas, para que probemos el arco y terminemos el certamen de una vez, después de ofrecer muslos a Apolo, famoso por su arco.»

Así dijo Antínoo, y les agradó su palabra. Así que los heraldos vertieron agua sobre sus manos y unos jóvenes coronaban 270 con vino las cráteras y lo distribuyeron entre todos haciendo una primera ofrenda en las copas. Y después que hubieron hecho libación y bebido cuanto quiso su apetito, les dijo meditando engaños el muy astuto Odiseo:

«Escuchadme, pretendientes de la ilustre reina, mientras os digo lo que el corazón me ordena dentro del pecho. Me dirijo principalmente a Eurímaco y Antínoo, semejante a un dios, puesto que él ha dicho oportunamente que dejéis ahora el arco y os volváis a los dioses, que al amanecer la divinidad 280 dará fuerzas al que quisiere. Vamos, dadme el pulimentado arco para que pueda probar con vosotros mi fuerza y mis brazos, para ver si tengo todavía el vigor cual antes tenía en mis flexibles miembros, o ya me lo han destruido la vida errante y la falta de cuidados.»

Así dijo, y todos ellos se indignaron sobremanera temiendo que lograse tender el pulido arco.

Entonces Antínoo le increpó y llamó por su nombre:

«¡Ah, miserable entre los forasteros, no tienes ni el más mínimo seso! ¿No te contentas con participar tranquilamente del festín con nosotros, los poderosos, y que no se te prive de nada del banquete, e incluso escuchar nuestras palabras y con- 290 versación? Ningún otro forastero ni mendigo escucha nuestras palabras. Te trastorna el vino, dulce como la miel, el que daña a quien lo arrebata con avidez y no lo bebe comedidamente. El vino perdió también al ilustre centauro Euritión en el palacio del muy noble Pirítoo cuando marchó al país de los Lapitas[281]. Cuando había dañado su mente con el vino, cometió enloquecido acciones indignas en la casa de Pirítoo, pero la indignación se apoderó de los héroes y se arrojaron sobre él, lo arrastraron afuera a través del vestíbulo y le cortaron orejas y nariz con cruel bronce. Y él, dañado en su mente, se marchó soportando su desgracia con ánimo demente. Por esto se produjo la contienda entre hombres y Centauros, y aquél fue el primero que encontró el mal para sí mismo por haberse cargado de vino.

»También a ti te anuncio una gran desgracia si tiendes el arco, pues no encontrarás afabilidad en nuestro pueblo y te enviaremos en negra nave al rey Equeto, azote de todos los mortales, y de allí no podrás escapar a salvo. Así que bebe tranquilo y no trates de rivalizar con hombres más jóvenes.»

Y la prudente Penélope se dirigió luego a él:

«Antínoo, no es decoroso ni justo ultrajar a los huéspedes de Telémaco, cualquiera que llegue a este palacio. ¿Crees que si el huésped lograra tender el arco, confiado en sus manos y fuerza, me llevaría a casa y haría su esposa? Ni siquiera él mismo alberga en su pecho tal esperanza. Que ninguno de vosotros coma con corazón acongojado por causa de éste, pues no parece cosa en modo alguno razonable.»

Y Eurímaco, hijo de Pólibo, le contestó:

«Hija de Icario, prudente Penélope, no creemos que éste te vaya a llevar, ni parece razonable, pero nos llenan de vergüenza las murmuraciones de hombres y mujeres, no sea que alguna vez el peor de los aqueos pueda decir: "En verdad son hombres muy inferiores los que pretenden a la esposa de un hombre irreprochable, pues no son capaces de tender el pulido arco; en cambio un mendigo cualquiera que llegó errante tendió fácilmente el arco y atravesó el hierro."

»Así dirá y tales reproches serán para nosotros.»

---

[281] Eran seres monstruosos, mitad hombre mitad caballo, nacidos de Ixión y de una nube que Zeus formó con la figura de Hera (cfr. Píndaro, *Pítica*, II.39 y ss.) La mitología conoce varios desmanes de los Centauros provocados por el vino. En la boda de Pirítoo con Hipodamia lo bebieron en demasía y Euritión trató de forzar a la novia. Al final fueron expulsados de Tesalia.

Y la prudente Penélope se dirigió a él:

«Eurímaco, no es posible en modo alguno que tengan buena fama en el pueblo quienes deshonran la casa de un varón principal y se la comen. ¿Por qué os hacéis merecedores de tales oprobios? Este forastero es muy alto y vigoroso y afirma ser hijo de un padre de noble linaje. Vamos, dadle el pulimentado arco, para que veamos. Os diré algo que se va a cumplir: si lograra tenderlo y Apolo le diera gloria, le vestiré de manto y túnica, hermosos vestidos, y le daré un agudo venablo para protección contra perros y hombres y una espada de doble filo; también le daré sandalias para sus pies y le enviaré a donde su corazón le empuje.» 340

Y Telémaco le habló discretamente:

«Madre mía, ninguno de los aqueos tiene más poder que yo para dar el arco o negárselo a quien yo quiera, ni cuantos gobiernan sobre la áspera Itaca ni cuantos en las islas de junto a la Elide, criadora de caballos. Ninguno de éstos me forzaría contra mi voluntad si yo quisiera de una vez dar este arco al extranjero para llevárselo. Conque, vamos, marcha a tu habitación y ocúpate de las labores que te son propias, el telar y la rueca, y ordena a tus esclavas que se apliquen a las suyas. El arco será cuestión de los hombres y principalmente de mí, de quien es el poder en este palacio»[282]. 350

Y ella volvió asombrada a su habitación poniendo en su pecho la prudente palabra de su hijo. Y luego que hubo subido al piso superior con sus siervas, rompió a llorar por Odiseo, su esposo, hasta que Atenea, de ojos brillantes, le echó dulce sueño sobre los párpados.

Entonces el divino porquero tomó el curvado arco y se disponía a llevarlo, cuando los pretendientes todos empezaron a amenazarlo en el palacio; y uno de los jóvenes arrogantes decía así: 360

«¿Adónde llevas el curvado arco, miserable porquero, insensato? Creo que bien pronto te van a comer lejos de aquí los pe-

---

[282] Cfr. I.356-64. Son dos pasajes similares en que Telémaco quiere imponer su autoridad en el palacio. Éste, sin embargo, es más adecuado a la situación: nos muestra a un Telémaco ya plenamente adulto y capaz de colaborar con su padre en la venganza.

rros, junto a las marranas que tú cuidabas, si Apolo y los demás dioses nos son propicios.»

Así dijeron, y éste dejó el arco en el mismo sitio atemorizado porque todos le amenazaban en el palacio. Pero Telémaco le dijo entre amenazas desde el otro lado:

«Abuelo, sigue adelante con el arco —no creo que hagas bien en obedecer a todos—, no sea que yo, con ser más joven, te persiga hasta el campo arrojándote piedras, pues soy más fuerte. ¡Ojalá fuera tan superior en manos y vigor a cuantos pretendientes están en mi casa! Pronto despediría de mi palacio a alguno para que se marchara vergonzosamente, pues maquinan maldades.»

Así dijo y todos los pretendientes se rieron dulcemente de él y abandonaron su terrible cólera contra Telémaco. El porquero llevó el arco por la habitación y poniéndose junto al prudente Odiseo se lo entregó. Luego llamó a la nodriza Euriclea y le dijo:

«Prudente Euriclea, Telémaco ordena que cierres bien las puertas del mégaron y que, si alguna de las siervas oye gemidos o golpes de hombres dentro de nuestras paredes, que no acuda a la puerta, que se quede en silencio junto a su labor.»

Así dijo; a Euriclea se le quedaron sin alas las palabras y cerró enseguida las puertas del mégaron, agradable para habitar.

Filetio salió sigilosamente y cerró enseguida las puertas del bien cercado patio. Había bajo el pórtico el cable de papiro de una curvada nave; con éste sujetó las puertas, entró y fue a sentarse en la silla de la que se había levantado mirando directamente a Odiseo.

Éste ya estaba manejando el arco, dándolo vueltas, probándolo por uno y otro lado no fuera que la carcoma hubiera roído el cuerno mientras su dueño estaba ausente.

Y uno de los pretendientes decía así, mirando al que tenía cerca:

«Desde luego es un hombre conocedor y entendido en arcos. Quizá también él tiene de éstos en casa o siente impulsos de construirlos, según lo mueve entre sus manos aquí y allá este vagabundo conocedor de desgracias.»

Y otro de los jóvenes arrogantes decía así:

«¡Ojalá consiguiera tanto provecho como va a conseguir tender el arco!»

Así decían los pretendientes. Entretanto el muy astuto Odiseo, luego que hubo palpado y examinado por todas partes el gran arco... Como cuando un hombre entendido en liras y canto consigue fácilmente tender la cuerda con una clavija nueva, atando a uno y otro lado la bien retorcida tripa de una oveja, así tendió Odiseo sin esfuerzo el gran arco. Luego lo tomó con su mano derecha, palpó la cuerda y ésta resonó semejante al 410 hermoso trino de una golondrina. Entonces les entró gran pesar a los pretendientes y se les tornó el color. Zeus retumbó con fuerza mostrando una señal y se llenó de alegría el sufridor, el divino Odiseo porque el hijo de Crono, de torcidos pensamientos, le había enviado un prodigio. Y tomó un agudo dardo que tenía suelto sobre la mesa, pues los otros estaban dentro del cóncavo carcaj, los que iban a probar pronto los aqueos. Lo acomodó en la encorvadura, tiró del nervio y de las barbas allí sentado, desde su misma silla, disparó el dardo 420 apuntando de frente y no marró ninguna de las hachas desde el primer agujero, pues la flecha de pesado bronce salió atravesándolas.

Entonces dijo a Telémaco:

«Telémaco, este huésped que tienes sentado en tu palacio no te cubre de vergüenza, que no he errado el blanco ni me he fatigado tratando de tender el arco. Todavía me queda vigor, no como me echan en cara los pretendientes por deshonrarme. Pero ya es hora de que los aqueos preparen su cena mientras haya luz y que luego se solacen con el canto y la lira, pues éstos son complemento de un banquete.» 430

Así dijo, e hizo una señal con las cejas. Telémaco se ciñó la aguda espada, el hijo del divino Odiseo; puso su mano sobre la lanza y se quedó en pie junto a su mismo sillón, armado de reluciente bronce.

Canto XXII

LA VENGANZA

Entonces el muy astuto Odiseo se despojó de sus andrajos, saltó al gran umbral con el arco y el carcaj lleno de flechas y las derramó ante sus pies diciendo a los pretendientes:

«Ya terminó este inofensivo certamen; ahora veré si acierto a otro blanco que no ha alcanzado ningún hombre y Apolo me concede gloria.»

Así dijo, y apuntó la amarga saeta contra Antínoo. Levantaba éste una hermosa copa de oro de doble asa y la tenía en sus manos para beber el vino. La muerte no se le había venido a las mientes, pues ¿quién creería que, entre tantos convidados, uno, por valiente que fuera, iba a causarle funesta muerte y negro destino? Pero Odiseo le acertó en la garganta y le clavó una flecha; la punta le atravesó en línea recta el delicado cuello, se desplomó hacia atrás, la copa se le cayó de la mano al ser alcanzado y al punto un grueso chorro de humana sangre brotó de su nariz. Rápidamente golpeó con el pie y apartó de sí la mesa, la comida cayó al suelo y se mancharon el pan y la carne asada.

Los pretendientes levantaron gran tumulto en el palacio al verlo caer, se levantaron de sus asientos lanzándose por la sala y miraban por todas las bien construidas paredes, pero no había en ellas escudo ni poderosa lanza que poder coger. E increparon a Odiseo con coléricas palabras:

«Forastero, haces mal en disparar el arco contra los hombres; ya no tendrás que afrontar más certámenes, pues te espe-

ra terrible muerte. Has matado a uno que era el más excelente
de los jóvenes de Itaca; te van a comer los buitres aquí   30
mismo.»

Así lo imaginaban todos, porque en verdad creían que lo
había matado involuntariamente; los necios no se daban cuenta de que también sobre ellos pendía el extremo de la muerte[283]. Y mirándolos torvamente les dijo el muy astuto Odiseo:

«Perros, no esperabais que volviera del pueblo troyano
cuando devastabais mi casa, forzabais a las esclavas y, estando
yo vivo, tratabais de seducir a mi esposa sin temer a los dioses
que habitan el ancho cielo ni venganza alguna de los hombres.   40
Ahora pende sobre vosotros todos el extremo de la muerte.»

Así habló y se apoderó de todos el pálido terror y buscaba
cada uno por dónde escapar a la escabrosa muerte. Eurímaco
fue el único que le contestó diciendo:

«Si de verdad eres Odiseo de Itaca que ha llegado, tienes razón en hablar así de las atrocidades que han cometido los
aqueos en el palacio y en el campo. Pero ya ha caído el causan-
te de todo, Antínoo; fue él quien tomó la iniciativa, no tanto
por intentar el matrimonio como por concebir otros proyectos   50
que el Cronida no llevó a cabo: reinar sobre el pueblo de la
bien construida Itaca tratando de matar a tu hijo con asechan-
zas. Ya ha muerto éste por su destino, perdona tú a tus conciu-
dadanos, que nosotros, para aplacarte públicamente, te com-
pensaremos de lo que se ha comido y bebido en el palacio esti-
mándolo en veinte bueyes cada uno por separado, y te devol-
veremos bronce y oro hasta que tu corazón se satisfaga; antes
de ello no se te puede reprochar que estés irritado.»

Y mirándole torvamente le dijo el muy astuto Odiseo: 60

«Eurímaco, aunque me dierais todos los bienes familiares y
añadierais otros, ni aun así contendría mis manos de matar
hasta que los pretendientes paguéis toda vuestra insolencia.
Ahora sólo os queda luchar conmigo o huir, si es que alguno
puede evitar la muerte y las Keres, pero creo que nadie escapará a la escabrosa muerte.

---

[283] Expresión de origen oscuro que probablemente significa «el extremo *que
es* la muerte». Pero cfr. R. B. Onians, ob. cit., págs. 310 y ss.

Así habló y las rodillas y el corazón de todos desfallecieron allí mismo. Eurímaco habló otra vez entre ellos y dijo:

«Amigos, no contendrá este hombre sus irresistibles manos, 70 sino que una vez que ha cogido el pulido arco y el carcaj lo disparará desde el pulido umbral hasta matarnos a todos. Pensemos en luchar; sacad las espadas, defendeos con las mesas de los dardos que causan rápida muerte. Unámonos todos contra él por si logramos arrojarlo del umbral y las puertas, vayamos por la ciudad y que se promueva gran alboroto: sería la última vez que manejara el arco.»

Así habló, y sacando la aguda espada de bronce, de doble filo, se lanzó contra él con horribles gritos. Al mismo tiempo 80 le disparó una saeta el divino Odiseo, y acertándole en el pecho, junto a la tetilla, le clavó la veloz flecha en el hígado. Se le cayó de la mano al suelo la espada y doblándose se desplomó sobre la mesa y derribó por tierra los manjares y la copa de doble asa. Golpeó el suelo con su frente, con espíritu conturbado, y sacudió la silla con ambos pies, y una niebla se esparció por sus ojos.

Anfínomo se fue derecho contra el ilustre Odiseo y sacó la aguda espada por si podía arrojarlo de la puerta, pero se le ade- 90 lantó Telémaco y le clavó por detrás la lanza de bronce entre los hombros y le atravesó el pecho. Cayó con estrépito y dio de bruces en el suelo. Telémaco se retiró dejando su lanza de larga sombra allí, en Anfínomo, por temor a que alguno de los aqueos le clavara la espada mientras él arrancaba la lanza de larga sombra o le hiriera al estar agachado. Echó a correr y llegó enseguida adonde estaba su padre y, poniéndose a su lado, 100 le dirigió aladas palabras: «Padre, voy a traerte un escudo y dos lanzas y un casco todo de bronce que se ajuste a tu cabeza. De paso me pondré yo las armas y daré otras al porquero y al boyero, que es mejor estar armados.»

Y le respondió el muy astuto Odiseo:

«Tráelas corriendo mientras tengo flechas para defenderme, no sea que me arrojen de la puerta al estar solo.»

Así habló, y Telémaco obedeció a su padre. Fue a la estancia donde estaban sus famosas armas y tomó cuatro escudos, ocho 110 lanzas y cuatro cascos de bronce con crines de caballo, los llevó y se puso enseguida al lado de su padre. Primero protegió él su cuerpo con el bronce y, cuando los dos siervos se habían puesto hermosas armaduras, se colocaron todos junto al prudente y astuto Odiseo.

Mientras tuvo flechas para defenderse, fue hiriendo sin interrupción a los pretendientes en su propia casa apuntando bien. Y caían uno tras otro. Pero cuando se le acabaron las flechas al soberano, una vez que las hubo disparado, apoyó el arco contra una columna del bien construido aposento, junto al 120 muro reluciente, y se cubrió los hombros con un escudo de cuatro pieles; en la robusta cabeza se colocó un labrado casco —el penacho de crines de caballo ondeaba terrible en lo alto—, y tomó dos poderosas lanzas guarnecidas con bronce.

Había en la bien construida pared un postigo[284] y en el umbral extremo de la sólida estancia había una salida hacia un corredor y estaba cerrado por batientes bien ajustados. Mandó Odiseo que lo custodiara el divino porquero manteniéndose 130 firme en él, pues era la única salida. Entonces Agelao les habló a todos con estas palabras:

«Amigos, ¿no habrá nadie que ascienda por el postigo, se lo diga a la gente y se produzca al punto un tumulto? Sería la última vez que éste manejara el arco.»

Y le respondió el cabrero Melantio:

«No es posible, Agelao de linaje divino; está muy cerca la hermosa puerta del patio y es difícil la salida al corredor; un solo hombre, que sea valiente, nos contendría a todos. Pero, vamos, os traeré armas de la despensa, pues creo que allí, y no en otro sitio, las colocaron Odiseo y su ilustre hijo.» 140

Así diciendo, subió el cabrero Melantio por una tronera[285] del

---

[284] Pasaje oscuro y debatido. Según la interpretación de A. J. B. Wace *(Companion...*, pág. 496), que se basa en la distribución del llamado «Palacio de las columnas» de Micenas, se trata de una sola salida, la *orsothýrē*, puerta lateral del mégaron que conduce a un pasillo *(laúrē)* por donde se accede a las habitaciones privadas. Ésta es la que manda vigilar Odiseo.

[285] Aparte de la *orsothýrē* o postigo, antes aludido, había unos «huecos» *(rhôges)* en el mégaron. Sobre estos misteriosos huecos que también daban acceso a las habitaciones privadas, se ha pensado que podrían ser ventanucos abiertos en una escalera que subía al piso superior o bien metopas huecas en el entablamento. Para a. J. B. Wace (ob. cit., pág. 497), estas interpretaciones son inadmisibles, porque a la dificultad de alcanzar tales huecos se añade la de pasar tantas

mégaron a la estancia de Odiseo, de donde tomó doce escudos, otras tantas lanzas e igual número de cascos de bronce con crines de caballo. Fue y se lo entregó rápidamente a los pretendientes. Entonces sí que desfallecieron las rodillas y el corazón de Odiseo cuando vio que se ponían las armas y blandían en sus manos las largas lanzas, pues ahora la empresa le parecía arriesgada. Y al punto dirigió a Telémaco aladas palabras: 150

«Telémaco, alguna de las mujeres del palacio, o Melantio, encienden contra nosotros combate funesto.»

Y le respondió Telémaco discretamente:

«Padre, yo tuve la culpa de ello, no hay otro culpable, que dejé abierta la bien ajustada puerta de la habitación, y su espía ha sido más hábil. Pero vete, divino Eumeo, y cierra la puerta de la despensa; y entérate de si quien hace esto es una mujer o Melantio, el hijo de Dolio, como yo creo.»

Mientras así hablaban entre sí, el cabrero Melantio volvió a   160
la estancia para traer hermosas armas, pero se dio cuenta el divino porquero y al punto dijo a Odiseo, que estaba cerca:

«Hijo de Laertes, de linaje divino, Odiseo rico en ardides, aquel hombre desconocido del que sospechábamos ha vuelto al aposento. Dime claramente si lo debo matar, en caso de vencerlo, o he de traértelo para que pague las muchas insolencias que ha cometido en tu casa.»

Y le respondió el muy astuto Odiseo:

«Yo y Telémaco contendremos en esta sala a los nobles pretendientes, a pesar de su mucho ardor. Vosotros ponedle atrás   170
pies y manos y metedlo en la habitación, cerrad la puerta y echándole una soga trenzada colgadlo de las vigas en lo alto de una columna, para que viva largo tiempo sufriendo fuertes dolores.»

Así habló, y ellos dos le escucharon y obedecieron, y, dirigiéndose a la estancia, le pasaron inadvertidos a Melantio, que estaba dentro. Éste buscaba armas en lo más recóndito de la   180
habitación y ellos montaron guardia a uno y otro lado de las jambas. Cuando atravesaba el umbral el cabrero Melantio, llevando en una mano un hermoso casco y en la otra un ancho

---

armas por ahí. El sugiere que podría tratarse de una balaustrada o galería soportada por las columnas que rodean el Hogar en el centro del mégaron.

escudo viejo, cubierto de moho, que el héroe Laertes solía llevar en su juventud y ahora se hallaba en el suelo con las correas rotas, se le echaron encima y lo arrastraron adentro por los pelos; lo echaron al suelo angustiado en su corazón y, poniéndole atrás pies y manos, se las ataron con doloroso nudo, como había mandado el hijo de Laertes, el divino y sufridor Odiseo; echaron a las vigas, en lo alto de una columna, la soga trenzada y burlándote le dijiste, porquero Eumeo:

«Ahora velarás toda la noche acostado en esta blanda cama que te mereces, y no te pasará inadvertida la llegada de la que nace de la mañana, de trono de oro, desde las corrientes de Océano, a la hora en que sueles traer las cabras a los pretendientes para preparar el almuerzo.»

Así quedó, suspendido de funesto nudo, y ellos dos se pusieron las armas, cerraron la brillante puerta y se dirigieron hacia el prudente y astuto Odiseo. Se detuvieron allí respirando ardor y eran cuatro los del umbral y muchos y valientes los de dentro. Y se les unió Atenea, la hija de Zeus, que tomó el aspecto y la voz de Méntor. Odiseo se alegró al verla y le dijo:

«Méntor, aparta de nosotros el infortunio, acuérdate del compañero amado que solía hacerte bien, pues eres de mi edad.»

Así habló, aunque sospechaba que era Atenea, la que empuja al combate. Y los pretendientes le hacían reproches en la sala, siendo Agelao Damastórida el primero en hablar:

«Méntor, que no te convenza Odiseo con sus palabras de luchar contra los pretendientes y ayudarle a él, pues que se cumplirá nuestro intento de esta manera: una vez que hayamos matado a éstos, al padre y al hijo, perecerás tú también por lo que tramas en el palacio y pagarás con tu cabeza. Y cuando seguemos vuestra violencia con el hierro, mezclaremos a los de Odiseo cuantos bienes posees dentro y fuera de tu palacio y no permitiremos que tus hijos ni hijas vivan en el palacio, ni que tu fiel esposa ande por la ciudad de Itaca.

Así hablo, Atenea se encolerizó más en su corazón y le hizo reproches a Odiseo con airadas palabras:

«Ya no hay en ti, Odiseo, aquel vigor y fuerza de cuando luchabas con los troyanos por Helena de blancos brazos, hija de ilustre padre, durante nueve años seguidos; diste muerte a mu-

chos hombres en combate cruel y por tu consejo se tomó la
ciudad de Príamo, de anchas calles. ¿Cómo es que ahora que   230
has llegado a tu casa y posesiones imploras ser valiente contra
los pretendientes? Ven aquí, amigo, ponte firme junto a mí y
mira mis obras, para que veas cómo es Méntor Alcímida para
devolverte los favores entre tus enemigos.»

Así habló, y es que no quería concederle todavía del todo la
indecisa victoria antes de probar el vigor y la fuerza de Odiseo
y su ilustre hijo. Conque se lanzó hacia arriba y fue a posarse
en una viga de la sala ennegrecida por el fuego, semejante a
una golondrina de frente.   240

Animaban a los contendientes Agelao Damastórida Euríno-
mo, Anfimedonte, Demoptólemo, Pisandro Polictórida y el
prudente Pólibo, pues eran los más valientes de cuantos pretendientes vivían y luchaban por sus vidas. A los demás los había derribado ya el arco y las numerosas flechas. A todos se dirigió Agelao con estas palabras:

«Amigos, ahora contendrá este hombre sus manos indómi-
tas, puesto que se ha ido Méntor tras decirle inútiles fanfarro-
nadas y han quedado solos al pie de las puertas. Conque no   250
lancéis todos a una las largas lanzas; vamos, disparad primero
los seis, por si Zeus nos concede de alguna manera que Odiseo
sea blanco de los disparos y conseguir gloria. De los otros no
habrá cuidado una vez que éste al menos haya caído.»

Así dijo, y dispararon todos como les ordenara, bien atentos, pero Atenea dejó sin efecto todos sus disparos. De éstos,
uno alcanzó la columna del bien construido mégaron, otro la
puerta sólidamente ajustada. De otro, la lanza de fresno, pesada por el bronce, fue a estrellarse contra el muro. Y una vez
que habían esquivado las lanzas de los pretendientes comenzó   260
a hablar entre ellos el sufridor, el divino Odiseo:

«Amigos, también yo ahora quisiera deciros que disparemos
contra la turba de los pretendientes, quienes, además de los
anteriores males, desean matarnos.»

Así dijo, y todos dispararon las afiladas lanzas apuntando de
frente. A Demoptólemo lo mató Odiseo, a Euríades Telémaco, a Elato el porquerizo y a Pisandro el que estaba al cuidado
de los bueyes. Así que luego todos a una mordieron el inmenso suelo mientras los otros pretendientes se retiraron hacia el   270

fondo del mégaron. Y ellos se lanzaron sobre los cadáveres y les quitaron las lanzas.

De nuevo los pretendientes dispararon las afiladas lanzas, bien atentos. Pero Atenea dejó sin efecto todos sus disparos. De ellos, uno alcanzó la columna del bien construido mégaron, otro la puerta sólidamente ajustada. De otro la lanza de freno, pesada por el bronce, fue a estrellarse contra el muro. Pero esta vez Anfimedonte hirió a Telémaco en la muñeca, levemente, y el bronce le dañó la superficie de la piel; Ctesipo rasguñó el hombro de Eumeo con la larga lanza por encima del escudo, y ésta, sobrevolando, cayó a tierra.   280

De nuevo los que rodeaban al prudente y astuto Odiseo dispararon las afiladas lanzas contra la turba de los pretendientes y de nuevo alcanzó a Euridamante, Odiseo, el destructor de ciudades, a Anfimedonte, Telémaco, y a Pólibo, el porquero, y luego alcanzó en el pecho a Ctesipo el que estaba al cuidado de los bueyes y jactándose le dijo:

«Politérsida, amigo de insultar, no digas nunca nada altanero cediendo a tu insensatez, antes bien cede la palabra a los dioses, puesto que en verdad son mejores con mucho. Este será para ti el don de hospitalidad por la patada que diste a Odiseo, semejante a un dios, cuando mendigaba por el palacio.»   290

Así dijo el que estaba al cuidado de los cuernitorcidos bueyes. Después Odiseo hirió de cerca al Damastórida con su larga lanza y Telémaco hirió de cerca con su lanza en medio de la ijada a Leócrito Evenórida, y el bronce le atravesó de parte a parte. Cayó de cabeza y dio de bruces en el suelo. Entonces Atenea levantó la égida, destructora para los mortales, desde lo alto del techo y sus corazones sintieron pánico[286]. Así que los unos huían por el mégaron como vacas de rebaño a las que persigue el movedizo tábano, lanzándose sobre ellas en la estación de la primavera, cuando los días son largos.   300

En cambio, los otros, como los buitres de retorcidas uñas y corvo pico bajan de los montes y caen sobre las aves que, asustadas por la llanura, tratan de remontarse hacia las nubes

---

[286] Aparte de la varita, que no le es propia (cfr. nota 208), Atenea utiliza la égida de Zeus, instrumento mágico que produce pánico en los combatientes (cfr. nota 53). Este pasaje imita a *Ilíada*, XV.306 y ss.

—éstos se lanzan sobre las aves y las matan, ya que no tienen defensa alguna ni posibilidad de huida y se alegran los hombres de la captura—, así golpeaban éstos a los pretendientes corriendo en círculo por la sala.

Y eran horribles los gemidos que se levantaban cuando las cabezas de los pretendientes golpeaban el suelo —y éste humeaba todo con sangre.

Fue entonces cuando Leodes se arrojó a las rodillas de Odiseo y asiéndolas le suplicaba con aladas palabras: 31(

«Te suplico asido a tus rodillas, Odiseo. Respétame y ten compasión de mí. Pues te aseguro que nunca dije ni hice nada insensato a mujer alguna en el palacio. Por el contrario, solía hacer desistir a cualquiera de los pretendientes que tratara de hacerlas, pero no me obedecían en alejar sus manos de la maldad. Por esto y por sus insensateces han atraído hacia sí un destino indigno y yo, sin haber hecho nada, yaceré con ellos por ser su arúspice, que no hay agradecimiento futuro para los que obran bien.»

Y mirándole torvamente le dijo el muy astuto Odiseo: 32(

«Si te precias de ser el arúspice de éstos, seguro que a menudo estabas pronto a suplicar en el palacio que el fin de mi dulce regreso fuera lejano, para atraer hacia ti a mi querida esposa y que te pariera hijos. Por esto no podrías escapar a la muerte de largos lamentos.»

Así diciendo, tomó con su ancha mano la espada que estaba en el suelo, la que Agelao había dejado caer al sucumbir. Con ella le atravesó el cuello por el centro y mientras todavía hablaba Leodes, su cabeza se mezcló con el polvo.

También el aedo Femio Terpíada trataba de evitar la negra 33(
Ker, el que cantaba a la fuerza entre los pretendientes. Estaba de pie sosteniendo entre sus manos la sonora lira junto al portillo, y dudaba entre salir desapercibido del mégaron y sentarse junto al altar del gran Zeus, protector del Hogar, donde Laertes y Odiseo habían quemado muchos muslos de reses, o lanzarse a las rodillas de Odiseo y suplicarle. Y mientras así pensaba, le pareció más ventajoso asirse a las rodillas de Odiseo Laertíada. Así que dejó en el suelo la curvada lira, entre la crá- 34(
tera y el sillón de clavos de plata, y se arrojó a las rodillas de Odiseo. Y asiéndolas, le suplicaba con aladas palabras:

«Te suplico asido a tus rodillas. Odiseo. Respétame y ten compasión de mí. Seguro que tendrás dolor en el futuro si matas a un aedo, a mí, que canto a dioses y hombres. Yo he aprendido por mí mismo, pero un dios ha soplado en mi mente toda clase de cantos. Creo que puedo cantar junto a ti como si fuera un dios. Por esto no trates de cortarme el cuello. También Telémaco, tu querido hijo, podría decirte que yo no venía 350 a tu casa ni de buen grado ni porque lo precisara, para cantar junto a los pretendientes en sus banquetes; mas ellos me arrastraban por la fuerza por ser más numerosos y fuertes.»

Así dijo, y la sagrada fuerza de Telémaco le oyó; así que luego dijo a su padre que estaba cerca:

«Detente y no hieras con el bronce a este inocente. También salvaremos al heraldo Medonte, que siempre, mientras fui niño, se cuidaba de mí en nuestro palacio, si es que no lo han matado ya Filetio o el porquero, o se ha enfrentado contigo cuando irrumpiste en la sala.» 360

Así habló, y Medonte, conocedor de pensamientos discretos, le oyó. Estaba tirado bajo un sillón y le cubría una piel recién cortada de buey, tratando de evitar la negra muerte. Enseguida saltó de debajo del sillón, se despojó de la piel de buey y se arrojó a las rodillas de Telémaco, y asiéndolas le suplicaba con aladas palabras:

«Amigo, ése soy yo; detente y di a tu padre que no me dañe con el agudo bronce, poderoso como es, irritado con los pretendientes quienes le consumieron los bienes en el palacio y no te respetaban a ti, inecios!» 370

Y sonriendo le dijo el muy astuto Odiseo:

«Cobra ánimos, ya que éste te ha protegido y salvado, para que sepas —y se lo digas a cualquier otro— que es mucho mejor una buena acción que una acción malvada. Conque salid del mégaron e id al patio alejándoos de la matanza tú y el afamado aedo, mientras que yo llevo a cabo en la sala lo que es menester.

Así dijo, y ambos salieron del mégaron y fueron a sentarse junto al altar del gran Zeus, mirando asombrados a uno y otro lado, temiendo siempre la muerte. 380

Entonces Odiseo examinó todo su palacio por si todavía quedaba vivo algún hombre tratando de evitar la negra muerte. Pero los vio a todos derribados entre polvo y sangre, tan numerosos como los peces a los que los pescadores sacan del canoso mar en su red de muchas mallas y depositan en la cóncava orilla —allí están todos sobre la arena añorando las olas del mar y el brillante Helios les arrebata la vida—; así estaban los pretendientes, hacinados uno sobre otro.

Entonces se dirigió a Telémaco el muy astuto Odiseo: 390

«Telémaco, vamos, llámame a la nodriza Euriclea para que le diga la palabra que tengo en mi interior.»

Así dijo; Telémaco obedeció a su padre y marchando hacia la puerta, dijo a la nodriza Euriclea:

«Ven acá, anciana, tú eres la vigilante de las esclavas en nuestro palacio; ven, te llama mi padre para decirte algo.»

Así dijo, y a ella se le quedó sin alas su palabra; abrió las puertas del mégaron, agradable para habitar, y se puso en camino, y luego la condujo Telémaco. 400

Encontró a Odiseo entre los cuerpos recién asesinados rociado de sangre ya coagulada, como un león que va de camino luego de haber engullido un toro salvaje —todo su pecho y su cara están manchados de sangre por todas partes y es terrible al mirarlo de frente. Así de manchado estaba Odiseo por sus brazos y piernas. Cuando la nodriza vio los cadáveres y la sangre a borbotones, arrancó a gritar, pues había visto una obra grande, pero Odiseo la contuvo y se lo impidió, por más que lo deseaba, y dirigiéndose a ella le dijo aladas palabras: 410

«Alégrate, anciana, en tu interior y no grites, que no es santo ufanarse ante hombres muertos. A éstos los ha domeñado la Moira de los dioses y sus obras insensatas, pues no respetaban a ninguno de los terrenos hombres, noble o del pueblo, que se llegara a ellos. Por esto y por sus insensateces han arrastrado hacia sí un destino vergonzoso. Conque, vamos, dime de las mujeres en el palacio quiénes me deshonran y quiénes son inocentes.»

Y al punto le contestó la nodriza Euriclea:

«Desde luego, hijo mío, te diré la verdad. Tienes en el palacio cincuenta esclavas a quienes hemos enseñado a realizar labores, a cardar lana y a soportar su esclavitud. Doce de éstas han incurrido en desvergüenza y no me honran a mí ni a la misma Penélope. Telémaco ha crecido sólo hace poco y su ma- 420 dre no le permitía dar órdenes a las esclavas. Pero voy a subir al piso de arriba para comunicárselo a tu esposa, a quien un dios ha infundido sueño.»

Y contestándole dijo el muy astuto Odiseo: 430

«No la despiertes todavía. Di a las mujeres que vengan aquí, a las que han realizado obras vergonzosas.»

Así dijo, y la anciana atravesó el mégaron para comunicárselo a las mujeres y ordenarlas que vinieran.

Entonces Odiseo, llamando hacia sí a Telémaco, al boyero y al porquero, les dirigió aladas palabras:

«Comenzad ya a llevar cadáveres y dad órdenes a las mujeres para que luego limpien con agua y agujereadas esponjas los hermosos sillones y las mesas. Cuando hayáis puesto en orden   440 todo el palacio sacad del sólido mégaron a las mujeres y matadlas con largas espadas entre la rotonda[287] y el hermoso cerco del patio, hasta que las arranquéis a todas la vida, para que se olviden de Afrodita, a la que poseían debajo de los pretendientes con quienes se unían en secreto.»

Así diciendo, llegaron las esclavas, todas en grupo, lanzando tristes lamentos y derramando abundantes lágrimas. Primero se llevaron los cadáveres y los pusieron bajo el pórtico del bien cercado patio, apoyándolos bien unos en otros, pues así lo había ordenado Odiseo que las apremiaba en persona. Y ellas los   450 llevaban por la fuerza. Luego limpiaron con agua y agujereadas esponjas los hermosos sillones y las mesas. Entretanto, Telémaco, el boyero y el porquero rasparon bien con espátulas el piso de la bien construida vivienda y las esclavas se lo llevaban y lo ponían fuera. Cuando habían puesto en orden todo el palacio, sacaron del sólido mégaron a las esclavas y las encerraron en un lugar estrecho, entre la rotonda y el hermoso cerco del patio, de donde no había posibilidad de huir.   460

Entonces, Telémaco comenzó entre ellos a hablar discretamente:

«No podría yo quitar la vida con muerte rápida a éstas que han vertido tanta deshonra sobre mi cabeza y la de mi padre cuando dormían con los pretendientes.»

---

[287] Ignoramos qué función podía tener esta edificación circular. En las excavaciones de los palacios micénicos no ha aparecido nada que se le parezca.

Así diciendo, ató el cable de una nave de azuloscura proa a una larga columna y rodeó con él la rotonda tensándolo hacia arriba de forma que ninguna llegara al suelo con los pies. Como cuando se precipitan los tordos de largas alas, o las palomas, hacia una red que está puesta en un matorral cuando se dirigen al nido —y en realidad las acoge un odioso lecho—, así las esclavas tenían sus cabezas en fila —y en torno a sus cuellos había lazos—, para que murieran de la forma más lamentable. Estuvieron agitando los pies entre convulsiones un rato, no mucho tiempo.

También sacaron a Melantio al vestíbulo y al patio, cortáronle la nariz y las orejas con cruel bronce, le arrancaron las vergüenzas para que se las comieran crudas los perros, y le cortaron manos y pies con ánimo irritado.

Luego que hubieron lavado sus manos y pies, volvieron al palacio junto a Odiseo, pues su trabajo estaba ya completo. Entonces dijo éste a su nodriza Euriclea:

«Tráeme azufre, anciana, remedio contra el mal, y también fuego, para que rocíe con azufre el mégaron; y luego ordena a Penélope que venga aquí en compañía de sus siervas. Ordena a todas las esclavas del palacio que vengan.»

Y luego le dijo su nodriza Euriclea:

«Sí, hijo mío, todo lo has dicho como te corresponde. Vamos, voy a traerte ropa, una túnica y un manto; no sigas en pie en el palacio cubriendo con harapos tus anchos hombros. Sería indignante.»

Y contestándole dijo el muy astuto Odiseo:

«Antes que nada he de tener fuego en mi palacio.»

Así dijo, y su nodriza Euriclea no le desobedeció. Llevó azufre y fuego y Odiseo roció por completo el mégaron, la sala y el patio.

Entonces la anciana atravesó el hermoso palacio de Odiseo para comunicárselo a las mujeres e incitarlas a que volvieran. Éstas salieron de la estancia llevando una antorcha entre sus manos, rodearon y dieron la bienvenida a Odiseo y abrazándole besaban su cabeza y hombros tomándole de las manos. Y a éste le entró un dulce deseo de llorar y gemir, pues reconocía a todas en su corazón.

Canto XXIII

PENÉLOPE RECONOCE A ODISEO

Entonces la anciana subió gozosa al piso de arriba para anunciar a la señora que estaba dentro su esposo, y sus rodillas se llenaban de fuerza y sus pies se levantaban del suelo.

Se detuvo sobre su cabeza y le dijo su palabra:

«Despierta, Penélope, hija mía, para que veas con tus propios ojos lo que esperas todos los días. Ha venido Odiseo, ha llegado a casa por fin, aunque tarde, y ha matado a los ilustres pretendientes, a los que afligían su casa comiéndose los bienes y haciendo de su hijo el objeto de sus violencias.»

Y se dirigió a ella la prudente Penélope: 10

«Nodriza querida, te han vuelto loca los dioses, los que pueden volver insensato a cualquiera, por muy sensato que sea, y hacer entrar en razón al de mente estúpida. Ellos te han dañado; antes eras equilibrada en tu mente.

»¿Por qué te burlas de mí, si tengo el ánimo quebrantado por el dolor, diciéndome estos extravíos y me despiertas del dulce sueño que me tenía encadenados los párpados? Jamás había dormido de tal modo desde que Odiseo marchó a la madita Ilión que no hay que nombrar.

»Pero vamos, baja ya y vuelve al mégaron. Porque si cual-   20
quiera otra de las mujeres que están a mi servicio hubiera venido a anunciarme esto y me hubiera despertado, seguro que la habría hecho volver al mégaron con palabra violenta. A ti, en cambio, te valdrá la vejez, por lo menos en esto.»

Y le contestó su nodriza Euriclea:

«No me burlo de ti en absoluto, hija mía, que en verdad ha llegado Odiseo, ha vuelto a casa como te anuncio y es el forastero a quien todos deshonraban en el mégaron. Telémaco sabía hace tiempo que ya estaba dentro, pero ocultó con prudencia los proyectos de su padre para que castigara la violencia de esos hombres altivos.»

Así dijo; invadió a Penélope la alegría y, saltando del lecho, abrazó a la anciana, dejó correr el llanto de sus párpados y hablándole dijo aladas palabras:

«Vamos, nodriza querida, dime la verdad, dime si de verdad ha llegado a casa como anuncias; dime cómo ha puesto sus manos sobre los pretendientes desvergonzados, solo como estaba, mientras que ellos permanecían dentro siempre en grupo.»

Y le contestó su nodriza Euriclea:

«No lo he visto, no me lo han dicho, sólo he oído el ruido de los que caían muertos. Nosotras permanecíamos asustadas en un rincón de la bien construida habitación —y la cerraban bien ajustadas puertas— hasta que tu hijo me llamó desde el mégaron, Telémaco, pues su padre le había mandado que me llamara. Después encontré a Odiseo en pie, entre los cuerpos recién asesinados que cubrían el firme suelo, hacinados unos sobre otros. Habrías gozado en tu ánimo si lo hubieras visto rociado de sangre y polvo como un léon. Ahora ya están todos amontonados en la puerta del patio mientas él rocía con azufre la hermosa sala, luego de encender un gran fuego, y me ha mandado que te llame. Vamos, sígueme, para que vuestros corazones alcancen la felicidad después de haber sufrido infinidad de pruebas. Ahora ya se ha cumplido este tu mayor anhelo: él ha llegado vivo y está en su hogar y te ha encontrado a ti y a su hijo en el palacio, y a los que le ultrajaban, a los pretendientes, a todos los ha hecho pagar en su palacio.»

Y le respondió la prudente Penélope:

«Nodriza querida, no eleves todavía tus súplicas ni te alegres en exceso. Sabes bien cuán bienvenido sería en el palacio para todos, y en especial para mí y para nuestro hijo, a quien engendramos, pero no es verdadera esta noticia que me anuncias, sino que uno de los inmortales ha dado muerte a los ilustres pretendientes, irritado por su insolencia dolorosa y sus malvadas acciones, pues no respetaban a ninguno de los hombres que pisan la tierra, ni al del pueblo ni al noble, cualquiera que se llegara a ellos. Por esto, por su maldad, han sufrido la desgracia, que lo que es Odiseo... éste ha perdido su regreso lejos de Acaya y ha perecido.»

Y le contestó su nodriza Euriclea:

«Hija mía, ¡qué palabra ha escapado del cerco de tus dientes! ¡Tú, que dices que no volverá jamás tu esposo, cuando ya está dentro, junto al hogar! Tu corazón ha sido siempre desconfiado, pero te voy a dar otra señal manifiesta: cuando le lavaba vi la herida que una vez le hizo un jabalí con su blanco colmillo; quise decírtelo, pero él me asió la boca con sus manos y no me lo permitió por la astucia de su mente. Vamos, sígueme, que yo misma me ofrezco en prenda y, si te engaño, mátame con la muerte más lamentable.»

Y le contestó la prudente Penélope:

«Nodriza querida, es difícil que tú descubras los designios de los dioses, que han nacido para siempre, por muy astuta que seas. Vayamos, pues, en busca de mi hijo para que yo vea a los pretendientes muertos y a quien los mató.»

Así dijo, y descendió del piso de arriba. Su corazón revolvía una y otra vez si interrogaría a su esposo desde lejos o se colocaría a su lado, le tomaría de las manos y le besaría la cabeza. Y cuando entró y traspasó el umbral de piedra se sentó frente a Odiseo junto al resplandor del fuego, en la pared de enfrente. Él se sentaba junto a una elevada columna con la vista baja esperando que le dijera algo su fuerte esposa cuando lo viera con sus ojos, pero ella permaneció sentada en silencio largo tiempo —pues el estupor alcanzaba su corazón. Unas veces le miraba fijamente al rostro y otras no lo reconocía por llevar en su cuerpo miserables vestidos.

Entonces Telémaco la reprendió, le dijo su palabra y la llamó por su nombre:

«Madre mía, mala madre, que tienes un corazón tan cruel. ¿Por qué te mantienes tan alejada de mi padre y no te sientas junto a él para interrogarle y enterarte de todo? Ninguna otra mujer se mantendría con ánimo tan tenaz apartada de su marido, cuando éste después de pasar innumerables calamidades

[373]

llega a su patria a los veinte años. Pero tu corazón es siempre más duro que la piedra.»

Y le contestó la prudente Penélope:

«Hijo mío, tengo el corazón pasmado dentro del pecho y no puedo pronunciar una sola palabra ni interrogarle, ni mirarle siquiera a la cara. Si en verdad es Odiseo y ha llegado a casa, nos reconoceremos mutuamente mejor, pues tenemos señales secretas para los demás que sólo nosotros dos conocemos.»　110

Así habló y sonrió el sufridor, el divino Odiseo, y al punto dirigió a Telémaco aladas palabras:

«Telémaco, deja a tu madre que me ponga a prueba en el palacio y así lo verá mejor. Como ahora estoy sucio y tengo sobre mi cuerpo vestidos míseros, no me honra y todavía no cree que yo sea aquél. Pero deliberemos antes de modo que resulte todo mejor, pues cualquiera que mata en el pueblo incluso a un hombre que no deja atrás muchos vengadores, se da a la fuga abandonando sus parientes y su tierra patria, pero yo he mata-　120 do a los defensores de la ciudad, a los más nobles mozos de Ítaca. Te invito a que consideres esto.»

Y le contestó Telémaco discretamente:

«Considéralo tú mismo, padre mío, pues dicen que tus decisiones son las mejores y ningún otro de los mortales hombres osaría rivalizar contigo. Nosotros te apoyaremos ardorosos y te aseguro que no nos faltará fuerza en cuanto esté de nuestra parte.»

Y le contestó y dijo el muy astuto Odiseo:

«Te voy a decir lo que me parece mejor. En primer lugar,　130 lavaos y vestid vuestras túnicas, y ordenad a las esclavas en el palacio que elijan ropas para ellas mismas. Después, que el divino aedo nos entone una alegre danza con su sonora lira, para que cualquiera piense que hay boda si lo oye desde fuera, ya sea un caminante o uno de nuestros vecinos; que no se extienda por la ciudad la noticia de la muerte de los pretendientes antes de que salgamos en dirección a nuestra finca, abundante en árboles. Una vez allí pensaremos qué cosa de provecho nos　140 va a conceder el Olímpico.»

Así habló, y al punto todos le escucharon y obedecieron. En primer lugar se lavaron y vistieron las túnicas, y las mujeres se adornaron. Luego, el divino aedo tomó su curvada lira y excitó en ellos el deseo del dulce canto y la ilustre danza. Y la gran mansión retumbaba con los pies de los hombres que danzaban y de las mujeres de lindos ceñidores.

Y uno que lo oyó desde fuera del palacio decía así:

«Seguro que se ha desposado ya alguien con la muy pretendida reina. ¡Desdichada!, no ha tenido valor para proteger con constancia la gran mansión de su legítimo esposo, hasta que llegara.»

Así decía uno, pero no sabían en verdad qué había pasado.

Después lavó a Odiseo, el de gran corazón, el ama de llaves Eurínome y lo ungió con aceite y puso a su alrededor una hermosa túnica y manto. Entonces derramó Atenea sobre su cabeza abundante gracia para que pareciera más alto y más ancho e hizo que cayeran de su cabeza ensortijados cabellos semejantes a la flor del jacinto. Como cuando derrama oro sobre plata un hombre entendido a quien Hefesto y Palas Atenea han enseñado toda clase de habilidad y lleva a término obras que agradan, así derramó la gracia sobre éste, sobre su cabeza y hombro[288]. Y salió de la bañera semejante en cuerpo a los inmortales.

Fue a sentarse de nuevo en el sillón, del que se había levantado, frente a su esposa, y le dirigió su palabra:

«Querida mía, los que tienen mansiones en el Olimpo te han puesto un corazón más inflexible que a las demás mujeres. Ninguna otra se mantendría con ánimo tan tenaz apartada de su marido cuando éste, después de pasar innumerables calamidades, llega a su patria a los veinte años. Vamos, nodriza, prepárame el lecho para que también yo me acueste, pues ésta tiene un corazón de hierro dentro del pecho.»

Y le contestó la prudente Penélope:

«Querido mío, no me tengo en mucho ni en poco ni me admiro en exceso, pero sé muy bien cómo eras cuando marchaste de Ítaca en la nave de largos remos. Vamos, Euriclea, prepara el labrado lecho fuera del sólido tálamo, el que construyó él mismo. Y una vez que hayáis puesto fuera el labrado lecho, disponed la cama —pieles, mantas y resplandecientes colchas.»

---

[288] Cfr. VI.230-5.

Así dijo poniendo a prueba a su esposo. Entonces Odiseo se dirigió irritado a su fiel esposa:

«Mujer, esta palabra que has dicho es dolorosa para mi corazón. ¿Quién me ha puesto la cama en otro sitio? Sería difícil incluso para uno muy hábil si no viniera un dios en persona y lo pusiera fácilmente en otro lugar; que de los hombres, ningún mortal viviente, ni aun en la flor de la edad, lo cambiaría fácilmente, pues hay una señal en el labrado lecho, y lo construí yo y nadie más. Había crecido dentro del patio un tronco de olivo de extensas hojas, robusto y floreciente, ancho como una columna. Edifiqué el dormitorio en torno a él, hasta acabarlo, con piedras espesas, y lo cubrí bien con un techo y le añadí puertas bien ajustadas, habilidosamente trabadas. Fue entonces cuando corté el follaje del olivo de extensas hojas; empecé a podar el tronco desde la raíz, lo pulí bien y habilidosamente con el bronce y lo igualé con la plomada, convirtiéndolo en pie de la cama, y luego lo taladré todo con el berbiquí. Comenzando por aquí lo pulimenté, hasta acabarlo, lo adorné con oro, plata y marfil y tensé dentro unas correas de piel de buey que brillaban de púrpura.

»Esta es la señal que te manifiesto, aunque no sé si mi lecho está todavía intacto, mujer, o si ya lo ha puesto algún hombre en otro sitio, cortando la base del olivo.»

Así dijo, y a ella se le aflojaron las rodillas y el corazón al reconocer las señales que le había manifestado claramente Odiseo. Corrió llorando hacia él y echó sus brazos alrededor del cuello de Odiseo; besó su cabeza y dijo:

«No te enojes conmigo, Odiseo, que en lo demás eres más sensato que el resto de los hombres. Los dioses nos han enviado el infortunio, ellos, que envidiaban que gozáramos de la juventud y llegáramos al umbral de la vejez uno al lado del otro. Por esto no te irrites ahora conmigo ni te enojes porque al principio, nada más verte, no te acogiera con amor. Pues continuamente mi corazón se estremecía dentro del pecho por temor a que alguno de los mortales se acercase a mí y me engañara con sus palabras, pues muchos conciben proyectos malvados para su provecho. Ni la argiva Helena, del linaje de Zeus, se hubiera unido a un extranjero en amor y cama, si hubiera sabido que los belicosos hijos de los aqueos habían de llevarla

190

200

210

220

de nuevo a casa, a su patria[289]. Fue un dios quien la impulsó a ejecutar una acción vergonzosa, que antes no había puesto en su mente esta lamentable ceguera por la que, por primera vez, se llegó a nosotros el dolor.

»Pero ahora que me has manifestado claramente las señales de nuestro lecho, que ningún otro mortal había visto sino sólo tú y yo —y una sola sierva, Actorís, la que me dio mi padre al venir yo aquí, la que nos vigilaba las puertas del labrado dormitorio—, ya tienes convencido a mi corazón, por muy inflexible que sea.»   230

Así habló, y a él se le levantó todavía más el deseo de llorar y lloraba abrazado a su deseada, a su fiel esposa. Como cuando la tierra aparece deseable a los ojos de los que nadan (a los que Poseidón ha destruido la bien construida nave en el ponto, impulsada por el viento y el recio oleaje; pocos han conseguido escapar del canoso mar nadando hacia el litoral y —cuajada su piel de costras de sal— consiguen llegar a tierra bienvenidos, después de huir de la desgracia), así de bienvenido era el esposo para Penélope, quien no dejaba de mirarlo y no acababa de soltar del todo sus blancos brazos del cuello.   240

Y se les hubiera aparecido Eos, de dedos de rosa, mientras se lamentaban, si la diosa de ojos brillantes, Atenea, no hubiera concebido otro proyecto: contuvo a la noche[290] en el otro extremo al tiempo que la prolongaba, y a Eos, de trono de oro, la empujó de nuevo hacia Océano y no permitía que unciera sus caballos de veloces pies, los que llevan la luz a los hombres, Lampo y Faetonte[291], los potros que conducen a Eos.

Entonces se dirigió a su esposa el muy astuto Odiseo:

«Mujer, no hemos llegado todavía a la meta de las pruebas,

---

[289] No parece muy clara la pertinencia de este ejemplo que aduce Penélope. Es posible que trate de exculparse de la frialdad inicial con Odiseo atribuyéndola a los dioses. En todo caso, es un buen ejemplo del proceso de rehabilitación moral de Helena cuyos ecos se perciben más de una vez en la *Odisea*.

[290] Resulta extraña esta alteración del orden normal del tiempo para tan insignificante fin. Sólo hay otro ejemplo en la Mitología griega cuando Zeus hizo que Helios invirtiera su curso para que Atreo reinara sobre Tiestes, cfr. Eurípides, *Electra*, vv. 726 y ss.

[291] Son dos nombres parlantes, «el que brilla» y «el que alumbra». No hay que confundir a este Faetonte con el hijo de Helios —o de Eos según Hesiodo, *Teogonía*, 986 y ss.

que aún tendremos un trabajo desmedido y difícil que es preci- 250
so que yo acabe del todo. Así me lo vaticinó el alma de Tiresias el día en que descendí a la morada de Hades, para inquirir
sobre el regreso de mis compañeros y el mío propio. Pero
vayamos a la cama, mujer, para gozar ya del dulce sueño acos-
tados.»

Y le contestó la prudente Penélope:

«Estará en tus manos el acostarte cuando así lo desee tu corazón, ahora que los dioses te han hecho volver a tu bien edificado palacio y a tu tierra patria. Pero puesto que has hecho
una consideración —y seguro que un dios la ha puesto en tu 260
mente—, vamos, dime la prueba que te espera, puesto que me
voy a enterar después, creo yo, y no es peor que lo sepa ahora
mismo.»

Y le contestó y dijo el muy astuto Odiseo:

«Querida mía, ¿por qué me apremias tanto a que te lo diga?
En fin, te lo voy a decir y no lo ocultaré, pero tu corazón no
se sentirá feliz; tampoco yo me alegro, puesto que me ha ordenado ir a muchas ciudades de mortales con un manejable remo
entre mis manos, hasta que llegue a los hombres que no conocen el mar ni comen alimentos aderezados con sal; tampoco 270
conocen estos hombres las naves de rojas mejillas ni los manejables remos que son alas para las naves. Y me dio esta señal
que no te voy a ocultar: cuando un caminante, al encontrarse
conmigo, diga que llevo un bieldo sobre mi ilustre hombro,
me ordenó que en ese momento clavara en tierra el remo,
ofreciera hermosos sacrificios al soberano Poseidón —un ca-
brito, un toro y un verraco semental de cerdas—, que volviera
a casa y ofreciera sagradas hecatombes a los dioses inmortales,
los que poseen el ancho cielo, a todos por orden. Y me sobre- 280
vendrá una muerte dulce, lejos del mar, de tal suerte que me
destruya abrumado por la vejez. Y a mi alrededor el pueblo
será feliz[292]. Me aseguró que todo esto se va a cumplir.»

Y se dirigió a él la prudente Penélope:

«Si los dioses nos conceden una vejez feliz, hay esperanza de
que tendremos medios de escapar a la desgracia.»

Así hablaban el uno con el otro. Entretanto, Eurínome y la

---

[292] Cfr. XI.121-37.

nodriza dispusieron la cama con ropa blanda bajo la luz de las
antorchas. Luego que hubieron preparado diligentemente el la- 290
brado lecho, la anciana se marchó a dormir a su habitación y
Eurínome, la camarera, los condujo mientras se dirigían al lecho con una antorcha en sus manos. Luego que los hubo conducido se volvió, y ellos llegaron de buen grado al lugar de su
antiguo lecho.

Después Telémaco, el boyero y el porquero hicieron descan-
sar a sus pies de la danza y fueron todos a acostarse por el
sombrío palacio.

Y cuando habían gozado del amor placentero, se compla- 300
cían los dos esposos contándose mutuamente, ella cuánto había soportado en el palacio, la divina entre las mujeres, contemplando la odiosa comparsa de los pretendientes que por
causa de ella degollaban en abundancia toros y gordas ovejas y
sacaban de las tinajas gran cantidad de vino; por su parte, Odiseo, de linaje divino, le contó cuántas penalidades había causado a los hombres y cuántas había padecido él mismo con fatiga. Penélope gozaba escuchándole y el sueño no cayó sobre
sus párpados hasta que le contara todo. Comenzó narrando[293] 310
cómo había sometido a los cícones y llegado después a la fértil
tierra de los Lotófagos, y cuánto le hizo al Cíclope y cómo se
vengó del castigo de sus ilustres compañeros a quienes aquél
se había comido sin compasión, y cómo llegó a Eolo, que lo
acogió y despidió afablemente, pero todavía no estaba decidido
que llegara a su patria, sino que una tempestad lo arrebató de
nuevo y lo llevaba por el ponto, lleno de peces, entre profundos lamentos; y cómo llegó a Telépilo de los Lestrígones, quienes destruyeron sus naves y a todos sus compañeros de buenas
grebas[294]. Sólo Odiseo consiguió escapar en la negra nave. 320

Le contó el engaño y la destreza de Circe y cómo bajó a la
sombría mansión de Hades para consultar al alma del tebano

---

[293] Hasta el v. 341 constituye un resumen completo y bastante ajustado, salvo algunos detalles, de todas las aventuras de Odiseo comprendidas en los cantos VIII-XIII, pero aquí, lógicamente, en orden cronológico. Algunos filólogos
han sugerido, desacertadamente, que podría tratarse de un resumen mnemotécnico para uso de rapsodas.

[294] No murieron todos. Quedaron los de la nave de Odiseo.

Tiresias con su nave de muchas filas de remeros —y vio a todos sus compañeros[295] y a su madre que lo había parido y criado de niño, y cómo oyó el rumor de las Sirenas de dulce canto y llegó a las Rocas Errantes[296] y a la terrible Caribdis y a Escila, a quien jamás han evitado incólumes los hombres. Y cómo sus compañeros mataron las vacas de Helios y cómo Zeus, el que truena arriba, disparó contra la rápida nave su humeante rayo —y todos sus compañeros perecieron juntos, pero él evitó a las funestas Keres. Y cómo llegó a la isla de Ogigia y a la ninfa Calipso, quien lo retuvo en cóncava cueva deseando que fuera su esposo; le alimentó y decía que lo haría inmortal y sin vejez para siempre, pero no persuadió a su corazón. Y cómo después de mucho sufrir llegó a los feacios, quienes le honraron de todo corazón como a un dios y lo condujeron en una nave a su tierra patria, después de regalarle bronce, oro en abundancia y vestidos.

Esta fue la última palabra que dijo cuando el dulce sueño, el que afloja los miembros, le asaltó desatando las preocupaciones de su corazón.

Entonces proyectó otra decisión Atenea, la diosa de ojos brillantes: cuando creyó que Odiseo ya había gozado del lecho de su esposa y del sueño, al punto hizo salir de Océano a la de trono de oro, a la que nace de la mañana, para que llevara la luz a los hombres. Entonces se levantó Odiseo del blando lecho y dirigió la palabra a su esposa:

«Mujer, ya estamos saturados ambos de pruebas inumerables; tú, llorando aquí mi penoso regreso y yo... a mí Zeus y los demás dioses me tenían encadenado con dolores lejos de aquí, de mi tierra patria, pero ahora que los dos hemos llegado al deseable lecho, tú has de cuidarme las riquezas que poseo en el palacio, que en cuanto a las ovejas que los altivos pretendientes me degollaron, muchas se las robaré yo mismo y otras me las darán los aqueos hasta que llenen mis establos. Mas ahora parto hacia la finca de muchos árboles para ver a mi noble padre que me está apenado. A ti, mujer, te encomiendo

---

295 No vio a *todos* sus compañeros, sino sólo a Elpenor.
296 En realidad, Odiseo evitó este camino que Circe le había señalado como alternativa de Escila y Caribdis, cfr. XII.60 y ss.

esto, ya que eres prudente: al levantarse el sol correrá la noticia de la matanza de los pretendientes en el palacio; sube al piso de arriba con las siervas y permanece allí, y no mires a nadie ni preguntes.»

Así dijo y vistió alrededor de sus hombros la hermosa armadura y apremió a Telémaco, al boyero y al porquero, ordenándoles que tomaran en sus manos los instrumentos de guerra. Éstos no le desobedecieron, se vistieron con el bronce, cerraron las puertas y salieron. Y los conducía Odiseo. Ya había luz 370 sobre la tierra, pero Atenea los cubrió con la noche y los condujo rápidamente fuera de la ciudad.

EL PACTO

Y Hermes llamaba a las almas de los pretendientes, el Cilenio[297], y tenía entre sus manos el hermoso caduceo de oro con el que hechiza los ojos de los hombres que quiere y de nuevo los despierta cuando duermen. Con éste los puso en movimiento y los conducía, y ellas le seguían estridiendo. Como cuando los murciélagos en lo más profundo de una cueva infinita revolotean estridentes cuando se desprende uno de la cadena y cae de la roca —pues se adhieren unos a otros— así iban ellas estridiendo todas juntas y las conducía Hermes, el Benéfico[298], por los sombríos senderos. Traspusieron las corrientes de Océano y la Roca Leúcade y atravesaron las puertas de Helios y el pueblo de los Sueños[299]; y pronto llegaron a un prado de asfódelo donde habitan las almas, imágenes de los difuntos.

10

---

[297] Cilenio es un epíteto local de Hermes en Arcadia donde se sitúa el monte Cilene. También aparece en el *Himno a Hermes*, v. 318.

[298] Es otro epíteto extraño de Hermes, aunque ya aparecía en *Ilíada*, XVI.185, y reaparece en Hesiodo, *Fragm.*, 137 West.

[299] Leúcade es el nombre de varios promontorios y ciudades costeras. Sin embargo, debe tratarse aquí de un nombre mítico, puesto que está «más allá de las corrientes de Océnao». Lo mismo hay que decir de «Las puertas de Helios» y del «Pueblo de los Sueños». Toda esta geografía infernal es ajena al resto de los poemas homéricos, así como el carácter de Psicopompo de Hermes y la forma en que bajan las almas al Hades. Toda esta parte, hasta el v. 204, es la llamada segunda Nekya y ya fue atetizada por Aristarco como señala el escoliasta. Cfr. Introducción.

Allí encontraron el alma del Pelida Aquiles y la de Patroclo y la del irreprochable Antíloco y la de Áyax, el más excelente en aspecto y cuerpo de los dánaos después del irreprochable hijo de Peleo. Todos se iban congregando en torno a éste; acercóse doliente el alma de Agamenón el Atrida y, a su alrededor, las de cuantos murieron con él en casa de Egisto y cumplieron su destino.

A éste se dirigió en primer lugar el alma del Pelida:

«Atrida, estábamos convencidos de que tú eras querido por Zeus, el que goza con el rayo, por encima de los demás héroes puesto que reinabas sobre muchos y fuertes hombres en el pueblo de los troyanos, donde sufrimos penalidades los aqueos. Sin embargo, también se había de poner a tu lado la luctuosa Moira, a la que nadie evita de los que han nacido. ¡Ojalá hubieras obtenido muerte y destino en el pueblo de los troyanos disfrutando de los honores con los que reinabas! Así te hubiera levantado una tumba el ejército panaqueo y habrías cobrado gran gloria también para tu hijo. Sin embargo, te había tocado en suerte perecer con la muerte más lamentable.»

Y le contestó a su vez el alma del Atrida:

«Dichoso hijo de Peleo, semejante a los dioses, Aquiles, tú que pereciste en Troya, lejos de Argos y en torno a ti sucumbían los mejores hijos de troyanos y aqueos luchando por tu cadáver, mientras tú yacías en medio de un torbellino de polvo ocupando un gran espacio, olvidado ya de conducir tu carro. Nosotros luchamos todo el día y no habríamos cesado de luchar en absoluto, si Zeus no lo hubiera impedido con una tempestad. Después, cuando te sacamos de la batalla y te llevamos a las naves, te pusimos en un lecho tras limpiar tu hermosa piel con agua tibia y con aceite, y en torno a ti todos los dánaos derramaban muchas, calientes lágrimas y se mesaban los cabellos.

»Entonces llegó tu madre del mar con las inmortales diosas marinas, después de oír la noticia, y un lamento inmenso se levantó sobre el ponto. El temblor se apoderó de todos los aqueos y se habrían levantado para embarcarse en las cóncavas naves, si no los hubiera contenido un hombre sabedor de cosas muchas y antiguas, Néstor, cuyo consejo también antes parecía el mejor. Éste habló con buenos sentimientos hacia ellos y dijo: "Conteneos, argivos, no huyáis, hijos de los aqueos. Esta es su madre y viene del mar con las inmortales diosas marinas para encontrarse con su hijo muerto." Así habló y ellos contuvieron su huida temerosa.

»Entonces te rodearon llorando las hijas del viejo del mar y, lamentándose, te pusieron vestidos inmortales. Y las Musas, nueve en total[300], cantaban alternativamente un canto funerario con hermosa voz. En ese momento no habrías visto a ninguno de los argivos sin lágrimas: ¡tanto los conmovía la sonora Musa!

»Dieciocho noches te lloramos, e igualmente de día, los dioses inmortales y los mortales hombres. El día décimoctavo te entregamos al fuego y sacrificamos animales en torno tuyo, bien alimentados rebaños y cuernitorcidos bueyes. Tú ardías envuelto en vestiduras de dioses y en abundante aceite y dulce miel. Muchos héroes aqueos circularon con sus armas alrededor de tu pira mientras ardías, a pie y a caballo, y se levantaba un gran estrépito. Después, cuando te había quemado la llama de Hefesto, al amanecer, recogimos tus blancos huesos, Aquiles, envolviéndolos en vino sin mezcla y en aceite, pues tu madre nos donó un ánfora de oro —decía que era regalo de Dioniso[301] y obra del ilustre Hefesto. En ella están tus blancos huesos, ilustre Aquiles, mezclados con los del cadáver de Patroclo, el hijo de Menetio, y, separados, los de Antíloco a quien honrabas por encima de los demás compañeros, aunque después de Patroclo, muerto también. Y levantamos sobre ellos un monumento grande y perfecto el sagrado ejército de los guerreros argivos, junto al prominente litoral del vasto Helesponto. Así podrás ser visto de lejos, desde el mar, por los hombres que ahora viven y por los que vivirán después.

---

[300] Homero habitualmente habla de Musa en singular (cfr. I.1, VIII.73, 481, 488. Este es el primer pasaje donde se habla de Nueve —aunque más abajo vuelve al singular, que es, más bien, un colectivo. A partir de Hesiodo (*Teogonía*, 915) ya se las considera hijas de Zeus y de Mnemósine, y posteriormente se les dieron nombres y funciones. Pero Musa procede de *montya* y es, en el origen, una divinidad de las montañas.

[301] Es la segunda vez que se cita a Dióniso (la primera en XI.325). Es un dios que no goza de las simpatías de la aristocracia, y, por tanto, de la Épica, aunque sin duda en época homérica ya tenía una presencia importante en las capas populares.

»Tu madre, después de pedírselo a los dioses, instituyó un muy hermoso certamen para los mejores de los aqueos en medio de la concurrencia. Ya has asistido al funeral de muchos héroes, cuando al morir un rey los jóvenes se ciñen las armas y se establecen competiciones, pero sería sobre todo al ver aquel cuando habrías quedado estupefacto: ¡qué hermosísimo certamen estableció la diosa en tu honor, la diosa de los pies de plata, Tetis, pues eras muy querido de los dioses. Conque ni aún al morir has perdido tu nombre, sino que tu fama de nobleza llegará siempre a todos los hombres, Aquiles. En cambio a mí...!, ¿qué placer obtuve al concluir la guerra? Zeus me preparó durante el regreso una penosa muerte a manos de Egisto y de mi funesta esposa.»

Esto es lo que decían entre sí.

Y se les acercó el Mensajero, el Argifonte, conduciendo las almas de los pretendientes muertos a manos de Odiseo. Ambos se admiraron al verlos y se fueron derechos a ellos, y el alma de Agamenón, el Atrida, reconoció al querido hijo de Melaneo, el muy ilustre Anfimedonte, pues era huésped suyo cuando habitaba su palacio de Itaca. Así que se dirigió a éste en primer lugar el alma del Atrida:

«Anfimedonte, ¿qué os ha pasado para que os hundáis en la sombría tierra, hombres selectos todos y de la misma edad? Nadie que escogiera en la ciudad a los mejores hombres elegiría de otra manera. ¿Es que os ha sometido Poseidón en las naves levantado crueles vientos y enormes olas?; ¿o acaso os han destruido en tierra firme, en algún sitio, hombres enemigos cuando intentabais llevaros sus bueyes o sus hermosos rebaños de ovejas, o luchando por la ciudad y sus mujeres? Dímelo, puesto que te pregunto y me precio de ser tu huésped. ¿O no te acuerdas cuando llegué a vuestro palacio en compañía del divino Menelao para incitar a Odiseo a que nos acompañara a Ilión sobre las naves de buenos bancos? Durante un mes recorrimos el ancho mar y con dificultad convencimos a Odiseo, el destructor de ciudades»[302].

---

[302] Esta frase indica que Odiseo se negaba en un principio a ir a Troya. En los *Cantos chipriotas,* poema épico tardío cuyo argumento recoge la *Crestomatía* de Proclo, se afirmaba que Odiseo se fingió loco, pero que Palamedes descubrió su

Y le contestó el alma de Anfimedonte:

«Atrida, el más ilustre soberano de hombres, Agamenón, recuerdo todo eso tal como lo dices. Te voy a narrar cabalmente y con exactitud el funesto término de nuestra muerte, cómo fue urdido.

»Pretendíamos a la esposa de Odiseo, largo tiempo ausente, y ella ni se negaba al odiado matrimonio ni lo realizaba —pues meditaba para nosotros la muerte y la negra Ker—, sino que urdió en su interior este otro engaño: puso en el palacio un gran telar e hilaba, telar suave e inacabable. Y nos dijo a continuación: "Jóvenes pretendientes míos, puesto que ha muerto el divino Odiseo, aguardad, aunque deseéis mi boda, hasta que acabe este manto —no sea que se me pierdan los hilos—, este sudario para el héroe Laertes, para cuando le arrebate la luctuosa Moira de la muerte de largos lamentos, no sea que alguna de las aqueas en el pueblo se irrite conmigo si yace sin sudario el que poseyó mucho." Así habló y enseguida se convenció nuestro noble ánimo. Conque allí hilaba su gran telar durante el día y por la noche lo destejía, tras colocar antorchas a su lado. Así que su engaño pasó inadvertido durante tres años y convenció a los aqueos, pero cuando llegó el cuarto año y transcurrieron las estaciones, sucediéndose los meses, y se cumplieron muchos días, nos lo dijo una de las mujeres —ella lo sabía bien— y sorprendimos a ésta destejiendo su brillante tela.

»Así fue como tuvo que acabarla, y no voluntariamente sino por la fuerza[303]. Y cuando nos mostró el manto, tras haber hilado el gran telar, tras haberlo lavado, semejante al sol y a la luna, fue entonces cuando un funesto demón trajo de algún lado a Odiseo hasta los confines del campo donde habitaba su morada el porquero. Allí marchó también el querido hijo del divino Odiseo cuando llegó de vuelta de la arenosa Pilos en negra nave y entre los dos tramaron funesta muerte para los

astucia sirviéndose de Telémaco, recién nacido. Sin embargo, todo ello parece un intento de justificar *a priori* la ulterior enemistad entre ambos héroes. En este pasaje se dice que fueron a buscar a Odiseo *solamente* Agamenón y Menelao.

[303] Es la tercera vez que se cuenta la historia del telar, cfr. también II.93-100 y XIX.138-156.

pretendientes. Y llegaron a la muy ilustre ciudad, Odiseo el último, mientras que Telémaco le precedía. El porquero llevó a aquél con miserables vestidos en su cuerpo, semejante a un mendigo miserable y viejo apoyado en su bastón, y rodeaban su cuerpo tristes vestidos. Ninguno de nosotros pudo reconocer que era él al aparecer de repente, ni los que eran más mayores, sino que le maltratábamos con palabras insultantes y con golpes. Él entretanto soportaba ser golpeado e injuriado en su propio palacio con ánimo paciente; pero cuando le incitó la voluntad de Zeus, portador de égida, tomó las hermosas armas junto con Telémaco, las ocultó en la despensa y echó los cerrojos; después mandó con mucha astucia a su esposa que entregara a los pretendientes el arco y el ceniciento hierro como competición para nosotros, hombres de triste destino, y comienzo de la matanza[304].

»Ello fue que ninguno de nosotros pudo tender la cuerda del poderoso arco; que éramos del todo incapaces. Cuando el gran arco llegó a manos de Odiseo, todos nosotros voceábamos al porquero que no se lo entregara ni aunque le rogara insistentemente. Sólo Telémaco le animó y se lo ordenó. Así que le tomó en sus manos el sufridor, el divino Odiseo y tendió el arco con facilidad, hizo pasar la flecha por el hierro, fue a ponerse sobre el umbral y disparaba sus veloces saetas mirando a uno y otro lado que daba miedo. Alcanzó al rey Antínoo y luego iba lanzando sus funestos dardos a los demás, apuntando de frente, y ellos iban cayendo hacinados.

»Era evidente que alguno de los dioses les ayudaba, pues, cediendo a su ímpetu, nos mataban desde uno y otro lado de la sala. Y se levantó un vergonzoso gemido cuando nuestras cabezas golpeaban contra el pavimento y éste todo humeaba con sangre.

»Así perecimos, Agamenón, y nuestros cuerpos yacen aún descuidados en el palacio de Odiseo, pues todavía no lo saben nuestros parientes, quienes lavarían la sangre de nuestras heri-

160

170

180

---

[304] Este relato no responde a la *Odisea* que tenemos, por lo que algunos críticos han llegado a pensar que quizá pertenezca a una redacción primitiva en que Odiseo se da a conocer a Penélope y *juntos* traman la muerte de los pretendientes.

das y nos llorarían después de depositarnos, que éste es el honor que se tributa a los que han muerto.»

Y le contestó el alma del Atrida:

«¡Dichoso hijo de Laertes, muy astuto Odiseo, por fin has recuperado a tu esposa con tu gran valor! ¡Así de buenos eran los pensamientos de la irreprochable Penélope, la hija de Icario! ¡Así de bien se acordaba de Odiseo, de su esposo legítimo! Por eso la fama de su virtud no perecerá y los inmortales fabricarán un canto a los terrenos hombres en honor de la prudente Penélope. No preparó acciones malvadas como la hija de Tíndaro que mató a su esposo legítimo y un canto odioso correrá entre los hombres; ha creado una fama funesta para las mujeres, incluso para las que sean de buen obrar»[305].

Esto era lo que hablaban entre sí en la morada de Hades, bajo las cavernas de la tierra.

* * *

Entretanto, Odiseo y los suyos bajaron de la ciudad y enseguida llegaron al hermoso y bien cultivado campo que Laertes mismo había adquirido en otro tiempo, después de haber sufrido mucho. Allí tenía una mansión y, rodeándola por completo, corría un cobertizo en el que comían, descansaban y pasaban la noche los esclavos forzosos que le hacían la labor. También había una mujer, la anciana Sícele que cuidaba gentilmente al anciano en el campo, lejos de la ciudad.

Entonces dijo Odiseo su palabra a los esclavos y a su hijo:

«Vosotros entrad ya en la bien edificada casa y sacrificad para la cena el mejor de los cerdos, que yo, por mi parte, voy a poner a prueba a mi padre, a ver si me reconoce y distingue con sus ojos o no me reconoce por llevar mucho tiempo lejos.»

Así dijo y entregó a los esclavos sus armas, dignas de Ares.

---

[305] Aquí culmina la *sýncrisis* o comparación entre las familias de Odiseo y Agamenón que ha sido un *leit-motiv* de la obra. Por ello la segunda Nekya no sólo no es innecesaria, como pretenden algunos, sino que ofrece un paralelismo necesario a la primera: allí se narraba la muerte de Agamenón y se señalaba el carácter pérfido de Clitemnestra; aquí se narra el triunfo de Odiseo y se subraya la fidelidad de Penélope. Incluso el detalle de hacer colaborar a Penélope con Odiseo parece intencionado para oponerla a Clitemnestra.

Estos entraron rápidamente en la casa, mientras que Odiseo se 220
acercaba a la viña abundante en frutos para probar suerte.
Y no encontró a Dolio al descender a la gran huerta ni a ninguno de los esclavos ni de los hijos; habían marchado a recoger piedras para un muro que sirviera de cercado a la viña y
los conducía el anciano. Así que encontró solo a su padre aco-
llando un retoño en la bien cultivada viña. Vestía un manto
descolorido, zurcido, vergonzoso y alrededor de sus piernas tenía atadas unas mal cosidas grebas para evitar los arañazos; en
sus manos tenía unos guantes por causa de las zarzas y sobre 230
su cabeza una gorra de piel de cabra. Y hacía crecer sus dolores.

Cuando el sufridor, el divino Odiseo lo vio doblegado por la
vejez y con una gran pena en su interior, se puso bajo un elevado peral y derramaba lágrimas. Después dudó en su interior
entre besar y abrazar a su padre, y contarle detalladamente
cómo había venido y llegado por fin a su tierra patria, o preguntarle primero y probarle en cada detalle. Y mientras meditaba, le pareció más ventajoso tentarle primero con palabras 240
mordaces; así que se fue derecho hacia él el divino Odiseo. En
este momento el anciano mantenía la cabeza baja y acollaba un
retoño, y poniéndose a su lado le dijo su ilustre hijo:

«Anciano, no eres inexperto en cultivar el huerto, que tiene
un buen cultivo y nada en tu jardín está descuidado, ni la planta ni la higuera ni la vid ni el olivo ni el peral ni la legumbre.
Pero te voy a decir otra cosa, no pongas la cólera en tu ánimo:
tu propio cuerpo no tiene un buen cultivo, sino una triste vejez al tiempo que estás escuálido y vestido indecorosamente. 250
No, por indolencia al menos no se despreocupa de ti tu dueño
y no hay nada de servil que sobresalga en ti al mirar tu forma y
estatura, pues más bien te pareces a un rey o a uno que duerme muellemente después que se ha lavado y comido, que ésta
es la costumbre de los ancianos. Pero, vamos, dime esto —e
infórmame con verdad—: ¿de qué hombre eres esclavo?, ¿de
quién es el huerto que cultivas? Respóndeme también a esto
con la verdad, para cerciorarme bien si esta tierra, a la que he
llegado, es Itaca como me ha dicho ese hombre con quien me 260
he encontrado al venir aquí (y no muy sensato, por cierto, que
no se atrevió a darme detalles ni a escuchar mi palabra cuando

le preguntaba si mi huésped vive en algún sitio, y aún existe, o ya ha muerto y está en la morada de Hades). Voy a decirte algo, atiende y escúchame: en cierta ocasión acogí en mi tierra a un hombre que había llegado a mí. Jamás otro mortal venido a mi casa desde lejanas tierras me fue más querido que él. Afirmaba con orgullo que su linaje procedía de Ítaca y que su padre era Laertes, el hijo de Arcisio. Lo conduje a mi casa y le acogí honrándole gentilmente, pues en ella había abundantes bienes. Le ofrecí dones de hospitalidad, los que le eran propios: le di siete talentos de oro bien trabajados, una crátera de plata adornada con flores, doce cobertores simples, otras tantas alfombras y el mismo número de hermosas túnicas y mantos. Aparte, le entregué cuatro mujeres conocedoras de labores brillantes, muy hermosas, las que él quiso escoger.»

Y le contestó su padre derramando lágrimas:

«Forastero, es cierto que has llegado a la tierra por la que preguntas, pero la dominan hombres insolentes e insensatos. Los dones que le ofreciste, con ser muchos, resultaron vanos, pues si lo hubieras encontrado vivo en el pueblo de Ítaca, te habría devuelto a casa después de compensarte bien con regalos y con una buena acogida; pues esto es lo establecido, quienquiera que sea el que empieza.

»Pero vamos, dime e infórmame con verdad: ¿cuántos años hace que diste hospitalidad a aquel huésped tuyo desgraciado, a mi hijo —si es que existió alguna vez—, al malhadado a quien han devorado los peces en el mar, lejos de los suyos y su tierra patria, o se ha convertido en presa de fieras y aves en tierra firme? Que no lo ha llorado su madre después de amortajarlo ni su padre, los que lo engendramos; ni su esposa de abundante dote, la prudente Penélope, ha llorado como es debido a su esposo junto al lecho después de cerrarle los ojos, pues éste es el honor que se tributa a los que han muerto.

»Dime ahora esto también tú con verdad para que yo lo sepa: ¿quién eres entre los hombres?, ¿dónde están tu ciudad y tus padres?, ¿dónde está detenida tu rápida nave, la que te ha conducido hasta aquí con tus divinos compañeros?; ¿o acaso has venido como pasajero en nave ajena y ellos se han marchado después de dejarte en tierra?»

Y le contestó y dijo el muy astuto Odiseo:

«Te voy a contar todo con detalle: soy de Alibante donde habito mi ilustre morada, hijo del rey Afidanto, hijo de Polipemón, y mi nombre propio es Epérito. Ello es que un demón me ha hecho llegar hasta aquí, aunque no quería, apartándome de Sicania[306]; mi nave está detenida junto al campo, lejos de la ciudad. Este es el quinto año desde que Odiseo marchó de allí y abandonó mi patria, el malhadado. Desde luego las aves le eran favorables cuando marchó, estaban a la derecha; con ellas yo me alegré y le despedí y él estaba alegre al marchar. Nuestro ánimo confiaba en que volveríamos a reunirnos en hospitalidad y entregarnos espléndidos presentes.» 310

Así habló y una negra nube de dolor envolvió a Laertes, tomó polvo de cenicienta tierra y lo derramó por su encanecida cabeza mientras gemía agitadamente. Entonces se conmovió el espíritu de Odiseo, le salió por las narices un ímpetu violento al ver a su padre y de un salto le abrazó y besó diciendo: 320

«Soy yo, padre, aquél por quien preguntas, yo que he llegado a los veinte años a mi tierra patria. Pero contén tu llanto y lamentos, pues te voy a decir una cosa —y es preciso que nos apresuremos ya—: he matado a los pretendientes en nuestro palacio vengando sus dolorosos ultrajes y sus malvadas acciones.»

Y le contestó Laertes diciendo:

«Si de verdad eres Odiseo, mi hijo, que has llegado aquí, muéstrame una señal clara para que me convenza.»

Y le contestó y dijo el muy astuto Odiseo: 330

«Contempla con tus ojos, en primer lugar, esta herida que me hizo un jabalí hundiéndome su blanco colmillo cuando fui al Parnaso. Tú y mi venerable madre me enviasteis a Autólico, padre de mi madre, para recibir los dones que me prometió al venir aquí afirmándolo con su cabeza. Es más, te voy a señalar los árboles de la bien cultivada huerta que me regalaste en cierta ocasión. Yo te pedía cada uno de ellos cuando era niño y te seguía por el huerto; íbamos caminando entre ellos y tú me

---

[306] Es el nombre que Homero da a Sicilia, aunque conocía también este último *(Sikelía)*, como se ve por la esclava de Laertes, llamada Sicele o siciliana, cfr. también XX.383.

decías el nombre de cada uno. Me diste trece perales, diez 340
manzanos y cuarenta higueras y designaste cincuenta hileras
de vides para dármelas, cada una de distinta sazón. Había en
ellas racimos de todas clases cuando las estaciones de Zeus
caían de lo alto.»

Así habló y se debilitaron las rodillas y el corazón de éste al
reconocer las claras señales que Odiseo le había mostrado;
echó los brazos alrededor de su hijo, y el sufridor, el divino
Odiseo le atrajo hacia sí desmayado. Cuando de nuevo tomó
aliento y su ánimo se le congregó dentro, contestó con pala- 350
bras y dijo:

«Padre Zeus, todavía estáis los dioses en el Olimpo si los
pretendientes han pagado de verdad su orgullosa insolencia.
Ahora, sin embargo, temo que los itacenses vengan aquí y en-
víen mensajeros por todas partes a las ciudades de los cefalenios.»

Y le contestó y dijo el muy astuto Odiseo:

«Cobra ánimos, no te preocupes de esto, pero vamos ya a la
mansión que está cerca del huerto. Ya he enviado por delante
a Telémaco con el boyero y el porquero para que preparen la 360
cena enseguida.»

Así hablando se encaminaron a su hermosa mansión. Cuando llegaron a la casa, agradable para habitar, encontraron a
Telémaco con el boyero y el porquero cortando abundantes
carnes y mezclando rojo vino. Entre tanto la sierva Sicele lavó
al magnánimo Laertes, le ungió con aceite y le puso una hermosa túnica. Entonces Atenea se puso a su lado y aumentó los
miembros del pastor de su pueblo e hizo que pareciera más
grande y ancho que antes. Salió éste de su baño y se admiró su 370
hijo cuando lo vio frente a sí semejante a los dioses inmortales.
Así que le habló dirigiéndole aladas palabras:

«Padre, sin duda uno de los dioses, que han nacido para
siempre, te ha hecho parecer superior en belleza y estatura.»

Y le contestó Laertes discretamente:

«¡Padre Zeus, Atenea y Apolo! ¡Ojalá me hubiera enfrentado ayer con los pretendientes en mi palacio, las armas sobre
mis hombros, como cuando me apoderé de la bien edificada 380
ciudadela de Nérito, promontorio del continente acaudillando
a los cefalenios! Seguro que habría aflojado las rodillas de mu-

chos de ellos en mi palacio y tú habrías gozado en tu interior.»

Esto es lo que se decían uno a otro. Y después que habían terminado de preparar y tenían dispuesta la cena, se sentaron por orden en sillas y sillones y echaron mano de la comida. Entonces se acercó el anciano Dolio y con él sus hijos cansados de trabajar, que los salió a llamar su madre, la vieja Sicele, quien los había alimentado y cuidaba gentilmente al anciano, luego que le hubo alcanzado la vejez.

Cuando vieron a Odiseo y lo reconocieron en su interior, se detuvieron embobados en la habitación. Entonces Odiseo les dijo tocándoles con dulces palabras:

«Anciano, siéntate a la cena y dejad ya de admiraros; que hace tiempo permanecemos en la sala, deseosos de echar mano a los alimentos, por esperaros.»

Así habló; Dolio se fue derecho a él extendiendo sus dos brazos, tomó la mano de Odiseo y se la besó junto a la muñeca. Y se dirigió a él con aladas palabras:

«Amigo, puesto que has vuelto a nosotros que mucho lo deseábamos, aunque no lo acabábamos de creer del todo —y los dioses mismos te han traído—, ¡salud!, seas bienvenido y que los dioses te concedan felicidad. Mas dime con verdad, para que lo sepa, si está enterada la prudente Penélope de tu llegada o le enviamos un mensajero.»

Y le contestó y dijo el muy astuto Odiseo:

«Anciano, ya lo sabe, ¿qué necesidad hay de que tú te ocupes de esto?»

Así dijo y se sentó de nuevo sobre su bien pulimentado asiento. De la misma forma también los hijos de Dolio daban la bienvenida al ilustre Odiseo con sus palabras y le tomaban de la mano, y luego se sentaron por orden junto a Dolio, su padre.

Así es como se ocupaban de comer en la casa, mientras Fama recorría mensajera la ciudad anunciando por todas partes la terrible muerte y Ker de los pretendientes. Luego que la oyeron los ciudadanos, venían cada uno de un sitio con gritos y lamentos ante el palacio de Odiseo, sacaban del palacio los cadáveres y cada uno enterraba a los suyos: en cambio a los de otras ciudades los depositaban en rápidas naves y los mandaban a los pescadores para que llevaran a cada uno a su casa.

Y luego marcharon todos juntos al ágora, acongojado su co-   420
razón.

Cuando todos se habían reunido y estaban ya congregados,
se levantó entre ellos Eupites para hablar —pues había en su
interior un dolor imborrable por su hijo Antínoo, el primero a
quien había matado el divino Odiseo—; derramando lágrimas
por él levantó su voz y dijo:

«Amigos, este hombre ha llevado a cabo una gran maldad
contra los aqueos: a unos se los llevó en las naves, a muchos y
buenos, perdiendo las cóncavas naves y a su pueblo; y a otros
los ha matado al llegar, a los mejores con mucho de los cefalenios. Conque, vamos, antes que llegue rápidamente a Pilos o a   430
la divina Elide, donde mandan los epeos, vayamos nosotros.
O estaremos avergonzados para siempre, pues esto es un baldón incluso para los venideros si se enteran; porque si no cas-
tigamos a los asesinos de nuestros hijos y hermanos, ya no me
sería grato vivir, sino que preferiría morir enseguida y tener
trato con los muertos. Vamos, que no se nos anticipen a atravesar el mar.»

Así habló derramando lágrimas y la lástima se apoderó de
todos los aqueos. Entonces se acercaron Medonte y el divino
aedo —pues el sueño les había abandonado[307]—, se detuvie-   440
ron en-medio de ellos y el estupor se apoderó de todos. Y habló entre ellos Medonte, conocedor de consejos discretos:

«Escuchadme ahora a mí, itacenses; Odiseo ha realizado estas acciones no sin la voluntad de los dioses. Yo mismo vi a
un dios inmortal apostado junto a Odiseo y era en todo parecido a Méntor. El dios inmortal se mostraba unas veces ante
Odiseo para animarle y otras agitaba a los pretendientes y se
lanzaba tras ellos por el mégaron, y ellos caían hacinados.»

Así habló y se apoderó de todos el pálido terror.   450

Entonces se levantó a hablar el anciano héroe Haliterses,
hijo de Mástor, pues sólo él veía el presente y el futuro; éste
habló con buenos sentimientos hacia ellos y dijo:

---

[307] La última vez que vimos a Medonte y al aedo (XXII.380) se habían ido
al altar de Zeus. La frase «el sueño les había abandonado» es una banal frase de
transición. También hay una pequeña inconsecuencia: Medonte no pudo ver la
muerte de los pretendientes porque estaba debajo de un sillón y cubierto por
una piel (cfr. XXII.361 y ss.).

«Escuchadme ahora a mí, itacenses, lo que voy a deciros. Para nuestra desgracia se han realizado estos hechos, pues ni a mí hicisteis caso ni a Méntor, pastor de su pueblo[308], para poner coto a las locuras de vuestros hijos, quienes realizaban una gran maldad con su funesta arrogancia, esquilmando las posesiones y deshonrando a la esposa del hombre más notable, pues creían que ya no regresaría. También ahora sucederá de esta forma, obedeced lo que os digo: no vayamos, no sea que alguien encuentre la desgracia y la atraiga sobre sí.»   460

Así habló y se levantó con gran tumulto más de la mitad de ellos, pero los demás se quedaron allí, pues no agradó a su ánimo la palabra, sino que obedecieron a Eupites. Y poco después se precipitaban en busca de sus armas. Después, cuando habían vestido el brillante bronce sobre su cuerpo, se congregaron delante de la ciudad de amplio espacio, y los capitaneaba Eupites con estupidez: afirmaba que vengaría el asesinato de   470 su hijo y que no iba a volver sino a cumplir allí mismo su destino.

Entonces Atenea se dirigió a Zeus, el hijo de Cronos[309]:

«Padre nuestro Cronida, el más excelso de los poderosos, dime, ya que te pregunto, qué esconde ahora tu mente. ¿Es que vas a levantar otra vez funesta guerra y terrible combate, o vas a establecer la amistad entre ambas partes?»

Y Zeus, el que reúne las nubes, le contestó:

«Hija mía, ¿por qué me preguntas esto? ¿No has concebido tú misma la decisión de que Odiseo se vengara de aquéllos al   480 volver? Obra como quieras, aunque te voy a decir lo que más conviene: una vez que el divino Odiseo ha castigado a los pretendientes, que hagan juramento de fidelidad y que reine él para siempre. Por nuestra parte, hagamos que se oldiven del asesinato de sus hijos y hermanos. Que se amen mutuamente y que haya paz y riqueza en abundancia.»

Así hablando, movió a Atenea ya antes deseosa de bajar, y ésta descendió lanzándose de las cumbres del Olimpo.

---

[308] Cfr. II.161-76 y 229-41.
[309] Este tránsito repentino de la asamblea itacense al Olimpo no tiene paralelo en Homero. Es otro rasgo que ha hecho sospechoso este canto a los analíticos, cfr. Introducción.

Y después que habían echado de sí el deseo del dulce alimento, comenzó a hablar entre ellos el sufridor, el divino Odiseo: 490

«Que salga alguien a ver, no sea que ya vengan cerca.»

Así habló y salió un hijo de Dolio, por cumplir lo mandado, y fue a ponerse sobre el umbral; vio a todos los otros acercarse y dijo enseguida a Odiseo aladas palabras:

«Ya están cerca, armémonos rápidamente.»

Así habló y se levantaron, vistieron sus armaduras los cuatro que iban con Odiseo y los seis hijos de Dolio. También Laertes y Dolio vistieron sus armas, guerreros a la fuerza, aunque ya estaban canosos. Cuando ya habían puesto alrededor de 500 su cuerpo el brillante bronce, abrieron las puertas y salieron afuera, y los capitaneaba Odiseo.

Entonces se les acercó la hija de Zeus, Atenea, semejante a Méntor en cuerpo y voz; al verla se alegró el divino Odiseo y al punto se dirigió a Telémaco, su querido hijo:

«Telémaco, recuerda esto cuando salgas a luchar con los hombres donde se distinguen los mejores: que no deshonres el linaje de tus padres, los que hemos sobresalido por toda la tierra hasta ahora en vigor y hombría.»

Y Telémaco le contestó discretamente: 510

«Verás si así lo desea tu ánimo, querido padre, que no voy a avergonzar tu linaje, como dices.»

Así habló; Laertes se alegró y dijo su palabra:

«¡Qué día éste para mí, dioses míos! ¡Qué alegría, mi hijo y mi nieto rivalizan en valentía!»

Y poniéndose a su lado le dijo la de ojos brillantes, Atenea:

«Arcisíada, el más amado de todos tus compañeros, suplica a la joven de ojos brillantes y a Zeus, su padre; blande tu lanza de larga sombra y arrójala.»

Así habló y le inculcó un gran valor Palas Atenea. Suplicando 520 do después a la hija de Zeus, el Grande, blandió y arrojó su lanza de larga sombra e hirió a Eupites[310] a través del casco de mejillas de bronce. El casco no detuvo a la lanza y ésta atrave-

---

[310] Eupites es el padre de Antínoo. Es lógico que sea él también el primero en morir en la refriega y que lo haga precisamente a manos de Laertes.

só el bronce de lado a lado; cayó aquél con gran estrépito y resonaron las armas sobre él.

Se lanzaron sobre los primeros combatientes Odiseo y su brillante hijo y los golpeaban con sus espadas; y habrían matado a todos y dejádolos sin retorno si Atenea, la hija de Zeus portador de égida, no hubiera gritado con su voz y contenido a todo el pueblo: 530

«Abandonad, itacenses, la dura contienda, para que os separéis sin derramar sangre»[311].

Así habló Atenea y el pálido terror se apoderó de ellos; volaron las armas de sus manos, aterrorizados como estaban, y cayeron al suelo al lanzar Atenea su voz. Y se volvieron a la ciudad deseosos de vivir.

Gritó horriblemente el sufridor, el divino Odiseo y se lanzó de un brinco como el águila que vuela alto. Entonces el Cronida arrojó ardiente rayo que cayó delante de la de ojos brillantes, la de poderoso padre, y ésta se dirigió a Odiseo: 540

«Hijo de Laertes, de linaje divino, Odiseo rico en ardides, contente, abandona la lucha igual para todos, no sea que el Cronida se irrite contigo, el que ve a lo ancho, Zeus.»

Así habló Atenea; él obedeció y se alegró en su ánimo. Y Palas Atenea, la hija de Zeus, portador de égida, estableció entre ellos un pacto para el futuro, semejante a Méntor en el cuerpo y en la voz.

---

[311] También es ajeno a Homero el que todo un ejército oiga la voz de un dios. El terror masivo lo suele producir Atenea con la égida, no con sus palabras, cfr. XXII.297 y ss.

ÍNDICE